# Julian
## Gore Vidal

"A subtle, provoking, enthralling book
. . . Mr. Vidal's ability to invoke a world
is amazing."
*The Christian Science Monitor*

---

"To the formidable task which Vidal sets
himself, he brings an easy and fluent gift
for narrative; a theatrical sense of scene
and dramatic occasion; and a revealing
eye and ear for character dilineation—to
say nothing of wide reading."
*Newsweek*

---

"A remarkably readable and revealing
novel—of ideas and an age."
*Newsday*

For Lucien Price

THE ROMAN EMPIRE
In The Fourth Century A.D.

0  50  100  200  300  400
MILES

SARMATIA

BLACK SEA

Hadrianopolis
Constantinople
Chalcedon    Heraclea
        Nicomedia        BITHYNIA
Nicaea    Ancyra    GALATIA    PONTUS    CAPPADOCIA    ARMENIA
Pergamon    Pessinus                Amida    CORDUENE
    ASIA        CAPPADOCIA    Caesarea        Bezabde
Ephesus    LYCAONIA    Nazianzus            Refaina    Nisibis    Ninus
        Tarsus    Mopsucrene    Edessa        Carrae    Singara
EAST        CILICIA    Hierapolis    Callinicum
        Antioch    Chalcis    Circesium    Dura    Anatho
RHODES    CYPRUS        SYRIA        Thilutha        Ctesiphon
ROMAN                    Anziachalce    Thilaba    Macepracta    Seleucia
        SEA            Tyre    Damascus        Barsanalcia    Pirisabora    Babylon
EMPIRE                    Orogendae    Maiozamalcha
    Alexandria    Pelusium                    ARABIA        Persian
                                                Gulf
EGYPT

RED SEA

# A NOTE

Robert Graves, when he came to publish his sequel to *I, Claudius*, remarked in a somewhat irritable preface that a good many reviewers seemed to think he had simply spun himself a novel from Suetonius's gossip, which looked to them like a very easy thing to do. In *Claudius the God*, Graves struck back with a long bibliography, listing nearly every relevant text which has survived from the ancient world. Unfortunately, I have not read as much as all that. But to anticipate those who might think that one's only source was the history of Ammianus Marcellinus (or even of Edward Gibbon), I have included at the end of the book a partial bibliography.

The Emperor Julian's life is remarkably well documented. Three volumes of his letters and essays survive, while such acquaintances as Libanius and Saint Gregory of Nazianzus wrote vivid accounts of him. Though I have written a novel, not a history, I have tried to stay with the facts, only occasionally shifting things around. For instance, it is unlikely that Priscus joined Julian in Gaul, but it is useful to the narrative to have him there.

Julian has always been something of an underground hero in Europe. His attempt to stop Christianity and revive Hellenism exerts still a romantic appeal, and he crops up in odd places, particularly during the Renaissance and again in the nineteenth century. Two such unlikely authors as Lorenzo de' Medici and Henrik Ibsen wrote plays about him. But aside from the unique adventure of Julian's life, what continues to fascinate is the fourth century itself. During the fifty years between the accession of Julian's uncle Constantine the Great and Julian's death at thirty-two, Christianity was established. For better or worse, we are today very much the result of what they were then.

In naming cities, I give the modern rather than the ancient name (Milan, not Mediolanum), except when the original name is more familiar to us (Ephesus, not Selçuk). Dates I put in our fashion, A.D. and B.C. Since Julian's court was a military one, I have used our own army's way of dating, i.e., 3 October 363. Currency is a tricky matter. No one is quite certain what the exact purchasing power of money was in the fourth century, but a gold solidus was probably worth about five dollars. Julian, Priscus and Libanius, the three narrators of this story, all wrote Greek. Their Latin was rather shaky, as they are quick to remind us, but they occasionally use Latin terms, much the way we do. For those readers who will search in vain for Julian's famous last words, "Thou hast conquered, Galilean!," he never said them. Theodoret must take credit for this fine rhetoric, composed a century after Julian's death.

I should like to thank the American Academy at Rome and the American School of Classical Studies at Athens for letting me use their libraries.

G. V.

# Youth

## I

*Libanius to Priscus*                    *Antioch, March [A.D.] 380*

Yesterday morning as I was about to enter the lecture hall, I was stopped by a Christian student who asked me in a voice eager with malice, "Have you heard about the Emperor Theodosius?"

I cleared my throat ready to investigate the nature of this question, but he was too quick for me. "He has been baptized a Christian."

I was noncommittal. Nowadays, one never knows who is a secret agent. Also, I was not particularly surprised at the news. When Theodosius fell ill last winter and the bishops arrived like vultures to pray over him, I knew that should he recover they would take full credit for having saved him. He survived. Now we have a Christian emperor in the East, to match Gratian, our Christian emperor in the West. It was inevitable.

I turned to go inside but the young man was hardly finished with his pleasant task. "Theodosius has also issued an edict. It was just read in front of the senate house. I heard it. Did you?"

"No. But I always enjoy imperial prose," I said politely.

"You may not enjoy this. The Emperor has declared heretic all those who do not follow the Nicene Creed."

"I'm afraid Christian theology is not really my subject. The edict hardly applies to those of us who are still faithful to philosophy."

"It applies to everyone in the East." He said this slowly, watching me all the while. "The Emperor has even appointed an Inquisitor to determine one's faith. The days of toleration are over."

I was speechless; the sun flared in my eyes; all things grew confused and I wondered if I was about to faint, or even die. But the voices of two colleagues recalled me. I could tell by the way they greeted me that they, too, had heard about the edict and were curious to know my reaction. I gave them no pleasure.

"Of course I expected it," I said. "The Empress Postuma wrote me only this week to say that . . ." I invented freely. I have not of course heard from the Empress in some months, but I thought that the enemy should be reminded to what extent I enjoy the favor

1

of Gratian and Postuma. It is humiliating to be forced to protect oneself in this way, but these are dangerous times.

I did not lecture yesterday. I went straight home. I am now living in Daphne, by the way, a charming suburb which I prefer to Antioch proper because of the quiet. As I get older, I find that the slightest sound in the night disturbs me and, once awake, I have difficulty falling asleep again. You can imagine how intolerable my old house in the city became. You remember the house; it was there that I gave the reception for the Emperor Julian when he . . . But I forget. You were not there, and you were much missed! My memory plays me odd tricks these days. Even worse, I tend to mislay the notes I jot down as reminders, or (terrible confession!) when I do find them, I am often unable to decipher my own handwriting. Age spares us nothing, old friend. Like ancient trees, we die from the top.

Except for occasional lectures, I seldom go into town, for the people, though my own, distress me with their loud voices and continual quarreling, their gambling and sensuality. They are hopelessly frivolous. Nights are made day with artificial light, while nearly all the men now use depilatories, which makes it difficult to tell them from women . . . to think how I once eulogized this city! But I suppose one must be tolerant, recalling that the Antiochenes are the victims of a demoralizingly sultry climate, the proximity of Asia and of course that pernicious Christian doctrine which asserts that a sprinkling of water (and a small donation) will wash away sin, again and again and again.

Now, my old friend, as I sit here in my study surrounded by our proscribed friends (I mean those books of Greece which made the mind of man), let me tell you what thoughts I had last night—a sleepless night not only because of the edict but because two cats saw fit to enliven my despair with the noise of lust (only an Egyptian would worship a cat). I am weary today but determined. *We must fight back.* What happens to us personally is not important, but what happens to civilization is a matter of desperate concern. During my sleepless night, I thought of various appeals that might be made to our new Emperor. I have a copy of the edict before me as I write. It is composed in bad bureaucratic Greek, the official style of the bishops, whose crudity of language is equaled only by the confusion of their thought. Not unlike those celebrated minutes of the council at—where was it? Chalcedon?—

answers to the questions they ask you. I despair of teaching anyone anything, least of all myself. I have not had a new idea since I was twenty-seven. That is why I don't publish my lectures. Also, too many of us publish out of vanity or to attract students. At seventy-five (I am nine, not a dozen, years older than you) I am an empty flagon. Tap me and you will hear an awful hollow sound. My head is a tomb quite as empty as the one Jesus is supposed to have walked away from. I incline now to Crates and the early Cynics, less to Plato and the rest. I am not in the least convinced that there is a Divine Oneness at the center of the universe, nor am I susceptible to magic, unlike Julian, who was hopelessly gullible. I often thought Maximus exploited his good-heartedness. But then I never could endure Maximus. How he used to waste Julian's time with his séances and arcane gibberish! I teased the Emperor about him once, but Julian only laughed and said, "Who knows through what door wisdom will walk?"

As to your publishing project, I am not at all certain that a sympathetic biography of Julian would have the slightest effect at this time. Theodosius is a military politician, impressed by bishops. He might of course sanction a biography of his predecessor simply because Julian is much admired to this day, though *not* for his philosophy. Julian is admired because he was young and handsome and the most successful general of our century. The people have a touching admiration for generals who win battles, which is why there are no heroes today. But if Theodosius did permit a biography, it would have to avoid the religious issue. The bishops would see to that. And for ferocity there is nothing on earth to equal a Christian bishop hunting "heresy," as they call any opinion contrary to their own. Especially confident are they on that subject where they are as ignorant as the rest of mankind. I mean death. Anyway, I don't want to fight them, because I am one and they are many. And though I am, as you so comfortingly suggest, old and near the end of my life, I enjoy amazingly good health. I am told that I look no different than I did at forty, and I am still capable of the sexual act at almost any time. This vitality repels Hippia, who has aged noticeably in the last few years, but it seems to please various young women in a certain quarter of Athens which you doubtless have heard of—in novels of the Milesian school!

Do I make myself clear? I have no wish to be burned alive or stoned or tacked up to the door of a Christian church, or "charnel house" as Julian used to call them. *You* may be as brave as you

5

like and I will applaud you in my heart. But I have no intention of writing a single sentence about Julian, fond as I was of him and alarmed as I am at the strange course our world has taken since the adventurer Constantine sold us to the bishops.

Julian's memoir was written during the last four months of his life. It was begun in March 363, at Hierapolis. Nearly every night during our invasion of Persia he would dictate recollections of his early life. The result is a bit helter-skelter, for both as a writer and as a man he was swift and impulsive. He once told me that he would like to compose an autobiography on the order of *Marcus Aurelius to Himself*, but he lacked that writer's discipline. Julian was also influenced by Xenophon's *The March Upcountry*, since Xenophon took much the same route we did seven centuries later. Julian's interest in history was always lively, and he was a great sightseer. The resulting memoir is something of a hybrid; even so, Julian was often an engaging writer, and if he was not better it is because it is hard to be emperor, philosopher and general all at once. He was also indiscreet about everyone. I hope you forgive him. I have done so. He suspected that he had very little time and he wanted to get everything said. As for his mysterious death, I have a theory as to what happened, which I will explain to you in due course.

I have never quite known what to do with this work. When Julian died, I took all his personal papers, suspecting that his Christian successors would destroy them. I had no right to these papers, of course, but I don't regret my theft. I told no one about the memoir until I was back safe in Antioch, where I must have mentioned it to you the day you read us your famous eulogy. I was so moved by your eloquence that I betrayed my own confidence.

I am now having a fair copy made of the manuscript. You are misinformed if you think copying is cheaper here than at Antioch. Quite the contrary. The estimated cost will run to eighty gold solidi, which I suggest you send by return post. On receipt of the full amount, I will send you the book to use as you see fit. Only do *not* mention to anyone that I had any connection with the matter. I have not the slightest desire to endure martyrdom at this time or ever.

I thought I had written you about your collection of letters. I did get the book and it was very thoughtful of you to send it to me. We are all in your debt for those letters, especially yours to

Julian. They are wise. I know of no other philosopher so sensible of posterity as to keep copies of *every* letter he writes, realizing that even his most trivial effusion has, in the context of the large body of his work, an eternal value. Hippia joins me in wishing you good health.

*Libanius to Priscus*                                      Antioch, April 380

You cannot imagine the pleasure I experienced when your letter was brought to me this evening. So eager was I to hear your voice again, as it were, that I fear I ripped the fastenings and tore the long-awaited page itself. But rest assured, your precious letter will be mended with glue and cherished, since any utterance of your genius is an essential reflection of the Hellenic spirit to be passed on to those who come after.

Let me say right off how pleased I am to learn of your unflagging sexual vigor. It is always inspiring to the rest of us to learn that in certain rare human beings the usual cycle of sad decline does not obtain. You have been indeed favored by the gods and in your obvious enjoyment of that favor will never sigh at eighty, as did Sophocles, "At last I am free of a cruel and insane master!" Your master is obviously a good companion, made even more enjoyable by Hippia's acquiescence. Not many wives of philosophers would allow their husbands freedom to consort with those deliciously civilized ladies of Athens whose evening parties used to delight me in my student days. Now of course my life is devoted to philosophy and affairs of state. I leave to younger men the charms of Aphrodite . . . to younger men and now, Priscus, to *you*, who have held at arm's length the villain time! Fortunate man! Fortunate girls to be so loved!

Since I wrote you last, I have not been idle. Through the office of the praetorian prefect at Constantinople, I have proposed myself for an audience with the Emperor. Theodosius has met very few people of our set, coming as he does from Spain, a country not noted for culture. He also belongs to a military family and there is no evidence that he has ever studied philosophy. Outside of politics, his principal interest is breeding sheep. But he is only thirty-three and his character, according to the best information available, is mild. *Though we should not count on this*. How often in the past have we been horrified by princes reputed to be good who, when raised to the throne of the world, have turned monstrous before our eyes? The late Valens for example, or Julian's own

7

brother, the Caesar Gallus, a charming youth who brought terror to the East. We must be on our guard, as always.

The question that now faces us is: how seriously will Theodosius enforce the edict? It is customary for emperors who listen to bishops to hurl insults at the very civilization that created them. They are inconsistent, but then logic has never been a strong point of the Christian faith. The extraordinary paradox is the collusion of our princes with the bishops. The emperors pride themselves on being first magistrates of the Roman imperium, through whose senate they exercise their power; and though in reality we have not been Roman for a century, nevertheless, the *form* persists, making it impossible, one would think, for any prince who calls himself Augustus to be Christian, certainly not as long as the Altar of Victory remains in the senate house at Rome. But confusions of this sort are as inconsequential to the Christian mind as clouds to a day in summer, and as a teacher I no longer try to refute them; since most of my students are Christian, I suppose I ought to be grateful that they have chosen to come to me to be taught that very philosophy their faith subverts. It is comedy, Priscus! It is tragedy!

Meanwhile, we can only wait to see what happens. The Emperor grows stronger in health every day, and it is thought that later this spring he may take the field against the Goths, who as usual are threatening the marches of Macedonia. If he decides to go north, that means he will not return to Constantinople till late summer or autumn, in which case I will have to attend him at Thessalonica or, worse, in the field. If so, I am confident the journey will be my last. For my health, unlike yours, continues to deteriorate. I have coughing fits which leave me weak and longing for the grave. I have also developed a curious rash on the backs of my hands and forearms which may be the result of eating a bad flounder last week (shades of Diogenes and the fatal raw octopus!), or it may be the outward sign of a corruption in the blood. How I wish Oribasius were in Antioch! He is the only physician I ever trusted, in which I follow Julian, who used to say, "The god Asklepios gave Oribasius secrets known only to heaven."

Over the years I have made a number of notes for a biography of Julian. I have them before me now. All that remains is the final organization of the material—and of course the memoir. Please send it to me as soon as the copy is ready. I shall work on it this summer, as I am no longer lecturing. I thought it wise to go into seclusion until we know which way the wind blows.

I don't need to tell you that Antioch has ignored the edict. Never in my memory has Antioch obeyed the imperial authority except at sword's point. I have often warned the local senate that emperors do not like disobedience, but our people feel that they are beyond law and reprisal. The folly of the clever is always greater than that of the dull. I tremble for Antioch, even though I am currently a beneficiary of its absence of reverence for the decrees of Caesar.

There have been no incidents so far. My Christian friends come to see me as usual (rather a large number of my old students are now bishops, a peculiar irony). Colleagues who are still lecturing tell me that their classes are much as usual. The next move is up to Theodosius, or, to be exact, up to the bishops. Luckily for us, they have been so busy for so long persecuting one another that we have been able to survive. But reading between the lines of the edict, I suspect a bloodbath. Theodosius has outlawed with particular venom the party of the late Presbyter Arius on the grounds that Galileans must now have a church with a single doctrine to be called universal . . . a *catholic* church, no less! To balance this, we must compose a true life of Julian. So let us together fashion one last wreath of Apollonian laurel to place upon the brow of philosophy, as a brave sign against the winter that threatens this stormy late season of the world. I want those who come after us to realize what hopes we had for life, and I want them to see how close our Julian came to arresting the disease of Galilee. Such a work, properly done, would be like a seed planted in the autumn to await the sun's awakening, and a new flowering.

Apparently, the cost of copying at Athens has gone up incredibly since I had some work done there last year. I find eighty gold solidi exorbitant for what you say is a fragment, or a book of moderate length. Only last summer I paid thirty solidi for a Plotinus which, in length, must be treble that of Julian's memoir. I send now by a friend who embarks tomorrow for Athens thirty gold solidi and this letter. Again my best wishes to the admirable Hippia, and to you, my old friend and fellow soldier in the wars of philosophy.

*Priscus to Libanius*                    *Athens, June 380*

I send you by my pupil Glaucon something less than half of the Emperor Julian's memoir. It cost me exactly thirty solidi to have this much copied. On receipt of the remaining fifty solidi I

9

shall send you the rest of the book. I can only assume that the copying you had done in Athens last summer was the work of an admirer who gave you a cut price as a sign of his esteem for your high contributions to philosophy and rhetoric.

I do not share your pessimism about the new Emperor. He is hardly what *we* would have picked had the choice been ours, but then the choice never has been ours. Julian's accession was the work of Fortune, a deity notable for her absence in human affairs. We can hardly hope to have another Julian in our lifetime. And that is that.

I have studied the edict since I wrote you last, and though it is somewhat sterner in tone than Constantine's, I suspect the only immediate victims will be those Christians who follow Arius. But I may be mistaken. I almost always am in political matters, a weakness no doubt of the philosophic temperament. However, what does give me hope was last year's appointment of the "poet" Ausonius as consul. Do you know him? I am sure you've read him. If not, you have a treat in store. I have lately become rather an expert on his career. He started life as the son of a well-to-do doctor in Bordeaux. His phenomenal luck began when the Emperor Valentinian made him tutor to his son Gratian. As Ausonius himself puts it, he "molded the tiny mind of the infant prince." When the prince became emperor, he rewarded his old tutor by making him praetorian prefect of Gaul as well as consul for last year. I mention all this because Ausonius is inclined favorably to us, and he exerts a considerable influence not only on Gratian (who is far too busy hunting wild boar in Gaul to distress us unduly) but on Theodosius as well. He is obviously the man for you to cultivate.

Not long ago I sent round to the library to see what they had by Ausonius. The slave returned with a wheelbarrow full of books. Ausonius must be read to be believed! As poet, no subject is too trivial for him; as courtier, no flattery too excessive. He did write one passable nature poem on the Moselle, but I'm not keen on rivers. The rest of his work is quite marvelous in its tedium. Particularly those verses he wrote at Valentinian's request. Among the subjects chosen by the Emperor were the source of the Danube (Ausonius did not locate it but he made a good try), Easter, and (best of all) four odes to the Emperor's four favorite horses. I had one of these equine odes copied out and Hippia reads it to me whenever I am depressed. It begins "Oh raven steed, whose fortune it is to spread the golden thighs and Mars-like firm convexities of divine Augustus . . ." I don't know when I have enjoyed a poem so much. I'll enclose a copy. Anyway, I suggest you see Ausonius as soon as possible. And of course you will remember to express admiration for his work! In a good cause hypocrisy becomes virtue.

I never go to evening parties. The quarter I referred to in my letter was *not* the elegant street of Sardes but the quarter of the prostitutes near the agora. I don't go to parties because I detest talking-women, especially our Athenian ladies who see themselves as heiresses to the age of Pericles. Their conversation is hopelessly pretentious and artificial. Their dinners are inedible, and for some reason they all tend to be rather squat with dark vestigial moustaches; no doubt Aphrodite's revenge on the talking-woman. I live very quietly at home with an occasional visit to the quarter.

Hippia and I get along rather better than we used to. Much of her charm for me has been her lifelong dislike of literature. She talks about servants and food and relatives, and I find her restful. Also, I have in the house a Gothic girl, bought when she was eleven. She is now a beautiful woman, tall and well made, with eyes gray as Athena's. She *never* talks. Eventually I shall buy her a husband and free them both as a reward for her serene acceptance of my attentions, which delight her far less than they do me. But that is often the case with the feminine half of Plato's ugliest beast. But then Plato disliked sexual intercourse between men and women. We tend of course to think of Plato as divine, but I am afraid he was rather like our old friend Iphicles, whose passion for youths has become so outrageous that he now lives day and night in the baths, where the boys call him the queen of philosophy.

I am sorry to hear that your health grows worse but that is to be expected at our age. The rash you refer to *does* sound like bad fish. I suggest a diet of bread and water, and not much of either. On receipt of the money, I will send you the balance of the memoir. It will disturb and sadden you. I shall be curious to see how you use this material. Hippia joins me in wishing for your good—or should I say better?—health.

You will note in the memoir that Julian invariably refers to the Christians as "Galileans" and to their churches as "charnel houses," this last a dig at their somewhat necrophile passion for the relics of dead men. I think it might be a good idea to alter the text, and reconvert those charnel houses into churches and those Galileans into Christians. Never offend an enemy in a small way.

Here and there in the text, I have made marginal notes. I hope you won't find them too irrelevant.

# II

*The Memoir of Julian Augustus*

From the example of my uncle the Emperor Constantine, called the Great, who died when I was six years old, I learned that it is dangerous to side with any party of the Galileans, for they mean to overthrow and veil those things that are truly holy. I can hardly remember Constantine, though I was once presented to him at the Sacred Palace. I dimly recall a giant, heavily scented, wearing a stiff jeweled robe. My older brother Gallus always said that I tried to pull his wig off. But Gallus had a cruel humor, and I doubt that this story was true. If I *had* tugged at the Emperor's wig, I would surely not have endeared myself to him, for he was as vain as a woman about his appearance; even his Galilean admirers admit to that.

From my mother Basilina I inherited my love of learning. I never knew her. She died shortly after my birth, 7 April 331. She was the daughter of the praetorian prefect Julius Julianus. From portraits I resemble her more than I do my father; I share with her a straight nose and rather full lips, unlike the imperial Flavians, who tend to have thin hooked noses and tight pursed mouths. The Emperor Constantius, my cousin and predecessor, was a typical Flavian, resembling his father Constantine, except that he was much shorter. But I did inherit the Flavian thick chest and neck, legacy of our Illyrian ancestors, who were men of the mountains. My mother, though Galilean, was devoted to literature. She was taught by the eunuch Mardonius, who was also my tutor.

From Mardonius, I learned to walk modestly with my eyes to the ground, not strutting or measuring the effect I was creating on others. I was also taught self-discipline in all things; he particularly tried to keep me from talking too much. Fortunately, now that I am Emperor everyone delights in my conversation! Mardonius also convinced me that time spent at the games or in the theatre was time wasted. And, finally, it was from Mardonius, a

Galilean who loved Hellenism too well, that I learned about Homer and Hesiod, Plato and Theophrastos. He was a good teacher, if severe.

From my cousin and predecessor, the Emperor Constantius, I learned to dissemble and disguise my true thoughts. A dreadful lesson, but had I not learned it I would not have lived past my twentieth year. In the year 337 Constantius murdered my father. His crime? Consanguinity. I was spared because I was six years old; my half-brother Gallus—who was eleven years old—was spared because he was sickly and not expected to live.

Yes, I was trying to imitate the style of *Marcus Aurelius to Himself*, and I have failed. Not only because I lack his purity and goodness but because while he was able to write of the good things he learned from a good family and good friends, I must write of those bitter things I learned from a family of murderers in an age diseased by the quarrels and intolerance of a sect whose purpose it is to overthrow that civilization whose first note was struck upon blind Homer's lyre. I am not Marcus Aurelius, in excellence or in experience. I must speak now in my own voice.

I never saw my mother. But I do recall my father. Julius Constantius was a tall imposing man. At least he seemed tall to me then. Actually, from his statues, I reckon him to have been somewhat shorter than I am now, and broader. He was most gentle with Gallus and me on those occasions when we saw him, which was not often for he was always traveling, attending to the various small tasks the Emperor set him. I should mention here that at one time my father was thought to have had a better right to the throne than his half-brother Constantine. But it was never his nature to protest. He was gentle; he was weak; he was destroyed.

On 22 May 337, Constantine died at Nicomedia, to his apparent surprise, since he had just taken the water cure at Helenopolis and all the omens suggested a long life. On his deathbed he sent for our cousin, Bishop Eusebius, to baptize him. Just before the Bishop arrived, Constantine is supposed to have said, rather nervously, "Let there be no mistake." I'm afraid that sounds exactly like him. He was not one to leave, as Aristophanes so wittily puts it, a single stone unturned. Constantine was never a true Galilean; he

13

merely used Christianity to extend his dominion over the world. He was a shrewd professional soldier, badly educated and not in the least interested in philosophy, though some perverse taste in him was hugely satisfied by doctrinal disputes; the mad haggling of bishops fascinated him.

According to Constantine's will, the empire was to be divided between his three surviving sons, each of whom had already been raised to the rank of Caesar. (Every schoolchild knows this but will they always?) To the twenty-one-year-old Constantine II went the prefecture of Gaul. To Constantius, twenty, the East. To Constans, sixteen, Italy and Illyricum. Each was to assume automatically the title Augustus. Surprisingly enough, this division of the world was carried out peaceably. After the funeral (which I was too young to attend), Constantine II withdrew immediately to his capital at Vienne. Constans set out for Milan. Constantius took over the Sacred Palace at Constantinople.

Then the murders began. Constantius maintained that there was a plot against his life, instigated by the children of Theodora, who had been legitimate wife to his grandfather Constantius Chlorus, whose concubine Helena, Constantine's mother, had been discarded when his father was raised to the purple. Yes, it all sounds a muddle to those who read of such matters, but to us, caught in the web, these relationships are as murderously plain as that of spider to fly.

Some say there was indeed such a plot, but I doubt it. I am certain that my father was in no way disloyal. He had not protested when his half-brother Constantine became emperor. Why should he protest the elevation of his son? In any case, during the course of that terrible summer, a dozen descendants of Theodora were secretly arrested and executed, among them my father.

The day of my father's arrest Mardonius and I had been out walking in the gardens of the Sacred Palace. I don't recall where Gallus was; probably sick in bed with fever. For some reason, when Mardonius and I returned to the house, we entered the front door instead of the back, our usual entrance.

It was a pleasant evening and, again contrary to custom, I went to my father where he sat in the atrium with his estate manager. I remember the white and scarlet roses that had been trained to grow in trellises between the columns. And—what else do I remember? The lion-footed chair. A round marble table. The dark-faced Spanish estate manager sitting on a stool to my father's left,

14

a sheaf of papers in his lap. As I dictate these words, I can suddenly remember everything. Yet until this moment—how strange—I had forgotten the roses and my father's face, which was—which is—all clear to me again. What a curious thing memory is! He was ruddy-faced, with small gray eyes, and on his left cheek there was a shallow pale scar, like a crescent.

"This," he said, turning to the manager, "is the best part of my estate. Guard him well." I had no idea what he was talking about. I am sure that I was embarrassed. It was rare at any time for my father to speak to me. Not for lack of affection but because he was even more shy and diffident than I, and not at all certain how to behave with children.

Birds—yes, I can hear them again—chattered in the branches of the trees. My father continued to speak of me, and I listened to the birds and looked at the fountain, aware that something strange impended. He said that Nicomedia was "safe," and I wondered what he meant by that. The estate manager agreed. They spoke of our cousin, Bishop Eusebius; he was also "safe." I stared at the fountain: Greek of the last century, a sea nymph on a dolphin whose mouth poured water into a basin. Remembering this, I realize now why I had a similar fountain installed in my garden when I was at Paris. Can one remember *everything* if one tries this hard? (Note: Have copy of fountain made for Constantinople if original can't be found.)

Then my father dismissed me with an awkward pat; no last word, no mark of undue affection; such is shyness.

While I was having supper, the soldiers came. Mardonius was terrified. I was so astonished by *his* fright that at first I could hardly understand what was happening. When I heard the soldiers in the atrium, I jumped to my feet. "What's that? Who's that?" I asked.

"Sit down," said Mardonius. "Don't move. Don't make a sound." His smooth beardless eunuch face with its thousand lines like a piece of crumpled silk had gone the color of a corpse. I broke away from him, in wonder at his fear. Clumsily, he tried to bar me from leaving the room, but now, more alarmed by his fear than by the noise of strange men in the house, I bolted past him to the empty atrium. In the vestibule beyond, a woman slave stood weeping. The front door was open. The porter clung to the frame as if he had been nailed to it. Through the woman's soft weeping, I heard the sound armed men make in a street: creaking

15

leather, dull clank of metal upon metal, and the hollow thud of thick-soled boots on stone.

The porter tried to stop me but I dodged past him into the street. Half a block away, I saw my father walking at the center of a formation of soldiers, led by a young tribune. Shouting, I ran after him. The soldiers did not halt but my father half-turned as he walked. His face was paler than the ashes of a wood fire. In a terrible voice, stern as Zeus, a voice I had never heard him use before, he said, "Go back! *Now!*"

I stopped dead in the center of the street, several yards from him. The tribune stopped, too, and looked at me curiously. Then my father turned on him and said peremptorily, "Go on. This is no sight for a child."

The tribune grinned. "We'll be back for him soon enough." Then the porter from our house seized me, and though I cried and fought, he carried me back into the house.

Several days later in one of the wine cellars of the Sacred Palace, my father was beheaded. No charges were made. There was no trial. I do not know where he was buried or if he was buried.


It is remarkable how many odd details come back to me as I write. For instance, the tribune's smile, which I had forgotten for twenty years. I find myself suddenly wondering: what ever became of *him*? Where is he today? Do I know him? Is he one of my generals? Could it have been Victor? Jovian? Each is the right age. No, better to let the past go, to preserve it only here upon the page. Vengeance must end somewhere, and what better place to stop than at the prince?

I soon discovered what my father had meant during that cryptic conversation with the estate manager. We were to be sent to our cousin Eusebius, bishop of Nicomedia. He was to be our guardian. The day after the arrest of our father, Mardonius hustled Gallus and me into a wagon with only our personal clothing. Except to change horses, we drove the fifty miles to Nicomedia without rest. Once we were stopped by mounted troops. With quavering voice, Mardonius told them that we were under the personal protection of the Emperor Constantius. They let us pass. We drove all day and all night.

That night! Gallus was suffering from the fever which nearly killed him. In his delirium, tortured by fever demons, he writhed on the pallet set for him on the wagon's floor. Mardonius put linen soaked in vinegar on his face—acrid odor of vinegar—yes, vinegar still recalls that terrible night to me. At one point I touched his face and found it hot as a damp cloth left in the sun to dry. His golden hair was dark with sweat; his arms flailed air; he shouted dream-words and wept.

Wide awake, I sat on the bench beside Mardonius as we jolted over country roads, the warm night as bright as day from a huge yellow moon that shone before us, like a beacon fire set for ships.

I spoke not at all that night. And though I was only six years old, I kept saying to myself: you are going to die; and I wondered what it was like to be dead. I think I became a philosopher that night, for in my youth and ignorance I was more curious than frightened. I suspect that I was even a bit thrilled by this desperate journey across unfamiliar country, with a gold moon blazing and Gallus writhing at my feet, begging me to give him a stick to fight the demons with.


We survived, to our surprise. For five years Gallus and I lived with Bishop Eusebius at Nicomedia and, later, at Constantinople. Eusebius was a grave old man, and though he did not like children he treated us kindly. More to the point, he forbade Constantius to come near us and Constantius obeyed him, for Eusebius was a great power in the Galilean hierarchy. Two years after he became our guardian he was made bishop of Constantinople, where in effect he governed the Eastern church until his death.

Children get used to anything. For a time we missed our father; then we forgot him. Mardonius was always with us, maintaining a link with the old life, and of course my mother's brother Count Julian often visited us. A charming bureaucrat with a taste for intrigue, he kept us informed of what was happening in the world. It was he who explained to us how Constantius was making himself sole master of the state. In the year 340 Constans and Constantine II disagreed. They went to war. Constantine II was ambushed at Aquileia and executed. Constans became sole ruler in the West. Then a general named Magnentius declared himself Augustus and drove Constans from Autun to the Pyrenees, where he was murdered in the winter of 350. The West was in chaos. While Magnentius was desperately trying to hold together his stolen empire, a general on the Danube named Vetranio declared *himself* emperor.

To give Constantius his due, he had a genius for civil war. He knew when to strike and, more important, *whom* to strike. He always won. I have often thought that had he lived he might have destroyed me in the same way that he had dealt with all the others. Faced with two usurpers, Constantius took the field in 350. Vetranio collapsed immediately and, unique in our history, was spared. Magnentius of course was defeated in the battle of Mursa, 28 September 352. This was one of the crucial moments in our history. To this day our army has not recovered from the loss of fifty-four thousand of our best troops.

Needless to say, I knew none of these emperors and usurpers. In fact, I don't recall ever meeting my cousins Constans and Constantine II. For that matter, I did not meet Constantius himself until I was sixteen years old; a meeting I shall presently describe in detail.

While princes schemed and fought, I was educated by Mardonius. He was a strict but inspiring teacher. I liked him. Gallus hated him, but then Gallus hated nearly everyone sooner or later. I recall once when I wanted to watch some chariot races, Mardonius said, "If you want games, read Homer. Nothing in life can equal what he wrote of games, or of anything else." Maddening injunction to a child, but wise. As it turned out, I was a grown man before I attended either the theatre or the arena, and then only because I did not want to give offense to others. Yes, I was something of a prig, and still am!

I have but one clear memory of Bishop Eusebius. It was the afternoon he decided to drill me himself in the life of the Nazarene. For hours we sat in a side chapel of the cathedral at Nicomedia while he questioned me. I was bored. The Bishop had a talent for explaining only those things one already knew, leaving mysterious those things one would like to have known. He was a heavy, pale old man, slow of speech and much too easy to follow. Simply for diversion, I stared at the ceiling, which was vaulted and divided into four sections, each dedicated to one of the seasons. In the most brilliant mosaic, flowers and vines, birds and fishes, were all intertwined. I knew that ceiling by heart for Gallus and I prayed three times a day in this particular chapel, and during those tedious prayers I used to imagine that I had the power to rise straight up in the air and enter that world of peacocks and palm trees and grape arbors, a gleaming world of gold where there was no sound but that of running water and birds singing—certainly no sermons, no prayers! A few years ago when Nicomedia was shattered by earthquake, my first question concerned the cathedral: did it still stand? Yes, I was told, but the roof had fallen in. And so my childhood's magic retreat is now rubble.

I must have been staring too obviously at the ceiling, for the Bishop suddenly asked me, "What is the most important of our Lord's teachings?"

Without thinking, I said, "Thou shalt not kill." I then rapidly quoted every relevant text from the new testament (much of which I knew by heart) and all that I could remember from the old. The Bishop had not expected this response. But he nodded appreciatively. "You have quoted well. But why do you think this commandment the most important?"

"Because had it been obeyed my father would be alive." I startled myself with the quickness of my own retort.

The Bishop's pale face was even ashier than usual. "Why do you say this?"

"Because it's true. The Emperor killed my father. Everybody knows that. And I suppose he shall kill Gallus and me, too, when he gets around to it." Boldness, once begun, is hard to check.

"The Emperor is a holy man," said the Bishop severely. "All the world admires his piety, his war against heresy, his support of the true faith."

This made me even more reckless. "Then if he is such a good Christian how could he kill so many members of his own family? After all, isn't it written in Matthew and again in Luke that..."

"You little fool!" The Bishop was furious. "Who has been telling you these things? Mardonius?"

I had sense enough to protect my tutor. "No, Bishop. But people talk about everything in front of us. I suppose they think we don't understand. Anyway it's all true, isn't it?"

The Bishop had regained his composure. His answer was slow and grim. "All that you need to know is that your cousin, the Emperor, is a devout and good man, and never forget that you are at his mercy." The Bishop then made me recite for four hours, as punishment for impudence. But the lesson I learned was not the one intended. All that I understood was that Constantius was a devout Christian. Yet he had killed his own flesh and blood. Therefore, if he could be both a good Christian and a murderer,

19

then there was something wrong with his religion. Needless to say, I no longer blame Constantius's faith for his misdeeds, any more than Hellenism should be held responsible for *my* shortcomings! Yet for a child this sort of harsh contradiction is disturbing, and not easily forgotten.

In the year 340 Eusebius was made bishop of Constantinople. As a result, Gallus and I divided our time between Nicomedia and the capital. Of the two, I preferred Constantinople.

Founded the year before I was born, Constantinople has no past; only a noisy present and a splendid future, if the auguries are to be believed. Constantine deliberately chose ancient Byzantium to be the capital of the Roman Empire, and then he created a new city in place of the old, and named the result—with characteristic modesty—after himself. Like most children of the city I delight in its vitality and raw newness. The air is always full of dust and the smell of mortar. The streets are loud with hammering. This confusion should be unpleasant, but it is invigorating. From day to day the city changes. Nearly all the familiar sights of my youth have been replaced by new buildings, new streets, new vistas, and I find it a marvelous thing to be—if only in this—at the beginning of something great rather than at the end.

In good weather, Mardonius used to take Gallus and me on walks around the city. "Statue hunts" we called them, because Mardonius was passionately interested in works of art and he would drag us from one end of the city to the other to look for them. I think we must have seen all ten thousand of the bronze and marble statues Constantine had stolen from every part of the world to decorate his city. Though one cannot approve his thefts (particularly those from Hellenic temples), the result has been that in and around the various arcades along Middle Street, the city's main thoroughfare, there are more important works of art than anywhere on earth, excepting Rome.

One of our expeditions took us to a Galilean charnel house, close by the Hippodrome. While Mardonius fussed with a map of the city, trying to get his bearings, Gallus and I threw bits of marble at a half-finished house across the street. There are always a satisfying number of things for a child to throw in the streets of Constantinople, chips of marble, splinters of wood, broken tile. The builders never clean up.

"Now here," said Mardonius, peering closely at the map, "should be the famous Nemesis of Pheidias acquired some years ago by the divine Constantine, and thought to be the original, though there are those who maintain it is a copy, but a copy made in the same century, in Parian marble, hence not Roman, hence not corrupt."

Suddenly the door to the charnel house was flung open and two old men ran out into the street, closely pursued by a dozen monks, armed with sticks. The old men got as far as the arcade where we were standing. Then the monks caught them, threw them to the ground and beat them, shouting all the while, "Heretic! Heretic!"

I turned with amazement to Mardonius. "Why are they hurting those men?"

Mardonius sighed. "Because they are heretics."

"Dirty Athanasians?" Gallus, older than I, was already acquainted with most of our new world's superstitions.

"I'm afraid so. We'd better go."

But I was curious. I wanted to know what an Athanasian was.

"Misguided fools who believe that Jesus and God are exactly the same . . ."

"When everybody knows they are only similar," said Gallus.

"Exactly. As Presbyter Arius—who was so much admired by your cousin the divine Emperor—taught us."

"They poisoned Presbyter Arius," said Gallus, already fiercely partisan. He picked up a rock. "Murdering heretics!" he yelled and hurled the stone with unfortunate accuracy at one of the old men. The monks paused in their congenial work to praise Gallus's marksmanship. Mardonius was furious, but only on grounds of rectitude.

"Gallus!" He gave my brother a good shake. "You are a prince, not a street brawler!" Grabbing us each firmly by an arm, Mardonius hurried us away. Needless to say, I was fascinated by all this.

"But surely those old men are harmless."

"Harmless? They murdered Presbyter Arius." Gallus's eyes shone with righteousness.

"Those two? *They* actually murdered him?"

"No," said Mardonius. "But they are followers of Bishop Athanasius . . ."

"The worst heretic that ever lived!" Gallus was always ecstatic when his own need for violence coincided with what others believed to be right action.

21

"And it is thought that Athanasius ordered Arius poisoned at a church council, some seven years ago. As a result, Athanasius was sent into exile by your divine uncle. And now, Julian, I must remind you for what is the hundredth—or is it the thousandth?—time, not to bite your nails."

I stopped biting my nails, a habit which I have not entirely broken myself of even today. "But aren't they all Christians?" I asked. "Don't they believe in Jesus and the gospels?"

"No!" said Gallus.

"Yes," said Mardonius. "They are Christians, too. But they are in error."

Even as a child I had a reasonably logical mind. "But if they are Christians, like us, then we must not fight them but turn the other cheek, and certainly nobody must kill anybody, because Jesus tells us that . . ."

"I'm afraid it is not as simple as all that," said Mardonius. But of course it was. Even a child could see the division between what the Galileans say they believe and what, in fact, they do believe, as demonstrated by their actions. A religion of brotherhood and mildness which daily murders those who disagree with its doctrines can only be thought hypocrite, or worse. Now for the purposes of my memoir it would be convenient to say that at this moment I ceased to be a Galilean. But unfortunately that would not be true. Though I was puzzled by what I had seen, I still believed, and my liberation from the Nazarene was a long time coming. But looking back, I suspect that the first chain was struck from my mind that day in the street when I saw two harmless old men set upon by monks.


In the summer I used to go to my maternal grandmother's estate in Bithynia. It was a small farm two miles from the sea. Just back of the house was a low hill from whose top there was a fine view of the sea of Marmora, while on the horizon's farthest curve to the north rose the towers of Constantinople. Here I spent many hours, reading and dreaming.

One afternoon, lulled by the murmuring of bees, the scent of thyme, the warm salt-laden air, I fell asleep and dreamed that I was having some sort of quarrel with Gallus. I wanted to escape him. So I began to run. As I ran, I took longer and longer steps until I began to bound like a deer. With each leap, I remained higher in the air until at last I was gliding over the countryside while the people below stared with wonder as I sailed over their heads, completely free. There is no dream quite so satisfying as the one of flying.

Suddenly in my pleasant voyage, I was aware that someone was calling my name. I looked about me but there was no one in sight, only pale clouds, blue sky, dark sea. I was gliding over the Marmora, toward Constantinople, when the voice sounded again.

"Who wants me?" I asked.

Then—I don't know how—but I realized that it was the sun who had spoken. Huge and gold above the city, the sun reached out fiery arms to me. And with an astonishingly poignant sense of coming home, I plunged straight into the blazing light. And awakened to find that the setting sun was indeed shining in my face. Dazzled, I got to my feet. I had been overwhelmed by light. I was also bewildered. Something important had happened. But what?

I told no one about this vision. However, some months later when Mardonius and I were alone together in the palace gardens overlooking the Bosphorus, I questioned him about the old religion. I began slyly: was everything Homer wrote true?

"Of course! Every word!"

"Then Zeus and Apollo and all the other gods must exist, because he says they do. And if they are real, then what became of them? Did Jesus destroy them?"

Poor Mardonius! He was a devoted classicist. He was also a Galilean. Like so many in those days, he was hopelessly divided. But he had his answer ready. "You must remember that Christ was not born when Homer lived. Wise as Homer was, there was no way for him to know the ultimate truth that we know. So he was forced to deal with the gods the people had always believed in . . ."

"False gods, according to Jesus, so if they're false then what Homer writes about them can't be true."

"Yet like all things, those gods are *manifestations* of the true." Mardonius shifted his ground. "Homer believed much as we believe. He worshipped the One God, the single principle of the universe. And I suspect he was aware that the One God can take many forms, and that the gods of Olympus are among them. After all, to this day God has many names because we have many languages and traditions, yet *he* is always the same."

23

"What are some of the old names?"

"Zeus, Helios the sun, Serapis . . ."

"The sun." My deity. "Apollo . . ." I began.

"Apollo also had many names, Helios, Companion of Mithras . . ."

"Apollo, Helios, Mithras," I repeated softly. From where we sat in the shady grove on the slope beneath the Daphne Palace, I could just catch a glimpse of my deity, impaled on the dark green bough of a cypress.

"Mithraism was most devilish of all the cults. In fact, there are still some active Mithraists, soldiers mostly, ignorant folk, though a few philosophers (or would-be philosophers) are drawn to Mithras, like Iamblichos . . . I met him once, a remarkably ugly man, a Syrian, from Chalcis, I think, he died a few years ago, much admired by a small circle, but I've always thought his prose unreasonably obscure. He pretended to be a disciple of Plato. And of course he maintained that Jesus was a false prophet and our trinity absurd. Then—utter madness—he invented a trinity of his own, based on Plato."

Carried away by his passion to explain, Mardonius was now hardly conscious of his rapt listener who understood perhaps every other word he spoke. Yet the general sense of what was being said was perfectly clear: Helios was an aspect of the One God, and there were those, like this mysterious Iamblichos, who still worshipped him.

"According to Iamblichos, there are three worlds, three realms of being, each presided over by the One God whose visible aspect is the sun. Now the first of these worlds is the *intelligible* world, which can be comprehended only by reason. You'll find all this in Plato, when we get to him, *if* you get to him at your present rate. The second world is an intermediary one (this is Iamblichos's invention); a world endowed with intelligence and governed by Helios-Mithras, with a number of assistants who turn out to be the old gods in various disguises, particularly Serapis to whom our souls return after death, Dionysos the fair, Hermes the intelligence of the universe, and Asklepios who actually lived, we think, and was a famous physician, worshipped by our ancestors as a savior and healer."

"Like Jesus?"

"Somewhat similar, yes. Finally, the third world is our world, the world of sense and perception. Between the three worlds, the

24

sun mediates. Light is good; darkness evil; and Mithras is the bridge, the link, between man and deity, light and dark. As you can see—or as you will see—only part of this comes from Plato. Most of it is Persian in origin, based on a Persian hero named Mithras who lived, if he lived, a thousand years ago. Fortunately, with the birth of Jesus and the mystery of the trinity all this nonsense ended."

"But the sun still exists."

"To be absolutely precise, at this moment the sun does *not* exist." Mardonius rose. "It's set and we're late for supper."

That is how I became aware of the One God. In a dream Helios-Mithras had called out to me and I had beheld, literally, the light. From that day on, I was no longer alone. The sun was my protector.

I must say that during those years I needed all the solace I could get for I was continually haunted by my predicament. Would I be put to death like my father? One of my recurrent daydreams was that Constantius and I would meet, quite by chance, on my grandmother's hill. In the dream the Emperor was always alone. He was stern but kind. We spoke of literature. He was delighted at my vast knowledge (I liked being praised for my reading). Then we became close friends, and the dream would end with him granting me my freedom to live out the rest of my life on my grandmother's farm, for one look into my eyes had convinced him that I was not worldly, that I wanted neither his throne nor revenge upon him for my father's death. Time and again in my imagination I would convince him with brilliant argument and he would invariably grant my wish, tears in his eyes at my sincerity and lack of guile.

How curious men are! I was indeed sincere at that time. I was exactly as I have described myself. I did not want power, or so I thought. I truly believed that I wanted to live obscurely. And then? I broke Constantius. I took the throne. Knowing this now, were I Constantius and he that dreamy boy on a Bithynian hill, I would have had that young philosopher's life on the spot. But then neither of us realized who I was, or what I would become.

# III

When I was eleven years old, my life again changed abruptly. One morning in May I was doing lessons with Mardonius. I was reciting Hesiod and making a good many mistakes, when Gallus came into the room.

"He's dead. The Bishop's dead. In the church. He died. Just like that!"

Mardonius drew a cross on his chest; so did I. A moment later we were joined by clergy, officials, servants. Everyone was stunned, and alarmed, for it is a great event when the bishop of Constantinople dies, and who succeeds him is a matter of national importance. The emperor—if he is Galilean—always has a hand in the choosing of a successor. But Constantius was a thousand miles away, on the borders of Persia. So for several weeks no bishop was appointed, and no one knew what to do with Gallus and me. Luckily, my uncle Count Julian was in the city, and the day after the funeral he came to see us.

"He's going to kill us, isn't he?" Under stress, Gallus could be reckless.

Count Julian's smile was not very convincing. "Certainly not. After all, you are the heirs of Constantine the Great."

"So was our father," said Gallus grimly. "And all the others."

"But the divine Augustus is your friend."

"Then why are we under arrest?" Gallus indicated the secret police who had arrived only that day; when Gallus and I had tried to go out, we were told politely to stay where we were "until further orders."

"They are for your protection."

"The only protection we need is from Constantius," said Gallus; but he lowered his voice. Though hot-tempered, he was not suicidal. Count Julian looked very nervous.

"That is not true, Gallus. Now listen to me carefully. Someone close to the Emperor, *very* close, has told me that Constantius believes that the reason he cannot have children is because he—because so many members of his own family were—because they, ah, *died!*"

26

"Yes, but since he's already committed enough murders to get him into hell, why stop at us? He has nothing to lose."

"Nothing to gain, either. After all, you are only children."

Gallus snorted. At sixteen he was physically a man, though in character he was still a child, a fierce destructive child.

"Believe me, you are safe." Count Julian was soothing. He was in an excellent mood, for he had just been appointed governor of Egypt, and I am afraid that was more on his mind than the fate of his nephews. But he did his best to comfort us, for which I at least was grateful. He left us with the hollow words, "You have nothing to fear."

When he was gone, Gallus deliberately smashed the cup he had used. Breaking things always gave Gallus physical relief; shattering this particular cup took on ritual significance. "He's like all the rest!" Gallus's voice cracked with anger as he stood there in the bright sun of a green May day, his long pale hair tangled across his brow, his startling blue eyes magnified with sudden tears. "There's no way out of this!"

I tried to say something hopeful but he rounded on me. "You're no loss, you little ape! But why do *I* have to die?" Why indeed? Everyone asks himself that question sooner or later. No one can ever love us quite so much as we love ourselves. Gallus saw no justice in a world where a beauty and vitality such as his could be pinched out as casually as a lamp wick. Of course fate is cruel. But children cannot accept this, nor men like Gallus who see all things as incidental to themselves. I loved Gallus. I hated him. During the first years of my life I was so entirely absorbed by him that I was hardly aware of myself at all except as I was reflected in those vivid blue eyes, which saw nothing of me nor much of anything else.

But Count Julian was right. Constantius *did* suffer remorse for his crimes. We were safe, for the time being. In due course a message arrived from the Chamberlain Eusebius. Gallus and I were to be sent to Macellum in Cappadocia "to continue your education."

"Education for *what*?" asked Gallus when this message had been read us. But Mardonius silenced him. "The Augustus is merciful. Never forget that he is now your father as well as your lord."

We departed for Macellum that same day. I was most upset, for Mardonius was not to accompany us. I don't know the motive

27

behind this act of petty cruelty except that as the Chamberlain Eusebius was also a eunuch and he might have thought that a fellow eunuch would prove to be too subtle an ally for us. Sniffling wretchedly, I was bundled into a wagon with Gallus.

Mardonius was also grief-stricken but he controlled himself. "We shall meet again," he said. "And when we do, I shall expect Gallus to know as much Hesiod as Julian." Mardonius stood stiffly in front of the bishop's palace as we drove off, escorted by a cohort of cavalry, just as if we were important princes, which we were, or important prisoners, which we also were. I sobbed. Gallus swore fierce oaths under his breath. In the street a crowd of people were gathered, eager for a glimpse of us. To get a close view one bold burgher thrust his head over the side of the wagon. Gallus promptly spat in the man's astonished face. Then Gallus covered his head with his cloak and would not take it off until we were outside the city gate. No one expected to see us alive again.

All travelers agree that Macellum is one of the beautiful places of the world. I hate it to this day. Macellum is not a town but an imperial residence originally used by the ancient Cappadocian kings as a hunting lodge. Constantine enlarged it so that it is now a complex of many buildings set in lonely woods at the foot of Mount Argaeus, some four hundred miles southeast of Constantinople. When Constantius inherited the principate, he acquired the lodge, along with a number of other properties in the neighborhood; in fact, our family's private income derives almost entirely form the Cappadocian crown lands.

Tonight when I was telling Priscus about my childhood, he said that it sounded enviable. "After all, you lived in a palace, with gardens, baths, fountains, a private chapel," he enjoys teasing me, "in the very best hunting country with nothing to do but read. You had the perfect life." Well, it was not perfect. Gallus and I might just as well have been hostages in a Persian prison. We had no one to talk to, except for a series of schoolmasters from nearby Caesarea. None stayed with us very long because of Gallus. He could not resist tormenting them. He got on better with our jailers, particularly the young officers. Gallus could be very winning when he wanted to be, and he soon had them training him in the use of sword and spear, shield and axe. Gallus was a natural athlete, with a gift for weaponry. I would have liked to practise with him but he preferred to keep his military companions to himself. "You

28

read your books," he said sharply. "I'm the one who's to be a soldier." So I read my books.

We were nominally in the charge of Bishop George of Cappadocia who lived at Caesarea. He visited us at least once a month, and it was he who insisted that our education be essentially Galilean. "Because there is no reason why *you* should not be a priest." He pointed a long finger at me. He was a small thin man whose lean face always looked in need of shaving.

While I was respectfully trying to think of a number of reasons why I should *not* become a priest, Gallus with an engaging smile said, "Julian dreams of the priesthood, Bishop. It's his whole life. He does nothing but read."

"I was that way myself at your age." Bishop George looked pleased at finding this likeness.

"But I read philosophy . . ." I began.

"So do we all, of course. But then we come to the story of Jesus which is the beginning and the end of knowledge. But I am sure you have had a good training already from your late cousin, my old friend, the Bishop Eusebius. Those of us who are *true* Christians miss him greatly." Bishop George began to pace up and down the room, snapping his fingers, a characteristic habit. Gallus grinned at me, very pleased with what he had done.

Bishop George suddenly spun round; the long finger was again pointed at me.

"*Homoiousios*. What does that mean?"

I knew. I rattled my answer like a crow taught to speak. "It means that Jesus the son is of *similar* substance to God the father."

"*Homoousios*. What does that mean?"

"That Jesus the son is of *one* substance with God the father."

"The difference?"

"In the first case, Jesus was created by the father *before* this world began. He is God's son by grace but *not* by nature."

"Why?"

"Because God is one. By definition singular. God cannot be many, as the late Presbyter Arius maintained at the council of Nicaea."

"Excellent." I received a series of finger-snappings as applause. "Now in the second case?"

"*Homoousios* is that pernicious doctrine"—I had been well-drilled by old Eusebius—"which maintains that the father and the son and the holy spirit are one and the same."

"Which cannot be!"

"Which cannot be," I chirruped obediently.

"Despite what happened at Nicaea."

"Where in the year 325 Bishop Athanasius of Alexandria..."

"A mere deacon at the time..."

"Opposed my cousin Bishop Eusebius as well as Presbyter Arius, and forced the council to accept the Athanasian doctrine that the father, son and holy spirit are one."

"*But* the battle is far from over. We are gaining ground every year. Our wise Augustus believes as we believe, as the late Presbyter Arius believed. Two years ago at Antioch we Eastern bishops met to support the true doctrine. This year we shall meet again at Sardica and, with the Emperor's aid, the true believers shall once and for all destroy the doctrine of Athanasius. My son, you are to be a priest. I can tell. You have the mark. You will be a great force in the church. Tomorrow I shall send you one of my deacons. He will give you religious instruction, both of you."

"But I'm to be a soldier," said Gallus, alarmed.

"A God-fearing soldier has the strength of twenty," said Bishop George automatically. "Besides, religious training will do you no harm." And curiously enough, it was Gallus who became the devout Galilean while I, as the world knows, returned to the old ways.

But at that time I was hardly a philosopher. I studied what I was told to study. The deacon who gave me instruction was most complimentary. "You have an extraordinary gift for analysis," he said one day when I was exploring with him John 14:25, the text on which the Arians base their case against the Athanasians. "You will have a distinguished future, I am sure."

"As a bishop?"

"Of course you will be a bishop since you are imperial. But there is something even more splendid than a bishop."

"A martyr?"

"Martyr and saint. You have the look of one."

I must say my boyish vanity was piqued. Largely because of this flattery, for several months I was confident that I had been especially chosen to save the world from error. Which, in a way, turned out to be true, to the horror of my early teachers.

Bishop George was an arrogant and difficult man but I got on with him, largely because he was interested in me. He was a devoted controversialist. Finding me passably intelligent, he saw

30

his opportunity. If I could be turned into a bishop, I would be a powerful ally for the Arians, who were already outnumbered by the Athanasians, despite the considerable help given them by Constantius. Today, of course, the "pernicious" doctrine of the three-in-one God has almost entirely prevailed, due to the efforts of Bishop Athanasius. Constantius alone kept the two parties in any sort of balance. Now that he is dead the victory of the Athanasians is only a matter of time. But today none of this matters since the Galileans are now but one of a number of religious sects, and by no means the largest. Their days of domination are over. Not only have I forbidden them to persecute us Hellenists; I have forbidden them to persecute one another. They find me intolerably cruel!"

Was I a true Galilean in those years at Macellum? There has been much speculation about this. I often wonder myself. The answer is not clear even to me. For a long time I believed what I was taught. I accepted the Arian thesis that the One God (whose existence we all accept) mysteriously produced a sort of son who was born a Jew, became a teacher, and was finally executed by the state for reasons which were never entirely clear to me, despite the best efforts of Bishop George to instruct me. But while I was studying the life of the Galilean I was also reading Plato, who was far more to my taste. After all, I was something of a literary snob. I had been taught the best Greek by Mardonius. I could not help but compare the barbarous back-country language of Matthew, Mark, Luke and John to the clear prose of Plato. Yet I accepted the Galilean legend as truth. After all, it was the religion of my family, and though I did not find it attractive I was unaware of any alternative until one afternoon when I was about fourteen. I had been sitting for two hours listening to the deacon sing me the songs of Presbyter Arius . . . yes, that great religious thinker wrote popular songs in order to influence the illiterate. To this day I can recall the words of half a dozen of his inane ballads which "proved" that the son was the son and the father was the father. Finally, the deacon finished; I praised his singing.

"It is the spirit which matters, not the voice," said the deacon, pleased with my compliment. Then—I don't know how it happened—Plotinus was mentioned. He was only a name to me. He was anathema to the deacon. "A would-be philosopher of the last century. A follower of Plato, or so he claimed. An enemy of the church, though there are some Christians who are foolish enough to regard him highly. He lived at Rome. He was a favorite of the

31

Emperor Gordian. He wrote six quite unintelligible books which his disciple Porphyry edited."

"Porphyry?" As though it were yesterday, I can remember hearing that name for the first time, seated opposite the angular deacon in one of the gardens at Macellum, high summer flowering all about us and the day hazy with heat.

"Even worse than Plotinus! Porphyry came from Tyre. He studied at Athens. He called himself a philosopher but of course he was merely an atheist. He attacked the church in fifteen volumes."

"On what grounds?"

"How should I know? I have never read his books. No Christian ought." The deacon was firm.

"But surely this Porphyry must have had *some* cause . . ."

"The devil entered him. That is cause enough."

By then I knew that I must read Plotinus and Porphyry. I wrote Bishop George a most politic letter, asking him to lend me the books of these "incorrigible" men. I wished to see, I said, the face of the enemy plain, and naturally I turned to the Bishop for guidance, not only because he was my religious mentor but because he had the best library in Cappadocia. I rather laid it on.

To my astonishment Bishop George immediately sent me the complete works of Plotinus as well as Porphyry's attack on Christianity. "Young as you are, I am sure that you will appreciate the folly of Porphyry. He was an intelligent man misled by a bad character. My predecessor, as bishop of Caesarea, wrote a splendid refutation of Porphyry, answering for all time the so-called 'inconsistencies' Porphyry claimed to have detected in scriptures. I am sending you the Bishop's works, too. I cannot tell you how pleased I am at the interest you are showing in sacred matters." What the good Bishop did not know was that the arguments of Porphyry were to form the basis for my own rejection of the Nazarene.

That same summer, Bishop George suggested that Gallus and I build a chapel at Macellum to be dedicated to Saint Mammas, a local shepherd whose remains were considered particularly potent: skin diseases were promptly cured by applying the saint's shinbone to the afflicted area. Bishop George thought it would be an inspiring gesture if Gallus and I were to build a charnel house for these scraps of dead shepherd. So all one summer Gallus and I worked on this project. I enjoyed laying brick. But Gallus hated prolonged effort of any kind, and I'm afraid he spent a good deal of time cursing Saint Mammas as we sweated in the sun. Shortly after we completed the chapel, the roof fell in. I am told that the Galileans now say that only *my* section of the building collapsed, because I was apostate. This is not true. The *whole* thing collapsed—because of faulty design.

At that time I neither believed nor disbelieved. Yet Porphyry's eloquent case against the Nazarene was now lodged in my head. When I tried to argue doctrinal points with Bishop George, I was swiftly discouraged with this sort of thing: "The very idea of the trinity is a mystery. Only through faith can it be understood, and then never entirely." I much preferred Plotinus, who four times in five years achieved that total consciousness of the One which is the ultimate goal of all religious practice. Despite Porphyry's wisdom, he experienced this heightened consciousness only once, at the age of sixty-eight. So far I have experienced it twice. I pray each day for yet another revelation.

Gallus and I had neither friends nor allies. Except for his dogged attempts to make me a priest, Bishop George showed no personal interest in either of us. Everyone else at Macellum treated us with nervous respect. We alarmed people; we reminded them of murder; we were such obvious victims.

I kept to my reading. I took little exercise though I was naturally strong, particularly in the arms. Gallus continued to surpass me at all games and physical feats. He was taller than I, beautifully made, with the face of a god. The soldiers assigned to guard us were infatuated with him, and he flirted shamelessly with them. They took him hunting whenever he chose and I suppose that he had affairs with some of them, though we were both involved much of the time with the same girl—or rather woman. She was the twenty-five-year-old wife of a civil servant who acted as comptroller to our household. She seduced me first, then Gallus. She was insatiable. Her husband was amenable; not that he had any choice. He used to giggle uncontrollably whenever he saw either of us. He was fat and small, and I remember asking her how she could bear to be touched by him.

"He has gifts," she said slyly. I can still recall how her black hair glistened as it fell over bare brown shoulders. Never before or since have I felt such smooth skin. I suppose she oiled herself but if she did she was an artist at it, for one's fingers never came

33

away thick with perfumed grease as happens so often with women of her sort. She was Antiochene. What else? Lovemaking is the only art the people of Antioch have ever taken seriously. She affected to find me attractive, but it was the golden Gallus who really enchanted her. He used to tell me with pride how "she does everything and I don't move." His passivity was baffling. But then I never undersood Gallus. Later when he turned monster, I was not surprised. He could have been anything at all because at heart he was nothing. Yet when he was in a room, all eyes watched him, for he was physically fascinating; men and women were equally attracted to him and since he felt nothing for anyone, every woman saw him as a challenge who must be made to love. So Gallus was able to take his pleasure as he chose . . . while hardly moving!

The Syrian woman was mistress to us both for three years. Though I am now celibate, I often think of her, especially at night. Where is she now? I don't dare inquire. She is probably fat and old, living in some provincial town and paying youths to sleep with her. But for a thousand days she was Aphrodite to my Adonis.

# IV

Five years passed. Little news of the outside world came to us. Sapor, the Great King of Persia, threatened our Eastern border, while the Germans infiltrated Gaul. That was all we knew. Politics was a forbidden subject. I studied Homer and Hesiod; read Plotinus and Porphyry; made love to the Antiochene; fought with Gallus, until one day I outwrestled him and he never challenged me again. He was a coward except when he was in a rage; then he would do anything.

As long as I could read, I was never entirely wretched. But I did long to see more of the world than Macellum. It is most unnatural for a youth to be brought up entirely by soldiers and slaves, none of whom dares to be fond of him. Gallus and I had each other for company but we were not true brothers in any but the family sense—and only *half*-brothers at that, for we had different mothers. We were like two potentially hostile animals in the same cage. Yet I was ravished by his beauty, and impressed by his energy. Gallus was always doing something which I wanted

34

to imitate. Sometimes he let me, but more often not, for he enjoyed tormenting me. It gave him particular pleasure to quarrel with me just before we were to go hunting. Then he could exclaim, "All right! You stay home. This is a day for men." And the soldiers would laugh at me and I would flee while the exuberant Gallus would ride forth to hunt, as dogs barked and horns sounded through the dark green woods. But when I was allowed to go with him, I was close to ecstasy.

One September afternoon Bishop George arrived unexpectedly at Macellum. We had not seen him for some months, because, according to the deacon, "It looks as though—now don't repeat a word of this!" (as if we two prisoners had anyone to confide in)—"Bishop George will be raised to the sea of Alexandria. Bishop Athanasius holds Alexandria only because the Emperor Constans of the West insisted upon it. But now the Emperor Constantius is arranging for Athanasius to be exiled again and if he is, *we* go to Alexandria!" The deacon was exalted at the thought.

But Bishop George said nothing to us about church politics when we joined him in the main hall of the hunting lodge. He had other, greater news. His sallow face was dark with excitement while his fingers snapped a sharp continuous accompaniment to his words, "The divine Augustus will visit you in ten days' time. He is on his way home from Antioch. He is making this side trip for the express purpose of seeing the two of you." I was too frightened to speak. It was Gallus who asked, "What does he want?"

The Bishop was impatient. "He is your cousin. Your guardian. Your emperor. He wants to see you. What else? To see what sort of men you've grown into. To see the result of your education. Now he will be particularly interested in your religious training. Therefore, I shall stay here until he arrives. We will review everything I have tried to teach you. This will mean, Gallus, a great deal of work for *you*. I suggest you put your mind to it, since your entire future may depend on the impression you make." And so does *yours*, Bishop, I remember thinking to myself, eager to include anyone I could in what I was certain would prove to be a harsh fate.

We studied hard. For hours on end the Bishop drilled us mercilessly. Fortunately I have an excellent memory and can learn—though not always understand!—a page at a glance. Between lessons, we tried to find out all that we could about Constantius's mood. Was he favorably disposed toward us? Were we to remain at Macellum? But the Bishop gave us no comfort. "The divine Augustus will do what is best, as he always does. You have nothing to fear, *if* you are loyal and obedient." But of course we had everything to fear. I did not sleep one night through during that time of waiting.

The day before Constantius was due to arrive, the imperial court came to Macellum. Some of the court had been with Constantius at Antioch; but most came directly from the Sacred Palace at Constantinople. All the chief officers of the state were to be lodged in the villa, while in the surrounding fields a hundred tents were pitched to accommodate the thousand clerks and notaries who conduct the business of the government.

At dawn the pageant began. Gallus and I stationed ourselves in the courtyard of the palace and gaped like two bumpkins. Neither of us had ever seen an imperial progress before, and in the general excitement and dazzle of that frosty autumn day we momentarily forgot our terror.

Bishop George stood in the doorway of the villa. He wore a jeweled chasuble, and held a silver crosier in one hand. To his left and right the military garrison of Macellum stood at attention to honor the great magnates of the Roman Empire. Some arrived on horseback, others in litters. Each was accompanied by a retinue of soldiers, clerks, eunuchs, slaves. All wore some variation of military dress, for ever since Diocletian the court has been military in its appearance, symbolic of Rome's beleaguered state.

The courtyard was soon crowded with clerks and slaves, horses and mules; only the area just in front of the door was kept clear. After each official dismounted, he would cross to the doorway, where Bishop George would then greet him with all his titles. The Bishop was a master of protocol. He knew exactly who everyone was and how he should be addressed, an enviable gift, since nowadays there are hundreds of subtle titles and distinctions. Highest in rank are the *clarissimi*. They include the two consuls for the year, all former consuls, the praetorian prefects, much of the senate. Next are the officials who are called *spectabiles*. Then the heads of government departments who are called *illustres*. But it is not easy to keep straight who is what, since an important minister of state like the quaestor (the emperor's legal adviser) is only an *illustris*, while the governor of an insignificant province may be a *clarissimus*. Also, the matter of the counts is confusing. In the old days, "count" was simply a courtesy title for any official or high-ranking officer who traveled in the emperor's entourage. But Constantine, with his Persian sense of hierarchy, made the title "count" a reward for important service. So some counts are *clarissimi* while others are merely *spectabiles*. It is amazing how obsessed otherwise sensible people are by these foolish titles. I have sat for hours in the company of grown men who could discuss nothing but who held what title and why he was unworthy of it. Yet a wise emperor can exert considerable pressure on ambitious men by the giving or withholding of these empty titles. Constantius was a master at this sort of thing. Unfortunately, since I find it hard to remember who is what, I call nearly everyone "my dear fellow," in imitation of Plato. This scandalizes the dignified.

First to arrive was the Count of the Sacred Largesse. It is his task to see that each province pays its taxes promptly on the first of every March. He also administers the government's salt monopoly and the provincial banks, as well as all state-owned factories, mines, and of course the mint. He is never a popular official, but he dies rich. He was followed by the Count of the Privy Purse, who administers the personal property of the imperial family. This official was accompanied by twenty slaves carrying chests of dark wood studded with metal; they contained the large sums of gold and silver the emperor must always travel with. Since Privy Purse is responsible for every coin, he tends to be a nervous, distracted figure, forever counting boxes. Next, the Count of the East, who governs Syria and Mesopotamia. Then the Master of the Offices, a very great man indeed. He administers the state transportation system and post; he is the head of the bureau of secret agents; he commands the palace guard; he arranges for audiences with the Emperor. Bishop George bowed particularly low to him.

For six years Gallus and I had seen no one except Bishop George and our guards. Now all at once there passed before us the whole power of the state. Our eyes were dazzled by glittering armor and elaborate cloaks, by the din of a thousand clerks and notaries who scurried about the courtyard, demanding their baggage, quarreling with one another, insisting on various prerogatives. These noisy clerks with their inky fingers and proud intelligent faces were the actual government of Rome, and they knew it.

The last official to arrive was the most important of all: the Grand Chamberlain of the Sacred Palace, the eunuch Eusebius. He was so large that it took two slaves to pull him out of his ivory and gold litter. He was tall, stout and very white. Beneath the peacock blue of his silk tunic one could see the rolls of flesh quiver as he moved. Of all the officers of state, only he wore civilian clothes. In fact, he looked like a winsome lady of fashion with mouth artfully rouged and hair arranged in long oiled ringlets. The gold thread of his cape flashed in the sunlight.

Eusebius looked about him with sharp eyes, and I knew suddenly that he was looking for us. Half hidden by a mound of saddlebags, Gallus and I tried to become invisible but though the Chamberlain had never seen either of us before, he knew immediately who we were. Gracefully, he motioned for us to join him. Like slaves anticipating a beating, we shuffled forward. Since we were not certain as to how to greet him, I attempted a military salute, which Gallus imitated. Eusebius smiled a tiny smile, exposing small dark teeth; several babyish dimples appeared in his full cheeks. He inclined his head; the neck fat creased; a long curl strayed across his brow.

"*Nobilissimi*," he said in a soft voice. This was an excellent omen. The title *nobilissimus* is used only for members of the imperial family. Bishop George never used this title with us nor did our guards. Now, apparently, our rank had been restored.

After a long scrutiny, Eusebius took each of us by a hand. I can still recall the soft dampness of his touch. "I have so looked forward to seeing you both! And how grown up you are! Especially the noble Gallus." Delicately he felt Gallus's chest. This sort of impertinence would ordinarily have sent my brother into a rage, but that day he was far too frightened. He also knew instinctively that his only protection was his beauty. Complaisantly he allowed the eunuch to caress him as we entered the villa.

Eusebius had the most beguiling voice and manner of anyone I have ever known. I should say something here about the voices of eunuchs. Actors and other people who try to mimic them invariably tend to pitch their voices high, and screech. Eunuchs seldom sound like that. If they did, who would ever find their company tolerable? And at a court one must be particularly pleasing in one's manners. In actual fact, the voice of a eunuch is like that of a particularly gentle child, and this appeals to the parent in both men and women. Thus subtly do they disarm us, for we tend to indulge them as we would a child, forgetting that their minds are as mature and twisted as their bodies are lacking. Eusebius spun his web about Gallus. He did not bother with me. I was too young.

Gallus and Eusebius dined alone together that night. The next day Gallus was Eusebius's devoted admirer. "He's also a friend," said Gallus. We were alone together in the baths. "He told me how he'd been getting reports about me for years. He knows everything I've ever done. He even knows about *her*." Gallus named the Antiochene, and giggled. "Eusebius says I'll be a great success at court. Not only am I good-looking but I have a well-developed intelligence, those are his exact words. He's positive he can talk the Emperor into letting me go free. He says it may take a little time but that he has some small influence with His Eternity, that's exactly how he put it. He's very interesting, though it's hard sometimes to figure out what he's talking about. He expects you to know all sorts of things you wouldn't have any way of knowing, buried in this damned place. Anyway Constantius does just as Eusebius tells him. Everyone says so. Which means if you have Eusebius on your side, that's half the battle. And I've got him."

"What did he say about me?" I asked. Gallus seldom strayed very far from his essential interest: himself.

"You? Why should he say anything about you?" Gallus ducked me in the cold pool. I pulled him in after me. He was slippery as a fish, but I managed to hold his head under water for a satisfactory length of time. At sixteen I was as strong as he was at twenty-one. He emerged sputtering and blue in the face. "He's going to make a monk out of you, that's what. Though if I have anything to say about it, you'll be a eunuch." He tried to kick me between the legs but slipped on the marble and fell. He cursed loudly, and I laughed. Then we were joined by slaves who helped us dress. Since Gallus was a man, the Master of the Offices had ruled that although he was not technically an officer, he could on this occasion wear the uniform of the household troops. Unfortunately, the *nobilissimus* Julian was merely a student and must dress accordingly. As a result, I looked quite insignificant beside my glittering half-brother. But I was perfectly happy to go unnoticed. Let Gallus shine. I preferred obscurity, and survival.

Constantius had arrived at noon and gone straight to his apartments. That was all anyone knew. He might be with us in a few minutes, a few hours, or not at all. Meanwhile, we waited nervously in the great hall of the villa. The rafters were hung with boughs of evergreen, and the ordinarily musty interior smelled of pine and eucalyptus. At one end of the hall, on a dais, a gold

39

throne had been set. To the right of the throne, but at floor level, was the ivory chair of the praetorian prefect of the East (he had arrived with the Emperor). According to rank, the officers of the state were arranged to the left and right of the throne. Just at the foot of the dais stood Bishop George in all his glory with Gallus on his right and me on his left.

Looking more than ever like a huge peacock, Eusebius stood at the door, surrounded by his staff of ushers. No one spoke or moved. We were like statues. Though the room was not hot, I was sweating nervously. I glanced at Gallus out of the corner of my eye; his mouth was twitching from the strain.

After what seemed days, we heard trumpets. Then the cry "Augustus!" which always precedes an emperor began, at first far off and faint; then closer, louder: "Augustus! Augustus!" My legs began to tremble. I was afraid I might be sick. Suddenly with a crash the double doors were flung open and there in the doorway stood Flavius Julius Constantius, Augustus of the East. With a gentle moan, Eusebius embraced Constantius's knees, melodiously murmuring soft words of ceremony not audible to the rest of us who were now prostrate, as the Lord of the World slowly and with extraordinary dignity crossed the room to his throne. I was too busy studying the mosaic floor to get even a glimpse of my imperial cousin. Not until the Master of the Offices gave the signal for everyone to rise was I able at last to observe my father's murderer.

Constantius was a man of overwhelming dignity. That was the most remarkable thing about him; even his most ordinary gestures seemed carefully rehearsed. Like the Emperor Augustus, he wore lifts in his sandals to make himself appear tall. He was clean-shaven, with large melancholy eyes. He had his father Constantine's large nose and thin, somewhat peevish mouth. The upper part of his body was impressively muscular but his legs were dwarfish. He wore the purple, a heavy robe which hung from shoulder to heel; on his head was a fillet of silver set with pearls.

Constantius sat very still on his throne as the Master of the Offices brought him Bishop George, who welcomed him to Macellum. Not once did the Emperor look at Gallus or me. The occasional ritual responses he made were said in such a low voice that none of us could make out the words.

Then the moment came. Bishop George led Gallus and me to the Master of the Offices, who in turn led us up to the dais and presented us formally to the Emperor. I was terrified. Without knowing how I got there, I found myself embracing Constantius' knees, as court etiquette requires.

From far off I heard the Emperor's voice, measured but rather higher-pitched than I had expected, "We are pleased to receive our most noble cousin Julian." A large callused hand reached down, gripped me firmly by the left elbow and helped me to rise.

For an instant I was so close to Constantius that I could make out every pore in his face, which was sunburned dark as a Persian's. I noticed the silkiness of his straight brown hair, only just beginning to turn gray. He was thirty-two, but I thought him ancient. I also remember thinking: what must it be like to be Emperor of Rome? to know that one's face on coins, on monuments, painted and sculptured, is known to all the world? And here—so close to me that I could feel the reciprocal warmth of his skin—was the original of that world-famous face, not bronze or marble but soft flesh and bone, like me, like any other man. And I wondered: what *is* it like to be the center of the world?

For the first time I experienced ambition. It came as a revelation. Only in communication with the One God have I known anything to equal it. How candid I am! I have never admitted to anyone that in my first encounter with Constantius, all that I could think was how much *I* should like the dominion of this earth! But my moment of madness was brief. I stammered a speech of loyalty, and took my place beside Gallus on the dais. I can remember nothing else that happened that day.

Constantius remained at Macellum for a week. He attended to the business of the state. He hunted. Bishop George had a long interview with him on the day he arrived, but then, to the Bishop's chagrin, Constantius ignored him. Though Gallus and I dined at the Emperor's table every evening, he never spoke to us.

I was beginning to fear the worst. But Gallus, who saw Eusebius every day said that the eunuch was optimistic. "He's positive we'll be allowed to come to court this year. At least I will. He also said there was talk in the Sacred Consistory that I be made Caesar for the East." Gallus glowed with excitement. "Then I could live at Antioch. I'd have my own court. After all, it's what one was born for!"

Gallus made a good impression on everyone—somewhat to my surprise, for he was always rather sullen with Bishop George and downright cruel to me and his teachers. But set among the great officers of the state, he was a different person. He laughed;

41

he flattered; he charmed. He was a natural courtier, and one by one he enchanted the members of the Sacred Consistory, as the Emperor's council is known. Only with Constantius did he make no headway. Our cousin was biding his time.

During the time the court was at Macellum, the junior officers and lesser officials dined in the main hall of the palace, while the Emperor and the magnates dined in the banqueting hall, which was somewhat smaller. In the hour before dinner everyone used to gather in the main hall to gossip. It was our first experience of a court. I found it bewildering, but Gallus took to it like a swan to water.

One evening Gallus allowed me to tag after him as he moved through that splendid company. Gallus was an excellent politician. He made friends not just with the magnates but also with the clerks and notaries who do the actual work of governing. He was shrewd. I of course was perfectly tongue-tied.

In the large hall, Gallus quickly gravitated to the group of officers with whom he had only that day gone hunting. I remember looking at these young men with wonder, for they had actually killed other men in battle in such faraway places as Germany and Mesopotamia. They were unusually self-contained and rather quiet, unlike the clerks and notaries, who were exceedingly talkative, eager to impress one with their knowledge of secret matters.

Gallus seemed particularly to like one tribune, an officer in his thirties named Victor (who is now one of my generals). Victor was—is—an impressive-looking man who speaks good Greek, though he comes from the Black Sea; he is bandy-legged and pale-eyed like so many Sarmatians. "Is this the most noble Julian?" he asked, turning to me.

Gallus introduced me in an offhand way to the company. I blushed and said nothing.

"Will you be serving with us in the household troops?" Victor asked.

Gallus answered for me. "No. He's going to be a priest."

Before I could deny this, Victor said quite seriously, "I can think of no life worthier than one in the service of God." I was struck by the simplicity with which he said this. No irony was intended.

Gallus was somewhat taken aback. "Not for me," he said finally.

"Nor for me, unfortunately," Victor gave me a sympathetic smile. "You must pray for us," he said.

42

Gallus changed the subject. While he talked hunting with Victor, I stood by silently, beginning to feel already like one of those Galilean monks or "solitaries" as they are called, which is rather a misnomer since no monk is ever solitary. They are the most gregarious set of men in the world, forever eating, guzzling and gossiping with one another. Most of them retire from the world in order to have a continuous party.

"Are you really going to become a priest?" The voice was low. I turned and saw a young man standing behind me. He had obviously been there for some time. I shook my head. "No," I said.

"Good." He smiled. He had sharp gray eyes beneath brows which met, giving him the look of one continually concentrating on some distant object. He wore civilian clothes, which was odd since at his age anyone of good family wears uniform at court.

"Who are you?" I asked.

"Oribasius of Pergamon, physician to the divine Augustus, who doesn't need me. Your cousin is the healthiest man I've ever met."

"I am happy to hear that!" I blazed sincerely. One's neck depended on this sort of response.

"It's a matter of diet," said Oribasius matter-of-factly. "He's a perfect example of the moderate life. He drinks almost no wine. He never overeats. He'll live forever."

"I pray that he does," I said, my heart sinking. What would *my* life be like, lived in the shadow of a never-dying, always suspicious Constantius?

"But why does your brother say you're going to be a priest?"

"Because I read books. He finds that strange."

"And he associates strangeness with the priesthood?"

I tried not to smile. "Something like that. But I should like to be a philosopher or a rhetorician. Apparently I have no gift for soldiering. At least Gallus says I haven't. But then, everything depends on the will of the divine Augustus."

"Yes," said Oribasius. He looked at me curiously. I recognized the look. I had seen it all my life. It meant: Are they going to kill this boy? And if they do, how interesting it all is! From birth I had been treated like a character in a tragic play.

"Do you like Macellum?"

"Would you, if you were me?" I had not meant to say this. But his look had irritated me and I suddenly rebelled at being treated like a mere thing, a victim, the dumb sacrifice in a bloody legend.

"No," said Oribasius evenly. "I would not."

"Well, then, you know how it is." But frightened now that I had said too much, I began to babble about the goodness of my cousin, the kindness of Bishop George, the beauty of Cappadocia. For all I knew, Oribasius was a secret agent. Luckily, one of the chamberlains came to announce the approach of the Emperor, and I hurriedly left the main hall and took my place at table.

I have recorded this meeting with Oribasius, since he was to become my closest friend. But I did not see him again at Macellum or, if I did, I don't remember him. He has told me since, "I've never seen anyone look so frightened as you."

When I told him that *my* memory of myself in those days was one of serene self-control, Oribasius laughed. "I was positive you were on the verge of madness. I even diagnosed you—incorrectly—as an epileptic."

"And what did you think of Gallus?"

"He was the one who appeared serene. I was quite impressed."

"And of course Gallus went mad."

"I don't claim to be infallible."

People never make the impression they think they make. But Oribasius was quite right in one thing: I *was* terrified.


My interview with Constantius occurred on the last day of his visit. Bishop George spent the morning coaching us in what to say. He was as nervous as we were; his career was at stake, too.

Gallus was admitted first to the sacred presence. During the half hour he was with the Emperor, I recall praying to every deity I could think of; even then I was eclectic!

At last the Master of the Offices, gorgeous in court robes, came to fetch me. He looked like an executioner. Bishop George rattled out a blessing. The Master gave me instructions in how I was to salute the Emperor and which formula of greeting I was to use. I muttered them over and over to myself as I swam—that was my exact sensation—into the presence of the Augustus.

Constantius was seated on an ordinary chair in the apse of the hall. Eusebius stood beside him, holding a sheaf of documents. On a stool at Constantius's feet sat Gallus, looking well-pleased with himself.

I went through the formula of homage, the words falling without thought from my lips. Constantius gave me a long, shrewd, curious look. Then he did not look at me again during the course of the interview. He was one of those men who could never look another in the eye. Nor should this characteristic be taken, necessarily, as a sign of weakness or bad conscience. I am rather like Constantius in this. I have always had difficulty looking into men's eyes. All rulers must. Why? Because of what we see: self-interest, greed, fear. It is not a pleasant sensation to know that merely by existing one inspires animal terror in others. Constantius was often evil in his actions but he took no pleasure in the pain of others. He was not a Caligula, nor a Gallus.

Constantius spoke to me rapidly and impersonally. "We have received heartening reports concerning the education of our most noble cousin Julian. Bishop George tells us that it is your wish to prepare for the priesthood." He paused, not so much to hear what I might say as to give proper weight to what he intended to say next. As it was, I was speechless.

Constantius continued, "You must know that your desire to serve God is pleasing to us. It is not usual for princes to remove themselves from the world, but then it is not usual for any man to be called by heaven." I suddenly saw with perfect clarity the prison I was to occupy. Deftly, Constantius spun his web. No priest could threaten him. I would be a priest. "Bishop George tells me that you have pondered deeply the disputes which— sadly—divide holy church. And he assures me that in your study of sacred matters you have seen the truth and believe, as all Christians ought, that the son is of like substance to the father, though not of the same substance. Naturally, as one of our family, you may not live as an ordinary holy man; responsibilities will be thrust upon you. For this reason your education must be continued at Constantinople. You are already a reader in the church. In Constantinople you can hope to become ordained, which will give us pleasure, as well as making you most pleasing to God who has summoned you to serve him. And so we salute our cousin and find him a worthy descendant of Claudius Gothicus, the founder of our house." That was all. Constantius gave me his hand to kiss. I never said a word beyond those required by court ceremonial. As I backed out of the room, I saw Gallus smile at Eusebius.

I wonder now what Constantius was thinking. I suspect that even then I may have puzzled him. Gallus was easily comprehended. But who was this silent youth who wanted to become a priest? I had planned to say all sorts of things to Constantius, but he had given me no opportunity. Surprisingly enough, he was nervous with everyone. He could hardly speak, except when he was able to speak, as it were, from the throne. Excepting his wife, Eusebia, and the Grand Chamberlain, he had no confidants. He was a curious man. Now that I am in his place I have more sympathy for him than I did, though no liking. His suspicious nature was obviously made worse by the fact that he was somewhat less intelligent than those he had to deal with. This added to his unease and made him humanly inaccessible. As a student he had failed rhetoric simply through slowness of mind. Later he took to writing poetry, which embarrassed everyone. His only "intellectual" exercise was Galilean disputes. I am told that he was quite good at this sort of thing, but any village quibbler can make a name for himself at a Galilean synod. Look at Athanasius!

I was relieved by this interview. Of course I did not want to become a priest, though if that were the price I had to pay for my life I was perfectly willing to pay it.

In a blaze of pageantry, Constantius departed. Gallus, Bishop George and I stood in the courtyard as he rode past. Mounted, he looked splendid and tall in his armor of chased gold. He acknowledged no one as he rode out of Macellum. In his cold way he was most impressive, and I still envy him his majesty. He could stand for hours in public looking neither to left nor right, motionless as a statue, which is what our ceremonial requires. It was the Emperor Diocletian who decided that we should become, in effect, if not in title, Asiatic kings, to be displayed on rare occasions like the gilded effigies of gods. Diocletian's motive was understandable, perhaps inevitable, for in the last century emperors were made and unmade frivolously, at the whim of the army. Diocletian felt that if it were to be set apart, made sacred in the eyes of the people and hedged round by awe-inspiring ritual, the army would have less occasion to treat us with easy contempt. To a certain extent, this policy has worked. Yet today whenever I ride forth in state and observe the awe in the faces of the people, an awe inspired not by me but by the theatricality of the occasion, I feel a perfect impostor and want to throw off my weight of gold and shout, "Do you want a statue or a man?" I don't, of course, because they would promptly reply, "A statue!"

As we watched the long procession make its way from the villa to the main highway, Gallus suddenly exclaimed, "What I'd give to go with them!"

"You will be gone soon enough, most noble Gallus." Bishop George had now taken to using our titles.

"When?" I asked.

Gallus answered. "In a few days. The Emperor promised. 'When all is ready, you will join us.' That's what he said. I shall be given a military command, and then . . . !" But Gallus was sufficiently wise not to mention his hopes for the future. Instead he gave me a dazzling smile. "And then," he repeated, with his usual malice, "*you'll* become a deacon."

"The beginning of a most holy career," said Bishop George, removing his silver headdress and handing it to an attendant. There was a red line around his brow where the crown had rested. "I wish I could continue with your education myself, but, alas, the divine Augustus has other plans for me." For an instant a look of pure delight illuminated that lean, somber face.

"Alexandria?" I asked.

He put his finger to his lips, and we went inside, each pleased with his fate: Gallus as Caesar in the East, George as bishop of Alexandria, and I . . . well, at least I would be able to continue my studies; better a live priest than a dead prince.

For the next few weeks we lived in hourly expectation of the imperial summons. But as the weeks became months, hope slowly died in each of us. We had been forgotten.

Bishop George promptly lost all interest in our education. We seldom saw him, and when we did his attitude was obscurely resentful, as if we were in some way responsible for his bad luck. Gallus was grim and prone to sudden outbursts of violence. If a brooch did not fasten properly, he would throw it on the floor and grind it under his heel. On the days when he spoke at all, he roared at everyone. But most of the time he was silent and glowering, his only interest the angry seduction of slave girls. I was not, I confess, in the best of spirits either, but at least I had Plotinus and Plato. I was able to study, and to wait.

One curious thing happened at this time. At the villa there were a number of Cappadocian youths, free-born country boys who worked in the stables as grooms and trainers. They were a cheerful lot and when I first came to Macellum I was allowed to play games with them. They were the only companions I ever had of my own age. I liked one in particular, Hilarius, a good-looking youth, two years older than I. He had a quick mind, and I remember trying to teach him to read when I was ten and already a pedagogue! But as we grew older, each became aware of his place, and intimacy ceased. Even so, I continued to interest myself in his welfare, and when he told me that he wanted to marry a girl in Caesarea whose father disapproved of the match, I was able to bring the father round. I also made Hilarius my personal groom.

One April morning when I sent for my horse, a strange groom brought it. Where was Hilarius? Out riding with the most noble Gallus. I was surprised. Gallus had his own groom, and we never used one another's servants. But then I thought no more about it. Quite happy to be alone, I rode toward the foothills of Mount Argaeus, enjoying the cool spring day. New leaves shone yellow-green against black branches and the earth steamed with a white mist as I rode toward a favorite spot where juniper and cedar grew around a natural spring.

At the approach to the clearing, I heard a sharp cry, like an animal in pain. Then I saw two horses tethered to a bent cedar tree at whose bole were strewn a man's clothes. Close by, hands and feet bound, the naked Hilarius lay on his belly while Gallus beat him with a riding crop. Every time the whip struck, Hilarius would cry out. Most extraordinary of all was the expression on Gallus's face. He was grinning with absolute pleasure, his face transfigured by the other's pain.

"Stop it!" I rode straight up to him. Startled, Gallus turned toward me. The boy called out to me to save him.

"Keep out of this." Gallus's voice was curiously hoarse.

"He's my groom," I said, rather irrelevantly, for if the boy had been disobedient then Gallus had quite as much right as I to punish him. "I said keep out of this! Go back!" Gallus aimed the whip at me but struck the flank of my horse instead. The horse reared. Gallus, alarmed, dropped the whip. In a fury myself, I rode straight at my brother, the way cavalrymen are taught to ride down foot soldiers. He bolted. I reined my horse just as he mounted his own. We faced one another for an instant, breathing hard. Gallus was still grinning, his teeth bared like a dog ready to snap.

I tried to be calm. With great effort I asked, "What did he do?"

To which Gallus answered, "*Nothing*!" Then with a laugh, he spurred his horse and was gone. To this day I can remember the way he said, "Nothing." Just as the Pythoness is filled with the spirit of Apollo, so my brother Gallus was possessed by evil. It was horrible.

I dismounted. I untied the boy, who was now sobbing and babbling how he had done nothing—again *nothing*!—when without a word of anger or reproach Gallus had ordered him to dismount and strip. Gallus had meant to beat him to death. I am sure of that.

I rode back to Macellum, ready to do murder myself. But when Gallus and I met that night at dinner, my anger had worn off and in its place I experienced something like fear. I could cope with almost any man. Young as I was, I had that much confidence in myself. But a demon was another matter; especially a demon that I did not understand.

All through dinner I stared at Gallus, who chose to be delightful, playful and charming; and nowhere in his smiling face could I find any hint of that sharp-toothed—I nearly wrote "fanged"—grin I had seen a few hours earlier. I almost began to wonder if perhaps I had dreamed the whole business. But when I visited Hilarius the next day and saw the scars on his back I knew that I had dreamt nothing. *Nothing*. The word haunts me to this day.

For the remainder of our time at Macellum, Gallus and I contrived never to be alone together. When we did speak to one another, it was always politely. We never mentioned what had happened in the clearing.

A month later a letter arrived from the Grand Chamberlain: the most noble Gallus was to proceed to his late mother's estate at Ephesus; here he was to remain at the Emperor's pleasure. Gallus was both elated and crestfallen. He was free of Macellum but he was still a prisoner, and there was no mention of his being made Caesar.

Gallus said good-bye to his officer friends at a dinner to which I was, surprisingly, invited. He made a pleasant speech, promising to remember his friends if he was ever to have a military command. Bishop George then presented him with a Galilean testament bound in massive silver. "Study it well, most noble Gallus. Outside the church there can be no salvation." How often have I heard that presumptuous line!

The next day when it was time for Gallus to say good-bye to me, he did so simply. "Pray for me, brother, as I pray for you."

"I shall. Good-bye, Gallus." And we parted, exactly like strangers who, having met for an evening in a post-house, take different roads the next day. After Gallus left, I wept, for the last time as a child. Yet I hated him. They say that to know oneself is to know all there is that is human. But of course no one can ever know himself. Nothing human is finally calculable; even to ourselves we are strange.

On 1 June 348, almost as an afterthought, orders concerning me were sent to Bishop George. I was to proceed to Constantinople. Though my uncle Julian was in Egypt, his household was at my disposal. I was to study philosophy under Ecebolius, a favorite of Constantius. There was no suggestion of the priesthood, which delighted me if not Bishop George. "I can't think why Augustus has changed his mind. He was quite positive when he was here."

"Perhaps he may have some other use for me," I said tentatively.

"What better use is there than the service of God?" Bishop George was in a bad temper. Athanasius was still at Alexandria, and it now looked as if George was doomed to spend the rest of his life in Cappadocia. With bad grace, he organized my departure.

It was a warm, misty day when I got into the carriage which was to take me to Constantinople. Just as I was about to depart, Bishop George asked me if I was certain that I had returned all the volumes of Plotinus to his library. His secretary had reported there was one missing. I swore that it had been returned only that morning (which was true: I had been hurriedly copying passages from it in a notebook). The Bishop then gave me his blessing and a Galilean testament, bound not in silver but in cheap leather; apparently I was not destined to be a Caesar! Yet I thanked him profusely and said farewell. The driver cracked his whip. The horses broke into a trot. For the first time in six years I was leaving the confines of Macellum. My childhood was over, and I was still alive.

# V

"And you like the poetry of Bacchylides, as well? Ah, we have extraordinary taste! No doubt of that." I was so overcome by Ecebolius's flattery that had he asked me then and there to leap off the top of my uncle Julian's house as a literary exercise, I would have done so gladly, with an appropriate quotation from

Hesiod as I fell. I chattered like a monkey as he examined me closely in Hesiod, Homer, Herodotus, Thucydides, and Theognis. For seven hours he listened as I recited from memory the many thousands of lines I had memorized at Macellum. He affected to be amazed. "I knew Bishop George was a splendid scholar—that enviable library! But I had no idea he was a teacher of such genius!" I beamed idiotically and kept on talking. I had at last found my tongue, and there are those who think I have not stopped talking since.

As a small child, I had studied at the Patricians' School with Ecebolius. So we quickly picked up where we had left off, almost as if nothing had changed, except that I was now a gawky adolescent with a beard thick on the chin, spotty on the upper lip, invisible on the cheeks. I looked frightful but I refused to shave. I am to be a philosopher, I said proudly; and that was that.

In Constantinople I was left largely to myself. I had only one audience with the Grand Chamberlain Eusebius. I say "audience," for not only did Eusebius exercise the actual power of the Emperor, he imitated his state. In fact, there used to be a joke that if one wanted anything done, Constantius was the man to see because he was reputed to have some influence with the Grand Chamberlain.

Eusebius received me in his suite at the Sacred Palace. He stood up to greet me (although he was the second most powerful man in this empire, he was only an *illustris* and I outranked him). He greeted me in that sweet child's voice of his and motioned for me to sit beside him. I noticed that his fat fingers shone with diamonds and Indian rubies, and he was drenched in attar of roses.

"Is the most noble Julian comfortable in his uncle's house?"

"Oh, yes, very comfortable."

"We thought he would prefer that to the . . . confinement of the Sacred Palace. But of course you are only a few yards away. You can visit us often. We hope you will." He gave me a dimpled smile.

I asked him when the Emperor would return.

"We have no idea. He is now at Nisibis. There are rumors that he may soon engage Sapor in a final battle. But you know as much as I." He made a flattering gesture of obeisance to me. "We have had excellent reports on your progress. Ecebolius tells us that you have a gift for rhetoric which is unusual for your age, though not—if I may say so—for one of your family." Nervous

51

as I was, I smiled at this hyperbole. Neither Constantius nor Gallus could develop an argument or even deliver a proper speech.

"Ecebolius proposes that you also take a course in grammar with Nicocles. I agree. These things are necessary to know, especially for one who may be raised very high." He let this sink in. As I gabbled my admiration of Nicocles and my passion for grammar, Eusebius studied me as though I were an actor in the theatre giving a recitation. I could see that he was curious about me. Gallus had obviously charmed him, but then Gallus was neither intelligent nor subtle; he posed no threat to the Grand Chamberlain. He could be governed, just as Constantius was governed. But who was this third prince, this half-grown youth with a patchy beard who talked too fast and used ten quotations where one would do? Eusebius had not yet made up his mind about me. So I did my best to convince him that I was harmless.

"My interest is philosophy. My goal the University of Athens, the lighthouse of the world. I should like to devote myself to literature, to philosophy. 'Men search out God and searching find him,' as Aeschylus wrote. But of course we know God now in a way our ancestors could not. Jesus came by special grace to save us. He is like his father *though not of the same substance*. Yet it is good to study the old ways. To speak out on every matter, even error. For as Euripides wrote, 'A slave is he who cannot speak his thought,' and who would be a slave, except to reason? Yet too great a love of reason might prove a trap, for as Horace wrote, 'Even the wise man is a fool if he seeks virtue itself beyond what is enough.'"

With some shame, I record the awful chatter I was capable of in those days. I was so uncertain of myself that I never made a personal observation about anything. Instead I spouted quotations. In this I resembled a great many contemporary Sophists who—having no ideas of their own—string together the unrelated sayings of the distinguished dead and think themselves as wise as those they quote. It is one thing to use text to illustrate a point one is making, but quite another to quote merely to demonstrate the excellence of one's memory. At seventeen I was the worst sort of Sophist. This probably saved my life. I bored Eusebius profoundly and we never fear those who bore us. By definition, a bore is predictable. If you think you know in advance what a man is apt to say or do, you are not apt to be disagreeably surprised by him. I am sure that in that one interview I inadvertently saved my life.

"We shall do everything we can to bring to the divine Augustus's attention your desire—*commendable* desire—to be enrolled at the University of Athens. At the moment you must continue your studies here. Also, I suggest . . ." He paused tactfully, his eyes taking in my schoolboy clothes as well as my fingers from which the ink had not been entirely washed. ". . . that you be instructed in the ways of the court. I shall send you Eutherius. Though an Armenian, he is a master of ceremony. He will acquaint you with the niceties of our arrangements twice . . . no, perhaps *three* times a week."

Eusebius rang a dainty silver bell. Then a familiar figure appeared in the doorway: my old tutor Mardonius. He looked no different than he had that day six years before when he said farewell to us in front of the bishop's house. We embraced emotionally.

Eusebius purred. "Mardonius is my right arm. He is chief of my secretarial bureau. A distinguished classicist, a loyal subject, a good Christian of impeccable faith." Eusebius sounded as if he were delivering a funeral oration. "He will show you out. Now if you will forgive me, most noble prince, I have a meeting with the Sacred Consistory." He rose. We saluted one another; then he withdrew, urging me to call on him at any time.

When Mardonius and I were alone together, I said gaily, "I'm sure you never thought you'd see me alive again!"

This was exactly the wrong thing to say. Poor Mardonius turned corpse-yellow. "Not here," he whispered. "The palace—secret agents—everywhere. Come." Talking of neutral matters, he led me through marble corridors to the main door of the palace. As we passed through the outer gate, the Scholarian guards saluted me, and I felt a momentary excitement which was not at all in the character I had just revealed to Eusebius.

My attendants were waiting for me under the arcade across the square. I motioned to them to remain where they were. Mardonius was brief. "I won't be able to see you again. I asked the Grand Chamberlain if I might instruct you in court ceremonial, but he said no. He made it very clear I am not to see you."

"What about this fellow he told me about, the Armenian?"

"Eutherius is a good man. You will like him. I don't think he has been sent to incriminate you, though of course he will make out regular reports. You must be careful what you say at all times. *Never* criticize the Emperor . . ."

"I know that much, Mardonius," I could not help but smile.

53

He was sounding exactly the way he used to. "I've managed to live this long."

"But this is Constantinople, not Macellum. This is the Sacred Palace which is a . . . a . . . *nothing* can describe it."

"Not even Homer?" I teased him. He smiled wanly. "Homer had no experience of this sort of viciousness and corruption."

"What do they mean to do with me?"

"The Emperor has not decided."

"Will Eusebius decide for him?"

"Perhaps. Keep on his good side. Appear to be harmless."

"Not difficult."

"And wait." Mardonius suddenly became his old self. "Incidentally, I read one of your themes. 'Alexander the Great in Egypt.' Too periphrastic. Also, a misquotation. From the Odyssey 16.187: 'No God am I. Why then do you liken me to the immortals?' You used the verb meaning 'to place among' rather than 'to liken.' I was humiliated when Eusebius showed me the mistake."

I apologized humbly. I was also amazed to realize that every schoolboy exercise of mine was on file in the Grand Chamberlain's office.

"That is how they will build their case for—or against—you." Mardonius frowned and the thousand wrinkles of his face suddenly looked like the shadow of a spider's web in the bright sun. "Be careful. Trust no one." He hurried back into the palace.

I remained the rest of that year at Constantinople. I had a sufficient income, left me by my grandmother who had died that summer. I was allowed to see her just before her death, but she did not recognize me. She spoke disjointedly. She shook with palsy and at times the shaking became so violent that she had to be strapped to her bed. When I left, she kissed me, murmuring, "Sweet, sweet."

By order of the Grand Chamberlain I was not allowed to associate with boys my own age or, for that matter, with anyone other than my instructors, Ecebolius and Nicocles, and the Armenian eunuch. Ecebolius is a man of much charm. But Nicocles I detested. He was a short, sparse grasshopper of a man. Many regard him as our age's first grammarian. But I always thought of him as *the enemy*. He did not like me either. I remember in particular one conversation with him. It is amusing in retrospect. "The most noble Julian is at an impressionable period in his life. He must be careful of those he listens to. The world is now full of false teachers. In religion we have the party of Athanasius, a most divisive group. In philosophy we have all sorts of mountebanks, like Libanius."

That was the first time I heard the name of the man who was to mean so much to me as thinker and teacher. Not very interested, I asked who Libanius was.

"An Antiochene—and we know what *they* are like. He studied at Athens. Then he came here to teach. That was about twelve years ago. He was young. He was bad-mannered to his colleagues, to those of us who were, if not wiser, at least more experienced than he." Nicocles made a sound like an insect's wings rustling on a summer day—laughter? "He was also tactless about religion. All the great teachers here are Christian. He was not. Like so many who go to Athens (and I deplore, if I may say so, *your* desire to study there), Libanius prefers the empty ways of our ancestors. He calls himself a Hellenist, preferring Plato to the gospels, Homer to the old testament. In his four years here he completely disrupted the academic community. He was always making trouble. Such a vain man! Why, he even prepared a paper for the Emperor on the teaching of Greek, suggesting *changes* in our curriculum! I'm glad to say he left us eight years ago, under a cloud."

"What sort of cloud?" I was oddly intrigued by this recital. Oddly, because academics everywhere are forever attacking one another, and I had long since learned that one must never believe what any teacher says of another.

"He was involved with a girl, the daughter of a senator. He was to give her private instruction in the classics. Instead, he made her pregnant. Her family complained. So the Emperor, to save the reputation of the girl and her family, a very important family (you would know who they are if I told you, which I must not) the Augustus exiled Libanius from the capital."

"Where is Libanius now?"

"At Nicomedia, where as usual he is making himself difficult. He has a passion to be noticed." The more Nicocles denounced Libanius, the more interested I became in him. I decided I must meet him. But how? Libanius could not come to Constantinople and I could not go to Nicomedia. Fortunately, I had an ally.

I liked the Armenian eunuch Eutherius as much as I disliked

55

Nicocles. Eutherius taught me court ceremonial three times a week. He was a grave man of natural dignity who did not look or sound like a eunuch. His beard was normal. His voice was low. He had been cut at the age of twenty, so he had known what it was to be a man. He once told me in grisly detail how he had almost died during the operation, "from loss of blood, because the older you are, the more dangerous the operation is. But I have been happy. I have had an interesting life. And there is something to be said for not wasting one's time in pursuit of sexual pleasure." But though this was true of Eutherius, it was not true of all eunuchs, especially those at the palace. Despite their incapacity, eunuchs are capable of sexual activity, as I one day witnessed, in a scene I shall describe in its proper place.

When I told Eutherius that I wanted to go to Nicomedia, he agreed to conduct the intricate negotiations with the Chamberlain's office. Letters were exchanged daily between my household and the palace. Eutherius was often in the absurd position of writing, first, my letter of request, and then Eusebius's elaborate letter of rejection. "It is good practice for me," said Eutherius wearily, as the months dragged on.

Shortly after New Year 349 Eusebius agreed to let me go to Nicomedia on condition that I not attend the lectures of Libanius. As Nicocles put it, "Just as we protect our young from those who suffer from the fever, so we must protect them from dangerous ideas, not to mention poor rhetoric. As stylist, Libanius has a tendency to facetiousness which you would find most boring. As philosopher, he is dangerously committed to the foolish past." To make sure that I would not cheat, Ecebolius was ordered to accompany me to Nicomedia.

Ecebolius and I arrived at Nicomedia in February 349. I enjoyed myself hugely that winter. I attended lectures. I listened to skilled Sophists debate. I met students of my own age. This was not always an easy matter, for they were terrified of me, while I hardly knew how to behave with them.

Libanius was much spoken of in the city. But I saw him only once. He was surrounded by students in one of the porticoes near the gymnasium of Trajan. He was a dark, rather handsome man. Ecebolius pointed him out, saying grimly, "Who else would imitate Socrates in everything but wisdom?"

"Is he so bad?"

"He is a troublemaker. Worse than that, he is a bad rhetorician. He never learned to speak properly. He simply chatters."

"But his writings are superb."

"How do you know?" Ecebolius looked at me sharply.

"I . . . from the others here. They talk about him." To this day Ecebolius does not know that I used to pay to have Libanius's lectures taken down in shorthand. Though Libanius had been warned not to approach me, he secretly sent me copies of his lectures, for which I paid him well.

"He can only corrupt," said Ecebolius. "Not only is he a poor model for style, he despises our religion. He is impious."

*Priscus*: That sounds just like Ecebolius, doesn't it? Of course when Julian became emperor, Ecebolius embraced Hellenism. Then when Valentinian and Valens became co-emperors, Ecebolius threw himself down in front of the Church of the Holy Apostles, crying, "Tread on me! I am as salt which has lost its savor!" I always wondered if anybody did tread on him. I should have liked to. He changed his religion five times in thirty years and died at a fine old age, honored by all. If there is a moral to his career, it eludes me.

I do recall that story about you and the senator's daughter. Is it true? I always suspected you were rather a lady's man, in your day of course.

*Libanius*: No, I shall not give Priscus the pleasure of an answer. I shall also suppress Julian's references to that old scandal. It serves no purpose to rake over the past in such a pointless way. I have always known that a story more or less along those lines was circulated about me, but this is the first time I have been confronted with it in all its malice. Envious Sophists will go to any lengths to tear down one's reputation. There was no "senator's daughter," at least not as described. The whole thing is absurd. For one thing, if I had been dismissed by the Emperor on such a charge, why was I then asked by the court to return to Constantinople in 353? Which I did, and remained there several years before coming home to Antioch.

I am far more irritated by Ecebolius's reference to my "facetiousness." That from him! I have always inclined to a grave—some feel too grave—style, only occasionally lightened by humor. Also, if I am as poor a stylist as he suggests, why am I the most imitated of living writers? Even in those days, a prince paid for my lecture notes! Incidentally, Julian says that he paid *me* for the lectures. That is not true. Julian paid one of my students who had a complete set of notes. He also engaged a shorthand writer to take down my conversation. I myself never took a penny from him. How tangled truth becomes.

*Julian Augustus*

Looking back, I seem to have followed a straight line toward my destiny. I moved from person to person as though each had been deliberately chosen for my instruction. But at the time I had only a pleasurable sense of freedom, nothing more. Nevertheless, the design of my life was taking shape and each wise man I met formed yet another link in that chain which leads toward the ultimate revelation which Plotinus has so beautifully described as "the flight of the alone to the Alone."

At Nicomedia I forged an important new link. Like most university towns, Nicomedia had a particular bath where the students assembled. The students' bath is usually the cheapest in town, though not always, for students have strange tastes and when they suddenly decide that such-and-such a tavern or bath or arcade is the one place where they most want to gather, they will then think nothing of cost or comfort.

I longed to go alone to the baths and mingle with students my own age, but Ecebolius always accompanied me. "The Chamberlain's orders," he would say, whenever we entered the baths, my two guards trailing us as though we were potential thieves in a marketplace. Even in the hot room, I would be flanked by sweating guards while Ecebolius hovered nearby to see that no one presented himself to me without first speaking to him. As a result, the students I wanted to meet were scared off.

But one morning Ecebolius awakened with the fever. "I must keep to my bed 'with only cruel pain for handmaid,'" he said, teeth chattering. I told him how sorry I was and then, utterly happy, I left for the baths. My guards promised that once inside they would not stick too closely to me. They realized how much I wanted to be anonymous, and in those days it was possible, for I was not well known in Nicomedia. I never went into the agora, and when I attended lectures I always came in last and sat at the back.

Students go to the baths in the morning, when the admission

price is cheapest. Shortly before noon I queued up and followed the mob into the changing room where I undressed at the opposite end from my two guards, who pretended to be soldiers on leave. As far as I know, I was not recognized.

Since the day was warm, I went outside to the palaestra; here the athletically inclined were doing exercises and playing games. Avoiding the inevitable group of old men who linger watchfully in the shade, I crossed to a lively-looking group, seated on a bench in the sun. They ignored me when I sat beside them.

"And you took the money?"

"I did. We all did. About a hundred of us."

"Then what happened?"

"We never went to his lectures."

"Was he angry?"

"Of course."

"But not as angry as he was when . . ."

". . . when all of us went *back* to Libanius!"

They laughed at what was in those days a famous story. Within a year of Libanius's arrival at Nicomedia, he was easily the most popular teacher in the city. This naturally enraged his rival Sophists, one of whom tried to buy Libanius's students away from him. The students took the man's money and continued to attend Libanius's lectures. It was a fine joke, until the furious Sophist applied to friends at court who had Libanius arrested on some spurious charge. Fortunately, he was soon freed.

*Libanius*: This was the beginning of my interest in penal reform. Over the years I have written a good deal on the subject, and there is some evidence that I am beginning to arouse the conscience of the East. At least our rulers are now aware of the barbarous conditions in which prisoners are held. I had never realized how truly hopeless our prison system is until I myself was incarcerated. But improvements are hard to make. Despite all evidence to the contrary, I do not think human beings are innately cruel, but they fear change of any kind. And now I am digressing.

Is this age? Just yesterday I had a most curious conversation on that subject with an old friend and colleague. I asked him why it was that nowadays whenever I address the assembly at Antioch, the senators cough and talk among themselves. I realize I am not a master of oratory, but after all what I have to say and the way in which I say it is—and I do not mean this immodestly—of

59

obvious interest to the world. I am the most famous living writer of Greek. As quaestor, I am official spokesman for my city. "So why do people stop listening when I start to speak? And why, when the session is over and I try to talk to various senators, and officials in the arcade, do they wander off when I am in mid-sentence, saying that they have appointments to keep, even though it is quite plain that they do not?"

"Because, my dear old friend, you have become—now you asked me to tell you the truth, remember that—a bore."

I was stunned. Of course as a professional teacher one tends to lecture rather than converse, but that is a habit most public men fall into. "But even so, I should have thought that *what* I was saying was of some interest. . . ."

"It is. It always is."

". . . rather than the *way* I say it, which may perhaps be over-explicit."

"You are too serious."

"No one can be too serious about what is important."

"Apparently the Antiochenes think otherwise."

We parted. I must say I have been thinking all day about what my colleague said. Have I aged so greatly? Have I lost my power to define and persuade? Am I too serious? I am suddenly tempted to write some sort of apologia for myself, to explain my unbecoming gravity. I must do something. . . . But scribbling these highly personal remarks on the back of Julian's memoirs is not the answer!

*Julian Augustus*

As I sat on the bench in the sun, reveling in warmth and anonymity, a dark man approached me. He gave me a close look. Then he said, "Macellum?"

At first I was annoyed at being recognized. But when I realized that this young man was the physician Oribasius, I was glad that he spoke to me. In no time at all we were talking as if we had known each other all our lives. Together we took the baths. In the circular hot room, as we scraped oil from one another, Oribasius told me that he had left the court.

"To practice privately?"

"No. Family affairs. My father died. And now I have to go home to Pergamon to settle the estate."

"How did you recognize me? It's been two years."

"I always remember faces, especially those of princes."

I motioned for him to lower his voice. Just opposite us two students were trying to overhear our conversation.

"Also," whispered Oribasius, "that awful beard of yours is a give-away."

"It's not very full yet," I said, tugging at it sadly.

"And everyone in Nicomedia knows that the most noble Julian is trying to grow a philosopher's beard."

"Well, at my age there's always hope."

After a plunge in the cold pool, we made our way to the hall of the tepidarium, where several hundred students were gathered, talking loudly, singing, occasionally wrestling, to the irritation of the bath attendants, who would then move swiftly among them, cracking heads with metal keys.

Oribasius promptly convinced me that I should come stay with him in Pergamon. "I've a big house and there's no one in it. You can also meet Aedesius. . . ."

Like everyone, I admired Aedesius. He was Pergamon's most famous philosopher, the teacher of Maximus and Priscus, and a friend of the late Iamblichos.

"You'll like Pergamon. Thousands of Sophists, arguing all day long. We even have a woman Sophist."

"A woman?"

"Well, perhaps she's a woman. There is a rumor she may be a goddess. You must ask her, since she started the rumor. Anyway, she gives lectures on philosophy, practices magic, predicts the future. You'll like her."

"But you don't?"

"But you will."

At that moment we were joined by the two young men from the hot room. One was tall and well built; his manner grave. The other was short and thin with a tight smile and quick black eyes. As they approached, my heart sank. I had been recognized. The short one introduced himself. "Gregory of Nazianzus, most noble Julian. And this is Basil. We are both from Cappadocia. We saw you the day the divine Augustus came to Macellum. We were in the crowd."

"Are you studying here?"

"No. We're on our way to Constantinople, to study with Nicocles. But Basil wanted to stop off here to attend the lectures of the impious Libanius."

Basil remonstrated mildly. "Libanius is not a Christian, but he is the best teacher of rhetoric in Nicomedia."

"Basil is not like *us*, most noble Julian," said Gregory. "He is much too tolerant."

I found myself liking Basil and disliking Gregory, I suppose because of that presumptuous "us." Gregory has always had too much of the courtier in him. But I have since come to like him, and today we are all three friends, despite religious differences. They were agreeable companions, and I still recall with pleasure that day we met when I was a student among students with no guardian to inhibit conversation. When it was finally time to leave the baths, I promised Oribasius that somehow or other I would join him in Pergamon. Meanwhile, Gregory and Basil agreed to dine with me. They were just the sort Ecebolius would approve of: devout Galileans with no interest in politics. But I knew instinctively that Oribasius would alarm Ecebolius. Oribasius had been at court and he moved in high circles. He was also rich and worldly and precisely the sort of friend a sequestered prince should not have. I decided to keep Oribasius my secret for the time being. This proved to be wise.

In January 350, Ecebolius and I got permission to move on to Pergamon. We made the three-hundred-mile trip in bitter cold. As we rode through the perpetual haze of steam from our own breath, I recall thinking, this must be what it is like to campaign in Germany or Sarmatia: barren countryside, icy roads, a black sky at noon, and soldiers behind me, their arms clattering in the stillness. I daydreamed about the military life, which was strange, for in those days I seldom thought of anything except philosophy and religion. I suspect that I was born a soldier and only "made" a philosopher.

At Pergamon, Ecebolius insisted we stay at the palace of the Greek kings, which had been made available to me. But when the prefect of the city (who had most graciously met us at the gate) hinted that I would have to pay for the maintenance of the palace, Ecebolius agreed that we were better off as guests of Oribasius, who had also met us at the gate, pretending not to know me but willing, as a good courtier, to put up the Emperor's cousin. In those days Oribasius was far richer than I and often lent me money when I was short of cash. We were like brothers.

Oribasius took delight in showing me his city. He knew my interest in temples (though I was not yet consciously a Hellenist), and we spent several days prowling through the deserted temples on the acropolis and across the Selinos River, which divides the city. Even then, I was struck by the sadness of once holy buildings now empty save for spiders and scorpions. Only the temple of Asklepios was kept up, and that was because the Asklepion is the center of the intellectual life of the city. It is a large enclave containing theatre, library, gymnasium, porticoes, gardens, and of course the circular temple to the god himself. Most of the buildings date from two centuries ago, when architecture was at its most splendid.

The various courtyards are filled with students at every hour of the day. The teachers sit inside the porticoes and talk. Each teacher has his own following. Unfortunately when we came to the portico where Aedesius was usually to be found, we were told that he was still ill.

"After all, he's over seventy," said a raffish youth, dressed as a New Cynic. "Why don't you go to Prusias's lectures? He's the coming man. Apparently first-rate. I'll take you to him." But Oribasius firmly extricated us from the young man's clutches. Cursing genially, the admirer of Prusias let us go. We started back to the agora.

"That's how a lot of students live in Pergamon. For each new pupil they bring to their teacher, they are paid so much a head." Just behind the old theater, Oribasius pointed to a small house in a narrow street. "Aedesius lives there."

I sent one of my guards to ask if the philosopher would receive me. After a long wait, a fat woman with a fine gray beard and spiky moustache came to the door and said firmly, "He can see no one."

"But when will he be able to?"

"Perhaps never," she said, and shut the door.

Oribasius laughed. "His wife. She's not as nice as she looks."

"But I must meet him."

"We'll arrange it somehow. Anyway, tonight I've something special for you."

That something special was the woman philosopher, Sosipatra. She was then in her forties but looked much younger. She was tall and though somewhat heavy, her face was still youthful and handsome.

63

When we arrived at her house, Sosipatra came straight to me, knowing exactly who I was without being told. "Most noble Julian, welcome to our house. And you too, Ecebolius. Oribasius, your father sends you greetings."

Oribasius looked alarmed, as well he might: his father had been dead three months. But Sosipatra was serious. "I spoke to him just now. He is well. He stands within the third arc of Helios, at a hundred-and-eighty-degree angle to the light. He advises you to sell the farm in Galatia. Not the one with the cedar grove. The other. With the stone house. Come in, most noble prince. You went to see Aedesius today but his wife turned you away. Nevertheless, my old friend *will* see you in a few days. He is sick at the moment but he will recover. He has four more years of life. A holy, good man."

I was quite overwhelmed, as she led me firmly by the hand into a dining room whose walls were decorated with pictures of the mysteries of Demeter. There were couches for us and a chair for her. Slaves helped us off with our sandals and washed our feet. We then arranged ourselves about the table. All the while, Sosipatra continued to talk in such a melodious voice that even Ecebolius, who did not much like the idea of her, was impressed.

"Do you know the beautiful story of Aedesius and his father? No? It is so characteristic. The father wanted his son to join him in the family business. But first he sent him to school at Athens. When Aedesius returned from school, he told his father that it was now impossible for him to go into business. He preferred to become a philosopher. Furious, his father drove him out of the house, shouting, 'What good does philosophy do you now?' To which Aedesius replied, 'It has taught me to revere my father, even as he drives me from his house.' From that moment on, Aedesius and his father were friends."

We were all edified by this story. Sosipatra was indeed a fountain of wisdom, and we were fortunate to drink of her depths.

*Priscus:* Did you ever meet this monster? I once spent a week with her and her husband at Pergamon. She never stopped talking. Even Aedesius, who was fond of her (I think he was once her lover), thought her ignorant, though he would never have admitted it. He, by the way, was an excellent man. After all, he was *my* teacher and am I not, after Libanius, the wisest man of our age?

*Libanius*: Irony?

*Priscus*: But though Sosipatra was hardly a philosopher, she was a remarkable magician. Even I came close to believing in her spells and predictions. She also had a sense of drama which was most exciting. Julian was completely taken in by her, and I date his fatal attraction to this sort of thing from that dinner party.

Incidentally, a friend of mine once had an affair with Sosipatra. When the act was over, she insisted that he burn incense to her as she lay among the tangled sheets. "For I am Aphrodite, goddess among men." He burned the incense but never went to bed with her again.

Maximus also thought that Sosipatra was divine, or at least "inhabited from time to time by the spirit of Aphrodite." Which made her sound rather like an inn. I always found her tedious. But she was often accurate in her predictions. Lucky guesses? Who knows? If the gods exist, which I doubt, might they not be every bit as boring as Sosipatra?

*Libanius*: As always, Priscus goes too far. But I rather agree with him about Sosipatra. She did talk too much. But then, who am I to criticize her when one of my oldest friends has just told me to my face that I bore all Antioch?

*Julian Augustus*

When the dinner was over, Sosipatra presented her sons to us. They were about my age. Two of them grew up to be speculators in grain, and most unsavory. The third, Anatolius, I heard news of only recently. Some years ago he attached himself to the temple of Serapis at Alexandria. After Bishop George destroyed the temple, Anatolius climbed onto a broken column and now stares continually at the sun. How I envy the purity of such a life! But that night at dinner, the future holy man seemed a very ordinary youth, with a slight stammer.

When the sons had withdrawn, Sosipatra sent for a tripod and incense. "And now you will want to know what the gods advise you to do. Where to go. With whom to study." She gave me a dazzling smile.

I blurted out, "I want to study here, with you." But she shook her head, to Ecebolius's relief. "I know my own future and a prince is no part of it. I wish it were otherwise," she added softly,

65

and I fell in love with her on the spot, as so many students had done before me.

Sosipatra lit the incense. She shut her eyes. She whispered a prayer. Then in a low voice she implored the Great Goddess to speak to us. Smoke filled the room. All things grew vague and indistinct. My head began to ache. Suddenly in a loud voice not her own, Sosipatra said, "Julian!"

I looked at her closely. Her eyes were half open but only the whites showed: she slept while the spirit possessed her. "You are loved by us beyond any man alive." That was puzzling. "Us" must mean the gods. But why should they love a Galilean who doubted their existence? Of course I had also begun to question the divinity of the Nazarene, which made me neither Hellenist nor Galilean, neither believer nor atheist. I was suspended somewhere between, waiting for a sign. Could this be it?

"You will rebuild our temples. You will cause the smoke of a thousand sacrifices to rise from a thousand altars. You shall be our servant and all men shall be *your* servants, as token of our love."

Ecebolius stirred nervously. "We must not listen to this," he murmured.

The voice continued serenely. "The way is dangerous. But we shall protect you, as we have protected you from the hour of your birth. Earthly glory shall be yours. And death when it comes in far Phrygia, by enemy steel, will be a hero's death, without painful lingering. Then you shall be with us forever, close to the One from whom all light flows, to whom all light returns. Oh, Julian, dear to us ... *Evil!*" The voice changed entirely. It became harsh. "Foul and profane! We bring you defeat. Despair. The Phrygian death is yours. But the tormented soul is ours forever, far from light!"

Sosipatra screamed. She began to writhe in her chair; her hands clutched at her throat as though to loosen some invisible bond. Words tumbled disjointedly from her mouth. She was a battle-ground between warring spirits. But at last the good prevailed, and she became tranquil.

"Ephesus," she said, and her voice was again soft and caressing. "At Ephesus you will find the door to light. Ecebolius, when you were a child you hid three coins in the garden of your uncle's house at Sirmium. One was a coin of the reign of Septimus Severus. A gardener dug up the coins and spent them. That coin of

66

Severus is now in Pergamon, in a tavern. Oribasius, your father insists you sell the property but hopes you will not make the same mistake you made last year when you leased the lower meadow to your Syrian neighbor, and he would not pay. Julian, beware the fate of Gallus. Remember... Hilarius!" She stopped. She became herself again. "My head aches," she said in a tired voice.

We were all quite shaken. I most of all for she had practically said that I would become emperor, which was treason, for no one may consult an oracle about the imperial succession, nor even speculate in private on such matters. Ecebolius had been rightly alarmed.

Sosipatra had no memory of what was said. She listened carefully as we told her what the goddess—and the other—had said. She was intrigued. "Obviously a great future for the most noble Julian."

"Of course," said Ecebolius nervously. "As a loyal prince of the imperial house . . ."

"Of course!" Sosipatra laughed. "We must say no more." Then she frowned. "I have no idea who the dark spirit was. But it is plain that the goddess was Cybele, and she wants you to honor her since she is the mother of all, and your protectress."

"It also seems indicated that Julian should avoid Phrygia," said Oribasius mischievously.

But Sosipatra took this quite seriously. "Yes. Julian will die in Phrygia, gloriously, in battle." She turned to me. "I don't understand the reference to your brother. Do you?"

I nodded, unable to speak, my head whirling with dangerous thoughts.

"The rest of it seems plain enough. You are to restore the worship of the true gods."

"It seems rather late in the day for that." Ecebolius had found his tongue at last. "And even if it were possible, Julian is a Christian. The imperial house is Christian. This makes him a most unlikely candidate for restoring the old ways."

"*Are* you unlikely?" Sosipatra fixed me with her great dark eyes.

I shook my head helplessly. "I don't know. I just wait for a sign."

"Perhaps *this* was the sign. Cybele herself spoke to you."

"So did something else," said Ecebolius.

"There is *always* the Other," said Sosipatra. "But light tran-

67

scends all things. As Macrobius wrote, 'The sun is the mind of the universe.' And nowhere, not even in the darkest pit of hell, is mind entirely absent."

"What is at Ephesus?" I asked suddenly.

Sosipatra gave me a long look. Then she said, "Maximus is there. He is waiting for you. He has been waiting for you since the day you were born."

Ecebolius stirred at this. "I am perfectly sure that Maximus would like nothing better than to instruct the prince, but, unfortunately for him, *I* was appointed by the Grand Chamberlain to supervise Julian's studies and I am not at all eager for my pupil to become involved with a notorious magician."

Sosipatra's voice was icy. "We think of Maximus as being something more than a 'notorious magician.' It is true that he can make the gods appear to him, but..."

"Actually appear?" I was fascinated.

"Actors, from the theatre," muttered Oribasius, "carefully rehearsed, tricks of lighting..."

Sosipatra smiled. "Oribasius! That is unworthy of you! What would your father say to that?"

"I have no idea. *You* see more of him nowadays than I do."

Sosipatra ignored this. She turned to me. "Maximus is no charlatan. If he were, I would have unmasked him years ago. Of course people question his powers. They should. One must not take anything on blind faith. Yet when he speaks to the gods..."

"He speaks to them, but do they really speak to *him*? That's more the point," said Ecebolius.

"They do. I was present once in Ephesus when a group of atheists questioned him, just as you have."

"Not to believe in Maximus does not make one an atheist." Ecebolius was growing irritated.

She continued through him. "Maximus asked us to meet him that night in the temple of Hecate. Now the temple has not been used in years. It is a simple building, containing a bronze statue of the goddess and nothing more, so there was no way for Maximus to... *prepare* a miracle." She looked sharply at Oribasius. "When we had all arrived, Maximus turned to the statue and said, 'Great Goddess, show these unbelievers a sign of your power.' There was a moment of silence. Then the bronze torches she held in her bronze hands burst into flame."

"Naphtha," said Oribasius.

"I must go to Ephesus," I said.

"But that was not all. The statue smiled at us. The bronze face smiled. Then Hecate laughed. I have never heard such a sound! All heaven seemed to mock us, as we fled from that place."

Sosipatra turned to Ecebolius. "He has no choice, you know. At Ephesus his life begins."

The next day I received word that Aedesius would see me. I found him lying on a cot, his bearded wife beside him. Aedesius was a small man who had once been fat, but now because of illness and age the skin hung from him in folds. It was hard to believe that this frail old man had once been the pupil of Iamblichos and actually present on that occasion when Iamblichos caused two divine youths to appear from twin pools in the rock at Gadara. Yet despite his fragility, Aedesius was alert and amiable. "Sosipatra tells me that you have a gift for philosophy."

"If a passion can be called a gift."

"Why not? Passion is a gift of the gods. She also tells me that you plan to go to Ephesus."

"Only if I cannot study with you."

"Too late for that." He sighed. "As you see, I am in poor health. She gives me four more years of this life. But I doubt that I shall last so long. Anyway, Maximus will be more to your taste. He was my student, you know. After Priscus of Athens, he was my best student. Of course Maximus prefers demonstration to argument, mysteries to books. But then there are many ways to truth. And from what Sosipatra tells me, he was born to be your guide. It is clearly destiny."

*Priscus*: It was clearly a plot. They were all in on it. Years later, Maximus admitted as much. "I knew all along I was the right teacher for Julian. Naturally, I never dreamed he would be emperor." He did not dream it; he willed it. "I saw him simply as a soul that I alone could lead to salvation." Maximus then got Sosipatra and Aedesius to recommend him to Julian, which they did. What an extraordinary crew they were! Except for Aedesius, there was not a philosopher in the lot.

From what I gather, Julian in those days was a highly intelligent youth who might have been "captured" for true philosophy. After all, he enjoyed learning. He was good at debate. Properly edu-

69

cated, he might have been another Porphyry or, taking into account his unfortunate birth, another Marcus Aurelius. But Maximus got to him first and exploited his one flaw: that craving for the vague and incomprehensible which is essentially Asiatic. It is certainly not Greek, even though we Greeks are in a noticeable intellectual decline. Did you know that thanks to the presence of so many foreign students in Athens, our people no longer speak pure Attic but a sort of argot, imprecise and ugly? Yet despite the barbarism which is slowly extinguishing "the light of the world," we Athenians still pride ourselves on being able to see things as they are. Show us a stone and we see a stone, not the universe. But like so many others nowadays, poor Julian wanted to believe that man's life is profoundly more significant than it is. His sickness was the sickness of our age. We want so much not to be extinguished at the end that we will go to any length to make conjurer-tricks for one another simply to obscure the bitter, secret knowledge that it is our fate not to be. If Maximus hadn't stolen Julian from us, the bishops would have got him. I am sure of that. At heart he was a Christian mystic gone wrong.

*Libanius*: Christian mystic! Had Priscus any religious sense he might by now have experienced that knowledge of oneness, neither "bitter" nor "secret," which Plotinus and Porphyry, Julian and I, each in his own way—mystically arrived at. Or failing that, had he been admitted to the mysteries of Eleusis just fourteen miles from his own house in Athens, he might have understood that since the soul *is*, there can be no question of its *not*-being.

But I agree with Priscus about Maximus. I was aware at the time of the magicians' plot to capture Julian, but since I was forbidden to speak to him I could hardly warn him. Yet they did Julian no lasting harm. He sometimes put too much faith in oracles and magic, but he always had a firm grip of logic and he excelled in philosophic argument. He was hardly a Christian mystic. Yet he was a mystic—something Priscus could never understand.

*Julian Augustus*

Ecebolius was eager to go to Ephesus, rather to my surprise; I had thought he would have wanted to keep me from Maximus. But he was compliant. "After all, *I* am your teacher, approved by the Emperor. You cannot officially study with Maximus, or anyone else. Not that I would object. Far from it. I am told Maximus is most inspiring, though hopelessly reactionary. But we hardly need worry about your being influenced at this late date. After all, you were taught Christian theology by two great bishops, Eusebius and George. What firmer foundation can any man have? By all means let us visit Ephesus. You will enjoy the intellectual life. And so shall I."

What Ecebolius had come to enjoy was playing Aristotle to my green Alexander. Everywhere we went, academics were curious to know me. That meant they got to know Ecebolius. In no time at all, he was proposing delicately that he "exchange" students with them. "Exchange" meant that they would send him students at Constantinople for which they would receive nothing except the possible favor of the prince. During our travels, Ecebolius made his fortune.

In a snowstorm we were met at the gates of Ephesus by the city prefect and the town council. They were all very nervous.

"It is a great honor for Ephesus to receive the most noble Julian," said the prefect. "We are here to serve him, as we have served the most noble Gallus, who has also honored us by his presence here." At the mention of Gallus, as though rehearsed, the councillors began to mutter, "Kind, good, wise, noble."

"Where is my brother?"

There was a tense pause. The prefect looked anxiously at the councillors. They looked at one another. There was a good deal of energetic brushing of snow from cloaks.

"Your brother," said the prefect, finally, "is at court. At Milan. He was summoned by the Emperor last month. There has been no word about him. None at all. Naturally, we hope for the best."

"And what is the best?"

"Why, that he be made Caesar." It was not necessary to inquire about the worst.

After due ceremony, we were led to the prefect's house, where I was to stay. Ecebolius was thrilled at the thought that I might soon be half-brother to a Caesar. But I was alarmed. My alarm became panic when later that night Oribasius told me that Gallus had been taken from Ephesus under arrest.

"Was he charged with anything?"

"The Emperor's pleasure. There was no charge. Most people expect him to be executed."

"Has he given any cause?"

Oribasius shrugged. "If he is executed, people will give a

71

hundred reasons why the Emperor did the right thing. If he is made Caesar, they will say they knew all along such wisdom and loyalty would be rewarded."

"If Gallus dies . . ." I shuddered.

"But you're not political."

"I was born 'political' and there is nothing I can do about it. First Gallus, then me."

"I should think you were safest of all, the scholar-prince."

"No one is safe." I felt the cold that night as I have never felt the cold before or since. I don't know what I should have done without Oribasius. He was the first friend I ever had. He is still the best friend I have, and I miss him here in Persia. Oribasius has always been particularly useful in finding out things I would have no way of knowing. People never speak candidly to princes, but Oribasius could get anyone to tell him anything, a trick learned practicing medicine. He inspires confidences.

Within a day of our arrival at Ephesus, Oribasius had obtained a full report on Gallus's life in the city. "He is feared. But he is admired."

"For his beauty?" I could not resist that. After all, I had spent my childhood hopelessly beguiled by that golden creature.

"He shares his beauty rather liberally with the wives of the local magnates."

"Naturally."

"He is thought to be intelligent."

"He is shrewd."

"Politically knowledgeable, very ambitious . . ."

"Yet unpopular and feared. Why?"

"A bad temper, occasionally violent."

"Yes." I thought of the cedar grove at Macellum.

"People fear him. They don't know why."

"Poor Gallus." I almost meant it, too. "What do they say about me?"

"They wish you would shave your beard."

"I thought it was looking rather decent lately. A bit like Hadrian's." I rubbed the now full growth affectionately. Only the color displeased me: it was even lighter than the hair on my head, which is light brown. To make the beard seem darker and glossier, I occasionally rubbed oil on it. Nowadays, as I go gray, the beard has mysteriously darkened. I am perfectly satisfied with the way it looks. No one else is.

"They also wonder what you are up to."

"Up to? I should have thought it perfectly plain. I am a student."

"We are Greeks in these parts." Oribasius grinned, looking very Greek. "We never think anything is what it seems to be."

"Well, I am not about to subvert the state," I said gloomily. "My only plot is how to survive."


In spite of himself, Ecebolius liked Oribasius. "Because we are really disobeying the Chamberlain, you know. He fixed your household at a certain size and made no allowance for a physician."

"But Oribasius is a very special physician."

"Granted, he helped my fever and banished 'pain's cruel hand-maid . . .'"

"He also has the advantage of being richer than I. He helps us pay the bills."

"True. Sad truth." Ecebolius has a healthy respect for money, and because of that I was able to keep Oribasius near me.

We were at Ephesus some days before I was able to see Maximus. He was in retreat, communing with the gods. But we received daily bulletins from his wife. Finally, on the eighth day, at about the second hour, a slave arrived to say that Maximus would be honored to receive me that afternoon. I prevailed on Ecebolius to allow me to make the visit alone. After much argument he gave in, but only on condition that I later write out for him a full account of everything that was said.

Maximus lived in a modest house on the slopes of Mount Pion, not far from the theatre which is carved out of its side. My guards left me at the door. A servant then showed me into an inner room where I was greeted by a thin, nervous woman.

"I am Placidia, wife of Maximus." She let go my robe whose hem she had kissed. "We are so sorry my husband could not see you earlier, but he has been beneath the earth, with the goddess Cybele." She motioned to a slave who handed her a lighted torch which she gave me. "My husband is still in darkness. He asks for you to join him there."

I took the torch and followed Placidia to a room of the house whose fourth wall was covered by a curtain which, when she pulled it back, revealed the mountainside and an opening in the rock. "You must go to him alone, most noble prince."

I entered the mountain. For what seemed hours (but must have

73

been only minutes), I stumbled toward a far-off gleam of light which marked the end of the passageway. At last I arrived at what looked to be a well-lit chamber cut in the rock, and filled with smoke. Eagerly, I stepped forward and came up hard against a solid wall, stubbing my toes. I thought I had gone mad. In front of me was a room. But I could not enter it. Then I heard the beautiful deep voice of Maximus: "See? The life of this world is all illusion and only the gods are real."

I turned to my left and saw the chamber I thought I had seen in front of me. The smoke was now gone. The room appeared to be empty. Yet the voice sounded as if the speaker were close beside me. "You tried to step into a mirror. In the same way, the ignorant try to enter the land of the blessed, only to be turned away by their own reflection. Without surrendering yourself, you may not thread the labyrinth at whose end exists the One."

My right foot hurt. I was cold. I was both impressed and irritated by the situation. "I am Julian," I said, "of the house of Constantine."

"I am Maximus, of the house of all the gods." Then he appeared suddenly at my elbow. He seemed to emerge from the rock. Maximus is tall and well proportioned, with a beard like a gray waterfall and the glowing eyes of a cat. He wore a green robe with curious markings. He took my hand. "Come in," he said. "There are wonders here."

The room was actually a natural grotto with stalactites hanging from the ceiling and, at its center, a natural pool of still dark water. Beside the pool was a bronze statue of Cybele, showing the goddess seated and holding in one hand the holy drum. Two stools were the only furnishings in the cave. He invited me to sit down.

"You will go on many journeys," said Maximus. My heart sank. He sounded like any soothsayer in the agora. "And I shall accompany you to the end."

"I could hope for no better teacher," I said formally, somewhat taken aback. He was presumptuous.

"Do not be alarmed, Julian . . ." He knew exactly what I was thinking. "I am not forcing myself upon you. Quite the contrary I am being forced. Just as you are. By something neither of us can control. Nor will it be easy, what we must do together. There is great danger for both of us. Especially for me. I dread being your teacher."

"But I had hoped . . ."

"I am your teacher," he concluded. "What is it that you would most like to know?"

"The truth."

"The truth of what?"

"Where do we come from and where do we go to, and what is the meaning of the journey?"

"You are Christian." He said this carefully, making neither a statement nor a question of it. Had there been a witness to this scene, I might have allowed a door in my mind to shut. As it was, I paused. I thought of Bishop George, interminably explaining "similar" as opposed to "same." I heard the deacon chanting the songs of Arius. I heard myself reading the lesson in the chapel at Macellum. Then suddenly I saw before me the leather-bound testament Bishop George had given me: "Thou shalt not revile the gods."

"No," said Maximus gravely. "For that way lies eternal darkness."

I was startled. "I said nothing."

"You quoted from the book of the Jews, from Exodus. 'Thou shalt not revile the gods.'"

"But I *said* nothing."

"You thought it."

"You can see into my thoughts?"

"When the gods give me the power, yes."

"Then look now, carefully, and tell me: am I Christian?"

"I cannot speak for you, nor tell you what I see."

"I believe there does exist a first maker, an absolute power . . ."

"Was it the same god who spoke to Moses 'mouth to mouth'?"

"So I have been taught."

"Yet that god was not absolute. He made the earth and heaven, men and beasts. But according to Moses, he did not make darkness or even matter, since the earth was already there before him, invisible and without form. He was merely the shaper of what already existed. Does one not prefer Plato's god, who caused this universe to come 'into being as a living creature, possessing soul and intelligence in very truth, both by the providence of god'?"

"From the *Timaeus*," I said automatically.

"And then there is the confusion between the book of the Jews and the book of the Nazarene. The god of the first is supposed to be the god of the second. Yet in the second he is father of the Nazarene . . ."

"By grace. They are of similar substance, but not the same."
Maximus laughed. "Well learned, my young Arian."

"I am Arian because I find it impossible to believe that God
was briefly a man executed for treason. Jesus was a prophet—a
son of God in some mysterious way—yes, but not the One God."

"Not even his deputy, despite the efforts of the extraordinary
Paul of Tarsus, who tried to prove that the tribal god of the Jews
was the universal One God, even though every word Paul says is
contradicted by the Jewish holy book. In letters to the Romans
and to the Galatians, Paul declared that the god of Moses is the
god not only of Jews but also of Gentiles. Yet the Jewish book
denies this in a hundred places. As their god said to Moses: 'Israel
is my son, my firstborn.' Now if this god of the Jews were indeed,
as Paul claimed, the One God, why then did he reserve for a single
unimportant race the anointing, the prophets and the law? Why
did he allow the rest of mankind to exist thousands of years in
darkness, worshipping falsely? Of course the Jews admit that he
is a 'jealous god.' But what an extraordinary thing for the absolute
to be! Jealous of what? And cruel, too, for he avenged the sins
of the fathers on guiltless children. Is not the creator described by
Homer and Plato more likely? that there is one being who encom-
passes all life—is all life—and from this essential source ema-
nates gods, demons, men? Or to quote the famous Orphic oracle
which the Galileans are beginning to appropriate for their own
use, 'Zeus, Hades, Helios, three gods in one Godhead.'"

"From the One many . . ." I began, but with Maximus one never
needs to finish sentences. He anticipates the trend of one's thought.

"How can the many be denied? Are all emotions alike? or does
each have characteristics peculiarly its own? And if each race has
its own qualities, are not those god-given? And, if not god-given,
would not these characteristics then be properly symbolized by a
specific national god? In the case of the Jews a jealous bad-
tempered patriarch. In the case of the effeminate, clever Syrians,
a god like Apollo. Or take the Germans and the Celts—who are
warlike and fierce—is it accident that they worship Ares, the war
god? Or is it inevitable? The early Romans were absorbed by
lawmaking and governing—their god? the king of gods, Zeus.
And each god has many aspects and many names, for there is as
much variety in heaven as there is among men. Some have asked:
did we create these gods or did they create us? That is an old
debate. Are we a dream in the mind of deity, or is each of us a

separate dreamer, evoking his own reality? Though one may not know for certain, all our senses tell us that a single creation does exist and we are contained by it forever. Now the Christians would impose one final rigid myth on what we know to be various and strange. No, not even myth, for the Nazarene existed as flesh while the gods we worship were never men; rather they are qualities and powers become poetry for our instruction. With the worship of the dead Jew, the poetry ceased. The Christians wish to replace our beautiful legends with the police record of a reforming Jewish rabbi. Out of this unlikely material they hope to make a final synthesis of all the religions ever known. They now appropriate our feast days. They transform local deities into saints. They borrow from our mystery rites, particulary those of Mithras. The priests of Mithras are called 'fathers.' So the Christians call *their* priests 'fathers.' They even imitate the tonsure, hoping to impress new converts with the familiar trappings of an older cult. Now they have started to call the Nazarene 'savior' and 'healer.' Why? Because one of the most beloved of our gods is Asklepios, whom we call 'savior' and 'healer.'"

"But there is nothing in Mithras to equal the Christian mystery." I argued for the devil. "What of the Eucharist, the taking of the bread and wine, when Christ said, 'He who eats of my body and drinks of my blood shall have eternal life.'"

Maximus smiled. "I betray no secret of Mithras when I tell you that we, too, partake of a symbolic meal, recalling the words of the Persian prophet Zarathustra, who said to those who worshipped the One God—and Mithras, 'He who eats of my body and drinks of my blood, so that he will be made one with me and I with him, the same shall know salvation. That was spoken six centuries before the birth of the Nazarene."

I was stunned. "Zarathustra was a man . . . ?"

"A prophet. He was stuck down in a temple by enemies. As he lay dying, he said, 'May God forgive you even as I do.' No, there is nothing sacred to us that the Galileans have not stolen. The main task of their innumerable councils is to try to make sense of all their borrowings. I don't envy them."

"I have read Porphyry . . ." I began.

"Then you are aware of how the Galileans contradict themselves."

"But what of the contradictions in Hellenism?"

"Old legends are bound to conflict. But then, we never think

77

of them as *literally* true. They are merely cryptic messages from the gods, who in turn are aspects of the One. We know that we must interpret them. Sometimes we succeed. Sometimes we fail. But the Christians hold to the literal truth of the book which was written about the Nazarene long after his death. Yet even that book so embarrasses them that they must continually alter its meaning. For instance, nowhere does it say that Jesus *was* God . . ."

"Except in John." I quoted: " 'And the Word was made flesh, and dwelt among us.' " I had not been five years a church reader for nothing.

"That is open to interpretation. What precisely was meant by 'Word'? Is it really, as they now pretend, the holy spirit who is also God who is also Jesus?—which brings us again to that triple impiety they call 'truth,' which in turn reminds us that the most noble Julian also wishes to know the truth."

"It is what I wish." I felt strange. The smoke from the torches was thick in the room. All things now appeared indistinct and unreal. Had the walls opened suddenly and the sun blazed down upon us, I should not have been surprised. But Maximus practiced no magic that day. He was matter-of-fact.

"No one can tell another man what is true. Truth is all around us. But each must find it in his own way. Plato is part of the truth. So is Homer. So is the story of the Jewish god if one ignores its arrogant claims. Truth is wherever man has glimpsed divinity. Theurgy can achieve this awakening. Poetry can. Or the gods themselves of their own volition can suddenly open our eyes."

"My eyes are shut."

"Yes."

"But I know what it is I want to find."

"But there is a wall in front of you, like the mirror you tried to walk into."

I looked at him very hard. "Maximus, show me a door, and not a mirror."

He was silent a long time. When he finally spoke, he did not look at me. Instead he studied the face of Cybele. "You are Christian."

"I am nothing."

"But you must be Christian, for that is the religion of your family."

"I must *appear* to be Christian. Nothing more."

"You do not fear being a hypocrite?"

78

"I fear not knowing the truth even more."

"Are you prepared to be admitted to the secret rites of Mithras?"

"Is that the way?"

"It is a way. If you are willing to make the attempt, I can lead you to the door. But you must cross through alone. I cannot help you past the gate."

"And after I pass through?"

"You will know what it is to die and be born again."

"Then you shall be my teacher, Maximus. And my guide."

"Of course I shall be." He smiled. "It is our fate. Remember what I said? We have no choice, either of us. Fate has intervened. Together we shall proceed to the end of the tragedy."

"Tragedy?"

"Human life is tragic: it ends in pain and death."

"But after the pain? after the death?"

"When you cross the threshold of Mithras, you will know what it is like to be beyond tragedy, to be beyond what is human, to be one with God."

*Priscus*: Interesting to observe Maximus in action. He *was* clever. I would have guessed that at their first meeting he would have done tricks. Made the statue of Cybele dance. Something like that. But no. He gives a shrewd attack on Christianity. Then he offers Julian Mithras, a religion bound to appeal to our hero. Mithras was always the favorite deity of Roman emperors, and of many soldiers to this day. Also, Maximus knew that he would be sure of a special relationship to Julian if he were the one who sponsored him during the rites.

There is now no doubt in my mind that at this point in Julian's life almost any of the mystery cults would have got him free of Christianity. He was eager to make the break. Yet it is hard to say quite why, since his mind tended to magic and superstition in precisely the same way the Christian mind does. Admittedly their worship of corpses did not appeal to him, but he was later to find manifestations of "the One" in even odder places. Had Julian been what he thought he was—a philosopher in the tradition of Plato—one might have understood his dislike of the Christian nonsense. He would have been like you and me. But Julian was concerned, finally, with the idea of personal immortality, the one obsession Christians share with those who are drawn to the old mystery cults.

Despite everything Julian wrote on the subject, I have never understood precisely why he turned against the religion of his family. After all, Christianity offered him nearly everything he needed. If he wanted to partake symbolically of the body of a god, why not remain with the Christians and eat their bread and drink their wine instead of reverting to the bread and wine of Mithras? It is not as if there was anything lacking in Christianity. The Christians have slyly incorporated most of the popular elements of Mithras and Demeter and Dionysos into their own rites. Modern Christianity is an encyclopedia of traditional superstition.

I suspect the origin of Julian's disaffection is in his family. Constantius was a passionate Christian, absorbed by doctrinal disputes. With good reason, Julian hated Constantius. Therefore, he hated Christianity. This puts the matter far too simply, yet I always tend to the obvious view of things since it is usually the correct one, though of course one can never get to the bottom of anything so mysterious as another man's character, and there is a mystery here.

Julian was Christian in everything except his tolerance of others. He was what the Christians would call a saint. Yet he swung fiercely away from the one religion which suited him perfectly, preferring its eclectic origins, which he then tried to systematize into a new combination quite as ridiculous as the synthesis he had rejected. It is a strange business and there is no satisfactory explanation for Julian's behavior. Of course he claimed that Bishop George's partisanship disgusted him as a boy, and that Porphyry and Plotinus opened his eyes to the absurdity of Christian claims. Well and good. But then why turn to something equally absurd? Granted, no educated man can accept the idea of a Jewish rebel as god. But having rejected that myth, how can one then believe that the Persian hero-god Mithras was born of light striking rock, on December 25th, with shepherds watching his birth? (I am told that the Christians have just added those shepherds to the birth of Jesus.) Or that Mithras lived in a fig tree which fed and clothed him, that he fought with the sun's first creation, the bull, that he was dragged by it (thus symbolizing man's suffering) until the bull escaped; finally, at the command of the sun god, Mithras stabs the bull with a knife and from the beast's body came flowers, herbs, wheat; from the blood, wine; from the seed, the first man and woman. Then Mithras is called up to heaven, after celebrating a sacramental last supper. Time's end will be a day of judgment when all will rise from their graves and evil will be destroyed while the good will live forever in the light of the sun.

Between the Mithraic story and its Christian sequel I see no essential difference. Admittedly, the Mithraic code of conduct is more admirable than the Christian. Mithraists believe that right action is better than contemplation. They favor old-fashioned virtues like courage and self-restraint. They were the first to teach that strength is gentleness. All of this is rather better than the Christian hysteria which vacillates between murder of heretics on the one hand and a cringing rejection of this world on the other. Nor can a Mithraist be absolved of sin by a sprinkle of water. Ethically, I find Mithras the best of all the mystery cults. But it is absurd to say it is any more "true" than its competitors. When one becomes absolute about myth and magic, the result can only be madness.

Julian speaks continually of his love of Hellenism. He honestly believed he loved Plato and reasonable discourse. Actually, what he craved was what so many desire in this falling time: assurance of personal immortality. He chose to reject the Christian way for reasons which I find obscure, while settling on an equal absurdity. Of course I am sympathetic to him. He dealt the Christians some good blows and that delighted me. But I cannot sympathize with his fear of extinction. Why is it so important to continue after death? We never question the demonstrable fact that before birth we did not exist, so why should we fear becoming once more what we were to begin with? I am in no hurry to depart. But I look on nothing as just that: *no thing*. How can one fear no thing?

As for the various ceremonies and trials the Mithraic initiate must undergo, the less said the better. I understand that one of the twelve tortures is the pulling out one by one of the pubic hairs, a most spiritual discipline. I was told that part of the ceremonies are conducted while everyone is roaring drunk and trying to jump over ditches blindfolded, a symbol no doubt of the bewildering life of the flesh. But men are impressed by secret rites, the more gruesome and repellent the better. How sad we are, how terrified to be men!

*Libanius*: It is not often one finds a philosopher so entirely lacking in the religious sense. It is like being born unable to perceive colors which are plain to everyone else. Priscus does have a logical mind and a precise way of stating things, but he is blind to what

81

truly matters. Like Julian, I was admitted to the Mithraic rites during my student days. The impression the mysteries made on me was profound, though I confess that the effect was not as revealing—for me—as it was for Julian. But I had never been a Christian, so I was not making a dramatic and dangerous break with the world I belonged to. However, for Julian it was a brave thing to do. Had Constantius learned of what he had done, it might have cost him his life. Fortunately, Maximus managed the affair so skillfully that Constantius never knew that at the age of nineteen his cousin ceased to be a Christian, in a cave beneath Mount Pion.

Priscus seems to have missed the point of the Mithraic mysteries, which does not surprise me. Priscus applauds our high ethical standards. We are grateful to him. But he finds the rites "repellent." Of course he knows about them only by hearsay, since no one who has been initiated may recount what happens in the cave. But though the "trials" are often disagreeable, the revelation is worth all the pain that one has borne. I for one cannot imagine a world without Mithras.

Priscus observes with his usual harsh candor that the Christians are gradually absorbing various aspects of the cult. A thought suddenly occurs to me: might not this be the way in which we finally conquer? Is it not possible that the absorber will become so like the absorbed that in time they will be us?

*Julian Augustus*

In March 351, I was admitted to the mysteries of Mithras. On that day I watched the rising of the sun; and I watched its setting, taking care to be unobserved, for since Constantius had made it illegal to pray to the sun, people had even been arrested for watching a sunset. Spies and informers were everywhere.

I had told Ecebolius that I intended to spend the day hunting on the slopes of Mount Pion. Since he hated hunting, he excused himself as I knew he would. He quoted Homer. I quoted Horace. He quoted Virgil, I quoted Theocritus. Together we used up nearly all of literature's references to hunting.

The next obstacle was the bodyguard. Twelve soldiers and one officer were assigned to my household. At all times I was attended by at least two men. What to do about them? It was Maximus who decided that since Mithras is the soldier's religion, at least two of the soldiers should prove sympathetic. Maximus was right. Of the twelve, five were Mithraists. It was then an easy matter to get two of the five assigned to me for the day. As Mithraic brothers, they were under the seal of secrecy.

An hour before dawn, Oribasius, the soldiers and I left the house. At the mountain's edge we were met by Maximus and nine fathers. In silence we climbed the slope. At a preordained spot, beneath a fig tree, we stopped and waited for the sun to rise.

The sky turned pale. The morning star shone blue. Dark clouds broke. Then just as the sun appeared on the horizon, a single shaft of light struck the rock behind us and I realized that it was not just ordinary rock, but a door into the mountainside. We prayed then to the sun and to his companion Mithras, our savior.

When the sun was at last above the horizon, Maximus opened the door into the mountain and we entered a small cave with seats carved out of the rock. Here Oribasius and I were told to wait while the fathers of Mithras withdrew into yet another cave, the inner sanctuary. Thus began the most momentous day of my life. The day of the honey and of the bread and the wine; the day of the seven gates and the seven planets; the day of challenges and of passwords; the day of prayer and, at its end (past Raven, Bride, Soldier, Lion, Persian, Courier of the Sun, and Father), the day of *Nama Nama Sebesio*.

*Libanius*: Of all the mysteries, excepting those at Eleusis, the Mithraic is the most inspiring, for in the course of it one actually experiences the folly of earthly vanity. At each of the seven stages, the initiate acts out what his soul will one day experience as it rises amongst the seven spheres, losing one by one its human faults. At Ares, the desire for war returns to its source; at Zeus, ambition is lost; at Aphrodite, sex, and so on until the soul is purged. Then . . . But *I* can say no more. *Nama Nama Sebesio*.

*Julian Augustus*

When the day ended, Oribasius and I stumbled from the cave, born again.

It was then that it happened. As I looked at the setting sun, I was possessed by light. What is given to few men was given to me. I saw the One. I was absorbed by Helios and my veins coursed not with blood but light.

I saw it all. I saw the simplicity at the heart of creation. The thing which is impossible to grasp without the help of divinity, for it is beyond language and beyond mind: yet it is so simple that

83

I marveled at how one could *not* have known what is always there, a part of us just as we are part of it. What happened inside the cave was a testing and a learning, but what happened to me outside the cave was revelation.

I saw the god himself as I knelt among sage bushes, the red slanting sunlight full in my face. I heard that which cannot be written or told and I saw that which cannot be recorded in words or images. Yet even now, years later, it is as vivid in retrospect as it was at the time. For I was chosen on that steep mountainside to do the great work in which I am now engaged: the restoration of the worship of the One God, in all his beautiful singularity.

I remained kneeling until the sun was gone. Then I knelt in darkness for what I am told was an hour. I knelt until Oribasius became alarmed and awakened me . . . or put me to sleep, for the "real" world ever since has seemed to me the dream while my vision of Helios is the reality.

"Are you all right?"

I nodded and got to my feet. "I have seen . . ." But I stopped. I could not say what I had seen. Even now, writing this memoir, I cannot describe what I experienced since there is nothing comparable in ordinary human experience.

But Maximus immediately recognized what had happened to me. "He has been chosen," he said. "He knows."

Silently we returned to the city. I did not want to talk to anyone, not even to Maximus, for I was still enfolded by wings of light. Even the back of my hand where I had received the sacred tattoo did not hurt me. But at the city gate my absorption was rudely shattered by a large crowd which surrounded me, shouting, "Great news!"

I was bewildered. All I could think was: has the god remained with me? is what I saw visible to all? I tried to speak to Maximus and Oribasius but we could not make ourselves heard.

At the prefect's house, I found Ecebolius with the town prefect and what looked to be the whole council. When they saw me, they fell to their knees. For an instant I thought it was indeed the end of the world and that I had been sent as messenger to separate the good from the bad. But Ecebolius quickly dispelled all thought of apocalypse.

"Most noble Julian, your brother . . ." All about us, men began to repeat Gallus's names and titles. ". . . has been raised by the divine Augustus to share with him the purple. Gallus is Caesar in the East. He is also to be married to Constantia, divine sister of the divine Augustus!"

There was loud cheering and eager hands touched my robe, my hands, my arms. Favors were requested, blessings demanded. Finally, I broke through the mob and got inside the house.

"But why are they all behaving like lunatics?" I turned on Ecebolius, as though it were his fault.

"Because you are now the brother of a reigning Caesar."

"Much good it will do them . . . or me." This was unwise, but it relieved me to say it.

"Surely you don't want them to love you for yourself?" Oribasius teased me. "You quite enjoyed the attention, until you heard the news."

"Only because I thought it was the sun . . ." I stopped myself just in time.

"The sun?" Ecebolius looked puzzled.

"Only the son of God should be treated in this fashion," said Maximus smoothly. "Men should not *worship* other men, not even princes."

Ecebolius nodded. "A relic of the bad old days, I'm afraid. The Augustus of Rome is of course 'divine' though not truly a god as men used to think. But come in, come in. The baths are ready. And the prefect is giving us a banquet to celebrate the good news."

So I beheld the One God on the same day that I learned my brother had been made Caesar. The omen was plain enough. Each was now set in his destiny. From that day on I was Hellenist or, as the Galileans like to call me (behind my back, of course!), apostate. And Gallus reigned in the East.

# VI

"Naturally the Caesar is concerned."

"But without cause."

"Without cause? You are a pupil of Maximus."

"I am also a pupil of Ecebolius."

"But he has not been with you for a year. Your brother feels that you are in need of a spiritual guide, especially now."

"But Maximus *is* responsible."

85

"Maximus is not a Christian. *Are you*?" The question came at me like a stone from a sling. I stared a long moment at the black-robed deacon Aetius of Antioch. He stared serenely back. I was close to panic. What did they know of me at Gallus's court?

"How can you doubt that I am a Christian?" I said finally. "I was instructed by two great bishops. I am a church reader. I attend every important church ceremony here at Pergamon." I looked at him, simulating righteousness doubted. "Where could such a rumor get started? If there is such a rumor."

"You cannot be seen too often in the company of a man like Maximus without people wondering."

"What shall I do?"

"Give him up." The answer was prompt.

"Is that my brother's order?"

"It is my suggestion. Your brother is concerned. That is all. He sent me here to question you. I have."

"Are you satisfied?"

Aetius smiled. "Nothing ever satisfies me, most noble Julian. But I shall tell the Caesar that you are a regular communicant of the church. I shall also tell him that you will no longer study with Maximus."

"If that is the wisest course, then that is the course I shall take." This ambiguity seemed to satisfy Aetius. My friends often tell me that I might have made a good lawyer.

As I escorted Aetius to the street, he looked about him and said, "The owner of this house..."

"...is Oribasius."

"An excellent physician."

"Is it wise for me to see him?" I could not resist this.

"A highly suitable companion," said Aetius smoothly. He paused at the door to the street. "Your brother, the Caesar, often wonders why you do not come to visit him at Antioch. He feels that court life might have a... 'polishing' effect upon you. The word is his, not mine."

"I'm afraid I was not made for a court, even one as celebrated as my brother's. I resist all attempts to polish me, and I detest politicians."

"A wise aversion."

"And a true one. I want only to live as I do, as a student."

"Studying to what end?"

"To know myself. What else?"

86

"Yes. What else?" Aetius got into his carriage. "Be very careful, most noble Julian. And remember: a prince has no friends. Ever."

"Thank you, Deacon."

Aetius departed. I went back into the house. Oribasius was waiting for me.

"You heard every word?" I hardly made a question of it. Oribasius and I have never had any secrets between us. On principle, he eavesdrops.

"We've been indiscreet, to say the least."

I nodded. I was gloomy. "I suppose I shall have to stop seeing Maximus, at least for a while."

"You might also insist that he not talk to everyone about his famous pupil."

I sighed. I knew that Maximus tended—tends—to trade on his relationship with me. Princes get very used to that. I don't resent it. In fact, I am happy if my friends prosper as a result of knowing me. I had learned Oribasius's lesson, and I do not expect to be loved for myself. After all, I don't love others for themselves, only for what they can teach me.

Since nothing is free, to each his price.

I summoned a secretary and wrote Maximus asking him to remain at Ephesus until further notice. I also wrote a note to the bishop of Pergamon to tell him that I would read the lesson on the following Sunday.

"Hypocrite," said Oribasius when the secretary had gone.

"A long-lived hypocrite is preferable to a dead . . . what?" I often have trouble finishing epigrams. Or rather I start one without having first thought through to the end, a bad habit.

"A dead *reader*. Aetius has a good deal of influence with Gallus, hasn't he?"

"So they say. He is his confessor. But who can control my brother?" Without thinking, I had lowered my voice to a whisper. For Gallus had become as suspicious of treason as Constantius. His spies were everywhere.

I blame Gallus's wife Constantia for the overt change in his character. She was Constantius's sister and took it for granted that conspiracy is the natural business of the human race. I never met this famous lady but I am told that she was as cruel as Gallus, and far more intelligent. She was also ambitious, which he was not. He was quite content to remain Caesar in the East. But she

87

wanted him to be the Augustus and she plotted the death of her own brother to achieve this end. As for Gallus, even now I cannot bear to write about his reign.

*Priscus*: I can. And you certainly can! After all, you were living at Antioch while that little beast was Caesar.

Curiously enough, Julian almost never mentioned Gallus to me, or to anyone. I have always had a theory—somewhat borne out by the memoir—that Julian was unnaturally attracted to his brother. He continually refers to his beauty. He also tends to write of him in that hurt tone one uses to describe a lover who has been cold. Julian professes to find mysterious what everyone else found only too obvious: Gallus's cruelty. Julian was naïve, as I find myself continually observing (if I repeat myself, do forgive me and blame it on our age).

Actually, the member of the family for whom I have the most sympathy is Constantius. He was quite a good ruler, you know. We tend to undervalue him because his intelligence was of the second rank, and his religious mania troubling. But he governed well, considering that he had problems of a sort which might have made any man a monster. He made some of his worst mistakes for the best of reasons, like creating Gallus Caesar.

It is significant that Julian blames Gallus's wife for the reign of terror in the East. I had always thought that they were equally to blame. But you lived through what must have been a terrible time. You doubtless know who was responsible for what.

*Libanius*: Yes, I do know. At the beginning, we all had great hopes for Gallus. I recall vividly Gallus's first appearance before the senate of Antioch. How hopeful we were! He was indeed as handsome as men say, though that day he was suffering from a heat rash, as fair people sometimes do in our sultry climate. But despite a mottled face, he carried himself well. He looked as one born to rule. He made us a most graceful speech. Afterwards, I was presented to him by my old friend Bishop Meletius.

"Oh, yes," Gallus frowned. "You are that teacher-fellow who denies God."

"I deny God nothing, Caesar. My heart is open to him at all times."

"Libanius is really most admirable, Caesar." Meletius always enjoyed making me suffer.

88

"I am sure he is." Then Gallus gave me a smile so dazzling that I was quite overwhelmed. "Come see me," he said, "and I shall personally convert you."

A few weeks later, to my surprise, I received an invitation to the palace. When I arrived at the appointed hour, I was shown into a large room where, side by side on a couch, lay Gallus and Constantia.

In the center of the room two nude boxers were pummeling one another to death. When I had recovered from my first shock at this indecent display, I tried to make my presence known. I coughed: I mumbled a greeting. But I was ignored. Gallus and Constantia were completely absorbed by the bloody spectacle. As the world knows, I hate gladiatorial demonstrations because they reduce men to the level of beasts—and I do not mean those unfortunates who are forced to perform. I mean those who watch.

I was particularly shocked by Constantia. It was hard to realize that this bright-eyed unwomanly spectator was the daughter of Constantine the Great, sister of the Augustus, wife of the Caesar. She seemed more like an unusually cruel courtesan. Yet she *was* distinguished-looking in the Flavian way—big jaw, large nose, gray eyes. As we watched the sweating, bloody men, she would occasionally shout to one or the other, "Kill him!" Whenever a particularly effective blow was dealt, she would gasp in a curiously intimate way, like a woman in the sexual act. Constantia was most alarming.

We watched those boxers until one man finally killed the other. As the loser fell, Gallus leapt from his couch and threw his arms around the bloody victor, as though he had done him some extraordinary service. Then Gallus began to kick the dead man, laughing and shouting gleefully. He looked perfectly deranged. I have never seen a man's face quite so revealing of the beast within.

"Stop it, Gallus!" Constantia had noticed me at last. She was on her feet.

"What?" He looked at her blankly. Then he saw me. "Oh, yes," he said. He straightened his tunic. Slaves came forward and removed the dead boxer. Constantia approached me with a radiant smile. "How happy we are to see the famous Libanius here, in our palace." I saluted her formally, noticing with some surprise that her normal voice was low and musical, and that her Greek was excellent. In an instant she had transformed herself from Fury to queen.

Gallus came forward and gave me his hand to kiss. I got blood on my lips.

"Good, very good," he said, eyes unfocused like a man drunk. Then without another word, the Caesar of the East and his queen swept past me and that was the end of the only private audience I was ever to have with either of them. I was most unnerved.

During the next few years the misdeeds of the couple were beyond anything since Caligula. To begin with, they were both eager for money. To further her political objectives Constantia needed all the gold she could amass. She tried everything: blackmail, the sale of public offices, confiscation. One of her fund-raising attempts involved a family I knew. It was a peculiar situation. When the daughter married an extremely handsome youth from Alexandria, her mother, an ordinarily demure matron—or so we all thought—promptly fell in love with him. For a year she tried unsuccessfully to seduce her son-in-law. Finally, he told her that if she did not stop importuning him, he would return to Alexandria. Quite out of her mind with rage, the woman went to Constantia and offered that noble queen a small fortune for the arrest and execution of her son-in-law. Constantia took the money; and the unfortunate youth was executed on a trumped-up charge. Then Constantia, who was not without a certain bitter humor, sent the matron her son-in-law's genitals with a brief note: "At last!" The woman lost her mind. Antioch was scandalized. And the days of terror began.

At times it seemed almost as if Gallus and Constantia had deliberately studied the lives of previous monsters with an eye to recreating old deeds of horror. Nero used to roam the streets at night with a band of rowdies, pretending he was an ordinary young buck on the town. So did Gallus. Caligula used to ask people what they thought of the emperor and if their answer was unflattering, he would butcher them on the spot. So did Gallus. Or tried to. Unfortunately for him, Antioch—unlike early imperial Rome—has the most elaborate street lighting in the world. Our night is like the noon in most cities, so Gallus was almost always recognized. As a result, the praetorian prefect of the East, Thalassios, was able to persuade him that not only was it unbecoming for a Caesar to rove the streets at night, it was also dangerous. Gallus abandoned his prowling.

During Gallus's third year as Caesar, there was a famine in Syria. When the food shortages at Antioch began, Gallus tried to fix prices at a level which would make it possible for everyone to buy grain. Even wise rulers from time to time make this mistake. It never works since the result is usually the precise opposite of the one intended. Grain is either held back from the market or bought up by speculators who resell it at a huge profit, increasing the famine. Men are like this and there is nothing to be done about them. The senate of Antioch has many faults, but its members are sound businessmen with an understanding of the market which is their life. They warned Gallus of the dangers of his policy. He ordered them to obey him. When they continued to resist him, he sent his own guards into the senate chamber, arrested the leading senators and condemned them to death.

Antioch had reason to be grateful to both Thalassios and Nebridius, the Count of the East. These two brave men told Gallus that if he went through with the executions, they would appeal to the Augustus and demand the Caesar's removal. It was a brave thing to do, and to everyone's surprise they carried the day. Gallus released the senators, and that was the end of the matter. For some months Antioch was relieved to know that in Thalassios the city had a defender. But then Thalassios died of fever. Of course it was rumored that he had been poisoned, but I happen to know that it was indeed the fever that he died of, as we shared the same doctor. But I do not mean to write the history of Gallus, which is so well known.

*Julian Augustus*

After Aetius's visit to me, I met Maximus only in secret. I arranged this by seeing to it that the guards who accompanied me were brothers in Mithras. I don't think I was once betrayed during the three years I lived with Oribasius at Pergamon. I also made a point of becoming a friend of the bishop of the city. With him, I observed every Galilean festival. I hated myself for this deception, but I had no choice.

During these years, I was free to travel wherever I pleased in the East. I could even visit Constantinople, though the Chamberlain's office suggested tactfully that I not live there since it was, after all, the imperial capital *without*, at present, an emperor in residence, which meant that any visit I chose to make could be construed as . . . I understood perfectly and stayed away.

My request for permission to go to Athens was rejected. I don't know why. Gallus sent me several invitations to come to Antioch, but I was always able to avoid accepting them. I think he was relieved not to have me near him. However, he was most conscientious in his role as older brother and guardian, not to mention ruler. I received weekly bulletins from him asking about my spiritual health. He was eager, he said, for me to be a devout and good man, like himself. I think he was perfectly sincere in his exhortations. His fault was a common one. He simply did not know what he was; he saw no flaw in himself, a not unusual blindness and preferable, on the whole, to being unable to find any virtue in oneself.

My friendship with Oribasius is the only intimate one I have ever had—the result, I suppose, of having never known the ordinary life of a family. Oribasius is both friend and brother, even though we are not much alike in disposition. He is skeptical and experimental, interested only in the material world. I am the opposite. He balances me. Or tries to. And I think at times I give him some inkling of what the metaphysical is like. For nearly four years we lived together, traveled together, studied together. We even shared a mistress for a time, though this caused some disturbance since I found, to my surprise, that I have a jealous nature. I had never forgiven the Antiochene at Macellum for preferring Gallus to me. Yet I should have. After all, Gallus was older and handsomer than I. Even so, I had been resentful. I did not realize to what extent, until I was again put in exactly the same situation. One afternoon I overheard Oribasius and our mutual mistress— a blue-eyed Gaul—making love. I heard their heavy breathing. I heard the leather thongs of the bed creak. Suddenly I wanted to murder them both. I knew then exactly what it was like to be Gallus, and I almost fainted at the violence of my own response. But the moment quickly passed and I was filled with shame.

During those years, Maximus taught me many things. He showed me mysteries. He made it possible for me to contemplate the One. He was the perfect teacher. Also, contrary to legend, he did not in any way try to excite my ambition. We never spoke of my becoming emperor. It was the one forbidden subject.

*Priscus*: This is simply not true. From certain things both Julian and Maximus said to me, I *know* that they were busy plotting to make Julian emperor. Maximus was not about to waste his time on a minor prince, nor was Oribasius—even though his friendship with Julian was genuine, or as genuine as anyone's relations can ever be with a prince.

I have been told of at least one séance where Maximus was advised by one of his invisible friends that Julian was destined to become emperor. I also know that Sosipatra and a number of other magicians were secret partisans. Of course, after Julian became emperor, every magician in Asia claimed to have had a hand in his success. I can't think why Julian wanted to deny what so many of us know to have been true. Perhaps to discourage others from plotting against *him*, as he plotted against Constantius.

*Libanius*: "Plotted" is the wrong word, though of course Julian is disingenuous in his narrative. I agree with Priscus that Maximus and Oribasius were already looking forward to the day when their friend would be, if not Augustus, at least Caesar. I am also perfectly certain that Maximus consulted forbidden oracles, and all the rest. Sosipatra told me as much a few years ago: "The goddess Cybele always favored Julian, and said so. We were all so grateful to her for her aid."

But I strongly doubt that there was any political plot. How could there be? Julian had very little money. He was guarded by a detachment of household troops whose commander was directly answerable to the Grand Chamberlain. Also, I do not believe that Julian at this point wanted the principate. He was a devoted student. He was terrified of the court. He had never commanded a single soldier in war or peace. How could he then, at the age of twenty, dream of becoming emperor? Or rather he might "dream"— in fact we know that he did—but he could hardly have *planned* to take the throne.

*Julian Augustus*

In the autumn of 353, Gallus made a state visit to Pergamon. It was the first time we had met since we were boys at Macellum. I stood with the town prefect and the local dignitaries in front of the senate house and watched Gallus receive the homage of the city.

During the five years since we had seen one another, I had become a man with a full beard. But Gallus had remained exactly as he was, the beautiful youth whom all admired. I confess that I had a return of the old emotion when he embraced me formally and I looked once again into those familiar blue eyes. What was

93

the old emotion? A loss of will, I should say. Whatever he wanted me to do I would do. Gallus, by existing, robbed me of strength.

"We are pleased to see once again our beloved and most noble brother." Gallus had by now completely assumed the imperial manner. Before I could reply, Gallus had turned to the bishop of Pergamon. "He is, we have heard, a pillar of the true church."

"Indeed, Caesar, the most noble Julian is a worthy son of holy church." I was extremely grateful to the bishop. Also, I was rather pleased that my efforts to appear a devout Galilean had been so successful.

Gallus then made a graceful speech to the city fathers, who were so charmed by him that they were obviously puzzled at how this enchanting creature had ever got the reputation of being a cruel and frivolous despot. Gallus could charm anyone, even me.

That night a dinner was given him at the prefect's palace. He behaved himself quite well, though I noticed that he did not cut his wine with water. As a result, he was drunk by the end of the evening. Yet he maintained his dignity and only a slight slowness of speech betrayed his state. Though I sat beside him during dinner, he did not speak to me once. All his efforts were bent on delighting the city prefect. I was miserable, wondering in what way I had managed to offend him. Oribasius, who sat across the room with the minor functionaries of the court, winked at me encouragingly. But I was not encouraged.

The dinner ended, Gallus suddenly turned to me and said, "You come with me." And so I followed him as he moved through the bowing courtiers to his bedroom, where two eunuchs were waiting for him.

I had never before seen the etiquette of a Caesar's bedchamber and I watched, fascinated, as the eunuchs, murmuring ceremonial phrases, undressed Gallus while he lolled in an ivory chair, completely unaware of them. He was without self-consciousness or modesty. When he was completely undressed, he waved them away with the command "Bring us wine!" Then while the wine was served us, he talked to me or rather *at* me. In the lamplight his face glowed red from drink and the blond hair looked white as it fell across his brow. The body, I noticed, though still beautifully shaped, was beginning to grow thick at the belly.

"Constantia wants to know you. She talks of you often. But of course she couldn't come here. One of us must always be at Antioch. Spies. Traitors. No one is honest. Do you realize that?

No one. You can never trust anyone, not even your own flesh and blood."

I tried to protest loyalty at this point. But Gallus ignored me. "All men are evil. I found that out early. They are born in sin, live in sin, die in sin. Only God can save us. I pray that he will save me." Gallus made the sign of a cross on his bare chest.

"But it is a fine thing in an evil world to be Caesar. From here," he indicated a height, "you can see them all. You can see them at their games. But they can't see you. Sometimes at night, I walk the streets in disguise. I listen to them. I watch them, knowing I can do anything to them I want and no one can touch me. If I want to rape a woman or kill a man in an alley, I can. Sometimes I do." He frowned. "But it is evil. I know it. I try not to. Yet I feel that when I do these things there is something higher which acts *through* me. I am a child of God. Unworthy as I am, he created me and to him I shall return. What I am, he wanted me to be. That is why I am good."

I must say I was stunned by this particular self-estimate. But my face showed only respectful interest.

"I build churches. I establish religious orders. I stamp out heresy wherever I find it. I am an active agent for the good. I must be. It is what I was born for. I can hardly believe you are my brother." He shifted his thought without a pause. He looked at me for the first time. The famous blue eyes were bloodshot in the full lamplight.

"*Half*-brother, Gallus."

"Even so. We are the same blood, which is what matters. That is what binds me to Constantius. And you to me. We are the chosen of God to do the work of his church on earth."

At this point an extraordinarily pretty girl slipped quietly into the room. Gallus did not acknowledge her presence, so neither did I. He continued to talk and drink, while she made love to him in front of me. I suppose it was the most embarrassing moment of my life. I tried not to watch. I looked at the ceiling. I looked at the floor. But my eyes continually strayed back to my brother as he reclined on the couch, hardly moving, as the girl with infinite skill and delicacy served him.

"Constantius will do anything I ask him. That is what blood means. He will also listen to his sister, my wife. She is the most important woman in the world. A perfect wife, a great queen."

95

He shifted his position on the couch so that his legs were spread apart.

"I hope you marry well. You could, you know. Constantius has another sister, Helena. She's much older than you, but that makes no difference when it is a matter of blood. Perhaps he will marry you to her. Perhaps he will even make you a Caesar, like me. Would that please you?"

I almost missed the question, my eyes riveted on what the girl was doing. Oribasius says that I am a prude. I suppose he is right. I know that I was sweating with nervous tension as I watched the ravishing of Gallus. "No," I stammered. "I have no wish to be Caesar. Only a student. I am perfectly happy."

"Everyone lies," said Gallus sadly. "Even you. Even flesh and blood. But there's very little chance of your being raised up. Very little. I have the East, Constantius the West. You are not needed. Do you have girls in your household?"

"One." My voice broke nervously.

"One!" He shook his head wonderingly. "And your friend? The one you live with?"

"Oribasius."

"Is he your lover?"

"No!"

"I wondered. It's perfectly all right. You're not Hadrian. What you do doesn't matter. Though if you like boys, I suggest you keep to slaves. It's politically dangerous to have anything to do with a man of your own class."

"I am not interested . . ." I began, but he continued right through me.

"Slaves are always best. Particularly stableboys and grooms." The blue eyes flashed suddenly: for an instant his face was transfigured by malice. He wanted me to recall what I had seen that day in the clearing. "But suit yourself. Anyway, my only advice to you, my only warning to you, not only as your brother but as your ruler . . ." He stopped suddenly and took a deep breath. The girl had finished. She got to her feet and stood in front of him, head bowed. He smiled, charmingly. Then he reached up and with all his strength struck her full in the face. She staggered back, but made no sound. Then at a gesture from him, she withdrew.

Gallus turned to me as though nothing had happened and picked up his sentence where he had left off. ". . . under no circumstances are you to see this magician Maximus. There are already enough

96

rumors that you may have lost your faith. I know that you haven't. How could you? We are of the house of Constantine the Great, the equal of the Apostles. We are the chosen of God. But even so . . ." He yawned. He lay back on the couch. "Even so . . ." he repeated and shut his eyes. I waited a moment for him to continue. But he was asleep.

The eunuchs reappeared. One placed a silk coverlet over Gallus. The other removed the wine. They acted as though what I had witnessed was a perfectly ordinary evening; perhaps it was. As Gallus began drunkenly to snore, I tiptoed from the room.

*Priscus*: I always thought Julian might have been a happier man had he been a bit more like Gallus. No one can say that Gallus did not enjoy himself. His was an exemplary life of complete self-indulgence. I could not be more envious of him.

*Libanius*: Obviously Priscus has found his ideal.

Within months of the state visit to Pergamon, Gallus fell. For two years the Emperor had been receiving disquieting reports about Gallus. Nebridius had told him bluntly that if Gallus were not removed as Caesar there would be civil war in Syria. In his last letter to Constantius, Thalassios had said much the same thing.

One final incident brought matters to a head. The food shortage had grown worse. The lower classes were rioting. Having failed at price fixing, Gallus determined to leave Antioch as quickly as possible. As pretext, he announced that he was planning to invade Persia (though he did not have sufficient troops to conquer a mud village on the Nile).

The day Gallus left the city, the senate met him in front of the memorial to Julius Caesar. A considerable crowd had also turned out to see him, but they were not interested in saying farewell to their Caesar. They wanted food, and they said so. They made the most terrible racket. I know. I was there. I have never seen such an angry mob. Behind a row of household troops with drawn swords, the Caesar and the senate exchanged formalities while all around us the mob roared, pressing closer and closer to where we stood. Even Gallus was alarmed.

Then Theophilus, the governor of Syria, came forward to make a speech to the Caesar. Now Theophilus was an excellent official but he was not popular. Why? Who knows? The Antiochenes are completely frivolous in public matters. If a cruel tyrant is witty,

97

they will adore him. But if their ruler is a good man, slow of speech, they will despise him. They despised Theophilus. They jeered his speech. Then the mob began to shout: "Food! Food!"

During this, I watched Gallus. At first he looked baffled; then— one could observe his very thought—crafty. He raised his hand for silence. But the shouting continued. So Theophilus motioned to the drummers, who set up an ominous rolling. The crowd fell silent.

Gallus spoke. "My good people, the heart of your Caesar grieves for you. Yet he is puzzled. You say you lack food. But why? There is food in Antioch. There is plenty of grain in the warehouses. Your Caesar put it there for you."

"Then give it to us!" A voice rang out.

Gallus shook his head. "But it is yours already. Your governor knows this." He turned to the stunned governor. "Theophilus, I have told you to feed the people. Why have you disobeyed me? Why have you been so cruel? Even if you are in league with the speculators, you must take pity on the people. The poor are hungry, Theophilus. Feed them!"

In all my long life I have never witnessed such a vicious scene. Gallus deliberately incited the people against his own governor. Then he rode off at the head of the legions, leaving us to the now violent mob. Like the rest of the senate, I bolted. Fortunately no one was hurt except Theophilus, who was torn to pieces. That day Gallus lost what small support he had among us.

When Constantius received news of the Theophilus affair, he realized at last that Gallus must be recalled. But it is easier to create a Caesar than to destroy one. Constantius knew that if he were to move against Gallus, there would be civil war. So Constantius proceeded cautiously. His first move was to order Gallus's army to rendezvous in Serbia preparatory to a campaign on the Danube. Inactive troops, said Constantius in a diplomatic letter to the Caesar, are prone to mutiny. So Gallus was left with only his personal guard and a single detachment of targeteers. Then Constantius instructed the prefect Domitian (until recently Count of the Sacred Largesse and a financial expert) to proceed to Syria, as though on a routine tour of the provinces. At Antioch, Domitian was to persuade Gallus to obey the Emperor's order to come to Milan "for consultation." Unfortunately, Domitian was vain and overbearing and perfectly confident that no one was so clever as he. I don't know why, but this seems to be a common trait of finance ministers.

Domitian arrived at Antioch to find Gallus again in residence, after a month's campaign on the Persian border. But instead of going first to the Caesar's palace as protocol requires, Domitian proceeded to military headquarters, announcing that he was too ill to come to court. For several weeks Domitian remained at headquarters, plotting against Gallus and sending back highly colored reports to the Emperor concerning the Caesar's doings. At last Gallus ordered Domitian to present himself at a meeting of the consistory. He did, and in a scene of unrivaled insolence, Domitian told Gallus that if he did not immediately obey the Emperor and go to Milan, "I shall personally order your supplies cut off." He then marched out of the palace and returned to headquarters, where he thought he was safe.

I was not present at that historic meeting of the Caesar's consistory, but I have been told by those who were there that it was an astonishing confrontation and that for once all sympathy was with the Caesar who had been insulted.

Gallus promptly struck back. He ordered Domitian arrested on a charge of lese majesty. To give the gloss of legitimacy to his arrest, he sent his legal adviser, the quaestor Montius, to instruct the troops in how to behave. Montius was an elderly man, with a passion for correct procedure. He told Gallus bluntly that the Caesar had no authority over a prefect engaged on the Emperor's business. Gallus ignored this advice.

Montius then appeared before the troops who had been called to assembly, and he told them that what Gallus intended to do was not only illegal but highly dangerous and that any soldier who obeyed the Caesar would be committing treason. "But should you decide to arrest the Emperor's prefect then I advise you first to overthrow the Emperor's statues, so that your revolt will at least be honest."

The troops were confused, to say the least. But not for long. When Gallus heard what Montius had done, he rushed to the assembly ground and harangued the troops as only he knew how to do.

"I am in danger. You are in danger. We are all in danger because of would-be usurpers, some of whom sit in my own consistory." And he turned fiercely on the courageous old Montius. "Yes, even the quaestor Montius is involved in this conspiracy. He plots against me, as well as against Constantius. He tells you that I may not arrest an insolent prefect because he is on imperial business. But I have the right to discipline any official in the East. I would be untrue to my oath to Constantius if I did not keep order in Antioch." And so on.

By the time Gallus had finished, the troops were with him. While he stood by, they murdered Montius. Next they marched on military headquarters. No attempt was made to resist them. They found Domitian in the commandant's private office on the second floor. They threw the wretched prefect down the stairs (which are very steep: I once badly twisted my ankle going up them). Then they dragged the bodies of Domitian and Montius side by side through the streets of Antioch.

Gallus was now thoroughly frightened. Though his troops were inadequate for controlling Antioch, he was in no position to resist Constantius, and it was perfectly plain that the two would soon be in open conflict. Yet Gallus still pretended to be carrying out the Emperor's orders when he declared martial law and arrested those whom he suspected of plotting against him. This turned out to be half the senate. I withdrew to Daphne during this troubled time.

Gallus set up a military tribunal and arraigned before it all those who had been accused of treason. During the trials Constantia sat behind a curtain listening to the testimony; every now and then she would poke her head into the courtroom to ask a question or to give an opinion. It was a ludicrous display. Hearsay was now accepted as fact, and no one was safe.

In a dyeshop a secret agent noticed a purple robe of the sort only an emperor may wear. It was immediately assumed that the cloak had been ordered by a would-be usurper. The shopowner wisely vanished but they found his files. Although there was no mention of a purple cloak having been ordered, the secret service did come up with a letter from a deacon inquiring when "the work will be ready." That was enough. "The work" was the purple cloak, according to the secret service, which had no other evidence. The guiltless deacon was arrested, tortured, tried, and put to death. This was typical of the "justice" at Gallus's court.

Having failed to persuade Gallus to come to Milan, Constantius ordered his sister Constantia to attend him. Confident that she could patch up the differences between her husband and her brother, she set out for Milan. But en route the lady died of fever, and that was the end for Gallus. Though he was by now perfectly willing to declare himself Augustus in the East, he lacked the military power to withstand Constantius. He was in a quandary.

Finally a letter arrived from Constantius that was most amiable in tone. The Emperor reminded Gallus that under Diocletian a Caesar *always* obeyed his Augustus, citing the famous case of the Caesar Galarius who walked a mile on foot because the Augustus Diocletian was displeased with him. This letter was delivered by Scudilo, a master diplomatist who told Gallus privately that Constantius wished him no harm.

Did Gallus believe this? It seems impossible. But he was by now a desperate man. He was also completely demoralized by his wife's death. To everyone's amazement, he agreed to go to Milan. However, he insisted on traveling by way of Constantinople, where as the reigning Caesar he presided over the games in the Hippodrome. But Julian describes this scene.

*Julian Augustus*

In the late autumn of 354 I learned of the sudden death of Constantia. I wrote Gallus a letter of condolence which was not answered. He was already having his difficulties at Antioch, where Constantius had earlier sent him a messenger who rudely ordered him to return to Milan. Gallus, quite rightly, refused to go. He knew what his fate would be. Instead he sent Constantia to the Emperor, hoping that she might make peace between them. But when she died of a fever in Bithynia, he knew that he must either obey Constantius or begin a civil war. Tricked by the eunuchs who assured him that he would be safe in Milan, Gallus set out for the West. On the way he sent me a message, ordering me to meet him at Constantinople. I obeyed.

*Libanius*: It is fascinating to observe how a man with Julian's objectivity and passion for truth can so blandly protect his brother's memory. Not one word about the murders of Montius and Domitian, nor any mention of the treason trials. I suspect Julian is more interested in constructing his case against Constantius than he is in telling what actually happened . . . a human failing.

*Julian Augustus*

I met Gallus at the back of the imperial box in the Hipprodome. The box is actually a two-story pavilion connected by a long corridor to the Sacred Palace. On the first floor there are rooms for musicians and minor functionaries; the second floor contains a suite of rooms used by the imperial family.

The horse races were going on when I arrived. Through the curtains which covered the door to the box, I could hear the crowd cheering its favorite drivers. Suddenly Gallus flung aside the curtain.

"Stay there," he said. He let the curtain fall. He was pale. His hands shook. His voice was low, his manner furtive. "Now listen to me. I know what people are saying: that I shall never return from Milan alive. But don't believe them. I am still Caesar." He gestured at the curtain. "You should have heard the way the crowd cheered me just now. They are with me. Also, I have an army waiting in Serbia, Theban troops who are loyal. Everything has been carefully planned. When they join me, I shall be ready to deal with Constantius." But his face revealed the uncertainty his words tried to dispel.

"You will go into rebellion?"

"I hope not. I hope for a truce. But who can tell? Now I wanted to see you to tell you that if anything should happen to me, go into a monastery. Take holy orders if you have to. That's the only way you will be safe. Then . . ." He looked suddenly quite lost. "Avenge me."

"But I am sure that the Emperor . . ." I started to gabble but I was interrupted by a stout red-faced man who saluted me cheerfully. "Most noble Julian, I am Count Lucillianus, attached to the Caesar as his . . ."

"Jailer!" Gallus grinned like a wolf.

"The Caesar enjoys making fun of me." He turned to Gallus. "The crowd is waiting for you to give the victor's crown to Thorax. He just won the chariot race."

Gallus turned abruptly and drew aside the curtain. For an instant he stood silhouetted against dazzling blue sky. The mob behind him sounded like a storm at sea.

"Isn't the most noble Julian joining us?" asked Lucillianus, aware that I had instinctively stepped back from the harsh light and sudden sound.

"No!" said Gallus. "He is to be a priest." Then he let the curtain fall behind him; and that was that.

\* \* \*

The rest of the story is well known. Gallus and his "jailers" took the overland route through Illyria. All troops were moved from the garrisons along the route, and Gallus could call on no one to support him. At Hadrianopolis, the Theban legions were indeed waiting, but Gallus was not allowed to see them. He was now a prisoner in all but name. Then in Austria, he was arrested by the infamous Count Barbatio, who had been until recently the commander of his own guard. Gallus was imprisoned at Histria; here his trial was held. The Grand Chamberlain Eusebius presided.

Gallus was indicted for all the crimes which had taken place in Syria during the four years of his reign. Most of the charges against him were absurd and the trial itself was a farce, but Constantius enjoyed the show of legality almost as much as he disliked the idea of justice. Gallus's only defense was to blame his wife for everything. This was unworthy of him; but then there was nothing that he could say or do which would save him. Also, by accusing Constantius's sister of a thousand crimes (she was guilty of many more), Gallus was able to strike one last blow at his implacable enemy. Furious at the form the defense took, Constantius ordered Gallus executed.

My brother's head was cut off early in the evening of 9 December 354. His arms were bound behind him as though he were a common criminal. He made no last statement. Or if he did, it has been suppressed. He was twenty-eight when he died. They say that in his last days he suffered terribly from bad dreams. Of the men of the imperial family, only Constantius and I were left.

On 1 January 355 a warrant was issued for my arrest. But by then I had joined a religious order at Nicomedia. I am sure that at first none of the monks knew who I was, for I had come to them with head shaved and I looked like any other novice. Oribasius also protected me. When the imperial messenger arrived at Pergamon to arrest me, Oribasius said that I had gone to Constantinople.

I was a monk for six weeks. I found the life surprisingly pleasant. I enjoyed the austerity and the mild physical labor. The monks themselves were not very inspiring. I suppose some must have had the religious sense but the majority were simply vagrants who had tired of the road and its discomforts. They treated the monastery as though it were some sort of hostel rather than a place to serve the One God. Yet they were easy to get along with, and had it not been for the Galilean rituals I could have been quite happy.

I don't suppose I shall ever know how I was discovered. Perhaps one of the monks recognized me or perhaps the secret agents in checking the rolls of the various monasteries for new arrivals had grown suspicious. No matter how it was done, it was done swiftly and efficiently. I was in the kitchen of the monastery, helping the baker to fire his oven, when a detachment of household troops came clattering in. Their commander saluted me. "The most noble Julian is to accompany us to Milan, by order of the Augustus."

I made no protest. The monks stared in silence as I was taken from them and marched through the cold streets of Nicomedia to the imperial palace. Here I was received by the city prefect. He was nervous. Under similar circumstances five years earlier, Gallus had been ordered to Milan and *he* had been made Caesar of the East. The same fate might befall me. It was hard for an official to know how to behave.

"Naturally, we regret these security precautions." The prefect indicated the guards. "But you will understand that the Grand Chamberlain's office was, as always, most specific. No details were omitted."

I was polite and noncommittal. I was also somewhat cheered to learn that my military escort was to be commanded by Victor, the same officer I had met at Macellum.

Victor was apologetic. "I don't enjoy this duty. I hope you realize that."

"Neither do I."

Victor frowned. "I particularly dislike taking a priest from a monastery."

"I am not exactly a priest."

"Even so, you were prepared to take orders. No one has the right to keep a man from God, not even the Emperor." Victor is a devout Galilean; at that time he was convinced that I was also one. I said nothing to disabuse him.

The next day we set out for Constantinople. Though I was treated like a prince, not a prisoner, I took it as a bad omen that we were to follow the same overland route to Italy that Gallus had taken a few months before.

As we were leaving Nicomedia, I noticed a head on a pike. I hardly glanced at it, since there is almost always the head of some felon or other on display at the main gate of every town.

"I am sorry," said Victor suddenly. "But we were ordered to use this gate."

"Sorry for what?"

"To lead you past your brother's head."

"Gallus?" I turned clear round in my saddle and looked again at the head. The face had been so mutilated that the features were unrecognizable, but there was no mistaking the blond hair, matted though it was with dirt and blood.

"The Emperor has had it displayed in every city in the East."

I shut my eyes, on the verge of nausea.

"Your brother had many good qualities," said Victor. "It was a pity." Ever since, I have respected Victor. In those days when secret agents were everywhere and no man was safe, it took courage to say something good of a man executed for treason. Victor was equally outspoken in my defense. It was his view that the two charges made against me by the Grand Chamberlain's office were not serious (that I had left Macellum without permission; that I had met Gallus in Constantinople when he was already accused of treason). Of the first charge I was innocent. The Grand Chamberlain himself had written Bishop George, giving me permission to go wherever I chose in the East. I had wisely kept a copy of this letter. As for the second charge, I had been summoned to Constantinople by the then reigning Caesar of the East. How could I refuse my lawful lord? "You have nothing to fear," said Victor. But I was not optimistic.

Since I was traveling as a prince, I was greeted at each city by the local dignitaries. Concerned as I was about my own fate, I was still able to take some pleasure in seeing new things. I was particularly pleased when Victor allowed me to visit Ilios, a modern city near the ruins of ancient Troy.

At Ilios I was taken round by the local bishop. At first my heart sank: a Galilean bishop was the last sort of person who would be interested in showing me the temples of the true gods. But to my surprise, Bishop Pegasius was an ardent Hellenist. In fact, *he* was the one who was surprised when I asked him if we might visit the temples of Hector and Achilles.

"But of course. Nothing would give me greater pleasure. But I am surprised that you are interested in old monuments."

"I am a child of Homer."

"So is every educated man. But we are also Christians. Your piety is well known to us even here." I could not be sure if he was being ironic or not. My friendship with Maximus was general knowledge and a good many Galileans were suspicious of me. On the other hand, my arrest in a monastery had given rise to a whole new legend: the priest-prince. In this role, I explained to the bishop that it was merely as a student of Homer that I wanted to see the famous temples our ancestors had built to those gods (false gods!) and heroes who had fought in this haunted place.

Pegasius took me first to the small temple which contains the famous bronze statue of Hector, said to be done from life. In the unroofed courtyard which surrounds the temple there also stands a colossal statue of Achilles, facing Hector in effigy as in life. To my astonishment, the altars in the courtyard were smoldering with sacrifice, while the statue of Hector shone from a recent anointing.

I turned to the Bishop. "What do these fires mean? Do the people still worship Hector?"

Pegasius was bland. "Of course they do. After all, it would be unnatural not to worship our brave men in the same way that we worship the martyrs who also lived here."

"I'm not sure it is the same thing," I said primly.

"Well, at least we have managed to preserve many beautiful works of art." Then Pegasius proceeded to show me the temples of Athena and Achilles, both in perfect repair. I noted, too, that whenever he passed the image of an old god, he did not hiss and make the sign of the cross the way most Galileans do, fearing contamination.

Pegasius proved to be a marvelous guide to Troy. I was particularly moved when he showed me the sarcophagus of Achilles. "There he lies, the fierce Achilles." He tapped the ancient marble. "A hero and a giant—actually, a giant. Some years ago we opened the tomb and found the bones of a man seven feet tall, and where his heel had been there was the head of an arrow."

It was awesome to be so close to the legendary past. Pegasius could see that I was impressed. Despite all efforts to the contrary, I am transparent as water. "Those were great days," he said softly.

"They will come again," I blurted out.

"I pray that you are right," said the bishop of Ilios. Today this same Pegasius is my high priest of Cappadocia. He was never a Galilean though he pretended to be one, thinking that by rising to a position of importance among that depraved sect he would be able to preserve the temples of our ancestors. Now he revels in his freedom.

*Priscus*: And *now* he revels in life at the Persian court, where, according to gossip, he is a convert to Persian sun worship. Julian took up with the oddest people.

*Julian Augustus*

At the beginning of February we arrived at Como, a town on a lake about thirty miles north of Milan. Here I remained as prisoner for six months. I was allowed to see no one except the servants who had come with me. Letters from Oribasius and Maximus were not delivered. I might as well have been dead. I consoled myself with reading the complete works of Pliny the Younger, who had lived at Como. I remember with what loathing I read his famous description of "darling Como." I hated the place, including the blue-green lake.

During this time I had no idea what was happening in the outside world, which was probably just as well for I was the subject of fierce debate in the Sacred Consistory. According to Eusebius: "He is another Gallus. He must be put to death." A majority of the Consistory agreed with the Chamberlain. Surprisingly enough, the opposition was led by the Empress Eusebia. Though she was not a member of the Consistory, she was able to make her views known. "Julian has committed no crime. His loyalty has never been seriously questioned. He is the last surviving male member of the imperial house. Until such time as we provide the Emperor with a son, Julian is heir to the principate. But should Julian be executed and should the Emperor then—heaven forbid—die without issue, the house of Constantine is at an end and there will be chaos in the empire."

Eusebia finally prevailed. But it took her six months of argument, during which time Constantius said not a word. He merely listened and brooded and waited.

At the beginning of June a court chamberlain arrived at Como. "The most noble Julian is to wait upon the divine Empress Eusebia." I was startled: the Empress, not the Emperor? I tried to question the chamberlain but he would say no more than that I was to be given a private audience; no, he could not tell me if the Emperor would receive me; no, he was not even certain that the Emperor was at Milan; he reveled in being uninformative.

We entered Milan through a door in one of the watchtowers. In complete secrecy, I was hurried through narrow back streets to a side entrance of the palace. Once inside the palace I was met

107

by chamberlains who took me straight to the apartment of the Empress.

Eusebia was handsomer than her portraits. The eyes and mouth, which appeared so severe when rendered in marble, in life were not severe at all, merely sad. A flame-colored robe set off her pale face and black hair. She was not much older than I.

"We are pleased to receive our cousin, the most noble Julian," she murmured formally. She motioned to one of her ladies-in-waiting, who came forward with a folding stool and placed it beside the Empress's silver chair.

"We hope our cousin enjoyed his stay at Lake Como."

"The lake is very beautiful, Augusta." At a gesture from her, I sat on the stool.

"Yes. The Emperor and I enjoy the lake."

For what seemed an eternity, we discussed that wretched lake. All the while she was studying me carefully. And I must say I was studying her. Eusebia was Constantius's second wife. His first wife had been Galla, the half-sister of Gallus. Galla had the same mother as Gallus, who had the same father as I, but I never knew her, and I don't think Gallus ever met his sister more than once or twice. When Galla died, Constantius promptly married Eusebia. It was said that he had always been in love with her. She came from an excellent consular family. She was a popular figure at court, and on more than one occasion she had saved innocent men from Constantius's eunuchs.

"We have been told that you are planning to become a priest."

"I was at a monastery, when I was . . . told to come to Milan." I started to stammer as I often do when I am nervous. The letter "m" gives me particular trouble.

"But do you seriously want to be a priest?"

"I don't know. I prefer philosophy, I think. I would like to live at Athens."

"You have no interest in politics?" She smiled as she said this, knowing what my answer must necessarily be.

"No! None, Augusta."

"Yet you have certain responsibilities to the state. You are imperial."

"The Augustus needs no help from me."

"That is not quite true." She clapped her hands and the two ladies-in-waiting withdrew, closing cedar doors softly behind them.

"Nothing is secret in a palace," she said. "One is never alone."

"Aren't we alone now?"

Eusebia clapped her hands again. Two eunuchs appeared from behind pillars at the opposite end of the room. She waved them away.

"They can hear but they cannot speak. A precaution. But then there are others listening whom one knows nothing about."

"The secret agents?"

She nodded. "Everything we say to one another in this room they can hear."

"But where . . . ?"

She smiled at my bewilderment. "Who knows where? But one knows they are always present."

"They even spy on you?"

"Especially on the Empress." She was serene. "It has always been like this in palaces. So remember to speak . . . carefully."

"Or not at all!"

She laughed. I found myself relaxing somewhat. I almost trusted her. She became serious. "The Emperor has given me permission to talk to you. He was reluctant. I don't need to tell you that since the Gallus affair, he has felt himself entirely surrounded by traitors. He trusts no one."

"But I . . ."

"He trusts you least of all." This was blunt. But I was grateful for her candor. "Against his own good judgment, he raised your brother up. Within months, Gallus and Constantia were plotting to usurp the throne."

"Are you so certain?"

"We have proof."

"I am told that secret agents often invent 'proof.'"

She shrugged. "In this case it was not necessary. Constantia was indiscreet. I never trusted her. But that is over with. You are now the potential threat."

"Easily solved," I said with more bitterness than I intended. "Execute me."

"There are those who advise this." She was as much to the point as I. "But I am not one. As you know, as the whole world knows, Constantius cannot have a child." Her face set bleakly. "I have been assured by my confessor that this is heaven's judgment upon my husband for having caused the deaths of so many members of his own family. Not that he wasn't justified," she added loyally. "But justified or not, there is a curse on those who kill

109

their own kind. That curse is on Constantius. He has no heir and I am certain that he will *never* have one, if he puts you to death."

There it was at last. My sense of relief was enormous, and perfectly visible in my face.

"Yes. You are safe. For the time being. But there still remains the problem of what to do with you. We had hoped you would take holy orders."

"If it is required, I shall." Yes, I said that. I am giving as honest an account as I can of my life. At that moment, I would have worshipped the ears of a mule to save my life.

But Eusebia was not insistent. "Your love of learning also seems genuine." She smiled. "Oh, we know whom you see, what books you read. There is very little that has escaped the attention of the Chamberlain's office."

"Then they know that it is my wish to be a philosopher."

"Yes. And I believe that the Emperor will grant you your wish."

"I shall be eternally grateful, and loyal. He has nothing to fear from me, ever..." I babbled on enthusiastically.

Eusebia watched me, amused. Then when I ran out of breath, she said, "Gallus made him much the same speech."

On that dampening note she rose, ending the interview. "I shall try to arrange an interview for you with the Emperor. It won't be easy. He is shy." At the time I found this hard to believe, but of course Eusebia was right. Constantius feared all human encounters. One of the reasons he was so fond of eunuchs was that, by and large, they are not quite human.

Two days later, I was visited by the Grand Chamberlain himself. I found it hard to believe that this enchanting creature with his caressing voice and dimpled smile was daily advising the Consistory to execute me. He quite filled the small apartment where I had been confined.

"Oh, you have grown, most noble Julian! In every way." Delicately Eusebius touched my face. "And your beard is now most *philosophic*. How Marcus Aurelius would have envied you!" For an instant one fat finger rested, light as a butterfly, on the tip of my beard. Then we stood face to face, beaming at one another; I with nerves, he with policy.

"I don't need to tell you how pleased I am to see you at court. We all are. This is where you belong, close to your own kind." My heart sank: was that to be my fate? a life at court where the eunuchs could keep an eye on me? A swift death was almost

110

preferable. "Now I suggest that when you see the divine Augustus, you will beg him to allow you to stay always at his side. He needs you."

I seized on the one fact. "The Emperor will see me?"

Eusebius nodded delightedly, as though he had been entirely responsible for my amazing good fortune. "Of course. Didn't you know? He made the decision at this morning's Consistory. We were all so pleased. Because we *want* you here. I have always said that there should be a place for you at the side of the Augustus. A high place."

"You flatter me," I murmured.

"I say only the truth. You are, after all, an ornament to the house of Constantine, and what better place has such a pure jewel to shine than in the diadem of the court?"

I swallowed this gravely and replied with equal insincerity, "I shall never forget what you have done for me and for my brother."

Tears came to Eusebius's eyes. His voice trembled. "It is my wish to serve you. That is all I ask for." He leaned forward—with some effort—and kissed my hand. The rhetoric of hate is often most effective when couched in the idiom of love. On a note of mutual admiration, we parted.

I was next instructed by one of the eunuchs in the court's etiquette, which was nearly as complicated as what one goes through during the Mithraic mysteries. There are a dozen set responses to an emperor's set questions or commands. There are bows and genuflections; steps to left and steps to right; alternative gestures should I be asked to approach the throne or merely to remain where I was. The eunuch loved his work. "Our ceremonies are among this world's marvels! More inspiring, in some ways, than the mass." I agreed to that.

The eunuch spread a diagram for me on a table. "This is the great hall where you will be received." He pointed. "Here sits the divine Constantius. And here you will enter." Every move either of us was to make was planned in advance like a dance. When I had finally learned my lesson, the eunuch folded his map with an exalted expression on his face. "We have considerably improved and refined court ceremonial since the divine Diocletian. I am sure that he never dreamed his heirs would be capable of such exquisite style as well as such profound symbolism, for we are now able to beautifully reflect the nature of the universe in a single ceremony lasting scarcely three hours!"

111

The cutting down of court ceremonies and the removal of the eunuchs was one of the first acts of my reign. It was certainly the most satisfactory.

Shortly after sundown, the Master of the Offices and his many ushers escorted me to the throne room. The Master of the Offices gave me last-minute instructions on how to behave in the sacred presence. But I did not listen. I was too busy preparing the speech I intended to make to Constantius. It was a masterpiece of eloquence. After all, I had been preparing it for ten years. Face to face, I intended to make Constantius my friend.

The Master of the Offices ushered me into a huge basilica which was once Diocletian's throne room. The Corinthian columns which line it are twice the usual height and the floor is of porphyry and green marble. The effect is most splendid, especially by artificial light. In the apse at the far end of the basilica stands the throne of Diocletian, an elaborate chair of ivory decorated with gold plaques. Needless to say, I remember everything about the room in which my fate was decided. Torches flared between the columns while on either side of the throne bronze lamps illuminated its occupant. Not counting my childhood encounter with Constantine, this was the first time I beheld an emperor in full state. I was not prepared for the theatricality of the scene.

Constantius sat very straight and still, his forearms resting on his knees in imitation of the Egyptian kings. He wore a heavy gold diadem set with huge square jewels. On one side of him stood Eusebius, on the other the praetorian prefect, while around the room the officials of the court were ranged.

I was officially presented to the Emperor. I paid him homage. Only once did I falter in the course of the ritual; when I did, the Master of the Offices was quick to whisper the correct formula in my ear.

If Constantius was curious about me, he did not betray it. His bronze face was empty of all expression as he spoke. "We receive our most noble cousin with pleasure." But there was no pleasure in that high-pitched voice. I felt myself suddenly blushing. "We give him leave to go to Athens to continue his studies." I glanced at Eusebius. Though his own grim advice had not prevailed, he gave me a small delighted nod as if to say, "We've won!"

"Also . . ." But then Constantius stopped talking. There is no other way to describe what happened. He simply stopped. The were no more words for me. I stared at him, wondering if I had

112

gone mad. Even the Master of the Offices was taken aback. Everyone had expected a full speech from Constantius as well as a response from me. But the audience was over. Constantius put out his hand for me to kiss. I did so. Then with the aid of the Master of the Offices, I walked backward to the entrance, bowing at regular intervals. Just as I was about to leave the presence, two squeaking bats swooped suddenly out of the shadowy ceiling, and darted straight toward Constantius. He did not move, even though one almost touched his face. As always, his self-control was marvelous. I have never known a man quite so deep or so cold.

I returned to my apartment to find a message from the Grand Chamberlain's office. I was to proceed at once to the port of Aquileia. My belongings had already been packed. My servants were ready. A military escort was standing by.

Within the hour, I was outside the walls of Milan. As I rode through the warm night, I prayed to Helios that I never see court or Emperor again.

# VII

I arrived at Piraeus, the port of Athens, shortly after sunrise 5 August 355. I remember every one of the forty-seven days I spent in Athens. They were the happiest days of my life, so far.

It was a windy dawn. In the east, light tore at the dark. Stars faded. The sea was rough. It was like the morning of the world. The ship creaked and shuddered as it struck against the pilings of the quay. I had half expected to see a detachment of troops waiting on the shore, ready to arrest me on some new charge. But there were no troops in sight, only foreign merchant ships and the usual bustle of a busy port. Slaves unloaded cargoes. Officials of the port moved solemnly from ship to ship. Men with carts and donkeys shouted to those just arrived, promising to get them to Athens faster than that youth who ran from Marathon to the city in four hours (and fell dead, one would like to retort, but irony is lost on drivers, even Greek drivers who know their Homer).

Barefoot students in shabby clothes moved in packs from ship to ship, trying to sign up newcomers for lectures. Each student was a proselytizer for his own teacher. There was a good deal of rancor as each of these youths went about trying to convince

113

would-be students (known as "foxes") that there was but one teacher in Athens worth listening to: his own. Fights often broke out between the factions. Even as I watched, two students actually manhandled a stranger; each grabbed an arm, and while one insisted that he attend the lectures of a certain Sophist, the other shouted that the Sophist was a fool and that only the wisdom of *his* teacher, a Cynic, was worth a student's time. Between them, they nearly tore the poor man in half. Nor would they let him go until he finally made it clear to them in broken Greek that he was an Egyptian cotton dealer and not at all interested in philosophy. Luckily, they did not get as far as my ship; so I was spared their attentions.

Usually when a member of the imperial family travels by sea, the dragon of our house flies at the mast. But since I was technically under "house arrest," I was in no way identified to the people, which was just as well. I wanted to be free in Athens, to wander unnoticed wherever I chose. But unfortunately a dozen soldiers had been assigned to me as permanent bodyguard (they were, in effect, my jailers) and their commanding officer was responsible for my safety. I felt some obligation to him, though not much.

I made a bold decision. While the servants were busy with the luggage and the men who guarded me were all gathered on the forward deck of the ship in sleepy conference with the officials of the port, I scribbled a note to my head jailer, telling him that I would meet him at the end of the day at the prefect's house. I left the note on one of our traveling chests. Then, student's cloak securely wrapped about me, I swung over the side of the ship and dropped unobserved onto the wharf.

It took a moment to become accustomed to the steadiness of earth. I am not a bad sailor but the monotony of a long voyage and the continual slap and fall of a ship at sea tire me. I am of earth, not water; air, not fire. I engaged a cart and driver after considerable haggling (I was able to bring the driver's cost down to half what he asked: good but not marvelous). Then I climbed into the little cart. Half standing, half sitting on the cart rail, I was borne over the rutted road to Athens.

The sun rose in a cloudless sky. Attic clarity is not just a metaphor; it is fact. The sky's blue was painful. One felt one could see straight to the farthest edge of the world if the mountain Hymettos, low and violet in the early light, had not blocked the view. The heat with each instant became more intense, but it was the dry heat of the desert, made pleasant by a soft wind from the sea.

My first reaction was delight at anonymity. No one stared at me. No one knew who I was. I looked a typical student with my beard and plain cloak. There were dozens like me. Some were in carts, most were on foot; all of them moving toward the same goal: Athens and the knowledge of the true.

On every side of me carts rattled and creaked, their drivers cursing and their contents, human or animal, complaining. The Athenian Greek is a lively fellow, though one looks in vain from face to face for a glimpse of Pericles or Alcibiades. As a race, they are much changed. They are no longer noble. They have been too often enslaved, and their blood mixed with that of barbarians. Yet I do not find them as sly and effeminate as certain Latin writers affect to. I think that the Old Roman tendency to look down on the Greeks is no more than a natural resentment of Greece's continuing superiority in those things which are important: philosophy and art. All that is good in Rome today was Greek. I find Cicero disingenuous when on one page he acknowledges his debt to Plato and then on the next speaks with contempt of the Greek character. He seems unaware of his own contradictions . . . doubtless because they were a commonplace in his society. Of course the Romans pretend *they* are children of Troy, but that nonsense was never taken too seriously. From time to time I have had a word or two to say about Roman character, not much of it flattering (my little work on the Caesars, though written much too quickly, has some point, I think). But then one must recall that even as I dictate these lines as Roman Emperor, I am really Greek. And I have been to Athens, the eye of Greece.

Athens. It has been eight years since I rode up to the city gate in a market cart, an anonymous student who gaped at the sights like any German come to town. My first glimpse of the acropolis was startling and splendid. It hovers over the city as though held in the hand of Zeus, who seems to say: "Look, children, at how your gods live!" Sunlight flashes off the metal shield of the colossal statue of Athena, guarding her city. Off to the left I recognized the steep pyramidal mountain of Lykabettos, a great pyramid of rock hurled to earth by Athena herself; to this day wolves dwell at its foot.

The driver turned abruptly into a new road. I nearly fell out of the cart. "Academy Road," he announced in the perfunctory loud voice of one used to talking to foreigners. I was impressed. The road from Athens to the Academy's grove is lined with ancient trees. It begins at the city's Dipylon Gate—which was straight ahead of us—and crosses through suburbs to the green-leafed academy of Aristotle.

The Dipylon Gate was as busy in the early morning as any other great city's gate might have been at noon. It is a double gate, as its name indicates, with two tall towers on the outside. Guards lolled in front, paying no attention to the carts and pedestrians who came and went. As we passed through the outer gate, our cart was suddenly surrounded by whores. Twenty or thirty women and girls of all ages rushed out of the shadows of the wall. They fought with one another to get close to the cart. They tugged at my cloak. They called me "Billy Goat," "Pan," "Satyr," and other less endearing terms. With the skill of an acrobat one pretty child of fourteen vaulted the railing of my cart and firmly grasped my beard in her fist. The soldiers laughed at my discomfort. With some effort I pried my beard free from her fingers, but not before her other hand had reached between my legs, to the delight of those watching. But the driver was expert at handling these girls. With a delicate flick of his whip, he snapped at her hand. It was withdrawn with a cry. She leapt to the ground. The other women jeered us. Their curses were vivid and splendid, Homeric! Then as we passed through the second gate they turned back, for a troop of cavalry had appeared at the outer gate. Like bees swarming in a garden, they surrounded the soldiers.

I arranged my tunic. The sharp tug of the girl's hand had had its effect upon me, and against my will I thought of lovemaking and wondered where the best girls in Athens might be found. I was not then, as I am now, celibate. Yet even in those days I believed that it was virtuous to mortify the flesh, for it is a fact that continence increases intellectual clarity. But I was also twenty-three years old and the flesh made demands on me in a way that the mind could not control. Youth is the body's time. Not a day passed in those years that I did not experience lust. Not a week passed that I did not assuage that lust. But I do not agree with those Dionysians who maintain that the sexual act draws men closer to the One God. If anything, it takes a man away from God, for in the act he is blind and thoughtless, no more than an animal engaged in the ceremony of creation. Yet to each stage of

116

one's life certain things are suitable and for a few weeks, eight years ago, I was young, and knew many girls. Even now in this hot Asiatic night, I recall with unease that brilliant time, and think of lovemaking. I notice that my secretary is blushing. Yet *he* is Greek!

The driver indicated a large ruin to the right. "Hadrian," he said. "Hadrian Augustus." Like all travelers, I am used to hearing guides refer to my famous predecessor. Even after two centuries he is the only emperor *every* man has heard of—because of his constant traveling, his continuous building and, sad to say, his ridiculous passion for the boy Antinoüs. I suppose that it is natural enough to like boys but it is not natural or seemly to love *anyone* with the excessive and undignified passion that Hadrian showed for Antinoüs. Fortunately, the boy was murdered before Hadrian could make him his heir. But in his grief Hadrian made himself and the Genius of Rome look absurd. He set up thousands of statues and dedicated innumerable temples to the dead boy. He even declared the pretty catamite a god! It was a shocking display and permanently shadows Hadrian's fame. For the first time in history, a Roman emperor was mocked and thought ridiculous. From every corner of the earth derisive laughter sounded. Yet except for this one lapse, I find Hadrian a sympathetic figure. He was much gifted, particularly in music. He was an adept at mysteries. He used to spend many hours at night studying the stars, searching for omens and portents, as do I. He also wore a beard. I like him best for that. That sounds petty, doesn't it? I surprise myself as I say it. But then liking and disliking, approval and disapproval depend on many trivial things. I dislike Hadrian's passion for Antinoüs because I cannot bear for a philosopher-emperor to be mocked by his subjects. But I like his beard. We are all so simple at heart that we become unfathomable to one another.

Just inside the wall of the city, I left my driver. Then like one who has gone to sleep over a book of history, I stepped into the past. I stood now on that ancient highway—known simply as The Road—which leads from gate to agora to acropolis beyond. I was now in history. In the present I was part of the past and, simul-

117

taneously, part of what is to come. Time opened his arms to me and in his serene embrace I saw the matter whole: a circle without beginning or end.

To the left of the gate was a fountain in which I washed the dust from my face and beard. Then I proceeded along The Road to the agora. I am told that Rome is infinitely more impressive than Athens. I don't know. I have never visited Rome. But I do know that Athens looks the way a city ought to look but seldom does. It is even better planned than Pergamon, at least at its center. Porticoes gleam in the bright sun. The intense blue sky sets off the red tile roofs and makes the faded paint of columns seem to glow.

The Athenian agora is a large rectangular area enclosed by long porticoes of great antiquity. The one on the right is dedicated to Zeus; the one on the left is of more recent date, the gift of a young king of Pergamon who studied here. In the center of the agora is the tall building of the University, first built by Agrippa in the time of Augustus. The original building—used as a music hall—collapsed mysteriously in the last century. I find the architecture pretentious, even its present somewhat de-Romanized version. But pretentious or not, this building was my center in Athens. For here the most distinguished philosophers lecture. Here I listened three times weekly to the great Prohaeresius, of whom more later.

Behind the University are two porticoes parallel to one another, the last being at the foot of the acropolis. To one's right, on a hill above the agora, is a small temple to Hephaestos surrounded by gardens gone to seed. Below this hill are the administrative buildings of Athens, the Archives, the Round House where the fifty governors of Athens meet—this last is a peculiar-looking structure with a steep roof which the Athenians, who give everything and everyone a nickname, call "the umbrella." There used to be many silver statues in the Round House but the Goths stole them in the last century.

Few people were abroad as the sun rose to noon. A faint breeze stirred the dust on the old pitted paving. Several important-looking men, togas draped ineptly about plump bodies, hurried toward the Bouleuterion. They had the self-absorbed air of politicians everywhere. Yet these men were the political heirs of Pericles and Demosthenes. I tried to remember that as I watched them hurry about their business.

Then I stepped into the cool shade of the Painted Portico. For

118

an instant my eyes were dazzled, the result of sudden dimness. Not for some time was I able to make out the famous painting of the Battle of Marathon which covers the entire long wall of the portico. But as my eyes grew used to the shade, I saw that the painting was indeed the marvel the world says it is. One can follow the battle's course by walking the length of the portico. Above the painting hang the round shields of the Persians, captured that day. The shields have been covered with pitch to preserve them. Looking at those relics of a battle fought eight hundred years before, I was much moved. Those young men and their slaves—yes, for the first time in history slaves fought beside their masters—together saved the world. More important, they fought of their own free will, unlike our soldiers, who are either conscripts or mercenaries. Even in times of peril, our people will not fight to protect their country. Money, not honor, is now the source of Roman power. When the money goes, the state will go. That is why Hellenism must be restored: to instill again in man that sense of his own worth which made civilization possible, and won the day at Marathon.

As I stood there looking up at the tarry shields, a youth approached me. He was bearded; his clothes were dirty; he wore a student's cloak and he looked a typical New Cynic of the sort I deplore. I have recently written at considerable length about these vagabonds. In the last few years the philosophy of Crates and Zeno has been taken over by idlers who, though they have no interest in philosophy, deliberately imitate the Cynics in such externals as not cutting their hair or beards, carrying sticks and wallets, and begging. But where the original Cynics despised wealth, sought virtue, questioned all things in order to find what was true, these imitators mock all things, including the true, using the mask of philosophy to disguise license and irresponsibility. Nowadays, any young man who does not choose to study or to work grows a beard, insults the gods, and calls himself Cynic. No wonder philosophy has earned the contempt of so many in this unhappy age.

Without ceremony, the New Cynic pointed at the wall. "That is Aeschylus," he said. I looked politely at the painting of a bearded soldier, no different from the others except for the famous name written above his head. The playwright is shown engaged in combat with a Persian. But though he is fighting for his life, his somber

119

face is turned toward us, as though to say: I know that I am immortal!

"The painter was self-conscious," I said neutrally, fully expecting to be asked for money and ready not to give it.

The Cynic grinned at me. Apparently he chose to regard neutrality as friendship. He tapped the painting. A flake of paint zigzagged to the ground. "One day the whole thing will disappear and then who will know what Marathon was like, when this picture's gone?" As he spoke, something stirred in my memory. I recognized the voice. Yet the face was completely strange to me. Confident now that we were friends, he turned from the painting to me. Had I just arrived in Athens? Yes. Was I a student? Yes. Was I a Cynic? No. Well, there was no cause to be so emphatic (smiling). He himself dressed as a Cynic only because he was poor. By the time this startling news had been revealed to me, we had climbed the steps to the temple of Hephaestos. Here the view of the agora is wide and elegant. In the clear noon light one could see beyond the city to the dark small windows of those houses which cluster at the foot of Hymettos.

"Beautiful," said my companion, making even that simple word sound ambiguous. "Though beauty . . ."

"Is absolute," I said firmly. Then to forestall Cynic chatter, I turned abruptly into the desolate garden of the temple. The place was overrun with weeds, while the temple itself was shabby and sad. But at least the Galileans have not turned it into a charnel house. Far better that a temple fall in ruins than be so desecrated. Better of course that it be restored.

My companion asked if I was hungry. I said no, which he took as yes (he tended not to listen to answers). He suggested we visit a tavern in the quarter just back of the temple. It was, he assured me, a place much frequented by students of the "better" sort. He was sure that I would enjoy it. Amused by his effrontery (and still intrigued by that voice which haunted me), I accompanied him through the narrow hot streets of the nearby quarter of the smiths, whose shops glowed blue as they hammered out metal in a blaring racket: metal struck metal in a swarm of sparks, like comets' tails.

The tavern was a low building with a sagging roof from which too many tiles had been removed by time and weather. I bent low to enter the main door. I was also forced to stoop inside, for the ceiling was too low for me and the beams were haphazard, even dangerous in the dim light. My companion had no difficulty stand-

120

ing straight. I winced at the heavy odor of rancid oil burning in pots on the stove.

Two trestle tables with benches filled the room. A dozen youths sat together close to the back door, which opened onto a dismal courtyard containing a dead olive tree which looked as though it had been sketched in silver on the whitewashed wall behind it.

My companion knew most of the other students. All were New Cynics, bearded, loud, disdainful, unread. They greeted us with cheerful obscenities. I felt uncomfortable but was determined to go through with my adventure. After all, this was what I had dreamed of. To be just one among many, even among New Cynics. The moment was unique, or so I thought. When asked who I was, they were told "*Not* a Cynic." They laughed good-naturedly. But then when they heard I was new to Athens, each made an effort to get me to attend lectures with his teacher. My companion rescued me. "He is already taken. He studies with Prohaeresius." I was surprised, for I had said nothing to my guide about Prohaeresius, and yet Prohaeresius was indeed the teacher of my choice. How did he know?

"I know all about you," he said mysteriously. "I read minds, tell fortunes." He was interrupted by one of the youths, who suggested that I shave my beard since otherwise I might be mistaken for a New Cynic and give them a bad name by my good behavior. This was considered witty in that room. Others debated whether or not I should be carried off to the baths to be scrubbed, the traditional hazing for new students, and one which I had every intention of avoiding. If necessary, I would invoke lese majesty!

But my guardian shoved the students away and sat me down at the opposite table close to the courtyard door, for which I was grateful. I am not particularly sensitive to odors, but on a blazing hot day the odor of unwashed students combined with thick smoke from old burning oil was almost too much for me. The tavernkeeper, making sure I had money (apparently my companion was deep in his debt), brought us cheese, bitter olives, old bread, sour wine. To my surprise, I was hungry. I ate quickly, without tasting. Suddenly I paused, aware that I was being stared at. I looked across the table at my companion. Yes?

"You have forgotten me, haven't you, Julian?"

Then I identified the familiar voice. I recognized Gregory of Nazianzus. We had been together at Pergamon. I burst out laughing and shook his hand. "How did such a dedicated Christian become a New Cynic?"

"Poverty, plain poverty." Gregory indicated the torn and dirty cloak, the unkempt beard. "And protection." He lowered his voice, indicating the students at the other table. "Christians are outnumbered in Athens. It's a detestable city. There is no faith, only argument and atheism."

"Then why are you here?"

He sighed. "The best teachers are here, the best instructors in rhetoric. Also, it is good to know the enemy, to be able to fight him with his own weapons."

I nodded and pretended agreement. I was not very brave in those days. But even though I could never be candid with Gregory, he was an amusing companion. He was as devoted to the Galilean nonsense as I was to the truth. I attributed this to his unfortunate childhood. His family are Cappadocian. They live in a small town some fifty miles southwest of Caesarea, the provincial capital. His mother was a most strong-willed woman named . . . I cannot recall her name, but I did meet her once a few years ago, and a most formidable creature she was. Passionate and proud and perfectly intolerant of everything not Galilean.

Gregory's father was part Jew and part Greek. As a result of his wife's relentless admonitions, he succumbed finally to the Galilean religion. According to Gregory, when his father was splashed with water by the bishop of Nazianzus, a great nimbus shone all round the convert. The bishop was so moved that he declared, "Here is my successor!" A most generous-minded man, that bishop! Most of us prefer *not* to name our successor. In due course, Gregory's father became bishop of Nazianzus. So his predecessor had the gift of prophesy, if nothing else.

All in a rush Gregory was telling me of himself. ". . . a terrible trip, by sea. Just before we got to Aegina, the storm struck us. I was sure the ship would sink. I was terrified. I'd never been (I still am not) baptized. So if I died like that at sea . . . Well, you must know yourself what I went through." He looked at me sharply. "Are you baptized?"

I said that I had been baptized as a child. I looked as reverent as possible when I said this.

"I prayed and prayed. Finally I fell asleep, exhausted. We all did. I dreamed that something loathsome, some sort of Fury, had come to take me to hell. Meanwhile, one of the cabin boys, a boy from Nazianzus, was dreaming that *he* saw—now this is *really* a miracle—*Mother walking upon the water*."

"His mother or your mother or the mother of Jesus?" I am afraid that I asked this out of mischief. I couldn't help myself.

But Gregory took the question straight. "*My* mother," he said. "The boy knew her, and there she was walking across that raging sea. Then she took the ship by its prow and drew it after her to a safe harbor. Which is exactly what happened. That very night the storm stopped. A Phoenician ship found us and towed us into the harbor of Rhodes." He sat back in triumph. "What do you think of *that*?"

"Your mother is a remarkable woman," I said accurately. Gregory agreed and talked at enthusiastic length about that stern virago. Then he told me of his adventures in Athens, of his poverty (this was a hint which I took: I gave him a good deal of money during the course of my stay), of our friend Basil who was also in Athens and was, I suspect, the reason for Gregory's attendance at the University. Wherever Basil went, Gregory followed. At Athens they were nicknamed "the Twins."

"I am expecting Basil now. We're both due at Prohaeresius's house this afternoon. We'll take you. You know we live together here. We study together. We argue almost as a team against the local Sophists. And we usually win." This was true. Both he and Basil were—are— eloquent. I deplore of course the uses to which their eloquence is put. Today they are most active as Galilean apologists, and I often wonder what they think of their old companion who governs the state. Nothing good, I fear. When I became emperor I asked them both to visit me at Constantinople. Gregory agreed to come, but never did. Basil refused. Of the two, I prefer Basil. He is plain, like me. He is misguided in his beliefs but honest. I suspect Gregory of self-seeking.

"Who is this?" Standing over us was a slender girl, with black intelligent eyes and a mouth that was as quick to sneer as to smile. Gregory introduced us; he said that I was from Cappadocia. She was Macrina, a niece of Prohaeresius.

"I like your beard," she said, sitting down without invitation. "It comes to a point. Most men's beards are like Gregory's, every which way. Yours suggests a plan. Will you study with my uncle?"

I said that I would. I was charmed by her. She wore her own version of a student's cloak, in faded blue linen. Her bare arms

123

were firm and darkened by the sun; strong fingers tore idly at the scraps of stale bread on the table; on the bench our thighs touched.

"You'll like my uncle. He's much the best teacher in this chattering place. But you'll hate Athens. I do! The splitting of hairs. The talk, talk, talk, and everyone trying to make a point, to pretend that all this talk means something."

"You are now listening to what is known as 'Macrina's Lament,'" said Gregory.

"But it's true just the same." She pointed to him like an actress in tragedy. "*They* are the worst: Gregory and Basil, the Twins of argument . . ."

Gregory brightened. "You should have heard Basil's argument yesterday when we were challenged on the virgin birth." Gregory turned to me. "As I told you, there are many atheists in Athens. And some of them have the devil's own cleverness. One in particular we despise . . ."

"One? You despise everybody, Gregory!" Macrina sipped wine from my cup, without invitation. "If ever there were a pair of bishops, it's those two. *You're* not a bishop, are you?" she challenged me agreeably.

I shook my head.

"Not even close," said Gregory, and I detected something sly in his voice.

"But a Christian?" asked Macrina.

"He must be," said Gregory smoothly. "He has to be."

"*Has* to be? Why? It's not illegal to be a Hellenist, is it? At least not yet."

I loved her deeply then. We were the same. I looked at her with sudden fondness as the fine if rather grubby fingers lifted and drained my cup.

"I mean he cannot be because . . ." I frowned at Gregory; he was not to tell her who I was. But he was on a different tack. ". . . because he is a brilliant student and anyone who truly loves learning loves God, loves Christ, loves the trinity."

"Well, I don't." She set the cup down hard. "I wonder if he does."

But I evaded. What had been Basil's defense of the virgin birth?

"He was challenged on the University steps, yesterday, shortly before noon." Gregory spoke precisely as though he were a historian giving the details of a battle all the world would want to

124

know about. "A Cynic, a true Cynic," he added for my benefit, "stopped Basil and said, 'you Christians claim that Christ was born of a virgin.' Basil said that we do not merely claim it, we proclaim it, for it is true. Our Lord was born without an earthly father. The Cynic then said that this was entirely against nature, that it was not possible for *any* creature to be born except through the union of male and female. Then Basil said—there was quite a large crowd gathered by now—Basil said, 'Vultures bring forth without coupling.' Well, you should have heard the applause and laughter! The Cynic went away and Basil was a hero, even among those students who have no faith."

"At least they knew Aristotle," I said mildly.

But Macrina was not impressed. "Just because vultures don't mate . . ."

"The female vulture is impregnated by the wind." Gregory is one of those people who must always embellish the other person's observation. Unfortunately, he is drawn to the obvious. He tells what everyone already knows. But Macrina was relentless.

"Even if vultures don't mate . . ."

"*Even*? But they don't mate. That is a fact."

"Has anyone ever seen a vulture made fertile by the wind?" Macrina was mischievous.

"I suppose someone must have." Gregory's round eyes became even rounder with irritation.

"But how could you tell? The wind is invisible. So how would you know which particular wind—if any—made the bird conceive?"

"She is perverse." Gregory turned to me, much annoyed. "Besides, if it were not true, Aristotle would not have said it was true and we would not all agree today that it is indeed the truth."

"I'm not sure of the logic of that," began Macrina thoughtfully.

"She'll be condemned for atheism one of these days." Gregory tried to sound playful; he failed.

Macrina laughed at him, a pleasant, low, unmalicious laugh. "All right. A vulture's eggs are laid by a virgin bird. Accepted. What has that to do with Christ's birth? Mary was not a vulture. She was a woman. Women conceive in only one way. I can't see that Basil's answer to the Cynic was so crushing. What is true of the vulture is not necessarily true of Mary."

"Basil's answer," said Gregory tightly, "was to the argument used by the Cynic when he said that *all* things are conceived by

125

male and female. Well, if *one* thing is not conceived in this fashion—and that was Basil's argument—then another might not be and . . ."

"But 'might not' is not an argument. I might suddenly grow wings and fly to Rome (I wish I could!) but I can't, I don't."

"There are no cases of human beings having wings, but there is . . ."

"Icarus and Daedalus," began the valiant Macrina, but we were saved by Basil's arrival. Gregory's face was dark with anger, and the girl was beside herself with amusement.

Basil and I greeted one another warmly. He had changed considerably since we were adolescents. He was now a fine-looking man, tall and somewhat thin; unlike Gregory, he wore his hair close-cropped. I teased him about this. "Short hair means a bishop."

Basil smiled his amiable smile and said in a soft voice, "'May that cup pass from me,'" a quotation from the Nazarene. But unlike the carpenter, Basil was sincere. Today he leads precisely the life that I should like for myself: withdrawn, ascetic, given to books and to prayer. He is a true contemplative and I admire him very much, despite his religion.

Macrina, having heard him call me Julian, suddenly said, "Isn't the Emperor's cousin, the one called Julian, supposed to come to Athens?"

Basil looked with surprise at Gregory, who motioned for him to be still. "Do *you* know the prince?" Macrina turned to me.

I nodded. "I know him. But not well." Solon's famous truth.

Macrina nodded. "But of course you would. You were all at Pergamon together. The Twins often discuss him."

I was embarrassed but amused. I have never been an eavesdropper, even in childhood. Not from any sense of virtue but because I really do not want to know what people think of me or, to be precise, what they say of me—often a different matter. I can usually imagine the unpleasant judgments, for we are what others need us to be. This is why our reputations change so often and so drastically, reflecting no particular change in us, merely a change in the mood of those who observe us. When things go well, an emperor is loved; badly, hated. I never need to look in a mirror. I see myself all too clearly in the eyes of those about me.

I was embarrassed not so much for what Macrina might say about me but for what she might reveal about Gregory and Basil. I would not have been surprised if they had a low opinion of me.

126

Intelligent youths of low birth tend to resent the intellectual pretensions of princes. In their place, I would.

Gregory looked downright alarmed. Basil's face was inscrutable. I tried to change the subject. I asked at what time her uncle would be receiving but she ignored the question. "It's their chief distinction, knowing Julian. They discuss him by the hour. They speculate on his chances of becoming emperor. Gregory thinks he *will* be emperor. Basil thinks Constantius will kill him."

Though Basil knew where the conversation was tending, he was fearless. "Macrina, how can you be so certain this is not one of the Emperor's secret agents?"

"Because you know him."

"We know criminals, too. Idolaters. Agents of the devil."

"Whoever saw a secret agent with that sort of beard? Besides, why should I care? *I'm* not plotting against the Emperor." She turned to me, black eyes glowing. "If you *are* a secret agent, you'll remember that, won't you? I worship the Emperor. My sun rises and sets in his divinity. Every time I see that beautiful face in marble, I want to weep, to cry out: Perfection, thou art Constantius!"

Gregory positively hissed, not at all sure how I would take this mockery. I was amused but uncomfortable. I confess it occurred to me that perhaps Gregory or Basil or even Macrina might indeed be a member of the secret police. If so, Macrina had already said quite enough to have us all executed. That would be the saddest fate of all: to die as the result of a joke!

"Don't be an old woman, Gregory!" Macrina turned to me. "These two dislike Julian. I can't think why. Jealousy, I suppose. Especially Gregory. He's very petty. Aren't you?" Gregory was now gray with terror. "They feel Julian is a dilettante and not serious. They say his love of learning is just affectation. Basil feels that his true calling is that of a general—if he lives, of course. But Gregory thinks he's far too scatterbrained even for that. Yet Gregory longs for Julian to be emperor. He wants to be friend to an emperor. You're both terribly worldly, deep down, aren't you?"

Gregory was speechless. Basil was alarmed but he showed courage. "I would deny only the part about 'worldly.' I want nothing *in* the world. In fact, next month I enter a monastery at Caesarea where I shall be as far from the world as I can be, this side of death."

127

Gregory rallied. "You do have a bitter tongue, Macrina." He turned to me, attempting lightness. "She invents everything. She loves to mock us. She is a pagan, of course. A true Athenian." He could hardly contain his loathing of the girl or his fear of me.

Macrina laughed at him. "Anyway, I'm curious to meet the prince." She turned to me. "Where will you live? With my uncle?"

I said no, that I would stay with friends. She nodded. "My uncle keeps a good house and never cheats. My father takes some of the overflow and though he's honest he hates all students deeply, hopelessly."

I laughed. The Twins laughed too, somewhat hollowly. Basil then proposed that we go to the house of Prohaeresius. I settled our account with the owner of the tavern. We went outside. In the hot dust of the street, Macrina whispered in my ear, "I have known all along that you were the prince."

*Priscus*: You will be aware of a number of ironies in what you have just read. The unspeakable Gregory is due to preside over the new Ecumenical Council. They say he will be the next bishop of Constantinople. How satisfying to glimpse this noble bishop in his ragged youth! Basil, who wanted only the contemplative life, now governs the church in Asia as bishop of Caesarea. I liked Basil during the brief period I knew him in Athens. He had a certain fire, and a good mind. He might have been a first-rate historian had he not decided to be a power in the church. But how can these young men resist the chance to rise? Philosophy offers them nothing; the church everything.

Julian was more wary of Gregory than I'd thought. But this could be hindsight. When Julian was writing his memoir, he asked me what I thought of Gregory and I assured him that if ever he had an enemy it was that jackal. Julian disagreed. But what I said apparently had some effect. As I have told you before, I want nothing to do with the publication of this memoir. Even so, if it is published, I shall delight in the effect it will have on the new bishop of Constantinople. He will not enjoy public reminder of his pseudo-Cynic youth.

It is also amusing to compare Gregory's actual behavior in Athens with his own account of those days which he has given us in the Invective he wrote shortly after Julian died. I have this work in front of me as I write. At almost no point is it honest. For instance, Gregory describes Julian's appearance in this way:

"His neck was unsteady, his shoulders always in motion, shrugging up and down like a pair of scales, his eyes rolling and glancing from side to side with an almost insane expression, his feet unsteady and stumbling, his nostrils breathing insolence and disdain, the expression of his face ridiculous, his bursts of laughter unrestrained and coming in noisy gusts, his nods of assent and dissent quite inappropriate, his speech stopping short and interrupted by his taking a breath, his questions without sense or order, his answers not a whit better than his questions . . ." This is not even good caricature. Of course Julian *did* talk too much; he was enormously eager to learn and to teach; he could often be silly. But he was hardly the spastic creature Gregory describes. The malice of a true Christian attempting to destroy an opponent is something unique in the world. No other religion ever considered it necessary to destroy others because they did not share the same beliefs. At worst, another man's belief might inspire amusement or contempt—the Egyptians and their animal gods, for instance. Yet those who worshipped the Bull did not try to murder those who worshipped the Snake, or to convert them by force from Snake to Bull. No evil ever entered the world quite so vividly or on such a vast scale as Christianity did. I don't need to tell you that my remarks are for your eyes alone and not for publication. I put them down now in this uncharacteristic way because I find myself more moved than I thought I would be as I recall that season in Athens, not only through the eyes of my own memory but through those of Julian.

Gregory also maintains that he knew even then that Julian was a Hellenist, secretly conspiring against Christianity. This is not true. Gregory might have guessed the first (though I doubt it); he certainly could not have *known* that Julian was conspiring against the state religion, since at that time Julian was hardly conspiring against anything. He was under constant surveillance. He wanted only to survive. Yet Gregory writes, "I used these very words about him: 'What an evil the Roman State is nourishing,' though I prefaced them by a wish that I might prove a false prophet." If Gregory had said this to anyone, it would have been treason, since Julian was the heir of Constantius. If Gregory ever made such a prophecy, it must have been whispered in Basil's ear when they were in bed together.

I find Julian's reference to Macrina amusing and disingenuous. In the proper place I shall tell you the true story, which you may

129

or may not use, as you see fit. Julian's version is true only up to a point. I suppose he wanted to protect her reputation, not to mention his own.

I see Macrina occasionally. She was always plain. She is now hideous. But so am I. So is all the world, old. But in her day Macrina was the most interesting girl in Athens.

*Julian Augustus*

Even today, Prohaeresius is a man I greatly admire. I say "even today" because he is a Galilean and has opposed my edict forbidding Galileans to teach the classics. Though I went out of my way to exempt him from this ban, he has gone into retirement. When I met him, he had been for forty years the city's most famous teacher of rhetoric. His house is a large one near the Ilissos River. At all hours it is—or was—crowded with students asking questions, answering questions.

At first I stood at the back of the crowded dim room and watched Prohaeresius as he sat comfortably in a large wooden chair. He was then eighty years of age: tall, vigorous, with a powerful chest, extraordinary black eyes, not unlike those of his niece Macrina. His hair was white and thick and curled richly upon his brow, like seafoam on a beach. He was in every way a handsome man, with a voice to match. In fact, he was such a master of eloquence that when my cousin Constans sent him on a mission to Rome, the Romans not only admitted that he was the most eloquent speaker they had ever heard, they set up a bronze statue to him in the forum, with the inscription: "From Rome, the Queen of Cities, to Prohaeresius, the King of Eloquence." I mention this to emphasize his gifts, for the people of the city of Rome are the most jaded and bored in the world. Or so everyone tells me. I have yet to see my capital city.

Prohaeresius was consoling a student who complained of poverty. "I make no case for poverty. But it is at least bearable in youth. Salt to the day. When I first came from Armenia to Athens, I lived with a friend in an attic, just off the Street of the Slaughterhouses. Between us we had one cloak and one blanket. In winter we broke the day in watches. When he went out, wearing the cloak, I would huddle under the blanket. When he came back, I would take the cloak while he kept warm in bed. You have no idea how good this is for one's style. I would prepare speeches of such eloquence that I brought tears to my own eyes as I declaimed

130

them into that old blanket, teeth chattering from the cold." There was an amused murmur. I had the sense that this was a favorite story, often told.

Then Gregory spoke to him in a low voice. Prohaeresius nodded and got to his feet. I was startled to see that he was nearer seven than six feet tall.

"We have a visitor," he said to the others. All eyes were turned to me and I looked nervously to the floor. "A scholar of some renown." Despite the irony of this, he said it amiably. "The cousin of a young friend of mine, now dead. Fellow scholars, the most noble Julian, heir to all the material world, as we are heirs to things spiritual, or try to be."

There was a moment of confusion. The students were uncertain whether to behave towards me as a member of the imperial family or as a student. Many of those who were seated rose; some bowed; others simply stared curiously. Macrina whispered in my ear, "Go on, you dummy! Speak to him!"

I pulled myself together and made a speech, very brief and to the point, or so I thought. Macrina told me later that it was interminable and pretentious. Fortunately, now that I am Emperor *all* my speeches are considered graceful and to the point. How one's style improves with greatness!

Prohaeresius then took me round among the students, introducing me to this one and that one. They were shy, even though I had carefully made the point that I intended to come and go at the University like any other student.

Prohaeresius continued his discourse a little while longer. Then he dismissed the students and led me into the atrium of his house. The sun slanted now from the west. From upstairs I could hear the laughter and scuffling of the students who boarded there. Occasionally they would come out on the gallery to get a glimpse of me. But when they caught me looking at *them*, they pretended they had business in someone else's room. I would have given a good deal to have lived anonymously in one of those bare rooms.

I was placed in the chair of honor beside the fountain, as Prohaeresius presented his wife Amphiclea to me. She is a sad woman who has never got over the deaths of two daughters. She spoke seldom. Obviously philosophy has been no consolation to her. I also met Macrina's father, Antolius, a boorish man who looked like an innkeeper, which he was. Macrina was not fond of him.

131

Basil and Gregory excused themselves. Gregory was most winning. He offered to take me to all the lectures; he would be my guide. Basil was equally pleasant though he said that he might have to excuse himself from most expeditions. "It's only a few months before I go back. I have a great deal to do, *if* I'm spared." And he pressed both hands to his middle, with a look of mock agony. "My liver feels as if Prometheus's vultures were tearing at it!"

"Stay out of drafts, then," I found myself saying too quickly, "or you may conceive and lay a vulture's egg!" Prohaeresius and Macrina both got the allusion and burst out laughing. Basil was not much amused and I regretted the quickness with which I had spoken. I often do this. It is a fault. Gregory shook my hand fondly; then he and Basil left. To this day he is probably afraid that I shall have my revenge on him for what he said about me. But I am not like that, as the world knows.

We drank wine in the garden. Prohaeresius asked me about matters at court. He was most interested in politics; in fact when my cousin Constans wanted to ennoble him as a sign of admiration, he offered Prohaeresius the honorary title of praetorian prefect. But the old man said that he preferred to be food comptroller for Athens (a significant title Constantius always reserved for himself). Then, exercising the authority that went with his title, he got the grain supply of several islands diverted to Athens. Needless to say, he is a hero to the city.

Prohaeresius was suspicious of me from the beginning. And for all his geniality he seemed by his questions to be trying to get me to confess to some obscure reason for visiting Athens. He spoke of the splendors of Milan and Rome, the vitality of Constantinople, the elegant viciousness of Antioch, the high intellectual tone of Pergamon and Nicomedia; he even praised Caesarea—"the Metropolis of Letters," as Gregory always refers to it, and not humorously. Any one of these cities, Prohaeresius declared, ought to attract me more than Athens. I told him bluntly that I had come to see him.

"And the beautiful city?" Macrina suddenly interrupted.

"And the beautiful city," I repeated dutifully.

Prohaeresius rose suddenly. "Let us take a walk by the river," he said. "Just the two of us."

At the Ilissos we stopped opposite the Kallirrhoe Fountain, a sort of stone island so hollowed and shaped by nature that it does indeed resemble a fountain; from it is drawn sacred water. We sat on the bank, among long grass brown from August heat. Plane trees sheltered us from the setting sun. The day was golden; the air still. All around us students read or slept. Across the river, above a row of dusty trees, rose Hymettos. I was euphoric.

"My dear boy," Prohaeresius addressed me now without ceremony as father to son. "You are close to the fire."

It was a most unexpected beginning. I lay full length on the thick brown turf while he sat cross-legged beside me, very erect, his back to the bole of a plane tree. I looked up at him, noting how rounded and youthful the neck was, how firm the jaw line for one so old.

"Fire? The sun's? The earth's?"

Prohaeresius smiled. "Neither. Nor hell's fire, as the Christians say."

"As you believe?" I was not certain to what extent he was a Galilean; even now, I don't know. He has always been evasive. I cannot believe such a fine teacher and Hellenist could be one of them, but anything is possible, as the gods daily demonstrate.

"We are not ready for that dialogue just yet," he said. He gestured toward the swift shrunken river at our feet. "There, by the way, is where Plato's Phaidros is set. They had good talk that day, and on this same bank."

"Shall we equal it?"

"Someday, perhaps." He paused. I waited, as though for an omen. "You will be emperor one day." The old man said this evenly, as though stating fact.

"I don't want to be. I doubt if I shall be. Remember that of all our family, only Constantius and I are left. As the others went, so I shall go. That's why I'm here. I wanted to see Athens first."

"Perhaps you mean that. But I . . . well, I confess to a weakness for oracles." He paused significantly. That was enough. One word more and he would have committed treason. It is forbidden by law to consult an oracle concerning the emperor—an excellent law, by the way, for who would ever obey a ruler the date of whose death was known and whose successor had been identified? I must say that I was shocked at the old man's candor. But also pleased that he felt he could trust me.

"Is it predicted?" I was as bold as he. I incriminated myself, hoping to prove to him my own good faith.

He nodded. "Not the day, not the year, merely the fact. But it will be tragedy."

"For me? Or for the state?"

"No one knows. The oracle was not explicit." He smiled. "They seldom are. I wonder why we put such faith in them."

"Because the gods *do* speak to us in dreams and reveries. That is a fact. Both Homer and Plato . . ."

"Perhaps they do. Anyway, the habit of believing is an old one . . . I knew all your family." Idly he plucked at the brown grass with thick-veined hands. "Constans was weak. But he had good qualities. He was not the equal of Constantius, of course. You are."

"Don't say that."

"I merely observe." He turned to me suddenly. "Now it is my guess, Julian, that you mean to restore the worship of the old gods."

My breath stopped. "You presume too much." My voice shook despite a hardness of tone which would have done justice to Constantius himself. Sooner or later one learns the Caesarian trick: that abrupt shift in tone which is harsh reminder of the rod and axe we wield over all men.

"I hope that I do," said the old man, serenely.

"I'm sorry. I shouldn't have spoken like that. You are the master."

He shook his head. "No, *you* are the master, or will be soon. I want only to be useful. To warn you that despite what your teacher Maximus may say, the Christians have won."

"I don't believe it!" Fiercely and tactlessly I reminded him that only a small part of the Roman population was actually Galilean.

"Why do you call them Galileans?" he asked, interrupting my harangue.

"Because Galilee was where *he* came from!"

Prohaeresius saw through me. "You fear the word 'Christian,'" he said, "for it suggests that those who call themselves that are indeed followers of a king, a great lord."

"A mere name cannot affect *what* they are," I evaded him. But he is right. The name is a danger to us.

I resumed my argument: most of the civilized world is neither Hellenist nor Galilean, but suspended in between. With good reason, a majority of the people hate the Galileans. Too many innocents have been slaughtered in their mindless doctrinal quarrels.

134

I need only mention the murder of Bishop George at Alexandria to recall vividly to those who read this the savagery of that religion not only toward its enemies (whom they term "impious") but also toward its own followers.

Prohaeresius tried to argue with me, but though he is the world's most eloquent man, I would not listen to him. Also, he was uncharacteristically artless in his defense of the Galileans, which made me suspect he was not one of them. Like so many, he is in a limbo between Hellenism and the new death cult. Nor do I think he is merely playing it safe. He is truly puzzled. The old gods do *seem* to have failed us, and I have always accepted the possibility that they have withdrawn from human affairs, terrible as that is to contemplate. But mind has not failed us. Philosophy has not failed us. From Homer to Plato to Iamblichos the true gods continue to be defined in their many aspects and powers: multiplicity contained by the One, all emanating from truth. Or as Plotinus wrote: "Of its nature the soul loves God and longs to be at one with him." As long as the soul of man exists, there is God. It is all so clear.

I realized that I was making a speech to a master of eloquence, but I could not stop myself. Dozing students sat up and looked at me curiously, convinced I was mad, for I was waving my arms in great arcs as I am prone to do when passionate. Prohaeresius took it all in good part.

"Believe what you must," he said at last.

"But you believe, too! You believe in what I believe. You must or you could not teach as you do."

"I see it differently. That is all. But try to be practical. The thing has taken hold. The Christians govern the world through Constantius. They have had almost thirty years of wealth and power. They will not surrender easily. You come too late, Julian. Of course if you were Constantine and this were forty years ago and we were pondering these same problems, then I might say to you: 'Strike! Outlaw them! Rebuild the temples!' But now is not then. You are not Constantine. They have the world. The best one can hope to do is civilize them. That is why I teach. That is why I can never help you."

I respected him that day. I respect him now. If he is still alive when this campaign is ended, I shall want to talk to him again. How we all long to make conversions!

Like two conspirators, we returned to his house. We now had

a bond between us which could not be broken, for each had told the other true and dangerous things. Fear defined our friendship and gave it savor.

In the dim atrium, students were again gathered, talking strenuously all at once as students will. When they saw us enter, they fell silent. I daresay the sight of me alarmed them. But Prohaeresius told them I was to be treated as just another student.

"Not that he is, of course, in spite of the beard and the old clothes." They laughed. "He is different from us." I was about to say that even members of Constantine's family have some (if not much) resemblance to the human family, when he said: "He is a true philosopher. He has *chosen* to be what we *must* be." This was accepted with some delight. Not until a day later did the irony of what he said occur to me.

Macrina took me by the arm and said, "You must meet Priscus. He is the most disagreeable man in Athens."

Priscus sat on a stool, surrounded by students. He is a lean, cold-faced man, nearly as tall as Prohaeresius. He rose when we approached him and murmured, "Welcome." I was pleased to meet this great teacher whom I had long known by reputation, for he is as famous for his wit as he is for his ambiguities. He is also completely without enthusiasm, which right off made him a good foil for me since I am often excited by the trivial. We were friends from the start. He is with me now in Persia.

"Try to pin him down," said Macrina, turning to me, her hand on Priscus's lean arm as though presenting him to me for a bout of wrestling, "on *anything*. We think of him as the master of evasion. He never argues."

With a look of distaste which I have come to know so well (and fear when it is turned on me!), Priscus got his arm loose from Macrina's grasp. "Why should I argue? I know what *I* know. And others are always quick to tell me what *they* know, or think they know. There is no need for confrontation."

"But surely you must find that new thoughts occur in argument?" I was naïve, of course; I pressed him hard. "After all, Socrates led others to wisdom through argument and conversation."

"The two are not quite the same thing. I teach through conversation, or try to. But *argument* is a vice in this city. Glib men can almost always score points off wiser but less well-spoken men. Nowadays style in speaking is everything; content nothing.

Most of the Sophists are actors—worse, they are lawyers. And the young men pay to hear them perform, like street singers."

"Priscus attacks me!" Prohaeresius had joined us. He was amused at what was obviously an old discussion.

"You know what I think." Priscus was severe. "You are the worst of the lot because you are the best performer." He turned to me. "He is so eloquent that every Sophist in Athens hates him."

"All but you," observed Macrina.

Priscus ignored her. "A few years ago his confreres decided that he was too popular. So they bribed the proconsul..."

"Careful," said Macrina. "We must not speak of bribed officials in front of what may one day be the greatest official of them all."

"Bribed the proconsul," said Priscus as though she had not spoken, "to exile our host. This was done. But then the proconsul retired and was succeeded by a younger man who was so indignant at what had happened that he allowed Prophaeresius to return. But the Sophists did not give up easily. They continued to plot against their master. So the proconsul held a meeting at the University..."

"At my uncle's suggestion."

Prophaeresius was amused. "Macrina allows us no secrets. Yes, I put him up to it. I wanted to get my enemies all together in one place in order that I might..."

"Dispatch them," said Macrina.

"*Win* them," said her uncle.

"Beat them," said Macrina.

Priscus continued. "It was a formidable display. Everyone was gathered in the main hall of the University. Friends were nervous. Enemies were active. The proconsul arrived. He took charge of the assembly. He announced that a theme should be proposed for Prohaeresius to argue. Any theme. The assembly could choose it. At first no one said a word."

"Until my uncle saw two of his very worst enemies skulking in the back. He called on them to set a theme. They tried to escape, but the proconsul ordered his guards to bring them back."

Priscus looked dour indeed. "It was the guards, I suggest, that won the day for virtue."

"The honeyed tongue of Priscus!" The old man laughed. "You may be right. Though I suspect the bad judgment of the enemy helped most, for they set me a theme of remarkable obscenity and limited scope."

137

"Which side of a woman is the most pleasing, front or back." Macrina grinned.

"But he accepted the challenge," said Priscus. "He spoke with such effectiveness that the audience maintained a Pythagorean silence."

"He also insisted that shorthand reporters from the law court take down every word." In an oblique way, Macrina was proud of her uncle's prowess. "He also insisted there be no applause."

"It was a memorable speech," Priscus continued. "First, he presented the argument in all its particulars. Then he took one side . . . the front. After an hour, he said, 'Now observe carefully whether I remember all the arguments that I used earlier.' He then repeated the speech in all its intricate detail, only this time he took the opposite point of view . . . the back. In spite of the proconsul's order, applause filled the hall. It was the greatest triumph of memory and eloquence heard in our time."

"And . . . ?" Prohaeresius knew that Priscus would not finish without a sudden twist to the knife.

"*And*? Your enemies were completely routed and where before they despised you, now they hate you." Priscus turned to me. "They nearly had his life the next year. They still plot against him."

"Which proves?" Prohaeresius was as curious as I to learn what Priscus was up to.

"That victories in argument are useless. They are showy. What is spoken always causes more anger than any silence. Debate of this sort convinces no one. Aside from the jealousies such a victory arouses, there is the problem of the vanquished. I speak now of philosophers. The one who is defeated, even if he realizes at last that he is fighting truth, suffers from having been publicly proved wrong. He then becomes savage and is apt to end by hating philosophy. I would prefer not to lose anyone for civilization."

"Well said," Prohaeresius agreed.

"Or, perhaps," said the devilish Macrina, "you yourself don't want to lose an argument, knowing that you are apt to turn bitter as a result of public humiliation. Oh, Priscus, you are vain! You won't compete for fear you might not win. As it is, none of us knows how wise you are. Silence is his legend, Prince. And he is all the greater for that. Each time Prohaeresius speaks he limits himself, for words limit everything, being themselves limited. That's why Priscus is wisest of all: silence cannot be judged.

Silence masks all things or *no* thing. Only Priscus can tell us what his silence conceals, but since he won't, we suspect him great."

Priscus did not answer. Macrina was the only woman I have ever known who could speak with so many odd twistings and turnings. Irony is not usual to woman, but then Macrina was not in any way usual. Before we had an opportunity to see if Priscus could answer her, we were interrupted by the arrival of my bodyguard, as well as an officer of the proconsul's staff. Word had already spread throughout Athens that I was at the house of Prohaeresius. I was again taken into custody.

*Priscus*: Macrina was a bitch. We all detested her, but because she was the niece of Prohaeresius we endured her. Julian's description of our first meeting is not accurate. That is to say, what he remembers is not what I remember. For instance, he says that his bodyguard arrived *before* I answered Macrina. This is not true. I told her then and there that my silence masked compassion for the intellectual shortcomings of others since I did not wish to wound anyone, even her. This caused some laughter. *Then* the guards arrived.

For the historic record I should give my first impression of Julian. He was a handsome youth, thick in the chest like all his family, muscular, a gift of nature since in those days he seldom exercised. He was far too busy talking. Gregory was not entirely inaccurate when he described Julian's breathless and continual conversation. In fact, I used to say to him, "How can you expect to learn anything when you do all the talking?" He would laugh excitedly and say, "But I talk and listen at the same time. That is *my* art!" Which perhaps was true. I was always surprised at how much he did absorb.

Not until I read the memoir did I know about the conversation with Prohaeresius. I never suspected the old man of such cunning, or boldness. It was a dangerous thing to admit to a strange prince that he had consulted an oracle. But he always had a weakness for oracles.

I never liked the old man much. I always felt he had too much of the demagogue in him and too little of the philosopher. He also took his role as a great old man seriously. He made speeches on any subject, anywhere. He cultivated princes the way bishops cultivate relics. He was a formidable orator, but his writings were banal.

Let me tell you something about Macrina since Julian is not candid and if I don't tell you you will never know. They had a love affair which was the talk of the city. Macrina behaved with her usual clownishness, discussing the affair with everyone in intimate detail. She declared that Julian was a formidable lover, indicating that her own experience had been considerable. Actually, she was probably a virgin when they met. There were not many men of her set who would have made the effort to make her a non-virgin. After all, Athens is famous for the complaisance of its girls, and not many men like to bed a talking-woman, especially when there are so many quiet ones to choose from. I am positive that Julian was Macrina's first lover.

There was a funny story going around at about this time, no doubt apocryphal. Julian and Macrina were overheard while making love. Apparently all during the act each one continued to talk. Macrina is supposed to have confuted the Pythagoreans while Julian restated the Platonic powers, all this before and during orgasm. They were well matched.

Julian seldom mentioned Macrina to me. He was embarrassed, knowing that I knew of the affair. The last time we spoke of her was in Persia when he was writing the memoir. He wanted to know what had become of her, whom she had married, how she looked. I told him that she was somewhat heavy, that she had married an Alexandrian merchant who lived in Piraeus, that she has three children. I did not tell him that the oldest child was his son.

Yes. That is the famous scandal. Some seven months after Julian left Athens, Macrina gave birth. During the pregnancy she stayed with her father. Despite her daring ways she was surprisingly conventional in this matter. She was desperate for a husband even though it was widely known that the bastard was Julian's and therefore a mark of honor for the mother. Luckily, the Alexandrian married her and declared the child was his.

I saw the boy occasionally while he was growing up. He is now in his twenties and looks somewhat like his father, which makes it hard for me to be with him. Stoic though I am, in certain memories there is pain. Fortunately, the boy lives now in Alexandria, where he runs his stepfather's trading office. He has, Macrina once told me, no interest in philosophy. He is a devout Christian. So that is the end of the house of Constantine. Did Julian know that he had a son? I think not. Macrina swears she never told him, and I almost believe her.

A few years ago I met Macrina in what we Athenians call the Roman agora. We greeted one another amiably, and sat together on the steps of the water-clock tower. I asked about her son.

"He is beautiful. He looks exactly like his father, an emperor, a god!" Macrina has lost none of her old fierce flow of language, though the edge to her wit is somewhat blunted. "But I don't regret it."

"The resemblance? Or being the mother of Julian's son?"

She did not answer. She looked absently across the agora, crowded as always with lawyers and tax collectors. Her dark eyes were as glittering as ever, though her face has grown jowly and the heavy bosom fallen with maternity and age. She turned to me abruptly. "He wanted to marry me. Did you know that, Priscus? I could have been Empress of Rome. What a thought! Would you have liked that? Do you think I would have been ... decorative? Certainly *unusual*. How many empresses have been philosophers in their own right? It would have been amusing. I should have worn a lot of jewelry, even though I detest ornaments. Look at me!" She tugged at the simple garment she wore. Despite her husband's wealth, Macrina wore no rings, no brooches, no combs in her hair, no jewels in her ears. "But empresses must look the part. They have no choice. Of course I should have had a bad character. I would have modeled myself on Messalina."

"You? Insatiable?" I could not help laughing.

"Absolutely!" The old edge returned briefly; the black eyes were humorous. "I'm a faithful wife now because I am fat and no one wants me. At least no one *I* would want wants me. But I'm drawn to beauty. I should love to be a whore! Except I'd want to choose the clientele, which is why I should have loved being empress! History would have loved me, too! Macrina the Insatiable!"

Anyone who saw us on those steps would have thought: what an eminently respectable couple! An old philosopher and a dignified matron, solemnly discussing the price of wheat or the bishop's latest sermon. Instead Macrina was intoning a hymn to lust.

"What would Julian have thought?" I managed to interject before she gave too many specific details of her appetite. It is curious how little interested we are in the sexual desires of those who do not attract us.

141

"I wonder," she paused. "I'm not sure he would have minded. No. No. No, he *would* have minded. Oh, not out of jealousy. I don't think he was capable of that. He simply disliked excess. So do I, for that matter, but then I have never had the chance to be excessive, except in food, of course." She patted herself. "You see the result? Of course I could still be a beauty in Persia. They revel in fat women." Then: "Did he ever mention me to you? Later? When you were with him in Persia?"

I shook my head. I'm not certain why I lied to her, unless dislike is sufficient motive.

"No. I suppose he wouldn't." She did not seem distressed. One must admire the strength of her egotism. "Before he went back to Milan, he told me that if he lived he would marry me. Contrary to gossip, he did *not* know that I was pregnant then. I never told him. But I did tell him that I wanted to be his wife, although if Constantius had other plans for him (which of course he did) I would not grieve. Oh, I was a formidable girl!"

"Did you ever hear from him again?"

She shook her head. "Not even a letter. But shortly after he became Emperor he told the new proconsul of Greece to come see me and ask if there was anything I wanted. I shall never forget the look of surprise on the proconsul's face when he saw me. One look assured him that Julian could not have had any amatory interest in this fat lady. He was puzzled, poor man. Do you think Julian knew about our son? It was not the best-kept secret."

I said I did not think so. And I do not think so. I certainly never told him, and who else would have dared?

"Did you know Julian's wife?"

I nodded. "In Gaul. She was much older than he. And very plain."

"So I've heard. I was never jealous. After all, he was forced to marry her. Was he really celibate after she died?"

"As far as I know."

"He was strange! I'm sure the Christians would have made a saint out of him if he had been one of theirs, and his poor bones would be curing liver complaints at this very moment. Well, that is all over, isn't it?" She glanced at the water clock behind us. "I'm late. How much do *you* bribe the tax assessor?"

"Hippia looks after those matters."

"Women *are* better at such things. It has to do with details. We delight in them. We are children of the magpie." She rose

142

heavily, with some difficulty. She steadied herself against the white marble wall of the tower. "Yes, I should have liked to have been empress of Rome."

"I doubt it. If you had been empress, you would be dead by now. The Christians would have killed you."

"Do you think I would have minded *that*?" She turned full on me and the large black eyes blazed like obsidian in the sun. "Don't you realize—can't you tell just by looking at me, my dear wise old Priscus—that not a day has passed in twenty years I haven't wished I were dead!"

Macrina left me on the steps. As I watched the blunt figure waddle through the crowd toward the magistrate's office, I recalled her as she had been years before and I must say for a moment I was touched by the urgency of that cry from the heart. But it does not alter the fact that she was and is a sublimely disagreeable woman. I've not talked to her since that day, though we always nod when we see one another in the street.

# VIII

*Julian Augustus*

A week after I arrived in Athens I met the Hierophant of Greece. Since I did not want the proconsul to know of this meeting, it was arranged to take place in the Library of Hadrian, a not much frequented building midway between the Roman and the Athenian agoras.

At noon I arrived at the library and went straight to the north reading room, enjoying as I always do the musty dry odor of papyrus and ink which comes from the tall niches where the scrolls and codices are kept. The high room with its coffered ceiling (for which we must thank Antinoüs's protector) was empty. Here I waited for the Hierophant. I was extremely nervous, for he is the holiest of all men. I am forbidden by law to write his name but I can say that he belongs to the family of the Eumolpidae, one of the two families from which Hierophants were traditionally drawn. He is not only High Priest of Greece, he is custodian and interpreter of the mysteries of Eleusis which go back at least two thousand years, if not to the beginning of our race. Those of us who have been admitted to the mysteries may not tell what we have seen or what we know. Even so, as Pindar wrote: "Happy is he who, having seen these rites, goes below the hollow earth; for he knows the end of life and he knows the god-sent beginning." Sophocles described initiates as "Thrice-happy mortals, who having seen those rites depart for Hades; for them alone is it granted to have true life there; to the rest, evil." I quote from memory. (Note to secretary: Correct quotations, if they are wrong.)

Eleusis is a city fourteen miles from Athens. For two thousand years the mysteries have been celebrated in that place, for it was at Eleusis that Persephone returned from the underworld to which she had been stolen by the death-god Hades and made his queen. When Persephone first vanished, her mother Demeter, the harvest goddess, sought her for nine days, neither eating nor drinking. (As I tell this story initiates will see the mystery unfold. But no one else may know what is meant.) On the tenth day Demeter came to Eleusis. She was received by the king and queen, who gave her a pitcher of barley water flavored with mint which she drank all at once. When the king's oldest son said, "How greedily you drink!" Demeter turned him into a lizard. But then, remorseful over what she had done, she conferred great powers upon the king's youngest son, Triptolemus. She gave him seed grain, a wooden plow and a chariot drawn by serpents; he then traveled the earth teaching men agriculture. She did this for him not only to make up for what in her anger she had done to his brother, but also because Triptolemus was able to tell her what had happened to her daughter. He had been in the fields when the earth suddenly opened before him. Then a chariot drawn by black horses appeared, coming from the sea. The driver was Hades; in his arms he held Persephone. As the chariot careened at full speed into the cavern, the earth closed over them. Now Hades is brother to Zeus, king of the gods, and he had stolen the girl with Zeus's connivance. When Demeter learned this, she took her revenge. She bade the trees not to bear fruit and the earth not to flower. Suddenly, the world was barren. Men starved. Zeus capitulated: if Persephone had not yet eaten the food of the dead, she might return to her mother. As it turned out, Persephone had eaten seven pomegranate seeds and this was enough to keep her forever in the underworld. But Zeus arranged a compromise. Six months of the year she would remain with Hades, as queen of Tartarus. The remaining six months she would join her mother in the world above. That is why the cold barren time of the year is six months and the warm

144

fruitful time six months. Demeter also gave the fig tree to Attica, and forbade the cultivation of beans. This holy story is acted out in the course of the mysteries. I cannot say more about it. The origin of the ceremony goes back to Crete and, some say, to Libya. It is possible that those places knew similar mysteries, but it is a fact that Eleusis is the actual place where Persephone returned from the underworld. I have myself seen the cavern from which she emerged.

Now: for those who have been initiated, I have in the lines above given in the form of a narrative a clear view of what happens after death. Through number and symbol, I have in a page revealed everything. But the profane may not unravel the mystery. They will merely note that I have told an old story of the old gods.

The Hierophant entered the reading room. He is a short plump man, not in the least impressive to look at. He saluted me gravely. His voice is powerful and he speaks old Greek exactly the way it was spoken two thousand years ago, for in the long descent of his family the same words have been repeated in exactly the same way from generation to generation. It is awesome to think that Homer heard what we still hear.

"I have been busy. I am sorry. But this is the sacred month. The mysteries begin in a week." So he began prosaically.

I told him that I wished to be initiated into *all* the mysteries: the lesser, the greater, and the highest. I realized that this would be difficult to arrange on such short notice, but I had not much time.

"It can be done, of course. But you will need to study hard. Have you a good memory?"

I said that I still retained most of Homer. He reminded me that the mysteries last for nine days and that there are many passwords, hymns and prayers which must be learned before the highest mystery can be revealed. "You must not falter." The Hierophant was stern. I said that I thought I could learn what I needed to know in a week, for I did indeed have a good memory; at least it is good when properly inspired.

I was candid. I told him that if I lived, it was my hope to support Hellenism in its war with the Galileans.

He was abrupt. "It is too late," he said, echoing Prohaeresius. "Nothing you can do will change what is about to happen."

I had not expected such a response. "Do you *know* the future?"

145

"I am Hierophant," he said simply. "The *last* Hierophant of Greece. I know many things, all tragic."

I refused to accept this. "But how can you be the last? Why, for centuries . . ."

"Prince, these things are written at the beginning. No one may tamper with fate. When I die, I shall be succeeded not by a member of our family but by a priest from another sect. He will be in name, but not in fact, the final Hierophant. Then the temple of Eleusis will be destroyed—all the temples in all of Greece will be destroyed. The barbarians will come. The Christians will prevail. Darkness will fall."

"Forever?"

"Who can say? The goddess has shown me no more than what I have told you. With me, the true line ends. With the next Hierophant, the mysteries themselves will end."

"I cannot believe it!"

"That alters nothing."

"But if I were to become Emperor . . ."

"It would make no difference."

"Then obviously, I shall *not* become Emperor."

I smiled at this subtlety, for we had got around the law forbidding prophecy.

"Whether you are Emperor or not, Eleusis will be in ruins before the century is done."

I looked at him closely. We were sitting on a long bench beneath a high latticed window. Lozenges of light superimposed their own designs upon the tiled floor at our feet. Despite his terrible conviction, this small fat man with his protuberant eyes and fat hands was perfectly composed. I have never known such self-containment, even in Constantius.

"I refuse to believe," I said at last, "that there is nothing we can do."

He shrugged. "We shall go on as long as we can, as we always have." He looked at me solemnly. "You must remember that because the mysteries come to an end makes them no less true. Those who were initiated will at least be fortunate in the underworld. Of course one pities those who come after us. But what is to be must be." He rose with dignity; his small plump body held tightly erect, as though by will he might stiffen the soft flesh. "I shall instruct you myself. We shall need several hours a day. Come to my house tonight." With a small bow he withdrew.

During the weeks that followed, we saw each other every day. Yet I came to know the Hierophant no better. On any subject not connected with the mysteries, he refused to speak. I gave up talking to him, accepting him as what he was: a palpable link with the holy past but not a human companion.

I need not describe the celebrations which precede the initiation, since they are known to everyone. Though I may not describe the mysteries themselves, I can say that in this particular year more people took part in the festivities than usual, to the chagrin of the Galileans.

The whole business takes nine days. The first day was hot and enervating. The proclamation was made and the sacred objects brought from Eleusis to the Eleusinion, a small temple at the foot of the acropolis where—among other interesting things—there is a complete list of Alcibiade's personal property, seized when he profaned the mysteries one drunken night by imitating on a street corner the Hierophant's secret rites. The sacred objects are contained in several jars tied with red ribbons. They are put in the Eleusinion, to be returned to Eleusis during the main procession, which is on the fifth day.

On the second day, we bathed in the sea and washed the pig each of us had bought for sacrifice. I chose the beach at Phaleron, and nearly lost the pig I had bought for six drachmae. It is an amazing sight to watch several thousand people bathing in the sea, each with a squealing pig.

The third day is one of sacrifice, and a long night.

The fourth day is sacred to Asklepios; one stays at home.

On the fifth day the procession starts from the Dipylon Gate to Eleusis.

It was a lovely sight. An image of the god Iacchos, son of Demeter, is borne in a wooden carriage at the procession's head. This part of the ceremony is sacred to him. Though all are supposed to walk to Eleusis, most of the well-to-do are carried in litters. I walked. My bodyguards complained, but I was exalted. I was crowned with myrtle and I carried not only the sacred branches tied with wool but also, according to tradition, new clothes in a bundle on a stick over my shoulder. Macrina accompanied me.

The day was cloudy, which made the journey pleasanter than it usually is at that time of the year. All told, there were perhaps a thousand of us in the procession, not counting the curious, which include a number of Galileans who shouted atheist curses at us.

On the outskirts of Athens, just off the main road, Macrina pointed to a complex of old buildings. "That is the most famous brothel in Greece," she said with her usual delight in such things. "The Shrine of Aphrodite." Apparently, people come from all over the world to visit the shrine, where for a price they enjoy the "priestesses." They pretend it is religion. Actually, it is mass prostitution. I could not disapprove more.

Just beyond the shrine there is an old bridge. Here the ordeal begins. On the bridge's parapet sit men with faces covered by hoods. It is their traditional function to remind important people of their faults and to condemn their pride. I consoled myself by remembering that Hadrian and Marcus Aurelius had preceded me on this bridge. If they had survived humiliation, so could I.

"It won't be bad." Macrina tried to be reassuring. "They're much too frightened of Constantius." But I recalled how Hadrian had been jeered for his love of Antinoüs, and Hadrian was a reigning emperor, not mere cousin to one. I was sweating as we reached the bridge. All eyes were upon me. The hooded men—at least thirty of them—had just finished tormenting a local magistrate. They turned now to me. Macrina held my arm tight. Heart beating fast and eyes cast down, I walked slowly over the bridge. The jeering curses were formidable. At first I tried not to listen, but then I recalled that this humiliation is an essential part of the mysteries: to rid oneself of pride. I listened. I was accused mostly of falseness and pretension. I was not a true scholar. I was a *poseur*. I looked like a goat. I was a coward and afraid to serve in the army (this was unexpected). I hated the Galileans. This made me nervous indeed but happily, it was said only once. After all, my tormentors were of the true religion and not apt to hold my dislike of the Galileans against me.

Finally, the bridge was crossed. The ordeal ended. Feeling purged and relieved (the worst is never so bad as one fears), I walked the rest of the way to Eleusis, with Macrina grumbling at my side. I'm afraid she taunted me quite as much as the men on the bridge. But as I drew closer to the mysteries, I was filled with such a sense of expectancy that nothing could disturb my mood.

It was night when we arrived at Eleusis. The city is a small one on the Saronic Gulf, with a view of the island of Salamis. Like most cities whose principal source of revenue is strangers, Eleusis is full of inns and cookshops and tradesmen eager to sell copies of sacred objects at ridiculously high prices. It is a wonder that any place remains sacred, considering the inevitable presence of those whose livelihood depends on cheating strangers. I am told that Delphi is even worse than Eleusis; while Jerusalem—which is of course "sacred" to the Galileans—is now a most distressing place to visit.

Torches blazed in every street of the town. Night was like day. Innkeepers solicited us, and at every street corner, men told of places to eat. Even vice was proposed, which shows how debased the local population is, for they should know better than anyone that during the pilgrims' three days in Eleusis, they must fast, remain continent, and touch neither the body of one dead or that of a woman who has just given birth; eggs and beans are also forbidden us, even after the first day's fast.

Macrina and I followed the crowd to where the mysteries were enacted. Homer has described how the original temple was at the foot of the acropolis, in much the same spot as the present temple, or Telesterion as it is called. This night everything was illuminated in honor of the Great Mysteries.

The entrance to the sacred enclosure is through a gate, even more noble than the Dipylon at Athens. We entered, passing through a roped-off section where guards and priests made sure that we were indeed initiates, remarkable by our dress and certain signs. The gate is so cunningly arranged that anyone looking through can see no more than a few yards of the sacred way; any further view of the Telesterion is broken by the large blank wall of the Ploutonion, a temple built over the original passage to Hades from which Persephone appeared.

Eyes smarting from torch smoke, Macrina and I ascended the sacred way, pausing first at the Kallichoros Well. I was overcome with awe, for this is the same well described by Homer. It is old beyond memory. It was here in the time when the gods walked the earth that the women of Eleusis danced in honor of Demeter. The opening of the well is several steps below the main terrace, and faced with magnificent marble. Near it stands a large basin containing sacred water. I bathed my hands and began to know Demeter and her grief. I was so moved that I almost neglected to pay the priestess the one drachma for the experience.

Next we entered the Ploutonion, which is set in a rocky hollow of the acropolis. The elmwood doors were shut to us, but the altar outside, cut in living rock, was illuminated.

Finally we came to the long stoa of Philon, which fronts the

149

Telesterion. Beyond this blue-paved portico the blank façade of the holiest building on earth is set against the acropolis, which provides its fourth wall. There are greater and more splendid temples in the world, but there is none which quite inspires one's reverence in the way the Telesterion does, for it has been holy since almost the first day of man, a creation of that beautiful lost world when the gods, not beleaguered, lived among us, and earth was simple and men good.

Since we were not yet initiates, we could not enter the Telesterion. At this point we were joined by two priests who led us to the house where the Eumolpidae have lived for a thousand years. We were to spend the night there. The Hierophant, however, did not join us. On this night of nights, he fasted and meditated.

Macrina and I sat up until dawn. "You must be admitted to the mysteries," I scolded her, as I had done before.

But she was perverse. "How can I? I'm not one thing or the other. I don't like the Christians because they are cruel. I don't like the mysteries and all the rest because I don't believe anything can help us when we are dead. Either we continue in some way, or we stop. But no matter what happens, it is beyond our control and there is no way of making a bargain with the gods. Consider the Christians, who believe there is a single god . . ."

"In three parts!"

"Well, yours is in a thousand bits. Anyway, if by some chance the Christians *are* right, then all this"—she gestured toward the Telesterion—"is wrong and you will go to their hell rather than to your Elysium."

"But the Galileans *are* wrong."

"Who can say?"

"Homer. Thousands of years of the true faith. Are we to believe there was no god until the appearance of a rabble-rousing carpenter three hundred years ago? It is beyond sense to think that the greatest age of man was godless."

"You must argue with the Twins," said Macrina; then we spoke of matters which I shall not record.

The next three days were beyond imagination. I was admitted to all of the mysteries, including the final and most secret. I saw that which is *enacted*, that which is *shown* and that which is *spoken*. I saw the passion of Demeter, the descent of Persephone to the underworld, the giving of grain to man. I saw the world as it is and the world that is to come. I lost my fear of death in the

150

Telesterion when, in a blaze of light, I looked upon the sacred objects. *It was true*. More than this I cannot write. It is forbidden to reveal anything that one sees and hears during the two nights spent in the Telesterion. But I will make one general comment, a dissent from Aristotle, who wrote: "The initiated do not learn anything so much as feel certain emotions and are put into a certain frame of mind." First of all, one must question the proposition that a new emotion is not something learned. I should think that it was. In any case, I have yet to meet anyone who has been initiated at Eleusis who did not learn new things not only about the life we live now but the one to follow. There is such a logic to what is revealed on those two nights that one is astonished not to have understood it before—which proves to me the truth of what is seen, heard and demonstrated. We are part of a never-ending cycle, a luminous spiral of life, lost and regained, of death to life to . . . but now I begin to tell too much.

*Priscus*: He tells altogether too much. But that was his charm, except when he goes on altogether too long and becomes tedious. I know that you were initiated at Eleusis and doubtless feel much as he did about what is revealed there. I don't. It is possible that if I had gone through all the nonsense of initiation, I *might* have had a revelation. But I doubt it. There are some natures too coarse to apprehend the mysteries. Mine is one. Nowadays of course we can write with a certain freedom of the mysteries since they are drawing to an end. The Emperor is expected to shut down the Telesterion as soon as he feels the time is politically right. Naturally, the bishops lust for the destruction of Eleusis, which to me is the only argument for preserving it.

I am cool to the mysteries because I find them vague and full of unjustified hope. I do not want to be nothing next year or next minute or whenever this long life of mine comes to its end (of course it does not seem at all long to *me*, not long enough by half!) Yet I suspect that "nothing" is my fate. Should it be otherwise, what can I do about it? To believe as poor Julian did that he was among the elect as a result of a nine-day ceremony, costing some fifteen drachmae, not counting extras, is to fall into the same nonsense we accuse the Christians of when we score their bitter exclusivity and lunatic superstition.

I had no idea Macrina was so sensible until I read Julian's account of their conversation at Eleusis. She might have made him a good wife. I had always assumed she only told him what he wanted to hear, like any other woman. She was rare, in her way; but not to my taste.

The remainder of Julian's stay in Athens was uneventful. He was personally popular. The Sophists all tried to curry favor with him. It is remarkable how men supposedly dedicated to philosophy and things of the mind are drawn to power; affecting scorn for the mighty, they are inevitably attracted to those who rule. When the powerful man is as amiable and philosophy-loving as Julian, the resulting attempt to capture him is all the more unseemly.

*Libanius*: How typical of Priscus! He can hardly restrain his jealousy of me, and his resentment of my influence over Julian. Yet my interest in Julian was *not* self-seeking. How could it be? When I turned down the title of praetorian perfect. I said that the title Sophist was good enough for me. My gesture is still much remembered not only here in Antioch but everywhere philosophy is valued. Those of us who wish to lead others to wisdom respond to any questioning soul, prince or beggar. Sometimes, as in the case of Maximus, Julian showed bad judgment, but by and large he cultivated the best minds of our era. I also find Priscus's remarks about Eleusis distasteful, even atheistic. Cicero, who was hardly superstitious, wrote that if all else Athens had brought the world was swept away, the mysteries alone would be enough to place mankind forever in Athen's debt. Priscus has got worse with age. Envy festers. He was never a true philosopher. I find myself pitying him as I read his bitter commentary.

*Priscus*: In any case, when Julian looked with adoration at that sheaf of wheat which is revealed with such solemnity at the highest moment of the ceremony . . .

*Libanius*: This is absolute blasphemy! These things must not be revealed. Priscus will suffer for this in the next world, while whoever betrayed to him our high secret will sink forever in dung. It is appalling!

*Priscus*: . . . he felt duly elated, believing that as the wheat withers, dies and is reborn, so it is with us. But is the analogy correct? I would say no. For one thing, it is not the *same* sheaf of wheat that grows from the seed. It is a new sheaf of wheat, which would suggest that our immortality, such as it is, is between our legs. Our seed does indeed make a new man but he is not us. The son is not the father. The father is put in the ground and that is the end of him. The son is a different man who will one day make yet another man and so on—perhaps forever—yet the individual consciousness stops.

*Libanius*: I hate Priscus! He is worse than a Christian. Homer believed. Was Homer wrong? Of course not.

*Priscus*: Julian did nothing to offend the Christians in Athens, though it was fairly well known that he tended toward philosophy. But he was discreet. On at least one occasion he attended church.

The Hierophant liked him but thought he was doomed, or so he told me years later. The Hierophant was an interesting man. But of course you knew him for you were admitted to the mysteries during his reign. He realized with extraordinary clarity that our old world was ended. There were times I think when he took pleasure in knowing he was the last of a line that extended back two thousand years. Men are odd. If they cannot be first, they don't in the least mind being last.

*Julian Augustus*

Those marvelous days in Athens came to an abrupt end when an imperial messenger arrived with orders that I attend Constantius at Milan. No reason was given. I assumed that I was to be executed. Just such a message had been delivered to Gallus. I confess now to a moment of weakness. Walking alone in the agora, I considered flight. Should I disappear in the back streets of Athens? Change my name? Shave my head? Or should I take to the road like a New Cynic and walk to Pergamon or Nicomedia and lose myself among students, hide until I was forgotten, assumed dead, no longer dangerous?

Suddenly I opened my arms to Athena. I looked up to her statue on the acropolis, much to the astonishment of the passersby (this took place in front of the Library of Pantainos). I prayed that I be allowed to remain in Athena's city, preferring death on the spot to departure. But the goddess did not answer. Sadly I dropped my arms. Just at that moment, Gregory emerged from the library and approached me with his wolf's grin.

"You're leaving us," he said. There are no secrets in Athens.

153

I told him that I was reluctant to go but the Emperor's will must be done.

"You'll be back," he said, taking my arm familiarly.

"I hope so."

"And you'll be the Caesar then, a man of state, with a diadem and guards and courtiers! It will be interesting to see just how our Julian changes when he is set over us like a god."

"I shall be the same," I promised, sure of death.

"Remember old friends in your hour of greatness." A scroll hidden in Gregory's belt dropped to the pavement. Blushing, he picked it up.

"I have a special permit," he stammered. "I can withdraw books, certain books, approved books..."

I laughed at his embarrassment. He knew that I knew that the Pantainos Library never allows any book to be taken from the reading room. I said I would tell no one.

The proconsul treated me decently. He was a good man, but frightened. I recognized at once in his face the look of the official who does not know if one is about to be executed or raised to the throne. It must be cruelly perplexing for such men. If they are kind, they are then vulnerable to a later charge of conspiracy; if they are harsh, they may live to find their victim great and vindictive. The proconsul steered a middle course; he was correct; he was conscientious; he arranged for my departure the next morning.

My last evening in Athens is still too painful to describe. I spent it with Macrina. I vowed to return if I could. Next day, at first light, I left the city. I did not trust myself to look back at Athena's temple floating in air, or at the sun-struck violet line of Hymettos. Eyes to the east and the morning sun, I made the sad journey to Piraeus and the sea.

# IX

It was mid-October when I arrived in Milan. The weather was dry and the air so clear that one could see with perfect clarity those blue alps which separate civilization from barbarism, our world of sun form that melancholy green forest where dwells Rome's nemesis.

Just before the city's gate we were met by one of Constantius's eunuchs, a gorgeous fellow with many chins and an effortless sneer. He did not salute me as is proper, a bad omen. He gave the commander of my guard a letter from the Emperor. When I saw this, I began to recite the first of the passwords I should need when I arrived in the kingdom of the dead. But I was not to be dispatched just yet. Instead I was taken to a house in one of the suburbs. Here I was imprisoned.

Imprisonment exactly describes my state. I was under heavy guard. During the day, I was allowed to stroll in the atrium. But at night I was locked in my bedroom. No one could visit me, not that there was anyone in Milan I wanted to see or who wanted to see me, excepting the Empress Eusebia. Of my household, I was allowed to keep only two boys and two men. The rest were transferred to the imperial palace. There was no one I could talk to. That was the greatest hardship of all. I should have been pleased to have had even a eunuch for company!

Why was I treated this way? I have since pieced the story together. While I was in Athens, a general named Silvanus was proclaimed Augustus in Gaul. I am convinced that at heart he was innocent of any serious desire to take the purple, but the enmity of the court eunuchs drove him to rebellion.

As soon as this happened, Constantius arrested me because he was afraid that I might take advantage of the defection of Gaul to rise against him in Attica. As it turned out, before I reached Milan, Silvanus was dead at Cologne. Constantius's luck in civil war had proved itself again.

But the death of Silvanus did not solve the problem of Julian. While I was locked up in that suburban villa, the old debate was reopened. Eusebius wanted me put to death. Eusebia did not. Constantius kept his own counsel.

I prepared several letters to Eusebia, begging her to intercede with the Emperor that I might be allowed to return to Athens. But I finally decided not to send her any message, for Constantius's suspicions were easily aroused, to say the least, and any exchange between his wife and his heir presumptive would not only be known to him but would doubtless turn him against both of us. I did the wise thing.

At dawn, on the thirteenth day of my captivity, my life altered forever. I was awakened by a slave banging on the bedroom door. "Get up, Lord! Get up! A message from the Augustus!" Fully clothed, I leapt out of bed. I then reminded the slave that until someone unlocked the door I could hardly receive the imperial messenger.

The door flew open. The commander of my guard was beaming. I knew then that the divine will had begun its work. I was to be spared.

"A messenger, sir. The Emperor will receive you tonight."

I stepped into the atrium and got my first taste of what it is like to be in favor. The house was now full of strangers. Fat eunuchs in gaudy silk; clerks from various government offices; tailors; sandalmakers; barbers; youthful officers drawn to what might be a new sun and source of honor. It was dizzying.

The messenger from Constantius was no other than Arintheus, who serves with me now in Persia. He is remarkably beautiful, and the army loves him in that fervent way armies have of loving handsome officers. He is auburn-haired and blue-eyed, with a strong, supple body. He is completely uneducated, but brave and shrewd in warfare. His only vice is an excessive fondness for boys, a practice I usually find unseemly in generals. But the men are amused by his sensuality. Also, he is a cavalry man and among cavalry men pederasty is a tradition. I must say that day when Arintheus approached me, blue eyes flashing and ruddy face grinning, I nearly mistook him for Hermes himself, streaming glory from Olympus as he came to save his unworthy son. Arintheus saluted me briskly; then he read aloud the letter summoning me for audience. When he had finished reading (with some difficulty, for he has never found reading easy), he put the message away, gave me his most winning smile and said, "When you are Caesar, don't forget me. Take me with you. I prefer action." He patted his sword hilt. I dithered like a fool. He departed.

Then began a new struggle. My beard would have to go, also

156

my student's clothes. I was now a prince, not a philosopher. So for the first time in my life my beard was shaved. It was like losing an arm. Two barbers worked on me while I sat in a chair in the center of the atrium as the morning sun shone on a spectacle which, looking back, was perfectly ludicrous. There was I, an awkward twenty-three-year-old philosophy student, late of the University of Athens, being turned into a courtier.

A slave girl trimmed my toenails and scrubbed my feet, to my embarrassment. Another worked on my hands, exclaiming at the inkiness of my fingers. The barber who shaved my beard also tried to shave my chest but I stopped him with an oath. We compromised by letting him trim the hair in my nostrils. When he was finished, he brought me a mirror. I was quite unable to recognize the youth who stared wide-eyed from the polished metal—and it *was* a youth, not a man as I had thought, for the beard had been deceptive, giving me an undeserved look of wisdom and age. Without it, I resembled any other youngster at court

I was then bathed, oiled, perfumed and elaborately dressed. My flesh shrank from the lascivious touch of silk, which makes the body uncomfortably aware of itself. Today I never wear silk, preferring coarse linen or wool.

I have only a vague memory of the rest of that day. I was carried to the palace through crowded streets. The people stared at me curiously, uncertain whether or not it was right to applaud. I looked straight ahead as I had been instructed to do when on view. I tried not to hear conversations in the street. Desperately I tried to recall the eunuch's instructions.

At the edge of the city's main square the palace, gray and forbidding behind its Corinthian colonnade, rose before me like fate itself. Troops were drawn up in full dress on either side of the main door. When I stepped out of the litter, they saluted.

Several hundreds of the people of Milan drew close to examine me. In every city there is a special class whose only apparent function is to gather in public places and look at famous men. They are neither friendly nor unfriendly, merely interested. An elephant would have pleased them most, but since there was no elephant, the mysterious Prince Julian would have to do. Few of them could identify me. None was certain just what relation I was to the Emperor. It is amazing how little we are known to our subjects. I know of places on the boundaries of the empire where they believe Augustus himself still reigns, that he is a great magician who may not die. Of course, the fact each of us calls himself Augustus is a deliberate attempt to suggest that the continuity of power emanating from Rome is the one constant in a world of flux. Yet even in the cities where there is widespread literacy, the average citizen is often uncertain about who the ruler is. Several times already I have been addressed as Constantius by nervous delegations, while one old man actually thought I was Constantine and complimented me on how little I had changed since the battle at the Mulvian bridge!

Inside the palace, curiosity was mingled with excitement and anticipation. I was in favor. I read my good fortune in every face. In the vestibule they paid me homage. Heads bobbed; smiles flashed; my hand was wrung with warmth, kissed with hope. It was disgusting ... in retrospect. At the time, it was marvelous proof that I was to live for a while longer.

I was delivered to the Master of the Offices, who gave me a final whispered briefing. Then, to the noise of horns, I entered the throne room.

Constantius wore the purple. The robe fell stiffly to his crimson shoes. In one hand he held an ivory staff, while the other rested on the arm of the throne, palm upward, holding the golden orb. As usual, he stared straight before him, unaware of anything except what was in his direct line of vision. He looked ill. His eyes were dark-circled, and his face was somewhat blotchy, as though from too much wine; yet he was abstemious. On a throne at floor level sat Eusebia, blazing with jewels. Though she too played statue, she managed to suggest sympathetic humanity. When she saw me, the sad mouth parted slightly.

To left and right, in full court dress, were the members of the Sacred Consistory. All stared at me as I slowly crossed to the throne, eyes downcast. October light streamed through high windows. The odor of incense was heavy in the room. I felt a child again, and this was Constantine. For a moment, the room swam before my eyes. Then Constantius spoke the first line of the ritual greeting. I answered, and prostrated myself at his feet. I kissed the purple, and was raised up. Like two actors we played our scene impersonally until it was done; then I was given a stool next to Eusebia.

I sat very still, looking straight ahead, aware of Eusebia next to me. I could smell the flowery scent of her robes. But neither of us looked at the other.

Ambassadors were received, generals appointed, titles bestowed. The audience ended when the emperor stood up. The rest of us dropped to our knees. Stiff-legged and swaying slightly from the weight of his robes and jewelry, Constantius marched off to the palace living quarters, followed by Eusebia. The moment the green bronze doors shut behind them, as though from a magician's spell, we were all set free.

Courtiers surrounded me and asked a thousand questions: Would I be made Caesar? Where would I live? Did I need any service? I had only to command. I answered as demurely and noncommittally as I could. Then my enemy Eusebius approached, his yellow moonface gravely respectful. Silk robes whispered as the heavy body bowed to me. "Lord, you are to dine with the sacred family." An excited whisper went through the court. This was the highest recognition. I was exalted in all eyes. Though my own first reaction was: dinner means poison.

"I shall escort you to the sacred quarters." Eusebius led me to the bronze doors through which the imperial couple had just passed. We did not speak until we were alone in the corridor beyond.

"You should know, Lord, that I have always, in every way, assured the Augustus of your loyalty to him."

"I know that you have." I lied with equal dignity.

"There are those in the Sacred Consistory who are your enemies." He gestured for a guard to open a small oaken door. We passed through. "But I have always opposed them. As you know, I had hoped all along that you would take your rightful place here at court. And though there are some who think that the title Caesar should lapse because your brother . . ." He allowed that sentence to go unfinished. "I have urged his Eternity to make you Caesar."

"I do not seek such honor," I murmured, looking about me with some interest. The palace at Milan is a large rambling building. Originally it was a military governor's rather modest headquarters. In the last century when Rome ceased to be a practical center for the West, the palace was enlarged to become an imperial residence. Because of the German tribes, the emperors had to be close to the Alps. Also, the farther an emperor is from the city of Rome the longer his reign is apt to be, for the populace of that city is notoriously fickle and arrogant, with a long memory of the emperors it has overthrown. None of us stays for long at Rome if he can help it.

Constantine enlarged the palace in Milan, building the state

159

rooms, while Constantius added the second-floor living quarters through which we now walked. These rooms look out on a large inner court. I personally prefer the old-fashioned form of architecture, with small private rooms arranged about an atrium, but Constantius was a modernist in architecture as well as in religion. I find such rooms too large, and of course ruinously expensive to heat.

Guards and eunuchs stood at every door, arrogant yet servile. A court is the most depressing place on earth. Wherever there is a throne, one may observe in rich detail every folly and wickedness of which man is capable, enameled with manners and gilded with hypocrisy. I keep court in the field. In residence, I keep as little as possible.

At the final door, Eusebius left me with a deep bow. Guards opened the door, and I stepped into the private dining room. Constantius reclined on one of the two couches within whose right angle was the table. Opposite him Eusebia sat in an ivory chair. I bowed low to both of them, intoning the proper formula.

Constantius mumbled his response. Then he waved me to the couch beside him.

"You look better without that damned beard."

I blushed as I took my place on the couch. Eusebia smiled encouragingly. "I rather liked the beard," she said.

"That's because you're an atheist, too."

My heart missed a beat. But it was only the Emperor's heavy wit.

"She likes these high-sounding, low-living Cynics." He indicated his wife with a knotty ringed hand. "She's always reading them. Not good for women to read." I said something agreeable, grateful to find him in a good mood. Constantius had removed his diadem and outer robes, and he looked almost human, quite unlike the statue he had appeared earlier.

Wine was brought me and though I seldom drink it full strength, this day I drank deep, to overcome nervousness.

"Who does he look like?" Constantius had been examining me curiously, like a new slave or horse. "Without that beard?"

Eusebia frowned, pretending to be thoughtful. One gives away nothing in dealing with a tyrant, even if the tyrant is one's husband.

The Emperor answered his own question. "Constans. You look just like him. Just like my brother." My heart sank. Constantius had always been thought to have had a hand in his brother's death.

But there was no significance to this remark, either. Constantius, at his ease, tended to be literal and rather simple.

I said that I had been too young to recall what my late cousin had looked like.

"Much the best of the three of us. Tall. Like our father." Constantius was much concerned with his own shortness.

An elaborate dinner was served us, and I tasted everything, for to refuse any dish would show that one suspected the Emperor of treachery. It was an ordeal, and my stomach nearly rebelled.

Constantius led the conversation, as emperors are supposed to do—unless they are given to philosophic debate like me, in which case I must speak very fast at my own table to be heard.

I was asked about my studies at Athens. I described them, ending "I could spend the rest of my life there." As I said this, I noticed that Eusebia frowned imperceptibly: a signal that I was not to speak of student life.

But Constantius had not been listening. He lay now flat on his back, belching softly and kneading his barrel-like stomach with one hand. When he spoke, he did so with eyes shut.

"I am the first Augustus to reign alone since my father, who was himself the first to reign alone in this century. But he never intended for just one of us to rule. Any more than Diocletian intended for any one of *his* successors to govern alone." Constantius raised himself on one elbow and looked at me with those curiously mournful eyes which were his most attractive yet most puzzling feature. They were the eyes of a poet who had seen all the tragedy in this world and knows what is to come in the next. Yet the good effect of those eyes was entirely undone by a peevish mouth.

Who could ever know Constantius? I certainly did not. I hated him, but Eusebia loved him—I think—and she was a woman who would not have cared for what was evil. Like the rest of us, Constantius was many men in the body of one.

"The world is too big for one person to govern it." My heart beat faster for I knew now what was to come. "I cannot be everywhere. Yet the imperial power *must* be everywhere. Things have a habit of going wrong all at once. As soon as the German tribes get loose in the north, the Persians attack in the south. At times I think they must plan it. If I march to the East, I'm immediately threatened in the West. If one general rises up against me, then I must deal with at least two more traitors at the same time. The

161

empire is big. Distances are great. Our enemies many." He tore off a roast duck's leg and chewed it, all the time looking at me with those melting eyes.

"I mean to hold the state together. I shall not sacrifice one city to the barbarians, one town, one field!" The high-pitched voice almost cracked. "I mean to hold the state for our family. We won it. We must maintain it. And that is why we must be loyal to one another." How that phrase from those cruel lips struck me! I dared not look at him.

"Julian," the voice was lower now. "I intend to make you Caesar, and my heir until such time as I have a son."

"Lord..." was all I could say. Tears unexpectedly filled my eyes. I shall never know if I *wanted* my fate. Yet when it came to me, a secret line snapped within and the perilous voyage began.

Eusebia congratulated me. I don't recall what was said. More wine was brought and Constantius, in a jovial mood, told me how the astrologists preferred 6 November to any other day in the month. He also insisted that I study military strategy, while assembling a household suitable to my new rank. I was to have a salary. It would not be large, he said, understating the matter considerably: if I had not had a small income from my mother's estate, I would have starved to death that first year. My cousin could never be accused of generosity.

Constantius almost smiled at me. "Now," he said, "I have a surprise for you." The surprise was his sister Helena. She entered the room with great dignity. I had never met her, though I had seen her at a distance during my first visit to Milan.

Helena was not an attractive woman. She was short, inclined to stoutness, with the short legs and long torso of Constantius. By one of those unlucky chances, her face was the face of her father Constantine the Great. It was almost alarming: the same broad cheeks, the thin proud mouth, the large nose, the huge full jaw, an imperial portrait re-created in a middle-aged woman. Yet despite this unfortunate resemblance, she was otherwise most feminine with an agreeable soft voice. (I have always hated women with shrill voices.) She moved modestly, even shyly. At the time I knew nothing about her except that she was ten years older than I, and that she was Constantius's favorite sister.

After formally acknowledging our greetings, Helena took her place in the vacant chair. She was obviously under considerable strain. So was I, for I knew exactly what was going to happen next. I had always known that something like this was apt to be my fate, but I had put it as much as possible out of my mind. Now the moment was at hand.

"We do you the honor," said Constantius, "of bestowing our own beloved sister upon you as your wife and consort, a human and tangible link between our crowns." He had obviously prepared this sentence in advance. I wondered if he had spoken thus to Gallus when he gave him Constantia in marriage.

Helena looked at the floor. I am afraid I turned scarlet, Eusebia watched me, amused but guarded. She who had been my friend and ally could now quite easily become my enemy. I was aware of this, even then. Or do I write now with hindsight? In any case, it was perfectly plain that should Helena have a child and Eusebia remain barren, my child would be Constantius's heir. The four of us were now caught like flies in a spider's web.

I have no clear idea what I said to Constantius. I am sure that I stammered. Helena later said that I was most eloquent, though unable to look at her during my speech of acceptance. Doubtless I was thinking of my conjugal duties. Never did a woman attract me less. Yet we would have to have a child. This sort of burden is the usual fate of princes and I daresay it is a small price to pay for greatness, though at the time it seems larger than it ought.

Helena was a good woman but our moments of intimacy were rare, unsatisfactory, and somewhat pathetic, for I did want to please her. But it was never pleasant, making love to a bust of Constantine. Though I could not make her happy, I did not make her suffer, and I think we became friends.

The dinner ended when Constantius swung his short bowed legs to the floor, and stretched till his bones cracked. Then without a word to any of us, he left the room. Eusebia gave me a half-smile. She put her hand out to Helena and together the two women withdrew, leaving me staring at the pheasant's eggs which an artist-cook had arranged in a beautifully feathered nest as final course. It was an extraordinary moment. I had entered the room a proscribed student. I left it as Caesar and husband. The change was dizzying.


I believe it is true of most courts that the principal figures seldom see one another. This is partly due to choice. The fewer the meetings, the less chance of something untoward happening.

But more to the point, it suits the courtiers to keep the great people apart, thereby increasing the importance of intermediaries who are then able to hurry from one wing of the palace to another, making mischief and policy as they go.

The court of Constantius was in many ways the worst since Domitian. The eunuchs were all-powerful. They kept everyone from the Emperor. If a man displeased a eunuch, he was doomed and Mercurius, "the count of dreams," would be called in or Paul "the chain" (the one so called because he was a genius at finding obscure links to a never-end-ending chain of treason while the other specialized in the analysis of seemingly harmless dreams which, invariably, upon scrutiny, revealed treasonable intent). Since Constantius would listen only to the eunuchs, injustice flourished. No one was safe, including the great figures themselves, particularly those like myself who were blood heirs to the principate.

I have often felt when studying history that not enough is made of the importance of those intermediaries who so often do the actual governing. We tend to think of courts as wheels at whose center is the emperor, from whom, like spokes, all those who serve him extend, drawing their power directly from his central presence. The truth is otherwise. Hardly anyone was allowed to come close to Constantius. Only the eunuch Eusebius saw him daily. As a result, factions within the court could form and reform, irrelevant to the nominal power.

In reading accounts of those weeks at Milan, one would think that Constantius and I saw each other daily, discussing high policy, military strategy and sharing, as it were, a family life. Actually, I saw the Emperor only four times in one month. The first encounter I have described; the second was at my investiture as Caesar.

I was created Caesar 6 November 355, the year when Arbetio and Lollianus were consuls. I will say one thing for Constantius. He had an artist's gift for ceremony. Though I like to think I surpass him in many ways, I know I shall never be able to create the sense of awful majesty he could whenever he chose. One *knew* this was the Augustus when he appeared before a crowd. When I appear, the people are not in the least impressed. I believe they have a certain affection for me. I don't in the least alarm them. They think I look like a professor of rhetoric. They are quite right. I do.

At the far end of the main square, a high wooden platform had been decorated with the eagles of Rome and the dragons of our house. The square itself was filled with soldiers in full military dress.

As I was led by the generals of the army to the platform, I was conscious that every muscle in my body ached, for I had been practicing daily with sword and javelin. I was exhausted, and I'm afraid that my instructors had nothing but contempt for me. They thought me a bookish fool who knew nothing of weaponry and preferred talk to war. Of course they were courteous to my face, but behind my back I often heard soft mocking laughter. Incidentally, I was surprised to discover how little I can endure mockery. One of the best consolations of philosophy is that it supposedly prepares one for the contempt of others. Some philosophers even revel in the dislike of the vulgar. Not I. Perhaps there *is* something to the idea of blood and inheritance. After all I am descended from three emperors. To be thought weak and womanish by hearty young officers was unbearable to me. Grimly, I made up my mind to surpass them in every way. Unfortunately, at this moment my primacy was more wish than fact. I had done too much to fast. As a result, I was even clumsier than usual.

The moment I reached the base of the platform, horns were sounded. Cheering began. A path opened through the legions, and Constantius appeared in his gilded state carriage; he wore a dragon-shaped gold helmet and the purple. As he passed me, I caught his eye and got a look as blind as Homer's! In public, the emperor does not see mere men.

Slowly Constantius climbed the steps to the platform, his short bowed legs slightly diminishing the majesty of his presence. From the platform, he received the cheer of the legions. Then he motioned for me to join him. With a sense of one going to his own execution, I climbed the steep wooden steps and took my place at the side of Constantius . . . I almost wrote at the side of history, for I was now legend. For better or worse, I had become a part of that long chronicle which began with Julius Caesar and whose end none can foresee.

I looked out over the massed troops. This was my first look at an army, and I confess to reveling in the sight. All thought of philosophy went clear out of my head as the dragon pennants fluttered in the autumn wind, and the eagles below us dipped as the salute was given.

Constantius reached out and took my right hand in his. His grip was firm and callused. I glanced at him out of the corner of my eye, conscious something was not right: he was half a head taller than I. I looked down and saw that he was standing on a footstool. Constantius neglected no detail which might enhance his majesty.

Constantius spoke to the legions. His high-pitched voice carried well. The Latin he used was that of the army, but it was easy to understand. He had memorized his speech. "We stand before you, valiant defenders of our country, to avenge the common cause. How this is to be done, I put to you not as soldiers but as impartial judges. After the death of those rebellious tyrants whom mad fury drove to seize the state, the savages to the north, thinking that this great empire was weak and in confusion, crossed into Gaul. They are there now. Only you and we, in perfect accord, can turn them back. The choice is yours. Here stands before you our cousin Julian, honored for his modesty, as dear to us for that as for the ties of blood; a young man of conspicuous ability whom I desire to make Caesar if you will confirm him . . ."

At this point, though in mid-sentence, Constantius was stopped by various voices declaring that it was clearly the will of God, not of man, that I be raised to the rank of Caesar. I quite agreed, though the God they had in mind and the One who did indeed raise me up were not the same. Nevertheless, I admired the skill with which Constantius had staged the scene. The voices rang out as though spontaneous (actually, everything had been carefully rehearsed). Constantius remained very still while they spoke, as though listening to an oracle. My hand in his grew sweaty; but he never relaxed the firm grip. When there was silence again, he nodded gravely to the legions. "Your response is enough. I see that I have your approval."

He let go of my hand. He motioned for two generals to join us on the platform. One carried a wreath; the other a purple robe. They stood behind us.

"This young man's quiet strength and temperate behavior" (he emphasized the word "temperate" to reassure them that I was not Gallus) "should be imitated rather than proclaimed; his excellent disposition, trained in all good arts, I concur in by the very fact that I have chosen to elevate him. So now with the immediate favor of the God of heaven, I invest him with this imperial robe."

The cloak was put about my shoulders. Constantius arranged it at the neck. Only once did he look me in the eye as we faced one another, he on his footstool and I with my back to the legions.

The look he gave me was curiously furtive and undecided, in sharp contrast to the easy majesty of his movements and the serene power of his voice.

Constantius was a man in terror of his life. I saw it plain in those great eyes. As he put the wreath on my head, he shut his eyes for an instant, like a man who flinches in anticipation of a surgeon's knife. Then he took my right hand again and turned me around that I might face the legions. But before they could salute me, he raised his arm. He had more to say. Though he spoke as though to me, he looked straight at them. Not certain which way to turn, I looked half at him and half toward the soldiers in the square.

"Brother, dearest to me of all men, you have received in your prime the glorious flower of your origin. Yet I must admit you add to my own glory, for I seem myself more truly great in bestowing almost equal power" (the "almost" was heavily rendered) "on a noble prince who is my kinsman than through that power itself. Come, then, to share in pain and perils, undertake the defense of Gaul, relieve its afflicted regions with every bounty. And should it be necessary to engage with the enemy, take your place with the standard-bearers. Go forth yourself, a brave man ready to lead men equally brave. You and I will stand by one another with firm and steadfast affection, and together—if God grants our prayers— we shall rule over a pacified world with moderation and conscientiousness. You will be present with me always in my thoughts, and I will not fail you in anything you undertake. Now go, with haste, with the prayers of all of us, to defend with your honor the post assigned you by Rome herself, and God's appointment! Hail, Caesar!"

This last he said in a loud voice which was immediately echoed by the legions. It was like a burst of thunder. I had sufficient presence of mind to respond: "Hail, Augustus!" The men repeated this, too. I saluted Constantius. Then I turned and saluted the legions. This was against all protocol. Generals do *not* salute their men. The standards, yes; the legions, no. But my gesture was sincerely tactless. After the first astonishment, the legions roared their approval of me and struck their shields hard against their armored knees: the highest tribute they may render a man. It is also the loudest. I thought I would be deaf forever as the clatter rang through the square. More terrible, however, is the army's

167

disapproval, when they roll their spears back and forth against their shields, as prelude to mutiny.

I could feel Constantius stiffen beside me. This was more than he anticipated. I am sure that he was positive that my gesture to the legions had been premeditated. But the deed was done. And I was Caesar.

Abruptly, Constantius left the platform. I followed him. There was a moment of confusion as he got into his carriage. He looked down at me for a long moment. Then he motioned for me to join him. I clambered in beside him and, side by side, we rode through the cheering legions. I felt a sudden affection for them all. We had been united as though in marriage, and like so many arranged marriages, odd though this one was, it proved to be happy.

The carriage moved slowly through the square to the palace. Constantius said nothing to me, and I dared not speak to him, unhappily aware that in this carriage there was no footstool and I was taller than he, a second bad omen. I murmured to myself a line from the *Illiad*: "By purple death I'm seized, and fate supreme." Inside the palace courtyard Constantius and I parted without a word. I did not see him again for several days.

My first act as Caesar was to send for Oribasius, who was at Athens. He had arrived there only a week after my recall. I also wrote Maximus and Priscus, inviting them to join me. Meanwhile, I continued military practice. I also learned as much as possible about the administration of Gaul.

During this time I saw none of the imperial family, including my soon-to-be wife. Yet the day of the wedding had been set and the inevitable documents were brought to me to be studied. I was given a meticulous ground plan of the chapel and my position from moment to moment during the ceremony was precisely traced.

I had but one friend at court, Eutherius, the Armenian eunuch who had taught me at Constantinople. Every evening we would study various documents and memoranda. It was his task, he said, to make an administrator of me.

The night before my wedding, Eutherius came to me with the news that I was to leave for Gaul the first week in December.

"To what city?"

"Vienne. You'll be there for the winter. Then in the spring you will take the field." He looked at me closely. "Does it seem strange to you to be a general?"

"Strange!" I exploded. "Insane!"

He raised his hand in some alarm, indicating the shadows where guards stood and informers listened, always hopeful of catching me at treason.

I lowered my voice. "Of course it is strange. I've never seen a battle. I've never commanded a single soldier, much less an army. But..."

"But?"

"But I'm not afraid." I did not say what I really felt: that I looked forward to military adventures.

"I am relieved." Eutherius smiled. "Because I have just been appointed grand chamberlain at the court of the Caesar Julian. I go with you to Gaul."

This was marvelous news. I embraced him warmly, babbling happily until he was forced to say, "Roman gravity, Caesar. Please. You are far too Asiatic."

I laughed. "It can't be helped. I *am* Asiatic..."

Suddenly, Eutherius was on his feet. With a speed which I would not have thought possible for one of his age, he darted into the shadowed archway just opposite us. A moment later he reappeared with a dark, richly dressed man.

"Caesar," said Eutherius with grim ceremony, "allow me to present Paul, of the secret service. He has come to pay your greatness homage."

I was hardly startled. I had been under surveillance all my life. The presence of the government's chief secret agent merely reminded me that the higher I rose the more important it was for Constantius to have me watched.

"We are always pleased to receive the Emperor's agents," I said politely.

Paul was imperturbable. His eyes shone in the lamplight; his hook nose made him resemble some great bird of prey. He bowed. He spoke with a slight Spanish accent. "I was on my way to the east wing. To report to Rufinus, the praetorian prefect."

"This is not the usual way to the east wing," said Eutherius amiably.

"What can I say?" Paul spread his hands, bird's talons ready to seize.

169

"You *can* say good-night, Paul, and report to the praetorian prefect that you heard nothing useful," I said.

Paul bowed. "I report only what I hear, Caesar." He was carefully insolent.

"Stay longer," I said, "and you will hear the beginning of your death."

That shook him, though my boldness was perfect bluff. I had no power. One word from him and I could be brought down. Yet I knew that if I was to be Caesar I would have to assert myself or earn the fatal contempt of eunuchs and spies. Paul withdrew.

I turned to Eutherius. "Was I too Asiatic?" I teased him, though my heart pounded.

He shook his head. "Perhaps that is the wisest way to handle him. Anyway, you are safe for the moment."

"But he is constructing one of his chains."

"Perhaps he will trap himself."

I nodded. Paul had been a prime mover in the plot which had destroyed my brother. That night in the palace at Milan I began my own plot.


My wedding day . . . what a strange thing for a celibate to write! It seems impossible now that I could ever have been a husband. Yet I became one on 13 November 355. I shall not describe the atrocious Galilean rites. It is enough to say that I endured them, heavy with purple and glittering with state jewels which I later sold in Gaul to buy soldiers.

After the ceremony, there were the usual celebrations and games in our honor. Helena delighted in all the panoply of rank; in this she resembled her brother. I was merely dutiful and did what was expected of me. A few days after the ceremony I was summoned to an audience with Eusebia.

"What do you think of the world now?" Eusebia's eyes gleamed with mischief.

"I owe it all to you," I said warmly.

"And how do you find Helena?"

"She is my wife," I said formally; again the conspiratorial look.

"She is very . . . handsome," said Eusebia, with an edge of malice.

"Noble, I should say." I almost burst out laughing. But there is a rule to these games.

"You will leave soon."

"I'm glad," I said. Then added. "Not that I look forward to leaving . . ." I could not say "you" so I said "Milan."

She shook her head. "This is not your sort of place. It's not mine either, but . . ." She left what was serious unsaid. Then: "You will go into winter quarters at Vienne. Money . . ."

"Will be scarce." The Grand Chamberlain had already told me that I would have to maintain myself and household on my salary as Caesar. Additional funds could not be granted at this time.

"Luckily, you are frugal."

"Helena is not."

"Helena has her own money," said Eusebia sharply. "She should use it. She owns half of Rome."

I was relieved to hear this, and said so.

"It is my hope," said Eusebia, "that you will soon have a son, not only for yourself but for us."

I admired her boldness. This was the one thing Eusebia did *not* want me to have, since it would endanger her own position. Rather than accept my son as his heir, Constantius was capable of divorcing Eusebia and taking a new wife who could give him what he most desired.

"It is my hope," I answered evenly, "that *you* will be blessed with many children."

But she did not believe me either. The interview now turned painful. No matter what either of us said, it sounded false. Yet I believe she did indeed wish me well, except in that one matter.

Finally, we got off the subject and she revealed to me the state of Constantius's mind. "I speak to you candidly." An admission that neither of us had been speaking candidly before. The sad face looked sadder still, while her long hands nervously fingered the folds of her robe. "He is divided. He cannot make up his mind about you. Naturally, there are those who tell him that you wish to overthrow him."

"Not true!" I began to protest but she stopped me.

"I know it is not true."

"And it *never* will be true!" I believed myself.

"Be tolerant. Constantius has had to face many enemies. It is only natural that he fear you."

"Then why won't he let me go back to Athens, where I am no danger?"

"Because he needs you more than he fears you." She looked

171

at me, suddenly frightened. "Julian, we are in danger of losing all Gaul."

I stared at her dumbly.

"This morning Constantius had a message from the praetorian prefect at Vienne. I don't know what it said. But I suspect the worst. We have already lost the cities of the Rhine. Should the Germans attack this winter, it is the end of Gaul, unless . . ." She held her hand above the flame of the alabaster lamp. The flesh glowed. "Julian, help me!" For a stupid moment I thought she had burned her hand. "You *must* be loyal to us. You must help us!"

"I swear by all the gods, by Helios, by . . ."

She stopped me, unaware that in my sincerity I had sworn by the true gods. "Be patient with him. He will always be suspicious of you. That is his nature. But as long as I live, you are safe. If something should happen to me . . ." This was the first inkling I had that Eusebia was ill. "Be loyal to him anyway."

I forgot what I said. Doubtless more protestations of loyalty, all sincere. When I rose to go, she said, "I have a gift for you. You will see it on the day you leave."

I thanked her and left. Despite all that Eusebia did to hurt me in the next two years, I still love her. After all I owe her not only the principate but my life.


At dawn on the first of December I left Milan for Gaul. I said farewell to Helena, who was to join me later at Vienne. We both behaved according to the special protocol the eunuchs have devised governing a Caesar's farewell to his new wife as he goes to a beleaguered province. Then, accompanied by the newly arrived Oribasius, I went down to the courtyard of the palace to place myself at the head of my army.

Outside in the frosty air, some three hundred foot soldiers and a score of cavalry were drawn up. I took this to be my personal bodyguard. I was about to ask the whereabouts of the army of Gaul when I was joined by Eutherius. He was frowning. "I've just spoken to the Grand Chamberlain. There has been a last-minute change in plans. Your legions have been assigned to the Danube."

I indicated the men in the courtyard. "Is *this* my army?"

"I am afraid so, Caesar."

I have never in my life been so angry. Only the arrival of Constantius prevented me from saying the unsayable. I saluted the Emperor; gravely, he returned the salute. Then he mounted a black horse and I mounted a white one. His personal guard (twice the size of my "army") fell into place behind him. My troops and household brought up the rear. Thus the Augustus and his Caesar launched the power of Rome against the barbarians. It was ludicrous.

The few citizens who were up and around at this hour cheered us dutifully. We made a particularly fine impression at the vegetable market which is just inside the city gate. The farm women waved their carrots and turnips at us, and thought us a brave sight.

Neither Constantius nor I spoke until we were out on the main road, the high Alps visible to us across the Lombard Plain. He had agreed to escort me as far as the two columns which stand on either side of the road midway between Lumello and Pavia. He had obviously decided this would give us sufficient time for a good talk. It did.

Constantius began with, "We have great confidence in Florentius, our praetorian prefect at Gaul." This was an announcement; there was no invitation for me to comment.

Of course he has confidence in Florentius, I thought savagely, otherwise he would have had him murdered by now. But I said, "Yes, Augustus." And waited. We rode a few more yards. Occasionally our armored legs touched, metal striking metal, and each would shrink instinctively from the other. The touch of another man has always disturbed me; the touch of my father's murderer alarmed me.

We passed a number of carts containing poultry; they had pulled off the road at our approach. When the peasants saw the Emperor, they fell flat on their bellies, as though blinded by the sight of that sacred figure. Constantius ignored them.

"We are fond of our sister Helena." This was also launched upon the dry cool air in an oracular tone.

"She is dear to me, too, Augustus." I replied. I was afraid he was going to lecture me on my marital duties, but he made no further mention of Helena.

Constantius was constructing a case. His occasional flat sentences, suitable for carving in marble, were all part of an edifice created to contain me. I was to obey the praetorian prefect of Gaul, even though as Caesar I was his superior. I was to remember that

173

Helena's first loyalty was to her brother and ruler, not to her husband. So far, I understood him clearly.

"We have heard from your military instructor that you show promise."

"I shall not fail you, Augustus. But it was my understanding that I was to go to Gaul with an army, not an escort."

Constantius ignored this. "You have come to soldiering late. I hope you are able to learn what you will need to know."

This was not optimistic, but not unnatural. There was no reason for anyone to suspect that a philosophy student should show *any* talent for war. Curiously enough, I had every confidence in myself because I knew that the gods would not desert me now they had raised me up. But my cousin had no way of knowing my feelings, or judging my capacity. He merely saw a young untried soldier about to go into battle against the fiercest fighters in the world.

"At all times remember that we are divine in the eyes of the people and sacred to heaven."

I took the "we" to mean Constantius and myself, though he may have been merely reminding me of his own rank. "I shall remember, Augustus." I always called him by his proper title, though he much preferred Lord, a title I despise and do not use for it means that one is the master of other men, rather than simply first among them.

"Control your generals." Though he still sounded as if he were repeating maxims, I could tell that now he was on the verge of actual advice, if not conversation. "No officer should be admitted to senatorial rank. All officers must be under strict civilian control. Any governor of any province outranks any general sent to him. No officer must be allowed to take part in civil affairs. Our praetorian prefects are set over all military and civil officials. That is why the administration of the empire runs as smoothly as it does."

Needless to say, I did not remark that the collapse of Gaul was hardly a sign of smooth administration. But in principle Constantius's advice was good and I tend still to follow it. There is no denying that he had a gift for administration.

"In matters of taxes, take whatever is owing us. Show no mercy to the cities and villages which are delinquent in meeting payments. It is their nature to complain. Assume that your taxgatherers are honest unless proved otherwise. They are *never* honest, but no one has yet found a way to correct their abuses. As long as they return to you the larger part of what they collect, be satisfied."

174

I was later to revise the system of taxation in Gaul, disproving everything he said. But all that in its proper place.

"Control the generals." He repeated this suddenly as if he'd forgotten he had already said it to me. Then he turned and looked at me for the first time that day. It was startling. No longer was he the sun god on his charger. This was my cousin, my enemy, my lord, source of my greatness and potential source of my death. "You must know what I mean," he said, sounding like a man, not an oracle. "You have seen the state disrupted. Our high place threatened. Provinces wrecked. Cities destroyed. Armies wasted. The barbarians seizing our lands, because we were too busy fighting one another to protect ourselves from the true enemy. Well, Caesar, remember this: allow no general sufficient power to raise an army against you. You have seen what I have had to suffer. Usurper after usurper has wasted our power. Be on your guard."

"I will, Augustus."

Then he said, very slowly, his eyes on mine, "As I am on *my* guard." He looked away when he saw that his meaning was quite clear. Then he added for good measure, "We have never yet lost so much as a foot of earth to any usurper, nor will we ever."

"As long as I live, Augustus, you shall have at least one arm to fight for you."

We rode until midday. Then at the two columns we stopped. It was a fine brisk noon and despite the chill in the air, the sun was hot and we were all sweating under our armor. A halt was ordered.

Constantius and I dismounted and he motioned for me to accompany him into a hard stubbled field. Except for our troops, no one was in sight. In every country peasants vanish when they see armed men coming; all soldiers are the enemy, I wish one could change that.

Constantius walked ahead of me toward a small ruined shrine to Hermes which stood at the edge of the field (a favorable omen, Hermes has always watched over me). Behind us, our men watered horses, rearranged armor, swore and chattered, pleased by the good weather. Just as Constantius entered the shrine, I broke a dead flower off its stalk. Then I followed him inside the shrine, which smelled of human excrement. Constantius was urinating on the floor. Even in this, he was grave and majestic.

"It is a pity," I heard myself saying, aware as I spoke that I was breaking protocol, "what has happened to these old temples."

175

"A pity? They should all be torn down." He rearranged his clothes. "I hate the sight of them."

"Of course," I muttered.

"I shall leave you here," he said. We stood facing one another. Though I deliberately stooped, I could not help but look down on him. He edged away from me, instinctively searching for higher ground.

"Whatever you need, you shall have. Call on me. Also, depend on our praetorian prefect. He represents us. You will find the legions of Vienne alert, ready for a spring campaign. So prepare yourself."

He handed me a thick document. "Instructions. To be read at your leisure." He paused. Then he remembered something. "The Empress has made you a gift. It is with your baggage. A library, I believe."

I was effusive in my gratitude. I said words but Constantius did not listen. He moved to the door. He paused; he turned; he tried to speak to me. I blushed. I wanted to reach out and take his hand and tell him not to fear me, but I did not dare. Neither of us was ever able to face the other.

When Constantius finally spoke, his voice broke with tension. "If this should come to you . . ." Awkwardly he gestured at himself to indicate the principate of the world, "Remember . . ." Then his voice stopped as if a strangler's thumb had blocked the windpipe. He could not go on. Words had failed him again, and me.

I have often wondered what it was he meant to say; what it was I should remember. That life is short? Dominion bitter? No. Constantius was not a profound man. I doubt if he had been about to offer me any startling insight. But as I think back on that scene in the ruined shrine (and I think of it often, I even dream of it). I suspect that all he meant to say was, "Remember me." If that is what you meant, cousin, then I have, in every sense, remembered you.

Constantius left the shrine. As soon as his back was to me, I placed the withered flower on the profaned floor and whispered a quick prayer to Hermes. Then I followed the Emperor across the field to the road.

Once mounted, we exchanged formal farewells, and Constantius rode back to Milan, the dragon banner streaming in the cool wind before him. We never saw one another again.

# Caesar

## X

At Turin, as I received city officials in the law court, a messenger arrived from Florentius, the praetorian prefect of Gaul. The prefect thought that the Caesar should know that some weeks ago Cologne had fallen to the Germans, and the Rhine was theirs. The military situation was, Florentius wrote with what almost seemed satisfaction, grave. The German King Chnodomar had sworn to drive every Roman from Gaul within the year. This was the bad news Constantius had not told me.

While the reception continued, Oribasius and I withdrew to the prefect's office to study the report. For some inexplicable reason the only bust to adorn the room was that of the Emperor Vitellius, a fat porker who reigned several months in the year of Nero's death. Why Vitellius? Was the official a descendant? Did he admire the fat neck, the huge jowls of the man who was known as the greatest glutton of his day? To such irrelevances does the mind tend to fly in moments of panic. And I was panicky.

"Constantius sent me here to die. That's why I was given no army."

"But surely he doesn't want to lose Gaul."

"What does he care for Gaul? As long as he can have his court, his eunuchs, his bishops, what more does he need?" This was not accurate; in his way, Constantius was a patriot. But in my bitterness there was no stopping me. I denounced Constantius recklessly and furiously. I committed treason with every breath. When I had finished, Oribasius said, "The Emperor must have a plan. It can't be that simple. What are those instructions he gave you?"

I had forgotten all about the packet I had been given on the road to Turin. It was still in my wallet. Eagerly, I undid the fastenings. I read quickly, with growing astonishment. "Etiquette!" I shouted finally, throwing the document across the room. "How to receive an ambassador. How to give a dinner party. There are even recipes!" Oribasius burst out laughing, but I was too far gone to find any humor in the situation.

"We'll escape!" I said at last.

"Escape?" Oribasius looked at me as if I had gone mad.

177

"Yes, escape." Curious . . . I never thought I would be able to write any of this. "We can desert together, you and I. It will be easy. Nothing but a piece of cloth to throw away." I tugged at the purple that I wore. "Then we let our beards grow, and back to Athens. Philosophy for me, medicine for you."

"No." He said it flatly.

"Why not? Constantius will be glad to see the end of me."

"But he won't know it's the end of you. He'll think you have gone to plot against him, raise an army, become usurper."

"But he won't find me."

Oribasius laughed. "How can *you* hide in Athens? Even with a new beard and student's clothes, you are the same Julian everyone met a few months ago with Prohaeresius."

"Then it won't be Athens. I'll find a city where I'm not known. Antioch. I can hide in Antioch. I'll study with Libanius."

"And do you think Libanius could hold his tongue? His vanity would betray you in a day."

*Libanius*: I shall say here that I never found Oribasius particularly sympathetic. Apparently, he felt the same about me. He is of course very famous nowadays (if he is still alive); but medical friends tell me that his seventy-volume encyclopedia of medicine is nothing but a vast plagiarism from Galen. After Julian's death, he was exiled and went to the court of Persia, where I am told his is worshipped by the Persians as a god; he must have enjoyed this, for he was always vain. Also avaricious: he once charged me *five gold solidi* for a single treatment for gout. I could not walk for a month after.

*Julian Augustus*

"Then I shall find a city where no one has ever seen me or heard of me."

"Farthest Thule. Wherever you go, officials will know who you are."

"*Complete* disguise? A new name?"

"You forget the secret agents. Besides, how will you live?"

"I can teach, become a tutor . . ."

"A slave?"

"If necessary, why not? In a proper household, a slave can be happy. I could teach the young men. I would have time to write, to lecture . . ."

178

"From the purple to a slave?" He said it with slow cold wonder.

"What do you think I am *now*?" I exploded, I raged. I lamented. When I finally stopped for lack of breath, Oribasius said, "You will continue into Gaul, Caesar. You will put down the German tribes, or die in the attempt."

"No."

"Then be a slave, Julian." It was the first time he had called me by my name since I had been raised to Caesar. Then he left me alone in the office, where I sat like a fool, mouth ajar, the hoglike face of Vitellius peering at me from above the doorway . . . even after three centuries in stone, he looked hungry.

I folded the letter into many squares, each smaller than the other. I thought hard. I prayed to Hermes. I went to the latticed windows and looked for the sun, my peculiar deity. I searched for a sign. At last it came. From the setting sun, light suddenly shone in my face. Yes, out of the west where Gaul was. Helios blazed dark-gold in my eyes. I was to follow my god, and if death was what he required of me, then that would be my offering. If victory, then that would be our glory. Also, it was perfectly plain that I could not escape even if I wanted to. I had indeed been seized by purple death.

I returned to the citizens of Turin as though nothing had happened. As I received their homage, Oribasius looked at me questioningly. I winked. He was relieved.

The next morning we continued our journey. The weather in the mountains was not yet cold, nor was there any snow except on the highest slopes. Even the soldiers, a remarkably complaining lot of Galileans, admitted that God must be with us. He should have been: they prayed incessantly. It was all they were good for.

When we crossed into Gaul, an interesting thing happened. All up and down our route my coming had been excitedly reported, for I was the first legitimate Caesar to be seen in Gaul for many years. I say "legitimate" because Gaul, traditionally, is the place for usurpers. There had been three in a decade. Each had worn the purple. Each had minted coinage. Each had accepted the oath of fealty. Each had been struck down by Constantius or fate. Now a true Caesar was at last in Gaul, and the people took heart.

Early one evening we entered our first Gallic village, set high in the mountains. The villagers were gathered along the main street to cheer me. As decoration, they had tied many wreaths of fir and pine between the houses on either side of the road. As Hermes is my witness, one of the wreaths broke loose and fell upon my head, where it fitted as close as a crown. I came to a dead halt, not certain what had happened. My first reaction was that I had been struck by a branch. Then I raised my hand and felt the wreath. The villagers were wide-eyed. Even my slovenly troops were impressed. Eutherius who was beside me murmured, "Even the gods mean for you to be crowned."

I did not answer him, nor did I remove the wreath. Pretending that nothing had happened, I continued through the village while the inhabitants cheered me with a new intensity.

Oribasius said, "By tomorrow everyone in Gaul will know of this."

I nodded. "And by the next day Constantius will know." But even this thought could not depress me. I was now in a fine mood, reflecting the brilliant winter day, not to mention the love the gods had shown me.

My passage through the Gallic towns was triumphal. The weather held until we arrived at the gates of Vienne. Then black clouds rolled out of the north and a sharp wind blew. One could smell snow upon the air. Bundled in cloaks, we crossed the winter-black Rhone and entered the city at about the third hour. Cold as it was, the streets were crowded and once again there was the remarkable response. I could not understand it. Constantius inspired awe and fear but I seemed only to evoke love . . .I do not mention this out of vanity but only as a puzzling fact. For all these people knew, I might be another Gallus. Yet there they were, cheering me as though I had won some important battle or increased the supply of grain. It was inexplicable but exhilarating.

Just as I came opposite the temple of Augustus and Livia, an old blind woman was thrust forward by the crowd. She fell against my horse. Guards pushed her back; she fell again. "Help her," I ordered.

They got her to her feet. In a loud voice she asked, "Who is this?" Someone shouted, "It is the Caesar Julian!" Then she raised her blind eyes to heaven and in the voice of a Pythoness proclaimed, "He will restore the temples of the gods!" Startled, I spurred my horse through the crowd, her words still ringing in my ears.

I met Florentius in the main hall of the palace, which was to be my residence, though "palace" was hardly the word for this not very large villa. Florentius received me courteously. Yes, he

180

received me, rather than the other way around, and he made it perfectly clear from the beginning that this was his province, not mine, even though I was Caesar and he merely praetorian prefect.

"Welcome to Gaul, Caesar," he said, as we saluted one another. He had not thought it worth while to call in the city's magistrates or, for that matter, any officials. Several military men attended him, and that was all. Oribasius was my only attendant.

"A warm welcome for a cold season, Prefect," I said. "The people at least seem pleased that I have come." I stressed the "at least."

"*All* of us are pleased that Augustus has seen fit to elevate you and to send you to us as a sign of his interest in the matter of Gaul." Florentius was a small swarthy man with sharp features. I particularly recall his sinewy forearms, which were black with hairs, more like a monkey's than a man's.

"Augustus will indeed be pleased to learn that you approve his actions," I said dryly. Then I walked past him to where the room's single chair was placed on a small dais. I sat down. I could see this had some effect. The military men exchanged glances. Florentius, however, was imperturbable, even though I was sitting in his chair.

"Present the officers, Prefect." I was as cool as my disposition ever allows me to be.

Florentius did so. The first officer was Marcellus, chief of staff of the army of Gaul. He saluted me perfunctorily. The next officer was Nevitta, a powerfully built Frank, blue-eyed, loud-voiced, a remarkable commander who serves with me now in Persia. But that day in Vienne, he treated me with such obvious disdain that I realized I would have to respond in kind, or lose all pretense of authority. Either I was Caesar or I was lost.

I turned to Florentius. I spoke carefully. "We are not so far from Milan that the respect due to the Caesar can be omitted. Field conditions do not prevail in a provincial capital, despite the reverses of our armies on the Rhine. Instruct your officers, Prefect, in their duty to us. Show them by your example what we are."

Constantius could not have done it better, and in truth I meant every word of this arrogant speech. I was convinced that I had come to Gaul to die, and I meant to die in the most honorable way possible, upholding to the end the great title that was mine.

Florentius looked astonished. The officers looked frightened. Oribasius was impressed . . . curious how much we enjoy those

181

rare moments when we can by some public act impress an old friend.

In his confusion, Florentius took too long to react. So in careful imitation of Constantius, I raised my right arm and pointed with forefinger to the floor in front of me, and in a hard voice said, "We wear the purple."

The military men with a clatter of armor dropped to their knees. Florentius, with a look of singular venom, followed suit. He kissed the robe. With that gesture, hostilities between us began. They were to continue for five years.

Constantius never meant me to take actual command of the province. I was to be a ceremonial figure, reminding the Gauls by my presence that Constantius had committed, if not a full army, at least his flesh and blood to the task of rallying a frightened people to the defense of the province. Florentius wielded all actual power. He was in direct charge of the army at Vienne and his personal courier service held together the various legions scattered about Gaul. Most of them incidentally, were trapped in fortresses, for the Germans had laid siege to every sizable town and military installation from the Rhine to the North Sea.

Only last year, in going through Constantius's secret archives— a fascinating if at times depressing experience, rather like hearing what people say behind one's back—I came across his instructions to Florentius. Now that I have read them I am more tolerant of the prefect; he was merely carrying out orders. Constantius wrote— I am paraphrasing, for the documents are all at Constantinople— that this "dearly beloved kinsman the Caesar Julian" was to be looked upon as a cadet in the art of war and as a novice in the business of government. Florentius was to be that dedicated tutor, to instruct, edify and guard him against evil companions and wrong judgments. In other words, I was to be put to school. Military matters were to be kept from me. I was to be watched for signs of *ambitio*, as the Romans say, a word no other language has devised, meaning that sort of worldly ambition which is injurious to the balance of the state.

My first year in Gaul did teach me a good deal, not only in the art of war but also in the arts of concealment and patience. I became a second Ulysses, biding my time. I was not allowed to attend the military council. But from time to time I was briefed on the general military situation. I was not encouraged by what I was told. Though the army of Gaul was considerable. Florentius had no intention of committing it in battle.

We did nothing. Fortunately our enemy Chnodomar did nothing either; his promised offensive never materialized. He declared himself quite pleased to control the Rhine and our largest cities. I was eager to engage him, but I did not command a single soldier, excepting my doughty Italian bodyguard. I was also in need of money. My salary as Caesar was supposed to be paid by the quarter, but the Count of the Sacred Largesse was always late in making payments. I lived entirely on credit my first year in Gaul, and credit was not easily come by when there were daily rumors that I was in disfavor and might be recalled at any moment. I was also irritated to discover that the villa where I lived was *not* the palace of the Caesar but a sort of guest house where official visitors were housed. The city palace was on the Rhone; and here Florentius and his considerable court were richly housed. He lived like the Caesar, I lived like a poor relation. But there were compensations. I had Oribasius with me, as well as Priscus, who arrived in March from Athens.

*Priscus*: I should add a bit to Julian's account of his relations with Florentius. The praetorian prefect was avaricious but capable. More to the point, he was following the Emperor's instructions to the letter. I always thought Julian was unduly bitter about him. Of course, on several public occasions the prefect humiliated him. I remember one military review when there was no place for Julian on the dais. So the Caesar was forced to watch "his" troops from the crowd, surrounded by old women selling sausages. That was probably Florentius's revenge for Julian's behavior at their first meeting.

To Constantius's credit . . . why is one always trying to find good things to say about the bad? Is it our uneasy knowledge that their version of us would be precisely the same as ours of them, from another viewpoint and a conflicting interest? In any case, Constantius was perfectly correct in not allowing a youth with no military or administrative experience to take over the direction of a difficult war which older and supposedly wiser soldiers had nearly lost. No one could have known then that Julian was a military genius, except possibly himself. I almost find myself

183

believing in that Helios of his when I contemplate his Gallic victories.

But at this time he lived much as a student in the villa next to the city wall. His "court," as it had to be termed, was no more than a hundred people, counting slaves. We dined meagerly. There was never enough wine. But the conversation was good. Oribasius kept us all amused as well as healthy. He was, even then, compiling remedies from every witch he could find, and trying them out on us. Eutherius was also an amiable companion.

I note with some amusement that though Julian mentions specifically my joining him at Vienne, he says nothing of the far more important person who arrived at the new year: his wife Helena. I was not present when she came to Vienne but I am told that she arrived with a luxurious suite of hairdressers, seamstresses, cooks, eunuchs, and wagonloads of fine clothes and jewels. I don't think she ever got over the shock of the cold depressing villa. But Julian was always very kind to her, though somewhat absent-minded. He would start to leave a table without her, or openly make plans for a visit to a nearby town and then forget to include her in the arrangements. I think she liked him a good deal more than he liked her. Not that he disliked her; rather, he was profoundly indifferent. I doubt if he performed his conjugal duties often. Even so, she was twice pregnant in the four years they were married.

My chief memory of Helena is her valiant attempts not to look bored when Julian was talking excitedly about those things which interested him and mystified her. Fortunately, she had learned the royal art of yawning without opening the mouth; but if one watched her very carefully, whenever there was talk of Plato or Iamblichos or you, my dear Libanius (great triad!), one could see her nostrils dilate suspiciously from time to time. I am certain that we literally bored Helena to death.

*Libanius*: I cannot imagine anyone finding it remarkable that Julian should speak of Plato, Iamblichos and myself as being of a quality. But one can always trust Priscus to be envious. "Great triad!" indeed! Simply because he had failed as a philosopher and a teacher, he would like to bring down all his contemporaries to his own level. Well, he will fail in that, too.

It is not easy to understand the Gauls. Their ways are strange to us, despite their many years as Roman subjects. I think they are the handsomest of the world's people. Both men and women are tall and fair-skinned, often with blue eyes and blond hair. They are forever washing their clothes and bodies. One can go from one end of the province to the other without seeing a man or woman in soiled or ragged clothes. Laundry hangs drying beside every hovel, no matter how poor.

But despite their beauty, they are remarkably quarrelsome. Both men and women speak with curiously loud voices, braying their vowels and sounding hard their consonants. Whenever I gave justice, I used to be deafened by the rival lawyers and claimants, all bellowing like wounded bulls. They boast that in a fight one Gaul is worth ten Italians. I'm afraid this is true. They love battle. They have both the strength and heart for it. And their women love fighting, too. It is not at all unusual for a Gaul in the heat of battle to call to his wife to aid him. When she does, his strength increases tenfold. With my own eyes I have seen Gallic women attack the enemy, teeth gnashing, necks corded with veins, large white arms revolving like the crosspiece of a windmill, while their feet kick like shots discharged by catapult. They are formidable.

The Gallic men take pride in military service, unlike the Italians, who think nothing of cutting off their own thumbs to thwart the state's recruiting officers. Gauls, however, delight in bloodletting, and they would be the greatest of all soldiers but for two reasons: they do not take well to military discipline, and they are drunks. At the most inconvenient moments a commander of Gallic troops is apt to find his soldiers mad with drink, under the excuse that such and such a day is holy and must be marked with a little wine or one of those powerful drinks they brew from grain and vegetables.

I shall not describe my campaigns in Gaul, for I have already published an account of them which flatterers declare is the equal of Julius Caesar's *Commentaries*. I will say that I put more care into writing about the Gallic wars than I did in fighting them! But I shall record some of the things which I could not reveal at the time.

* * *

The winter 355-356 was a painful one for me. I had no authority. I was ignored by the praetorian prefect. I had no duties, except to make an occasional progress through the countryside. Yet whenever I did show myself to the Gauls, I attracted large crowds. Even on the frostiest winter days, the people would come from miles around to look at me, and cheer me on. I was much moved even though I was aware that often as not they hailed me not as Julian Caesar but as *Julius* Caesar. Indeed, there was a legend among the peasants that the great Julius had once vowed that he would return from the grave to protect Gaul from its enemies; many thought the time had now come for the dead general to keep his promise, and that I was he.

Out of these progresses came several unexpected victories for us. One town, besieged by Germans, took heart at the presence of the Caesar, and the townspeople drove the enemy from their fields. Another town in Aquitania, defended only by old men, repulsed a German attack, shouting my name as warcry and talisman of victory.

In Aquitania I fought my first "battle." We were passing two abreast through a thick forest, when a band of Germans fell upon us. For a moment I was afraid my Italians would break and run. But they held their ground. That is all one needs when taken by surprise. In those few minutes of attack an alert commander can rally his troops and strike back, if they hold fast initially.

Fortunately, we were at the forest's edge. I ordered the men at the front to divert the Germans while the men at the rear got through the forest to the open plain. In a matter of minutes, our men were free of the woods. There were no casualties. Then, when we began to get the better of the Germans, they promptly fled: first one, then another, then several at a time.

Suddenly I heard myself shouting, "After them! Cut them off!" My troops obeyed. The Germans were now in full flight, back into the forest. "A silver piece for every German head!" I shouted. This bloodthirsty cry was taken up by my officers. It was the incentive needed. Roaring with excitement and greed, my troops fell upon the enemy. By the end of the day, a hundred German heads had been brought to me.

I have described this engagement not because it was of military importance—it was not—but because this was my first taste of battle. Unlike nearly all my predecessors (not to mention any conscientious patrician), I was quite without military experience.

I had never even seen a man killed in battle. I had always preferred peace to war, study to action, life to death. Yet there I was shouting myself hoarse on the edge of a Gallic forest, with a small hill of bloody human heads in front of me. Was I sickened? or ashamed? Neither. I was excited in a way that men who choose to serve Aphrodite are excited by love. I still prefer philosophy to war, but nothing else. How I came to be like this is a mystery whose origin must be divine, determined by that fierce sun who is the genesis of all men and the protector of kings.

As we rode back to Vienne in the pale winter light, I trembled with an excitement that was close to joy, for I knew now that I would survive. Until that moment, I had not been certain of myself. For all that I knew, I might have been a coward or, worse, too paralyzed by the confusion of the moment to make those swift decisions without which no battle was ever won. Yet when the shouting had begun and the blood flowed, I was exalted. I saw what had to be done with perfect clarity, and I did it.

This skirmish was not taken very seriously at Vienne. What was taken seriously, however, was the fact that Constantius had named me his fellow consul for the new year. It was his eighth consulship, my first. I was pleased, but only moderately. I have never understood why men so value this ancient title. The consul has no power (unless he also happens to be emperor), yet ambitious men will spend a fortune to be admitted to consular rank. Of course, one's name will be known forever, since all dates are figured by consulates. Even so, I am not much drawn to any form which has lost its meaning. Yet at my investiture, Florentius was almost civil, which was something gained. In a private meeting, he told me, "We plan an offensive in the late spring. You will, if you choose, take part."

"As commander?"

"Caesar commands all of Gaul."

"Caesar is most sensible of his high place. But am I to *lead* the armies? Am I to plan the war?"

"You will be our guide in all things, Caesar." He was evasive. Clearly, he was not about to give up control of the province. But a beginning was made. The wall was breached. Now it was up to me to exploit this small change for the better.

When Florentius had departed, I sent for Sallust, my military adviser. He had been assigned to me when I first arrived in Gaul and I am forever in Constantius's debt for having brought the two of us together. Sallust is both Roman soldier and Greek philosopher. What higher compliment can I give him? When we met, Sallust was in his late forties. He is tall, slow of speech but swift of mind; he comes of an ancient Roman family and like so many Romans of the aristocracy he has never wavered in his allegiance to the true gods. A close friend of such distinguished Hellenists as Symmachus and Praetextatus, he published some years ago a classic defense of our religion. *On the Gods and the World.* As Maximus is my guide to mysteries and Libanius my model for literary style, so Sallust remains my ideal of what a man should be.

Sallust was as pleased as I by the news. Together we studied a map of Gaul, and decided that the best move would be to strike directly at Strasbourg. This large city not only commanded a considerable part of the Rhine; it was also being used as a center of operations by King Chnodomar. Its recapture would greatly strengthen us and weaken the enemy.

"There is a lesson in this," said Sallust suddenly.

"In what?"

"Why are the Germans in Gaul?"

"Plunder. Desire for more territory. Why do the barbarian tribes ever move from place to place?"

"They are in Gaul because Constantius invited the tribes to help him against Magnentius. They helped him. And then they remained in Gaul."

The point was well taken. One must never appeal for help to barbarians. Engage them as mercenaries, bribe them if that is the only way to keep the peace, but *never* allow a tribe to move into Roman territory for eventually they will attempt to seize what is Roman for themselves. Even as Sallust and I were talking, Constantius was on the Danube, fighting two rebel tribes he had once allowed to settle there.

Sallust then told me that there was conclusive evidence that Florentius was dealing secretly with certain of the German chiefs. Some he paid on the sly to remain where they were; others paid him not to disturb their present holdings. Carefully Sallust and I constructed our case against Florentius.


In May the plan to strike directly at Strasbourg was submitted by Sallust and me to Florentius and his general, Marcellus. It was promptly dismissed. We argued. We begged. We promised victory. But they would not listen.

"We are not yet ready to commit the army to a major battle. This is not the time." As Marcellus was provincial commander-in-chief, I was forced to obey.

"At what time," I asked, looking about the council chamber (we were in the prefect's palace), "will we be able to obey the Emperor and drive the Germans out of Gaul?"

Florentius was suave. His manner to me, although still condescending, was more cautious than before. Obviously, I was not to fall without careful effort on his part.

"May I propose to the Caesar a compromise?" Florentius played with a delicate purse of deerskin, containing *his* god, gold. "We have not the men for a major campaign. Until the Emperor sends reinforcements, which he is not apt to do this year since he is already committed on the Danube, we must confine ourselves to holding what we have, and to regaining what we can, without too much risk."

Florentius clapped his hands, and a secretary who was squatting against a wall sprang to his feet. Florentius was most imperial in his ways, but then, praetorian prefects are important men. At this time Florentius governed Morocco, Spain, Gaul and Britain. The secretary held up a map of Gaul.

Florentius pointed to a town called Autun, just north of us. "We have received news that the town is besieged." I almost asked why I had not been told before, but I held my tongue. "Now if the Caesar chooses, he might—with General Sallust—" Florentius addressed a small crooked smile at Sallust, whose face remained politely attentive—"relieve Autun. It is an old city. The walls were once impregnable but they are now in considerable disrepair, like nearly all our defenses, I'm afraid. There is not much of a garrison but the townspeople are valiant."

I told him quickly that nothing would please me more. I would go immediately to the relief of Autun.

"Of course," said Florentius, "it will take several weeks to equip your troops, in assemble supplies, to . . ."

"One good thing," Marcellus interrupted, "you won't have to worry about siege engines. Even if the Germans capture the city before you get there, they won't occupy it. They never do."

"But what about Cologne and Strasbourg?"

"Destroyed," said Marcellus, with almost as much pleasure as

189

if he personally had done the destroying. "But not *occupied*. The Germans are frightened of cities. They won't stay in one overnight."

"Their custom," said Florentius, "is to occupy the countryside around a city and starve the inhabitants. When the city finally capitulates, they burn it and move on."

"How many troops will I be allowed?"

"We are not certain just yet. There are other . . . contingencies." Florentius shifted from hand to hand the purse of gold. "But in a few weeks we shall know and then the Caesar may begin his first . . . Gallic war." This gibe was crude but I had learned not to show offense.

"Then see to it, Prefect," I said, as royally as possible, and accompanied by Sallust I left the palace.

As we walked through the city streets to my villa, not even the memory of Florentius's contempt could shatter the delight I took in the thought of action. "Just one successful campaign and Constantius will give me the whole army!"

"Perhaps." Sallust was thoughtful. We crossed the square, where carts from the countryside were gathering with the first of the season's produce. Two guards followed me at a discreet distance. Though I was Caesar, the townspeople were by now quite used to seeing me wander alone in the streets and where before they had done me frightened obeisance, they now greeted me— respectfull of course—as a neighbor.

"Only . . ." Sallust stopped.

"Only if I have too great a victory, Constantius will see to it that I never command an army again."

"Exactly."

I shrugged. "I must take my chances. Besides, after the Danube, Constantius will have to face the Persians. He'll have no choice except to trust me. There's no one else. If I can hold Gaul, then he must let me."

"But suppose he does not go against Persia? Suppose he moves against *you*?"

"Suppose I am struck dead by . . . that cart?" And we both leaped to the side of the road as a bullock cart rumbled past us while its driver loudly cursed it and us and the gods who had made him late for market. "It will be all right, Sallust," I said as we approached the villa. "I have had signs."

Sallust accepted this, for he knew that I was under the special protection of Hermes, who is the swift intelligence of the universe.

# XI

On 22 June I left Vienne at the head of an army of twelve thousand men—cuirassiers, crossbowmen and infantry. The whole town came out to see us off. Florentius radiated irony, while Marcellus could hardly disguise his amusement. I am sure that they thought this was the last they would see of me. Helena bade me farewell with stoic dignity. She was the essence of a Roman matron, quite prepared for me to return upon my shield.

It was a sunny day as we rode out of the city. On my right was Sallust and on my left Oribasius. Directly in front of me a standard bearer carried a hideously lifelike image of Constantius, crowned and wearing the imperial robe. My cousin had recently sent me this effigy, with a long set of instructions on how I was to show it off. He also reminded me that I had not been sent to Gaul as monarch but as a representative of the Emperor whose principal task was to display the imperial robe and image to the people. Despite this small humiliation, I was in high spirits as we took to the road.

We arrived at Autun 26 June. On that same day I defeated the Germans and set the city free. *Note to secretary:* At this point insert relevant chapter from my book, *The Gallic Wars*. It should be that section which covers the campaign from Autun to Auxerre to Troyes to Rheims, where I passed the month of August.

*Priscus:* As Julian described, Sallust on his right, Oribasius on his left, and myself just behind. His official account of the campaign is generally accurate. From Julius Caesar on, commanders tend to give themselves the best of it in their memoirs, but Julian was usually honest. Of course he tended not to mention his mistakes. He does not tell how he lost the better part of a legion through carelessness: he sent them through a forest where he had been warned that there were Germans . . . and there *were* Germans.

191

But in general, Julian was a cautious commander. He seldom committed a man unless he was certain that the odds were in his favor. Or so the experts assure us. I know práctically nothing of military matters, even though I served with Julian both in Gaul and Persia. I was not of course a soldier, though I did fight from time to time, with no pleasure. I experienced none of that blood lust he referred to some pages back, a rather surprising admission because in conversation Julian never once admitted to a liking for war.

Sallust took care of all details. He was most capable and in every way an admirable man. Too admirable, perhaps? One often had the feeling that he was playing a part (usually that of Marcus Aurelius); he was invariably demure and diffident and modest and sensible, all those things the world believes it admires. Which is the point. Less self-conscious men invariably have traits we do not admire. The good and the bad are all mixed together. Sallust was all good. That must have taken intense self-discipline as well as the awareness that he was indeed trying to be something he was not. But no matter what his motives, he was impressive, and a good influence on Julian.

Julian lifted the siege at Autun. He then marched north to Auxerre. He rested there a few days. He always took every possible opportunity to refresh his troops, unlike so many generals who drive them past their strength. From Auxerre we moved to Troyes. This was a difficult journey. We were continually harassed by Germans. They are a frightening-looking people, tall and muscular, with long hair dyed bright red, a tribal custom. They dress pretty much like us, wearing armor pilfered from Roman corpses. In open country, they are easily vanquished, but in forests they are dangerous.

At Troyes we spent several hours outside the walls trying to explain to the frightened garrison that we were not Germans and that this was indeed the Caesar. Finally Julian himself, with that "hideously lifelike" image of Constantius beside him, ordered the people to open the gates.

We stayed at Troyes a day. Then we moved on to Rheims. Julian had previously agreed with Florentius that the main army of Gaul would be concentrated there in August, preparatory to retaking Cologne. So Marcellus was already at Rheims when we got there. Shortly after we arrived, a military council was called.

Weary from the long ride and longing for the baths, I accompanied Julian and Sallust to the meeting.

Marcellus was hardly pleased to find Julian so obviously thriving on military life. When Julian inquired if the troops were ready, he was told that they were not. When would they be ready? Evasion. Finally: a major offensive was not possible this year.

Then Julian rose and lied with the genius of a Ulysses. I could hardly believe my ears. He spoke first in sorrow. "I had hoped to find all of you here eager and ready to fight the tribes. Instead, I find nothing is planned and we are on the defensive as usual." Marcellus began to mutter dangerously but Julian was in full flow. You know what he was like when the spirit (often identified as Helios) was upon him.

"I was sent here, General, by the divine Emperor to show his image to the barbarians. I was also sent here to recover the cities *you* have lost. I was sent here to drive the savages back to their forests beyond the Rhine. I was sworn as Caesar to conquer them or to die."

"But Caesar, we . . ." That was all Marcellus was allowed to say. As Julian talked through him, he withdrew a document from his tunic. It was the booklet on etiquette that Constantius had given him. "Do you see this, General? All of you?" Julian waved it like a standard in the air. No one could tell what it was exactly, but the imperial seal was perfectly visible.

"It is from the divine Emperor. It is to me. It arrived by special messenger at Autun. It contains orders. We are to regain Cologne. Those are his commands and we are his slaves. We have no choice but to obey."

There was consternation on Marcellus's side of the council table. No one had heard of these instructions for the excellent reason that they did not exist. But the bold lie worked largely because Marcellus was a true politician in the sense that could not admit that there was anything which he ought to know that in fact he did not know. He gave Julian the army.

*Julian Augustus*

At Rheims I reviewed the legions as they marched through the city gates, all of us sweating in the hot August sun. It was a lowering day, humid and ill-omened. As I stood on the platform outside the city gate, gnats whirring about my head and sweat trickling down my face, a message from Vienne was handed to

193

me. It was a brief note from Florentius. My wife had been delivered of a boy who had died shortly afterwards. She was in good health. That was all.

It is an odd thing to be the father of a son and the grieving father of a dead son, all in the same instant. I handed the letter to Sallust. Then I turned back to the legions who were marching rhythmically now in Pyrrhic measure to the sound of pipes.

*Priscus*: The midwife cut too short the child's umbilical cord. We later learned that she had been paid to do this by the Empress Eusebia. Yet I never heard Julian refer to Eusebia in any but the most glowing terms. It is sad how tangled the relations among princes become . . . What a ridiculous statement! We are all in the habit of censuring the great, as if we were popular playwrights, when in fact ordinary folk are quite as devious and as willful and as desperate to survive (if not to prevail) as are the great; particularly philosophers.

Julian skips the rest of that year's campaign with a note that a section from his earlier book will be inserted. That will be your task. Personally, I find his book on the Gallic wars almost as boring as Julius Caesar's. I say "almost" because a description of something one has lived through can never be entirely dull. But descriptions of battles soon pall. I would suggest—although you have not asked for my literary advice—that you keep the military inserts to a minimum.

Julian's autumn campaign was a success. He fought a set battle at Brumath which strategists regard as a model of brilliant warfare. I wouldn't know. At the time I thought it confusing, but it opened the road to Cologne. That part of the world, by the way, is quite lovely, especially a spot called the Confluence, where—obviously—two rivers join, the Moselle and the Rhine, at a town called Remagen—ours; just past Remagen is an old Roman tower which commands the countryside. Not far from Remagen is Cologne, which to everyone's amazement Julian regained, after a brief battle.

We remained at Cologne all of September. Julian was in excellent form. Several of the Frankish chiefs paid him court and he both charmed and awed them, a rare gift which he apparently shared, if one is to trust Cicero, with Julius Caesar.

A light note of consequence: Oribasius bet me one gold piece that Constantius would take revenge on Julian for lying to Marcellus. I bet him that he would not. I won the gold piece. We then spent the winter at Sens, a depressing provincial town north of Vienne. It was nearly the last winter for all of us.

*Julian Augustus*

After the victories described, I went into winter quarters at a pleasant town called Sens whose particular virtue was that it kept me at a proper distance from Florentius at Vienne and Marcellus at Rheims.

During those months Helena kept much to herself. She had several ladies with her from the court at Milan and I think that she was reasonably content, though she was not in good health: because of her age, the birth had been a difficult one. I was always ill at ease with Helena. I could hardly forget that she was the sister of my enemy. For a long time I was uncertain to which of us she was loyal. I do know that she kept up a considerable correspondence with her brother (since destroyed; by whom? very mysterious); as a result, I was careful to say nothing in her presence which might make Constantius suspicious. This self-restraint was a considerable burden for me.

Only once did Helena reveal that she had some idea of what was in my mind and heart. It was in December. We had dined frugally in my office, which was easier to heat than the state apartments. Several braziers gave forth sufficient heat—at least for me; Priscus used to complain bitterly of my meanness in this regard. Helena sat with her ladies at the opposite end of the room, listening to one of the women sing Greek songs, while Oribasius, Sallust, Priscus and I reclined on couches at the other end of the room.

We spoke idly at first, as one does after supper. We touched on the military situation. It was not good. Despite my victory at Cologne, Florentius had left me with only two legions. The rest of my army had been recalled to Rheims and Vienne. I was in the same position I had been my first winter at Vienne, a prince with no principality. Only now I carried a larger burden. But as the old saying goes, "A packsaddle is put on an ox; that is surely no burden for me." It was my task not only to hold Sens but to protect the neighboring villages from the German tribes who were, even in the dead of winter, moving restlessly from town to town, burning and pillaging. In fact, Chnodomar himself had sworn that he would hang me before the spring thaw. To garrison the nearby towns, I was obliged to give up two-thirds of the soldiers under my command. Added to this, we were faced with an unusual number of desertions, especially among the Italian soldiers.

"Any man who deserts should be executed," said Sallust, "publicly, before the legions."

"It is remarkably difficult, General," said Priscus in his sly way, "to execute a deserter. First, you must catch him."

"The only solution," I said, "is victory. If we are successful, the men will be loyal. There are few deserters in a winning army."

"But we are neither winning nor an army," said Priscus with unpleasant accuracy.

"Which is exactly what the Emperor wants." Oribasius spoke too loudly. I silenced him with a gesture. Helena had heard this but she made no sign.

"I am sure the divine Emperor, my cousin and colleague, is eager for us to succeed in driving the Germans from Gaul." Actually, I had received no word from Constantius since taking up residence at Sens. I assumed that he was angry with me for not returning to Vienne.

Then Priscus asked me to read from the panegyric I was writing on Eusebia. I sent for a notary, who brought me the manuscript. I read a few pages, not liking it at all. The work was rough. I said so.

"Probably," said the wicked Priscus, "because it is nearly sincere."

The others laughed. At Vienne I had written a lengthy panegyric of Constantius which—if I say so myself—was a masterpiece, carefully ordered and beautifully composed. The art of panegyric does not necessarily exclude honesty, though one's true feelings are perfectly irrelevant to the final composition, which is artifice, not truth. Even Constantius realized that I had created something marvelous and wrote me a letter in his own hand, filled with misspellings and errors of syntax. I then tried to write a panegyric on Eusebia, and found it difficult; no doubt, as Priscus suggested, because of my true regard for the subject. Also, I was honor bound not to reveal to what extent she had saved my life. This was limiting.

While we were talking amiably, I heard far off the uneasy neighing of horses but thought nothing of it. Then Oribasius mentioned those Hebrew books which the Galileans refer to as the old testament. This was a favorite subject with me. So much so that I forgot Helena was in the room. "I admire the Jews because of their devotion to a single god. I also admire them because of their self-discipline. But I deplore the way they interpret their god. He is supposed to be universal, but he is interested only in them. . . ."

"Christ," said my wife suddenly, "was sent by God to all of us."

There was an embarrassed silence.

"The issue," I said finally, with great gentleness, "is just that: would the One God intervene in such a way?"

"We believe that he did."

The room was now completely still save for the far-off sound of horses. My companions were on edge.

"Yet is it not written in the so-called gospel of John, that 'out of Galilee arises no prophet'?"

"God is God, not a prophet," said Helena.

"But the idea of the Nazarene's mission, in his own words, is taken from the old testament, which is Jewish, which says that a prophet—messiah—will one day come to the Jews, but not God himself."

"That is a difficulty," she admitted.

"In fact," and I was stupidly blunt, "there is almost no connection between what the Galileans believe and what the Nazarene preached. More to the point, I see nothing in the Jewish text that would allow for such a monstrosity as the triple god. The Jews were monotheists. The Galileans are atheists."

I had gone too far. Helena rose, bowed, and withdrew, accompanied by her ladies.

My companions were alarmed. Priscus spoke first. "What a gift you have, Caesar, for making the difficult impossible!"

The others agreed. I asked their forgiveness. "Anyway," I said, not believing my own words, "we can trust Helena."

"I hope so." Sallust was gloomy.

"One must be true to what is true," I said, wishing as I so often do that I had held my tongue.

There was a sudden shouting in the streets. We all sprang to our feet. We had hardly got to the door when an officer arrived to report that Sens was being attacked. Elsewhere I describe what happened and I shall not repeat it here.

*Priscus*: We were besieged for a month. A number of our deserters had gone over to the Germans and reported on our weakness. Encouraged by this, and excited at the thought of capturing a Roman Caesar, King Chnodomar marched on Sens. It was a difficult time and we owed our lives, finally, to Julian's energy and intelligence. Though he could not make us cheerful or even confident, he at least kept us dutiful and modestly hopeful.

That night the call to arms was sounded. Men rushed to their posts on the battlements. The Germans could be seen less than half a mile away, illuminated by burning farmhouses. It had been the neighing of farm horses that had disturbed our after-dinner conversation. Had the Germans been quieter, they might have taken the city. Fortunately for us, every last one of them was drunk.

During the next few days, Julian's mood changed from almost boisterous excitement to grim rage. He was positive that he had been deliberately abandoned. This suspicion was confirmed when a messenger arrived from Rheims to say that Marcellus would not come to our aid; he pleaded weakness. He also insisted that Julian had sufficient men to repulse the Germans.

Our rations were nearly gone when the Germans departed as suddenly as they had arrived. Long sieges bored them. Julian immediately sent to Vienne for supplies. He then recalled all his troops to Sens and the remainder of the winter was passed, if not in comfort, at least without fear of sudden annihilation. Julian also wrote Constantius a full account of Marcellus's refusal to come to his aid. It was a splendid document. I know; Sallust and I helped to write it. So splendid was it, in fact, that unlike most state papers this one had an effect. Marcellus was recalled to Milan and after a short interval Julian finally got what he wanted, the command of the armies of Gaul.

The year 357 was the making of Julian as a world hero. In the spring, when the grain was ripe, he proceeded to Rheims, where he learned that Barbatio, the commander of the Roman infantry, was on his way to Augst with twenty-five thousand troops and seven river boats. He was to assist Julian in a final drive against the Germans. But before a plan could be devised, a tribe called the Laeti passed through our territory and laid siege to Lyon, burning all the countryside around. Julian quickly sent three squadrons of light cavalry to relieve that city. He also set a watch on the three roads radiating from Lyon, in order to ambush the savages when they fled. Unfortunately, Barbatio's troops allowed the Germans to get through because a tribune of targeteers, named Cella, acting under Barbatio's orders, prevented the cavalry commander from attacking. Why? Barbatio was eager for Julian to fail. He was also to some extent in league with the German tribes. Julian ordered Cella and his staff cashiered; only the cavalry commander was let off. He was, incidentally, Valentinian, our future emperor.

By now the Germans were alarmed. They tried to block our progress to the Rhine by felling great trees across the roads. They took refuge on the islands in the Rhine, where they used to bellow all sorts of insults at us, and at night sing the most melancholy songs. When Julian asked Barbatio for his seven ships, they were promptly and mysteriously burned. So Julian, always inventive, ordered the light-armored auxiliaries of the Cornuti Legion to swim out to one of the islands, using their wooden shields as rafts. This worked. They killed the German defenders and then, using German boats, attacked the other islands. The savages then abandoned the remaining islands and fled into the eastern forest.

Julian next restored the fortress at Savernes, an important installation because it stands directly in the path of anyone intent on the conquest of central Gaul. He then harvested the crops the Germans had planted. This gave him twenty days' rations. He was now ready to face King Chnodomar. His only obstacle was Barbatio. Happily for us, this extraordinary creature was attacked by the Germans just north of Augst. Though Barbatio had a large, well-disciplined army, he fled in a panic back to Augst and promptly announced that he had won a famous victory and, though it was only July, he went into winter quarters. That was the end of him for a year. We were much relieved.

With thirteen thousand men, Julian marched directly on Strasbourg. A few miles from the city, Chnodomar sent Julian an embassy commanding him to quit Gaul since this was now "German country, won by German arms and valor." Julian laughed at the king's convoys. But Chnodomar was not a man to be taken lightly. Ever since he defeated the Caesar Decentius, he had been free to come and go in Gaul as though it were indeed his own

199

kingdom. Now, encouraged by the collapse of Barbatio, he was positive he would again be victorious.

The issue was resolved, as we all know, and I am sure you will insert of this point Julian's account of the Battle of Strasbourg. I think it is almost the best of his writings—and you know my prejudice against military commentaries! Only the garrulousness of age makes me go on as I have about these months in Gaul. I do it partly to inform you and partly—to be honest—to see how much memory I have left; more than I thought. One detail which came back to me just as I wrote the word "memory": while riding outside the walls of a Gallic town, I saw a cemetery where several of the graves were covered with fishnets. I asked one of the native soldiers what this meant. "It is to keep the ghosts of mothers who die in childbirth from stealing back their children." There is a lot of interesting folklore in that part of the world and I hope some latter-day Herodotus will record it before the people become so completely Romanized that the old customs are forgotten.

Incidentally, it was at this time that Helena was recalled to Rome, where Constantius was celebrating not only his first triumph but his first visit to the capital. She was again pregnant, and again she lost her baby, this time through a miscarriage brought on by a potion Eusebia gave her.

As for the famous Battle of Strasbourg, I can add very little to what Julian himself wrote.

*Libanius*: Then why do you? Priscus keeps protesting he can add little and then adds too much. He has aged. He always used to be brief, to the point of being laconic, but now . . . !

*Priscus*: My own memories of that day in August are quite vivid and surprisingly full, considering the fact that I have no memory of what happened last year, or even this morning.

Julian had submitted his plan of battle to Florentius at Vienne and to our surprise it was approved. No one will know what Florentius's motives were. I suspect the fact that Julian had thirteen thousand troops while the German army numbered some thirty-five thousand might have had something to do with it.

On the morning of 14 August we stopped some twenty miles from the Rhine, on whose banks Chnodomar had assembled his army. I recall that day as one of the hottest I have ever experienced. The heat was even worse than Persia, for it was damp. Also, the air swarmed with insects, and I sneezed continually as I always do at that time of year, the result of humors rising from the rank earth.

I was at Julian's side through most of the battle, more as ornament than as soldier, though I did lay about me from time to time simply to avoid being killed. Julian made a good speech to the army. His speeches, though never particularly brilliant, did have the gift of striking precisely the right note with the men. I have often wondered how such a bookish young man could have learned to talk with such ease to some of the most formidably ignorant and prejudiced men on earth. Yet he did. His cultured voice would become harsh, his manner royal; the content modest, the effect inspiring.

Julian sat his horse, with his standard-bearer beside him holding a spear on which the imperial dragon fluttered in the hot wind, purple and ominous. The infantry filled the narrow declivity at the foot of the hill where Julian and his staff were posted, all knee deep in ripened grain, for we were in the midst of a large farm.

Trumpets blared in unison. Squadrons of cavalry, cuirassiers and archers moved in from left and right until Julian was surrounded. When at last they were all assembled and silent, he spoke to them. He was never more subtle though his manner was vigorous and forthright. He wanted to persuade them to fight immediately, but knowing that they were tired and hot from the sun, he realized that he would have to trick them into wanting what he wanted.

"The thing we most care for is the safety of our men, and though we are eager to engage the enemy, we also realize that rashness can be dangerous and caution a virtue. Though we are all young men and inclined to be impetuous, as Caesar I must be the one to move warily, though—as you know—I am far from being timid. Now here is our situation. It is almost noon. The heat is terrible. It will get worse. We are all of us tired from a long march. We are not certain of sufficient water this side of the Rhine. The enemy is fresh, and waiting. So I suggest that we erect pickets, that we eat and sleep and make ready for battle tomorrow, when, if it be God's will, we shall strike at first light and with our eagles in the advance, drive the Germans from Roman soil . . ."

But the legions interrupted him. They gnashed their teeth, a terrible sound, and struck their spears against their shields.

Then one of the standard-bearers shouted, "Forward, Caesar!

201

Follow your star!" He turned dramatically to the legions, "We have a general who will win! So if it be God's will, we shall free Gaul this day! Hail, Caesar!"

This was all that was needed. As the legions cheered, Julian gave the order to prepare for battle. After this, I had him to myself for a moment. We were so close to one another that our stirrups clashed. "A fine speech," I said. "Suitable for history."

He grinned like a schoolboy. "How did you like the standard-bearer's speech?"

"Exactly what was required."

"I coached him in it last night, with gestures." Then Julian deployed his troops. The Germans were already in battle formation. To left and right as far as the eye could see, their forces lined the river. In their first rank was King Chnodomar, a big man with a great belly who wore a scarlet plume in his helmet.

At noon, Julian ordered the attack. The Germans had dug a number of trenches in our path and there, hidden by green boughs, archers suddenly fired at the legions who halted in consternation. They did not retreat; but they did not advance.

Julian was now in his element. Voice cracking with tension, he darted from squadron to squadron, legion to legion. He drove the men to attack. Those who fell back, he threatened. I cannot remember exactly what he said, but the burden of it was: these are savages, these are the spoilers of Gaul, *now* is the chance to break them, this is the moment we have waited for! He also used a wily approach for those who seemed bent on retreat. "I beg you, don't follow the enemy too closely! Stop at the Rhine! Let them drown. But you be careful!"

For me, the day was confusion. In the course of that sweltering afternoon, the battle was several times in doubt. At one point our cavalry broke; they would have fled had they not come up against a solid wall of infantry reserves behind them. My most vivid memory is of the German faces. I have never seen anything like them, nor hope to again in this world. Should there be a hell, I am sure that I shall spend it entirely in the company of Germans in battle. Their dyed red hair is worn long, and hangs about the face like a lion's mane. They grind their teeth and shout words which are not words but sounds of rage. Their eyes are quite mad and staring, the veins thick in their necks. I suspect many of them were drunk but not drunk enough to lose their ferocity. I killed several, and was myself nearly killed.

202

After the Germans had split our cavalry, they turned on the infantry, thinking to overwhelm them by sheer numbers. But they did not reckon with the two best legions of Rome: the Cornuti and the Bracchiati. These men in tortoise formation, heads masked by their shields, steadily advanced into German horde. This was the crisis of the battle, just as Oribasius maintains that there is a crisis in a fever when all at once it is decided whether the sick man lives or dies. We lived. The Germans died. It was a great—a sickening—butchery. Wounded and dying men lay four and five deep on the river bank; some were suffocated by the bodies above them; some literally drowned in blood. I was never again to see a day quite like that one, for which I am thankful.

Suddenly, as though by some signal (but it was merely instinct; other witnesses of war have noticed this same phenomenon), the Germans broke for the river. Our men followed. It was a lurid sight. The savages desperately tried to swim to the other side. At one point, and this is no chronicler's exaggeration, the Rhine was indeed red with blood.

It was now late afternoon. Aching in every muscle and trembling from what I had seen and done, I found Julian and his staff already encamped on a high bluff beside the river. Julian's tent had been pitched in a grove of ash trees, and though his face was black with sweat and dust; he seemed fresh as when he began the day. He embraced me warmly.

"Now we're all here!" he exclaimed. "And still alive." We drank wine as the shadows of the trees around us lengthened, and Sallust reported that we had lost four officers and two hundred and forty-three men. No one could reckon the German losses but the next day they were figured to be somewhere between five and six thousand. It was the greatest victory for Roman arms in Gaul since Julius Caesar. Difficult though it is for me to delight in military affairs, I could not help but be caught up by the general excitement, which increased when shortly before midnight King Chnodomar himself was brought to us, arms pinned behind him, great belly sagging, eyes white with terror. The Germans lack true pride, as others have so often remarked. In victory they are overbearing; in defeat cringing. The king threw himself at Julian's feet, moaning his submission. The next day Julian sent him to Constantius, who had him imprisoned in Rome's Castra Peregrina on the Caelian Hill, where he died of old age. All in all, a better fate than was to befall his conqueror.

Julian records nothing of the rest of the year. He decently buried the Gallic dead. He returned to Savernes. He ordered captives and booty to be taken to Metz. Then he crossed the Rhine into German territory. He seized all livestock and grain; he burned the houses, which are built exactly like ours even though the Germans are supposed to prefer living in forest huts—so much for legend. Then we penetrated those awesome vast woods which fill the center of Europe. There is nothing like them in the world. The trees are so dense that only a dim green light ever penetrates to the ground. Trees as old as time make passage difficult. Here the savage tribes are safe from attack, for what stranger could find his way through that green labyrinth? and who would want to conquer those haunted woods? Except the Emperor Trajan. We stumbled upon one of his abandoned forts, and Julian had it rebuilt and garrisoned. Then we crossed the Rhine once more and went into winter quarters at Paris, a city which the Roman always refer to, with their usual elegance, as Mudtown.

# XII

*Julian Augustus*

Of the cities of Gaul, I like Paris the best and I spent three contented winters there. The town is on a small island in the River Seine. Wooden bridges connect it to both banks where the towns-people cultivate the land. It is lovely green country where almost anything will grow, even fig trees. My first winter I set out a dozen (jacketed in straw) and all but one survived. Of course the Paris winters are not as cold as those at Sens or Vienne because the nearness of the ocean warms the air. As a result, the Seine seldom freezes over; and its water—as anyone knows who has ever visited there—is remarkably sweet and good to drink. The town is built of wood and brick, with a fair-sized prefect's palace which I used as headquarters. From my second-floor study, I could see the water as it divided at the island's sharp tip, like the sea breaking on a ship's prow. In fact, if one stares hard enough at that point in the river one has a curious sense of movement, of indeed being on a ship in full sail, the green shore rushing past.

As for the Parisians, they are a hardworking people who delight in the theatre and (alas) in Galilean ceremonies. In the winter they are townsfolk, and in the summer peasants. By the most remarkable good luck, they combine the best rather than the worst aspects of the two estates. We got on very well together, the Parisians and I.

Relations with Florentius grew worse. At every turn he tried to undermine my authority. Finally I fell out with him over money. Because of the German invasion, the landowners had suffered great losses. Year after year, whole harvests had been destroyed, buildings burned, livestock stolen. To lessen the burden of men already bankrupt, I proposed that both the poll tax and the land tax be reduced from twenty-five to seven gold pieces a year. Florentius vetoed this, countering with an outrageous proposal that a special levy be raised against all property, to defray the cost of *my* campaign! Not only was this proposed tax unjust, it would have caused a revolt.

Now although Florentius controlled the administration and civil service, as resident Caesar, no measure was legal without my seal. So when Florentius sent me the proposed capital levy, I sent it back to him unsigned. I also enclosed a long memorandum reviewing the financial situation of Gaul, proving by exact figures that more than sufficient revenue was now being raised through the conventional forms of taxation. I also reminded him that many provinces had been wrecked before by such measures as he proposed—particularly Illyricum.

Messengers spent the winter dashing back and forth along the icy roads from Paris to Vienne. The capital levy was dropped, but Florentius was still determined to raise taxes. When he sent me a proposal to increase the land tax, I would not sign it. In fact, I tore it up and told the messenger to return the pieces to the praetorian prefect, with my compliments.

Florentius then appealed to Constantius, who wrote me a surprisingly mild letter. Part of it read: "You must realize, my dear brother, that it hurts us if you undermine confidence in our appointed officers of state at Gaul. Florentius has his faults, although youthful impetuosity is not one of them." (I was now quite hardened to this sort of insult.) "He is a capable administrator with great experience, particularly in the field of taxation. We have every confidence in him, nor can we in all honesty disapprove any effort toward increasing the state's revenue at a time when the empire is threatened both on the Danube and in Mesopotamia. We recommend to our brother that he be less zealous in his attempts to gain favor with the Gauls, and more helpful in our prefect's honest attempts to finance your defense of the province."

A year earlier I would have bowed to Constantius without question. I would also have been furious at the reference to my victory at Strasbourg as a mere "defense of the province," but I was learning wisdom. I also knew that if I were to succeed in Gaul, I needed the wholehearted support of the people. Already they looked to me as their defender, not only against the savages but against the avarice of Florentius.

I wrote Constantius that though I accepted his judgment in all things, we could not hope to hold the province by increasing the taxes of ruined men. I said that unless the Emperor directly ordered me to sign the tax increase, I would not allow it to take effect.

There was consternation at Paris. We waited several weeks for some answer. The betting, I am told, was rather heavily in favor of my being recalled. But I was not. By not answering, Constantius condoned my action. I then reduced taxes. So grateful and astonished were the provincials that we obtained our full tax revenue *before* the usual time of payment. Today, Gaul is on a sound financial basis. I mean to make similar tax reforms elsewhere.

I am told that Constantius was shattered by the news of my victory at Strasbourg. He was even more distressed when I sent him King Chnodomar in chains, as visible proof of my victory. But men have a way of evading hard fact, especially emperors who are surrounded by toadies who invariably tell them what they want to hear. The court nicknamed me 'Victorinus' to emphasize the tininess—in their eyes—of my victory. Later in the winter, I was astonished to read how Constantius had personally taken Strasbourg and pacified Gaul. Proclamations of *his* great victory were read in every corner of the empire, with no mention of me. I have since been told by those who were at Milan that Constantius eventually came to believe that he had indeed been in Strasbourg that hot August day and with his own hands made captive the German king. On the throne of the world, any delusion can become fact.

The only sad matter that winter was my wife's health. She had another miscarriage while visiting Rome, and she complained continually of pain in the stomach. Oribasius did his best for her but although he could lessen the pain, he could not cure her.

My own health—since I seem never to refer to the subject—is invariably good. Partly because I eat and drink sparingly, and partly because our family is of strong stock. But I did come near to death that winter. It happened in February. As I have said, my quarters in the governor's palace overlooked the river, and my rooms were not equipped with the usual heating through the floor. As a result, I was always slightly cold. But I endured this, realizing that I was hardening myself for days in the field. My wife used to beg me to use braziers but I refused, pointing out that if the rooms were overheated, the damp walls would steam, making the air poisonous.

But one evening I could bear the cold no longer. I was reading late—poetry, as I recall. I summoned my secretary and ordered a brazier of hot coals. It was brought. I continued to read. Soothed by the lapping of the river beneath my window, I got drowsier and drowsier. Then I fainted. The fumes from the coal combined with the steam from the walls nearly suffocated me.

Fortunately, one of the guards, seeing steam escape from underneath the door, broke in and dragged me into the corridor where I finally came to. I vomited for hours. Oribasius said a few more minutes in that room and I would have been dead. So my Spartan habits saved my life; though some, of course, would say it was my stinginess! Curiously enough, thinking back on that night, I cannot help but reflect what a pleasant death it might have been. One moment reading Pindar, the next a pleasant drowsiness, and then the end. Every day I pray to Helios that my death when it comes be as swift and as painless as that night's beginning.

My days were full. I gave justice or, as some say, merely executed the law, since there is no true justice that is man-made. I conferred daily on administrative problems with the various officers of the province, and each month I personally paid the salaries of the high officials. This is an ancient custom and I have always meant to investigate its origins. They date, I suspect, from the early Republic. Among those I personally paid were the secret agents. Though I disapproved of them—and knew that their main occupation at Paris was watching me and reporting on my movements to Milan—I usually concealed my dislike. Except on one occasion.

I sat at a table covered with hides. Gold in various piles was set before me. When it came time to pay the chief agent, Gaudentius, he reached forward and took the gold for himself, not waiting for me to give it to him. Even his fellow agents were startled by this rude gesture, to which I responded: "You see, gentlemen, it is seizing, not accepting, that agents understand." This was much quoted.

Evenings were spent, first, in business, then in sleep and, finally, the best part, late at night, talking philosophy and literature with friends, who used to wonder how I could so quickly fall asleep and then awake at exactly the hour I wanted. I don't know myself how this is done but I have always been able to do it. If I tell myself I wish to awaken in the first hour of the night, I shall—to the minute. I attribute this lucky gift to Hermes. But Oribasius thinks it has to do with something in my brain and he wants to take a look at it when I am dead!

Sallust was a considerable historian and drilled me extensively in both domestic and foreign history. We particularly studied the era of Diocletian, for it was he who renewed the empire in the last century and his reforms are still with us.

One of our continuing arguments concerns Diocletian's edict which ordered all men to remain for life at whatever happened to be their craft or labor; also, their descendants must continue in the same way: a farmer's son must be a farmer, a cobbler's son must be a cobbler, and the punishment for changing one's estate is severe. Sallust maintained, as did Diocletian, that this law was necessary for social stability. In the old days, people drifted from city to city, living on doles or through crime. As a result, production of all things was inadequate. Diocletian not only stabilized production but he even tried to set prices for food and other essentials. This last failed, which was a pity. A few months ago I myself tried to set the price of grain at Antioch, and though I have for the moment failed, I think in time this sort of manipulation will succeed.

Priscus took the view that Diocletian's law was too rigid. He thought the people should be allowed to change their lot *if* they showed sufficient capacity. But who is to judge their capacity? He was never able to answer this. Oribasius proposed that the court send out commissions to the main cities to examine the young men to determine which ones showed ability. I pointed out that the corruption involved would be formidable; not to mention the impossibility of judging thousands correctly. Personally, I believe that the lower orders do, on occasion, produce men of ability and I believe that that ability, if it is sufficiently great, will be somehow recognized and used. For one thing, there is always the army. A farmer's son who is ambitious can join the army, which is—in the old Greek sense—the most democratic of institutions: anyone can rise through the ranks, no matter how humble his origins. Priscus responded to this by saying that not every one of ability is inclined to warfare. I was forced to agree that there is indeed some hardship for a man whose talents might be for literature or for the law, but as Sallust was quick to point out, the law schools at Beirut and Constantinople are crowded, and the civil service has more "capable" candidates than it can find jobs for. We have quite enough lawyers.

Priscus thinks that there should be widespread literacy. Sallust thinks not, on the grounds that a knowledge of literature would only make the humble dissatisfied with their condition. I am of two minds. A superficial education would be worse than none: envy and idleness would be encouraged. But a full education would open every man's eyes to the nature of human existence; and we are all of us brothers, as Epictetus reminds us. I have not yet made up my mind as to this problem. It is doubly difficult because of language. To educate anyone properly he must be taught Greek. Yet in a supposedly Hellenic city like Antioch, less than half the population knows Greek; the rest speak one or another of the Semitic languages. The same is true of Alexandria and the cities of Asia. A further complication is the matter of Latin. The language of both law and army is Latin, while that of literature and administration is Greek. As a result, an educated man must be bilingual. If he were the son, say, of a Syrian tailor in Antioch he would have to be trilingual. Just learning languages would take up most of his time. I know. As much as I have studied Latin, I can still hardly read it. And though I speak the military jargon easily, it bears little relation to Cicero whom I read in Greek translation! So we argued among ourselves in the best of spirits through the winter and a most beautiful spring which covered the banks of the Seine with flowers, and reminded us, in life, what Eleusis shows us in mystery.

At the beginning of June the idyll ended. Constantius transferred Sallust to army headquarters at Milan. He cut off my right arm. My response: grief, rage, and, finally, in imitation of the philosophers, I composed a long essay on the gods, and dedicated it to Sallust.

Insert account of that summer's campaign.

*Priscus*: That year's campaign was a troublesome one. Constantius had neglected to supply Julian with money to pay his troops. Also, supplies were short and what grain Julian could amass, he was forced to render into hardtack, not the sort of ration calculated to please troops already exhausted from much fighting. Julian was so short of funds that on at least one occasion when a soldier asked him for what the men call "shave money" or "the barber's due," he was not able to give the man even one small coin.

Julian moved north to Flanders. In a most guileful way, he conquered a Frankish tribe which occupied the city of Tongres. Then he defeated a German tribe called the Chornevi who dwell at the mouth of the Rhine. After that he marched to the Meuse River and restored three of our ruined fortresses. At this point, the food gave out. The local harvest was late, and the troops were on the verge of mutiny. They jeered Julian in public and called him "Asiatic" and "Greekling." But he comported himself with dignity, stripped the countryside of what food there was, and quelled the mutiny.

Next Julian built a pontoon bridge across the Rhine and we crossed over into the country of the German king, Suomarius . . . but all that is in the military history. After this short campaign, we recrossed the Rhine and returned to Paris for the winter.

*Julian Augustus*

Our second winter in Paris was even more agreeable than the first, though I missed Sallust more than I could say—but then I *did* say it, in panegyric prose! I still had no money. I was watched and reported on by the secret agent Gaudentius. My wife continued to be ill. Yet despite all this, I was content. I had grown used to governing, and I no longer thought wistfully of a private life, teaching at Athens. I was well pleased to be Caesar in Gaul.

The principal event of the winter was the first major trial I was to preside over. Numerius, governor of Gallia Narbonensis (one of the Mediterranean provinces), was accused of embezzling state funds. Enemies had prepared a damning case against him. He was brought to Paris for trial. It was a fascinating experience for me and almost as interesting for the Parisians as their beloved theatre, for I allowed the public to attend the trial.

Day after day the hall of justice was crowded. It was soon apparent that there was no proper evidence against Numerius. He

210

was a striking-looking man, tall and stately. He chose to defend himself against Delphidius, the public prosecutor. Now Delphidius is one of the most vigorous speakers and cunning legal minds in the empire but even he could not make evidence out of air, though he certainly tried, using his own breath.

Numerius had made political enemies, as we all do, and they had trumped up charges against him in the hope that I might remove him. Point by point Numerius refuted every charge against him so skillfully that Delphidius finally turned to me and shouted angrily. "Can anyone, great Caesar, *ever* be found guilty if all he must do is deny the charge?" To which I answered in one of those rare unpremeditated bursts in which—at least so I like to think—the gods speak through me: "Can anyone ever be found innocent, if all you must do is accuse him?" There was a sudden silence in the hall. Then a great burst of applause, and that was the end of the trial.

I tell this story out of vanity, of course. I am very pleased with what I—or Hermes—said. But to be honest, I am not the best judge in the world. Often when I think I am making some subtle point, I am actually only spreading confusion. Yet I mention this story because it demonstrates, I believe, the true basis of law. Those of the earth's governors who have been tyrants have always presumed that if a man is *thought* guilty then he must be guilty because why otherwise would he find himself in such a situation. Now any tyrant knows that a man may be perfectly blameless but have powerful enemies (very often the tyrant himself is chief among them), which is why I prefer to place the burden of proof on the accuser rather than on the accused.

Helena was somewhat better that winter. She was particularly animated whenever she discussed her visit to Rome. "Do you think we shall ever be able to live there?" she asked me one day, when—rather unusually—we found ourselves dining alone.

"That is for your brother to decide," I said. "Personally, I like Gaul. I could be quite happy living here the rest of my life."

"In *Paris*?" The way she said it revealed how much she hated our life.

"Yes, but then who knows what will happen next year, next week?"

"You would love the house in Via Nomentana," she said wistfully. "I have the most beautiful gardens..."

"Better than ours? Here?" We were quite proud in Paris of the many flowers and fruit trees that grew with small effort.

"Infinitely!" she sighed. "I should so much like to go back."

"I'm sorry." This was an awkward moment and I silently cursed whoever it was had contrived for us to be alone together for a meal. I don't think it ever happened again.

"My brother respects you." This was also unusual. We seldom spoke of Constantius. "He only fears that you will... listen to wrong advice." She put the case tactfully.

"He has nothing to fear," I said. "Either from me or my advisers. I have no intention of usurping the throne. I want only to do what I was sent here to do: pacify Gaul. And I may say your brother has not made it easy for me."

"Perhaps *he* listens to bad advisers." That was the most she would admit.

I nodded grimly. "And I can name them, starting with Eusebius..."

She broke in, "You have one friend at court." She pushed her plate from her, as though clearing a place for something new to be set down. "The Empress."

"I know..." I began. But Helena stopped me with a strange look; for the first time in our marriage she struck an intimate note. "Eusebia loves you." Helena said this in such a way that I could not precisely tell what she meant by that overused and always ambivalent verb. "Her love is constant," she went on, adding but not defining. "While she lives, you are safe. Of course, that may not be long." Her voice shifted; she became more ordinary, more of a woman telling gossip. "The night we arrived at Rome, there was a reception for Constantius in the palace on the Palatine. The senate of Rome and all the consulars were present. I've never seen anything quite so splendid. My brother meant it when he said, 'This is the great moment of my life!' I suppose it always is when a Roman emperor first comes to Rome. Anyway, Constantius wore the crown, and Eusebia sat beside him. She seemed tired but no one suspected she was ill. Then during the Emperor's reply to the senate's welcome, she turned deathly pale. She tried to rise but her robes were too heavy for her. Since everyone was watching Constantius, hardly anyone noticed her. But I did. I was the first to see the blood flow from her mouth. Then she fell backwards

212

onto the floor. She was unconscious when they carried her from the room."

I was appalled. Not only at this bad news, but at Helena's pleasure in Eusebia's pain. "Naturally, my brother—all of us—were concerned. But in a few days she was all right. And of course she was most kind to me when it came *my* turn to . . . bleed. All through my labor, Eusebia was beside me. She could not have been more kind. She even arranged for our dead child to be buried in Constantia's mausoleum. She was as thoughtful as though I were her own sister . . . instead of her enemy." Helena flung this last word at me, and got to her feet. I was startled by the quality of her rage.

"Your friend, your protectress, killed both our children." Helena was now at the door. She spoke with complete calm, like a Sophist who has studied exactly what and how he will say a written speech. "You pride yourself on your philosophy, your love of harmony and balance. Well, how do you measure *this* in your scales? Two children here." She held up her left hand. "Eusebia here." She held up her right hand and made the scales even.

I did not answer her. How could I? Then Helena left the room. We never spoke of this matter again, but I respected her passion, realizing that one can never entirely know another human being even though one has shared the same bed and the same life.

A month later, we received word that Eusebia was dead.


While I wintered at Gaul, Constantius was a thousand miles away at Sirmium, a large city on the border between Dacia and Illyricum. Unlike me, he had a troubled winter. First Eusebia died. Then, though he managed to put down the Sarmatians for a second time, the Danube was far from pacified. The tribes were constantly on the move, causing much damage to us. Constantius, however, issued a proclamation declaring that as victor once again over the Sarmatians, he was for a *second* time taking the title of "Sarmaticus." He did not say how he wished to be styled but Priscus thought we should refer to him as Constantius Sarmaticus Sarmaticus.

My own relations with Constantius were no worse than usual. Actually, his reverses tended to keep his mind off me. I do know that he always referred contemptuously to my "success" in Gaul. In fact, Eusebius used to delight in thinking up epithets for me, knowing that they would amuse his master. Among the ones repeated to me—and it is amazing how much princes are told if they choose to listen—"chattering mule," "ape in purple," "Greekish pedant," and "nanny goat" because I had let my beard grow again.

Men are curious when it comes to fashion. Since Constantine and his heirs were clean-shaven, everyone must now be clean-shaven, especially high officials. I always answer those who criticize my beard by pointing out that Hadrian and *his* successors were all bearded, and that I consider their age superior to ours. Actually, my beard is resented because philosophy is resented. Philosophers wear beards; Julian wears a beard; therefore Julian is a philosopher and may well share with that subversive tribe sentiments hostile to the superstitions of the Galileans.

I have elsewhere described that year's campaign. In brief, I rebuilt seven ruined towns on or near the Rhine, restored granaries and garrisoned them. The towns were: Fort Hercules, Schenkenschanz, Kellen, Nuys, Andernach, Bonn and Bingen. All were regained without great effort.

At Bingen, I had a surprise. The praetorian prefect Florentius, whom I had not seen for more than two years, suddenly appeared at the head of his army to assist me in my task. Since the campaign was nearly over, I could do no more than thank him for the graciousness of his gesture and extort as much grain and gold as I could from him. We had an amusing interview.

Both our camps were pitched outside Bingen. I chose to live in my tent since the town was in considerable turmoil with rebuilding, while the praetorian prefect's army was encamped to the south of me, close to the river. Florentius requested audience the day after our armies had converged. I granted it to him, noting with some pleasure that Florentius now came to me instead of insisting that I attend him.

Florentius arrived at sundown. I received him inside my tent, alone. He saluted me with unusual ceremony. He was noticeably changed. There was no ironic reference to my Spartan quarters. He was plainly nervous. But why?

We sat in folding chairs near the opening of the tent through which came the golden light of a summer evening. Birds sang. The noise of the army about us was constant but soothing. In the distance one could see, just above the green of woods, the gray

214

walls of Bingen. Florentius began the dialogue. "You know, Caesar, that Persia is now in arms against us."

I said that I knew only what was common knowledge, that an embassy Constantius had sent to Sapor had failed.

"I'm afraid it's worse than that." His nervous gaze flitted here and there like a bird searching for a branch to light on. His hands trembled. "Several months ago Sapor marched on Mesopotamia. He laid siege to Amida."

I was surprised, not so much that Sapor had attacked us as I was that the news had been kept from me. Ordinarily not a head can fall in the empire that word of it does not circulate thousands of miles in an instant, like the wind—no, swifter, like the sun's rays. No one knows how it is that news travels faster than men and horses, but it does. Yet this news had not. I said as much.

Florentius gestured. "The Augustus," he said. "He has kept the matter as secret as possible. You know how he is."

It was part of Florentius's task in dealing with me to make subtly derogatory remarks about Constantius, hoping to lure me into expressing treasonable sentiments. But I never fell into this trap, and he knew that I never would; yet we continued to play the familiar game, rather like those old men one sees in the villages who sit hour after hour, year after year, playing draughts with one another, making the same moves and countermoves to the end of their lives.

I was puzzled. "Why would he want to keep the matter secret?"

"Because, Caesar, it is a disaster." Florentius withdrew his purse of doeskin and fingered his gold. "Amida has been destroyed."

I could not have been more affected if he had said that Antioch or even Constantinople had fallen to the barbarians. Amida was the most important of our border cities, and supposedly impregnable.

"The city was besieged for twenty-three days. I have a full account for you, if you want to study it. There were seven legions inside the city walls. Those troops, plus the inhabitants, meant that one hundred and twenty thousand people were crowded in a single small space. They suffered from plague, hunger, thirst. Sapor himself fought in the first ranks. Fortunately, we fought better, and Sapor lost thirty thousand men."

"But we lost Amida?"

"Yes, Caesar."

"What now?"

"The Augustus plans to move to Antioch for the winter. Next spring he will launch a major offensive against Persia. He has sworn to recover Amida."

"And Sapor?"

"He has withdrawn to Ctesiphon to prepare . . . who knows for what?"

We sat in silence as the light fell behind the trees. The warm air was full of the smell of cooking. Men laughed. Metal struck metal. Horses whinnied; a soldier's dog barked. I thought of Amida, destroyed.

"Naturally, the Augustus will want all the troops he can muster." I said this first, knowing that was why Florentius had come to see me.

"Yes, Caesar."

"Has he specified *what* he will want from me?"

"No, Caesar. Not yet."

"I have, all-told, twenty-three thousand men, as you know."

"Yes, Caesar. I know."

"Most of my men are Gallic volunteers. They joined me on condition that they fight only in Gaul for the protection of their own country."

"I am aware of that, Caesar. But they are also Roman soldiers. They have taken the oath of allegiance to the Emperor. They must obey him."

"Even so, I cannot guarantee how they will act if word I gave them should be broken."

"Let that be my responsibility, Caesar." Florentius put away the purse.

"Nothing in Gaul can be done without me, Prefect. *All* responsibility is mine." I let that hard statement fall between us like a slab of marble dropping into place.

"Such is the will of Caesar," said Florentius politely, with only the slightest trace of his usual irony. We both rose. At the opening to the tent, he paused. "Might I see the agent Gaudentius?"

"Haven't you already talked to him?" I was as bland as he. "But of course you may. Ask my chamberlain. He'll know where to find him. I'm sure you will find Gaudentius in excellent health, and informative, as always."

Florentius saluted me. Then he disappeared into the twilight. I sat alone for a long time. It was my duty to let Constantius have whatever troops he wanted; yet if I sent the Gauls to Asia I would have broken my word to them. I would also be fatally weakened as a commander. What to do?

In the next few days, every detail of the fall of Amida was known to the army. We also learned that Constantius had dispatched Paul "the chain" to the Orient to conduct treason trials. It was Constantius's inevitable reaction. Any defeat must be the work of traitors. For a season, Paul wreaked havoc in Asia, and many blameless men were exiled or executed.

The remainder of that summer I spent on the Rhine, treating with the German kings, sometimes severely, sometimes generously. The Germans are innately treacherous, and their word means nothing. They are unfathomable. If we had taken their forest-country away from them, I might understand their constant duplicity: love for one's own land is common to all, even to barbarians. But it was not *their* land and cities we took from them, but our own, held by us for centuries and ravaged by them. Yet whenever a treaty could be broken, they would break it. Whenever any dishonorable thing might be done, it was done.

Why are the Germans like this? I don't know. They are difficult to understand, even those who have been educated by us (ever since Julius Caesar we have taken kings' sons as hostages and civilized them, but to no avail). They are wild by nature. They love fighting as much as Greeks and Romans hate it.

To govern at all, it was necessary for me to obtain a reputation for strictness. I achieved it. I executed kings who broke their word. I crossed the Rhine whenever I chose. I was hard. I was just. Slowly it dawned upon the Germans that I meant to keep them to their side of the Rhine and that any man who chose to rise against me would be struck down. When I left Gaul, the province was at peace.

# XIII

My third and last winter at Paris was crucial. I had heard nothing from Constantius directly or indirectly since the meeting with Florentius. The prefect preferred to stay at Vienne while I remained at Paris. We did not meet, though documents continually passed between us. Aware that there might soon be a crisis in our affairs, I proposed at one point that Florentius join me for the winter at

Paris. But he declined. Obviously he wanted to keep what authority he could. In principle I was the master of Britain, Gaul, Spain and Morocco. In fact Florentius administered that part of Gaul which is south of Vienne, as well as Spain and Morocco. I controlled Britain. For the time being, we had tacitly agreed not to interfere in each other's territories.

Helena's health grew worse, and when the cold weather came, she took to her bed. The pains increased. I sent for Oribasius. He was not hopeful. "I'm afraid the best I can do is keep her out of pain. She has a tumor of the stomach. There is nothing to be done." And he told me of a new herb he had discovered which caused the flesh to lose sensation.

Oribasius was a comforting companion. So was Priscus, though he kept threatening to go home. His wife Hippia had sent him several angry letters, and he longed for Athens, though he denied it. Priscus always likes to appear more unfeeling than he actually is. Eutherius was a constant source of intelligence. But except for these three friends, I was quite isolated. My chief of staff Lupicinus, who had replaced Sallust, was arrogant and ignorant, while Sintula, the cavalry commander, was hardly company. Nevitta, that splendid officer, I kept at Cologne, to guard the Rhine.

Rather desperately, I wrote letters to old friends, inviting them to Paris. To those who liked to hunt I promised whole packs of deer and a clement season. To philosophers I praised the delights of Parisian intellectual life, though there was none except for the Galilean bishop and his entourage, from whom I kept my distance. But no one came. Even Maximus was unable to make the journey, though he wrote me often, in a code of his own devising.

At about this time, November or December, I had a prophetic dream. In the third watch of the night I fell asleep, tired from dictating the notes which later became my commentary on the Battle of Strasbourg. As often happens when I have something specific on my mind, I dreamed first of the battle. Then the battle vanished, as things do in dreams, and I found myself in a large room at the center of which grew a tall tree; at the time this seemed perfectly natural. But then the tree fell to the floor, and I noticed that a smaller tree was growing among its roots, and that the smaller tree had not been uprooted by its parent's fall. "The tree is dead," I heard myself say. "And now the smaller one will die, too." And I was filled with a pity all out of proportion to the event. Suddenly I was aware of a man beside me. He took my arm. But though I could not make out his face, he did not seem strange. "Don't despair." He pointed. "See? The small tree's root is in the ground. As long as it is there, it will grow, even more securely than before."

Then the dream ended, and I knew that I had spoken to my patron deity, Hermes.

When I told Oribasius of this, he interpreted it as meaning that Constantius would fall while I would flourish, my roots in the All-Seeing One. Needless to say, we kept this dream a secret. Men were regularly executed for innocent dreams and mine was hardly innocent. It was prophecy.

In December our quiet court was interrupted by the news that the Picts and Scots who inhabit the north of Britain were menacing the border. Our governor begged for reinforcements. I was in a quandary. I had few enough troops as it was and I knew that my chances of keeping even those were slim for it was everywhere rumored that the Caesar at Gaul was to be stripped of his army the day Constantius took the field against Persia. But Britain was of great economic importance to us. Since so many Gallic farms had been ravaged by the Germans, we were forced that year to rely on British grain to feed the people.

I took counsel and it was decided that Lupicinus must go immediately to Britain. He was a good commander, though we used often to wonder whether he was more covetous than cruel, or more cruel than covetous.

On the day that Lupicinus arrived in Britain, the tribune Decentius, an imperial state secretary, arrived at Paris with a considerable retinue of lawyers and fiscal agents. Before coming to me, he had spent several days in Vienne with Florentius. I did not take this well, since it is usual to pay homage first to the Caesar.

Decentius was an exhausted man when he arrived. So I allowed him to sit while he read me the Emperor's letter. The tone was friendly, but it was absolute in its demands. I was to send Constantius the Aeruli, the Batavians, the Celts and the Petulantes— the best of my legions—as well as three hundred men from each of the remaining legions. They were to start for Antioch without delay, in time for a spring offensive against Persia.

When Decentius finished, I said as calmly as I could, "He wants slightly more than half my army."

"Yes, Caesar. It will be a difficult war in Persia. Perhaps a decisive one."

"Has the Emperor considered the effect this will have upon the Germans? My army is small enough to begin with. If I am allowed less than twelve thousand soldiers—and those the worst—the German tribes are sure to rise again."

"But the Augustus was led to understand by your own reports that Gaul has been pacified for a generation, because of your great victories." I wondered whether Decentius had thought of this on the spur of the moment or whether Constantius had instructed him ever so gently to prick me.

"No province is ever entirely pacified. As long as there is a German alive, we are in danger."

"But no *immediate* danger, Caesar. You would agree to that?"

"No, Tribune, I would not. Also, at this moment, there is serious trouble in Britain."

"There are always troubles, Caesar. Nevertheless, in the prosecution of the war against Persia, the Augustus feels he must have the best of all *his* armies with him. He feels . . ."

"Is he aware of the vow I made the Gallic soldiers: that they were not to fight outside the province?"

"Your vow to them is superseded by the oath they took to the Augustus." This was stated with a sharp legality.

"True, but I must warn you, Tribune, there is a chance of mutiny."

He looked at me intently. I knew what he was thinking. Will this supposedly unambitious Caesar now see his chance to stage a mutiny and usurp the West? Courtiers never take things at face value. When I said the troops *might* mutiny, he took this as a threat that I would, if provoked, incite them to revolt.

"I am," I said carefully, "loyal to Constantius. I shall do as I am told. I merely warn you that there may be trouble. Meanwhile, we must wait at least a month before the troops can be sent to the East."

"Augustus has said immediately . . ." Decentius began.

I interrupted. "Tribune, as we sit here, the legions he asked for are now at sea, bound for Britain." And I told him about Lupicinus. But then to demonstrate my good faith, I allowed him to listen as I dictated a letter to Lupicinus ordering him back from Britain. This done I sent Decentius to Sintula and gave orders that the Tribune was to be obeyed in every way. By the end of the week, some of my best soldiers had departed for Antioch. The subtle Decentius must have promised them various bounties, for they left in better humor than I thought possible.

Now there are those who believe that at this point I planned to disobey Constantius and set myself up as the Augustus of the West. This is not true. I will not deny that I did *think* of it as a possibility—it would have been impossible not to. After all, through my efforts, the Rhine was secure and I governed a third of the world. Even so, I was not eager to break with Constantius. He was stronger than I. It was as simple as that. Also, I had no desire to challenge my cousin in that one field where he was preeminent: keeping his throne.

But I was considerably shaken when Decentius insisted that I order all the remaining troops in Gaul to come to Paris so that he might choose the best for the Persian campaign. We argued several days about this. Not until I threatened to abdicate did Decentius agree to maintain the Rhine garrisons at full strength. I then ordered the army of Gaul to converge on Paris. All obeyed me, except Lupicinus, who wrote to say that he could not possibly return to Paris before April. Decentius complained bitterly, but there was nothing to be done.

By the second week in February when the legions were encamped on both sides of the river, Decentius dropped his courtly mask. He no longer wheedled; he ordered. Eutherius was with me when the Tribune finally pounded the table and shouted, "If you won't speak to the legions, I will, in Constantius's name!" I told him mildly that there was no need for him either to shout at me or to do my work. I then dismissed him. Eutherius and I were left alone in the council chamber. We looked at one another; he concerned, I wretched.

"Well, old friend," I said at last, "what do I do?"

"As you are told. Unless . . ." He paused.

I shook my head. "No, I won't go into rebellion."

"Then tell the men that you have been ordered to send them east. The rest," he said this slowly, with emphasis, "is up to them."

The next day was 12 February. I was up at daybreak. I gave orders to my household that a dinner be prepared for all officers that evening. It was to be a sumptuous affair. I ordered the best wine from the palace cellars. All sorts of fowl and livestock were to be prepared. Though I pride myself on the austerity of my table, this time I chose to be lavish.

221

I then set out to make the rounds of the army, accompanied only by my standard-bearer. Our breaths were frosty as we clattered across the wooden bridge to the left bank. Slowly I made my way through the camp. I spoke to the men, singly, in groups. It was good-humored talk, and I soon had an idea of their mood. They were well-disposed toward me, and suspicious of Constantius. There are no secrets in an army.

When I came to the encampment of the Petulantes, my own favorite among the legions, I paused to talk to a large group. We chatted lightly but guardedly. Finally, one of them stepped forward, with a letter in his hand. He saluted me. "Caesar, none of us can read." There was some laughter at this broad deception. Well over half the Petulantes are reasonably literate. "When we got here, we found this on the door of the church." He pointed to a nearby charnel house, a temple of Vesta converted by Galileans. "Read it to us, Caesar."

"If I can," I said amiably. "It's Latin, and I'm only an Asiatic, a Greekling . . ." Mention of two of the pleasanter nicknames they have for me made them laugh. The letter was in soldier-Latin. I started to read. "Men of the Petulantes, we are about to be sent to the ends of the earth like criminals . . ." I stopped, blinded for a moment by the pale sun to which I had turned almost instinctively, as though for guidance. The men shouted grimly, "Go on, Caesar!" They already knew the contents of the anonymous letter. I shook my head and said firmly, "This is treason against the Emperor."

I threw the letter to the ground and wheeled my horse about. "But not against *you!*" shouted the man who had given me the letter. I spurred my horse and with the standard-bearer lagging behind, I galloped back to the island. To this day I do not know who wrote the letter; naturally, I have been accused of having written it myself.

Shortly after noon the officers arrived at the palace. I received them in the great banqueting hall which had been made to look quite festive on such short notice. Evergreen boughs festooned walls and rafters while coal-burning braziers cut the chill. It was the most costly banquet of my career thus far. Helena was too ill to join us, so I did the honors alone. Decentius sat on my right, watching me carefully. But I neither said nor did anything remarkable.

When the officers had begun to grow boisterous with wine,

Decentius said, "Now is the time to tell them that they must leave within the week."

I made one last attempt. "Tribune, in April the legions from Britain will be here. If we wait until then..."

"Caesar," Decentius shifted from presumptuousness to guileful reasonableness, "if you wait until then, people will say that the British legions forced you to obey the Augustus, but if you carry out your orders *now*, they will say it was of your own choice, and that you are indeed master of Gaul, not to mention loyal to the Augustus."

There was no doubting the truth of this. I felt the trap spring. I surrendered. I agreed to make the announcement at the end of the dinner. Did I have any secret design? I think not. Yet at important moments in one's life there is a tendency to do instinctively the necessary thing to survive.

During the banquet, I was saluted repeatedly by minor officers, in violation of etiquette. At one point, Eutherius murmured in my ear, "You have broken every rule governing Caesar's table." I smiled wanly. This was an old joke between us. "Caesar's table" was a euphemism for the restrictions put on me by Constantius.

At the end of the dinner, I said a few words to the officers, who were now in a mood for anything from riot to battle. I told them that I had never known better troops. I told them that for the first time in my life I envied Constantius, for he was about to receive the world's best soldiers into his own army. There was muttering at this, but no more. I was careful not to play too much on their emotions. I chose not to provoke them.

*Priscus*: Yet.

*Julian Augustus*

After many tearful embraces, the banquet ended. I accompanied the officers as far as the square in front of the palace. Just to the right of the main door, there is a high stone tribunal from which proclamations are read. I stood at the foot of it, while the officers milled somewhat unsteadily about me. As I said good-bye to this one and that one, I noticed that a large crowd had gathered in the arcades which border the square on two sides. When the people recognized me, they rushed forward. Quickly my guards drew swords and made a ring about me. But the crowd was not hostile. They were mostly women and children. They implored me not to send their husbands away. One woman waved a baby in front of me like a screaming flag. "Don't send his father away! He's all we have!"

Others shouted, "You promised us, Caesar! You promised!"

Unable to bear their cries, I turned away. At the door to the palace, Decentius was deep in conversation with the secret agent Gaudentius. They broke off guiltily when they saw me approaching. "An old friend," said Decentius.

"I am certain of that," I said sharply. I motioned to the crowd. "Do you hear them?"

Decentius looked at me blankly for a moment. Then he looked toward the square. "Oh, yes. Yes. That's quite usual in the provinces. The women always complain when the men are ordered away. When you have been in the army as long as I have, you won't even notice them."

"I am afraid I find it hard *not* to notice. You see, I did promise them..."

But Decentius had heard quite enough of my famous promise. "My dear Caesar," he said, and his tone was that of a father, "these women will each have found a new man by the time the warm weather comes round. They are animals. Nothing more."

I left him in the square and went straight to my study on the second floor. I sent for Priscus, Oribasius and Eutherius. While waiting for them to arrive, I tried to read but I could not concentrate. I counted the tiles in the floor. I paced up and down. Finally, I opened the window on the Seine and looked out. The cold air was refreshing. My face burned as though I had the fever. My hands trembled. I took deep breaths, and started to count the blocks of broken ice as they floated downstream. I prayed to Helios.

Eutherius was the first to come. I shut the window. I motioned for him to sit in my chair. Because of his size no other chair would hold him and he tended to break stools.

"It is a plot," he said. "Constantius has an army of nearly a hundred thousand men in Syria. Your Gauls will hardly make much difference."

"But they will to me, if I lose them."

"They will to you. And that is the plot. He wants you destroyed."

I was surprised at Eutherius. Of all my friends and advisers he was the one who invariably preached caution. He loved good form, justice, the orderly processes of the state at peace. He was not made for treason. But he had changed.

"You believe this?"

Eutherius nodded, the small black eyes glittered like the eyes of an Egyptian statue.

"Then what shall I do?"

At this point Oribasius and Priscus entered. They heard my question. Oribasius answered for Eutherius. "Rebel," he said promptly. That was, I swear by Helios, Mithras and my own Hermes, the first treasonable word that had ever passed openly among us. There was dead silence. Priscus sat on the edge of my heavy wood table. Oribasius stood at the room's center, staring intently at me. I turned to Priscus.

"What do you think?"

"You must consider everything. Can you remain in Gaul without those troops? If you can, what is Constantius apt to do? Will he remove you? Or will he be too occupied in Persia to do anything at all? I suspect," and Priscus answered his own question, "that you have heard the last from Constantius for some time. He must retake Amida and defeat Sapor. That may be his life's work. Meanwhile, you are master of the West and, should he die, emperor."

Eutherius nodded. "That is the *sensible* point of view, of course." He smiled. "Because it has been my own point of view all along. Yet I think the situation is a good deal more serious than that. You forget Florentius. My agents tell me that he is to be given full authority in Gaul as soon as Caesar loses his army. When that happens, there is nothing we can do but submit. Frankly, I think it better to resist now than to wait and be destroyed by Florentius."

While they talked among themselves, I retreated again to the window and watched the sun, a bitter winter orange, fall in the west. Night fires blossomed on the river banks. What to do? There was a sudden pounding at the door. Angrily, I opened it, declaring, "No one is to disturb us..."

But there stood Decentius, pale and distressed. "A thousand apologies, Caesar," he saluted hurriedly. "I should not have disturbed you, but they are here!"

"*Who* is *where*?"

"Can't you hear them?" Decentius was chattering with fright. We all fell silent and listened to the far-off sound of men shouting and women wailing.

"Mutiny!" said Oribasius. He ran to the window and looked out. Though one ordinarily sees only the river and the tip of the island from my window, by craning one's head it is just possible to see the wooden bridge to the north. "It's the Celtic Legion. They're crossing to the island!"

As I joined him at the window, there was a shout from just below us. "Caesar!" I looked down and saw a squad of infantry with swords drawn. They waved to me cheerfully but their voices were threatening. "Don't let us go, Caesar. Keep us here!"

One of the men, a tall fierce Celt with a blond moustache and a blind white eye, thrust his sword toward me and in a voice hoarse from many battles roared "Hail, Augustus! Hail, Julian Augustus!" The others took up the cry. I stepped back from the window. Decentius turned to me. "This is treason! Arrest those men!"

But I pushed him to one side and hurried to one of the rooms which look out on the square. I peered through a crack in the shutter. The square was filled with troops and they were by no means all drunk, as I had first suspected. This was indeed rebellion.

In front of the palace, my personal guard stood with drawn swords and leveled spears, but the mob seemed in no mood to do violence. Instead, they shouted my name, demanded my presence, declared their loyalty. Then, as if by signal—who knows how these things suddenly start? I suspect Hermes—they began to chant, first one group, then another, then the entire crowd: "Augustus! Augustus! Julian Augustus!"

I turned from the window.

"Attack them!" said Decentius. "Show them the Emperor's image. They won't dare defy that."

"We have four hundred troops in the palace," I said. "There are some twenty thousand men out there. Even an inexperienced soldier like myself avoids such odds. As for the imperial image, I'm afraid they will hack it to bits."

"Treason!" was all Decentius could say.

"Treason," I replied reasonably, as though identifying a particular star for one who wishes to know the nature of the heavens. Decentius rushed from the room.

We looked at one another, the word "Augustus" falling regularly on our ears like surf upon the beach.

"You will have to accept," said Eutherius.

"You who always preach caution tell me this?"

Eutherius nodded. Oribasius was even more emphatic. "Go on. You have nothing to lose now."

Priscus was cautious. "My interest, Caesar, is philosophy, not politics. If I were you, I would wait."

"For what?" Oribasius turned on him indignantly.

"To see what happens," said Priscus ambiguously. "To wait for a sign."

I accepted this in the spirit Priscus meant it. He understood me. He knew that unless I believed I had heaven's revealed blessing, I could not act with full force.

"Very well," I motioned to the door. "Oribasius, see to the guard. Make sure no one is admitted to the palace. Eutherius, keep an eye on our friend the Tribune. Don't let him out of your sight. Priscus, pray for me." On that we parted.

In the main corridor, one of my wife's ladies was waiting for me. She was close to hysteria. "Caesar, they're going to kill us, all of us!" I took her by the shoulders and shook her till her teeth chattered; in fact, she bit her lower lip, which had a most calming effect. She then told me that my wife was asking for me.

Helena's bedroom was dimly lit and unbearably warm. Her illness made her crave heat. A heavy odor of incense and musk filled the room, yet it could not disguise the sweet-sharp odor of the dissolution of the flesh. I hated visiting Helena, and thought myself contemptible for this aversion.

Helena lay in bed, a prayer book on the coverlet. Beside her stood the bishop of Paris, a solemn charlatan who was her closest friend and adviser. He saluted me. "I daresay that the Caesar will want to speak to the Queen alone . . ."

You have dared say it, Bishop. And it is true." The Bishop withdrew in a swirl of splendid robes, chanting loudly, as though we were a congregation.

I sat beside the bed. Helena was pale and she had lost much weight. Her eyes had grown large, as eyes appear to do when the face thins. She was a sickly yellow in the lamplight, and yet in a way she looked more appealing in her illness than ever she did in health. She no longer resembled the vigorous, hard-jawed Constantine. She was a woman now, delicate and melancholy, and I felt a sudden surge of feeling as I took her hand, hot with fever and delicate as a dead bird's wing.

"I am sorry I was too ill for the reception . . ." she began.

I cut her off. "It was of no importance. How is the pain?"

227

Her free hand touched her stomach reflexively. "Better," she said, and lied. "Oribasius finds me a new herb every day. And I take whatever he finds. I tell him he must make me his collaborator when he writes his encyclopedia." I tried not to look at her stomach, which curved large beneath the coverlet as though she were in the last month of pregnancy. For a moment neither of us spoke; then the silence was broken by the rhythmic chanting: "Augustus!" She turned toward me.

"They have been shouting for hours."

I nodded. "They are angry because the Emperor wants them to fight in Persia."

"They call you Augustus." She looked at me very hard.

"They don't mean it."

"They do," she said flatly. "They want you for Emperor."

"I've refused to show myself to them. Anyway, now it's dark, they'll soon get cold and bored and go away, and tomorrow they will do as they're told. Sintula has already gone, you know. He left yesterday with two legions." I talked fast, but she would not be put off.

"Will you take what they have offered?"

I paused, uncertain what to say. Finally, neutrally, "It would be treason."

"Traitors who prevail are patriots. Usurpers who succeed are divine emperors."

I still could not tell what she wanted me to do. "Emperors are not made," I said at last, "by a few thousand troops in a small provincial city."

"Why not? After all, it is God's will that raises us up, as it is God's will that . . . throws us down." She looked away and again her hand strayed to the seat of her mortality. "Those few soldiers are enough, *if* it is meant to be."

"What do you want me to do?" For the first and only time I asked her a direct question, as one person to another; and I did wish to know her answer.

"Tonight? I don't know. This may not be the moment. You must judge that. But I do know that you are meant to be Emperor of Rome."

Our eyes met and we studied one another as though the face of each was new and unexplored. I responded with equal candor. "I know it, too," I said. "I have had dreams. There have been signs."

228

"Then *take* it!" She said this with unexpected force.

"Now? An act of treason? Against your brother?"

"My brother and his wife killed our two children. My loyalty has . . . shifted to my cousin, who is my husband." She smiled on the word "shifted" but her great eyes were solemn.

"Curious," I said finally. "I always thought you preferred him to me."

"I did. I did. Until that last visit to Rome. You know, he tried to keep me there after the baby died. He said that there might be difficulties for you in Gaul."

"But you came back."

"I came back."

"Leaving your beloved villa?"

"Leaving that was hardest of all!" She smiled.

Then she indicated the window and the city beyond. "Now the difficulties he promised have begun. You must decide very soon."

"Yes." I rose.

"Decentius was here," she said suddenly.

I was startled. "When?"

"Just before the reception for your officers. He wanted to know if I would like to return to Rome. He said the Gallic legions would escort me as far as Milan."

"He is sly."

"Yes. I told him I chose to stay. He was disappointed." She laughed softly. "Of course even if I wanted to go, I cannot travel . . . again."

"Don't say that. One day we shall go to Rome together."

"I want that more than anything," she said. "But be quick about it . . ."

"I will be quick," I said. "I swear it."

I kissed her brow, holding my breath so as not to catch the scent of death. She clutched at me suddenly with all her strength, as though she were suffering a sharp spasm of pain. Then she let me go. "What a pity I was so much older than you."

I did not answer. I grasped her hands in silence. Then I left.

The Bishop was in the anteroom with the ladies. "The Queen is improved, don't you think, Caesar?"

"Yes, I do." I was curt. I tried to get past him. But the Bishop had more to say.

"She is of course concerned by that mob outside. We all are.

229

Most frightening. A terrible lapse of discipline. One hopes that the Caesar will dismiss this rabble with stern words."

"The Caesar will do what the Caesar must." I pushed past him into the main gallery. Servants rushed here and there, as though on urgent business. The ushers kept to their posts, but even they had lost their usual aplomb. All eyes were on me, wondering what I would do. As I crossed to the room which overlooks the square, I nearly stumbled over Gaudentius, lurking in the shadows. I was pleased to see that he was frightened.

"Caesar! The Tribune Decentius asks for audience. He is in the council chamber. They are all there. They want to know what you intend to do. We are completely surrounded. No one can escape . . ."

"Tell the Tribune I am going to bed. I shall be happy to see him in the morning." Before the agent could recover himself, I was halfway down the gallery to my own room. Outside my door stood the chief usher. I told him I was not to be disturbed unless there was an attack on the palace. I then went to my room and bolted the door after me.

It was a long night. I read. I prayed. I thought. I have never before nor since been so undecided. Everything seemed to me to be premature; events were pushing me faster than I chose to go. Yet would a moment like this come again? How often is an emperor spontaneously made? We all know of ambitious generals who have staged "popular" coronations for themselves; yet these seldom occur without the general's active collusion. I am sure that Julius Caesar very carefully instructed his friend to offer him the crown in public, simply to see what the reaction might be. Now that same crown had come to me, without my asking.

Still undecided, I slept. I dreamed and, as often happens, I found in dreaming what I must do awake. I was seated in my consular chair, quite alone, when a figure appeared to me, dressed as the guardian spirit of the state, so often depicted in the old Republic. He spoke to me. "I have watched you for a long time, Julian. And for a long time I have wished to raise you even higher than you are now. But each time I have tried, I have been rebuffed. Now I must warn you. If you turn me away again, when so many men's voices are raised in agreement with me, I shall leave you as you are. But remember this: *if I go now, I shall never return.*"

I awakened in a cold sweat and leapt from my bed; my own room was suddenly strange and menacing, as sometimes happens when we have dreamed deeply. Was I awake or not? I opened the window; icy air restored me. The stars were fading. The east was pale.

The mob was still gathered in the square. They had built bonfires. From time to time they chanted "Augustus!" I made up my mind. I summoned my bodyservant. He dressed me in the purple. Then I went out into the gallery.

Apparently I was the only one who had slept that night. Men and women still scurried through rooms and corridors, like mice seeking holes. In the council chamber I found Decentius and most of my advisers. As I entered, Eutherius was saying in his most calming voice, "Everything rests now with the will of Caesar. There is nothing we can do to affect that . . ."

"Precisely," I said. The room came to attention. Decentius, haggard, needing a shave, crossed to me and declared: "Only you can stop them! You must tell them to obey the Emperor. They will listen to you."

"I intend to speak to them now." I smiled at Eutherius. "You may all attend me on the tribunal . . . if you like."

Decentius seemed not to want this honor. But my friends did. Together we went to the main door of the palace.

"Be prepared," I said, "for anything. And don't be startled by anything I say." Then I motioned to the frightened guards to slip the bolt and open the gate.

With a deep breath, I stepped out into the square. When the mob saw me, they began to cheer. Quickly I climbed the steps to the tribunal, my companions close behind me. Then my personal guard, swords drawn, surrounded the tribunal. The mob drew back. I waved for silence; it was a long time coming. When at last I spoke, I was temperate.

"You are angry. You have reason to be. And I take your side in this matter. What you want, I promise to get for you. But without revolution. You prefer service in your native land to the dangers of a foreign country and a distant war. So be it. Go each of you to his home and take with you my promise that none of you shall serve beyond the Alps. I assume full responsibility for this decision. I shall explain it to the Augustus, and I know that he will listen to me, for he is reasonable and just."

With this speech, I dispatched my duty to Constantius. Honor was satisfied. Now what would happen? There was an instant of silence, and then shouts of "Augustus!" began again; also, insults to Constantius—and a few to me for weakness. The mob pushed closer and closer to the platform. I remained absolutely still, looking across the square to the place where day was coming, gray and cold above the houses of the town.

Eutherius whispered in my ear, "You must accept. They'll kill you if you don't." I made no answer. I waited. I knew what was to come. I saw what was about to happen as clearly as I had seen the spirit of Rome in my dream. In fact, that whole morning was like a continuation of the night's dream.

First, my guards broke and scattered as the mob pushed against the tribunal. One soldier climbed onto the back of another and seized me by the arm. I made no effort to resist. Then—again as in a dream but that pleasant sort of dream where one knows one is dreaming and has no fear—I fell into the mob. Hands, arms, shoulders broke my fall. All around me the deafening cry "Augustus!" sounded; strong in my nostrils was the smell of sweat and of garlic, as hard bodies forced me up from the ground where I lay, lifted me up high above them all like a sacrifice to the sun.

In full view of the mob, the fiercest of the men seized me. "Accept!" he shouted, sword's point held to my heart. I looked him in the face, saw red broken veins on the nose, smelled wine on his breath; that one glance was like a lifetime's acquaintance. Then in a matter-of-fact voice I said, "I accept."

The roar was tremendous. An infantryman's shield was placed under me and I was borne around the square like a Gallic or a German king. Thus was I made Augustus not by Romans nor according to Roman custom, but by barbarians, and according to their ritual.

I was returned to the tribunal. Then someone shouted that I must wear the diadem. Now I did not possess a crown of any sort. It would have been worth my life to have owned one. I told the mob this.

"Get one from your wife!" shouted a cavalryman. The mob laughed good-naturedly. Worried that my life's great moment might turn unexpectedly into low foolery, I answered quickly, "You don't want an emperor who wears a woman's jewels."

This went down well enough. Then a tall fellow named Marius, standard-bearer to the Petulantes, clambered onto the platform. He took from his neck the ring of metal which supports the chain that holds the regimental eagle in its place. He jerked the circlet free of the chain; then, holding the ring of metal high over my head, he shouted: "Hail, Julian Augustus!" As the mob repeated the phrase, Marius placed the battered circlet on my head.

The thing was done. I motioned for silence, and got it. "You have this day made a solemn choice. I promise you that as long as I live you shall not regret it." Then recalling the usual form in these matters, I said, "To each man here today I give five gold pieces and a pound of silver. May heaven bless this day, and what we have together done."

Then I descended the steps of the tribunal two at a time and darted into the palace.

# XIV

I went straight to my wife's room. She had already been told what had happened. She was sitting up in bed, attended by several women. Her hair had been combed and her sallow face was cruelly mocked by rouge. The women withdrew.

"It is done," I said.

"Good." She held my hands and for a moment I felt strength in her fingers. "Now there will be war."

I nodded. "But not immediately. I shall tell Constantius that this was none of my doing, and it was not. If he is wise, he will accept me as Augustus in the West."

"He won't." She let go my hands.

"I hope he does."

She was staring at me with eyes half-shut (her vision had never been good and to see things clearly she was forced to squint). At last she murmured. "Julian Augustus."

I smiled. "By grace of a mob in the main square of a provincial town."

"By the grace of God," she corrected me.

"I think so. I believe so."

She was suddenly practical. "While you were in the square, one of my officers came to tell me there is a plot to murder you. Here. In the palace."

I did not take this too seriously. "I am well guarded."

She shook her head. "I trust this man. He is my best officer." Like all ladies of the imperial house, Helena not only had her own servants and attendants but her own bodyguard.

"I shall look into it." I rose to go.

"Decentius is behind the plot."

"Naturally."

As I crossed to the door, she said in a loud voice, "Hail Augustus!" I turned and laughed, and said, "Hail, Augusta!" Helena smiled. I had never seen her as happy as she was at that moment.

Next I went to the council chamber, where all of my court was assembled, including Decentius.

I came straight to the point. "You are all witnesses that I did not in any way arouse the soldiers. Nor did I ask for this honor they have done me—illegally." There was a murmur of disappointment in the chamber. Decentius began to look hopeful. I gave him a friendly smile; I continued. "I shall report all of this to the Augustus, describing exactly what happened, and I shall pledge him, as always, my loyalty not only as a a colleague but as a kinsman." Everyone was now quite puzzled. Decentius stepped forward.

"If that is . . . Caesar's decision." He was very bold to call me "Caesar" but I respected his loyalty to his master. "Then Caesar must discipline his own troops. He must do as the Augustus wants, and send them to the East."

"My dear Tribune . . ." I sounded even to myself like the most honey-tongued of lawyers. "I am willing to give my life for the Emperor in any battle against barbarians. But I will not give it in this way. I have no intention of being murdered by an army I have devoted five years to training, an army which loves me perhaps too much and their Emperor too little. No, I shall not take back what they have given me." I suddenly recalled that I still wore the metal circlet. I took it off and held it up. "A piece of military equipment, no more." I let the circlet drop on the table in front of me. "Nor do I have any intention of sending them East. For one thing, Tribune, they will not go. No matter what I or anyone says."

"Then, Caesar, do you mean to go against the Augustus?" Decentius was stony.

I shook my head. "I shall try to obey him. But that may not be possible. We shall write Constantius today. But even better than our writing will be your own description of what happened here in Paris. I am sure that once you have explained to him our true situation, he will be sympathetic." There was a murmur of laughter.

"Very well, Caesar. Have I your permission to go?"

"You have it," I said.

Decentius saluted and left the chamber.

Then tired as I was, I called a meeting of the consistory. We spent the morning dictating a long letter to Constantius. In brief, I said that I had not incited the troops, that they had threatened me with death if I did not take the title Augustus, that I had accepted for fear they might select someone else, another Magnentius or Silvanus. I then requested that the legions be kept in Gaul. I promised, however, to send Constantius all the Spanish horses he needed (there had been some correspondence already on this subject), as well as a number of targeteers from the tribe of Laeti on the Rhine: good soldiers, eager for war. I requested that a new praetorian prefect be appointed; the other officers of state would be selected by me, as is usual. I ended with the hope that only harmony prevail between us, and so on.

There was a good deal of discussion as to how I should style myself. My own view prevailed. I signed the letter "Caesar," not "Augustus."

Eutherius offered to take the letter himself to Constantinople. Since he was my best advocate, I let him go.

The next few days were turmoil. Decentius left for Vienne. Eutherius departed for Constantinople. I sent Gaudentius packing During this period, I did not show myself in public, nor wear the diadem, nor style myself Augustus. This was a time for caution.

Though I had sent several messages to Florentius, I had heard nothing from Vienne except conflicting rumors: Florentius planned to take the field against me in the spring. Florentius had been recalled. Florentius was withdrawing to Spain, to Britain, to Morocco. In the absence of any word from the praetorian prefect himself, I replaced every governor in Gaul with men of my own choosing, and thus assured the loyalty of the cities

*Priscus*: Julian skips that spring and summer, I suppose because much of it is covered in his military history.

That spring, while we were at Paris, Constantius moved to Caesarea. There he assembled an army for the campaign against Persia. He was very good at assembling armies. His problem was that he never quite knew what to do with an army once he'd got

235

it all together. He was joined at Caesarea first by Decentius, then by Florentius who had fled Gaul, leaving his family to shift for themselves. To everyone's surprise, Julian later allowed the family to join Florentius, transporting them at state expense. Julian was determined to be merciful. He saw himself in the line of Marcus Aurelius. Actually, he was greater than that self-consciously good man. For one thing, he had a harder task than his predecessor. Julian came at the end of a world, not at its zenith. That is important, isn't it, Libanius, my fellow relic? We are given our place in time as we are given our eyes: weak, strong, clear, squinting, the thing is not ours to choose. Well, this has been a squinting, walleyed time to be born in. Fortunately, when most eyes see distortion as a matter of course, nothing bizarre is thought out of the way, and only a clear vision is abnormal.

Poor Eutherius had a most difficult embassy. Everything went wrong for him on the road. Because of his rank as chamberlain to Caesar he was necessarily accompanied at many stages by other important officials. You know how it is when one travels at state expense. It is marvelous of course because it costs nothing, one gets the best horses, there is always a place to spend the night, and brigands seldom assault guests of the state. *But* one must contend with the highly placed bores (who are contending with us!). There is always the general who recalls old battles. The bishop who sputters at the thought of his colleagues' "heresies." The governor who was honest and can prove it as he returns home with a retinue of several hundred heavily burdened pack horses.

Eutherius was taken over by officials. By now the world knew what had happened, and Julian's chamberlain was wined and dined so much en route that he lost many days' travel. Finally, braving storms at sea and the snows of Illyricum, he crossed to Constantinople only to learn that the Augustus was at Caesarea. So the embassy wearily pressed on. The chamberlain was received in late March.

Julian told me that Eutherius told him that he had never seen Constantius in such a rage. He fully expected to be slaughtered on the spot. But—luckily for Julian—Constantius was trapped. Though his every instinct (and his political cunning was always astute) told him that he must strike at Julian as soon as possible, he could not because Sapor was in Mesopotamia. Constantius was forced to stay in Asia. So he dismissed Eutherius noncommittally;

he also gave a letter to the Tribune Leonas to be delivered to Julian personally.

As luck would have it, the day Leonas arrived in Paris, Julian was to take part in some sort of festival which was to be heavily attended not only by the troops but by the Parisians. Now Julian dearly loved showing off in front of a crowd, an unexpected trait in a philosopher. Knowing pretty much what was in the letter, Julian presented Leonas to the mob, telling them why he was in Paris. Then, in front of thousands, Julian read the letter aloud from beginning to end. When he came to the part where he was ordered to remain in his rank as Caesar, the crowd roared back as though rehearsed. "Augustus! Julian Augustus!"

The next day Julian gave Leonas a letter for Constantius; I gather it was conciliatory; among other things, he accepted Constantius's appointment of the quaestor Nebridius as praetorian prefect, and he signed himself "Caesar." One ought to have all his letters at hand. I suppose they can be found in the archives at Constantinople, although I am not sure what the current policy is as to his papers. Some years ago when a student of mine—a Christian—wanted to examine certain of Julian's state papers, he was not allowed to see them. In fact, the chamberlain's office was most suspicious, which *is* suspicious. But that was in Valens's time. Maybe things have changed. You will doubtless find out when you edit these papers.

In June Julian took the field against those Franks who live near Kellen; they were the last of the tribes to molest Gaul. Despite the bad roads and thick forests that protected their home across the Rhine, he defeated them easily. But I was not with him. Just before he took to the field, I departed for Athens.

The day I was to leave, I went to say good-bye to Julian in his study, a room always referred to by his friends as the Frigidarium. I have never known a room to be so cold. But Julian seemed not to mind it. And of course after he nearly suffocated that first winter, he never heated the room properly again. In warm weather, however, it was pleasantly cool, and the last I saw of him at Paris was on a fine June day. I found Oribasius also waiting outside the study door.

"He has a bishop with him," said Oribasius.

"No doubt converting him."

"No doubt."

Then the door opened and a scowling, red-faced man sailed past us.

Julian came to the door and pulled us inside. His eyes gleamed. He had obviously been enjoying himself. "You should have heard him!"

"What sort of bishop is he?" I asked. "Arian or Athanasian or . . ."

"Political. That was Epictetus, bishop of Civitavecchia. His interests, I suspect, are secular rather than religious. Constantius sent him to me, with a most extraordinary message." Julian threw himself on the military cot by the window. (Though he nowhere in his memoir mentions it, he often dictated while lying down; after reading some of his late-night essays, I used to accuse him of talking in his sleep. To which he would answer, "In sleep the gods speak to us, so what I say in my sleep must be divine.")

"My colleague, the Augustus, proposes that if I step down as Caesar, abandon the army of Gaul, return to Constantinople as a private person, my life will be safe."

Both Oribasius and I laughed; but I was uneasy. "It's absurd, of course," I said, "yet what is the alternative if you don't?"

"The bishop was not specific. The implication is that sooner or later Constantius will deal with me."

"Much later," said Oribasius. "He is having his difficulties in Persia. It will be at least a year before he can march against us."

Julian shook his head. "I'm not sure." He swung his legs over the cot and reached over to a nearby folding table on which lay the usual sheaf of agents' reports. "All sorts of news." He tapped the papers. "Here is an order we intercepted from Constantius to the prefect of Italy: gather three million bushels of wheat, have them ground at Bregentz—that's on Lake Constance—and store the grain in several cities, all on the border of Gaul. Then there's another order for wheat to be stored on the Italian side of the Cottian Alps. He means to invade Gaul. There's no doubt of that."

"But when?" Even though I was leaving and would soon be safe (not being a hero, my constant interest is the preservation of my own life), I did care what happened to my friend.

"Who knows? We can only hope Sapor involves him in a major campaign. Meanwhile, *I* have all that grain." He grinned like a boy. "I've ordered it confiscated and held for my own use." He paused; then: "All I need is a year."

"And after that?" I looked at him closely, for Julian had never before spoken of any time other than the immediate future. As well as we knew him, none of us had any idea of the extent of his ambition, or the nature of his long-range plan.

He answered cautiously, again flat on his back, one hand tugging at his youthful beard, which glinted gold as fox fur in the bright June light. "In one year I shall be secure in Gaul, *and* in Italy." Now it was out. To cross the Alps would indeed mean war.

"I have no choice," he said. "If I stay here, if I remain as I am, he will have my head." He indicated the papers on the table. "There is a report here that he is negotiating with the Scythians to come into Gaul. Typical, of course. To destroy me he'll wreck Gaul a second time, fill it again with savages and *never* regain it." He sat up. "Next spring, my friends, I take the field against Constantius."

All that I could think to say, finally, was, "He has ten times the army you have. He controls Italy, Africa, Illyricum, Asia ”

"I know." Julian was unexpectedly calm. Ordinarily, such a conversation would have had him on his feet, arms waving, eyes flashing, words tumbling over one another in his excitement. I think I was more impressed by his unusual gravity than by what he said. "But if we move swiftly, gathering strength as we go, I can take all of Europe in three months."

"Then you must face the largest army on earth, at Constantinople." Oribasius looked unhappy.

"I believe I shall win. Anyway, better to die at the head of an army than perish here and be known to history as the *fourth* usurper Constantius put down. Besides, this contest is between the Galileans and the true gods, and we shall win it because I was chosen to win it." He said this so quietly, so lacking in his usual exuberance that there was nothing left for us to say; sooner tell the rain to stop on a spring morning in Gaul.

Then he was his old self. "So now Priscus deserts us! Just as the battle lines are drawn, he retreats to Athens ”

"Cowardice is my prevailing characteristic," I said.

"And uxoriousness," said Oribasius slyly. "Priscus longs for the powerful arms of Hippia . . ."

"And the company of my children, who are now at an age to embarrass me not only intellectually but financially."

"Will you need money?" Julian, even at his poorest—and at this point he was unable to pay his household expenses—was always generous to friends. Maximus took him for a considerable fortune . . . and Maximus was one of the reasons I was leaving Gaul: he was rumored to have accepted Julian's offer to join him in the spring. I could not face that.

I told Julian I had all the money I needed. He then gave me his personal medallion, or *tessura*, which allowed me to travel free of charge anywhere in the West. We made a most warm farewell. He seemed perfectly certain of his own victory, although in the memoir he betrays an anxiety which one would never have suspected from his behavior, proving that our Julian had at last grown up. For once he kept his own counsel.

Julian and Oribasius saw me off in the afternoon carriage which left from the palace door for Vienne. As I got into the wagon with its usual complement of bishops and secret agents, Julian whispered in my ear, "We shall meet in Constantinople." That was the last I saw of him until we did indeed meet in Constantinople, to my surprise. I thought he would be dead before the autumn.

*Julian Augustus*

I should here sum up what I did in Gaul during the four years I was actively Caesar. Three times I crossed the Rhine. One thousand persons who were held as captives on the farther bank I took back. In two battles and one siege I captured ten thousand prisoners, men in the prime of life. During those years, I sent Constantius four levies of excellent infantry, three more of infantry (not so good), and two very distinguished squadrons of cavalry. I recovered every place held or besieged by the barbarians, some fifty towns.

After strengthening our defenses as far as Augst, I proceeded late in the summer to Vienne by way of Besançon. All told, I spent three months in the field that summer.

I had hoped to find Maximus at Besançon. There was a rumor that he was there, waiting for me. But though I had the agents look everywhere, he was not to be found. I did have a curious experience in Besançon while strolling about the city, quite alone, enjoying the sights. There is a fine view from the citadel, which is situated on a high rock. The place is well protected, not only by its eminence but by the River Doubs which circles it like a moat.

Besançon is a small town now, but it was once an important city and there are many abandoned temples, relics of a better time.

Standing in front of the ruined temple of Zeus, I saw a man dressed as a Cynic. I was so positive that it was Maximus that I came up behind him—as boys do, I'm afraid—and clapped him on the shoulder to startle him. I succeeded. He turned about and to my embarrassment it was not Maximus at all but a fellow I had once met at Prohaeresius's house. Both of us blushed and stammered. Then he saluted me, and said, "How great is Caesar to remember the friend of his youth, a humble philosopher, a mere seeker of truth . . ."

"Welcome to Gaul," I said, not letting on I had mistaken him for another. "You must dine with me." And thus I attached to my court for several months one of the most extraordinary bores I have ever known. Oribasius teases me about it to this day. But I never had the heart to dismiss the man, so he sat with us night after night, ruining all conversation. Why do I find it difficult simply to say, "No!" Why am I so timid? I envy the tyrants. Also, why do I tell this story when it is my purpose to describe only crucial events? Because I am reluctant to describe the state of my own mind that winter at Vienne when, like Julius Caesar before me, I decided to cross the Alps. I have always said that I acted in self-defense, that I did not want to usurp the throne, that I wanted only to be recognized by Constantius as legitimate Augustus in the West. Yet I must say I find it impossible to describe what I really felt. Only historians can ever be certain of one's motives! Nevertheless, I do mean to record the truth, no matter how painful or in what a bad light it puts me.

I entered Vienne about the first of October. I moved into the praetorian prefect's palace. I now had a personal retinue of nearly a thousand men and women, slaves and soldiers. Heaven knows how these households expand, but they do, and they are ruinously expensive even for emperors . . . even? *especially* for emperors! I installed Nebridius, the new praetorian prefect, in my old villa by the wall. He was a good enough fellow who wisely kept to himself.

At this time I made an important decision. In all public places it is the law that the image of the Emperor, either painted or in the round, be displayed. Oaths are sworn to it. No legal decision is binding unless made in the sight of his image. And so the ubiquitous face of Constantius, with its soulful eyes and pinched mouth, looked down on every official in the West, including me.

241

My first day in Vienne, I ordered that my own portrait, *as Augustus*, be placed beside his. Now the two of us stared, side by side, at litigants and lawyers. I am told that we were known as "man and wife," since I looked the man with a beard and he, with his jewelry and smooth face, seemed the woman.

I was bombarded all through the summer with letters from Constantius. Why had I detained Lupicinus? Why had I stolen grain belonging to the prefecture of Italy? Where were the troops I had promised? The horses? Why did I style myself Augustus? I was ordered to report immediately to Constantius at Antioch. He even prescribed the household I might bring with me: no more than a hundred soldiers, five eunuchs . . . he delighted in making lists. Yet to every denunciatory letter I made soft answer, always signing myself "Caesar."

While I was assembling the army of Gaul, Constantius was having his difficulties with Arsaces, that most unreliable king of Armenia, who was suspected of dealing with the Persians on the sly. I have since read the secret transcript of the meeting between Arsaces and Constantius. It was shocking. Arsaces got everything he asked for in exchange for remaining as he ought to be in the first place: loyal to us who support not only his throne but his country's independence. Constantius was hopeless at negotiations. To seal this "reunion" (there is no word to describe holding an ally to a course to which honor and treaty have already committed him), Constantius gave Arsaces as wife the daughter of the old praetorian prefect Ablabius. Her name is Olympia, and she was once supposed to marry Constantius, which made her the nearest thing he had to an unmarried female relation. She is now queen of Armenia, a devout Galilean and hostile to me.

During this exchange between the Emperor and the Armenian, there was much talk of me. It is a strange experience to read literal transcripts of conversations in which one is discussed like a character in an epic.

Arsaces brought up the subject: would Julian march against the Emperor? Constantius thought it unlikely. If I did, at a signal from him, the German tribes would attack me on the Rhine. Then, should I survive them, Scythians would bar my way to the East, not to mention the loyal armies of Italy and Illyricum.

Arsaces wanted to know if it was true that Julian's victories in Gaul surpassed those of Julius Caesar. Constantius responded angrily: "All that was done in Gaul was done by my generals,

acting on the orders of my praetorian prefect, who obeys me."
Constantius then went on to declare that he himself had achieved
every victory, despite my hopeless muddling. In fact, I was so
incompetent that Constantius was himself forced to take personal
command of the army in order to win the famous victory of Strasbourg!

I must say I trembled with rage when I read those lines. Yes,
I am vain. There is nothing to be done about it. I want credit. I
want honor. I want fame. But I want only what is mine. I was
amazed at Constantius's boldness. How could he lie with such
recklessness? Arsaces must have known that Constantius was on
the Danube becoming Sarmaticus Sarmaticus, while I was freeing
Gaul. I rather suspect that Arsaces *did* know the Emperor was
lying, for in the transcript he swiftly changed the subject.

I was particularly struck by one passage about myself (how
hungrily we read about ourselves!). Constantius said that I had no
gift for soldiering: I was a pedant who should have been left at
the University of Athens. Arsaces remarked that the pedant seemed
to have made a remarkable court of fellow pedants for himself at
Paris. He even named them. Constantius said that he approved of
the company I kept for schoolteachers would keep me so occupied
with books and idle dispute that I would not have time to ponder
treason. He offered to show Arsaces the "cringing" letter in which
I declared my loyalty to him, while rejecting the title "Augustus."
Arsaces said that he would indeed like copies, and they were
prepared. I wonder if Constantius showed him *all* the correspondence? I will blush when I think of that Armenian reading my
highly politic and conciliatory (but hardly "cringing") letters.

Then Arsaces said, "I mention the men at Julian's court because
there is a rumor that they are all of them atheists." Surprisingly,
Constantius seemed not at all interested in this. He merely remarked
that schoolteachers tend to be unreliable, dirty, greedy, impious,
beard-wearing . . . all of them Cynics, he said largely. But Arsaces
was obviously concerned; he hoped that Julian was a true Galilean
Constantius said that he was certain I was but that it made little
difference, since after the Persian campaign I would cease to exist.
They then talked of other matters.

Constantius next proceeded south to Melitena, Locatena and
Samarath. He crossed the Euphrates and made for Edessa, a large
city of Mesopotamia, sixty miles west of the ruins of Amida, now
Sapor's by right of conquest. Daily Constantius's army grew larger

243

and larger, but he did nothing with it. Finally, as autumn began, he marched to Amida. In sight of the troops, he wept; not a particularly helpful gesture in a war. That was the same day that Ursulus, the Count of the Sacred Largesse, made his much-quoted remark, "See how bravely our citizens are protected by those soldiers, whose pay is bankrupting us!" This sardonic remark later cost him his life. One sympathizes with treasurers, but one must honor soldiers, especially those who fought at Amida against impossible odds.

From Amida, Constantius crept some thirty miles southeast to Bezabde, a Persian town on the Tigris. He laid siege to the town, but because of the ardor of the Persians and his own incompetence, Bezabde withstood every sort of assault. Then came the rainy season. Those who were there have since told me that the thunder and lightning was appalling. Our men were demoralized by what they took to be heaven's anger—and perhaps it was, directed at Constantius. Also, there were innumerable rainbows, which means that the goddess Iris has been sent down from heaven to effect some important change in human affairs. Constantius abandoned the siege and withdrew to Antioch for the winter.

Meanwhile, I was getting my own affairs in order at Vienne. I sent for various wise men and prophets, including the Hierophant of Greece. I consulted oracles and sacred books; I made sacrifices to the gods . . . in secret, of course, for Vienne is a city dominated by Galileans. All signs agreed that I would prevail and that Constantius would fall. Yet I did not neglect the practical. Every prophecy is always open to interpretation and if it turnes out that its meaning was other than what one thought, it is not the fault of the gods but of us who have misinterpreted their signs. Cicero has written well on this. I particularly credit dreams, agreeing with Aristotle that important messages from heaven are often sent to men as they sleep, though to dream meaningfully it is necessary for the eyes beneath the lids to be turned neither to left nor right but set straight ahead, often difficult to arrange.

At the end of October, during consistory, Oribasius sent me a message. I must go straight to my wife. She was dying.

Eyes shut, Helena lay on her bed. She was emaciated except for her stomach, which was grotesquely large beneath the coverlet. Oribasius was at her side while the bishops of Vienne and Paris chanted and prayed. I took Helena's hand, now cool, soon cold. It is a grisly miracle when the soul leaves the body, taunting us

244

with the unimportance of that flesh which in life so entirely enslaves us, since it *is* us, or seems to be.

"Julian." She spoke in an ordinary voice.

I found I could say nothing, only murmur sounds of compassion. Yet I suffered with her even though I hardly knew her. We were royal animals, yoked by the same master to pull a golden carriage. Now one animal had fallen between the traces.

"They tell me I am dying." Before I could give ritual comfort, she said, "I don't mind. I'm not afraid. Only do remember that the new wing on the east has only a temporary roof. There wasn't time to have the right sort of tiles made. You know the ones I mean. They are called, I think, Patrician tiles. Anyway, the steward knows what to buy. The temporary ones will have to be replaced *before* the spring rains. I have had estimates made of the cost. It will be expensive, but we can take it out of my private account in Rome. The new mosaic work could be spoiled should there be a great deal of rain, which there is apt to be this time of year in Rome." With those words, Helena died, thinking of her beloved villa in the Via Nomentana.

The bishops looked at me furiously as though I had in some way spoiled their fun. Then they set to praying, very loud. I left the room. In the outer hall I found Helena's women.

"The Queen is dead." I felt nothing. They began to wail.

"Prepare her," I said sternly, "and save your tears."

They went inside the bedroom. Oribasius put his hand on my shoulder. I looked about me at all the things Helena had owned, worn, touched.

"I don't know," I said at last, with true wonder, "*what* I feel."

"You should feel relief. She suffered. Now it's over."

I nodded. "We are toys, and a divine child takes us up and puts us down, and breaks us when he chooses."

So my marriage ended. Helena's body was sent to Rome and she is buried in the same mausoleum as her sister Constantia and our son. I also remembered to give orders to replace the tiles in the villa. Helena was forty-two when she died. I was twenty-eight. The day after her death I took the vow of celibacy, as an offering to Cybele for her continued favor.

# XV

On 6 November 360, I celebrated my fifth year as Caesar, my "quinquennial," as the Romans call it.

I thought it wise to make a great event of this occasion. It is well known that I detest what goes on in hippodromes, whether games, fighting or the slaughter of animals. But there are certain things one must do in a high place and the giving of games is one of the most important. If the games are a success, one enjoys popularity with the mob. If not, not. It's as simple as that. Though I have many times cursed those consuls of the old Republic who started this boring and costly business, I always do what is expected of me as well as I can with the means at hand.

I am told that the games at Vienne were a success. I cannot judge. I attended them as little as possible. But when I did appear, it was as Augustus. I wore a heavy gold crown which I am now quite used to, justifying it to myself as a symbol of the sun, which is God. I looked quite imperial that year. Even Oribasius was satisfied; he could never endure the old purple fillet I usually wore in public. "You look like a gymnasium director," he would complain.

Constantius and I exchanged polite letters on the death of Helena. Then in December I received the announcement that Constantius had married a lady of Antioch called Faustina. I sent him congratulations. Meanwhile, each of us prepared for civil war.

A number of significant things happened in December. One afternoon while I was practicing with shield and sword (I do this nearly every day, because I came late to soldiering and must work harder than most to toughen muscles and learn the subtleties of combat), my shield broke loose from both the handle and the strap, and fell to the ground with a crash in full view of the Petulantes with whom I took exercise. Before anyone could interpret this as an ill omen, I said loudly, "Look!" And I held up the handle which I still clutched. "I have what I was holding!" This was taken to mean that I would hold Gaul, no matter what happened. But I was puzzled until that night when I dreamt that I saw again the guardian deity of Rome. He came to my bedside, and he spoke very plainly, in verse:

> When Zeus the noble Aquarius shall reach
> And Saturn come to Virgo's twenty-fifth degree,
> Then shall Constantius, K. of Asia, of this life so sweet,
> The end attain with heaviness and grief.

This was as clear a statement as one could hope for from the gods. The next morning I told Oribasius, and he in turn called in Mastara, the best of the Etruscan astrologers. He cast Constantius's horoscope and found that the Emperor would indeed be dead within a few months. He even set the date as some time in June 361. But in spite of this celestial assurance, I took no chances. I continued to prepare for war.

I liked the praetorian prefect, Nebridius, though he did not like me, for the very reason I liked him: he was faithful to his master and I honored him for that. Yet despite his loyalty to Constantius, he did not conspire against me. Because of this, I allowed him to carry out the ceremonial functions of praetorian prefect, though nothing more. Yet despite our cordial relations, he was always on the lookout for ways to trap me. He devised an excellent embarrassment.

On 6 January, the Galileans celebrate something called the feast of the Epiphany. It is the day the Galilean is supposed to have been baptized. Suspecting my dislike of the Galileans, Nebridius announced to the city that I would attend the feast of the Epiphany at the Vienne charnel house, a brand-new basilica paid for by Helena's numerous gifts to the bishops. I was furious but dared not show it. I am sorry to say Oribasius was amused at my predicament.

Grimly, I did what I had to do. I spent two hours meditating on the thighbone of some villain who had been eaten by lions at Rome, while the bishop delivered a considerable sermon at me, praying that I would throw the weight of my majesty against the enemy Arians. He even turned political by suggesting that as Constantius was Arian and I *possibly* Athanasian, the line might then be drawn between us in all things, and the side of "truth" (also the side of the majority, he added pointedly) would prevail, supporting my throne like columns, I believe was his metaphor, or it may have been holy caryatids. When it came time to pray,

247

my words were addressed to the Galilean but my heart spoke to Zeus.

The winter was a time of waiting. I was now ready to march. All that I needed was a sign from heaven. Though the prefect at Rome would not allow my emissaries to consult the Sibylline books, a friendly priest of the old order was able to look at a part of that book which describes our period. According to his secret report, I would indeed be the next emperor. My reign would be stormy but long. That is all I ask for: time. Time to make an old world young again, to make winter spring, to free the One God from the triple monster of the atheists. Give me twenty years, O, Helios, and I will fill the earth with praise for your light, and illuminate the dark windings of Hades' kingdom! Even as Persephone returned to Demeter, so shall our time's living-dead return to your arms, which are light, which is life, which is all!

In April I learned that the German tribe of King Vadomar had crossed the Rhine and was devastating the area near Raetia. This was particularly puzzling news because two years before we had negotiated a "final" peace with Vadomar. He had no grievance against us. He was a cultivated man, educated at Milan. He was by nature cautious. To any show of force he always responded with a thousand apologies and a quick withdrawal to his own side of the river. That Vadomar was now actively in the field against me could mean only one thing. He was acting on Constantius's orders.

I sent Vadomar one of my counts, a man called Libino. He was a good soldier and negotiator, or so I thought. I sent him with half a legion and orders to reason with Vadomar. Should reason fail, threats of extinction were in order. Libino got as far as Sechingen on the Rhine. There the Germans surrounded him. Unfortunately, Libino was eager for battle, even though his mission was only to negotiate. Like a fool, he ordered his men to attack. Five minutes later, Libino himself was hacked in two by a German sword, and his men, outnumbered five to one, were massacred.

I then dispatched the Petulantes to the Rhine only to find that the savages had faded into their forests, as mysteriously as they had appeared. For the moment all was peaceful on the Rhine. Now ordinarily I would have taken this for what it seemed to be: a single raid by restless tribesmen, conducted without the knowledge of Vadomar, who all the while was writing me long and eloquent letters, offering to punish his own people, *if* of course the guilty ones were his. He even sent a gift of money to the family of the dead Libino.

I did not believe Vadomar, but I was willing to forget the matter until one of the border guards intercepted a German messenger bound for the East. The messenger was found to be carrying a letter from Vadomar to Constantius. I quote from it: "Your will is being done, Lord, and your Caesar who lacks discipline will be chastened." That was all I needed. I promptly sent one of my notaries, a clever chap named Philogius, to join the Petulantes who were still at Sechingen, close to the country of Vadomar.

*Libanius*: I feel compelled to note that this same "clever chap named Philogius" has just been appointed Count of the East by Theodosius. He is a dedicated Christian and no one knows how we shall fare under his rule. If only Julian had sent *him* instead of the long-forgotten Libino to that fatal rendezvous on the Rhine! But then, were it not he, fate would no doubt find us a worse Philogius. The Count arrived in Antioch early this month. I saw him for the first time yesterday in the senate. He moved amongst us like a swan who has found himself in a particularly small and distasteful pond. Do I dare mention Julian to him?

*Julian Augustus*

I gave Philogius sealed instructions. If he encountered Vadomar on *our* side of the Rhine, he was to open the letter and do as he was told. Otherwise, the letter was to be destroyed. I was fairly certain that he would see Vadomar, who often traveled in our territory, visiting Roman friends. Like so many German nobles, he was in some ways more Roman than the Romans.

Philogius met Vadomar at a reception given by a local contractor. Philogius invited the king to dinner the next day at the officers' mess of the Petulantes. Vadomar said that he would be delighted to dine with such distinguished men. When he arrived for dinner, Philogius excused himself, saying that he had forgotten to give certain instructions to the cook. He then read my letter. In it I commanded him to arrest Vadomar for high treason. Philogius did so, to the astonishment of his guest.

A week later, Vadomar was brought to me at Vienne. I received him alone in my study. He is a handsome, blue-eyed man, with a face red from hard drink and cold winters. But his manners are

249

as polished as any Roman courtier's. He speaks excellent Greek. He was very frightened.

"You have made a bad choice, King," I said.

He stammered: he did not know what I meant. I gave him the letter we had intercepted. The red face became blotchy.

"I did as I was told, Augustus . . ."

"In the letter you call me Caesar."

"No, no, Augustus. That is, I *had* to when I wrote to him. He'd ordered me to attack you. What could I do?"

"You might have honored your treaty with me. Or you might have made a better choice, as I suggested originally. You might have chosen me instead of Constantius as your master."

"But I do, great Lord. I do *now*! I always have. Only . . ."

"Don't!" I stopped him with a gesture. I take no pleasure in seeing another man grovel before me. "Actually, you—and your correspondence—have been very useful to me." I took the letter back from him. "I now have proof that not only does Constantius mean to destroy me, he incites the barbarians against his own people. Now I know what to do, and how to do it."

"But what will you do, Augustus?" Vadomar was momentarily distracted from his own fate.

"Do? I shall exile you to Spain." He fell on his face in gratitude, and it was with difficulty that I extricated myself from his embrace, and turned him over to the guards.

I sent for Oribasius. I have never been so elated in my life. "We're ready!" I shouted when he joined me. "Everything is ready!" I don't recall now what else I said. I suppose I "babbled," as Priscus calls my talk during seizures of enthusiasm. I do remember that Oribasius, always the most conservative of advisers, agreed entirely with me. It was now or never. There remained only one possible obstacle, the mood of the legions. Some were still adamant about leaving Gaul.

Together we studied the military roster. Those units prone to mutiny we sent as permanent garrisons to the farther cities of Gaul. The remainder would assemble at full strength on 25 June, when it would be my task to rouse them for the war against Constantius. Never was an orator given greater challenge. I rehearsed my speech every day for three weeks. Oribasius coached me until he too knew every word by heart.

At dawn on the 25th, Oribasius and I met with several officers of like mind in a small chapel off the council chamber. There I

250

made special offering to Bellona, goddess of battles. The omens were propitious. Then, nervous at the thought of the speech ahead, I went forth in full regalia to review the legions who were gathered in a field outside the city, just beyond the gate through which I had arrived in Vienne five years before, a green boy with a handful of troops who knew only how to pray. I thought of this as I made my way to the stone tribunal, my neck rigid beneath its burden of gold.

I do not have a copy of this speech with me. In fact, my chief secretary seems to have packed none of my personal files though I *especially* asked that they be brought with us, knowing that I would be composing this memoir in Persia. Nevertheless, I recall most of what I said, even down to the gestures which I find myself reproducing as I repeat the words I said two years ago. I will not weary the reader with a catalogue of gestures, nor every word of the peroration. I will only say that I was at my best.

First, I addressed the army as "Noble soldiers." This is an unusual way to style an army, and it caused much comment. Yet I wanted to emphasize to them their importance to me and my respect for them. I spoke of all that we had done together against the Germans and the Franks. "But now that I am Augustus, I shall, with your support and that of the Deity—should fortune honor us—aim at greater things. To forestall those in the East who wish us ill, I propose that while the garrisons of Illyricum are still small, we take possession of all Dacia and then decide what more must be done. In support of this plan, I want, under oath, your promise of a lasting and faithful accord. For my part, I will do all that I can to avoid both weakness and timidity. I also swear that I will undertake nothing that does not contribute to us all. I only beg you: do nothing to hurt private citizens, for we are known to the world not only as the victors of the Rhine but as men whose right conduct in victory had made half a world prosperous and free."

There was more in this vein. At the end, by various cries and loud oaths, they swore that they would follow me to the end of the earth, something of an exaggeration since their immediate interest was the spoils to be got as the result of what they knew would be an easy campaign in Dacia.

When I asked them to swear the oath of allegiance to me as Augustus, they did so, swords to their throats. Then I turned to the officers and officials gathered about the stone tribunal:

"Will you, too, swear allegiance to me, in God's name?" I

251

asked according to ritual. All swore, except Nebridius. There was a menacing growl from the troops.

"You will not swear allegiance to me, Prefect?"

"No, Caesar. I have already sworn an oath to uphold the Emperor. Since he still lives, I cannot swear again without jeopardizing my soul." His voice trembled, but not his will.

Only I heard his whole speech, for on the word "Caesar" the men roared their anger. Swords were drawn. A legionnaire grabbed Nebridius by the neck and was about to throw him in the dust when I quickly stepped down from the tribunal and put myself between the soldier and the prefect. Nebridius, pale as death, clung to my knees. I removed my cloak and threw it over him: the ancient gesture which means a man has the protection of the emperor. Then I shouted to the legions. "He will suffer quite enough when we are masters of Rome!" This bit of demagoguery distracted the men, and I ordered Nebridius taken under guard to the palace.

I then reviewed the troops. It was a fine sight, and all the doubts which had tormented me in the night were dispelled by the blue-green summer day and the sight of twenty thousand men marching in rhythmic unison to the Pyrrhic measure. It is at such moments that one realizes war is an essential aspect of deity, and that the communion of an army is a mystery in its way quite as beautiful as that of Eleusis. For a moment all hearts beat to the same music. We were one and there was nothing on earth we could not do!

When I returned to the palace, I sent for the stubborn Nebridius. I exiled him to Tuscany. He had expected death. With tears in his eyes he said, "Caesar, give me your hand. Let me . . . in gratitude . . ." But I pulled back.

"There would be no honor nor sign of affection for me to give to my friends, if I gave *you* my hand." That was the end of Nebridius in Gaul.


On 3 July I took the field against Constantius. The omens were excellent and the weather fair.

We moved east to Augst, where I called a staff meeting. As usual, I had kept my plans to myself; not even Oribasius knew what I intended, though we rode together, ate together and chattered like schoolboys.

With me as commanders were Nevitta—the great Frank whom I come to admire more and more as I know him; Jovinus, a competent officer; Gomoarius, a man I did not trust, for he was the one who betrayed his commander Vetranio when he rebelled against Constantius; Mamertinus, a good secretary; Dagalaif, perhaps the best commander of cavalry in the history of the Roman army. I began with the announcement that Sallust was now on his way to Vienne to act as praetorian prefect; he would govern in my place. This was well received. Sallust is admired not only by me but by all men.

"I now have certain appointments to make." I did not have to consult the sheet of paper before me. I got the disagreeable task over with first. "Gomoarius, I remove you as commander of cavalry. That post goes to Nevitta." There was silence. Gomoarius said nothing. All knew my motive. We are a small family, the military, despite the size of the empire. We all know one another's faults and virtues. "Jovinus, I make you quaestor; Mamertinus, treasurer; Dagalaif, commander of the household troops."

Then I went over the map on the folding table. "We are outnumbered ten to one by the combined armies of Illyricum and Italy. Fortunately, those armies are not combined. They consist mostly of garrison troops, while ours is an aggressive army, used to swift attack. Now, what is our best course of action?" I paused. They took my question for the rhetoric it was. "When in doubt, imitate Alexander. Whenever his army was seriously outnumbered, he would disperse his troops in such a way as to give the impression that he had far more men than anyone knew. Therefore I mean to split the army in three sections. We shall seem to be attacking from every direction.

"Jovinus will take the direct route to Italy." I pointed to the map. "You will notice I have marked the main roads for you. Spread out along them. I want everyone to see you. Nevitta, you take the middle course, due east through Raetia. I shall take the remainder of the army and go north through the Black Forest to the Danube. Then east and south along the Danube, straight to Sirmium. Whoever holds Sirmium controls Illyricum and the approach to Constantinople." I turned to Nevitta. "You and I will rendezvous at Sirmium, no later than October."

None objected to my plan. Incidentally, for those who may get the impression from history that divine emperors are never contradicted by those who serve them, I should note that such is not the case in the field. Though the emperor's word is final, any commander is free to argue with him as much as he likes until the war plan is actually set in motion. Personally, I have always encouraged debate. Often as not it deteriorates into quibbling, but occasionally one's strategy is improved. This time, however, there was little discussion, only the usual arguments as to who got what legion. The next day the army was divided, and the conquest of the West began.

The Black Forest is a strange and ominous place. Seeing it from within made me understand the Germans better. "The place is haunted; perverse demons lurk in every shadow . . . and what shadows! Even at noon, the forest is so dim that it is like being drowned in a deep green whispering sea. As we rode over quiet trails, the legions, two abreast, wound like some slow sea serpent on the ocean floor. Fortunately, we had reliable guides who knew every twist and turn of the forest. I cannot think how, for there were no markers of any kind; yet they knew their way through the green maze. For days on end we never saw the sun, until I despaired of ever seeing my god again.


By the middle of August we were in the wild but beautiful valley of the Danube. Though the river is not as impressive to look at as the Rhine, it is far less treacherous to navigate. So I decided to make the rest of the journey by water.

At a village on the south bank, we halted and I ordered boats built. While this was being done, I received the fealty of the local tribes. They were amazed to see a Roman emperor (even a not quite legitimate one!) so far north. When they discovered that I meant them no harm, they were most cooperative and offered to act as river pilots. They are a handsome, fair-skinned people, somewhat shy.

Meanwhile, messengers from Jovinus arrived, with good news. Milan had fallen. He also wrote me the latest news of Constantius. Sapor had advanced to the Tigris. Constantius had then withdrawn to Edessa, where he was now holed up, avoiding battle. I was amused to note that he had appointed Florentius praetorian prefect of Illyricum. I was obviously poor Florentius's nemesis. I had sent him out of Gaul; soon I would drive him from Illyricum. I believe of all those who hate me, he must hate me the most. He certainly has the best reason!

We sailed down the Danube through a golden country, rich with harvest. We paused at none of the towns or fortresses which became more numerous the farther south we went. There was no time to waste. If I took Sirmium, all these towns would be mine by right, but if I paused to lay siege to each I should never be done fighting. Most of the natives were well disposed toward us; but then none was put to the test.

In early October, at night, with the moon waning, we reached Bonmunster, nineteen miles north of Sirmium. It is a small town, with no garrison. Late as it was, I ordered all men ashore. We pitched camp on the bank of the river.

I do not know if it is common to all in my place, but it was my experience as a usurper (and one must call me by that blunt name) that everywhere I went well-wishers and informers flocked to me like bees to honey, until I was forced to devise a screening process to examine each would-be ally and determine if he could be used. Most proved to be sincere; but then I proved to be victorious!

Before the moon had set, I had learned that Count Lucillianus was at Sirmium, with a considerable army and orders to destroy me. However, Lucillianus did not expect me in the vicinity for another week, and so he slept now at Sirmium.


As soon as I had heard these reports, I sent for Dagalaif. I ordered him to go straight to Sirmium with a hundred men; he was to seize Lucillianus and bring him back. This was a considerable assignment, but I knew from spies that the city was no more than usually guarded and that the palace where Lucillianus was staying was close to the gate. At night our men would look no different from any other imperial troops; there would be no problem entering the city. For the rest, I counted on Dagalaif's boldness and ingenuity.

After Dagalaif had left, Oribasius and I strolled together on the river bank. It was a warm night. In the black sky a misshapen moon, like a worn marble head, made all the country silver. Behind us the fires and torches of the camp burned. The men were quiet; they had orders to make no unnecessary noise; only the horses occasionally disobeyed me, with sharp sudden whinnies. At the top of the river bank we stopped.

"I like this," I said, turning to Oribasius, who was seated now on a rock, staring at the bright diagonal the moonlight made across the slow deep water.

Oribasius looked up at me. The moon was so bright that I could make out his features. "This?" He frowned. "Do you mean the river? or war? or travel?"

"Life." I sat on the damp ground beside him and crossed my legs, muddying the purple I wore. "Not war. Nor travel. Just this. Right now." I sighed. "I can hardly believe we have crossed nearly half the world. I feel like the wind, without a body, invisible."

He laughed. "You are probably the most visible man on earth, and the most feared."

"Feared," I repeated, wondering if I would ever take satisfaction from the knowledge that men's lives and fortunes could be taken away from them at a nod of my head. No, I cannot enjoy that sort of power; it is not what I want.

"What *do* you want?" Oribasius had divined my mood, as he so often does.

"To restore the gods."

"But if they are real and do exist . . ."

"They are real! There is no 'if'! They do exist!" I was fierce.

His laughter stopped me. "Then they exist. But if they exist, they are always present, and so there's no need to 'restore' them."

"But we must worship what God tells us to."

"So the Christians say."

"Ah, but theirs is a false god, and I mean to destroy them."

Oribasius stiffened at the word "destroy." "*Kill* them?"

"No. I shall not allow them the pleasure of martyrdom. Besides, at the rate they kill one another, it would be gratuitous for me to intervene. No, I shall fight them with reason and example. I shall reopen the temples and reorganize the priesthood. We shall put Hellenism on such a footing that people will choose it of their own free will."

"I wonder." Oribasius was thoughtful. "They are rich, well-organized. Most important, they educate the children."

"We shall do the same!" I was thinking as I spoke; I had no plan. "Even better, we could take the schools away from them."

"If you could . . ."

"The Emperor can."

"It might work. Otherwise . . ."

"Otherwise?"

"You would have to reign as a bloody tyrant and even then you'd lose."

"I am not so pessimistic." But Oribasius had put an idea into my head, one which will save us all. Curiously enough, though we had often spoken of what it would be like when I became emperor, none of us had ever really considered in much detail what form the contest between Hellenism and the Galileans would take. We agreed that when I could I would publicly repudiate the Nazarene, but none of us had thought what the reaction might be, particularly from the common people of whom perhaps half are Galilean. Only the army is truly religious. The men worship Mithras. There are few Galileans in the ranks, though a third of the officers believe in the triple monster.

We talked until it was morning. Just as the sun appeared over the world's edge, like an omen, Dagalaif returned to camp with Count Lucillianus as prisoner.

I hurried to my tent. There on the ground in his nightclothes was Lucillianus, trussed like a chicken. He was terrified. For a moment I looked down on the shivering body, recalling that the last time I had seen him he had been my brother's jailer. Then I loosened his bonds and raised him to his feet. This friendly gesture somewhat relieved his anxiety. He is a large man, given to peculiar diets. For years he would eat only udder of sow; at least that is the story one hears.

"We are happy you could attend us on such short notice, Count." I was formal but agreeable.

"If only I had known, Caesar . . . I mean Augustus . . . I should have met you myself . . ."

"And put me to death, like Gallus?"

"Those were my orders, Augustus, but you may depend on my loyalty to you in this dispute. I have always been loyal. I have always preferred you to the Emp—to *him* at Antioch."

"We accept your loyalty, your troops, your city of Sirmium, and the prefecture of Illyricum."

He gasped but bowed. "Such is the will of Augustus. All these are yours."

"Thank you, Count." I was in an excellent mood. Lucillianus is the sort of man who does not think ahead—witness his failure to anticipate my arrival—and men who do not think ahead tend to accept what is; they never conspire.

I said, "Now swear your oath to me." He swore; and kissed

257

the purple, getting a bit of Danube mud on his face. "You will retain your rank, Count, and serve in my army."

Lucillianus's recovery was swift. "If I may say so, Lord, it is a very rash thing you have done, coming here with such a small army in the midst of someone else's territory."

"Reserve, my dear Count, your wisdom for Constantius. I have given you my hand not to make you my counsellor but less afraid." I turned to Mamertinus. "Give the word to the army. We march to Sirmium."

Sirmium is a large city, hightly suitable for an imperial capital, standing as it does upon the border between the prefecture of Illyricum and the diocese of Dacia—the westernmost country of the prefecture of the East. I was now at the beginning of the territory traditionally assigned to the Augustus of the East.

I had warned my officers that there might be incidents. I did not expect the city to surrender without token resistance, even though its commander was now with us, riding at my side.

But to my astonishment, we were met outside the gates by a vast crowd of men, women and children, carrying chains of flowers, boughs of trees and numerous sacred objects. I was hailed as Augustus with the most extraordinary enthusiasm.

I turned to Lucillianus and shouted to him above the din, "Did you arrange this?"

He shook his head. He was too stupid to lie. "No, Augustus. I don't know who arranged it . . ."

"Legend!" said Oribasius. "They know you'll win. They always do."

A large bouquet of flowers hit me in the face. Eyes stinging, I swept it aside; a blood-red poppy caught in my beard. Men and women kissed my robe, my legs, my horse. Thus was I escorted into the capital of Illyricum while the grapes were still green. It was the first great city ever to fall to me, twice the size of Strasbourg or Cologne or even Treves. The date was 3 October, 361.

I went straight to the palace, and to business. I received the senate of the city. I allayed their fears. They swore loyalty to me, as did the legions within the city. I ordered a week of chariot races next day to amuse the populace, one of the burdens the conquered invariably put upon the conqueror. With great pleasure, I received Nevitta who, true to his promise, arrived at Sirmium after a victorious passage through Raetia. The West was ours.

I called a staff meeting, and we discussed our next move. Some

258

favored marching straight to Constantinople, two hundred miles distant. Dagalaif argued that with Constantius in Antioch, Constantinople would fall to us without a battle. Nevitta was not so certain. He was afraid that Constantius was probably already on the march from Antioch to the capital. If this were so, we were hardly a match for what was, in fact, the largest army on earth. I agreed with Nevitta. We would remain where we were for the winter.

I entrusted to Nevitta the defense of the Succi Pass, a narrow defile in the high mountains that separate Thrace from Illyricum. Whoever holds this pass is safe from attack by land. I then sent two of the Sirmium legions to Aquileia, to hold that important seaport for us. With the main part of the army I withdrew some fifty miles southeast to Nish (where Constantine was born); here I went into winter quarters.

The weeks at Nish were busy ones. Every night I dictated until dawn. I was determined to present my case against Constantius as clearly as possible for all to read and comprehend. I sent a lengthy message to the Roman senate. I also composed separate letters for the senates of Sparta, Corinth and Athens, explaining what I had done and what I intended to do. Heavily but justly, I placed the blame for all that had happened on Constantius. Then— though Oribasius warned me not to—I assured the various senates that I intended to restore the worship of the old gods, making the point that I personally imitated them in order that, by having the fewest possible needs, I might do good to the greatest possible number. These letters were read at every public gathering. They made a profound and favorable impression.

During this period I planned an amphibious attack on Constantinople to take place as soon as the winds favored us. We were in a good position militarily. At Succi we controlled the land approach to the West. At Aquileia we controlled the sea approach to northern Italy. I felt reasonably secure, and was confident that before civil war broke out, Constantius would come to terms with me. But my sense of security was rudely shattered when I learned that the two legions I had sent to Aquileia had promptly gone over to Constantius. The port was now his; and I was vulnerable to an attack by sea. Since I was not able to leave Nish and Nevitta could not leave Succi, my only hope was Jovinus, who was in Austria en route to Nish. I sent him a frantic message: proceed immediately to Aquileia. My situation was now most precarious. Constantius

259

could at any time land an army at Aquileia and cut me off from Italy and Gaul. I was in despair, confident that the gods had deserted me. But they had not. At the last moment, they intervened.

On the night of 20 November I was working late. Lamps filled with cheap oil smoked abominably. The three night secretaries sat at a long table, mountains of parchment stacked in front of them. At a separate table I was writing a letter to my uncle Julian, trying to reassure him—and myself—that victory was certain. I had just finished the letter, with one of those postscripts even old friends say they cannot decipher, when I heard footsteps quickly approaching. Without ceremony the door flew open. The clerks and I leapt to our feet. One never knows if assassins are at hand. But it was Oribasius, out of breath, a letter in his hand.

"It's happened!" he gasped. Then he did something he had never done before. He dropped on his knees before me, offered me the letter. "This is for you . . . Augustus."

I read the first line. Then the words blurred together and I could read no more. "Constantius is dead." As I said those extraordinary words, the clerks one by one fell to their knees. Then, as in a dream, the room began to fill with people. All knew what had happened. All paid me silent homage for I had, miraculously, with the stopping of one man's breath, become sole Augustus, Emperor of Rome, Lord of the world. To my astonishment, I wept.

# *Augustus*

## XVI

*Priscus*: That is the way it happened. At least that is the way Julian *says* it happened. As you must gather, he omits a number of details. To read his account one would think that there had been no resistance at all to him, other than from the wicked Constantius. This was hardly true. I should say that a majority of the "responsible" men in the empire preferred Constantius to Julian, nor was this on religious grounds, since Julian's passion for Hellenism was not generally known as of November 361. I am sure you will want to state matters as they actually were. Your famous balance would be seriously deranged if you were to record that Julian's success was the result of a popular uprising against Constantius. It was not—despite the impression you gave in your justly celebrated oration at the time of Julian's death. But then the great wings of a memorial, like those of a panegyric, are not expected to be clipped by tedious fact.

*Libanius*: How typical!

*Priscus*: Julian notes in passing that he sent various messages to different cities. Indeed he did! He must have composed at least a dozen lengthy harangues, addressed variously to the senates at Rome and Constantinople—a not unnatural precaution—but then an equal number of *apologias* were sent to such cities as Corinth and Sparta, as if they still mattered in the scale of power. Their poor backwoods town councils must have been astonished to receive an emperor's homage.

I was present at the senate in Athens when the message to us was read. Since I know that you want only the truth, I must tell you that the letter was not well received, and of all cities Athens was most inclined to Julian.

I sat beside Prohaeresius while the message was read. The old man was amused, but cautious. So was I. Of course, everyone in Athens was aware that I had only recently come from Julian; even so, I was firm in saying that I knew nothing of his plans. I even praised Constantius on several public occasions. After all, Constantius might have lived. Julian might have been defeated. *I* might have been executed for treason. Like everyone else, I prefer to avoid undue distress at the hands of tyrants.

We were all quite nervous at the beginning of the message. (If you don't have a copy of this address, I will send you mine, free of charge.) Naturally, we were flattered by Julian's references to our ancient past, as well as respectful of his quite skillful mastery of rhetoric, even though he was prone to clichés, especially when he was tired or writing too fast. He could seldom prepare a message without "Xerxes defying nature," or trotting out that damned "oak tree" which no contemporary writer seems able to avoid.

But after a good beginning, Julian then denounced Constantius. He named all the murders. He made a point of Constantius's infertility (not knowing that Constantius's new wife Faustina was pregnant). He denounced the eunuchs, particularly Eusebius. He gave us a considerable autobiography, generally accurate, ending with the statement that he was now in the field because no one could trust the word of Constantius, since it was, he declared (relying again on a familiar phrase), "written in ashes." At this point the senators of Athens began to clear their throats and scruff their sandals on the floor, always a bad sign.

At the end of the message there was no discussion. The senate, wisely, went on to other matters. No one had the courage to behave as the senate at Rome did when they were read their letter, and Tertullus, the city's prefect, shouted, "We demand reverence for Constantius, who raised you up!"

When the senate adjourned, Prohaeresius and I left the chamber together. No one spoke to anyone else. Then—as now—the secret service was ubiquitous. We knew nothing except that Julian was somewhere in the Balkans, that the West *appeared* to be his, and that Constantius was moving against him with a superior army. It was not easy to know how to behave. Our sort is forever courted by usurpers and asked to join in this or that undertaking. Since no one can know the future, it is quite easy to pick the wrong side. The death of Maximus was instructive, wasn't it, old friend?

But of course we are all so used to these sudden changes in government that there is almost an etiquette in how one responds to invitations which could as easily turn out disastrous as advantageous. First, one appears to ponder the request with grave attention; then one pleads a personal problem; finally, one does nothing.

262

That is how you and I have managed to live to be so old in such a stormy time.

I recall vividly my walk with Prohaeresius. It must have been some time in the second week of November. The weather was cold, the wind sharp, the afternoon clouds more thick than usual. Absently, Prohaeresius put his arm through mine. We hurried through the crowd which had gathered outside the senate house. Not till we were past the temple of Hephaestos did he speak. "*You* know him. What will happen?"

"I think he will win."

"How can he? Constantius has the army. The people are with him. They're certainly not with your . . . *our* young student. The senate's mood was perfectly plain."

"I think he will win, that's all." But I was by no means as confident as I sounded.

"The oracles . . ." But the old man stopped. He was not about to give himself away to me. "Come home with me."

I accepted, not yet eager for Hippia's company. My marriage, always unhappy, was at this time unbearable: Hippia was still furious at me for having spent nearly three years in Paris, despite the money I had been able to send her. Today, however, after fifty years of mutual loathing, we are quite dependent on one another. Habit is stronger than hate.

I was surprised to find Macrina at Prohaeresius's house. She had not been much in evidence since the birth of her child (ostensibly sired by the businessman husband). She had gained a little weight, which was attractive.

Macrina greeted us in the inner court. She was ecstatic. "It's happened! He's all right!"

"What has happened? Who is all right?" Prohaeresius was irritable.

"Julian is Emperor!"

That is how we got the news at Athens. Apparently, the formal message to the senate had been delayed. But Julian had written Prohaeresius and me, taking it for granted that we had already heard the news. We were both invited to attend him at Constantinople.

Macrina was exultant. "We must all go to court. Every one of us. We'll all live in Constantinople. No more Athens. No more grubby students . . ."

263

"No more grubby husband?" I could not resist this. She stopped talking.

Prohaeresius, who had been studying the letter, frowned. "He says, 'I worship the true gods openly and all the troops with me worship them. I have offered the gods many oxen as thanks-offerings for my victory, and I shall soon restore their worship in all its purity.'" The old man looked at us grimly. "So he means to do what he said he would do."

"Why not?" Macrina was sharp. "He can't be worse than the bishops."

"Except that now he's Emperor there won't be an ox left in the world!" I believe I was the first to make what was soon a universal joke: Julian's sacrifices were so rich that he was nicknamed "Bull-Burner."

Unlike Macrina and me, Prohaeresius was in a dark mood. "I see only trouble for us," he said.

"Trouble?" When you are the man the Emperor most admires?" Macrina was unbelieving. "Nonsense. It'll be the making of all you schoolteachers. He'll be another Marcus Aurelius. Well, Septimus Severus, anyway."

"Julian is better than Marcus Aurelius," I said, and I meant it. Marcus Aurelius has been enormously overrated as a philosopher. People—especially scholars—are so thrilled that an emperor can even write his own name that they tend to exaggerate the value of his literary productions. If you or I had written those *Meditations*, they would not, I am certain, be considered of any great value. They are certainly inferior to your own superb *pensées*.

Not for several weeks did we know the details of Constantius's death, or in what manner the succession had been assured. Julian gives his version of what happened.


*Julian Augustus*

As far as I can make out, Constantius had been in poor health for some months. He had chronic stomach trouble, a family weakness from which I alone seem to be exempt (so far!). As soon as I had been given the news, I sent everyone out of the room except Oribasius. Then the two officers from the Consistory were brought to me. My first question was the obvious one: "How did he die?"

"Of a fever, Augustus." The older officer, Aligildus, did most of the telling.

264

"Had there been omens?" I particularly wanted to know because I had myself received a number of mysterious signs during the previous weeks. It is good to be scientific about these things. Might not an omen observed to be malign by Constantius appear simultaneously to me as benign?

"Many, Augustus. For several weeks in the field he had been disturbed by waking-dreams and nightmares. On one occasion, he thought he saw the ghost of his father, the great Constantine, carrying in his arms a child, a handsome, strong child which Constantius took and held on his lap."

I turned with wonder to Oribasius. "Is Constantius *my* creator?" For it was plain enough that I was the child in the dream.

"Then the boy seized the orb Constantius held in his right hand . . ."

"The world," I murmured.

". . . and threw it out of sight!" Aligildus paused.

I nodded. "I understand the dream. Did *he*?"

"Yes, Augustus. Shortly afterward, when we came to Antioch, the Emperor told Eusebius that he had a sense that something which had always been with him was gone."

"The Spirit of Rome. These are the signs," I said to Oribasius. Like so many who deal too much in the material world, Oribasius puts little stock in omens and dreams. Yet I think even he was impressed by what he had heard. I quoted Menander, "A spirit is given each man at birth to direct his course." Then I asked about my cousin's last days.

"He spent most of the summer at Antioch, assembling an army to . . ." Aligildus paused, ill at ease.

"To use against me." I was amiable. Why not? Heaven was on my side.

"Yes, Lord. Then in the autumn, after many dreams and bad omens, Constantius left Antioch for the north. Three miles outside of the city in a suburb . . ."

"Called Hippocephalus," said Theolaif, the other officer, reminding us that he too was messenger and witness. "We saw, on the right-hand side of the road, at noon, the headless corpse of a man *facing west*."

A chill ran through me. I hope that when my star falls I shall be spared the torment of such signs.

"From that moment on, Lord, the Emperor was not himself. We hurried on to Tarsus, where he came down with a fever."

"But he could not stop," said Thcolaif, suddenly inspired: the deaths of princes and the malignity of Fate obsess us all. "I know. I was with him. I rode beside him. I said, 'Lord, stop here. Wait. In a few days you will be well.' But he looked at me with glazed eyes, his face dark with fever. He swayed in the saddle. I steadied him with my hand and felt *his* hand, hot and dry. 'No,' he said, and his tongue was dry, too. He could hardly speak. 'We go on. We go on. We go on.' Three times he said that. And we went on."

Aligildus continued, "When we came to the springs at Mopsucrene, he was delirious. We put him to bed. In the night he sweated and the next morning he seemed better. He gave orders to leave. We obeyed, reluctantly. But when the army was ready to move, he was delirious. Constantius was ill three days, his body so hot that it was painful to touch him. Yet he had moments of clarity. In one of those moments, he made his will. This is it." Aligildus handed me a sealed letter which I did not open.

"How was he, at the end?"

"When he was conscious, he was angry."

"At me?"

"No, Lord, at death, for taking him in his prime, for taking him from his young wife."

"It is bitter," I said formally. Who is so inhuman as not to feel *something* at a man's death? even at that of an enemy.

"Then, shortly before dawn on the third of November, he asked to be baptized, like his father. After the ceremony, he tried to sit up. He tried to speak. He choked. He died. He was forty-five years old," added Aligildus, as though he were making a funeral address.

"In the twenty-fifth year of his principate," I noted, in the same style.

"Pray, Augustus," said Oribasius suddenly, "*you* reign as long."

We were silent for a moment. I tried to remember how Constantius looked and failed. When a famous man dies one tends to remember only the sculpture, especially when there is so much of it. I can recall Constantius's monuments but not his living face, not even those great dark eyes which are to my memory blank spaces cut in marble.

"Where is the Chamberlain Eusebius?"

"Still at the Springs. The court waits upon your orders." Aligildus for the first time sounded uncertain. "You, Augustus, are the heir legitimate." He pointed to the letter that I held in my hand.

"There was no . . . objection in the Consistory?"

"None, Lord!" The two men spoke as one.

I rose. "Tomorrow you will return to the Springs. Tell the Consistory that I shall meet them as soon as possible at Constantinople. See that the body of my cousin is brought home for a proper burial, and that his widow is treated with all the honor due her rank." The officers saluted, and departed.

Then Oribasius and I opened the will. It was short and to the point, unlike the usual imperial prose. One knew that a man had dictated it, not a lawyer.

"The Caesar Julian at my death is raised legitimately" (even on his deathbed he could not resist this jab) "to the principate of Rome. He will find my stewardship has been faithful. Despite much treason within the empire and formidable enemies without, the state has prospered in my reign and the borders are secure."

I looked at Oribasius, amused. "I wonder how they feel about that in Amida."

I read on. "We entrust to our most noble cousin and heir our young wife Faustina. She is provided for in a separate testament, and it is our final prayer that our most noble cousin and heir will respect the terms of that will and carry them out as befits a great prince who can afford to show mercy to the weak . . ."

I paused. "Once I tried to make that same speech to him."

Oribasius looked at me oddly. "He spared you," he said.

"Yes. To his regret." I hurried through the rest of the document. There were a number of bequests to retainers and friends. One particularly struck me. "I cannot recommend to my most noble cousin and heir a wiser counsellor or one more loyal than the Grand Chamberlain Eusebius." Even Oribasius laughed at this. Then, at the very last, Constantius spoke directly to me. "We have had differences, the Caesar Julian and I, but I think that he will find when he fills my place that the earth seems not so big as he thought it was from his previous place or from any other place, saving this summit where there can be but one man and a single responsibility for all men, and great decisions to be made, often in haste and sometimes regretted. We are not to be understood by any except our own kind. My most noble cousin and heir will know what I mean when he takes up the orb I have let go. Now in death I am his constant brother in the purple and from whatever

267

place God sees fit to put my soul I shall observe his deeds with fellow-feeling and hope that as he comes to know the singularity of his new estate—and his cruel isolation—he will understand if not forgive his predecessor, who wanted only the stability of the state, the just execution of the law, and the true worship of that God from whom come all our lives and to whom all must return. Julian, pray for me."

That was it. Oribasius and I looked at one another, unable to believe that this crude and touching document was the work of a man who had governed the world for a quarter century.

"He was strong." I could think of nothing more to say.

The next day I ordered a sacrifice to the gods. The legions were most enthusiastic, not only at my accession (and the avoidance of a civil war), but at being allowed to pray to the old gods openly. Many of them were fellow brothers in Mithras.

*Priscus*: This is quite untrue. In actual fact there was a near-mutiny when the sacrifices were ordered, especially among the officers. At this time Julian was very much under the influence of a Gaul names Aprunculus, who had foretold Constantius's death by discovering an ox liver with two lobes, which meant that . . . et cetera. As a reward for having found that double liver, Aprunculus was made governor of Gallia Narbonensis. It was said at the time that a *quadruple* liver might have got him all of Gaul.

Aprunculus persuaded Julian to place the images of the gods next to his own image so that when each man came to throw incense on the fire as homage to the emperor, he also did reverence, like it or not, to the gods. This caused a good deal of bad feeling, none of which Julian notes.

*Julian Augustus*

Less than a week later, I gave the order to proceed to Constantinople. I will not dwell on the elation of those days. Even the cold winter—and it was the coldest in many years—did not depress us.

In a blizzard, we filed through the pass of Succi and descended into Thrace. From there we proceeded to the ancient city of Philippopolis where we stayed overnight. Then we moved south to Heraclea, a town fifty miles southwest of Constantinople where, shortly before midday, to my astonishment, most of the senate and the Sacred Consistory were gathered in the main square.

I was hardly prepared for such a greeting. I was tired, dirty, and I desperately needed to relieve myself. Imagine then the new emperor, eyes twitching with fatigue, hands, legs, face streaked with dust, bladder full, receiving the slow, measured, stately acclamation of the senate. Looking back, I laugh; at the time, I was hard pressed to be gracious.

I dismounted at one end of the square and crossed to the prefect's house. The Scholarian Guards made an aisle for me. They are called Scholarian because their barracks are in the front portico—the "school"—of the Sacred Palace. I studied my new troops with a cold eye. They were smartly turned out; most were Germans . . . what else? They studied me, too. They were both curious and alarmed, which is as it should be. Too often in the past emperors have been frightened of the guard.

I climbed the steps to the prefect's house. There, all in a row, were the officers of the empire. As I approached, they fell to their knees. I asked them to rise. I hate the sight of men old enough to be my grandfather prostrate before me. Recently I tried to simplify the court's ceremonies but the senate would not allow it, so used are they to servitude. They argue that since the Great King of Persia keeps similar state, I must, too, or appear less awesome in men's eyes. Nonsense. But there are too many important changes to be made to worry about court ceremonial.

The first official to greet me was Arbetio, who had been consul in the year I was made Caesar. He is a vigorous, hard-faced man of forty; born a peasant, he became a soldier, rising to commander of cavalry and the consulship. He wants my place, just as he wanted Constantius's place. Now there are two ways to handle such a man. One is to kill him. The other is to keep him near one, safely employed, always watched. I chose the latter for I have found that if someone is reasonably honest and well-meaning—though he has treated one badly—he should be forgiven. When men are honest in public life we must be on good terms with them, even though they have treated us badly in a private capacity; while if they are dishonest in public affairs, even though they are personally devoted to us, they must be dismissed.

Arbetio welcomed me in the name of the senate, though he was not its chief officer.

"We are here to do as the Augustus wills." The proud loud voice belied the words. "In everything."

". . . and to prepare for his entering the city as our Lord!" I

269

turned when I heard those words and there, approaching me from a crowd of senators, was Julian, my uncle. He was trembling with excitement (and infirmity, for he suffered from a recurrent fever, souvenir of his days as governor of Egypt). I embraced him warmly. We had not seen each other for seven years, though we had corresponded as regularly as we dared. My uncle had aged alarmingly; his face was haggard, the yellow skin loose, eyes deep-set, but, even so, this day he was transfigured with delight. I kept my arm through his as I addressed the crowd.

"I am moved at your gesture, since it is not usual for the senate to leave their city to meet the first citizen. Rather it is the first citizen who must come to you, to his peers, who share with him the task of governing, and I shall be with you shortly in your own house to do you the homage you deserve. Meanwhile, I make only one announcement: I shall accept no coronation money from the provinces, imitating in this Hadrian and Antoninus Pius. The empire is too poor at present to make me a gift." There was applause. Then after a few more ungraceful remarks, I pleaded fatigue, and excused myself. The town prefect bowed me into the building, stammering, stumbling, getting in my way, until at last I shouted, "In Hermes's name, where do you piss?" Thus graciously did the new Emperor of Rome come to the East.

The prefect's house had a small private bath and while I soaked in the hot pool, taking deep breaths of steam, my uncle Julian discussed the political situation.

"When Constantius died, Eusebius sounded out several members of the Consistory to see if they would accept Arbetio as emperor, or Procopius . . . or me." My uncle smiled shyly at this. He wanted me to hear this from his own lips rather than from an informer.

"Naturally," I said, watching the dust from my beard float like a gray cloud into the corner of the pool where a Negro slave stood, ready to scrub me with towels and sponges, unaware that I never let bath attendants touch me.

"What did the Consistory say to all this?"

"That you were the Emperor, by blood and by choice."

"As well as being only a few hundred miles away."

"Exactly."

"Where is Eusebius?"

"At the palace, preparing for your arrival. He is still Grand Chamberlain." My uncle smiled.

I submerged for a moment, eyes tight shut, soaking my head. When I came to the surface, Oribasius was sitting on the bench beside my uncle.

"That is no way to approach the sacred presence." And I splashed Oribasius very satisfactorily. He laughed. My uncle Julian laughed, too, for I had soaked him as well. Then I was alarmed. In just this way are monsters born. First, the tyrant plays harmless games: splashes senators in the bath, serves wooden food to dinner guests, plays practical jokes; and no matter what he says and does, everyone laughs and flatters him, finds witty his most inane remarks. Then the small jokes begin to pall. On day he finds it amusing to rape another man's wife, as the husband watches, or the husband as the wife looks on, or to torture them both, or to kill them. When the killing begins, the emperor is no longer a man but a beast, and we have had too many beasts already on the throne of the world. Vehemently, I apologized for splashing my uncle. I even apologized for splashing Oribasius, though he is like my own brother. Neither guessed the significance of this guilty outburst.

Oribasius told me that the Consistory wanted to know whom I intended to appoint as consuls for the coming year.

"Uncle, what about you?"

"I can't afford the consulship." It was a sign of my uncle's wealth that he always complained of poverty. Actually, the consulship is not so expensive as it used to be. Nowadays, the two consuls pool their resources for the games they must sponsor, while the emperor usually helps them from the Privy Purse.

"I don't think *you'd* like it, Oribasius."

"No, Augustus, I would not."

"Mamertinus," I said, swimming to the far side of the pool.

Both my uncle and Oribasius approved. "He's a distinguished rhetorician," said my uncle. "Of good family, a popular choice..."

"And Nevitta!" I dove under the water as I said this. When I came up for air, I could see that Oribasius was amused and my uncle horrified.

"But he is...he is..."

I nodded. "A Frank. A barbarian."

I got out of the bath. The slave wrapped me in a large towel. I broke away from him before he could start pummeling me. "He is also one of our best generals. He will be a continual reminder to the East that my power rests securely in the West."

"No one will ever accuse you of consistency." Oribasius grinned.

Only the month before at Nish, I had denounced Constantius for appointing barbarians to prefectures. Now I was making one consul. There is nothing harder politically than to have to reverse yourself publicly. But where Constantius would rather die than ever admit to a mistake, I was quite willing to look a bit foolish, and do the right thing.

"We shall deny," I said with much grandeur, "that I ever criticized the appointment of barbarians to high office."

"Your letter to the Spartan senate was a forgery?"

"In every detail."

Oribasius and I laughed but my uncle looked pained. "At least," he said, "name only Mamertinus today. Besides, it's the custom to name one consul at a time, so name him for the East. Later you can announce the . . . the other man for the West."

"So be it, Uncle!" And together we went into the dressing room where I put on the purple.

The Consistory was almost at full strength, some forty officers of state, who received me ceremoniously at the town hall. Arbetio escorted me to my ivory chair. To my left and right were the empty consular chairs. One for Florentius, who had—has—vanished from the face of the earth; the other for Taurus, who fled to Antioch when I first came into Illyricum.

I greeted the Consistory politely. I noted the absence of the consuls, remarking that as a new year was about to begin, there would soon be two new consuls. One would be Mamertinus. This was received with every appearance of satisfaction. I then made a number of additions to the Consistory. When I had finished, Arbetio begged to address me. Heart sinking, I granted him leave.

Slowly, solemnly, as though *he* were the Augustus, Arbetio moved to the center of the room, just in front of my chair. He cleared his throat. "Lord, there are those who have plotted against you." A sharp intake of breath was heard all round the room. After all, there was hardly a man present who had *not* conspired against me. It had been their duty. "Those men are still at large. Some in high places. Lord, there are also those who conspired against your most noble brother, the Caesar Gallus. They, too, are at large. Some in high places."

I looked about the room and saw several men "in high places" look most uneasy. There was the stout Palladius, chief marshal of Constantius's court. He had brought charges against Gallus. Next to him stood Evagrius, Count of the Privy Purse; he had helped

272

prepare the case against Gallus. And Saturninus, Steward of the Household . . . A dozen conspirators looked back at Arbetio and me. The question in every face was: Will this reign begin in blood?

It was Ursulus, Count of the Sacred Largesse, who spoke up boldly. "Augustus, are those of us who served the emperor *you* served so well, to suffer for having done our duty?"

"No!" I was firm.

But Arbetio turned his bleak, pale gaze upon Ursulus. "Yet, Augustus, those who have by *deed* hurt you and your brother, by *word* and by deed, must be condemned."

There was an uneasy murmur in the room. Yet Ursulus stood his ground. He was a handsome fleshy man with a quick wit and quicker tongue. "The Consistory are relieved, Lord, that only those who are truly guilty will be charged."

"They shall be charged," said Arbetio, speaking for me, which I did not like, "if it be our Lord's will."

"It is our will." I said the traditional phrase in Latin.

"Who shall compose this court, Lord? and where shall it sit?"

Now I should have stopped Arbetio at that moment. But I was tired from the long journey and languorous from a hot bath (*never* try to do any business immediately after bathing). I was unprepared for a strong will with a plan, and Arbetio had a plan, alas. Meanwhile, Ursulus proposed: "Since the Emperor Hadrian, the Consistory has been our highest court. So let the guilty be judged here, by us who are responsible for the business of the state."

"But, Count," and Arbetio's voice was cold in its correctness, "the Consistory is still that of the late emperor, *not* of our new lord. I am sure the Augustus will want his own tribunal, as he will in time want his own Consistory." This was undeniable.

I motioned to one of the secretaries to pay close attention as I spoke. "The court will be headed by Salutius Secundus." This went over very well. As praetorian prefect of the East he is known for his sense of justice. I then named Mamertinus, Agilo, Nevitta, Jovinus, and Arbetio to the court. It was, in short, a military tribunal. I then ordered them to meet at Chalcedon, across the Bosphorus from Constantinople. Thus began the treason trials. I shall—sadly—refer to them later.

On 11 December 361 I entered Constantinople as Roman Emperor. Snow fell at slow intervals and the great flakes turned like feathers in air so still that the day was almost warm. The sky was low and the color of tarnished silver. There was no color that day in nature, only in man, but what color! It was a day of splendor.

In front of the Golden Gate, close to the sea of Marmora, the Scholarians in full dress uniform stood at attention. On each of the brick towers at either side of the gate, the dragons were unfurled. The green bronze gates were shut. As custom demanded, I dismounted a few yards from the wall. The commander of the Scholarians gave me a silver hammer. With it I struck the bronze gate three times. From within, came the voice of the city's prefect. "Who goes there?"

"Julian Augustus," I replied in a loud voice. "A citizen of the city."

"Enter Julian Augustus."

The bronze gates swung open noiselessly and there before me in the inner courtyard stood the prefect of the city—and some two thousand men of senatorial rank. The Sacred Consistory was also there, having preceded me into the capital the night before. Quite alone, I passed through the gate and took possession of the City of Constantine.

Trumpets sounded. The people cheered. I was particularly struck by the brightness of the clothes they wore. I don't know whether it was the white setting which made the reds and greens, the yellows and blues almost unbearably vivid, or the fact that I had been away too long in northern countries where all colors are as muted and as dim as the forests in which the people live. But this was not the misty north. This was Constantinople, and despite the legend that we are the New Rome (and like that republican city, austere, stern, virtuous), we are not Rome at all. We are Asia. I thought of this as I was helped into the gold chariot of Constantine, recalling with amusement Eutherius's constant complaint, "You are hopelessly Asiatic!" Well, I am Asiatic! And I was home at last.

As flakes of snow settled in my hair and beard, I rode down Middle Street. Everywhere I looked I saw changes. The city had altered completely in the few years I had been away. For one thing, it has outgrown the wall of Constantine. What were once open fields are now crowded suburbs, and one day I shall have to go to the expense of building a new wall to contain these suburbs, which, incidentally, are not carefully laid out in the way the city was but simply created helter-skelter by contractors interested only in a quick profit.

Colonnades line Middle Street from one end to the other. The arcades were crowded with people who cheered me ecstatically. Why? Because they loved me? No. Because I was a novelty. The people tire of the same ruler, no matter how excellent. They had got bored with Constantius and they wanted a change of program and I was it.

Suddenly I heard what sounded like thunder at my back. For a moment I took it as an omen that Zeus had approved me. Then I realized it was not thunder but my army singing the marching song of Julius Caesar's troops: *"Ecce Caesar nunc triumphat, Qui subegit Gallias!"* It is the sound of war itself, and of all earthly glory.

The prefect of the city walked beside my chariot and tried to point out the new buildings, but I could not hear him for the noise of the mob. Even so, it was exhilarating to see so much activity, in contrast to old cities like Athens and Milan where a new building is a rarity. When an old house collapses in Athens, the occupants simply move into another one, for there are far more houses than people. But everything in Constantinople is brand-new, including the population, which is now—the prefect shouted to me just as we entered the Forum of Constantine—close to a million people, counting slaves and foreigners.

The colossal statue of Constantine at the center of the oval forum always gives me a shock. I can never get used to it. On a tall column of porphyry, my uncle set up a statue of Apollo, stolen I believe from Delos. He then knocked the head off this masterpiece and substituted his own likeness, an inferior piece of work by any standard and so badly joined that there is a dark ring where head and neck meet. The people refer to this monument as "old dirty neck." On the head there is a monstrous halo of seven bronze rays, perfect blasphemy, not only to the true gods but to the Galilean as well. Constantine saw himself as both Galilean and as incarnation of the sun god. He was most ambitious. I am told he doted on this particular statue and used to look at it every chance he got; he even pretended that the Apollonian body was his own!

We then entered that section of Middle Street which is called Imperial Way and leads into the Augusteum, a large porticoed square which was the center of the city when it was called Byzantium. In the middle of the Augusteum, Constantine set up a large statue of his mother Helena. She is seated on a throne and looks quite severe; in one hand she holds a piece of wood said to have been a part of the cross to which the Galilean was nailed. My great-aunt had a passion for relics: she was also infinitely gullible. There is not a Charnel house in the city to which she did not give some sliver of wood, shred of cloth, bit of bone said to have been associated in one way or another with that unfortunate rabbi and his family.

To my astonishment, the entire north side of the square was taken up by the basilica of a charnel house so new that the scaffolding had not yet been removed from the front. The prefect beamed cheerfully at me, thinking I would be pleased.

"Augustus may recall the old church that was here? the small one the Great Constantine dedicated to Holy Wisdom? Well, the Emperor Constantius has had it enlarged. In fact, only last summer he rededicated it."

I said nothing but immediately vowed to turn their Saint Sophia into a temple to Athena. It would never do to have a Galilean monument right at my front door (the main entrance to the palace is on the south side of the square, just opposite the charnel house). To the east is the senate house to which the senators were now repairing. The senate's usual quorum is fifty, but today all two thousand were present, elbowing one another as they hurried up the slippery steps.

The square was now jammed with people, and no one knew what to do next. The prefect was used to being given his orders by the palace chamberlains, who were, if nothing else, masters of pageantry. But today the chamberlains were in hiding and neither the prefect nor I knew what to do. I'm afraid between us we made rather a botch of things.

My chariot had stopped at the Milion, a covered monument from which all distances in the empire are measured. Yes, we counterfeit Rome in this, too; in everything, even to the seven hills.

"The senate waits for you, Lord," said the prefect nervously.

"Waits for me? They're still trying to get inside the senate house!"

"Perhaps the Augustus would prefer to receive them in the palace?"

I shook my head, vowing that never again would I enter a city without preparation. No one knew where to go or what to do. I saw several of my commanders arguing with the Scholarians, who did not know them, while ancient senators slipped and fell in the slush. It was a mess, and a bad omen. Already I was handling matters less well than Constantius.

I pulled myself together. "Prefect, while the senate meets I shall make sacrifice."

The prefect indicated Saint Sophia. "The bishop should be inside, Augustus. If he's not, I can send for him."

"Sacrifice to the true gods," I said firmly.

"But . . . *where*?" The poor man was bewildered, with good reason. After all, Constantinople is a new city, dedicated to Jesus, and there are no temples except for three small ones on the old Byzantine acropolis. They would have to do. I motioned to those members of my entourage who had got through the guards and together we made a small ragged procession to the low hill where stood the shabby and deserted temples of Apollo, Artemis and Aphrodite.

In the dank filthy temple of Apollo, I gave thanks to Helios and to all the gods, while the townspeople crowded round outside, amused by this first show of imperial eccentricity. As I sacrificed, I swore to Apollo that I would rebuild his temple.

*Libanius*: A few weeks ago the Emperor Theodosius gave the temple of Apollo to his praetorian prefect, as a coach house!

*Julian Augustus*

I then sent Mamertinus, as consul-designate, to tell the senate that I should not address them until the first of January, out of deference to my predecessor, whose body was already on its way to the city for interment. Through a now gusty blizzard, I made my way to the palace, entering through the Chalkê Gate, whose vestibule is covered with a bronze roof. Just over the gate, I noticed a new painting of Constantine. He is shown with his three sons. At their feet, a dragon, javelin in its side, sinks into the pit: the true gods slain. Above the emperor's head is a cross. A nice coat of whitewash should do the trick.

On either side of the gate, the Scholarian Guards are quartered. They saluted smartly. I ordered their commander to house and feed my military retinue. Then I crossed the inner court and entered the main part of the palace. In the great hall I found Eusebius

277

with his eunuchs, notaries, slaves, secret agents, at least two hundred men and half-men, all waiting for me in a room which was as bright and as warm as a summer's day. I have never seen so richly dressed a group in my life, nor smelled so much expensive perfume.

I stood in the doorway and shook snow from my cloak as a dog shakes water from his back. All present fell to the floor with exquisite grace, and Eusebius humbly kissed the hem of my robe. I looked down for one long moment at that large body which resembled one of those African beasts Egypt sends us for the games. Eusebius glittered with jewels and smelled of lilies. This was the creature who had tried to destroy me, as he had destroyed my brother.

"Get up, Chamberlain." I said briskly, I motioned for the others to do the same. With some difficulty, Eusebius got to his feet. He looked at me shyly, with appealing eyes. Though he was terrified, years of training at court and a consummate skill at negotiating served him well; not once did his voice falter nor his poise desert him.

"Lord," he whispered, "all is in readiness. The bedrooms, the kitchens, the rooms of assembly, the robes, the jewels . . ."

"Thank you, Chamberlain."

"An inventory will be presented to the Lord of the World tomorrow."

"Good, and now . . ."

"Whatever he wishes, our Lord need only command." The voice that whispered in my ear was confiding and intimate.

I stepped away from him. "Show me my apartments."

Eusebius clapped his hands. The hall emptied. I followed the eunuch up white marble stairs to the second floor, where, through latticed windows, one can see the splendid gardens which descend in shallow terraces to the sea of Marmora. Off to the right is the mansion of the Persian Prince Ormisda who defected to us in 323, as well as the group of small buildings or pavilions known as the Daphne Palace; here the emperors hold audience.

It was strange to be in Constantius's rooms. I was particularly moved when I saw the inlaid silver bed where my cousin had slept, and no doubt dreamed uneasily of me. Now he is gone and the room is mine. I wonder: who will sleep here after me? My reverie was interrupted by Eusebius, who cleared his throat nervously. I looked at him blankly. Then I said, "Tell Oribasius I want to see him."

"Is that *all*, Lord?"

"That is all, Chamberlain."

Face grave and perfectly controlled, Eusebius withdrew. That evening he was arrested for high treason and sent to Chalcedon to stand trial.

Together Oribasius and I explored the palace, to the consternation of the staff, who had never before seen an emperor stray from the strict round prescribed for him by ceremonial. I was particularly interested in seeing the palace of Daphne. So Oribasius and I, escorted by no more than a dozen guards, pounded on the door of the little palace. A nervous eunuch opened it and showed us into the throne room where, years before, I had seen Constantine on a day when all our family was together; now all are dead but me. The room was as splendid as I remembered, including, I'm afraid, the jewel-encrusted cross which covers the entire ceiling I should like to remove it, but traditionalists argue that no matter what the state's religion it should be kept simply because my uncle put it there. Perhaps they are right.

The old eunuch who had shown us into the room said that he remembered the day I was presented to my uncle.

"You were a handsome child, Lord, and we knew even then that you would be our master." Naturally!

We also explored the banquet hall, with its arched triklinos at one end where, on a dais, the imperial family dine. The floor is particularly handsome, inlaid with different-colored marbles from every province of the empire. While we were gaping like countryfolk, the Master of the Offices appeared, accompanied by a tall lean officer. After gently chiding me for having escaped him, the Master indicated the officer, a commander of cavalry named Jovian. "He has just arrived, Augustus, with the sacred remains of the Lord Constantius."

Jovian saluted me; he is a good-humored unintelligent man who serves with me now in Persia. I thanked him for his efforts and assigned him to temporary duty with the Scholarians. I then called a Consistory where, among other matters, we planned the funeral of Constantius. It was the last ceremony the eunuchs conducted and I am happy to say it went off without a hitch. He had loved them; they loved him. It was fitting that their last task at court should have been the funeral of their patron.

*　*　*

Constantius's funeral was held in what the Galileans call the Church of the Holy Apostles, which is situated on the fourth of the city's hills. Just back of the basilica, Constantine had put up a round mausoleum, much like the one of Augustus at Rome. Here lie his remains, and those of his three sons. May the earth rest lightly on them.

To my surprise, I was quite moved at the funeral of my life's enemy. For one thing, since I am celibate, our line ends with Constantius. But that's not quite true: his widow Faustina was then pregnant. I saw her at a distance, heavily veiled among the mourners. Several days later I granted her an audience.

I received Faustina in Constantius's dressing room, which I use as an office because it is lined with cupboards originally built to hold his many robes and tunics. I now use the cupboards for books.

When Faustina entered, I rose and greeted her as a kinswoman. She knelt. I raised her up. I offered her a chair. We both sat.

Faustina is a vivacious woman, with a high arched Syrian nose, blue-black hair and gray eyes, testament to some Gothic or Thessalian ancestor. She was clearly frightened, though I did my best to put her at her ease.

"I hope you don't mind my receiving you here." I indicated the row of tailor's dummies which still lined one wall, mute reminder of the body they were intended to represent.

"Wherever my Lord chooses," she said formally. Then she smiled. "Besides, I have never been inside the Sacred Palace before."

"That's right. You were married at Antioch."

"Yes, Lord."

"I am sorry."

"It was the will of heaven."

I agreed that indeed it was. "Where will you live, Princess?" I had decided to style her thus. "Augusta" would have been out of the question.

"If it pleases my Lord, at Antioch. Quietly. In retirement. With my family. Alone." She dropped each phrase like a coin at my feet.

"You may live wherever you please, Princess. After all, you are my last kinswoman and . . ." As tactfully as possible, I indicated her swelling stomach beneath black robes, ". . . you bear the last child of our house. That is a great responsibility. Were it not for you, the Flavians would come to an end."

For a moment, I saw fear and suspicion in the gray eyes; then she lowered her head and a faint color rose in her neck. "I hope, Lord, you will have many children."

"None," I said flatly. "Your son—or daughter—alone must continue the line."

"When my husband was dying, he said that you would be just and merciful, Lord."

"We understood each other," I said. But then I could not help adding. "Up to a point."

"I am free to go?"

"You are perfectly free. Constantius's bequests to you shall be honored." I rose. "Let me know when the child is born." She kissed the purple; and we parted.

I get regular reports on her from Antioch. She is thought to be proud and difficult but not given to conspiracy. She dislikes me not allowing her the title of Augusta. Her child, incidentally, turned out to be a girl, much to my relief. She is named Flavia Maxima Faustina. It will be interesting to see what happens to her.

*Libanius*: Flavia—or Constantia Postuma as we call her—is a lady of the greatest charm, very like her mother, and a most intimate friend of mine. She of course married the Emperor Gratian and they reside now in Treves. So the daughter became what her mother did not, a reigning Augusta. Faustina is extraordinarily proud of her daughter, though when I saw her last month she was somewhat hurt at not having been invited to join the Empress in the West. Apparently the thoughtful child felt that the journey would be too taxing for her mother. Also, as I told Faustina: children *do* tend to live their own lives and we must be tolerant. I even loaned her the only copy I have of my little essay on "The Duty to Parents." Which reminds me that she has not returned it.

As for the Emperor Gratian, he is everyone's hero, although (alas!) he is a devout Christian. When he was raised to the principate, he refused the title of Pontifex Maximus, the first emperor in our history to do so, a most ominous sign. As a matter of record, last year when Gratian selected Theodosius to be Augustus of the East, he gave his mother-in-law Faustina the honorary title Augusta. We were all tremendously pleased.

When Faustina left, I sent for a barber. My hair had not been cut since Gaul, and I was beginning to look quite savage, more Pan than philosopher. I was studying the palace roster when what looked like the Persian ambassador entered the room. I nearly got to my feet, so awed was I by the spectacle: gold rings, jeweled brooch, curled hair. But this was not an ambassador. This was the barber. My response was weak. "I sent for a barber, not a tax collector," I said. But the man took this serenely, as an imperial pleasantry.

He chattered freely. He told me that he had an annual salary, paid by the treasury; he also earned twenty loaves of bread a day, as well as fodder for twenty pack animals. Yet he felt himself underpaid, he said, as he trimmed my beard, gracefully deploring the fact that I like it to come to a point. I held my tongue until he had left; then I dictated a memorandum dismissing all barbers, cooks, and other supernumeraries from my service.

I was engaged in this pleasant task when Oribasius joined me. He listened with amusement while I roared and waved my arms, getting more and more upset as I thought about the court I had inherited. When I had finally run out of breath, Oribasius reported that he had been exploring the barracks of the Scholarian Guards. It seems that the men slept on *feather mattresses*! Their mess was sumptuous, and their goblets were a good deal heavier than their swords. As a sideline, some conducted a traffic in jewels, either stolen or extorted from rich merchants whom they regularly terrorized, demanding protection money. As if this were not bad enough, the guardsmen had formed a glee club and regularly hired themselves out to private parties where they sang *love songs*!

I'm afraid I was screaming with anguish by the time Oribasius had finished. He always takes pleasure in arousing me, deliberately adding detail to detail just to watch the veins in my forehead throb. Then after he has roused me to a blind rage, he takes my pulse and tells me that if I'm not careful I shall have a stroke. I will, too, one day.

I was all for clearing out the barracks at once. But he thought it would be better to do it gradually. "Besides, there is far worse going on in the palace."

"Worse!" I raised my eyes to Helios. "I don't expect soldiers to be philosophers. I know they steal. But singing love songs, feather mattresses . . ."

"It's not the soldiers. It's the eunuchs." But he said nothing more, indicating the secretaries. Sworn though they are to secrecy, one must always be careful what one says in front of any witness.

"Later," Oribasius whispered.

We were suddenly aware of a great babble from below. The Master of the Offices entered, breathing hard. "Lord, the Egyptian delegation begs your presence, humbly, graciously..." At this point the noise below began to sound like a riot.

"Is this usual, Master?"

"Oh, Lord, but Egyptians..."

"...are noisy?"

"Yes, Lord."

"And the praetorian prefect is unable to handle them?"

"Exactly, Lord. He told them you could not see them and..."
There was a noise of breaking pottery, and a few high-pitched screams.

"Are the Egyptians always like this, Master?"

"Often, Lord."

Much amused, I followed the Master of the Offices downstairs to the praetorian prefect's audience chamber. Just as I was about to enter the hall, a half dozen attendants appeared from nowhere. One arranged my hair; another my beard; my cloak was redraped; a diadem was set on my head. Then the Master of the Offices and what was now a considerable retinue opened the doors and, feeling rather like Constantius, I entered the prefect's chamber.

I should explain that Egyptians are easily the most tiresome of my subjects, if one wishes to generalize... and who does not? Their bad reputation was not gained for nothing. They particularly delight in litigation. Sometimes a family will conduct a lawsuit for a century, simply for the pleasure of making trouble. This particular delegation had come to see Constantius in Antioch, but he was gone before they arrived. They pursued him to the Springs, where death mercifully saved him from them. Then, hearing that a new emperor would soon be in Constantinople, they had come straight to me. Their complaint? A thousand suits against our government in Egypt.

They swarmed about me—they were of every color, from pale Greek to black Numidian—and they all talked at once, quite unimpressed by my greatness. The praetorian prefect looked at me across the room; hopefully, he made the sign of the knife. But I was more amused than offended.

283

With some difficulty, I got their attention. "Justice," I shouted, "will be done each of you!" This occasioned both cheers and groans. Apparently, some felt things were going much too easily. "But," I said firmly, "no redress can be given here. Only at Chalcedon, across the Bosphorus. That is where the treasury is, where such matters are decided." I was now improvising quite freely, to the amazement of the prefect. "You will all be taken there at my expense." A rapturous sigh from the delegation. "And tomorrow I shall join you and examine in detail each suit. If I find any of you has been injured, I shall know what to do." There was a pleased response, and I slipped out of the room.

The Master of the Offices was distressed. "But tomorrow is impossible! And the treasury is here, not there."

"Get the whole lot of them to Chalcedon. Then tell the boatmen that no Egyptian is to be brought back to the city."

For the first time I felt that I had earned the respect of the Master of the Offices. The Egyptians stayed at Chalcedon a month, annoying the local officials. Then they went home.

*Priscus*: You will note that though Julian referred some while back to the treason trials at Chalcedon and promised to discuss them, he never mentions the subject again. Of course he did not have the chance to go over any of these notes, but I am not sure that even if he had caught the omission he would have been at all candid. The whole business was shameful, and he knew it.

Arbetio arrested a dozen of Constantius's high officials. They were all friends of Arbetio, but that did not prevent him from charging each with high treason. Why? Because any one of these officers of state might have compromised him. Arbetio wanted to be emperor; he had tried to persuade Eusebius to recognize him as Constantius's heir. As a result, he was now a man with a purpose: the covering of his own tracks.

Although Salutius Secundus was officially president of the court, Arbetio was in charge. He was a tiger among sheep. Palladius, a blameless official who had been chief marshal to the court, was charged with having conspired against Gallus; on no evidence at all, Palladius was exiled to Britain along with Florentius (a chamberlain, not our friend from Gaul). Also exiled—again on no evidence—were Evagrius (former Count of the Privy Purse), Saturninus (former Steward of the Sacred Household), Cyrinus (a private secretary). Even more shocking was the exile of the consul

Taurus, whose only fault was that he had joined his rightful lord Constantius when Julian marched into Illyricum. Public opinion was particularly scandalized to read a proclamation which began, "In the year of the consulate of Taurus and Florentius, Taurus was found guilty of treason." That sort of thing is not done, except by the most reckless of tyrants.

The praetorian prefect Florentius was condemned to death, properly, I think. He did indeed try to destroy Julian, though if one wanted to be absolutely just (and who does in political matters?), he acted only upon Constantius's orders. Fortunately for him, his trial was conducted *in absentia*. He had wisely disappeared the day Constantius died and he did not reappear until some months after Julian's death. He lived to a great age and died at Milan, rich and contented. Some live to be old; some are struck down too soon. Julian of course would have said it was inexorable Fate, but I know better. It is nothing, absolutely nothing. There is no design to any of it.

Paul "the chain," Mercurius "the count of dreams" and Gaudentius were all put to death, as was proper. Eusebius also was executed, and his vast property reverted to the crown from which he had stolen it.

Then the outrage occurred. Of all the public men in our timorous time, Ursulus alone had the courage always to say what he thought was right, despite consequences. He understood Arbetio perfectly. He deplored the trials. He said so. To everyone's amazement, Arbetio had Ursulus arrested.

The trial was an abomination. I am told by those who were present that Ursulus tongue-lashed Arbetio, mocked his ambition, dared the court to find him either disloyal to Julian or in any way connected with Gallus's death. I say that I was "told" this because I was not able to read about it: the records of the trial have vanished. But I *was* able to talk frankly to Mamertinus, who had been a horrified witness of this grim farce. He told me what happened, making no excuse for himself. Like all the rest, including Julian, he was led by the willful Arbetio, and must share in the guilt.

Forged testimony was prepared against Ursulus, but the forgeries were so clumsy that he was able to have them thrown out as evidence. At this point even Arbetio might have given up, but he had one last weapon in reserve. The trial was a military one, held in the camp of two legions. Now Ursulus was supremely unpopular with the army because of that bitter remark he made when, surveying the ruins of Amida, he said, "See how bravely our citizens are protected by those soldiers, whose pay is bankrupting us!"

Suddenly Arbetio threw this quotation in Ursulus's face. Immediately the officers and men who were present at the trial made a loud racket, demanding Ursulus's head. They got it. He was executed within the hour.

This was the talk of the city when I arrived in January. I questioned Julian about the trial; he was evasive. "I didn't know what was happening. I put the whole thing in Salutius's hands. I was as surprised as anyone."

"But they acted in your name..."

"Every village notary acts in my name. Am I responsible for all injustice?"

"But surely you had to give permission for the execution. Under Roman law..."

"The military court acted on its own initiative. I didn't know."

"Then every member of the court was guilty of treason for using your power of life and death illegally."

"The court was not illegal. They were duly constituted by imperial edict..."

"Then they *must* have informed you before the execution and if they did..."

"*I did not know!*" Julian was furious. I never mentioned the subject again. But when we were in Persia he brought up the matter, on his own. We had been talking about the idea of justice when suddenly Julian said, "The hardest thing I ever did was to allow a court to condemn an innocent man."

"Ursulus?"

He nodded. He had quite forgotten he had once told me that he had known nothing of the Chalcedon proceedings. "The army wanted him dead. There was nothing I could do. When the court found him guilty of high treason—even though he was innocent— I had to let the sentence stand."

"To appease the army? or Arbetio?"

"Both. I was not sure of myself then. I needed every bit of support I could get. But if that trial were today, I would free Ursulus and indict Arbetio."

"But yesterday is not today, and Ursulus is dead."

"I'm sorry," said Julian, and that was the end of that chapter.

It is one of the few instances I know where Julian was weak and in his weakness bad. But how might *we* have acted in his place? Differently? I think not. One good thing: Julian did not confiscate Ursulus's estate as law requires in the case of a traitor. The property all went to the dead man's daughter.

*Libanius*: Priscus seems unduly sentimental in this matter. As he himself admits, he did not study the transcript of the trial, so how could he know what sort of evidence was presented against Ursulus? Unlike Priscus, I should never predict my own behavior in any circumstance until I knew precisely what the given facts were. Is not all conduct based on this sort of empiricism? or have I misled three generations of pupils?

*Julian Augustus*

I had heard all my life about what went on in the eunuchs' quarters of the Sacred Palace. But I tend to discount gossip, having been myself the subject of so much, most of it fantastic. I confess I did not really want any rumors confirmed, but Oribasius insisted that we see for ourselves. So I got myself up in a hooded robe while Oribasius disguised himself as a Syrian merchant with oiled ringlets and glossy false beard.

Shortly before midnight, we left my apartment, by way of a private staircase. Outside the palace we found ourselves in a small courtyard, bright with moonlight. Like shadowy conspirators, we crossed to the opposite wing of the palace where the eunuchs and minor officials lived. We slipped inside the portico. At the third door from the south, Oribasius stopped, and rapped three times. A muffled voice said, "What is the time?"

"The time is ours," said Oribasius. This was the correct password. The door opened just wide enough for us to enter. A dwarf greeted us and pointed to the dimly lit stairs. "They're just starting."

Oribasius gave him a coin. On the second-floor gallery deaf mute slaves showed us into what had been Eusebius's dining hall. It was almost as splendid as my own! Against the walls of the room some fifty eunuchs reclined on couches. They were so gorgeously dressed that they looked like bales of silk on display. In front of each couch a table was set, piled with food. Even for an evening of what (in my innocence) I took to be music, the eunuchs needed their food.

At the end of the room there were chairs and benches for what were known as "friends of the court." Here sat a number of Scholarian officers, drinking heavily. I was completely mystified but dared not speak for fear someone would recognize my voice. As Mardonius—that *good* eunuch—used to say: "Julian has no lyre, only a brazen trumpet."

We sat down in the front row, next to a centurion of the Herculani. He was already quite drunk. He nudged me in the ribs. "Don't look so gloomy! And take that hood off, makes you look like a dirty Christ-y!" This was considered high wit, and there was a good deal of laughter at my expense. But the glib Oribasius rescued me. "Poor fellow's from the country, doesn't dare show his patched tunic." Oribasius's accent was pure Antioch. I was most impressed.

"He part of the show?" The centurion pushed his face close to mine, his breath like the last dregs from a skin of wine. I pulled back, hand to my hood.

"No," said Oribasius. "A friend of Phalaris." This impressed the centurion, who left me alone. Oribasius whispered in my ear. "Phalaris is our host. He's there. In the center." Phalaris was large and sullen, with a pursed mouth. I knew that I had seen him before, but I could not place him. Oribasius explained. "He's in charge of the kitchen. Which makes him—now that Eusebius is dead—the richest man at court."

I sighed. The emperor is hugely robbed by his servants.

Cymbals were struck. A long line of Scholarians filed into the room. They halted before Phalaris and gave him a parody of the imperial salute. I started angrily to my feet, but Oribasius held me back. With a gesture quite as majestic as any of Constantius's, Phalaris acknowledged the salute. The soldiers then took their places against the wall and, at a signal from their leader, they sang a love song! But there was worse to come.

Fifty shabbily dressed youths entered the hall. They moved awkwardly and seemed not to know what to do until a Scholarian shoved one of them to his knees in front of Phalaris; all followed suit. The eunuch then motioned for them to sit on the floor directly in front of us. I was completely baffled. These youths were obviously not entertainers. They looked like ordinary workmen of the sort one sees in every city, hanging about the arcades, eyeing women.

Next, the same number of young girls were herded into the room. All around me the "friends of the court" breathed satisfaction. The girls were uncommonly pretty, and terrified. After a slow tour of the hall, they were ordered to sit on the floor beside the young men. They too wore ordinary clothes, which meant that they were neither prostitutes nor entertainers. I saw that the eunuchs were studying the girls with almost as much interest as were the men about me. I thought this surprising, but Oribasius assures me that the desire for women remains cruelly strong in eunuchs, especially in those gelded after puberty. Incapacity does not prevent lust.

Musicians appeared and played while a troupe of Syrian cotylists danced. I suppose they were good. They moved violently, made astonishing leaps in the air, did lewd things with the cups which are a part of their "art." While all eyes watched them, I tapped the shoulder of the boy who sat just in front of me. He gave a nervous start, and turned around, pale with fright. He had the fair skin and gray eyes of Macedonia. His hands were large and calloused, the nails black with soot. I took him to be a metalworker's apprentice, at the most eighteen years old.

"Sir?" His light voice cracked with tension.

"Why are you here?"

"I don't know, sir."

"But how did you get here?"

"They..." He motioned to the Scholarians. "I was coming home from the silver market, where I work, and they stopped me and made me go with them."

"Did they tell you why?"

"No, sir. They won't kill us, will they?" There is no terror to equal that of the ignorant in a strange place.

"No," I said firmly. "They won't hurt you."

The Syrian dancers were followed by what looked to be priestesses of the Egyptian cult of Syra. Though I recognized many of the ritual gestures, I suspect that these women were not actually priestesses but prostitutes, imitating the sacred erotic dances. It was, after all, a night of travesty. Every stage of the mysteries was acted out, including the ceremony of abundance with its wooden phalluses. This last brought loud applause from the "friends of the court," and ecstatic sighs and giggles from the eunuchs. Though the cult of Syra does not much appeal to me, I was offended to see its mysteries profaned.

After the "priestesses" had finished their dance, several burly Scholarians motioned for the girls and youths to parade in pairs

289

before the reclining eunuchs, much the way young people stroll on feast days in provincial towns. For some minutes they moved, tense, self-conscious, trapped. Then Phalaris motioned for a particular girl and youth to approach him. This was a signal for the other eunuchs to choose pairs. They did so, hissing like angry geese.

Suddenly Phalaris reached up and tore the girl's dress at the shoulder; it fell to her knees. Those about me gasped with excitement. I was too stunned to move. When the girl tried to pull her dress back in place, Phalaris tugged at it again and this time the cheap material split and came away in his hand. Like a sacrifice, she stood, naked, arms crossed on her breast. Phalaris then turned to the boy and lifted up his tunic as far as the belly. Loud laughter; the youth wore nothing underneath. Phalaris then pulled both girl and boy, the one pale and the other red with embarrassment, onto the couch, his fat arms girdling each.

Meanwhile, the other eunuchs had stripped their terrified prey. None resisted, although one young man, inadvertently shying from a eunuch's grasp, was cracked hard across the buttocks by the flat of a Scholarian's sword. The rest submitted.

As I watched, I had the sense of having witnessed something similar. This monstrous scene contained a baffling familiar element. Not until days later did I recall what it was: children opening presents. The eunuchs were like greedy children. They tore the clothes off their victims in the same way children tear wrappings from a gift, passionately eager to see what is inside. Stubby eunuch fingers explored the strange bodies as though they were toys; they were particularly fascinated by the sex, male and female. Imagine fifty huge babies allowed people for playthings and one can begin to apprehend what I saw that night.

I might have sat there forever, turned to astonished stone, if I had not noticed the boy I had talked to earlier. He was stretched across a eunuch's lap while a frightened girl poured dippers of honey over his belly, the eunuch fondling him all the while, preparatory to heaven alone knew what vice. That was enough.

I had got as far as the center of the room when one of the Scholarians grabbed me roughly by the shoulder. The hood fell back from my head. One look at my face was enough. The music stopped, instrument by instrument. No one moved. No one spoke. Only the young people stared at me dumbly and without interest. I motioned to a tribune who sat on the first row. He was the highest-ranking officer present. Trembling, he saluted me. I indicated the boys and girls and in a low voice that only he could hear, I said, "Send them home." Then I pointed to Phalaris. "Arrest the eunuchs. Confine all Scholarians present to barracks." In a silence as complete as any I have ever heard, Oribasius and I left the banquet hall.

Oribasius feels that I took the entire thing too seriously because I am celibate. But that is not the reason. It is the basis of a lawful society that no man (much less half-man) has the power to subject another citizen to his will. If the young people had been voluntary prostitutes, I would have forgiven the eunuchs. But what was done that night—and many other nights, I discovered—was lawless and cruel.

*Priscus*: Julian often used to talk about that night in the eunuchs' quarters. He was naïve to be so upset. Palace eunuchs are distressing in their habits and what he saw was hardly a revelation. Naturally, it is not pleasant to think of such things going on in the Sacred Palace, but then there are perhaps twenty thousand people associated with the court, which makes the palace a world in itself, and like the world. But nothing could stop Julian when he had made up his mind. He sacked the lot and as a result, life in the palace was quite unbearable. For one thing, no one knew where anything was. Every day search parties were sent out to explore the cellars and attics, and of course a number of new scandals came to light, including a sizable counterfeiters' mint which had been set up in the cellar of the Daphne Palace by several enterprising Scholarians.

There were certain aspects of life which Julian never faced if he could help it. The sexual impulse was one. He pretended to be shocked at the way the eunuchs commandeered ordinary citizens for their pleasure. Of course this is a bad thing, contrary to the laws and customs of a decent society. It should not be allowed. Naturally. But is it *astonishing*? Julian writes—and used to talk—as though the evil he had witnessed was some sort of unparalleled horror, which it was not.

I finally asked him once if he had any idea what his own armies did in the German and Frankish villages. Wasn't he aware that no man, woman or child was safe from their lust? Julian responded vaguely, deploring the brutality of war in general. But I pressed him until he admitted that though he had *heard* of such things happening (I know of at least a dozen cases of rape he was forced personally to punish), he had always accepted them as a concomitant of war. Though this was disingenuous, Julian was often surprisingly innocent. His celibacy after Helena's death was not a pose, as so many (including myself) suspected at the time. He was quite genuine in his mortification of the flesh, which explained his dislike of being touched and his avoidance of any place where the human body was revealed, particularly public baths.

I think what most distressed him about the behavior of the eunuchs was the knowledge that not only had he the power to do the same but that he *wanted* to. This recognition of his own nature horrified him. Note that as he lingers over the scene, what most strikes him is not so much the demonstration of lust but the power to do what one likes with another, and that other not a slave but free. Our Julian—like all of us—had a touch of Tiberius in him, and he hated it.

For twenty years now I have been haunted by one detail, the pouring of honey on the genitals of the smith's apprentice. What exactly *was* the eunuch's plan? What was the girl supposed to do? And why honey? I have theories of course, but I shall never know for certain since Julian ended the party much too soon. I am confident of one thing: the eunuch was a cook and accustomed to basting game birds with honey. He was obviously reverting to habit.

*Libanius*: The lechery of Priscus is an unexpected development of his senescence. I am not aware of any "touch of Tiberius" in myself, rather the contrary.

# XVII

*Julian Augustus*

Constantius seldom addressed the senate for the excellent reason that he could not speak for any length of time without stammering or making some error in logic or grammar. As a result, he almost never set foot in the senate house. He preferred to summon the senate to the throne room in the Daphne Palace where he could address them informally, on those rare occasions when he dealt with them at all.

I returned to the old ways, imitating Augustus, who was content to be first citizen. On January first I walked across the square to attend the senate merely as a member. The conscript fathers affected to be pleased by my gesture, and for the remaining months that I was in the city I often attended their sessions. I don't need to add that whatever I did, I always spoke!

It is customary for new consuls taking office to sponsor games and entertainments. Mamertinus gave us three days of chariot races in the Hippodrome which I attended as a courtesy to him. I found the races interminable but I enjoyed the crowds. They always greeted me with an earsplitting roar, and I was told that not once in twenty-five years had Constantius evoked such an affectionate response. Since several people told me this perhaps it is true and not mere flattery.

While attending the first day's races, I examined with some interest the various works of art Constantine had placed along the center of the track: obelisks, columns, bronze memorials. One of them is particularly beautiful: three bronze snakes intertwine to form a tall column upon which a golden tripod supports a golden bowl dedicated by the Greeks to Apollo at Delphi as a thanksgiving for their victory over Persia. Constantine stole even the holiest of relics to decorate his city. One day I shall send them all back to their original homes. But thinking of Delphi gave me an idea. I turned to Oribasius. "We should consult the oracle."

"Which oracle?" Oribasius maintains that between soothsayers, oracles and sacrifices, I have terrified the future into submission.

"Delphi! The only oracle."

"Does it still exist?"

"Find out."

Oribasius laughed. "Shall I go now, before the games are over?"

"No. But you want to visit Greece anyway. If you do, visit the oracle and consult the Pythoness."

So it was agreed. We were wondering what form my question to the oracle should take, when a number of slaves were brought forward to receive their freedom. This is an ancient custom, to celebrate the new year and the accession of new consuls. The slaves lined up before the imperial box and I eagerly said the legal formula which made them free. There was a startled gasp from the crowd. I was bewildered. Mamertinus who sat on my right was much amused. "Augustus, the consul is supposed to free the slaves, just as the consul gives the games." Greatly embarrassed,

I shouted to the people, "I hereby fine myself ten pounds of gold for usurping the consul's function!" This was received with much laughter and cheering, and I think it made a good impression.

On 4 February 362 I declared religious freedom in the world. Anyone could worship any god in any way he chose. The cult of the Galileans was no longer the state's religion, nor were Galilean priests exempt from paying taxes and the usual municipal duties. I also recalled all the bishops who had been sent into exile by Constantius. I even allowed the terrible Athanasius to return to Alexandria, though I did not mean for him to be bishop again. Among those who returned from exile was Actius, who had given a good report of me to Gallus. I shall always be grateful to him.

Soon after I had taken possession of the capital, I was faced with a most disagreeable crisis. My old teacher Bishop George had finally succeeded Athanasius as bishop of Alexandria. Not surprisingly, George proved to be an unpopular prelate. He was highhanded and arbitrary with everyone. Matters came to a head when he destroyed a Mithraeum, saying that he intended to build a charnel house on its foundation. When our brothers rightfully protested this sacrilege, he retaliated by displaying all sorts of human skulls and bones as well as obscene objects, declaring falsely that he had found these "proofs" of human sacrifice buried in the Mithraeum. It was an ugly business.

George also incurred the wrath of the Athanasians by his single-minded persecution of all those who had followed the teachings of the bishop. The Alexandrians could not endure him. When word finally came that his protector Constantius was dead, the mob stormed the bishop's palace and murdered George; his body was then tied to a camel and dragged through the city to the beach, where it was burned and the ashes thrown into the sea. This happened on 24 December. When I heard about it, I wrote the people of the city a harsh letter, threatening reprisals. Their officials were most apologetic and promised to keep the peace. Not long after, Athanasius appeared in the city with a great mob of fanatics and resumed his old place as bishop. Almost his first gesture was to "baptize" the wife of my governor. This was too much. I banished Athanasius, making it clear that a return from exile did not mean a return to power for deposed bishops, especially those who are resourceful enemies of Hellenism.

At about this time I acquired George's library, easily one of the best in Asia. I am rather sentimental about that library, for his were the actual books which had shaped my own mind. I am traveling at this moment with George's set of Plotinus. The rest of the books I left at Constantinople as a nucleus for the Julian library.

The Edict of 4 February had a good effect, though there was much complaint from the Arian bishops, who felt that by allowing their Athanasian brethren to return, I was insuring doctrinal quarrels which would inevitably weaken the Galilean organization. Exactly! They are now at one another's throats. I have also insisted that all lands and buildings which over the years the Galileans seized from us be restored. I realize that this will cause some hardship, but there is no other way of getting the thing done. I am quite prepared for trouble.

On 22 February I issued another edict, reserving to myself alone the right to use the public transport. The bishops, hurrying here and there at the state's expense, had wrecked the system. *Note*: At this point list all edicts for the year, as well as government appointments. They are of course on permanent file at the Record Office, but even so one must be thorough. Meanwhile, I want only to touch on the high points of those six months in Constantinople.

Late in February I learned, quite by accident, that Vettius Agorius Praetextatus and his wife were in the city. He is the leader of the Hellenist party at Rome while his wife, Aconia Paulina, has been admitted to every mystery available to women as well as being high priestess of Hecate. I was eager to meet them.

Praetextatus is a slight, frail man, with flowing white hair and delicate small features. His wife is somewhat taller than her husband and as red-faced and robust as a Gaul, though she is of the purest Roman stock. They are most enthusiastic at what I am doing, particularly Aconia Paulina. "We have had a remarkable response at our temple of Hecate. Truly remarkable. And all due to you. Why, last year in Rome we could hardly get anyone to undergo initiation but now . . . well, I have received reports from Milan, Alexandria, Athens . . . *everywhere*, that the women are flocking to us! We are second only to Isis in enrollment, and though I am devoted to the Isis cult (in fact, I am an initiate,

295

second degree, I think Hecate has always drawn a better class of women. I only hope we shall be able to open a temple right here."

"You shall! You shall!" I was delighted. "I want every god represented in the capital!"

Aconia Paulina beamed. Praetextatus smiled gravely. "Every day," he said softly, "every waking hour, we pray for your success."

For at least an hour the three of us celebrated that unity which only those who have been initiated into the mysteries can know. We were as one. Then I got down to business.

"If we are to defeat the Galileans we must, very simply, have a comparable organization."

Praetextatus was dubious. "We have often discussed this at Rome and until recently we thought we were at least holding our own. At heart, Rome is anti-Christian. The senate is certainly Hellenist." He paused and looked out the window, as though searching for Zeus himself in the rain clouds rolling in from the sea. "You see, Augustus, we are not one organization like the Galileans. We are many. Also, we are voluntary. We do not have the support of the government . . ."

"You do now."

". . . now, yes, but is now too late? Also, our appeal is essentially to the individual, at least in the mysteries. Each man who is initiated undergoes the experience alone. At Eleusis it is the single soul which confronts eternity."

"But there is also the sense of fellowship with other initiates! Look at us! You and I are brothers in Mithras . . ."

"That is not the same thing as belonging to an open congregation, our conduct governed by priests who are quite as interested in property and political power as they are in religion."

"I agree." I tapped the papers in front of me. "And I suggest we fight them on their own ground. I plan a world priesthood, governed by the Roman Pontifex Maximus. We shall divide the world into administrative units, the way the Galileans have done— and each diocese will have its own hierarchy of priests under a single high priest, responsible to me."

They were impressed. Aconia Paulina wanted to know if all cults would be represented in the priesthood. I said yes. Every god and goddess known to the people, no matter in what guise or under what strange name, would be worshipped, for multiplicity is the nature of life. We all believe—even the Galileans, despite their confused doctrine of trinity—that there is a single Godhead from which all life, divine and mortal, descends and to which all life must return. We may not know this creator, though his outward symbol is the sun. But through intermediaries, human and divine, he speaks to us, shows us aspects of himself, prepares us for the next stage of the journey. "To find the father and maker of all is hard," as Socrates said. "And having found him it is impossible to utter him." Yet as Aeschylus wrote with equal wisdom, "men search out god and *searching* find him." The search is the whole point to philosophy and to the religious experience. It is a part of the Galilean impiety to proclaim that the search ended three hundred years ago when a young rabbi was executed for treason. But according to Paul of Tarsus, Jesus was no ordinary rabbi nor even messiah; he was the One God himself who rose from the dead in order to judge the world *immediately*. In fact, Jesus is quoted as having assured his followers that some of them would still be alive when the day of judging arrived. But one by one the disciples died in the natural course and we are still waiting for that promised day. Meanwhile, the bishops amass property, persecute one another, and otherwise revel in this life, while the state is weakened and on our borders the barbarians gather like winter wolves, waiting for us to stagger in our weakness, and to fall. I see this as plainly as I see my hand as it crosses the page (for this part I do not entrust to any secretary). To stop the chariot as it careens into the sun, *that* is what I was born to do.

I explained my plans to Praetextatus. Some I have already put into effect. Others must wait until I return from Persia.

The failure of Hellenism has been, largely, a matter of organization. Rome never tried to impose any sort of worship upon the countries it conquered and civilized; in fact, quite the contrary. Rome was eclectic. All religions were given an equal opportunity and even Isis—after some resistance—was worshipped at Rome. As a result we have a hundred important gods and a dozen mysteries. Certain rites are—or were—supported by the state because they involved the genius of Rome. But no attempt was ever made to coordinate the worship of Zeus on the Capitol with, let us say, the Vestals who kept the sacred fire in the old forum. As time passed our rites became, and one must admit it bluntly, merely form, a reassuring reminder of the great age of the city, a token gesture to the old gods who were thought to have founded and guided Rome from a village by the Tiber to world empire. Yet

297

from the beginning, there were always those who mocked. A senator of the old Republic once asked an augur how he was able to get through a ceremony of divination without laughing. I am not so light-minded, though I concede that many of our rites have lost their meaning over the centuries; witness those temples at Rome where certain verses learned by rote are chanted year in and year out, yet no one, including the priests, knows what they mean, for they are in the early language of the Etruscans, long since forgotten.

As the religious forms of the state became more and more rigid and perfunctory, the people were drawn to the mystery cults, many of them Asiatic in origin. At Eleusis or in the various caves of Mithras, they were able to get a vision of what this life can be, as well as a foretaste of the one that follows. There are, then, three sorts of religious experiences. The ancient rites, which are essentially propitiatory. The mysteries, which purge the soul and allow us to glimpse eternity. And philosophy, which attempts not only to define the material world but to suggest practical ways to the good life, as well as attempting to synthesize (as Iamblichos does so beautifully) all true religion in a single comprehensive system.

Now into this most satisfactory—at least potentially—of worlds, came the Galileans. They base *their* religion on the idea of a single god, as though that were a novelty: from Homer to Julian, Hellenes have been monotheist. Now this single god, according to the largest of the Galilean sects, sent his son (conceived of a virgin, like so many other Asiatic gods) to preach to the world, to suffer, to rise from the dead, to judge mankind on a day which was supposed to have dawned more than three hundred years ago. Now I have studied as carefully as any bishop the writings of those who knew the Galilean, or said they did. They are composed in bad Greek, which I should have thought would have been enough to put off any educated man, while the story they tell is confused, to say the least (following Porphyry I have discovered some sixty-four palpable contradictions and absurdities).

The actual life story of the Galilean has vanished. But I have had an interesting time trying to piece it together. Until thirty years ago, the archives at Rome contained a number of contemporary reports on his life. They have since disappeared, destroyed by order of Constantine. It is of course an old and bitter joke that the Nazarene himself was not a Christian. He was something quite else, I have talked to antiquarians who knew about the file in the archives; several had either read it or knew people who had. Jesus was, simply, a reforming Jewish priest, exclusive as the Jews are, with no interest in proselytizing outside the small world of the Jews. His troubles with Rome were not religious (when did Rome ever persecute anyone for religious belief?) but political. This Jesus thought he was the messiah. Now the messiah is a sort of Jewish hero who, according to legend, will one day establish a Jewish empire prior to the end of the world. He is certainly *not* a god, much less the One God's son. The messiah has been the subject of many Jewish prophecies, and Jesus carefully acted out each prophetic requirement in order to make himself resemble this hero (the messiah would enter Jerusalem on an ass; so did he, et cetera). But the thing went wrong. The people did not support him. His god forsook him. He turned to violence. With a large band of rebels, he seized the temple, announcing that he had come with a sword. What his god would not do for him he must do for himself. So at the end he was neither a god nor even the Jewish messiah but a rebel who tried to make himself king of the Jews. Quite correctly, our governor executed him.

We must never forget that *in his own words*, Jesus was a Jew who believed in the Law of Moses. This means he could not be the son of God (the purest sort of blasphemy), much less God himself, temporarily earthbound. There is nothing in the book of the Jews which prepares us for a messiah's kinship with Jehovah. Only by continual reinterpretation and convenient "revelations" have the Galileans been able to change this reformer-rabbi's career into a parody of one of our own gods, creating a passion of death and rebirth quite inconceivable to one who kept the law of Moses . . . not to mention disgusting to us who have worshipped not men who were executed in time but symbolic figures like Mithras and Osiris and Adonis whose *literal* existence does not matter but whose mysterious legend and revelation are everything.

The moral preachings of the Galilean, though often incoherently recorded, are beyond criticism. He preaches honesty, sobriety, goodness, and a kind of asceticism. In other words, he was a quite ordinary Jewish rabbi, with Pharisee tendencies. In a crude way he resembles Marcus Aurelius. Compared to Plato or Aristotle, he is a child.

It is the wonder of our age how this simple-minded provincial priest was so extraordinarily transformed into a god by Paul of

299

Tarsus who outdid all quacks and cheats that ever existed any-where. As Porphyry wrote so sharply in the last century, "The gods have declared Christ to have been most pious; he has become immortal and by them his memory is cherished. Whereas, the Christians are a polluted set, contaminated and enmeshed in error." It is even worse now. By the time Constantine, Constantius and the horde of bishops got through with Jesus, little of his original message was left. Every time they hold a synod they move further away from the man's original teaching. The conception of the triple god is their latest masterpiece.

One reason why the Galileans grow ever more powerful and dangerous to us is their continual assimilation of our rites and holy days. Since they rightly regard Mithraism as their chief rival, they have for some years now been taking over various aspects of the Mithraic rite and incorporating them into their own ceremonies. Some critics believe that gradual absorption of our forms and prayers is fairly recent. But I date it from the very beginning. In at least one of the biographies of the Galileans there is a strange anecdote which his followers are never able to explain (and they are usually nothing if not ingenious at making sense of nonsense). The Galilean goes to a fig tree to pick its fruit. But as it is not the season for bearing, the tree was barren. In a fit of temper, the Galilean blasts the tree with magic, killing it. Now the fig tree is sacred to Mithras: as a youth, it was his home, his source of food and clothing. I suggest that the apologist who wrote that passage in the first century did so deliberately, inventing it or recording it, no matter which, as a sign that the Galilean would destroy the worship of Mithras as easily as he had destroyed the sacred tree.

But I do not mean here in the pages of what is supposed to be a chronicle to give my familiar arguments against the Galileans. They may be found in the several essays I have published on the subject.

Praetextatus and I worked closely together all that winter in Constantinople. I found both him and his wife enormously knowl-edgeable on religious matters. But whenever I spoke of practical matters, Praetextatus would lose interest. So quite alone, I set about reorganizing ... no, organizing Hellenism. The Galileans have received much credit for giving charity to anyone who asks for it. We are now doing the same. Their priests impress the ignorant with their so-called holy lives. I now insist that our priests be *truly* holy. I have given them full instructions on how to comport themselves in public and private. Though Praetextatus lacked inspiration, he worked diligently with me on these plans. But Aconia was no help at all. She does not, as the saying goes, grow on one. I am afraid that her only interest is her own salvation. She regards religion as a sort of lottery, and if she takes a chance on each of the gods, the law of averages ought to favor her to pick the right one who will save her soul. Though what eternity would want with Aconia Paulina, I don't know.

*Priscus*: Bravo Julian!

Though Julian makes no mention of it, at about this time our old friend Maximus made his triumphant entry into Constantinople. I was not there when he arrived, but I certainly heard enough about it. When he became emperor, Julian invited every philosopher and magician in the empire to court. And just about all of them came. Only his Christian "friends" stayed away. Basil was being holy in Cappadocia; I don't think Gregory was invited. It might be interesting to check the Record Office about Gregory because I seem to recall a most flattering letter he wrote Julian at about this time, but perhaps I dreamed it ... Only last week I called Hippia by my mother's name, after half a century of marriage! I am of course losing my mind. But why not? When death comes, it will have nothing to take but a withered sack of bones, for the memory of Priscus, which is Priscus, will long since have flown.

Several times, Julian tried to get Maximus to leave Ephesus and come to Gaul, but the omens were never right. I'm sure they weren't! Maximus was not about to ally himself to what most people thought would be the losing side of a rebellion. But when an invitation finally came from the Sacred Palace, Maximus was ready. He arrived in Constantinople while Julian was at the senate house. Incidentally, Julian was in his element with that body, though I'm not sure they enjoyed him as much as he did them. The senate usually cannot muster a quorum. But with an emperor present, the senate chamber threatened to burst. The conscript fathers sat on one another's laps while Julian joked, prayed, exhorted and, all in all, got quite a lot of work done, for there was nothing which he did not concern himself with.

During the six months he was at Constantinople, Julian built a harbor at the foot of the palace. He exempted all men with thirteen children or more from paying taxes: he was much concerned at our declining birthrate. I can't think why. It is not as if there were not too many people on earth as it is and to make more of them will simply dilute the breed. But he was disturbed by the fact that the barbarians increase in numbers while we decrease. He also confirmed our old friend Sallust as praetorian prefect of Gaul, though he clearly would have liked to have him close by. He made this personal sacrifice because there was no one else he could trust to protect the West, and he was right, as each year confirms. Today Gaul is still secure while the Goths are now just a few days' march from this house in Athens where I sit, writing of old things, and remembering more than I thought.

Julian was in the middle of an impassioned speech when Maximus appeared in the door of the senate chamber. The great "philosopher" was dressed in green silk robes covered with cabalistic designs; his long gray beard was perfumed and his shaggy eyebrows were carefully combed—I've actually seen him comb them to give the effect of two perfect arches. He carried his magic staff carved from dragon's bone, or some such nonsense. The senators were shocked, for no one but a senator may enter during session; certainly, no one may enter when the emperor is speaking. But Julian, seeing Maximus, stopped in mid-sentence and ran, arms outstretched, to embrace that old charlatan. I'm glad I was not there.

Julian then presented Maximus to the senate, calling him the world's wisest and holiest man and stressing what an honor it was for all present to be able to do homage to such a man. Needless to say, everyone was scandalized. Maximus and his wife were given an entire wing of the Sacred Palace for their own court; and there were now two emperors in Constantinople. Maximus's wife did a considerable business on her own as a sort of unofficial Master of the Offices, arranging audiences with the Emperor and granting petitions. They made a fortune in those months. They were a rare couple.

Though I am not in the habit of laughing at anyone's death, I still chuckle to myself when I think of *her* death. Do you know the story? After the Persian campaign when Maximus was first in trouble, he decided to commit suicide. His wife agreed that this was the correct thing to do. She also insisted on killing herself. With her usual brisk efficiency, she put their affairs in order; bought poison and composed farewell letters of enormous length. Then, gravely, they said good-bye to one another. She drank first and promptly died. Maximus lost his nerve, and survived. To this day I find myself smiling whenever I think of that preposterous couple.

*Julian Augustus*

At the beginning of April, for my own amusement, I summoned the bishops to the palace. After all, I am Pontifex Maximus and all religion is my province, though I would not have the temerity to say to any priests what Constantius said to the bishops at the synod of Milan in 355: "My will shall be your guiding line!"

I received the Galileans in the Daphne Palace. I wore the diadem and I held the orb. (Galileans are always impressed by the ritual show of power.) It was a remarkable occasion. Nearly a thousand bishops were present, including those whom I had recalled from exile. As a result, there are often two bishops for one see. This makes for much bitter wrangling. They are not gentle, these priests of the Nazarene.

At first the bishops were afraid of me, but I put them at their ease. I told them that I was not a persecutor, though others before me had been, not all of them emperors. This was directed at several militant bishops who had, by violence, destroyed their enemies.

"No one," I said, "shall ever be hurt by me because of his faith." There was a general easing of tension. But they were still wary. "Of course I should like to convince you that I am right. But since what is true is as plain as the sun, if you will not see it, you will not see it. But I cannot allow you to hurt others, as you have done for so many years. I will not list the crimes you have committed, or permitted. The murders, the thieving, the viciousness more usual to the beasts of the field than to priests, even of the wrong god."

I held up a thick sheaf of documents. "Here are your latest crimes. Murders requested, and property requested ... oh, how you love the riches of this world! Yet your religion preaches that you should not resist injury or go to law or even hold property, much less steal it! You have been taught to consider nothing your own, except your place in the other and better world. Yet you wear jewels, rich robes, build huge basilicas, all in *this* world, not the next. You were taught to despise money, yet you amass it. When done an injury, real or imagined, you were told not to retaliate, that it was wrong to return evil for evil. Yet you battle with one another in lawless mobs, torturing and killing those you

303

disapprove of. You have endangered not only the true religion but the security of the state whose chief magistrate I am, by heaven's will. You are not worthy even of the Nazarene. If you cannot live by those precepts which you are willing to defend with the knife and with poison" (a reference to the poisoning of Arius by Athanasius), "what *are* you then but hypocrites?"

All through this there had been mumbling. Now there was a fine Galilean eruption. They began to shout and rant, shaking their fists not only at me—which is treason—but at one another—which is folly, for they ought to be united against the common enemy. I tried to speak but I could not be heard, and *my* voice can be heard by an entire army out-of-doors! The tribune of the Scholarians looked alarmed, but I motioned to him to do nothing.

Finally, like the bull of Mithras, I bellowed, "The Franks and Germans listened when I spoke!" This had a quieting effect. They remembered where they were.

I was then all mildness. I apologized for having spoken harshly. It was only because I had such respect for the words of the Nazarene, as well as for the strict law of the Jews which he—as a Jew—sought only to extol. This caused a slight but brief murmur. I then said that I was willing to give the Nazarene a place among the gods between Isis and Dionysos, but that no man who had the slightest reverence for the unique creator of the universe could possibly conceive that this provincial wonder-worker could have been the creator himself. Before they could start their monkey-chatter, I spoke quickly and loudly. "Yet I am willing to believe he is a manifestation of the One, a healer, much like Asklepios, and as such, I am willing to honor him."

I then repeated what I had written in the Edict of 4 February. There was to be universal toleration. The Galileans could do as they pleased among their own kind though they were not to persecute each other, much less Hellenists. I suggested that they be less greedy in the acquiring of property. I admitted that I was causing them hardship when I asked for the return of temple lands, but I pointed out that they had done us considerable hardship when they had stolen them. I suggested that if they were less contemptuous of our ancient myths—Kronos swallowing his children—we might be less rude about their triple god and his virgin-birth.

"After all, as educated men, we should realize that myths always stand for other things. They are toys for children teething. The man knows that the toy horse is not a true horse but merely suggests

304

the idea of a horse to a baby's mind. When we pray before the statue of Zeus, though the statue contains him as everything must, the statue is not the god himself but only a suggestion of him. Surely, as fellow priests, we can be frank with one another about these grown-up matters.

"Now I must ask you to keep the peace in the cities. If you do not, as chief magistrate I shall discipline you. But you have nothing to fear from me as Pontifex Maximus, *if* you behave with propriety and obey the civil laws and conduct your disputes without resorting, as you have in the past, to fire and the knife. Preach only the Nazarene's words and we shall be able to live with one another. But of course you are not content with those few words. You add new things daily. You nibble at Hellenism, you appropriate our holy days, our ceremonies, all in the name of a Jew who knew them not. You rob us, and reject us, while quoting the arrogant Cyprian who said that outside your faith there can be no salvation! Is one to believe that a thousand generations of men, among them Plato and Homer, are lost because they did not worship a Jew who was supposed to be god? a man not born when the world began? You invite us to believe that the One God is not only 'jealous,' as the Jews say, but evil? I am afraid it takes extraordinary self-delusion to believe such things. But I am not here to criticize you, only to ask you to keep the peace and never to forget that the greatness of our world was the gift of other gods and a different, more subtle philosophy, reflecting the variety in nature."

An ancient bishop got to his feet. He wore the simple robes of a holy man rather than those of a prince. "There is but One God. Only one from the beginning of time."

"I agree. And he may take as many forms as he chooses for he is all powerful."

"Only one form has the One God." The old voice though thin was firm.

"Was this One God revealed in the holy book of the Jews?"

"He was, Augustus. And he remains."

"Did not Moses say in the book called Deuteronomy that 'You shall not add to the word I have given you, nor take away from it?' And did he not curse anyone who does not abide by the Law God gave him?"

There was a pause. The bishops were subtle men and they were perfectly aware that I had set some sort of trap for them, but they

305

were forced to proceed according to their holy book, for nothing in this part of it is remotely ambiguous.

"All that you say Moses said is not only true but eternal."

"Then," I let the trap snap shut, "why do you alter the Law to suit yourselves? In a thousand ways you have perverted not only Moses but the Nazarene and you have done it ever since the day the blasphemous Paul of Tarsus said 'Christ is the end of the Law!' You are neither Hebrew nor Galilean but opportunists."

The storm broke. The bishops were on their feet shouting sacred texts, insults, threats. For a moment I thought they were going to attack me on the throne, but even in their fury they kept within bounds.

I rose and crossed to the door at the back, ignored by the bishops who were now abusing one another as well as me. As I was about to leave the room, the ancient bishop who had challenged me suddenly barred my way. He was Maris of Chalcedon. I have never seen such malevolence in a human face.

"You are cursed!" He nearly spat in my face. The Scholarian tribune drew his sword but I motioned for him to stand back.

"By you perhaps, but not by God." I was mild, even Galilean.

"Apostate!" He hurled the word at me.

I smiled. "Not I. You. I worship as men have worshipped since time began. It is you who have abandoned not only philosophy but God himself."

"You will burn in hell!"

"Beware, old man, *you* are the one in danger. All of you. Don't think that the several generations which have passed since the Nazarene died count for more than an instant in eternity. The past does not cease because you ignore it. What you worship is evil. You have chosen division, cruelty, superstition. Well, I mean to stop the illness, to cut out the cancer, to strengthen the state . . . Now step aside, my good fellow, and let me pass."

He stepped not aside but directly in my path. The tribune of the Scholarians said suddenly, "He is blind, Augustus."

The old man nodded. "And glad that I cannot see you, Apostate."

"You must ask the Nazarene to restore your sight. If he loves you, it is a simple matter." With this, I stepped around him. As I did, he made a hissing noise, the sort old women make when they fear the presence of an evil demon. He also made the sign of the cross on his forehead. I responded to this gracious gesture by making the sign which wards off the evil eye, but it was lost on him.

*   *   *

Spring came early to the city. It was an exciting time, full of new things accomplished. I attended the senate regularly. I was the first emperor since Augustus to act simply as a member of that body rather than as its lord and dictator. Priscus thinks they detest me for my taking part in their debates; perhaps he's right, but even if they do, it is always good to restore meaning to ancient institutions.

I made many reforms. I removed all Galileans from the Scholarian Guard. I refused to allow any Galilean to be governor of a province. There was some outcry at this. But I am right. A governor who sympathizes with the Galileans can hardly be expected to carry out my edicts, particularly those which have to do with the rebuilding of temples. Several senators took me to task in debate: why if I was so tolerant of all religions did I persecute Galilean officials? For obvious reasons my answer was more sophistic than honest.

"Do the conscript fathers agree that a governor must uphold the laws of the state?" There was agreement. "Are not there certain crimes—such as treason—which carry with them the death penalty?" Again agreement. "Would you also agree that no man could be an effective governor who did not have the right to sentence the guilty to death?" A few had now got the drift of my argument. "Well, then how can a Galilean be a governor when he is expressly enjoined by the Nazarene never to take another man's life, as you may read in that book which is said to be by Matthew, Chapter XXVI, verse 52, and again in the work of the writer John?" Always use their own weapons against them; they use ours against us.

I removed the cross from all military and civil insignia, as well as from the coins I minted, substituting instead images of the gods. I addressed everyone as "my good fellow," imitating Socrates. Finally, I took direct charge of the army. The emperor of course is commander-in-chief, but if he is not an experienced soldier he can never be more than a sort of totem or sacred image, the actual business of war being left to the field commanders. But with my own Gallic troops as core, I was able to dominate the army, aided by the officers I had brought with me from Gaul, particularly Nevitta, Dagalaif, and Jovinus; from the old army of the East, I retained Victor, Arintheus and my cousin Procopius.

Curiously enough, I heard nothing directly from Sapor when

307

I became Emperor. This was a serious breach of etiquette, for the Roman and Persian rulers always exchange ritual greeting upon the accession of one or the other. Yet there was only silence from Ctesiphon. But I did learn something about Sapor when a most opulent and curious embassy arrived in the city at the beginning of May. The ambassadors were a brown-skinned, delicate little people from Ceylon, an island off the coast of India. They brought rich gifts. They wished to establish trade with us, and we were most receptive. Their ambassador told me that Sapor had followed closely my campaigns in Gaul and feared me. How strange to think that an Oriental king at the edge of the world should know all about my conquests three thousand miles away! But then I know quite a lot about him. Sapor and I have more in common with one another than we do with our own intimates, for we share the same sort of responsibility and the same awesome power. If I take him captive, we should have much to talk about.

I planned a winter campaign, recalling the old saying that in cold weather "a Persian won't draw his hand from his cloak." Unfortunately, as it turned out, I was several months off schedule. But meanwhile, Nevitta trained the troops and their spirits were high; even the Celts did not mind the East as much as they thought they would.

During this time, I got to know the Persian Prince Ormisda. He is a half-brother of Sapor, and the Persian throne is rightfully his. But when he was a boy Sapor exiled him. After a brief stay at the court of Armenia, Ormisda attached himself to us. For forty years (he is sixty) he has dreamed of only one thing, a Roman conquest of Persia that would place him on the throne. Constantine, Constantius and myself have all used him as a soldier and as a source of information. But of the three I am the first to try and make his dream a reality. Meanwhile, he is invaluable to me. He has many secret partisans at the court of Ctesiphon; he is a fine soldier who fought with Constantine in Europe; and of course he always used to accompany Constantius whenever that bold warrior would assemble the Eastern army for a march to the Euphrates. Once at the river's edge, the Emperor would make camp and wait until Sapor and the Persian army appeared. As soon as the enemy was in view, Constantius would then withdraw with superb dignity to Antioch or Tarsus and go into winter quarters. These military pageants got to be a most depressing joke.

Ormisda was in despair, until I became emperor. Now he is content. As I write these lines, he is almost Great King of Persia.

In my leisure time—there was no leisure!—I sat up late with friends and we talked of a thousand things. I was particularly close to Maximus; in fact, it was like old times in Ephesus. As always, he was the link between the gods and me. I recall one evening as being particularly significant; even revelatory.

A number of us were gathered on the garden terrace of the Daphne Palace. It was a warm night, and there was a splendid view of the sea of Marmora, glittering in the full moon's light. Flowering trees and shrubs filled the air with fragrance. Far off the lights of the city flickered at the sea's edge. The night was still, except for us and the cry of an occasional guard as he challenged strangers.

Ormisda seemed eager to speak to me; I motioned for him to come with me to the far end of the terrace. Here we sat on a ledge among roses in their first bloom.

"Sapor does not want a war, Augustus." Ormisda still speaks with a heavy Persian accent despite a lifetime among us.

"So the Singhalese embassy tells me." I was noncommittal; I beat a war-tattoo with my heels on the ledge.

"Do you know what the Persians call you?"

"I can imagine." I sighed. It is amazing how one's intimates enjoy repeating the terrible things said of us. In ancient times those who brought bad news were promptly put to death: one of the pleasures of classical tyranny!

"The thunderbolt."

"Because I am the agent of Zeus?"

"Because of the speed with which you crossed Europe and surprised the army at Sirmium."

I was pleased. "It's as good as a battle won to be feared by your enemy."

"They fear 'the thunderbolt.'"

"But then Constantius's army fears Sapor. So the fears are now balanced."

Ormisda came to the point. "They will do everything possible to placate you. I am told by . . ." He gestured delicately with his rose. He knew that I knew he maintained close connections with the dissident party in Persia. ". . . that Sapor is willing to withdraw from the border, to leave Mesopotamia. Almost anything you ask, he will do."

I looked at him gravely. He looked at me. A long moment. Then I smiled. "I promise you to listen to no embassy."

"But I did not suggest that, Augustus."

"No embassy. No treaty. Only war to the end. That is a holy vow."

"I believe you, Lord. I thank you." He spoke softly, in his curiously accented Greek.

"And if the gods are with us, I shall crown you myself at Ctesiphon, with Sapor as . . ."

"Footstool!" Ormisda laughed, referring to a particularly grue-some custom of the Persian kings, who skin captured rulers and stuff them for cushions. Then Praetextatus joined us on the ledge. As much as I esteem him, I find his company sometimes burden-some. He has no lightness in him, only a constant noble gravity. Yet in religious matters, I could not manage without him.

"Are we making progress?" That was my usual greeting to him.

"I hope so, Augustus. I believe so. Only last week my wife initiated a hundred local ladies into Hecate's mysteries."

"Wonderful!" And it was, for women are the operatives of religion and though they seldom possess the true religious sense, they are excellent at getting things done and making converts. The early Galileans devoted much time to flattering slave-women in order to win over their mistresses. Even at Rome today, it is not uncommon for senators to uphold fiercely the old gods in the senate only to come home to a house filled with Galilean women, singing Galilean songs.

"When I leave for the south, Praetextatus, I shall want you to fill an important post for me."

"What is that, Augustus?" Noble as he was, I detected that sudden alertness in the face which I have come to recognize as the premonitory look of one who hopes to be raised up.

"If it suits you, I mean to make you proconsul of Greece." It suited him beautifully, and at great length he thanked me. I then gave him instructions to be as useful as he could to such old friends as Prohaeresius and his niece Macrina.

After this, I left the ledge of roses and walked down a flight of shallow steps, breathing the night air with some delight, aware how little opportunity I now have, simply, to be. For one whose essential interest is philosophy I have managed to be almost every-thing else: soldier, administrator, lawyer . . . whatever is *not* con-templative I am it!

310

Maximus was standing at the foot of the steps in the shadow of a tall cypress. He was looking at the moon. In his hand he held a small staff which, from time to time, he held up to the sky, shifting it this way and that, the shadow crossing his face, drained now of color in the pale light.

"What are the omens?" I stayed outside the circle of the tree, not wanting to disturb what could have been a spell. Maximus did not answer for some minutes as he continued to study the staff and the moon from various angles.

"Good," he said at last, stepping outside the circle of the tree's shadow. "At almost any time this year the omens are good. No matter what you attempt, you will succeed."

"We have come a long way," I said idly, looking down at the city, and the sea beyond. It is awesome to think that everything is one's own, at least for the brief space of a life—which is why I have always the sense I must hurry to get things done, that there is hardly any time at all for a man to impress his quality and passion upon a world which will continue after him, as unconcerned as it was when it preceded him. Each day that I live I say to myself: the visible world is mine, use it, change it, but be quick, for the night comes all too fast and nothing is ever entirely finished, nothing.

"You have made Praetextatus proconsul of Greece."

Once again Maximus knew what—until a few moments before—only I had known. Does he read my mind, the way the Chaldeans do? or does he get instruction from his private genius? No matter *what* his method, he can always anticipate not only my mood but my administrative appointments!

*Priscus*: Julian was often willfully gullible. Maximus had been standing just below the ledge when the announcement was made. He did not need to consult "his private genius," just his ears. As a matter of fact Maximus's ears *did* resemble those of a fox: long, pointed and slightly bent forward. He was a notorious eavesdropper, proving that nature is always considerate in putting together a man. Though as philosophers, we might argue that a man born with the ears of a fox might then be impelled to become an eavesdropper.

*Julian Augustus*

"I saw something interesting tonight." Maximus took me by the arm and led me along the terrace to a bench which faces the

311

sea. Several small ships were making for the new harbor I am building just to the north. We could hear the long cry of sailors across the waters, and the response from the harbor. "Safe landing," I prayed to Poseidon out of habit. We sat down.

"All the signs for several weeks have pointed to a marvelous victory for you—for us." He indicated my star, which shone at that moment in the west.

I nodded. "I have had good signs, too."

"Yesterday—while praying to Cybele—the goddess spoke to me."

I was impressed. Maximus speaks often to gods of the lower rank (and of course to demons of every sort) but very seldom does he hear the voice of Cybele, the Great Mother, Earth herself.

Maximus was excited, though he tried to disguise it. He had every reason to be exultant, for to speak with Cybele is an extraordinary feat. No, not feat, for one cannot storm heaven; rather, a beautiful sign that the prime movers of the universe now thought him ready and worthy to receive their messages.

"I was praying in her shrine. Down there." He pointed to the makeshift temple I had built near the Daphne Palace. "The chapel was dark, as prescribed. The incense heavy. Her image dim by the light of a single lamp. I prayed as I always pray to her . . ."

"The full verses? to the seventh power?"

He nodded. "Everything, as prescribed. But then, instead of the usual silence and comfort, I felt terror, as if I had strayed to the edge of a precipice. A coldness such as I had never felt before came over me. I thought I might faint, die. Had I offended her? Was I doomed? But then she spoke. The light from the lamp suddenly flared and revealed her image, but it was no longer bronze, *it was she!*"

I murmured a prayer to myself, chilled by his account.

"'Maximus,' she called my name and her voice was like a silver bell. I hailed her by her titles. Then she spoke. 'He whom you love is well loved by me.'"

I could hardly move or breathe while Maximus spoke. It was as if I myself were now listening to the voice of this goddess.

"'He whom the gods love as their true son will be Lord of all the earth.'"

"Persia . . . ?" I whispered. "Did she mean Persia?"

But Maximus continued in the voice of the goddess.

312

"'. . . of all the earth. For we shall send him a second spirit to aid him in the long marches.'"

"Hermes?"

"'One who is now with us shall be with him until he reaches the end of the earth and finishes the work which that spirit began, for our glory,'" Maximus stopped, as though he had come to the end of a page.

There was a long silence. I waited, then Maximus turned to me, eyes flashing, beard like water flowing in the moonlight. "Alexander!" He breathed the name. "You are to finish his work."

"In Persia?"

"And India and all that lies to the farthest east!" Maximus took the edge of my cloak in his hand and held it to his lips, the gesture of a suppliant doing homage. "You are Alexander."

"If this is true . . ."

"*If!* You have heard her words."

"Then we shall break Sapor."

"And after that nothing shall stand in your way from Persia to the eastern ocean. She asks only that you restore her temple at Pessinus."

"Gladly!"

Maximus made a secret and holy gesture to my star. I did the same. Then we were interrupted by Priscus, who said in his loud clear voice, "Stargazing again?"

*Priscus:* If I had known what they were up to, I should have had a good deal more to say in my "loud clear voice." From certain things Julian let slip during the Persian campaign I did get the impression that he believed he was in some spectacular way supported by the gods, but I had no idea that he actually thought he was Alexander, or at least had the ghost of Alexander tucked inside of him, located somewhere between the heart and the liver. This particular madness explains a good deal about the last stages of that campaign when Julian-Alexander began to act very peculiarly indeed. Personally, if I were a general, I would not like to be inhabited by another general, especially one who went insane! But Maximus was capable of anything; and Julian never doubted him.

This is all there is to the Constantinople section of the memoir. Julian intended to give a full account of all his edicts and appointments, but he never got round to it. You can doubtless obtain this material from the Record Office.

313

In May, Julian left Constantinople, to tour Galatia and Cappadocia, en route to his winter quarters at Antioch. Though he said nothing publicly, everyone knew that the Eastern army would assemble at Antioch, in readiness for the invasion of Persia.

I stayed on in Constantinople because I was hard pressed for money at this time. Unlike Maximus and his wife, who were making a fortune out of their imperial protégé, I asked for nothing and I got nothing. Julian never thought of money unless you did. Then he was generous. Fortunately, I was able to give a series of lectures at the University. Old Nicocles was most helpful in getting me pupils. You knew him, didn't you? But of course. He forced you to leave the city back in the 40's. A sad business. But Nicocles was a good friend to me and I was soon able to send Hippia quite a large amount of money. Also, Julian allowed me to live at the Sacred Palace while I taught, so my personal expenses were slight.

One interesting detail: just before Julian left for Antioch, Oribasius returned from Greece. He was significantly silent and there was no longer any talk of restoring Apollo's temple. It was not until many years later that Oribasius told me what had happened at Delphi, the so-called "navel of the earth."

Oribasius found modern Delphi very sad indeed. The works of art which had once decorated the numerous shrines are all gone. Constantine alone stole 2700 statues. There is no sight quite so forlorn as acres of empty pedestals. The town was deserted except for a few tattered Cynics, who offered to show Oribasius about. I've never visited Delphi myself, but one has always heard that the people who lived there were the most rapacious on earth, even worse than the tradesmen at Eleusis. I cannot say that I feel particularly sorry for them now. They had a thousand years of robbing visitors. It was unreasonable to think that this arrangement would last forever.

I suspect Oribasius disliked all religion, much the way I do. But where I prefer the mind of man to any sort of magic, Oribasius preferred the body. What he could not see and touch did not interest him. He was an unusual friend for a prince. His only passion was medicine, which I have always regarded as a branch of magic, though his approach to it was blessedly matter-of-fact. Have you noticed that whenever a physician prescribes such-and-such a treatment, and one follows it and is cured, he is always slightly surprised? Everything a doctor does is guess-work. That is why he must be as good at acting as any Sophist; his cures depend entirely upon a convincing show of authority.

At the temple of Apollo, Oribasius called out, "Where is the priest?" No answer. He went inside. Part of the roof had fallen in: dust was everywhere. Just behind the pedestal where the god's statue had been, he found a sleeping priest with a half-empty skin of wine beside him. It took Oribasius some minutes to wake the man. When told that Oribasius was the Emperor's envoy, he became quite nervous. "It's been a bad season for the temple, very bad. Our revenues are gone. We don't even get the few visitors we had last year. But you must tell the Augustus that we still go about our holy tasks, even though there's no money to fix the roof, or to pay for sacrifices." He got to his feet, swaying from drink.

Oribasius asked about the oracle.

"Oh, we're still functioning. We have an excellent Pythoness. She's rather old but she gets good results. Apollo talks to her all the time, she says. We're quite pleased with her work. I'm sure you'll find her satisfactory. Naturally, you'll want to talk to her. I'll go ask when she can receive you. She has bad days, you know . . ." He gestured vaguely. Then he disappeared down a steep flight of steps.

Oribasius examined the temple. All the famous statues were gone, including the one of Homer which used to be by the door. Incidentally, Julian found this particular statue in a storeroom of the Sacred Palace, and had it set up in his library. I've seen it myself: a fine work, the face full of sadness, Homeric in fact.

The priest returned to say that the Pythoness would consult the oracle the following day. Meanwhile, the usual propitiatory ceremonies must be enacted, particularly the sacrifice. The priest salivated at the word.

Next day, Oribasius and the priest sacrificed a goat on the altar outside the temple. As soon as the animal was dead, the priest sprinkled it with holy water and the legs trembled, supposedly a good sign. After this, they entered the temple and descended the steep steps to the crypt. Against his will, Oribasius found the whole nonsense most impressive.

They sat in a sort of waiting room cut in rock. Opposite them was a door which led into the cell of the god. Here, from a fissure in the earth, steam rises; here, too, is the navel of the world— the omphalos—a round stone said to have been flung to earth by Zeus.

The priestess entered from the temple. She looked at neither priest nor visitor. According to Oribasius, she was immensely old and shrunken and toothless.

"She is now pure," whispered the priest. "She has just bathed in the Kastalian spring." The Pythoness threw a number of laurel leaves and barley meal on a brazier; the room filled with an acrid smoke. "Now she is making the air pure," said the priest. Then Oribasius, eyes streaming with tears from the smoke, followed the Pythoness into the inner cell where, for a thousand years, Apollo has spoken to man. Just beside the omphalos was a tripod, on which the Pythoness sat, cross-legged, her face bent over the steam as it escaped from the earth below her. She muttered incantations.

"All right," whispered the priest. "She is ready to hear you."

In a loud voice Oribasius said: "I come from Flavius Claudius Julianus, Augustus and Pontifex Maximus. He does homage to the god Apollo, and to all the true gods."

The Pythoness sang softly to herself during this, her attention fixed on the steam at the foot of the tripod.

"The Augustus wishes guidance from the god Apollo. He will do whatever he is commanded."

"The question?" The old voice was thin and indistinct.

"Shall the Emperor restore the holy temple of Delphi?"

For a long moment the only sound in the shrine was the faint hissing noise steam makes escaping rock. That sound is possibly the origin of the legend that the earth goddess Ge had a son who was a serpent called Python. The serpent controlled the oracle until Apollo killed him and threw the body down a crevice. The steam is supposed to come from the corpse. The hissing sound is the serpent's dying voice.

At last the Pythoness stirred. She took several deep breaths of steam. She gasped; she coughed; she rolled her eyes; she clung with claw-like hands to the top of the tripod, rocking back and forth. Then she was motionless. When she finally spoke, her voice was firm and distinct despite the absence of teeth.

"Tell the King: on earth has fallen the glorious dwelling, and the water-springs that spoke are still. Nothing is left the god, no roof, no shelter, and in his hand the prophet laurel flowers no more."

That was all. The Pythoness shut her eyes. She seemed to sleep. Oribasius and the priest departed. The priest was distraught.

"I don't believe it," he said. "Of course Apollo wants his temple rebuilt. I can't think what got into her. Of course these messages are always open to interpretation. Sometimes they are deliberately perverse, and obscure . . ." But it was no good.

I asked Oribasius what Julian said when he was told the oracle. "Nothing," said Oribasius. "Except to ask me to mention it to no one."

Personally, I am certain that the priestess was in the pay of the Christians. They knew what importance Julian set by oracles, especially this one. Why do I think they had a hand in the prophecy? Because if the priestess was genuine she would have done everything possible to see that Delphi was restored. She would not have admitted in so many words that the game was up. And to speak *against* the interests of her own establishment meant that she had been made a better offer. Of course I do not believe—as Julian did—that Apollo speaks to us through a succession of ladies who have fits from breathing steam. The whole thing was always a fake. But this time I am positive it was a double fake. Oribasius rather agreed with me when I told him my theory.

As I said, Julian left Constantinople in high spirits and I did not see him again for some months. When I did, I noticed a great change in his mood. The euphoria of Constantinople was gone. He was uneasy and touchy and of course he hated Antioch, which he describes.

# XVIII

*Julian Augustus*

On 10 May I left Constantinople for Antioch. All omens were favorable. The weather was good, though far too dry for that time of year. Instead of going straight south to Syria, I swung to the east, passing through Phrygia and Galatia. I pretended that I wanted to see for myself what these territories were like so that I might have some firsthand knowledge of their problems when it came time for the tax reforms the new Count of the Sacred Largesses, Felix, insisted that I make. But my actual motive was to visit the temple of Cybele at Pessinus and there make solemn offering to my patroness.

I was accompanied by the Petulantes and Scholarians. The

remainder of the army of the East was to gather at Antioch in the autumn. For a number of reasons, I had decided to postpone the invasion of Persia to the following spring. This would give me half a year at Antioch to train the troops and to put in effect various civil and religious reforms. Of my close friends only Maximus accompanied me on this progress. Priscus remained in Constantinople, while Oribasius preferred to make his own way to Antioch, stopping at out-of-the-way villages to look for cures— and he accuses me of liking magic!

It was good to be on the move again, even though, try as I might to reduce my retinue, it was still large and cumbersome. Half the Sacred Consistory attended me, as well as most of the administrative staff of the Sacred Palace. I was particularly bored— yet impressed—by Count Felix, who was acknowledged to be the most brilliant juggler of figures in the empire, a reputation he never allowed me to forget, since his vanity was boundless. Whenever I would rather timidly try to recall my own experiences with the finances of Gaul, he would point a long finger at me and in the tone of master to schoolboy, define the extent of my ignorance, the folly of my instincts, and the need I had of his advice which was invariably: never forgive tax arrears. I came to dread his tall crane-like figure as it approached me after each Consistory, the long dour face set primly in a mask of false patience. But Felix was remarkable in his grasp of detail and, like it or not, I learned a good deal from him.

We crossed the Bosphorus on a fine spring day. The countryside was yellow with wild flowers and the warm air smelled of honey. We passed by Chalcedon but did not enter the city. At Libyssa, I paused to look at the grave of Hannibal. Like my predecessors, I honor him. I particularly admire him as a soldier, for his campaigns in Italy were perhaps the most remarkable of all time, excepting always those of Alexander. No one will ever know why Hannibal failed to take Rome—which is proof to me that the gods on that occasion intervened to save Rome from its most resourceful enemy. The grave is shabby: only a plain marble *stele* records the death of the exile.

We then proceeded to Nicomedia. This was a sad occasion, for Nicomedia is now in ruins. On 24 August 358 earthquakes destroyed half the city. It was the worst natural disaster in our time.

We reached the outskirts of Nicomedia in the late afternoon.

318

Here I was met by the senate of the city, all in darkest mourning. As we passed through streets filled with rubble, I nearly wept; so many familiar sights were gone or altered beyond recognition. Along the street to the palace the people stood, intent and watchful. Every now and then one would step forward to kiss my hand or touch the purple. Some I recognized as fellow students from the University, others as people I had observed in the forum. It was a wretched day.

I granted Nicomedia a considerable sum of money for rebuilding. Felix thought I was setting a bad precedent, but I pointed out to him that this was not just any city but a former world capital, made memorable by the fact that it was here on 24 February 303, Diocletian launched his edict against the Galileans, ordering their charnel houses razed and their communities dissolved. Unfortunately, Diocletian retired two years later and his work was not completed. If it had been . . . but that is wishful thinking. To me has fallen the same task, now doubly difficult, for the enemy have had half a century in which to establish themselves not only among the ignorant but in the Sacred Palace itself.

I could not wait to get away from Nicomedia. As soon as it was decently possible, I bade farewell to the senate, I should note here that everywhere I went I set about restoring the temples, and it was not easy. Most of them are in ruins or occupied by Galileans. To make matters worse, the priesthood in many places has completely died out. Provinces like Cappadocia are now entirely atheist.

Yet I forced no one. Instead, I argued. I reasoned. Occasionally, I confess, I bribed the people to honor as they ought to honor their constant deities. I was criticized for this, particularly by Count Felix, who has no interest in religious matters and thought it folly to give anything to local temples, much less to the people themselves. But I felt it was worth doing. No matter what impels a man to pray to a god, the fact that he performs the ritual act is itself an act of worship and a beginning, even though his heart is false. I do not delude myself that I made many converts. Though I spoke at length to many groups in Galatia, Cappadocia, Cilicia, I convinced only a few. I am perfectly aware of this. Yet one must begin somewhere, even if it means talking to stones. I now realize that the business of restoration will be slow, but it will be sure. Meanwhile, the Galileans are hopelessly divided, and in their division is our hope.

319

At Pessinus I went straight to the temple of Cybele, at the foot of the town's acropolis. The temple is very old and very impressive, but in disrepair. It has been a holy place ever since the statue of the goddess fell from heaven. This was about the time she gave birth to her son, the legendary King Midas, who built the first sanctuary, in honor of his mother. The myth that everything Midas touched turned to gold, though symbolically fascinating—and certainly cautionary!—was probably based on the fact that the countryside around Pessinus is rich in iron. Midas was one of the first to make and sell weapons of iron and this made him fabulously rich. What he touched indeed turned to metal, but the metal was iron. In the side of the acropolis, next to Midas's tomb, I saw with my own eyes the world's first foundry, given to the king by his mother.

I offered a great sacrifice to Cybele, but the townspeople would not take part in the ceremonies even though I offered them a bounty, to the horror of Count Felix. More than ever I relied on Maximus, who is in constant communication with the goddess. It was he who found me Arsacius, a Hellenist whom I appointed High Priest of Galatia. Arsacius is old and garrulous, but he gets things done. In less than a week he had enrolled some twenty priests in the service of Cybele. On several occasions I lectured them at length on the necessity of proving themselves to be as virtuous in all their dealings as the Galileans *claim* to be in theirs. I particularly forbade them to attend the theatre, enter taverns, or involve themselves in shady business deals. I also ordered them to set up hostels for the poor and to be particularly generous to those who are Galilean. I then assigned to the diocese of Galatia an annual allowance of 30,000 sacks of grain and 60,000 pints of wine, one fifth to be used for the poor who serve the priests, and the rest to be given to strangers and beggars, since "from Zeus come all strangers and beggars, and a gift, though small, is precious." That quotation is *not* from the Nazarene, but from our own Homer!

My last night in Pessinus, I sat up late with Maximus, discussing the nature of the Great Mother Goddess. He was more than usually eloquent and I was more than usually inspired by him, and of course by her spirit. Cybele is the first of the gods, the mother of all; and though I do not approve of eunuchs in politics, I have only veneration for those of her priests who, imitating Attis, castrate themselves in order to serve the goddess completely. After Maximus left me, I was so keyed up that I began to dictate a hymn to the Mother of the Gods. I completed it before morning. Maximus thinks it easily my best work in that vein.

Next we moved on to Ancyra. Here I was besieged by a thousand litigants. It was like a visit to Egypt. I did my best to give justice, but my temper was getting short. Reports of religious dissension were coming in from all sides. Some of our own people, excessively zealous, were damaging Galilean property, while the Galileans were doing everything possible to prevent us from reopening the temples. Sooner or later I knew that I would have to make a stand and by some harsh gesture convince the Galileans that I meant to be obeyed. But for the moment, I reasoned and argued. I promised Pessinus funds for public works, *if* the townspeople would support the temple of Cybele. I refused to visit Nisibis until they became less hostile to Hellenism. I deposed several bishops and warned the remainder that there was to be no interference with my plans. I don't know what I should have done without Maximus. He was always at my side; his energy never flagged; he was always a source of consolation, and I needed consoling.

At Ancyra I lost my temper. I had spent three days in the courthouse, listening to men lie about one another. The creative lengths to which human malice will go quite inspire awe. One man, determined to destroy a business rival, came to me every day bringing new charges against his enemy. Each was promptly dismissed. Finally, the accuser declared in a ringing voice, "He has committed high treason, Augustus. He aspires to your place."

This got my full attention. "What evidence do you have?"

"Two weeks ago he ordered a silk robe, of *purple!*" Everyone gasped with horror at this lese majesty. I could stand it no longer. I pulled off my red shoes and flung them as hard as I could at the idiot's head. "Then give him these shoes! They go with the purple." The terrified rogue fell prone in front of me. "And then remind him—and yourself—that it takes more than clothes to be an emperor!" I was not particularly pleased with myself for this outburst, but I was under great tension.

From Ancyra I moved west and south. At what they call the Gates, a mountain pass connecting Cappadocia and Cilicia, I was met by Celsus, governor of Cilicia. I had known him slightly in Athens, where he had been a fellow student. He was also a disciple of Libanius. I'm afraid that I was so overjoyed to see a friendly

321

Hellenic face that I kissed him in full view of the Petulantes. Then I let him ride beside me in my carriage as far as Tarsus. In a strange country, surrounded by hostile people, one clings to mere acquaintances as though they were brothers. That day I would gladly have made Celsus praetorian prefect of the East, simply to show my pleasure in talking to someone who believed as I did.

On the road to Tarsus, Celsus told me many things. He was not optimistic about my revival of Hellenism, but he felt that, given time, we might prevail. He did agree with me that the Galileans would eventually kill one another off.

We also discussed the most important political problem in the empire: the town councils or senates.

Everywhere I have traveled as emperor, I am met by crowds of well-to-do citizens begging me to exempt them from serving in their local councils. What was once the highest honor a provincial might aspire to is now a cruel burden, because the councils are responsible for raising taxes. This means that in a year of poor harvest when the people are unable to pay their taxes, the members of the local council must make up the tax deficit out of their own pockets. Not unnaturally, no one wants to serve on a town council. The only alternative would be to govern directly through imperial decree, and that is not practical for obvious reasons. The whole thing is a mess and no emperor has known how to handle it. I don't. Like my predecessors, I give rousing speeches to those concerned. I tell them that it is a great honor to govern a city and that the state would perish without the cooperation of its worthiest citizens. But the burghers still beg for exemption from public service and I can't blame them. One solution of course is *not* to hold the councils responsible for the collection of taxes. But that would cut the state's revenue in half, which we cannot afford. Someone must see to tax-collecting and who should be better qualified than the leading citizens of the community? So I have chosen to reinvigorate the councils rather than change the system drastically. One way to distribute the responsibility more fairly is to allow no exemptions from service in the councils. Under Constantius both the Galilean priests and the military were exempt. I have changed this, making more rather than fewer citizens available for service. There have been a good many repercussions, but I think in time the communities will be strengthened. It is certainly an intolerable state of affairs when men of property refuse to be senators in a famous city like Antioch.

322

I stayed a number of days at Tarsus, a pleasant town on a lake, connected by canal with the sea. Celsus assembled an interesting group of philosophers to meet me, and we had several enjoyable discussions. The modern Tarsians are quite worthy of their predecessors, the great Stoics of six centuries ago. I even went swimming one afternoon in the Cydnus River, despite the fact that Alexander was almost killed after *his* swim in that river. Although Tarsus is predominantly Galilean (there are innumerable memorials to the devilish Paul who was born here), I found the inhabitants reasonable and simple in their ways. I was almost sad when it came time to leave. But I consoled myself with the thought that I was exchanging Tarsus for Antioch, the Queen of the East. I shudder now when I recall my excitement.

I arrived at Antioch in the last week of July, on a hot humid day. Just outside the city I encountered a large crowd of men and women. Naturally, I thought they had come to welcome me, and I was about to make them a speech of thanks. But they ignored me, calling out strange words, while waving branches in the air.

I looked about for my uncle Julian, but there was no official in sight, only this mob which kept singing rhythmically that "a new star had risen in the east." I'm afraid that I took this to be a reference to myself. One gets used to all sorts of hyperbole. But when I tried to speak to them, they ignored me, their eyes on heaven. At the North Gate the praetorian prefect, Salutius Secundus, my uncle and the senate welcomed me officially. The instant the formal exchanges were finished, I asked, "What is this crowd?"

My uncle was apologetic. Of all days to come to Antioch, I had arrived on that of the festival which commemorates the death of Adonis, the lover of Aphrodite. Adonis is one of the principal gods of Syria, and Maximus and I should have known that this was the day sacred to him. But the mistake was made and there was nothing to be done about it. So I made my entrance into Antioch amid cries and groans and funeral keening, quite spoiling my first impression of the city which, after all, is a beautiful place inhabited by scum. No, that is not fair. They have their ways and I have mine. I am dog to their cat.

The North Gate is a massive affair made of Egyptian granite. Past the gate, one's first view of the city is dazzling, for the main street is two miles long and lined with double porticoes built in

323

the reign of Tiberius. Nowhere else in the world can you walk beneath a portico for two miles. The street itself is paved with granite and so laid out that it always gets a breeze from the sea, twenty miles away. Always a breeze . . . except on this day. The air was stifling. The sun oppressive. Sweat streaming from beneath my helmet, I rode grimly toward the forum, while the people remained within their shady porticoes, occasionally moaning that Adonis was dead.

As I rode, I looked about me curiously. To the left is Mount Silpius, which rises abruptly from the plain. Most of the city is contained between the Orontes River on the west and Silpius on the east and south. The finest villas are on the mountain's slopes, where there is morning shade, luxurious gardens, and a fine view of the sea. One of the Seleucid kings, during a year of plague, carved a colossal head in the rock just above the city. It is called the Charonion and it broods over the city like some evil spirit. One sees it from almost every quarter. The natives admire it. I don't, for it represents to me Antioch.

The forum of Tiberius contains a large statue of that emperor as well as an elaborate marble and mosaic nymphaeum built over a spring whose waters Alexander claimed were sweeter than his mother's milk. I drank from it and found the water was good, but then I was extremely thirsty, as Alexander no doubt had been. I cannot recall the taste of my mother's milk, but since Alexander's mother was bitter in all things, no doubt her milk was, too.

Then, accompanied by city officials, I entered the main square of the island in the river where, just opposite the impressive façade of the imperial palace, stands a brand-new charnel house, begun by Constantine and finished by Constantius. It is octagonal in shape and capped with a gilded dome. The building is known as the Golden House and I must confess that it is a most beautiful example of modern architecture. Even *I* like it, and I am no modernist. In front of the charnel house stood Bishop Meletius and his fellow priests. We greeted one another politely. Then I entered the palace, most of which was built by Diocletian, who invariably reproduced the same building wherever he was: a rectangle based on a military camp. But in recent years my family has added so much to the old palace that the original austere design has been completely obscured by new buildings and elaborate gardens. Within the palace compound there are baths, chapels, pavilions and, best of all, an oval riding track surrounded by evergreens, a great convenience for me.

I was greeted by the palace chamberlain, an ancient eunuch who was terrified that I would do to him what I had done to the eunuchs in Constantinople. But I put his mind at rest. All that I demanded, I said, was decent behavior. If I was well served, I would make no changes. Needless to say, I was looked after superbly, an improvement over my last weeks in Constantinople when my bed was often not made and dinner was never on time. There is something to be said for being comfortable, at least when one is not in the field.

I chose an apartment for myself high above the river, with a roofed terrace where I could sit or stroll in the open air, and look across the western plain to the sea. Here I spent most of my time. During the day, I received visitors and worked; in the evening, I was joined by friends. Close to the palace is the Hippodrome, one of the largest in the East. Yes, I did my duty. I attended the games when I had to, though I never stayed for more than six races.

There was much ceremonial. I received the senate. I listened to testimonials, I attended the theatre. I made graceful speeches, though Priscus claims that no matter how secular the occasion, sooner or later I get on to the subject of religion! I reviewed the troops who were already there, and made plans for the reception of the legions which had not yet arrived. To the horror of Count Felix, I remitted one fifth of all tax arrears in Syria, on the reasonable ground that since we did not stand much chance of getting these revenues anyway, why not do the popular thing? And I was most popular—for about three months.

In August during a meeting of the Sacred Consistory I received word that Sapor had sent me a messenger with an important letter. I turned to Ormisda who happened to be attending the Consistory that day. "Will he want peace or war?"

"My brother always wants both. Peace for himself. War for you. When you are disarmed, he will arm. When you are armed, he will . . . write you letters."

The messenger was brought before the Consistory. He was not a Persian but a well-to-do Syrian merchant who had business dealings with Persia. He had just come from Ctesiphon. He knew nothing of politics. He had been asked to deliver a letter. That was all. But a Persian had accompanied him, in order to take my answer back to the Great King. I asked for the Persian to be brought to us. He turned out to be a tall gaunt nobleman, with a face as composed as statuary. Only once did he betray emotion: when Ormisda addressed him in his native tongue. Startled, he answered. Then when he realized who Ormisda was, his mouth set. He was silent. I asked Ormisda what he had said to him. "I inquired about his father. I know his family," said Ormisda mildly.

"He seems not to admire you. Perhaps we can change that." I gave Ormisda the letter and he read it rapidly in the soft sibilant Persian tongue. Then he translated. Briefly, Sapor wished to send me an embassy. Nothing more; but the implication was plain. "He wants peace, Augustus," said Ormisda. "He is afraid." He handed me the letter. I let it drop to the floor, an affront to a fellow sovereign. I turned to Ormisda.

"Tell the Persian that there is no need for Sapor to send us an embassy, since he will see me soon enough at Ctesiphon."

The war was now officially resumed.


At Antioch I dictated ten, even twenty, hours at a stretch, until my voice gave out; then I would whisper as best I could. Still there was not enough time to do what I had to do. The reaction to the two February edicts has not been good. The Galileans in Caesarea set fire to the local temple of Fortune. I fined the city and changed its name back to Mazaca; it does not deserve the title of Caesarea. I received private information from Alexandria that my enemy, Bishop Athanasius, has not left the city, though I had expressly banished him from Egypt. Instead he is living hidden in the house of an extremely rich and beautiful Greek woman who, my informant suggests, is his mistress. If this is so, we have a splendid weapon to use against him, since much of his authority derives from the so-called holiness of his life. I have given orders that he be kept under surveillance until the right moment comes for us to expose his venery. When Athanasius was told that I had exiled him, he is supposed to have said, "It is a little cloud which soon will pass." He is remarkably confident.

I also ordered the Serapion at Alexandria rebuilt, and I restored to it the ancient Nilometer which is used to record the levels of the Nile. The Galileans had moved the Nilometer to one of their own buildings. I moved it back. During this time I strengthened the Antioch senate by adding to it (despite their piteous protests) two hundred of the richest men in the city.

In September, with Maximus's help, I composed the most important edict of my reign so far: concerning education. I have always felt that much of the success the Galileans have had was due to their mastery of Hellenic writing and argument. Skilled in *our* religion, they turn our own weapons against us. Now we never ask our priests to teach the writings of Matthew, Mark, Luke and John, and not merely because they wrote bad Greek. No. Our priests do not believe in the Nazarene-god. Therefore why should we offend those who do believe in him by teaching the work of his apologists? But Galileans teach our classics in every university in the world. They teach them as models of style and wit, while discarding what they say as untrue. This is intolerable. I therefore decreed that no Galilean be allowed to teach the classics. Naturally, the sternness of this law has been resented and I am sorry for the hurt it has caused certain admirable men. But I had no choice. Either the line is clearly drawn between the gods of Homer on the one hand and the followers of the dead Jew on the other, or we shall be quite absorbed in the general atheism of the day. Friends of mine disagree with me; Priscus, in particular. But Maximus and I stood firm. At first I made no exceptions to the law, but then I modified it to allow Prohaeresius at Athens and Marius Victorinus at Rome to continue teaching. Both accepted gladly. In Constantinople my old teacher Ecebolius forsook the Galilean madness, and in a most eloquent declaration returned to the true gods.

*Priscus*: Julian is here misrepresenting everything. Ecebolius we know about. Whatever the reigning emperor worshipped, Ecebolius adored. Now I was not at Athens when the edict took effect, the Prohacresius told me later that he himself promptly stopped teaching. Later, when his personal exemption arrived, he still refused to teach, declaring that though the edict was highly unjust, if it was to be law, it must at least be consistent. This sounds rather braver than, in fact, it was, for the day the edict was published Prohaeresius paid a visit to his old friend the Hierophant. I don't know how the Hierophant did it, but he had a genius for guessing the future. He was the only soothsayer who ever impressed me. By the way, he has just predicted the destruction of all the temples in Greece within *this* decade. I don't know whether he

327

means by Theodosius or by the Goths. From the way the tribes are gathering on our borders, I suspect the latter.

Anyway, Prohaeresius had a chat with the Hierophant. Now obviously he could not ask him directly about Julian's life expectancy. That was treason. But he could ask about one of Julian's pet projects: the reassessment of all Achaian real estate in order that the land taxes might be lowered. Prohaeresius pretended to be worried about some property his wife owned. Should she sell it now? or wait until the tax went into effect? Sell it now, said the Hierophant (no breathing from a steaming rock or magic spells), the tax cut will not take place. Prohaeresius then knew that Julian's reign would be short.

Julian was quite right when he said that I opposed the Edict on Education. I thought it cruel, as well as impossible to regulate. At least half the good teachers in the universities are Christian. Who could replace them? But Julian at this period was more and more showing the strain of his huge work. In a way, it was a pity that he was not a Tiberius, or even a Diocletian. He had turned butcher, he might have got his way. Though the Christians declare that their blood is semen, an emperor whose sole intent is their destruction might succeed through violence, especially if he were at the same time creating an attractive alternative religion. But Julian had made up his mind that he would be a true philosopher. He would win through argument and example. That was his mistake. One has only to examine what the Christians believe to realize that reason is not their strong point. Only the knife might have converted them to Julian's beliefs. But, good man that he was, his blade was sheathed.

Despite Julian's resolve to be serene, the continual bad news from the provinces affected him. He grew irritable and began to retaliate. The Edict on Education was, he thought, a terminal blow. If he had lived, it *might* have worked, though I doubt it. At heart he was too mild to have made it stick. In all of this he was constantly egged on by Maximus, who was at his most insufferable those months in Antioch.

*Libanius*: For once Priscus and I are in complete agreement. Maximus was neither Sophist nor philosopher, neither lawyer nor teacher. He was a magician. Now I have never *not* believed in magic (after all, there is so much that is familiar which we cannot

328

comprehend), but the magic of Maximus was obvious fakery and the influence he exerted over Julian was deplorable.

*Julian Augustus*

There was one amusing sequel to the Edict on Education ... the only one, as far as I was concerned. Two literary hacks, a father and son named Apollinaris, immediately rewrote the testaments of the Galilean and the old book of the Jews as Greek tragedies and plays! In this way they hoped to get around the edict and be able to teach classic Greek. I read several of these monstrous works and I must say, crude as they were, they read rather better than the originals. The new testament they rewrote as a series of Socratic dialogues, imitating Plato (but in anapests!), while the old book of the Jews was compressed into twenty-four chapters from Alpha to Omega, rendered in deadly dactyl.

The works of the Apollinarises were sent to me for comment by a very nervous bishop at Caesarea ... I mean Mazaca. I sent him back a letter of one sentence: "I read; I understood; I condemn." Just before I left Antioch I got a reply to this letter from my old friend Basil (I have several times asked him to court but he will not come). Basil's letter was also one sentence: "You have read but you have not understood, for if you had understood you would not have condemned." No one can accuse Basil of time serving!

I shall not describe at any length the people of Antioch. Their bad character is too well known. They are quarrelsome, effeminate and frivolous; they are devotees of horse races, gambling and pederasty. The city is of course beautiful and well favored by climate and geography. There is a large Syrian population which lives in its own quarter down by the river, just opposite the island. To visit that quarter is like going to Persia, so Oriental are the people in costume and appearance. There is also a considerable Jewish population in the south section of the city and along the road to Daphne; the Jews are mostly farmers who received land as a reward for military service. I shall have more to say about them later.

During my first "popular" weeks, I made all the usual appearances. I presided at the Hippodrome, and was laughed at for my beard. But the laugh was good-natured. I also attended the theatre, which is built into the side of Mount Silpius, following a natural curve in the hill. The performance was Aeschylus so I did not feel my time wasted. Generally, I am required to attend comedies. Since most of the emperors have been rather light-minded, theatre managers tend to save their most idiotic farces for imperial patrons. Constantine loved Menander. Constantius probably liked farce though no one knows since it was his policy never to laugh or smile in public. But I suspect that the fast-spoken old Greek of the comedies with its many puns and plays on words probably bewildered him. My uncle Julian, as Count of the East, was at least able to spare me comedies. I enjoyed the Aeschylus very much. It was his *Prometheus*.

A good part of my time was passed in the law courts. There was the usual log-jam of cases, aggravated by my presence. When litigants know that an emperor is coming to their city, they all try to get him for judge, believing that he is impartial (rightfully) and tending to leniency because he wishes to curry favor with the mob (in my case, wrongfully).

Though emperors tend to be more merciful than local magistrates, a few lawyers inevitably press their luck too hard and at one time or another we all make some angry judgment we later wish we hadn't. Aware of this tendency in myself, I instructed the city prefect to stop me whenever he thought I was becoming too emotional or irrelevant. After he overcame his first shyness, he was very useful to me, and kept my prow to the course, as the saying goes.

As a matter of private curiosity, I did ask each litigant what his religion was, and I believe most of them answered honestly. Quite a few admitted to being Galilean when it would have helped their case (so it was believed) to lie to me. But since it was soon known that I never allowed my own religious preferences to affect my judgment, many of those who appeared before me declared themselves Galileans in the most passionate way, demanding I persecute those not of their persuasion.

In Antioch the Galileans are divided between blind followers of Arius and semi-blind followers; they quarrel incessantly. There are of course good Hellenists in the city, but they are ineffective. *Potentially* there are many who agree with us, but we make no headway, for the Antiochenes cannot be bothered with serious religion. They like the Nazarene because he "forgives" their sins and crimes with a splash of water . . . even though there is no record of this water having cured even a wart! One interesting paradox I mentioned to Bishop Meletius. We met only twice; once cautiously, once angrily. On the first and cautious occasion, Meletius told me that the city was devoutly Galilean not only because Paul of Tarsus himself had converted so many of the people but also because it was at Antioch that the presumptuous word "Christian" was first used to describe the Galileans.

"Then why, Bishop, if your people are so devoted to the Nazarene, does the entire city celebrate the death of Adonis? one of *our* gods?"

Meletius shrugged. "Old customs are hard to break."

"So is an ancient faith."

"They regard it merely as a festival."

"Yet they break the law the Nazarene preaches: Thou shalt have no other god but me."

"Augustus, we do not condone what they do."

"I cannot believe it is possible for a Galilean to worship both Adonis and the dead man you call god."

"One day we hope to persuade them to forsake *all* impious festivals."

"Unless of course I have succeeded in persuading them to worship the One God."

"The many gods of paganism?"

"Each one is an aspect of the One."

"Ours *is* the One."

"But isn't it written in the book of the Jews—which you believe to be holy because the Nazarene thought it holy..."

"It is holy, Augustus."

"... written that the most high god of the Jews was a jealous god..."

"It is written and so he is."

"But was he not also by his own definition the god only of the Jews?"

"He is all embracing..."

"No, Bishop. He was the *particular* god of the Jews, as Athena was the goddess of Athens. He did not claim to be the One God, only a particular and jealous god, limited to one unimportant tribe. Well, if he is limited then he cannot, by definition, be the One God, who, you will agree with me, can have no limitation, since he is in everything and all things comprise him."

I was particularly vehement at this period, for I was doing research for my book *Against the Galileans*, in which, following Porphyry, I make a considerable case against the atheists. The

331

bishops of course tend to dismiss the many contradictions in their holy books as signs of a divine mystery rather than plain proof that theirs is a man-made religion, suitable for slaves and uneducated women.

Right to the end of my stay in Antioch, I was popular in the law courts, if nowhere else. The people often burst into applause at my decisions. Now I realize that I am in some ways very vain. I enjoy applause. Of course most men are like this, excepting perhaps the greatest of philosophers. But I think I am capable of discerning true admiration from false. The people of Antioch like making a noise, and they are guileful flatterers. One day I decided to let them know that I was on to them. After I had given a lengthy judgment on a peculiarly difficult case, the courtroom burst into frantic applause, and there were many cries of "Perfect justice!"

To which I answered, "I ought to be overjoyed at your praise for my good judgment. But I am not. For I know—sadly—that though you can praise me for being right, you have not the power to blame me for being wrong."


When I was first in Antioch, I was not able to do anything I wanted to do. My time was taken up with administrative tasks, and the settling in of the court. It was not until October that I was able to go to the suburb of Daphne and worship at the temple of Apollo. I had made several attempts to go there but urgent business always kept me in the city. At last all preparations were made. The schedule called for a dawn sacrifice at the temple of Zeus Philios in the old quarter of Antioch; then, to the amazement of the Antiochenes, I announced that I would walk the five miles to Daphne, like any other pilgrim.

When the day came, I was awakened before dawn. Accompanied by Maximus and Oribasius (who grumbled at the early hour), I crossed the bridge to the Syrian quarter. I was accompanied only by archers, as though I were a simple city magistrate. I had hoped to escape notice, but of course the whole quarter knew that I was to give sacrifice at dawn.

We entered the Syrian quarter, with its crowded narrow streets. Here on the river bank the original Antioch was founded almost seven hundred years ago by a general of Alexander's. The temple of Zeus Philios is one of the few remaining from that time. It is small and completely surrounded by a market whose thousand carts beneath awnings make it a colorful, if unholy sight. Luckily, the temple has never been entirely abandoned. Even the Galileans respect it because of its association with the founding of the city.

As the archers made a path for me through the crowded market, I carefully kept my hands under my cloak; since they had been cleansed according to ritual, I could not touch anything. The market people ignored me. Not even an emperor could disturb the important work of selling.

But at the temple a large mob was gathered. They cheered me gaily. Brown hands reached out to touch me. It is the thing I hate most about my place: hands forever grasping at one's clothes. Sometimes it is done merely for the thrill of having touched the purple, but usually the hands belong to those who are diseased and believe that the living body of an emperor is a powerful cure. The result is that emperors are peculiarly prone to contagious diseases. So if the knife does not end our progress in this world, the hand of a sick subject will. Diocletian and Constantius never allowed the common people to come within a dozen feet of them. I may yet imitate them, on hygienic grounds!

The altar in front of the temple was already garlanded and ready. Of the two priests who held the white bull, one looked suspiciously like a butcher. We are short of priests. On the steps of the temple, just back of the altar, the leading Hellenists of the city were gathered, with my uncle Julian at their head. He looked quite cadaverous and coughed almost continuously, but otherwise, he was in excellent spirits. "All is ready, Augustus," he said, joining me at the altar.

The crowd was noisy, good-humored and perfectly oblivious to the religious significance of what was happening. Be calm, I murmured to myself, betray nothing. The archers arranged themselves in a semicircle about the altar, making sure that I would not be touched during the ceremony. Behind us the market continued about its business, as noisy as a senate discussing taxes.

I turned to Maximus and asked him in ritual phrases if he would assist me. He responded that he would. The bull was brought forward. I looked at it with a most professional eye. I suppose I have performed ten thousand sacrifices and there is little I do not know about auguries. Everything is significant, even the way the bull walks as it is led to the altar. This bull was unusually large. He had obviously been drugged, a practice most priests tolerate though purists argue that drugging makes the pre-sacrifice move-

333

ments meaningless. Yet even drugged, one can tell a good deal. The bull moved unsteadily. One leg was weak. He stumbled. A bad omen.

I took the ritual knife. I said what must be said. Then I cut the bull's throat in a single clean gesture. At least that went well. The blood gushed. I was covered with it, and that was also good.

Through all of this, the priests made the appropriate gestures and responses and I repeated the formula of offering as I had done so many times before. The mob was now quiet, interested, I suppose, in an ancient ceremony which many of them had never seen before.

When it came time for the augury, my hand hesitated. Some demon tried to prevent me from seizing the bull's liver. I prayed to Helios. Just as I did, the sun rose behind Mount Silpius. Light streamed on either side of the mountain, though its shadow still fell across the morning city. I plunged my hand into the entrails and withdrew the liver.

The omen was appalling. Parts of the liver were dry with disease. I examined it carefully. In the "house of war" and in the "house of love" death was the omen. I did not dare look at Maximus. But I knew he had seen what I had seen. Entirely by rote, I continued the ceremony, held the sacrifice aloft to Zeus, studied the entrails with Maximus, repeated the old formulas. Then I went inside to complete the ceremonies.

To my horror the temple was crowded with sightseers; worse, they applauded as I entered. I stopped dead in my tracks at this impiety and said, "This is a temple, not a theatre!" I had now made a complete hash out of the ceremony. If even one word is misplaced in a prayer, the entire ritual must begin again from the beginning. By speaking to the crowd, I had broken the chain that links the Pontifex Maximus with the gods. Cursing under my breath, I gave orders to clear the temple, and to begin again.

The second bull—undrugged—tried to bolt just as I raised the knife, again the worst of omens. But at least the liver was normal, and the ceremony was completed satisfactorily. Nevertheless, in the worst of moods, I began my walk to Daphne not in the cool of early morning as I had planned but in the full heat of noon.

Maximus and Oribasius walked beside me. My uncle, pleading illness, was carried beside us in a litter. The archers cleared a way for us and though crowds occasionally gathered along the route, they did not try to touch me; nor was there much importuning, though as always there was that man who suddenly throws himself at one's feet and begs for imperial favor. I don't know how he manages it, but no matter whether one is in Gaul or Italy or Asia, he always breaks through every guard and lands at one's feet. Patiently, I take his name and try to do something for him—if he is not, as so many are, merely mad.

Depressed and nervous as I was, the walk to Daphne was a lovely distraction. The road follows more or less the course of the Orontes River. The earth is rich and because there is an abundance of water the gardens along the way are among the most beautiful in the world. In fact, their owners hold an annual competition to see whose garden is the most various and pleasing. This year, despite practically no rainfall, the gardens were as dazzling as ever, watered by underground springs.

There are of course many fine villas along the way, and an unusual number of inns, built originally for the thousands of pilgrims who used to come from all over the world to worship at the temple of Apollo. But now there are few pilgrims and the inns are devoted almost entirely to providing shelter for lovers. Once holy, Daphne is now notorious for the amorousness of its visitors.

Halfway to the suburb, my uncle suggested we stop at an inn kept by a former slave of his. I must say it was an attractive place, set back from the road and hidden from view by a hedge of laurel.

We sat outside at a long table beneath a vine trellis heavy with dusty purple grapes whose thick scent attracted humming bees. The innkeeper brought us earthen jugs of fruit juice mixed with honey, and we drank thirstily. It was the first pleasing moment in a bad day. Only my uncle's health disturbed me. His hands shook as he drank. From time to time he would grimace in pain. Yet he never allowed his body's discomfort to interfere with his conversation, which was, as always, lucid and courtly.

"You will find the temple in fairly good condition," he said. "The old priesthood was disbanded some years ago, but there is still a high priest in residence. Naturally, he is most excited at your coming."

Maximus shook his head sadly and tugged at his beard. "When I was here as a boy there were a thousand priests, daily sacrifices, crowded inns . . ."

I am always amazed at how much Maximus has traveled. There is hardly a holy place in the world he has not visited, from that

335

Paphian rock where Aphrodite came from the sea to the precise place on the bank of the Nile where Isis found the head of Osiris.

"I'm afraid you'll find Daphne changed," said my uncle. "But we should be able to get things going again. After all, everyone wants to visit Daphne, if only for the waters and the beauty of the place. It is perfect except for one thing..."

I finished his sentence, a bad habit of mine. I interrupt everyone, including myself. "Except for the charnel house my brother Gallus saw fit to build to contain the bones of... what was that criminal's name?"

"The late Bishop Babylas, executed by the Emperor Decius." My uncle's hand shook and he spilled fruit juice on his tunic. I pretended not to notice. But Oribasius, who had been carefully dissecting a large honey bee with a fruit knife, reached across the table and felt my uncle's wrist. "Drink the waters today," said Oribasius at last.

"I have not been well," said my uncle, apologetically, death in his face. I have noticed that the eyes of men who are dying of natural ailments tend to be unnaturally brilliant. They have a kind of straining look as though they want to see everything there is to see before they go. I liked my uncle, and wanted him to live.

As for Daphne, I can only say that it is quite as beautiful as one has always heard. The town is set among gardens and springs. Nearby is the famous grove of cypresses planted centuries ago by Seleucus, at the command of Apollo. The trees are now so tall and dense that their branches form a roof against the sun, and one can walk for hours on end in the cool shade. Daphne has always been sacred; first to Hercules, then to Apollo. It was here that Apollo pursued the nymph Daphne. When she appealed to Zeus to save her, Zeus changed her into a laurel tree. I have seen this tree myself. It is incredibly old and gnarled, yet each spring it puts forth new shoots, reminding us that held by magic within its ancient grasp a girl sleeps, always young. One may also visit the grove where Paris was required to judge which of three goddesses was the most beautiful.

I went quickly through the ceremony of welcome in the town square. Then instead of going straight to the palace, I went sightseeing with Maximus and Oribasius while my uncle went on to the temple of Apollo to prepare for the sacrifice.

I was particularly impressed by the variety of limestone springs. They flow freely in every weather. Hadrian—yes, he was here,

336

too—built a large reservoir at the Saramanna Spring with a colonnade; here one can sit on a marble seat and enjoy the cool air that spring-water brings with it from the earth below. I also saw the famous Kastalian Spring which was once an oracle of Apollo. When Hadrian was a private citizen he inquired about his future by dropping a laurel leaf into the water. The leaf returned to him a moment later marked with the single word "Augustus." When Hadrian eventually became the Augustus, he had the spring sealed with marble on the reasonable ground that others might learn what he had learned and this was not in the best interest of the state. I plan to reopen the spring, *if* the omens are propitious.

The town prefect tactlessly showed us the basilica which contains the remains of the criminal Babylas. I was saddened to see quite a long line of sightseers waiting to be admitted. They believe the bones of this dead *man* have a curative power, yet they will not go near Apollo's springs! Next to the charnel house there is a large factory manufacturing Galilean curios. Apparently, this business is run at a considerable profit. How superstitious people are!

It was late afternoon when we arrived at the temple of Apollo. A large crowd had gathered outside, but none had come to do homage to the god. They were all sightseers.

I went inside. It took my eyes a moment to accustom themselves to the shadowy interior. At last I could make out the marvelous collossus of Apollo. I could also see that no preparations had been made for a sacrifice. Just as I turned to go, two figures hurried towards me from the far end of the temple. One was my uncle. The other was a stout man carrying a cumbersome sack.

According to my breathless uncle, this was the high priest of Apollo. High priest! He was a local handyman who had been entrusted by the town council to keep the temple swept and to make sure it was not used as a home for the poor, or as a convenience for lovers, or for those with a full bladder. Lacking any other attendant, *he* was the god's priest.

"Naturally, Lord, we have no money. I wasn't able to get us a proper white bull or even goat . . . and a goat does just as well, I always say, if it's not old and stringy. But knowing you'd be here, I brought you this from home. She's the last I've got. Not too tough, I'd say." With that he removed a furious gray goose from the sack he was holding.

Aware that I was ready to roar, my uncle spoke quickly. "This

337

will do nicely, high priest. For now. But tomorrow we'll have a proper ceremony. You must see how many former priests you can find. I'll take care of all expenses. We can rehearse them in the morning. Then . . ." He chattered on until I had controlled myself. I thanked the oaf politely for his efforts, said a prayer to the god and departed, the goose unsacrificed.

Fortunately, I found prompt distraction at the palace. The great Libanius had arrived from Antioch. This was our first meeting and I must admit that I was thrilled. He is a noble-looking man, with a gray beard and eyes pale with cataracts. He is going blind, but like the philosopher he is, he makes no complaint. We had a long talk that night, and almost every night that I was in Syria. I was only too pleased to appoint him quaestor, an office which he very much wanted.

*Libanius*: It is curious how people's memories err. I *never* requested the post of quaestor. What I did request—at the insistence of the senate of Antioch—was the right to be able to argue the city's case before the Sacred Consistory. I had done a good deal of this in the past, trying to justify the deeds—often misdeeds!—of my fellow citizens. Even before the awful 22 October, I sensed that there would be serious trouble between emperor and city, and since my love for each was as equal as two things can be, I felt that I might be able to keep the peace. My fellow senators agreed. Julian agreed. And I take some credit for saving Antioch from what, under any other emperor, might have been a bloodbath. In any case, Julian made me quaestor on *his own initiative*. I did not ask for the post, nor for any post. After all, I later turned down the title "praetorian prefect," a fact the world knows. I have never coveted titles or official honors.

In my dealings with Julian I was precisely the opposite of Maximus. I made no attempt to win favor. I never once asked for an audience, except when I was acting as spokesman for the city. Julian has not recorded how we met but I shall, for my behavior at the beginning permanently set the tone of our personal relationship, doomed to be so short.

When Julian first came to Antioch, I confess that I expected to be sent for immediately. We had corresponded for years. At Nicomedia, he had had my lectures taken down in shorthand. He had based his prose style on my own, and there is no higher compliment than that. But weeks passed and I was not sent for.

338

Later he apologized by saying that he had been much too distraught to see me. I understood of course. Yet I confess I was like a proud father who wanted more than anything else to delight in the success of his gifted son. Naturally, I saw him when he addressed our senate, but we did not meet though he referred to me in his speech as "principal ornament of the crown of the East!" I was thought to be in high favor after this, but there was still no summons to the palace.

Not until late October did I receive an invitation from Julian, asking me to dine with him that day. I replied that I never lunch because of fragile health, which is true: a heavy meal during the heat of a day invariably brings on headache. He then invited me to join him the following week at Daphne, and I accepted.

As the record plainly shows I did not "run after" him; rather, *he* ran after me. He mentions the cataracts in my eyes. I had not realized they were so noticeable. In those days I could see fairly well. Now of course I am practically blind.

I was enchanted with Julian, as most men were. He flattered one outrageously, but there was always enough good sense in his flattery to make it more agreeable than not.

Unfortunately, he enjoyed sitting up all night and I don't; as a result, I was forever excusing myself just as he was getting a second wind. Even so, we still found time to discuss my work in considerable detail and I was gratified to discover how much of it he had memorized. We also discussed Iamblichos and Plato.

*Julian Augustus*

I finally made a proper sacrifice to Apollo, offering up a thousand white birds. This occupied most of one day. Then I entered the temple to consult the oracle. I asked certain questions, which I may not record, but the priestess would not answer. She was silent for nearly an hour; then she spoke with the god's voice: "Bones and carrion. I cannot be heard. There is blood in the sacred spring." That was all. That was enough. I knew what had to be done.

As I left the temple, there was a crowd gathered in front of it. They applauded me. I paused and looked across the way to the charnel house, the cause of the pollution. I turned to my uncle. "Tomorrow I want the bones of that Galilean, Babylas, removed."

"Babylas, removed?" My uncle looked distressed. "But this is

339

one of their most famous shrines. People come from all over Asia to touch the remains of Saint . . . of the bishop."

"They can still touch them all they like. But not here. Not in Daphne. This place is sacred to Apollo."

"There will be trouble, Augustus."

"There will be even more trouble if Apollo is not obeyed."

Glumly, my uncle bowed, and crossed to the charnel house across the square.

As I was about to get into my litter, I noticed a group of Jewish elders standing on the edge of the crowd. I signaled for them to come forward. One proved to be a priest. He was an old man, and I teased him. "Why didn't you join me in the sacrifice?"

"Augustus knows we may not." The priest was stiff; his companions were nervous. In the past emperors had often slaughtered Jews for not observing the rituals of state.

"But surely you prefer Apollo to . . . that!" I pointed to the charnel house across the square.

The old man smiled. "Augustus must know that this is one of the few choices we have never been forced to make."

"But we have at least a common enemy," I said, quite aware that since my voice could be heard by those nearby, every word I said would soon be repeated from the Tigris to the Thames. The old man did not answer, but he smiled again. I continued, "You should at least make occasional sacrifice. After all, your High God is a true god."

"We may sacrifice in only one place, Augustus. At the temple of Jerusalem."

"But that temple has been destroyed."

"So we no longer make sacrifice."

"But if the temple were rebuilt?"

"Then we should offer up thanksgiving to our God."

I got into my litter, a plan half-made. "Come see me at Antioch."

The Nazarene predicted that the temple of the Jews would be forever destroyed; after his death the temple was burned by Titus. If I rebuild it, the Nazarene will be proved a false prophet. With some pleasure, I have given orders that the temple be restored. Also, what better allies can one have against the Galileans than the Jews, who must contemplate with daily horror the perversion of their holy book by the followers of the man-god?

340

*Priscus*: Julian does not again refer to this matter, but when he gave orders for the Jewish temple to be rebuilt, there was consternation among the Christians. They hate the Jews, partly because they feel guilty for having stolen their god from them, but mostly because they realize that the Jews know better than anyone what perfect nonsense the whole Christian mishmash is. Now if the Jewish temple were rebuilt, not only would Jesus be proved a false prophet but the Christians would again have a formidable rival at Jerusalem. Something had to be done. And it was.

I got the true story from my old friend Alypius, who was in charge of the project. He had been vice-prefect in Britain when Julian was Caesar. Looking for a new assignment, Alypius came to Antioch and we saw a good deal of one another, for he was as much given to the pleasures of the flesh as am—as *was*—I. One night we visited every brothel in Singon Street. But I shall spare you the idle boasting of an old man.

*Libanius*: For this small favor, I thank heaven.

*Priscus*: Julian sent Alypius to Jerusalem to rebuild the temple. He had *carte blanche*. With the help of the governor, they started work, to the delight of the local Jews, who agreed to raise all necessary money. Then the famous "miracle" happened. One morning balls of flame flared among the stones and a sudden fierce north wind caused them to roll about, terrifying the workmen who fled. That was the end of that. Alypius later discovered that the Galileans had placed buckets of naphtha in the ruins, so arranged that if one was lit all the others would catch fire, too, giving the impression of fire-demons scurrying about.

The north wind was not planned; it is of course possible that Jesus sent the wind to ensure his reputation as a prophet, but I think coincidence is more likely. Plans were made to start rebuilding in the spring, but by then it was too late.

*Julian Augustus*

The next day was 22 October. At dawn, a thousand Galileans assembled to remove the pieces of the late Babylas from the shrine Gallus had built for them. It was all carefully planned. I know because on that same day I too returned to the city and saw the procession.

The Galileans—men and women—wore mourning as they

341

reverently escorted the stone casket which contained the criminal's remains. None looked at me. All eyes were cast down. But they sang ominous dirges for my benefit, particularly, "Damned are they who worship graven images, who preen themselves in idols." When I heard this, I spurred my horse and cantered past them, followed by my retinue. We kicked up a gratifying amount of dust, which somewhat inhibited the singers. In good spirits I arrived at Antioch.

The next day I learned what had happened in the night. My uncle was delegated to inform me. Everyone else was too frightened.

"Augustus . . ." My uncle's voice cracked with nervousness. I motioned for him to sit, but he stood, trembling.

I put down the letter I had been reading. "You should see Oribasius, Uncle, you look quite ill."

"The temple of Apollo . . ."

"He's got an herb the Persians use. He says the fever breaks overnight."

". . . was burned."

I stopped. Like so many who talk too much, I have learned how to take in what others are saying even when my own voice is overriding them. "Burned? The Galileans?"

My uncle gestured wretchedly. "No one knows. It started just before midnight. The whole thing's burned, gone."

"The statue of Apollo?"

"Destroyed. *They* claim it was a miracle."

I controlled myself. I have found that one's rage (which in little things is apt to make one quite senseless) at great moments sharpens the senses. "Send me their bishop," I said evenly. My uncle withdrew.

I sat a long time looking out across the plain. The sun hung in the west, red as blood. I allowed myself a vision of perfect tyranny. I saw blood in the streets of Antioch, blood splattered on walls, arcades, basilicas. I would kill and kill and kill! Ah, how I reveled in this vision! But the madness passed, and I remembered that I had weapons other than the sword.

Bishop Meletius is an elegant ironist, in the Alexandrian manner. For a Galilean prelate his Greek is unusually accomplished and he has a gift for rhetoric. But I gave him no opportunity to employ it. The instant he started to speak, I struck the table before me with my open hand. The sound was like a thunderbolt. I had

342

learned this trick from an Etruscan priest, who not only showed me how to make a terrifying sound with one's cupped hand but also how to splinter solid wood with one's bare fingers held rigid. I learned the first trick but have so far lacked the courage to attempt the second, though it was most impressive when the Etruscan did it and not in the least magic. Meletius gasped with alarm.

"You have burned one of the holiest temples in the world."

"Augustus, believe me, we do not..."

"Don't mock me! It is not coincidence that on the day the remains of your criminal predecessor were taken from Daphne to Antioch, our temple which has stood seven centuries was burned."

"Augustus, I knew nothing of it."

"Good! We are making progress. First, it was 'we.' Now it is 'I.' Excellent. I believe *you*. If I did not, I would this day provide a brand-new set of bones for your followers to worship." His face twitched uncontrollably. He has a tic of some sort. He tried to speak but no sound came. I knew then what it was the tyrants felt when they were in my place. Fury is indeed splendid and exhilarating, if dangerous to the soul.

"Tomorrow you are to deliver the guilty ones to the praetorian prefect. They will be given a fair trial. The see of Antioch will of course pay for the rebuilding of the temple. Meanwhile, since you Galileans have made it impossible for us to worship in our temple, we shall make it impossible for you to worship in yours. From this moment, your cathedral is shut. No services may be held. What treasures you have, we confiscate to defray the costs of restoring what you have burned."

I rose. "Bishop, I did not want this war between us. I have said it and I have meant it: all forms of worship will be tolerated by me. We ask for nothing but what was ours. We take nothing that is lawfully yours. But remember, priest, when you strike at me, you strike not only at earthly power—which is terrible enough—but at the true gods. And even if you think them not the true, even if you are bitterly atheist, by your behavior you disobey the teachings of your own Nazarene, whom you pretend to follow. You are hypocrites! You are cruel! You are ravenous! You are beasts!"

I had not meant to say so much, as usual. But I was not displeased that I had spoken out. Trembling and speechless, the Bishop departed. I daresay he will one day publish a long vitriolic sermon, claiming that he had spoken it to my face. Galileans take

343

pride in acts of defiance, especially if the enemy is an emperor. But their reckless denunciations are almost always the work of a later date and often as not composed by another hand.

I sent for Salutius and ordered him to shut down the Golden House. He already had theories about the burning and was confident that in a few days he would be able to arrest the ringleaders. He thought that Meletius was ignorant of the whole affair. I was not so certain; we shall probably never know.

A week later, there were a number of arrests. The man responsible for the burning was a young zealot named Theodore, who had been a presbyter in the charnel house at Daphne. While he was tortured, he sang the same hymn the Galileans sang to me on the road to Antioch. Though he did not confess, he was clearly guilty. Salutius then held a board of inquiry and to everyone's astonishment the so-called priest of Apollo (the one who had brought me the goose for sacrifice) swore by all the gods that the fire was indeed an accident and that the Galileans were not responsible. As watchman of the temple he has always been in their pay, but because he was known to Antioch as "priest of Apollo," his testimony managed to obscure the issue.

So far I have not had the heart to go back to Daphne. After all, I was one of the last to see that beautiful temple as it was. I don't think I could bear the sight of burned walls and scorched columns, roofed only by sky. Meanwhile the Golden House in Antioch will remain closed until our temple is rebuilt. There is much complaint. Good.

# XIX

*Priscus*: I arrived not long after the fire. My season of teaching ended with the old year, and I traveled from Constantinople to Antioch in eight days, which is excellent time. Julian had so completely reformed the state transportation system that travel was a pleasure. Not a bishop in sight, though there were several newly appointed high priests in the carriages and I confess I began to wonder if they were any improvement over the Christians. I suspect that had Julian lived, matters would have been just as they were under Constantius, only instead of being bored by quarrels about the nature of the trinity we would have had to listen to disputes about the nature of Zeus's sex life ... rather an improvement, come to think of it, but essentially the same thing.

I found Julian much changed. You of course were seeing a great deal of him then, but since you had not known him before, you could not have realized how nervous and ill-humored he had become. The burning of the temple was not only a sacrilege in his eyes, it was a direct affront to his sovereignty. He always did have trouble keeping in balance his two roles of philosopher and king. The one might forgive and mitigate, but the other *must* be served, if necessary with blood.

My first day in Antioch, Julian insisted I go with him to the theatre. "At least we can talk if the play is too foolish." Now it happens that I very much like comedy, particularly low farces. No joke is so old that it cannot delight me, if only by its dear familiarity. The comedy that night was *The Frogs* by Aristophanes. Julian hated it, even the rather good jokes about literary style which ought to have amused him. Julian was not without humor. He had a lively response to bores; some gift of mimicry; and he enjoyed laughing. But he was also conscious every moment of his sacred mission and this tended to put him on guard against any form of wit which might turn against himself; heroes cannot survive mockery and Julian was a true hero, perhaps the last our race shall put forth.

I was delighted to be in Antioch that day. I enjoy the languorous weather, the perfumed crowds, the wide streets ... As you can gather, I like the luxurious and "depraved" ways of your city. If I had the money, I would be living there right now. How I envy you!

I was in a fine mood when we arrived at the theatre. We all were. Even Julian was like his old self, talking rapidly, waving with good humor to the crowds that cheered him. But then from the cheaper seats came the ominous cry, "Augustus! Augustus!" And a chant began, "Everything plentiful, everything dear!" This kept on for half an hour, the voices growing louder until it seemed as if everyone in the theatre was bellowing those words. At last Julian motioned to the commander of the household troops, and a hundred guards appeared so swiftly that they gave the impression of being part of the program as they gathered about the Emperor with drawn swords. The chanting promptly ceased, and the play, rather dismally, began. The next day the food riots started, but then you, as quaestor, know far more about all this than I.

345

*Libanius*: One curious aspect of human society is that preventive measures are seldom taken to avert disaster, even when the exact nature of the approaching calamity is perfectly plain. In March when the rains did not fall, everyone knew that there would be a small harvest; by May, it was obvious that there would be a food shortage; by June, famine. But though we often discussed this in the senate—and the people in the markets talked of little else but the uncommon dryness of the season— no plans were made to buy grain from other countries. All of us knew what was going to happen, and no one did anything. There is a grim constant in this matter which might be worth a philosopher's while to investigate.

It was Julian's bad luck to come to Antioch just when the shortages began. But though he could in no way be blamed for either the dry weather or the city fathers' lack of foresight, the Antiochenes (whose emblem ought to be the scapegoat) immediately attributed the famine to him.

They claimed that the quartering and provisioning of his considerable army had driven up prices and made food scarce. This was true in a few commodities but not in grain, the essential food: grain for the army was imported directly from Egypt. Yet the people of the city were eager to abuse Julian. Why? Bishop Meletius had declared that Julian's fate was decided when he removed the bones of St. Babylas from Daphne. That strikes me as a rather special point of view. Meletius also maintains that the people of the city turned against him the day he shut down the cathedral. I doubt this. Some were shocked of course, but the Antiochenes are not devout Christians; they are not devout anything, except voluptuaries. Not wanting to blame themselves for the famine, they blamed Julian, who had made himself ridiculous in their eyes by his continual sacrifices and grandiose revivals of archaic ceremonies.

I confess that even at the time I felt Julian was overdoing it. On one day at Daphne, he sacrificed a thousand white birds, at heaven knows what expense! Then a hundred bulls were sacrificed to Zeus. Later, four hundred cows to Cybele. That was a particularly scandalous occasion. In recent years the rites of Cybele have been private affairs, involving as they do many ceremonies which are outrageous to ordinary morality. Julian decided to make the ceremonial public. Everyone was shocked at the ritual scourging of a hundred youths by the priestesses. To make matters worse, the youths had agreed to take part in the ceremony not out of faith but simply to curry favor with the Emperor, while the priestesses were almost all of them recent initiates. The result was unhappy. Several young men were seriously hurt and a number of priestesses fainted at the sight of so much blood. The ultimate rites were a confused obscenity.

But Julian grimly persisted on the ground that no matter how alarming some of these rites may appear to us, each is a part of our race's constant attempt to placate the gods. Every ancient ceremony has its own inner logic, and efficacy. The only fault I find with Julian is that he was in too great a hurry. He wanted everything restored at once. We were to return to the age of Augustus in a matter of months. Given years, I am sure he could have re-established the old religions. The people hunger for them. The Christians do not offer enough, though I must say they are outrageously bold in the way they adapt our most sacred rituals and festivals to their own ends. A clear sign that their religion is a false one, improvised by man in time, rather than born naturally of eternity.

From the beginning, the Christians tried to allay man's fear of death. Yet they have still not found a way to release that element in each of us which demands communion with the One. Our mysteries accomplish this, which is why they are the envy of the Christians and the enduring object of their spite. Now I am perfectly willing to grant that the Christian way is *one* way to knowing. But it is not the only way, as they declare. If it were, why would they be so eager to borrow from us? What most disturbs me is their curious hopelessness about *this* life, and the undue emphasis they put on the next. Of course eternity is larger than the brief span of man's life, but to live entirely within the idea of eternity is limiting to the spirit and makes man wretched in his day-to-day existence, since his eye must always be fixed not on this lovely world but on that dark door through which he must one day pass. The Christians are almost as death-minded as the original Egyptians, and I have yet to meet one, even my own pupil and beloved friend Basil, who has ever got from his faith that sense of joy and release, of oneness with creation and delight in what has been created, that a man receives when he has gone through those days and nights at Eleusis. It is the meagerness of Christian feeling that disconcerts me, their rejection of this world

347

in favor of a next which is—to be tactful—not entirely certain. Finally, one must oppose them because of their intellectual arrogance, which seems to me often like madness. We are told that there is only one way, one revelation: theirs. Nowhere in their tirades and warnings can one find the modesty or wisdom of a Plato, or that pristine world of flesh and spirit Homer sang of. From the beginning, curses and complaints have been the Christian style, inherited from the Jews, whose human and intellectual discipline is as admirable as their continuing bitterness is limiting and blighting.

I see nothing good ever coming of this religious system no matter how much it absorbs our ancient customs and puts to use for its own ends Hellenic wit and logic. Yet I have no doubt now that the Christians will prevail. Julian was our last hope, and he went too soon. Something large and harmful has now come into the life of this old world. One recalls, stoically, the injunction of Sophocles: "And ever shall this law hold good, nothing that is vast enters into the life of mortals without a curse."

It is also significant that this death cult should take hold just as the barbarians are gathering on our borders. It is fitting that if our world is to fall—and I am certain that it will—the heirs of those who had originally created this beautiful civilization and made great art should at the end be artless and worship a dead man and disdain this life for an unknown eternity behind the dark door. But I have given way to my worst fault! Prolixity! I have delivered myself of a small oration when I should have kept to the task at hand, Julian in Antioch.

Not only did the people regard Julian's continual round of sacrifice as wasteful and ridiculous: they were alarmed by the Gallic troops who used to attend every sacrifice, pretending to do honor to the gods but really waiting for the banquet of smoking meat which followed. The moment Julian left the temple, the soldiers would devour the sacrificed animals and guzzle wine until they became unconscious. Whenever a drunken legionnaire was carried like a corpse through the streets, the people would say, "The Emperor has been praying again." This did Hellenism little good in the eyes of the Antiochenes, who are so adept at vice that they never get drunk, and have the greatest contempt for those who do.

The trials of those supposedly responsible for the burning of the temple of Apollo also turned the city against Julian. As quaestor, I looked into the matter perhaps more closely than anyone. Now Julian honestly thought that the Christians had set the fire, but for once they were (probably) innocent. I talked many years later to the so-called priest of Apollo and he told me what he had *not* told the Board of Inquiry.

On 22 October, shortly after Julian left the temple precinct, the philosopher Asclepiades arrived, hoping to see the Emperor. Finding him gone, Asclepiades went inside and placed as an offering a small silver statue of the goddess Caelestis at the feet of Apollo, just inside the wood railing. He also lit a number of tapers and arranged them about the statue. Then he left. That was at sundown. Just before midnight, sparks from the expiring candles set fire to the railing. The season was dry; the night windy; the cedar wood ancient. The temple burned. Now if this fool had only told Julian the truth *before* the arrests, nothing would have happened, but he was almost as afraid of the Hellenic Emperor as he was of the Christians.

The whole episode was sad. Fortunately, no lives were lost. The Christians suffered nothing more serious than the shutting down of the cathedral. Later a number of bishops came to Julian to complain that he was causing them great hardship, to which he replied with some humor, "But it is your duty to bear these 'persecutions' patiently. You must turn the other cheek, for that is the command of your God."

*Julian Augustus*

Late in the autumn a large crowd appealed to me in a public place by chanting that though everything was plentiful, prices were far too high. This was a clear indictment of the wealthy class of Antioch, who will do anything to make money, even at the risk of starving their own people. Just seven years ago they had taken advantage of the same sort of situation, and the people had rebelled. Lives were lost, property destroyed. One would have thought that the burghers might have learned something from such recent history; but they had not.

The day after the demonstration, I sent for the leading men of the city. Before the meeting, I was briefed at length by Count Felix. We sat in the empty council chamber, a pile of papers on a table between us. A bronze statue of Diocletian looked disdainfully down at us. This was very much the sort of problem he used to enjoy wrestling with. I don't.

"These figures, Augustus, show a century of grain prices as they fluctuate not only from year to year but month to month." The count beamed with pleasure. He got from lists of numbers that same rapture others obtain from Plato or Homer. "I have even—as you will notice—made allowances for currency fluctuations. They are listed here." He tapped one of the parchments, and looked at me sharply to make sure that I was paying attention. I always felt with Count Felix that I was again a child and he Mardonius. But Felix was an excellent guide to the mysterious underworld of money. He believed, as did Diocletian, in fixing prices. He had all sorts of proof from past experiments that such a system would increase the general prosperity. When I was with him, he always convinced me that he was right. But then in matters of money anyone can, momentarily at least, convince me of anything. After a brilliant, yet to me largely unintelligible, discourse, Felix advised me to set the price of grain at one silver piece per ten measures, a fair price in Antioch. We would then rigorously hold the price at this level, preventing the merchants from taking advantage of the season's scarcity.

In principle I agreed with Felix. "But," I asked, "shouldn't we allow the senate to set the price themselves? to restrain their own people?"

Count Felix gave me the sort of pitying look Mardonius used to when I had made some particularly fatuous observation. "You cannot ask a wolf *not* to eat an unprotected sheep. It is his nature. Well, it is their nature to make as much profit as they can." I thought not. As it turned out, Felix was right.

At the appointed hour some three hundred of the leading burghers of Antioch were admitted to the council chamber. I kept Felix close beside me, as well as Salutius. As Count of the East my uncle Julian should have presided, but he was ill. The Antiochenes were a handsome, ceremonious, rather effeminate crew who smelled—though the day was hot—like three hundred gardens of Daphne; in that close room, their scent made my head ache.

I came straight to the point. I quoted that morning's price for grain. "You ask the people to pay three times what the grain is worth. Now food is scarce but not so scarce as that, unless what I've been told is true, that certain speculators are keeping their grain off the market until the people are hungry and desperate and will pay anything." Much clearing of throats at this, uneasy glances exchanged. "Naturally, I don't believe these stories. Why would the leaders of any city wish to exploit their own people? Foreigners, yes. Even the imperial court." Dead silence at this. "But not your own kind. For you are men, not beasts who devour their weaker fellows."

After thus soothing them, I carefully outlined Count Felix's plan. While I spoke, his lips moved, repeating silently along with me the exact arguments I had learned from him a few minutes before. The burghers were distraught. Not until I had thoroughly alarmed them, did I say, "But I know that I can trust you to do what is right." There was a long exhalation of breath at this. They were all relieved.

I was then answered by the city prefect. "You may depend on us, Lord, in all things. We shall—and I know I speak for every man here—hold the price of grain at its usual level, though it must be taken into account that there *is* a shortage . . ."

"How many bushels?" I broke in. The prefect conferred a moment with several hard-faced men.

"Four hundred thousand bushels, Lord."

I turned to Salutius. "Send to Chalcis and Hierapolis. They have the grain. Buy it from them at the usual cost." I looked up at Diocletian; the heavy face was majestic yet contemptuous; how he had despised the human race!

When the burghers of Antioch departed, Felix rounded on me. "You have done exactly the wrong thing! I know them better than you. They will hold the grain back. They will create a famine. Then they will sell, and every time you reason with them they'll tell you: but this is the way it is always done. Prices *always* find their proper level. Do nothing. Rely on the usual laws of the marketplace. Well, mark my words . . ." Felix's long forefinger had been sawing the air in front of me when suddenly he froze, an astonished look in his face.

"What's wrong?" I asked.

He looked at me vaguely. Then he touched his stomach. "The fish sauce, Augustus," he said, turning quite pale. "I should never touch it, especially in hot weather." He ran quickly to the door, in much distress. I'm afraid that Salutius and I laughed.

"My apologies, Augustus," he said. "But one greater than you calls!" On that light note Felix left us. An hour later he was found seated on the toilet, dead. I shall never have such a good tax adviser again.

* * *

Two weeks later I had a most unsettling vision. I had gone to pray at the temple of Zeus on Mount Kasios, which is in Seleucia, not far from Antioch. I arrived at the temple just before dawn. All preparations had been made for a sacrifice, and there was none of the confusion I had met with at Daphne. I was purified. I put on the sacred mantle. I said what must be said. The white bull was brought to the altar. As I lifted the knife, I fainted.

My uncle attributed this to the twenty-four hour fast which preceded the sacrifice. No matter what the cause, I was suddenly aware that I was in danger of my life. I was being warned. No, I did not see the face of Zeus or hear his voice, but as a black green sea engulfed me, I received a warning: death by violence was at hand. Oribasius brought me to, forcing my head between my knees until consciousness returned.

That night, two drunken soldiers were heard to say that no one need worry about a Persian campaign because my days were numbered. They were arrested. Eight more were implicated. They were all Galileans who had been incited to this action by various troublemakers, none of whom was ever named. I was to have been killed at the next day's military review, and Salutius made emperor.

Salutius was most embarrassed by this, but I assured him that I did not believe he was responsible for this hare-brained plot. "You could kill me so easily in far subtler ways," I said quite amiably, for I respect him.

"I have no desire to kill you, Augustus, if only because I would kill myself before I ever allowed anyone to make me emperor."

I laughed. "I felt that way once. But it is curious how rapidly one changes." Then I said to him with perfect seriousness, "Should I die, you might well be my personal choice to succeed me."

"No!" He was fierce in his rejection. "I would not accept the principate from Zeus himself."

I think I believe him. It is not that he is modest or feels himself inadequate, quite the contrary. But he does feel (and this I gather by what he does not say) that there is some sort of—I cannot find any but a most terrible word to describe his attitude—"curse" upon the principate. As a man, he would be spared it. Perhaps he is right.

The ten soldiers were executed. I used the military review

where I was to have been murdered as an occasion to announce that I would not make any further inquiry into the matter. I said that unlike my predecessor I was not afraid of sudden death by treachery. Why should I be when I had received a warning from Zeus himself? "I am protected by the gods. When they decide that my work is done then—and not until then—will they raise their shield. Meanwhile, it is a most dangerous thing to strike at me." This speech was much cheered, largely because the army was relieved to discover that I was not one of those relentless tyrants who wish to implicate as many as possible in acts of treason.

But while this matter ended well, my relations with the magnates of Antioch were rapidly deteriorating. Three months after our meeting, they had not only not fixed prices, they had kept off the market the grain I had myself imported from Hierapolis. Prices were sky-high: one *gold* solidus for ten bushels. The poor were starving. Riots were daily. I took action.

I set the price of grain at one silver piece for fifteen bushels, though the usual price was one for ten. To force the merchants to unload their hoarded grain, I threw onto the market an entire shipment of grain sent me from Egypt for the use of the troops. The merchants then retreated to the countryside, forcing up the price of grain in the villages, thinking that I would not know what they were doing. But they had not counted on thousands of country people flocking to the city to buy grain. Their game was fully exposed.

I was now ruling by imperial decree and military force. Even so, the burghers, confident of my restraint (which they of course took to be weakness), continued to rob the poor and exploit the famine they had themselves created.

I again sent the senate a message, ordering the burghers to obey me. At this point several of the wealthier members (my own appointees) saw fit publicly to question my knowledge of the "intricacies of trade." A report of this rebuke was sent me while the senate was still in session. I had had enough. In a rage, I sent troops to the senate house and arrested the entire body on a charge of treason. An hour later, thoroughly ashamed of myself, I rescinded the order, and the senators were let free.

Criticism of me now went underground. Rude songs were sung and anonymous diatribes copied and passed around. The worst was a savagely witty attack, composed in elegant anapests. Thousands were amused by it. I read it, with anger. These things always hurt no matter how used one is to abuse. I was called a bearded goat (as usual), a bull-butcher, an ape, a dwarf (though I am above the middle height), a meddler in religious ceremonies (yet I am Highest Priest).

I was so much affected by this attack that on the same day that I read it, I wrote an answer in the form of a satire called "Beard-Hater." This was written as though it were an attack by me upon myself, composed in the same style as the unknown author's work. Under the guise of satirizing myself, I made very plain my quarrel with the senate and people of Antioch, pointing out their faults, much as they had excoriated mine. I also gave a detailed account of how the speculators had deliberately brought on famine.

My friends were appalled when I published this work, but I do not in any way regret having done so. I was able to say a number of sharp and true things. Priscus thought the work ordinary and its publication a disaster. He particularly objected to my admitting that I had lice. But Libanius felt that I had scored a moral victory against my invisible traducers.

*Libanius*: I do regard "Beard-Hater" highly. It is beautifully composed and though there are echoes in it of many other writers (including myself!) I found it altogether impressive. Yet Julian somewhat misrepresents me in suggesting that I approved of the work and thought its effect good. How could I? It was an unheard-of gesture. Never before had an emperor attacked his own people with a *pamphlet*! The sword and the fire, yes, but not literature. Nor had any emperor ever before written a satire upon himself.

Antioch laughed. I remonstrated with friends and fellow senators, reminding them that the patience of even this unusual emperor could be strained too far. But though the arrest of the senate had certainly frightened them, the subsequent countermanding of the order had convinced them that Julian was mad, but in a harmless way. There is of course no such thing as a harmlessly mad emperor, but my constant exhortations were ignored. Luckily, I was able to save Antioch from Julian's wrath, for which I was credited at the time. All this, naturally, has been forgotten or twisted by malice into something other than the truth. There is nothing so swiftly lost as the public's memory of a good action. That is why great men insist on putting up monuments to themselves with their deeds carefully recorded, since those they saved will not honor them in life or in death. Heroes must see to their own fame. No one else will.

I should note—I *will* note when I assemble this material for the final edition—that the senate did have a case against Julian. Though a few senators were speculators, most of them had not taken advantage of the famine. Their only fault had been negligence in not preparing for the scarcity, but if negligence in statesmen were a capital offense there would not be a head left in any senate in the world. When Julian's message was read to us, it was received most respectfully. Yet everyone agreed that his abrupt underpricing of grain would result in a worse shortage than the overpricing of the speculators. As it turned out, the senate was right. The grain which had been sold so dramatically below cost was soon gone, and the shortage was as bad as before.

I suspect Julian of wanting to make himself popular with the mob. He had hoped to win their support against the wealthy Christian element, but he failed. Our people can be bought rather cheaply, but they are far too frivolous to remain bought. Also, he neglected to hold down the price of other commodities, and it is the luxuries, finally, that are the key to the Antiochene heart. So his attempt at price-control was a failure, just as Diocletian's had been. Perhaps if Count Felix had lived the thing might have worked, for he was most brilliant in these matters and all his life had searched for a prince who could put into effect his quite elaborate system of economic controls. Myself, I tend to believe with the conservative element that inflation and scarcity must be endured periodically and that in time all things will come more or less to rights. But then I am neither trader nor fiscal agent . . . merely Stoic!

Count Felix, incidentally, had literary ambitions, and I once spent a pleasant afternoon with him at Daphne in the house of a mutual friend. The count read us a most entertaining set of verses on—I believe—the pleasures of agriculture. Odd because he was very much a city man. I remember his saying that my essay "For Aristophanes" had opened his eyes to a whole new view of that superb writer.

*Julian Augustus*

Shortly before noon on 2 December, a messenger came to me with the appalling news that once again Nicomedia had been struck by earthquake. Everything that had been rebuilt was thrown down. As soon as I heard the news I went outside. The day was dark

355

and cold, and a thin rain fell. I walked to the garden just north of the riding ring, and there I prayed to Zeus and to Poseidon. All day I prayed, while the rain continued to fall and the cold wind to rise. Not until sundown did I stop. Two days later I learned that the tremors ceased at exactly the moment I began my prayers in the garden. So what had been the worst of signs became the best: the gods still look favorably upon me, and answer my prayers.

A week later I was deeply saddened, though not surprised, to learn that my uncle Julian had died in his sleep. The Galileans promptly declared that he had been struck down by the Nazarene for having removed the treasure from the charnel house in Antioch. But of course his illness preceded this act by some years. Actually, I am surprised that he lived as long as he did, considering the gravity of his illness. I can only assume Asklepios must have blessed him.

I was fond of my uncle. He was a good and loyal functionary; he was also the last human link with my parents. His only fault was the common one of avarice. He could never get enough money. In fact, our last meeting was spoiled by a small quarrel about the Bithynian farm my grandmother had left me. He was furious when I gave it to a philosopher friend, even though the land was not worth one of the gold vases he used to display in his dining room. I seem to have missed the fault of avarice. I have no desire to own anything. No. On second thought, I am greedy about books. I do want to own them. I think I might commit a crime to possess a book. But otherwise, I am without this strange passion which seems to afflict most men, even philosophers, some close to me.

*Priscus*: An allusion to our friend Maximus. He was at this time buying real esate in Antioch with the money he obtained from selling offices and titles. Looking back on those days, I curse myself for not having feathered my own nest. Unlike Julian, I *am* rather greedy, but I am also proud and the excessiveness of my pride prevents me from asking anyone for anything. I cannot easily accept a gift. Yet I could steal, if I thought I would not be caught.

Julian's uncle was an amiable man, though overzealous as an official. He once told me that his sister Basilina, Julian's mother, had been extraordinarily ambitious. When she was pregnant with Julian, he asked her what sort of life she wanted for her child, and she replied, "There is only one life for a son of mine. He must be emperor."

Julian used to describe his mother (from hearsay) as having been quite blond. She was indeed. According to her brother, she was an albino. I once made love to an albino girl in Constantinople. She had the most extraordinary blood-red eyes, like an animal's. The hair of course was absolutely white, including the pubic hair. I believe she was called Helena.

*Libanius*: How interesting!

*Julian Augustus*

On 1 January 363, I became consul for the fourth time in association with Sallust. Naturally, there were many complaints, since Sallust was not of senatorial rank. But I ignored custom. Sallust is my right arm at Gaul. I also appointed Rufinus Aradius as Count on the East and filled a number of other offices, mostly in the West. I was now ready for the Persian campaign. I waited only upon the weather.

On the Kalends of January I went to the temple of the Genius of Rome to make sacrifice. Here, on the steps, were assembled most of the city's priests and high officials. As I was completing the ritual, I happened to look up just as one of the priests fell the length of the steps, later I learned that the priest who had fallen was not only the oldest but he had fallen from the highest step, dead of a heart attack.

By nightfall all Antioch had interpreted this to mean that he who is highest (oldest) in the state will fall from his great place (the top step), dead. So my days are supposed to be numbered But I interpret the omen another way. The dead priest was on the top stair. Our highest rank is consul. There are two consuls. The dead priest was the *oldest* priest. Sallust is many years my senior. If either of us dies, the omen suggests it will be Sallust, not I. Of course the whole thing might possibly have no significance at all. Perhaps I should listen more to Priscus, who does not believe in signs.

*Priscus*: Indeed I don't! I am sure that if the gods (who probably don't exist) really wanted to speak to us, they could find a better messenger than the liver of a bull or the collapse of an old priest during a ceremony. But Julian was an absolute madman on this subject, and I must say, even though I don't believe in omens, I was impressed by the number of disasters reported. Among them:

357

the second earthquake at Nicomedia, the fire in the Jewish temple, the burning of the temple of Apollo, and as if all these "signs" were not bad enough, Julian sent to Rome for a consultation of the Sibylline books. As we all know, these "books" are a grab bag of old saws and meaningless epithets, much rewritten at moments of crisis. But bogus or not, their message to him was clear: Do not go beyond the boundaries of the empire this year. I never heard him reinterpret that sentence. I can't think why I am recording all this. *I* don't believe any of it, but then Julian did, which is the point. True or false, these signs affected his actions.

There was one more bit of nonsense. The day that Julian left Antioch for Persia, an earthquake shook Constantinople. I told Maximus that if he told Julian what had happened, I would kill him. As far as I know, he never said a word.

*Julian Augustus*

Late in February I completed plans for the Persian campaign. Word was sent the legions that we would start moving east during the first week of March. I also sent a message to Tarsus, instructing the governor that his city would be my winter quarters, as I would not return to Antioch. My private letter to the governor was immediately known to the senate of Antioch, and they were most contrite. Would I not reconsider? I would not. And so I was ready to depart, in good spirits, except for the fact that Oribasius, suddenly ill of fever, was not able to accompany me. This was a blow. But I shall see him later in the year at Tarsus.

The day before I left Antioch, I had a final meeting with Libanius. Getting to know this wise man was perhaps the only good experience I had in that terrible city. He had been unable to attend a dinner I had given the night before, because of gout. But the next day he felt somewhat better and was able to join me while I was exercising at the riding ring.

It was the first spring-like day. Air warm, sky vaporous blue, first flowers small but vivid among winter grass. I was practicing swordplay with Arintheus and though we had both started the exercise in full winter uniform, by the time Libanius had joined us, we were half-stripped and sweating freely in the sun.

Libanius sat benignly on a stool while we banged at one another. Arintheus has the body of a god and is far more agile than I, but my arms are stronger than his, so we are well matched. Besides

358

it is not humanly possible for a mere army commander to defeat an emperor, even in mock combat.

Finally, Arintheus, with a mighty cry, struck my shield a fierce blow which caused me to stagger back. He was almost upon me with his blunt practice sword when I raised my hand majestically and said, "We must receive the quaestor Libanius."

"As usual, when I'm winning," said Arintheus, throwing his weapons to the nearest soldier to catch. Then, wearing only undershorts, he sauntered off.

"The young Alcibiades," said Libanius, appreciatively, watching the muscular figure as it disappeared into the barracks.

I wrapped myself in a cloak, breathing hard. "Let's hope he doesn't take to treason like the original." I sat in my folding chair. There was a long pause. Aware then that Libanius had something private to say to me, I motioned for the guards to fall back to the edge of the riding ring.

Libanius was unexpectedly nervous. To put him at his ease, I asked him a question about philosophy. Answering me, he recovered his poise. Even so, it was some time before he got the courage to say, "Augustus, I have a son. A boy of five. His mother . . ." He stopped, embarrassed.

"His mother is a slave?"

"A freedwoman. She *was* my slave."

I was amused by this unexpected sign of vigor in one in whom I had thought such things had long since been forgotten. But then Libanius had rather a scandalous reputation when he first taught at Constantinople. He was often in trouble with young girls of good family (and young boys, too), if one is to believe his envious rivals. I do and I don't. There is usually *some* truth to gossip, except when it concerns me!

"This child—his name is Cimon—cannot of course be made my legal heir. Up til now I've been able to provide for him. But when I die, he'll be penniless, no better than a slave. In fact, he could be sold into slavery if he were not protected."

"You want me to recognize him as your legal heir?"

"Yes, Augustus. The law of course . . ."

". . . is quite clear. It cannot be done. But *I* can get round it by special decree. Make out a deposition, and I'll present it myself to the Consistory." He thanked me profusely. I had never before seen Libanius humanly moved; it was most impressive. Usually, he is entirely the philosopher, serene and explicit, his only passion that for ideas. But now he was a father, and I was touched.

We then spoke of the coming campaign. I asked him to come with me, but he pleaded infirmity and I was forced to agree that a man with failing sight and severe gout would find life in the field torture.

"But I do wish, my dear friend" (now that Libanius was no longer a subject asking a favor of his ruler, he reverted to being teacher with pupil), "you would reconsider this military adventure."

"Reconsider? I have no choice. We are at war."

"We have been at war for many years with Persia. But war does not necessarily mean invasion this year."

"But the omens . . ."

"The omens are not good. I have heard about the Sibylline books."

There are no secrets. I cursed silently to myself, wondering who had betrayed me. I had expressly forbidden the priests from Rome to tell anyone what the books advised. "I have reinterpreted the prophecy," I said flatly. "Besides, both Delphi and Delos are favorable."

"Augustus." He was now solemn. "I am sure that you will defeat Persia. I have perfect faith in your destiny. I only wish that you would put off going until next year. You have set in motion a hundred reforms. Now you must see to it that they take effect. Otherwise, the Galileans will undo everything the moment you are out of sight. You cannot control them from the field or even from the ruins of Ctesiphon."

Libanius is right of course and I continually worry, particularly now, at what is happening in my absence. But I told him what I believe to be true: that as conqueror of Persia I would be more than ever awesome to the Galileans, who would see in my victory a clear sign of heaven's favor to me. This useful end is worth a few months' confusion at home.

Libanius was not convinced, but he said no more and we talked of other matters. I find him inspiring, though somewhat long-winded, a traditional fault of great teachers. I am sure that I would be long-winded, too, except for the fact that in conversation I can never sustain any subject for very long. I shift rapidly from point to point, expecting those who are listening to fill in the gaps. They often don't. But in talking with Libanius there are no gaps or incompleted sentences. Listening to him is like being read to from a very long book, but what a splendid book!

Since I am writing these notes as history as well as for my own amusement, I should perhaps set down the reasons for this present war with Persia. One of the faults of most historians is that they take too much for granted. They assume that the reader must know the common things they know; therefore, they tell only the *un*common things, details ferreted out of archives and from private conversations. It is frustrating to read most history, because so many times one can see the author hovering on the verge of explaining some important fact and then shying away out of fear of dullness; everyone knows *that*, the author says to himself, and I won't bore the reader (and myself) by telling him what he already knows.

But if one is writing to be read a hundred years from now or, with luck (and a continued interest in one's period), even a thousand years, like great Homer, then all those things we take so much for granted today will be quite unknown to those who come after. So we must explain things that every schoolboy now living knows. For instance, everyone knows that Constantius would not eat fruit, but is it likely that anyone will know—or care—in the next century? Yet it is a point to be made about him, and worth exploring on religious grounds.

I confess that I do have some hope of being read by the future, not because of my negligible literary art nor because of my deeds (though I hope they will be great), but because I am an emperor and I mean to be candid. Such autobiographies cannot help but be interesting. Marcus Aurelius is the supreme example. But the others memoirs which have come down to us are also interesting, especially the commentaries of Julius Caesar and the fascinating if calculated memoirs of Octavian Augustus. Even Tiberius's clumsy autobiography is interesting, particularly his attack on Sejanus...

There! I have strayed from my point. I ask the pardon of my poor secretary, who can barely keep his eyes open as I talk, faster and faster, for in my fatigue I often have the most extraordinary bursts of clarity. At such moments the gods are near; my beloved Hermes hovers at my side. But in the interest of good form, I shall of course revise all that I have dictated, cutting out those parts where I tend to ramble.

The future will want to know why I am invading Persia. I am

quite sure that there are many at this very moment who do not understand what I am trying to do. It is of course taken for granted that we must protect our boundaries and occasionally annex new provinces. Though Salutius and the literary men who are with me know how this war started, I am confident that neither Nevitta nor Arintheus has the slightest idea why I have taken the field against Sapor. Nor do they care. They think I want plunder and the military glory, because that is what *they* want. Well, I am not without a certain love of worldly glory—though I deplore it in myself—but that is not why I must prosecute this war. Persia (or Parthia as we ceremonially call it in imitation of our ancestors) has always been the traditional enemy of Rome. There have been occasional generations of peace, but for the most part we have been in conflict ever since the wars against Mithridates brought Rome to Parthia's border four centuries ago.

The present war began in an almost frivolous way. Some thirty years ago an adventurer named Metradorus made an expedition to India. He was received generously by the king of India, who presented him with a number of gifts from the king to the Emperor Constantine. As I piece together the story, this Metradorus was a singular liar and schemer. When he returned home he gave Constantine the Indian presents but claimed that they were his own gifts to the emperor. Then, afraid that Constantine might wonder why there was no gift from the king of India, Metradorus declared that there had indeed been many rich gifts, but that the Persians had confiscated them en route, in the name of Sapor.

Constantine, partly out of greed, partly out of policy, wrote Sapor, demanding that he return the gifts. Sapor did not deign to answer him. Constantine sent another angry letter (copies are to be found in the Sacred Archives). Finally, Sapor answered: he demanded Mesopotamia and Armenia as rightful territories of the Persian crown; there was no mention of the presents. Constantine declared war on Sapor, but before he could take the field he was dead.

For most of Constantius's reign, Sapor was relatively inactive. He had political problems in his own country. But then in 358, he sent Constantius a most arrogant embassy, again demanding Mesopotamia and Armenia. Much alarmed, Constantius sent an embassy to Ctesiphon, headed by Count Lucillianus and my cousin Procopius. Our ambassadors were duly alarmed by Sapor, and they advised Constantius to maintain the *status quo*. But even this was not possible when Sapor laid siege to the border city of Amida, leading his army in person; an innovation, by the way, for in the old days the Great King never appeared in battle, his life being considered too sacred to risk in combat.

Amida fell. It was a terrible defeat for Rome. Sapor was surprisingly merciful to the inhabitants. Even so, we have lost an important city, and our border defenses are dangerously weakened. When I succeeded Constantius, I looked through all his military papers and talked with his commanders, but I could not find what if any plan he had for defeating Sapor. I was forced to start from the beginning. Now I am ready.

It is my plan to conquer Persia in three months. I have no alternative. For if I fail none of the reforms I have proposed will ever come to pass, nor can our state long survive between the continual harassment of the Goths on our borders to the north and the Persians to the east. Also, and I confess it honestly, I want the title *Parthicus* after my name and an arch to my memory in the forum at Rome. Not since Alexander has a Greek or Roman commander conquered Persia, although some, like Pompey, pretended to, after small victories. I dream of equaling Alexander. No, I must be honest: I dream of surpassing him! And are we not one, in any case? I want India. I want China beyond. Upon the shore of that blood-dark sea to the farthest east, I would set the dragon standard and not simply for the glory (though the very thought of it makes me dizzy . . . oh, where is philosophy now?), but to bring the truth about the gods to all those lands bending toward the sun, the god from whom all life flows. Also, Persia is to me a holy land, the first home of Mithras and Zarathustra. It will be, for me, a homecoming.

I always keep a biography of Alexander at my bedside. It is remarkable how many of us have used the deeds of that extraordinary youth as a standard of measurement for ourselves. Julius Caesar wept at Alexander's tomb because, already older than the boy was at his death, he had not yet begun a conquest of the world. Octavian Augustus opened the tomb and looked a long time at the mummy's face. The body was well preserved, he tells us in his autobiography, and he says that he would have recognized Alexander from his portraits. Withered and brown in death, the face was set in an expression of such rage that despite all the centuries which separated the living politician from the dead god, the cool Octavian knew for the first time what fear was, and he

363

ordered the sarcophagus sealed. Years later, it was reopened by the beast Caligula, who stole the shield and breastplate from the tomb and dressed up as Alexander, but there all likeness ceased. Each of my predecessors longed to equal this dead boy. None did. Now I shall!

*Priscus*: There it is. The memoir of Julian. You were present of course when he left the city on 5 March. I can still hear in memory your witty citizens chanting "Felix Julian *Augustus*," meaning that after Count Felix and his uncle Julian, the Augustus was next to die.

The army marched east across the Euphrates to Carrae. Here Julian split it in two. Thirty thousand men under his cousin Procopius and Duke Sebastian were sent on to Armenia. There they would rendezvous with King Arsaces. Then with the Armenian troops as auxiliaries, they would seize Media, and strike for Ctesiphon where they would meet us. With the remaining thirty-five thousand troops, Julian started to go south along the Tigris. But he was wily. In a surprise maneuver, he retraced his steps to Callinicum on the Euphrates and then moved directly toward Ctesiphon, the Persian capital, some four hundred miles south. Sapor was demoralized by this feint. But all that is military history. It is generally agreed that Julian moved armies faster than any general since Julius Caesar.

Though Julian never had the chance to shape the memoir, I suspect he would have left it just the way it was. He hated rewriting. *He* never filled a gap if he could help it. I could fill quite a few about those days in Antioch, but I refrain since you were there, too, and can rely on your own excellent memory. He was by no means finished with the chronicle of his life, any more than he was finished with living it. He intended to write an account of his Persian campaign and the notes he made during those last months are fascinating.

I hope my occasional commentary has not been too burdensome. I think it is always good to get as many viewpoints as possible of the same event, since there is no such thing as absolute human truth. You should be pleased at Julian's final reference to you. He admired you tremendously. I cannot think what he meant when he called you "long-winded." You are merely thorough. But then Julian was often like a child whose span of attention is capricious. I shall be very curious to see what you do with this memoir.

364

By the way, whatever happened to your son Cimon? Did Julian make him your legal heir? Naturally, one has heard of Cimon's exploits as a lawyer, but I never realized he was a child of yours. You are full of surprises.

*Libanius to Priscus*                                    *Antioch, July 380*

I have been working for some weeks on my preface to the memoir of Julian, which will, I hope, set this work in its proper historical frame. May I say that your notes have been of the greatest—perhaps even decisive—value to me? Just this morning as I was reviewing the last pages of the work, so tragically cut short, I noticed a phrase of yours which had escaped my attention. You say that Julian was planning to write an account of his Persian campaign. You then add "the notes he made during those last months are fascinating." Is there more text? I had thought the memoir was all that was left. Do let me know, for I am impatient to start a final "shaping" of the work.

Yesterday I paid a call on my old friend Bishop Meletius. You recall him, I am sure, from your visit here. He is much aged and rather fragile, but he has kept all his wits. I intimated that I might be doing a new work on Julian, using previously unpublished material. He thinks this might be a mistake. "Theodosius is a Spaniard," he said, meaning, I suppose, that the Emperor has all the stern uncompromising violence of that race. "It is one thing to send him a graceful essay 'On Avenging Julian,' whose merit was literary rather than political," (I thought my work highly political), "but it is quite something else to challenge the Church, especially now that the Emperor has been saved by Christ." I never know if Meletius is serious or not. His tendency to be ironic has so increased with age that he seems never to mean what he says.

Meletius also told me that the Emperor expects to be in Constantinople this autumn. So I shall wait until then to see him. I also learned that the poisonous Gregory, now a bishop, is urging that a new Ecumenical Council meet next year, probably in the capital. There is also talk that he is angling to be made bishop of Constantinople. No doubt of it, his career has been a success. But then those people usually do well. I extend my best wishes to your wife Hippia, and of course to yourself.

*Added*: Julian died before he was able to legitimize my son. Due to religious bigotry and the continuing perseverance of academic enemies, none of Julian's successors was willing to do the humane thing in this matter. I now pin my hopes—without much hope—on Theodosius.

*Priscus to Libanius*                    *Athens, September 380*

You must forgive me for not answering your letter earlier, but I have been ill. A mild stroke has drawn down the side of my mouth in a peculiarly sinister way. I now look like one of the infernal deities and countryfolk make the sign to ward off the evil eye when they see me tottering along the road to the Academy. Happily, my mind is not affected. If it is, then—equally happily—I don't know it. So all's well.

It is now definite that Theodosius will spend the winter at Constantinople and you ought to go see him. It's only a ten-day journey. He is reasonable, I am told, but much impressed by his miraculous recovery. Whether he would sanction your project is another matter, but you can lose nothing by trying. He won't eat you. Also your being a friend of the Empress in the West will do you no harm. She is most active politically and, some say, had a hand in her husband's raising Theodosius to the purple. Use her name freely. But then I hardly need advise the famous quaestor of Antioch in how to put a case!

Yes, Julian left a considerable journal describing the day-by-day campaign. I have been annotating it with a thought *perhaps* of publication, though I should need at least some of your courage to go through with it, for this work is far more dangerous than the memoir. Julian knew all about the plot against his life; as did I. I also know what he did not, the identity of his murderer.

I have nearly finished the work of annotation. I have been slowed up recently as a result of my stroke, but I hope to get at it soon again. If I decide not to publish, I should of course be pleased to sell you the work at the same price you paid for the memoir. The cost of copying is still what it was here at Athens. If anything, it has gone up.

I hope your vision is not any worse; at our age nothing gets better. My student Glaucon was delighted to meet you last spring when he delivered the manuscript, but saddened to find your sight so greatly impaired. Oribasius used to have a nonsurgical cure for cataract, but I have forgotten it. Look in his encyclopedia. It should

366

be in the latest edition, but if you don't have that, look it up in Galen. That's probably where *he* got it from.

Hippia sends you her best wishes, as always. She is eternal. She will bury us all. She certainly looks forward to burying me. We spend quite a lot of time eyeing one another, each speculating on which will outlast the other. Until this stroke, I thought I had a clear edge. Now I'm not so sure. She was quite thrilled when I was sick, and gay as a girl for several days "looking after" me.

*Libanius*: On top of everything else, Priscus is a thief. Our agreement was plain. I was to get everything Julian left for the original price. Then he holds back the most important work of all and there is nothing I can do but submit to this robbery and pay the price! I must say I hope Hippia will soon be a widow. Priscus is a terrible man!

*Priscus to Libanius*                    *Athens, October 380*
Here is the journal, as I promised. I have done extensive notes, which you are free to use in any way you like. I have been somewhat weakened as a result of my stroke, but so far neither my memory nor the ability to string together sentences seems to be affected. Some of these notes have been dictated, as you will notice when you see Hippia's childish handwriting. I pay her to be my secretary. She will do anything for money. To this day she denounces me for not having made us a fortune when, as a friend of Julian's, it would have been so easy, as you well know. Though of course *your* fortune was made long before Julian became Emperor. I was much impressed the first time I visited you at your Antioch mansion and you told me, with perfect casualness, that you had just sent a cargo ship to Crete. Fortunate Cimon to have such a wealthy father! I am sure Theodosius will legitimize him for you.

I have talked—very discreetly—to several people close to the court and they agree that the Emperor would *probably* stop publication of any work which showed Julian in too favorable a light. Needless to say, I did not mention that there was both a memoir and a journal in existence. But it is perfectly plain that if Theodosius and his bishops knew about these works they would do everything possible to destroy them, just as they labor so devotedly to distort the history of Julian's reign. It is the perquisite of power to invent its own past. Julian must be obliterated or at least made monster before the Christian Empire can properly be born. I don't mean to sound discouraging, but there it is.

I must confess that I'm relieved to have got Julian's papers out of my house and into your most capable hands. I tell you these things simply to put you on your guard, for one of those I talked to at some length was the celebrated Ausonius, who is very much in favor at court. I flattered him unmercifully when he visited here last month.

Ausonius is a small stately man who gives an impression of great dignity and power until he starts to speak. Then one knows he is simply one of us, a nervous clerk, embarrassingly anxious to be admired. He also stammers. He was pleased, he told us in his speech at the proconsul's reception, to be in such a distinguished assemblage of intellectuals and magistrates, particularly because he liked to think of himself as a "sort of bridge between the two." We wagged our tails fiercely at this to show that we loved him and wanted favors. When he finished, he nicely took my arm and told me how much he admired me. What could I do but quote his own poetry to him?

"I have always admired you, P-P-Priscus, and I am g-g-glad to find you still alive and well."

"So am I, Consul." I beamed down at the absurd figure in its consular robe. I then praised his many books, and he praised my many silences. The academicians all about us watched me with a quite satisfying envy. Then, rather skillfully I think, I brought Julian into the conversation.

Ausonius frowned. "We aren't very happy with him of course. Not at all. No, *not* at all."

I murmured the ancient saw about the rarity of human happiness. Almost any quotation from Sophocles has a soothing effect.

"Theodosius is most displeased about the body. Most unhappy. But she insisted."

"What body? Who insisted?" I was at sea.

"His. Julian's. It's been m-m-moved. From Tarsus to Constantinople. The Emperor Gratian ordered it, or to be p-p-precise, his w-w-wife." P's, W's and M's are Ausonius's main obstacles. Having told you this, I shall no longer try to dramatize his speech.

After much spluttering, I learned that your friend the Empress Postuma, last of the Flavians, suddenly realized that her blood was also Julian's and that the new dynasty's legitimacy rests upon that frail fact. So Postuma got her husband Gratian to move Julian's

368

remains from Tarsus to the Church of the Holy Apostles at Constantinople. At this very moment Julian's body is lying beside Constantine's mother Helena. How each would have hated that proximity. Though Ausonius did not mention it, I suspect that both Postuma and Gratian are aware for the first time what a great man Julian was. They live in Gaul and for the Gauls Julian is the only emperor since Augustus. I am told by everyone who comes from there that he is still spoken of with awe and affection, and that the common people believe that he is not really dead but sleeping beneath a mountain, guarded by the dragon of his house, and should the West ever be in danger, Julian will awaken and come to the defense of the Rhine. It will take some doing to destroy his legend in Europe.

We spoke of you. Ausonius admires you. Who does not? He told me that Theodosius admired your "graceful" (!) essay "On Avenging Julian," but took it as a rhetorical exercise. I am sure that is not how you intended it, but I suggest you allow the imperial adjective to be your own.

"What would be the feeling in court if *I* were to publish a book about Julian, covering, say, the Persian campaign?"

Ausonius picked a word beginning with "m" and nearly choked to death. Finally, in bursts, he told me, "Never! Theodosius and Gratian both regard him as the devil. Only out of courtesy to Libanius, who is old, did Theodosius accept the essay. But nothing more. Ever! We don't mean to persecute pagans of course," (the "we" reminded me of Maximus; do all busy friends of princes use "we" in that awful way?) "but we shall make it as disagreeable as possible for them to worship in the old way. You've read the two edicts? There will be others. I can give no details of course. Premature."

"But Libanius *was* able to write a defense of Julian."

"Once. Only. We've also heard he's planning a book about Julian." (No, I did not tell him.) "Discourage him, as a friend. Also, there is a private matter he would like attended to. I'm not free to say what it is, but he has already sent us a request. Well, one hand washes the other, as they say. Do tell him." I suppose this refers to the matter of your natural son Cimon. Anyway, that is the gist of my talk with Ausonius. Perhaps you can do better yourself face to face with the Emperor.

Here then is the journal. Some of it is cryptic. There are many lacunae. I have tried to provide as many missing pieces as possible.

369

For weeks now I have been reliving that tragic time and I am amazed at how much I was able to recall when I set what is left of my mind to the task.

My mouth is still ominously twisted but vision and speech are unimpaired, to the surprise of my doctor. I almost wrote "disappointment." Doctors like for one's decline to be orderly and irrevocable. How is your gout? Your eyesight? Hippia, whose exquisite penmanship you have been reading, sends you her respects (she has given me such a sweet smile!), as do I.

# XX

*The Journal of Julian Augustus*
*Callinicum on the Euphrates*                          *27 March 363*

Waiting for the fleet. They should have been here when we arrived. Callinicum is a rich city, strongly fortified. Morale is good. Dictating this while riding in a carriage to the river. Today is the festival of the Mother of the Gods. There is a great ceremony at Rome. I hold a small one here. The sun is hot. People crowd about the carriage. I dictate to the secretary. I wave to the crowd. I am in ceremonial vestments. Maximus and Priscus are with me. The local priests are waiting at the riverbank. The people who crowd around are darkskinned with long thin arms that reach toward me like the tentacles of some twisting vine. They chatter, shrill as Egyptians.

*Priscus*: This is the first entry. Most of the journal is written in Julian's own hand. He usually wrote late at night, after he had finished dictating his memoir. I recall this particular day in Callinicum as one of the "good days." They were so few that each is relatively vivid in my mind.

Several thousand people lined the Euphrates when we arrived for the ceremony. A few were pious, most were merely curious. The Euphrates is a broad muddy river set in rolling country, at this season green.

Julian handled the ceremonies with his usual efficiency. This particular bit of nonsense involved the immersion and ritual washing of the carriage in which the image of the goddess is carried. Julian was thoroughly soaked but happy as he carried out his duties

370

as Pontifex Maximus. Later he gave us dinner (if mashed beans, native bread and fresh tough venison can be called dinner) in the prefect's house. We were all in excellent spirits.

As I wrote you in one of my letters (at least I *think* I wrote you: I often don't remember nowadays whether something I meant to say I did say or not), the generals were seldom a part of Julian's inner circle. For one thing, they don't stay up late; while Aristotle, as the beautiful Arintheus so often used to say, makes the military head ache. Nevertheless, these particular officers were superior men; and of course three of them became emperors.

The generals fell in two categories. The Christian-Asiatics and the Hellenist-Europeans. The first group had been loyal to Constantius; the second to Julian.

For the record, I give you my impression of the principal commanders.

## The Asiatics

Count Victor: In appearance, a typical Sarmatian, short, bandy-legged, with a large head, pale eyes slanted like a Hun's. He spoke both Greek and Latin with a barbarous accent. A devout Christian, he was profoundly contemptuous of Julian's philosopher friends. I always mistrusted him.

Arintheus: Julian has described him. Once his beauty has been noted, there is not much else to say. He and Victor led the Christian party.

Jovian: An extraordinarily tall man, even taller than I—or would have been had he ever stood up straight. He tended to eat and drink too much, though he never gained weight. He had the reputation for being stupid, and I see no reason for altering this common judgment. Jovian was well connected, which largely explains his later moment of glory. His father was the famous general Varronian, and his wife was the daughter of the egregious Count Lucillianus. I am told that Jovian had a monstrous child-hood, living under "field conditions" until he was seventeen. Old Varronian was an insufferable martinet. Jovian commanded the household troops.

## The Europeans

Nevitta: He was a large man, red-faced, blue-eyed, perhaps forty years old at the time. He was an illiterate boor but a fine

371

soldier and completely loyal to Julian. Even so, we all hated him. To his credit *he* hated no one. We were beneath his contempt.

Dagalaif: He was an amiable sort. Stocky and fair (are all good soldiers blond? shall we offer this as a topic of debate for our students?), Dagalaif spoke excellent Greek and Latin. He was a marvelous cavalryman and much of Julian's legendary swiftness was due to Dagalaif's ability to maneuver men and horses. He used to ask me for reading lists. He longed to be civilized. Three years later, when he was made consul, he wrote me a panegyric, with surprisingly few mistakes.

Salutius Secundus: A mild, elderly man. We got on famously, though he had almost no conversation. In that sea of youth our gray hairs and aging muscles called out to one another, like to like. As praetorian prefect he spared Julian many tedious details. He was an excellent administrator who would have made an admirable emperor.

Among others of the court, I should mention the chief marshal, Anatolius, a nice fat little man who managed to create quite a lot of confusion in a position where one is supposed to make order. Also, the notary Phosphorius, whose family forced him to enter the civil service. Solely through merit and hard work he rose to a place on the Consistory; his career was unique. I have never known another like it. As for Julian's philosopher friends, you met them all at Antioch. The only addition was the Etruscan high priest Mastara. He was exactly what you might think.

On the march, we would usually make camp at sundown. As soon as Julian's tent was raised, we would dine with him, Maximus and I, and sometimes one or another of the commanders. At first Julian was in marvelous spirits. He had every reason to be. Sapor was demoralized at the speed of our attack. The weather was good. The countryside was rich in grain that soon would come to harvest. All things promised well, except the omens.

Julian's tent was a plain affair, necessarily large but simply furnished, not half so comfortable as the tent of any of his generals. As I recall, there were two large folding tables, a number of folding chairs, stools, and several large chests containing state papers and the small library Julian always traveled with. There were several tripod lamps, although seldom was more than one lit at a time. Julian wondered if he was mean: yes, he *was* mean, but compared

372

to the lavish waste of his predecessors this was a virtuous fault. In a corner, his black lion-skinned bed was screened by a woven Persian rug.

Julian was invariably dictating when we presented ourselves. He would smile at us and indicate that we sit down without once breaking the flow of his thought. He did an amazing amount of work, nearly all of it necessary. He conducted a lot of business usually left to notaries or eunuchs. When he had completely exhausted one set of secretaries, he would send for another. All complained that he dictated too fast. And he did, as if he suspected there was hardly time to put on paper all the ideas he had in his brain. We know his famous postscripts. No sooner was a letter sealed than he would have it opened again so that he could scribble some afterthought in his own hand, apologizing with his usual phrase, "I write fast, without taking a breath." His fingers were always black with ink by the time we arrived for supper.

Before we ate, Maximus or I would read him Homer and he would wash his hands in a plain earthen jug, listening all the time. The meal was always simple. But then you know his crotchets about food. I usually had another dinner late that night. I am sure Maximus ate before. Sometimes we would be joined by Salutius, an intelligent man for a general, or by Arintheus, whom I always thought a bore. Incidentally, Arintheus was in Athens several years ago. I was shocked to see him. He is now stout and bald, and though he was no favorite of mine, I nearly wept at what time had done. But tears were stopped by his conversation, which had undergone no change. When he saw me at the proconsul's reception, he gave a loud empty laugh and shouted across the room in a voice hoarse from battle and wine, "That Aristotle of yours *still* makes my head ache!" And that I'm afraid is all that passed between us after so many years and so much history.

As I have said, the philosophers and warriors seldom mingled. That night in Callinicum was one of the few occasions when Julian's two worlds confronted one another.

I sat in a corner and watched Julian play his various roles. Up to a point, we all tend to assume different masks with different people. But Julian changed completely with each person. With the Gallic soldiers, he became a harsh-voiced, loud-laughing Gaul. With the Asiatics, he was graceful but remote, another Constantius. Not until he turned to a philosopher friend was he himself. *Himself?* We shall never know which was the true Julian, the abrupt military genius or the charming philosophy-mad student. Obviously he was both. Yet it was disquieting to watch him become a stranger before one's eyes, and an antipathetic one at that.

I was joined in my corner by Victor. He asked if he could sit down. I beamed fatuously. Why are we all so physically awed by soldiers? "By all means, Count," I dithered. He sat down heavily; he smelled of wine but he was not drunk.

"You're a long way from the Academy at Athens," he said.

I agreed. "But then Gaul was a long way, too, and the Battle of Strasbourg." Silently I cursed myself for having boasted of a military career. The ideal philosopher would have conducted the conversation entirely in his own terms; he would *never* compete in an alien field. But then I am not the ideal philosopher. Everyone says so.

"Yes . . . Gaul," he said, as though that were enough. I could not divine his mood or attitude. We were both silent, watching Maximus as he held a number of the young officers spellbound with some nonsense or other. His flowing beard was exquisitely combed and he wore a robe of saffron-yellow silk, the gift of a magician in China, or so he said. He probably found it in the market at Antioch.

"Can you make your gods appear?" asked Victor suddenly, "the way *he* does?" Because Victor would not dignify Maximus by giving him a name, my heart went out to him, briefly.

"No," I said. "The gods rather leave me alone. But then I make no effort to talk to them."

"Do you believe?" He spoke with such passionate urgency that I turned to look at him. I have never seen such cold eyes as those which stared at me beneath thick pale brows. It was like coming face to face with a lion.

"Believe in *what*?"

"Christ."

"I believe that he existed." I was myself again. "But I don't think of him as a god."

Victor was again the Roman commander. "It will be a long campaign," he said, as though speaking of the weather. "But we shall win it."

*Julian Augustus*                                                    *3 April*

We are at Circesium, ninety-eight miles south of Callinicum. We have been here two days. All goes well.

On 28 March while I was still at Callinicum, four tribes of Saracens appeared at the city's gate. Their princes wished to speak to me. Now the Saracens are among the most savage and unreliable of this world's races. They live in tents in the desert. They never build so much as a hut nor till an acre of ground. Restlessly, they roam through the deserts of Assyria, Egypt, Morocco. They live on game, wild birds, whatever grows of itself. Few have tasted grain or wine. They love warfare, but on their own terms. They are good at striking swiftly (their ponies and camels are especially bred for fleetness), but since they fight only for plunder, they are useless in a formal engagement. They are best at scouting and harassing an enemy.

Salutius did not want me to see them. "They will offer to help you. Then they will make the same offer to Sapor—if they haven't already—and betray you both."

"So we shall be on our guard." I was not in the least disturbed.

I received the Saracen princes. They are small, sinewy, dark from the sun. They wear full cloaks to their knees. Beneath their cloaks, they wear only leather drawers. Of the dozen princes, only one could speak Greek.

"We come, Lord, to pay homage to the ruler of the world." The Saracen then motioned to one of his fellows, who gave him an object wrapped in silk. The prince removed the silk to reveal a heavy gold crown. Hermes knows what king lost it to them. I took the crown and made them a little speech, to which the prince replied, "Lord, we wish to fight beside you in your war against Sapor. Our courage is known to all the desert. Our loyalty to our ruler is so far beyond that of the merely human that it partakes of the divine..." Salutius cleared his throat but I did not dare look at him. "Therefore, Lord, with us beside you in the desert, you need never fear..."

At that moment Nevitta broke into the meeting, to the horror of Anatolius. "Caesar, the fleet is here!" I'm afraid we all behaved like excited children. I turned the Saracens over to Salutius. Then, followed by the entire Consistory, I made my way to the docks where, as far as the eye could see, the river was filled with ships. 50 W.S., 64 P.B., 1403 C.S., Ct. Luc.

*Priscus*: This entry breaks off here. The abbreviations mean that there were 50 ships of war, 64 pontoon boats used for making bridges, 1403 cargo ships containing food, weapons, foundries, siege engines; Count Lucillianus was in charge of the fleet. As you will recall, he was the commander at Sirmium whom Dagalaif captured in the middle of the night. Though he was a ridiculous creature, Julian used him because he was an important strand in that web of men and families which governs the world. Despite the vastness of the empire, the actual rulers are a small, close-knit family. Every general knows or has heard of every other general, and they talk of nothing else except, "How is old Marcellus? still with the same wife? got a different post?"

Lucillianus was waiting at the riverbank when Julian and the Consistory arrived. He greeted Julian with meticulous ceremony and formally turned the fleet over to him. Suddenly Dagalaif said, "Lucillianus, where's your nightshirt?" Everyone laughed except Julian, who muttered, "Shut up, Dagalaif." I noticed that Lucillianus's son-in-law Jovian scowled. He was less than amused.

*Julian Augustus*                                             *4 April*

I have been working for three hours on my memoir. It is nearly dawn. My voice is hoarse. The secretaries have just gone. I scribble these random notes. We are still at Circesium. It is a large city, well fortified by Diocletian. The city occupies a promontory between the Euphrates River and the place where the Abora River empties into the Euphrates. The Abora is the traditional border between Rome and Persia. Circesium is our last important outpost. From now on we shall be in enemy country.

All night the troops have been crossing the river. The engineers are complaining because the river is swollen with spring rains. But engineers always complain. So far their pontoon bridge is holding. Scouts report no sign of the Persian army. The Saracens tell me that Sapor is astonished at the suddenness of our attack. Apparently, he did not expect us until May. That means he has not yet assembled his army. All of this is marvelous for us. Yet I am not so energetic and hopeful as I ought to be. For one thing, I have just received a long letter from Sallust at Paris. He is unimpressed by the good omens. He begs me not to cross into Persia. Like Libanius, he wishes I would remain at Constantinople and execute the reforms I have proposed. As usual he puts his case superbly, and I am thoroughly depressed.

Tonight I sent away everyone except Maximus. I showed him what Sallust had written, remarking that since Sallust was seldom wrong when it came to politics, we ought at least to consider his advice. Maximus agreed. He praised Sallust at extraordinary length and I wondered how I had ever got the impression they were not friends. For almost an hour Maximus and I discussed the pros and cons of the Persian campaign. We agreed it must continue; although Maximus pointed out that there were any number of precedents for assembling an army and then not using it. Constantius used to do this every year, maintaining that the assembling of an army is in itself a deterrent; perhaps it is.

"But then of course Sallust does not know what we know," I said at last, referring to Maximus's vision of Cybele.

"There is something else he does not know." Maximus fixed me with those luminous eyes which have looked upon so many secret and forbidden things. "Something I have not told even you."

There was a long silence. I knew Maximus well enough not to hurry him. I waited, heart's blood pounding in my ears.

Maximus got to his feet. The robe of yellow silk fell about him in hieratic folds. In wavering lamplight he cast a huge shadow on the wall. I felt the imminence of some extraordinary force, that premonitory chill which signals the approach of deity. To ward off demons, Maximus drew a circle around us with his staff. Then he spoke.

"Last night, at the darkest hour, I summoned from the depths of Tartarus, Persephone herself, the Queen of all the Dead that are and ever shall be."

The lamps flickered; his shadow danced upon the wall; though the night was warm, I shivered with cold.

"I asked her the one question that must not be asked, but since the question concerned not me but you, not you but Rome, not Rome but the worship of the gods, I believed that I could ask this awful question without incurring the wrath of the Furies, or tangling the web of Fate."

I knew the question. I waited. I could hardly breathe. Maximus drew precautionary symbols on the floor, murmuring spells as he did.

"I asked. 'Dread Queen of Tartarus, tell me the place where your loyal son Julian will meet his death.'"

Maximus suddenly stopped. His hand went to his throat. He choked; he stumbled; only by clutching at his staff was he able to keep from falling. Something invisible wrestled with him. I did not move to help him for fear of breaking the power of the circle he had drawn. At last he was free. "Demons," he whispered. "But we have the highest power. Helios is our shield. . . . Persephone said, 'While all men mourn and all gods rejoice at a new hero come to Olympus, our beloved son Julian will die in Phrygia.'"

Maximus's voice faded as though from great weariness. I sat very still, cold as my own Phrygian death. Then Maximus clapped his hands and said in a matter-of-fact voice, "We are quite a long way from Phrygia, my dear fellow."

I laughed weakly, from relief. "And if I have my way, I shall never set foot in that province again." I then told Maximus that I had been told the same thing by Sosipatra. He was most surprised. He had not known.

"In any case, you see now why I am not concerned by Sallust's letter. Persephone has spoken to us. You know what few men have ever known, the place of your death."

"And the hour?"

". . . impossible, for that would be an affront to Fate herself. But we do know that you will survive the Persian campaign. If you survive it, that means you will have conquered."

"Like Alexander!" In a rush my confidence was restored. Am I not Alexander come again to finish the great work of bringing to the barbarous East the truth of Hellas? We cannot fail now.

*Priscus*: That was Maximus at his very best, and further proof that Sosipatra and Maximus were in league together. Maximus should have been an actor. But then he *was* an actor, and Julian was his devoted audience.

I don't remember much else about Circesium except that a supply master was executed because the grain barges he had promised for 4 April did not arrive. An hour after the wretch was put to death, the barges were sighted. It was an unpleasant business and Salutius, who had ordered the execution, was most unhappy at what he had done.

At dawn the next day, unable to sleep, I walked to the riverbank where Salutius sat in his praetorian prefect's chair, while the army laboriously crossed the pontoon bridge into Assyria, as that part of Persia is called. I remember that cool dawn as though it were today's. A pale pink light in the east, the Abora River muddy and swollen, the cavalry on the bridge, horses shying, men cursing, armor rattling. As far as the eye could see men waited, their armor gleaming like stars in the first light, their voices unnaturally sub-

378

dued, even apprehensive, for it had been many years since a Roman army had pursued the Great King into his own land.

I sat on a stool beside Salutius while aides came to him at regular intervals: could the Tertiaci Legion cross before the Victores, who weren't ready? in what order were the siege engines to be moved? were the Saracens to cross now with the cavalry or later with the infantry? Patiently, Salutius kept all things in order.

In between messengers, we chatted. I asked him bluntly what he thought of the campaign. He shrugged. "Militarily, we have nothing to fear from the Persians." He indicated the legions about us. "These are the best soldiers in the world, and the Emperor is the best general. We shall beat them in every battle."

"But they avoid battles. And this is their country. They know how to harass an enemy."

"Even so, we are the superior force. Only . . ."

"Only?" Salutius studied the list of legions which rested on his lap. "Only?" I repeated.

But at that moment a centurion rode up, cursing the Saracens, who insisted on crossing at the same time as the cavalry "with those damned wild horses of theirs!" Salutius soothed the man, effected a compromise, by which time a notary had come to tell me that the Emperor wished me to attend him. As I left, Salutius said, "Be on your guard, Priscus. We are not safe." An understatement, as it turned out.

*Julian Augustus*                                                    *6 April*

I crossed the Abora River yesterday afternoon. As Highest Priest I made sacrifice to Zeus. All omens were good except one: my horse nearly rode over the body of a quartermaster who had been executed by order of the praetorian prefect. Luckily, one of my aides pulled the horse to one side, nearly unseating me in the process.

We then rode some fifteen miles to a village called Zaitha, which means "olive tree" in Persian. The day was cool, and our spirits were high. Miles before we got to Zaitha we could see its principal monument, the tall circular mausoleum built for the Emperor Gordian. In 242 Gordian conducted a successful campaign against the Persians. Two years later he was murdered by his own men, who had been incited to mutiny by an Arab named Philip who became—briefly—emperor. A sad story, and typical. How often have emperors won great victories and saved the state only to be struck down by an unsuspected rival? Gordian decisively defeated the Persian king at Resaina, only to be murdered by Philip. As a result, a lasting victory over Persia was promptly thrown away by that pusillanimous Arab who wanted only to loot an empire gained by murder.

We stopped for an hour at the tomb, which is in good repair since the Persians respect monuments to the dead, while the roving Saracens fear all buildings. I offered a sacrifice to Gordian's spirit and prayed that I be spared his fate. I must get a biography of him. I know almost nothing of his life, except of course that he was a friend of Plotinus. Maximus says Gordian still haunts this part of the world, demanding vengeance. Unhappy spirit!

While we were still at the tomb, Nevitta got me to one side. He was troubled because, "The men believe this is the first time Romans have ever invaded Persia. They believe that . . ." he gestured to include all the south . . . "this country has a spell on it."

We were standing in the shadow of the tomb. I reached out my hand and touched the rough-hewn tufa. "Here is the proof that we have been in Persia before."

"Exactly, Emperor. They say that this old emperor was killed by Persian demons because he dared to cross the Abora River. They say lightning struck him dead. They say Persia is forbidden to us."

I was astonished. Nevitta, who fears no man, is frightened of demons. I spoke to him as teacher to child. "Nevitta, Gordian defeated the Great King in a battle one hundred and twenty years ago. Then he was killed by his own men. The Persians had nothing to do with his death. They are not demons. They are men. Men can be defeated, especially Persians. We have defeated Persians many times before."

Nevitta almost asked "when?" but then he thought better of it. After all, as a Roman consul he is expected to know something of Roman history. Yet as far as I know, he has never read a book of any kind, though in preparation for this campaign he told me, quite seriously, that he was studying Alexander. When I asked which biography he was reading, he said, *Alexander and the Wicked Magician*, a popular novel!

I reassured Nevitta. I told him about the victories of Lucullus, Pompey and Ventidius, Trajan, Verus and Severus. Apparently, these names had a somewhat familiar ring and he looked relieved.

I did not of course mention our defeats. "So tell the soldiers that their fear of the Persians is the result of Constantius's fear of war."

"You tell them, Emperor." Nevitta is the only man who addresses me by that military title. "They don't know these things. And there's a lot of talk about how bad things are going to be."

"The Galileans?"

Nevitta shrugged. "I don't know who starts it. But there's talk. You'd better give them one of your history lectures." That is the closest Nevitta ever comes to humor. I laughed to show that I appreciated his attempt.

"I'll speak to them when we get to Dura." Nevitta saluted and started to go. I stopped him.

"It might be useful . . ." I began. But then—I don't know why—I chose not to finish. "Tomorrow, Nevitta."

He left me alone in the shadow of the tomb. I had meant to ask him to find out who was spreading rumors. But I thought better of it. Nothing destroys the spirit of any army more quickly than the use of secret agents and midnight interrogations. Even so, I have been warned. I must be on guard.

We set out for Dura. We were only a few miles south of Zaitha when two horsemen appeared from the east, carrying something in a sling between them. At first I thought it was a man, but when they came close I saw that it was a dead lion of great size. Maximus whispered excitedly in my ear, "A king will die in Persia!" But I had already got the point to the omen quite on my own. I also refrained from making the obvious retort: "Which king?" But as this Persian lion was killed by Roman spears it seems likely that the Persian King Sapor will be killed by Roman arms.

This lion, incidentally, was the first I'd ever seen close-to; even in death, he was terrifying, with teeth long as my thumb and yellow eyes still glaring with life's hot rage. I ordered the lion skinned. I shall use its pelt for my bed.

As we continued toward Dura, the sun vanished, the sky turned gray, lightning flashed. A violent thunder storm broke. We were all soaked and chilled by the rain, but we continued our march.

Shortly before evening, Victor rode up to me. "Augustus, a soldier has been killed by lightning." Though Victor is a Galilean he has the usual military man's interest in omens. "The soldier was watering two horses at the river when the storm broke. He was just about to lead them back to his cohort when he was struck by lightning. He was killed instantly."

381

"What was his name?"

"Jovian, Augustus." I pretended to take this merely as an added detail. "Bury him," I said, and rode on. Maximus was the first to speak. "The sign is ambiguous. The fact he is named after the king of the gods, the thunderer Jove himself, does not necessarily mean that a king is involved." But I did not listen. This was a matter for the Etruscans.

We made camp on the outskirts of Dura, a long-deserted town whose houses of brick are slowly returning to the dust from which they were shaped by dead hands. The streets were empty except for herds of deer. I allowed the men to kill as many as they could for food. It was an amusing sight to see our best archers and cavalrymen careering through muddy streets in pursuit of the deer, who promptly fled to the river and, like seasoned troops obeying an agreed-upon plan, swam to the other side. In midstream the bargemen killed many of them with their oars.

That night Maximus, Priscus and I dined on fresh venison in my tent. Afterward we were joined by the Etruscan priests. Their chief is an elderly man named Mastara. He is held in high regard at Rome, where he used to be consultant to the senate. I record here, privately, that Mastara has been against this campaign from the beginning. He even interpreted the killing of the lion as unfavorable to me.

In general, the Etruscan religion is well known; in particular, it is obscure. From the beginning of time, the genius of the Etruscan religion has been its peculiar harmony with the natural forces of creation. The first revelation is known to all. Tages, a divine child, appeared in the field of a peasant named Tarchon, and dictated to him a holy book which is the basis of their religion. Later Vegoia, a young goddess, appeared during a ceremony to the thunder god and gave the priests a second book which contained instructions on how to interpret heavenly signs, particularly lightning. According to this book, the sky is divided into sixteen parts, each sacred to a particular god (though the same god may at times influence a section not his own). One can discover which god has manifested himself by the direction from which the lightning comes, the angle at which it strikes, and of course the place where it strikes.

Mastara wasted no time. He had already analyzed the death of the soldier Jovian. "Highest Priest, the lightning came from the ninth house." I knew what this meant even before he interpreted it. "The house of Ares. The house of war. At the eleventh hour Ares struck down the soldier Jovian beside the river to our west. That means a soldier from the west, a king, will be killed late in a war. We are now making projections as to the exact day and hour of this king's death. By tomorrow we should be able to tell you when this . . . warning shall become fact."

There it was. We were all quite still for several moments. Maximus sat opposite me, hand wound in his beard, eyes shut as though listening to some voice within. Priscus shifted his long frame uneasily on a hard bench. The Etruscans were motionless, their eyes downcast.

"The king," I said at last, "*could* be Sapor."

"Highest Priest, Sapor does not come from the west."

"Nor do I, to be exact." I was ready to quibble as people always do when a prophecy has gone against them. "I come from the north. The only kings hereabout who are from the west are the Saracen princes. My own interpretation is that one of them will die in battle."

"Then shall we continue with our projection, Highest Priest?" Mastara did not show emotion. He was a priest speaking to his superior, correct, demure, obedient.

"No," I said firmly. "I see no need. But to the extent that the army is apt to hear of your first interpretation, I must ask you to allow the second—and correct—interpretation to be generally known."

Mastara bowed. He and his priests departed. Priscus gave that dry chuckle of his. "I see now why the early emperors always insisted on being Highest Priest, too."

"I don't think I misinterpreted the sign." But realizing this sounded weak, I turned to Maximus for help. He opened his eyes. Then he leapt to his feet and turned first west then east then north then south. "Not even a Saracen!" he said abruptly. "Africa. Mauretania. *There* is the doomed king."

At first I wondered if perhaps Maximus was not trying deliberately to raise my spirits, but as he was in such an exuberant mood for the rest of the evening I now believe him. I have just written a letter to Sallust, asking him to send me news of the Mauretanian kings.

It is daybreak. I have not slept in twenty-four hours, nor will I sleep for another twelve. We must be on the march within the hour. I hear my servant Callistus outside the tent, giving the guard

383

the password. I must now make notes for the speech I give to the troops today. My head is empty. My eyes burn. How to begin?

*Priscus*: The speech was a success. If Julian was tired, he did not show it. Incidentally, in his description of that séance with the Etruscans he omits my remark to him, "What is the point of listening to soothsayers, if you won't believe what they tell you?" But Julian was very like the Christians who are able to make their holy book endorse anything they want it to.

Julian's speech had a good effect. In the briefest but most convincing way, he explained to the men how often Roman armies had won victories in this country and he warned them against listening to defeatists, particularly those who had been set among us by the Persians, whose cunning and treachery he emphasized. When he finished, there was a great racket of approval. The Gauls were vociferous, but the eastern legions were unenthusiastic, particularly Victor's cavalry. I mentioned this later to Julian. Yes, he had noticed it, too. "But they don't know me. The Gauls do. When they've won a few battles and looted a few cities they will love their leader." Julian the practical soldier, not the Hellenic humanist!

*Julian Augustus*                                      *14 April*
   L. Arin., Orm., Cav.; R. Nev. Tert., Pet., C., C. inf. J . . . Dag, Vic.; Van. 1500 sc.; Pyrr.; Luc. fleet; Anatha island: Luc. 1000? Waiting. Cyb. Mith. Her.

*Priscus*: I think I can interpret this entry. Julian is noting for himself our military order during the march south. On the right, skirting the riverbank, Nevitta commanded the Tertiaci, Petulantes and Celts. In the center Julian commanded the main part of the infantry—the baggage and the philosophers were also in the center. On the left—or east—Arintheus and Ormisda commanded the cavalry. Though Ormisda was an infantry general, in the field there is a good deal of shifting back and forth of high-ranking officers. Dagalaif and Victor brought up the rear, while 1500 mounted scouts ranged the countryside before us. Lucillianus commanded the fleet which accompanied us downriver.

"Anatha island: Luc. 1000?" refers to the first Persian stronghold we came to, a heavily fortified island in the middle of the river, four days' march from Dura. Julian sent Lucillianus with a thousand light-armed troops to make a night landing under the walls of the fortress. As there was also a heavy mist that evening, Julian hoped to take the island by surprise. But at dawn the mist suddenly lifted and a Persian soldier sent out to draw water, seeing Lucillianus's men, shouted a warning and that was the end of Julian's surprise attack.

A few hours later, Julian crossed over to the island. One look at those huge walls decided him against a siege. He would have to take the fort by other means. Incidentally, this was to be his policy during the whole campaign. Between the Roman border and Ctesiphon—a distance of more than three hundred miles— there were a dozen fortresses and walled cities. Julian had the power to take any one of them but at the cost of weeks' or even months' delay. He could not afford this. So he chose to isolate the fortresses, knowing that once the Great King fell all the cities would be his.

Julian sent word to the governor of Anatha that he would spare the lives of the garrison if they surrendered. The governor asked for a parley with Ormisda. Julian describes this in the next entry.

"Waiting." These notes were made late in the night of the fourteenth when Lucillianus was still hidden on the island.

"Cyb. Mith. Her." A prayer: Cybele, Mithras, Hermes.

## Julian Augustus                                    15 April

Anatha has surrendered! Our first victory on Persian soil. At noon the governor of the island, Pusaeus, asked me to send him Ormisda to work out the details of the surrender. I confess I was nervous while awaiting the outcome of the conference. Pusaeus could so easily murder Ormisda. But less than an hour after Ormisda entered the fortress, the gates swung open and a garlanded ox was led forth by a Persian priest as sign of peace. There was a great cheer from our legions. Then Ormisda and the governor appeared. Pusaeus is a dark intense man, reputedly a good soldier, (why else would he have been entrusted with this important fort?). He saluted me as he would have saluted the Great King, flat on his belly. Then, face full of dust, he asked me what I intended to do with the inhabitants of the town.

I motioned to Anatolius and his notaries to join us. Then I said, "Governor, since you have shown yourself friendly to us and honorable in your dealings, we shall, at our own expense, move your people to Syria, to the city of Chalcis, where they will be able to live as they have lived here."

He thanked me warmly, his head rolling about in the dirt until I told him to get up. Pusaeus then asked me if I would take him into the Roman army. I turned to Ormisda. "Should I?"

Ormisda's face is a sea of delicate responses; by the slightest quiver of a brow or the flaring of a nostril he is able to communicate without words. The face said: beware! The voice said, "Yes, but perhaps not here, perhaps with a garrison in Spain or Egypt." So I made Pusaeus a tribune and posted him to Egypt.

All this took place in the main square of Anatha, a town of wood and thatch and mud brick, exactly like every other town, Persian or Roman, in this part of the world. While we talked, the people passed by us. The women balanced rolls of bedding and clothing on their heads while the men carried weapons and cooking utensils. Suddenly a frail old man, supported by two women, approached us. He gave me the Roman salute and said in soldier-Latin: "Maximanus, foot soldier with the Ziannis, reporting for duty." He stood shakily at attention. I looked at him with wonder. "Where are you from? Who are you?"

"A Roman soldier, General. In the army of Galerius Augustus."

Salutius said flatly, "That's impossible. It's a hundred years since Galerius died."

"No, Prefect," said the old man (he still knew a praetorian prefect when he saw one), "Galerius was here sixty-six years ago. And I was with him. I was eighteen years old. I'd enlisted at Philippopolis in Thrace. We won great victories here."

"But why are you *still* here?" Easily the most fatuous question one could ask a man in his eighties. But I was quite overwhelmed by this relic of another age.

"I fell ill with the fever. My tribune, Decius—never got on with him—thought I was going to die. So he left me here with a family who said they'd bury me properly when the time came. Then the army left." He laughed, an old rooster cackling. "Well, they haven't buried me yet. You can see that, I guess! And *they're* all gone: Galerius, Decius, Marius . . . he was a good friend, but got the pox . . . he's gone, too. So the family here that was willing to bury me took me in and I married two of their daughters. Both good girls. Dead now. These are later wives." He indicated the women who stood, ready to support him should he stumble. "General, I beg one favor."

386

"Whatever I can grant," I said.

"I have sworn that I would die on Roman soil and be buried in Roman earth. Send me back to Thrace."

"So be it, soldier." I motioned for Anatolius to arrange the matter. The old man then kissed my hand and I looked down with wonder at the back of his shriveled neck, lined as old parchment and burned dark by the fierce suns of nearly a century. What must it be like to have lived so long? With some difficulty, his wives got him to his feet. He was breathing hard from the exertion. He looked at me curiously.

"You *are* the Emperor of Rome, aren't you?"

I nodded. "Do you doubt it?"

"No, no, Lord. They told me that the Roman general was also the Emperor and that's when I advised the town council to surrender. 'You haven't a chance,' I said, 'not when there's an Emperor on the loose and the Great King out there, hidden in the desert, frightened out of his wits. Better surrender,' I said. Didn't I, Pusaeus?"

"Yes, Augustus, he did say so."

"This Pusaeus is married to a grandchild of mine, which makes him partway to being Roman. They're a good people, you know, the Persians. I hate to see them hurt."

"We shall be as merciful as we can."

"I've had a good life here." He looked about him vaguely. Then his eye caught on the standard of the Zinnnis. "There's my legion! I must talk to those boys. I knew their fathers, *grandfathers* anyway. Yes..." He started to walk off but then, recalling me, he stopped. "Thank you, General."

"Thank you, soldier, for remaining loyal to Rome all these years."

"You know, General... Lord, I don't follow too much what happens in the world outside of the province here because there's so little news and what there is makes no sense because they're capital liars, the Persians. They can't help it, you know, they don't mean any harm by it. It's just their way. But I did hear word of a great emperor who they call Constantine. That's not you, is it?"

"No, but there was such an emperor and he was my uncle."

"Yes, yes." The old man was not listening. He frowned, trying to recall something. "There was also this young officer who was with us in 297... well-connected, he was, *his* name was Con-

387

stantine, too. I often wondered if it was the same fellow. Do you know if he was?"

Constantine had indeed served one year with Galerius in Persia. I nodded. "It could have been the same," I said.

"He looked a bit like you, only he was clean-shaven. A nice enough young chap, though we none of us thought he'd ever make a soldier, liked the girls and the soft life too much, but who doesn't?" He sighed contentedly. "So now I've seen three emperors, and I'll die on Roman soil. And where's the tribune Decius, I ask you? who used to give me such a hard time and left me here to die? Where is he? who remembers him, after all these years? But I'm alive and I've been talking to the Emperor, to Julius himself! Now that's a great thing, isn't it? So if you'll excuse me, General, I want to go chat with those Thracian lads; maybe one is a grandchild to Marius, though they say when they get the pox it makes the children stillborn or worse. He was a lovely friend, Marius."

The old man saluted me and, helped by the two old wives, he slowly crossed the square to the place where the standard of the Ziannis had been set up. I was much moved by this encounter, even though I had been called Julius!

When all the inhabitants had left Anatha, we set fire to the town. Then I returned to our camp on the riverbank to be greeted by the Saracens, who had just captured a number of Persian guerrilla fighters in the act of raiding our supplies. I gave the Saracens money to show my pleasure, and told them to continue to be on the alert. I also asked if the Saracen princes were safe. Yes.

It is late at night. I am pleasantly drowsy. Our first encounter with the enemy has been all that I could have wished it. If it were not for the rain which is falling and turning the floor of my tent to mud, I would be perfectly content.

*Priscus*: The rain that night was accompanied by winds. The next day, 16 April, at about the third hour, we were struck by a hurricane from the north. Tents were ripped by the wind, while the river, already swollen from spring rains, overflowed and several grain barges were wrecked. The dikes which control the flow of river water into irrigation ditches broke and some suspected the Persians of deliberately shutting the sluice gates in order to flood our camp. We shall never know if they did or not. Anyway, after two wet wretched days, we moved on.

Julian was in good spirits. We all were. The first Persian strong-hold was ours and the Great King's army had vanished. It was too good to be true.

Our army was stretched out over ten miles, much the same trick Julian used when he came from Gaul, to give the impression of a mighty host. Julian rode either at the head or at the rear of the army, the two places most apt to be harassed by guerrillas. But we did not come up against the Persians for some days. They kept to the opposite side of the river, watching us. Whenever we made as though to cross, they would disappear in the thickets of wormwood. Yet they were very much on the alert. When one of the Gauls—for reasons of his own—crossed over, he was butchered and his head placed on a long pole in full view of our army.

Incidentally, I lost my tent in the storm and for three nights I was forced to share quarters with Maximus. We were not happy with one another. Among other bad habits, he talked in his sleep. The first night we slept together, I found his mumbling so unbearable that I woke him up.

"I? Talking in my sleep?" He looked at me blearily, silver beard tangled like fleece wool before carding, face stupid with sleep. Then he remembered himself. "But of course I was talking. It is in sleep I converse with the gods."

"Then could you perhaps *whisper* to them? You're keeping me awake."

"I shall do my best." He later complained to Julian that my coughing had kept him awake! But I coughed hardly at all considering that I had caught a very bad cold as a result of being soaked in the storm. Julian was much amused at the thought of our sharing the same quarters.

*Julian Augustus*                                                22 April
17 April, Thilutha, Achaiachalca. 18 April, abandoned fort burned. 20 April, Baraxmalcha, cross river 7 miles to Diacira. Temple. grain. salt. bitumen springs. deserted. burned. to Ozogardana. deserted. burned. monument to Trajan. two days in camp. 22 April, attempt to ambush Ormisda. Warning. Persian army gathering tonight.

*Priscus*: Between 17 April and 20 April we passed three island fortresses. The first was Thilutha, a mountain peak jutting out of the water with a stronghold on the top of it. Julian sent a messenger

389

demanding surrender. The commandant sent back a most courteous answer. He would not surrender, but he swore to abide by the outcome of the Emperor's war with the Great King. Since we could not waste time in a siege, we accepted the commandant's reply. In return, the garrison saluted our fleet as it passed beneath the walls of the island. The same thing happened at Achaiachalca, another island fortress.

On 20 April we came to a deserted village called Baraxmalcha. At Ormisda's suggestion we then crossed the river and marched seven miles inland to Diacira, a rich market center. The city was deserted when we arrived. Fortunately, the warehouses were filled with grain and, most important, salt. Outside the town wall, Nevitta's soldiers found several women and put them to death. This did not sit well with me. I don't know if Julian knew about these murders or not. He was ruthless when it came to punishing disobedience and treachery, but he was not cruel, unlike Nevitta and the Gauls, who liked blood for its own sake.

Diacira was burned, as was the nearby town of Ozogardana where, incidentally, we found the remains of a tribunal of Trajan. Julian made this relic center to the camp that was pitched. We remained there for two days while the grain and salt taken from Diacira was loaded onto barges. During this time, Julian was busy with his generals and I did not see him at all.

I contented myself with the company of Anatolius (who was quite amusing, particularly about his failures as marshal of the court), the admirable Phosphorius, and Ammianus Marcellinus, whom I had met earlier at your house in Antioch. I liked him very much. He told me that we had first met at Rheims where he'd been on duty with one of Ursicinus's legions, though I'm afraid I don't recall that meeting. As you know, Ammianus is writing a history of Rome which he plans to bring up to date. Brave man! Some years ago he sent me an inscribed copy of the first ten books of his history, *in Latin*! Why he has chosen to write in that language, I don't know. After all, he comes from Antioch, doesn't he? And I seem to have got the impression that he was of good Greek family. But looking back, I can see that he was always something of a Romanophile. He used to spend most of his time with the European officers, and he rather disliked the Asiatics. As a historian, he has deliberately put himself in the line of Livy and Tacitus rather than that of Herodotus and Thucydides, showing that there is no accounting for taste. He wrote me recently to say

390

that he is living at Rome where, though he finds the literary world incredibly arid and pretentious, he means to make this mark. I wish him well. I haven't read much of his history but he seems to write Latin easily, so perhaps he has made the right choice. But what a curious old-fashioned thing to want to be, a *Roman* historian! He tells me that he is in regular correspondence with you. So I daresay the two of you will join forces when the time comes to publish the memoir.

The night of 22 April Ormisda was about to go reconnoitering when he was nearly ambushed by a cohort of the Persian army. Nobody knows how the Persians knew the exact hour he was to leave the camp, but they did. Ormisda was saved by the unexpected deepness of the river at that point. The enemy could not ford it due to the rains.

"Warning." I don't know what Julian means by this. Perhaps a counterspy warned Ormisda at the last moment. Or someone warned Julian of a plot against *his* life.

"Persian army gathering tonight." The next morning (23 April) we finally saw the Persian army. Several thousand horsemen and archers were assembled a mile from our encampment. In the morning's light their glittering chain mail made our eyes water. They were under the command of the Grand Vizier, who is second only to the Great King himself, a position somewhere between that of a Caesar and a praetorian prefect. Associated with the Vizier's army was a large band of Assanatic Saracens, a tribe renowned for cruelty.

At the second hour, Julian engaged the enemy. After much maneuvering, he got his infantry into position some yards from the Persian archers. Then before they could fire, he gave the order for an infantry charge at quick march. This maneuver startled the Persians just long enough for our men to neutralize their archers. Infantry shields were thrust against archers in such a way that the Persians could not take aim to fire. They broke and ran. The field was ours.

Julian was delighted. "Now our soldiers know the Persians are men just like ourselves!" He looked the perfect war god: face flushed, purple cloak stained with the blood of others, eyes bright with excitement. "Come along," he shouted to Maximus and the philosophers who were now coming up to what had been the front line. "Let's see the walls of Macepracta!"

None of us knew what Julian meant until he led us to a deserted village near the battlefield. Here we saw the remains of an ancient wall. Julian consulted a book. "This," he said, "is part of the original Assyrian wall. Xenophon saw it when he was here 764 years ago." Happily, our victorious general clambered over the stones, reading at the top of his voice from Xenophon's *March Upcountry*. We all looked dutifully on what had been a ruin even then, so long ago, but I'm afraid that after the stimulus (and terror) of battle, no one was in a mood for sightseeing. Finally, Julian led us back to the river.

On the outskirts of the encampment, a legion of household troops were gathered around a rock on which stood their Tribune, haranguing them. He was tall, thickly muscled, with fair hair. ". . . you fear the Persians! You say they are not men like us but demons! Don't deny it! I've heard you whispering at night like children afraid of the dark."

The Tribune's voice was strong. His face was ruddy and his eyes were—what else? blue. We dark-eyed people have lost the world to those with eyes like winter ice. He spoke with a slight German accent. "But now you've seen these demons close to. You beat them in battle. Were they so fierce? So huge? So terrible?"

There was a low murmur from the men about him: no, the Persians had not been superhuman. The Tribune was a splendid demagogue. I looked at Julian, who had bundled his cloak about his face as momentary disguise. He was watching the man with the alert interest of an actor or rhetorician studying a rival's performance.

"No. They are men like us. But *inferior* men. Look!" The Tribune motioned for one of his officers to step forward. The man was holding what looked at first to be a bundle of rags. But it was a dead Persian. The officer tossed the body to the Tribune. He caught it easily. The men gasped, impressed at the strength of these two men who handled a corpse as though it were a doll.

The Tribune with one hand held up the body by the neck. The dead Persian was slight, with a thin black moustache and a fierce display of teeth. His armor had been stripped away and the remains were clad only in a bloody tunic. "There he is! The Persian devil! *This* is what you were afraid of?" With his free hand, the Tribune tore the tunic away, revealing a slight, almost childlike body with a black crescent beneath the breast-bone where a lance had entered.

The Tribune shook the body, as a hunting dog will shake a hare. "Are you afraid of this?" There was a loud response of "No!"

392

Then great laughter at the sight of the hairless smooth body, so unlike us. The Tribune tossed the remains contemptuously to the ground. "Never again do I want to hear anyone whisper in the night that the Persians are devils! *We* are the men who will rule this land!" To loud cheering, the Tribune stepped down from his rock and walked straight into Julian. He saluted smartly, not at all taken aback. "A necessary speech, Augustus."

"An *excellent* speech, Valentinian." For as you have doubtless guessed, the Tribune was our future emperor. "I want all my commanders to give their troops the same . . . demonstration. First-rate."

The soldiers promptly vanished, as soldiers tend to the moment they realize the Emperor is among them.

Julian and his successor exchanged a few soldierly words. Then as we were about to move on, Valentinian motioned to a young cavalry officer who was standing nearby, wide-eyed at the sight of the Emperor. "Augustus, may I present to you my brother Valens?"

I often wonder what Julian would have thought if he had known that in less than a year those brothers, sons of an Austrian rope seller turned general, would be co-emperors of East and West. I suspect he would have approved of Valentinian, but Valens was a disaster. And the fact that both were Christian would hardly have pleased him. It certainly did not please us, did it? I nearly lost my life because of Valens. Maximus did lose his.

Then Julian left his successors, none aware of the future. If the gods exist, they are kind. Despite oracles and flashes of lightning, they tell us nothing. If they did, we could not bear it.

The next day we came to a place where the water of the Euphrates was drawn off into a network of irrigation canals. Some of these canals are a thousand years old and without them Persia would not be the rich country it is. There were those who wanted to divert the waters and cause the fields to dry up but Julian would not allow this, pointing out that we should soon be living off the produce of these same fields. At the beginning of the largest canal was a tall tower, marking the source of the Naharmalcha (Persian for "the king's river"), which flows into the Tigris below Ctesiphon. This river or canal was unusually swift from the rains. With difficulty, pontoon bridges were constructed. The infantry got across safely, but a number of pack animals were drowned in the current.

As I recall, there was some harassing of the cavalry by Persian scouts, but they were soon driven off by our Saracen outriders.

On 28 April, after an uneventful march, we came to Pirisabora, a large city with impressive high walls and towers burned by the sun to the buff color of a lion's skin. The river surrounds the city naturally on three sides. On the fourth, the inhabitants have dug a canal so that they are, in effect, an island and hard for an enemy to approach. At the center of the city on a high hill was a formidable inner fortress. I must say my heart sank when I saw it. The siege of such a place could take months.

Julian sent his usual message to the city: if they surrendered, he would spare the lives of the inhabitants. But Pirisabora was one of the important cities of Persia, and the answer of its commandant, Mamersides, was arrogant indeed. The city would not surrender. But Mamersides would speak to Ormisda (apparently they had been in secret correspondence with one another).

I was present when Ormisda, tall and glittering and very much a Persian king, rode to the moat which separated city from mainland. He reined in his horse at the water's edge. When the Persians on the wall recognized him, they began a loud jeering and hissing. They called him "traitor" and worse. I was close enough to Ormisda to see his sallow face set in harsh lines, but he did not move or in any other way show that he had heard. For a full half hour he endured their insults. Then, seeing that there was to be no dealing with these men, he motioned for his standard-bearer to join him. This caused an even louder tumult. Ormisda's standard was that of the Great King of Persia. Majestically, Ormisda withdrew, and Julian ordered a siege.

Unfortunately, Julian did not describe the siege and I don't remember much about it. Perhaps our friend Ammianus will record it. Military history is not really my forte. My chief memory of this siege was a series of quarrels with Maximus. I shall spare you the quarrels, since I've completely forgotten what they were about.

The city of Pirisabora fell on the second day, after much fighting. But the matter was not yet finished, for the army and the governor promptly took refuge on their mountain top and there, behind walls of bitumen and brick, strong as iron, they held fast. Julian himself led the first attack on the citadel, and was repulsed.

On the third day, Julian ordered a helepolis built. This is a tall wooden tower which is used to scale even the highest walls. There

394

is no defense against it, not even fire, for it is covered with wet hides. The helepolis was not needed. No sooner was it half assembled than Mamersides asked for a truce. He was lowered from the citadel by a rope which broke a few yards above the ground; he fractured both legs. Julian was merciful. All lives would be spared if the citadel was surrendered.

At sundown, some 2500 Persians, men and women, issued forth, singing a hymn of thanksgiving to the Great Lord who had spared their lives and would now reign mercifully over them. Then Pirisabora was burned to the ground. By this time, I was no longer speaking to Maximus.

*Julian Augustus*                                                                 *3 May*
3 squ. cav. Trib. killed. Viz. command. Standard lost! 2 Trib. cash. dec. Stand. regained. speech. 100 p. silv.

*Priscus:* I recall "3 squ. cav. Trib. killed, etc." vividly. The day after the burning of the city we all dined at midday with Julian. It was a pleasant meal and he was refighting the siege, as soldiers like to do, the "what-might-have-happened-if" kind of thing, when Anatolius came into the tent with the news that the Grand Vizier had personally put to flight three of our cavalry squadrons, killing one of the tribunes and capturing the regimental standard.

I thought Julian would have a stroke. He hurled his plate to the ground and rushed from the tent, shouting for a call-to-arms. Within the hour, the Vizier's force had been located, and our standard regained. Within three hours, the two surviving tribunes were cashiered and, of those who had fled before the enemy, ten were executed, according to the old law of decimation. I had never seen Julian so angry nor so much the classic general. He ordered the entire army to watch the execution. When it was done, he made a speech, warning against disobedience and cowardice, and reminding the army that should anyone surrender to the enemy, the Persians would hamstring him and leave him to die in the desert. Then he praised the troops for the victory at Pirisabora, and he gave each man a hundred pieces of silver.

Poor Julian! Having so little interest in money himself, he could never get sums right. He never knew the correct price for anything, including the common soldier's loyalty. At the mention of such a small sum, the army roared its displeasure and I was afraid they would mutiny right then and there. But Julian was not intimidated.

395

He told them sharply that he himself was a poor man and that the Roman nation was in straitened circumstances because so many of his predecessors had used gold to buy a false peace rather than iron to fight necessary wars. But he promised them that soon they would be at Ctesiphon and the treasure of all Persia would be theirs. This put them in a good humor, and they cheered him and clattered their shields.

*Julian Augustus*                                           *4 May*
   14 miles. Floods. Halt. Bridges.

*Priscus*: The Persians broke the river dikes to the south of us and we lost a day while boats and rafts were used to get across the many pools the river water made. The countryside had become a giant swamp. My chief memory is of giant blood-sucking leeches clinging to my legs as I waded through muddy waters.

*Julian Augustus*                                           *7 May*
   Maiozamalcha. Camp. Prepare siege. Ambush. Treason?

*Priscus*: Three days later we came to Maiozamalcha, another important city with great walls. Here Julian set up camp.
   "Ambush" refers to what happened that evening. Julian and several scouts made an inspection of the outer walls, to look for points of weakness. While they were passing under the walls, ten Persians slipped out of the city through a porter's gate and, crawling on their hands and knees, took Julian and his scouts by surprise. Two of them set upon Julian. He killed one, protecting himself from the other with his shield. In a matter of minutes the Persians were dead and Julian returned to camp, happy as a boy with the dead Persian's weapons for trophy.
   "Treason?" How did the Persians know about this scouting party? Julian was aware that his army was full of spies, not to mention those who wished him harm. He suspected treason, and he was right.
   The inhabitants of Maiozamalcha refused to surrender. So Julian settled in for a siege. He was now fearful of the Persian army which was supposed to be gathering just south of Ctesiphon. For added protection, he erected a double palisade around our camp.

Cavalry under the Grand Vizier attacked pack animals in the palm groves. No casualties for us. Several for them. Persians driven off. Countryside is heavily wooded and full of streams and pools. I always thought Persia was desert. How I should like to have the leisure to turn Herodotus and describe this part of the world! It is so beautiful Date palms and fruit trees abound. Fields are yellow-green with new grain. This year's harvest will be a good one, and ours!

I find particularly interesting the pools of naphtha, an oily flammable substance which bubbles up from the ground. This morning I ordered one of the pools lit. A column of fire leapt to heaven. The only way it can be put out is to smother the pool in sand; otherwise, it may burn for years. I left the pool afire as an offering to Helios.

Several prisoners from this morning's raid were brought to me. They are curious-looking creatures and I examined them with some attention, recalling one of the tribunes who recently showed his troops a Persian corpse, saying: "See what you feared? This is the Persian devil, all of seven feet tall with arms of bronze and breathing fire!" Then he showed them the remains of a fragile creature more like a boy than a man.

*Priscus*: Traditionally the reporting of speeches in historical texts is not meant to be literal. But my version of Valentinian's comments was accurate because I kept a few notes at the time, which I am using now in making this commentary. Yet here is Julian less than a week later already altering the text. History is idle gossip about a happening whose truth is lost the instant it has taken place. I offer you this banality for what it is: *the truth!*

*Julian Augustus*                                         *8 May*

The Persians I examined were cavalrymen. They are small, wiry, leaden-complexioned. Ormisda acted as interpreter Though they expected immediate death, they seemed without fear. One spoke for all of them, a flood of words. When he was finally out of breath, I asked Ormisda what he had said.

Ormisda shrugged, "Typically Persian." Ormisda was in his Greek mood. "He hopes we choke in our pride and that the moon will fall on our army and crush it and that the tribes of the desert will rise up from as far away as India and China to butcher us.

The Persian style of address is always a bit exaggerated, particularly the metaphors."

I laughed. I have always been more amused than not by Persian rhetoric. It is characteristic of eastern peoples to talk always with a mad extravagance. Even their diplomatic letters are often unintelligible because of Pindar-like excesses.

Ormisda replied in kind. The Persians listened contemptuously. They are handsome men with pointed smooth beards and eyebrows which tend to grow together. Their eyes are particularly expressive, black and deep. They are quite slender because of their austere diet. They eat only when they are hungry, and then very little. They seldom drink wine. Their only excess (aside from their conversation!) is women. Each man has as many concubines as he can afford. They do not like boys. They are most modest about their persons and it is considered shameful for a man to be seen by another relieving himself in a natural way. I rather wish our army would imitate their physical modesty. Yet for all their virtues, they are not a likable people. They are arrogant and boastful and revel in cruelty. The nobles terrorize the lower classes as well as the slaves, torturing or killing them as they please, and there is no law to protect the helpless, nor any idea of charity. Their laws are savage. For instance, if a man is guilty of a capital crime, not only is he executed but all of his family as well.

"They are hopeless," said Ormisda wearily when the captives were taken away. "The most foolish race on earth."

"But *you* are their Great King," I teased him. "And therefore the most foolish of all."

"I've lived too long among you," he said sadly.

"But as a ruler you should be all the better for that. You can change them."

"No change." He shook his head. "That is the point to Persia. As we were, we are; as we are, we shall be. When I am Great King (the Sun and Julian willing), I shall be Greek no longer. Plato will be forgotten. I shall be like Darius and Cyrus, like Xerxes and . . . yes, like my brother Sapor."

"An unreliable ally to Rome?" I asked this jokingly, but I was serious.

"What else? I am the heir to the Sassanides kings. We are cruel and extravagant." Then he smiled, winningly. "You'd be well-advised, Augustus, to kill *all* the Persians, including me."

"Impractical," I said, and changed the subject. But I was

impressed by what Ormisda said, and uneasy. Should I keep a Roman army at Ctesiphon and govern through a pro-consul? Or would we fail in this the way our ancestors failed with the Jews? I wish Sallust were here.

We spent the rest of the day with the staff, preparing for the siege of Maiozamalcha. The town is on high ground with a double wall. It is well-garrisoned. I have ordered a mining of the walls. This is a good exercise we have not yet tried. Nevitta and Dagalaif are at this moment digging tunnels beneath the walls. At dawn, Victor and a number of cavalry scouts will reconnoiter as far as Ctesiphon. There is a rumor the Great King's army is on its way to us from the east, but it is only rumor.

Everything goes too easily. Yet why should I be surprised? The gods are with me and the spirit of Alexander whispers: advance, to the farthest edge of the world!

*Priscus*: As usual the spirit of Alexander was overambitious. We had enough troubles taking Maiozamalcha, much less India and China. But at this time Julian was not mad, despite Maximus's best efforts. There was no immediate plan to conquer farthest Asia. Julian anticipated a short campaign in Persia, winter at Tarsus, and *then* an expedition to India.

Julian does not describe the siege and fall of Maiozamalcha and neither shall I. As I recall, the city was on a high bluff overlooking the river. To get to it one had to climb steep cliffs, eminently suited for defense. The first day a frontal assault was attempted. It failed. Meanwhile, tunnels were being dug beneath the walls.

The second day the siege engines were brought up. The air was filled with the roaring sound of rocks being catapulted against the walls. The sun burned fiercely. Defenders and attackers were soon exhausted. But Julian drove the men to the limit of their strength, for he had no time to waste in a siege so near Ctesiphon and the Great King's army. Finally, word came from the tunnel builders that they were ready to break into the city. That night, Julian attacked the walls with his army while the troops below ground entered the city through the floor of the back room of an empty tavern. The city surrendered.

# XXI

We have had excellent luck. Maiozamalcha fell with few casualties for us. I have just received Nabdates, the Persian commander. He hailed me as Lord of the World and I have spared his
life. This should make a good impression. If the Perisan lords
believe that I am merciful, they will be more apt to surrender
when overwhelmed. I hope so, since there is nothing so demoralizing for an army as to fight long sieges for unimportant cities.

Nabdates swears that he does not know where the Great King
is and I believe him. He suspects that Sapor is not at the capital
but somewhere to the south. In any case, we shall soon meet, the
Great King and I.

I write this in my tent beside the river. On its high hill the city
of Maiozamalcha burns like a torch in the black night. With difficulty I prevented a slaughter in the city. The Gauls regard Persian
resistance as an affront; they always do. Incidentally, they discovered several hundred women hidden in the citadel. They
promptly drew lots for them. At such times, the officers vanish
and the men take over. Quite by accident, I happened to be near
the square during the lottery.

The women were huddled together, along with the city's treasure: gold coins, ornaments, bolts of silk, whatever had been found
in the ruins had been brought together for a fair division. One of
the Petulantes, seeing me, shouted, "Something for Julian!" So I
joined the men on foot, like a legionnaire.

The centurion in charge of the lottery indicated one of the piles
of gold. "That's your share, soldier," he said, using the traditional
phrase. I thanked him and took a single piece of gold. Then the
men began to shout that I should take one of the women. They
know of course that I am celibate, and find this fact infinitely
comic. I refused amiably. But they kept pressing me. So I looked
at the crowd of wretched women, thinking to take a child and set
her free. But there was none, only a very handsome boy of about
ten. So I pointed to him. The men were delighted. Better a boy-
lover than a celibate on the throne!

The boy turned out to be a deaf-mute of great intelligence. The

400

signs he makes with his hands are swift and graceful and I find that I can understand him easily. I have made him my personal servant and he seems happy.

I am depressed tonight. Ordinarily, I would be exhilarated by victory. I can't think what is wrong. Perhaps it is the memoir. I have been dictating memories of my childhood at Macellum and remembering those years always puts me in a bad mood.

Interesting note: One of the men of the Herculani reports that at the height of the battle today he saw a huge man in strange armor climbing one of the siege ladders. Later he saw this same warrior in the thick of the fighting, but he could not identify him nor could any of the others who saw him. They are all certain that this warrior was the war god Ares himself. I must ask Maximus to find out.

*12 May*

It is afternoon. I am seated in the throne room of one of the Great King's palaces, a fine building in the Roman style, more like a country villa than a formal palace. Next to it is a fenced-in game preserve. Here all sorts of wild animals are kept in a wooded area . . . lions, boars and that truly terrible beast, the Persian bear. The men have just broken down the fences and are now hunting and killing the animals. I should have preferred for them not to indulge in this slaughter but they must be kept in a good mood, for we are close to Ctesiphon and the decisive battle.

Jovian has just come and gone. He brought me the skin of a lion he killed, quite a large beast. "A match for the one on your bed." I thanked Jovian warmly. Of the Galilean officers, he is the one I trust the most, possibly because he is the stupidest. I gave him some wine we had found in the cellar of the palace. He drank it so greedily that I gave him two more flagons to take with him when he left. He was most pleased and slightly drunk.

Priscus and I explored the palace together. It is both beautiful and comfortable, a combination Roman emperors are not used to. Apparently the servants fled shortly before we arrived, leaving a dinner still warm in the kitchen. I was about to taste the contents of one of the pots when the deaf-mute boy struck the ladle from my hand. Then *he* tasted the mess, indicating that I should beware of poison. I never think of such things. No, that is not true. I do occasionally wonder if my evening bowl of polenta contains my death, but I never hesitate to eat it. If that is to be my end, there

401

is nothing I can do about it. Fortunately, the dinner the Persians left us was not poisoned.

I have set the secretaries to work in the throne room, a cool dim room with latticed windows and a red lacquered throne on which I now sit scribbling. The Great King lives far more luxuriously than I. In one of the rooms we discovered hundreds of his silk robes . . . Priscus insists that I give them to Maximus.

Tonight I have planned a large dinner for the military staff. I have the beginnings of a plan for this last phase. Contrary to what historians may think, wars are mostly improvisation. One usually has an ultimate goal, but the means of attaining it cannot be determined in advance. That is why the favorite deity of generals—and of Rome—is Fortune.

*16 May*

Encamped for three days now at Coche. This is a village near the site of the now vanished city of Seleucia, built by Alexander's general. Farther on are the ruins of yet another city, destroyed in the last century by the Emperor Carus. I thought it good policy to show this to the men, demonstrating yet again how victorious Roman arms have been in Persia.

I am still struck by the beauty of the countryside. Flowers bloom; fruits ripen; there are many forests; much water. This is an idyllic part of the world and I am sad that so many of its cities must be put to the torch. But what men build they can rebuild. I am with the Stoics, who regard all life as an infinite series of growth and decline, each temporary terminus marked with the clean impartiality of fire.

Near the city Carus destroyed, there is a small lake which empties into the Tigris. Here we beheld a gruesome sight. Impaled on stakes were the entire family of Mamersides, the officer who surrendered Pirisabora to us. Thus cruelly does the Great King punish those who disobey him. It was horrible to see not only women but children put to death in this painful way.

While we were at the lake, Ormisda and his Persian court (he now has over a hundred Persians in attendance on him) appeared, with Nabdates, the governor of Maiozamalcha. Ormisda saluted me formally. Then he said, "Augustus, I have passed sentence of death on Nabdates."

I asked him why.

Ormisda was grim. "Before the siege, we had a private under-

402

standing. He was to surrender the city to us. It was all arranged. Then he broke his oath to me, the highest oath a Persian can swear. Therefore, as Great King, I *must* put him to death, by fire." I was impressed by Ormisda's manner. The closer we come to Ctesiphon, the more imperial and Persian he becomes. So I gave my assent, and the wretched man with his broken legs was dragged to the stake. I left before the burning began. I dislike all executions except those with the sword.

I write these lines seated on a bench in what looks to be some nobleman's park. It is a beautiful day; the sun is warm but not hot; as far as the eye can see the countryside is green and blooming. I am certain now of success. A messenger from Arintheus has just come and gone. A fortress some twenty miles to the east will not surrender.

I shall have to go there to determine whether or not there should be a siege. Now another messenger approaches. I feel lazy and comfortable. I would like to sit in this park forever. A warm south wind suddenly brings me the scent of flowers: roses?

*Priscus*: The second messenger probably brought him the bad news that three of Dagalaif's cohorts were set upon by the Persians at a town called Sabatha. While the cohorts were thus engaged, guerrillas sneaked up behind the army and slaughtered most of the pack animals and their attendants. This was a severe blow and Julian was furious with Dagalaif, who had left the beasts unguarded.

As for "the fortress some twenty miles to the east," which would not surrender, Julian rode too close to its walls and was nearly killed; his armor-bearer was wounded.

That night Julian ordered the siege engines to be put in place. Unfortunately, the moon was nearly full and night was like day. While the mantlets and turrets were being placed against the walls, the Persians suddenly threw open their gates and charged our siege troops with sword and javelin. They killed the better part of a cohort, as well as the tribune in command.

How do I remember all this so clearly? Because I have just received by post a rough draft of Ammianus Marcellinus's account of Julian's Persian campaign. I wrote him months ago to ask him if he had written anything about those days. In a covering letter, he says that he kept "untidy notes in Persia, as usual." I assume that his account is reliable. He is particularly good at describing military action. He ought to be. As a professional soldier, he served from Britain to Persia. I would send you his history, but since it is in Latin you won't be able to read it and I am sure that you wouldn't want to go to the expense of having it translated. By the way, he says that he intends to write the history of Julian's reign "just as it occurred." I suppose he means "deadpan," as though Julian's reign took place a thousand years ago and were not of any contemporary interest. I wish him luck.

Where was I? The mauling of one of our cohorts by the Persians. As soon as the Persians had done their bloody work, they escaped inside the fortress. The next day Julian threw the full force of his army against the fortress. After fierce fighting, it fell. Julian was physically exhausted by this engagement. I am told that he led the siege himself, fighting for thirteen hours without a break. I don't know because our camp was pitched ten miles away. We of the court rested comfortably while the soldiers fought.

What do I remember of that particular time? Not much. I used to play draughts with Anatolius. We would sit in front of his tent and play on a portable table whose top was inlaid with squares like a game board. Inside the tent, the clerks labored incessantly. The Emperor's correspondence is always kept up just as though he were at the palace in Constantinople. No matter how desperate the military situation, he must answer his mail.

Once when Anatolius and I were busy at draughts, Victor swept through the camp at the head of a column of light cavalry. We were nearly blinded by the dust. Anatolius was furious. "He does that deliberately! He knew we were sitting here!" He dabbed the dust from his eyes with the edge of his cloak.

"He behaves rather as the Gauls are supposed to." I said this to be challenging. Anatolius was usually close-mouthed about the various factions at court.

"He is a good deal worse than any Gaul. More ambitious, too."

"For the purple?"

"I can't say." Anatolius pursed his small mouth.

"What *do* you know?"

"Augustus knows what I know." He said no more. I then won four silver pieces from him, which he never paid me. That is the sort of historian I am.

*Julian Augustus*                                                  *19 May*

We are again spending the night in one of the Great King's palaces. This one is even handsomer and more luxurious than the hunting lodge. It is surrounded by a large park of cypresses in a countryside rich with vineyards and orchards. We are now at high summer. What a fine season to be at war!

Victor reports that he was able to ride up to the walls of Ctesiphon and no one stopped him. The gates were shut. The guards on the walls made no move to fire at his men. According to rumor, the Great King's army is still some miles to the south. We must now be ready to move fast. Once the capital falls, the war is over. Sapor will sue for peace. At the worst, he will risk everything in one set battle, and the Persians are not noted for their ability at conventional warfare. They are by nature marauders, like the Saracens.

I gave dinner to Maximus, Priscus, Anatolius and Ormisda. The dining room is particularly splendid with painted frescoes showing Sapor hunting lions and boars, all very realistic, the sort of painting I like though I have not much taste for these things. Even so, after two months of staring at the wall of a tent, one enjoys beauty.

I was surprised to find that Maximus is rather a connoisseur of art. This morning he made a careful tour of the palace, recommending to Anatolius what should be packed up and sent back to Constantinople. "But have you noticed, Augustus, how the paintings have only one subject? Killing. Animals in the chase. Men at war. Beast against beast." I hadn't noticed this, but it was quite true.

"That is because we regard killing as a necessary and sacred part of life," said Ormisda.

"So do we," said Priscus. "Only we pretend to abhor it."

I chose not to correct him. I was—am—in much too good a mood. I had bathed in the Great King's marble bath, and put on one of his fine linen tunics. Apparently we are the same height. I also found a strongbox containing a number of Sapor's personal ornaments, among them a gold ram's head helmet with the imperial ensign on it. I gave it to Ormisda.

"You may as well get used to wearing this," I said. He took it from me. Then he dropped to his knees and kissed my hand. "The House of Persia is grateful to you for all eternity."

"A generation of peace will do," I said dryly, wondering how long it would be before the Great King Ormisda would prove disloyal to Rome. Men are without gratitude, particularly kings.

Ormisda does not know it, but I have decided to maintain an army at Ctesiphon indefinitely.

While the philosophers amused themselves in debate, Ormisda and I met the generals in an adjoining room. On the table was a map of Ctesiphon which Ormisda had found in the Great King's library. He believes it reliable. Victor, Nevitta, Dagalaif, and Arintheus were present; also the chief engineer.

I came straight to the point. "There is no way for us to approach Ctesiphon by water." I pointed to the map. "We are within a triangle. Above us the King's River; behind us the Euphrates; in front of us the Tigris. The Euphrates and Tigris Rivers meet here, just south of Ctesiphon. But we can't sail from the Euphrates to the Tigris because Ctesiphon commands the Tigris at the natural juncture. Also, we'd hoped to use the King's River, which joins the Tigris *above* Ctesiphon, but that section of the channel is dry. We are left only one choice, to open up Trajan's canal." I pointed to a dotted line on the chart. "When Trajan was here, he dug a deep channel from the Euphrates to the Tigris, following the bed of an old Assyrian canal. The chief engineer has been studying this canal for the past two days. He believes it can be reopened."

The chief happily listed the many difficulties involved in opening the canal, the principal being a stone dam the Persians had built across the channel to prevent invaders from using it as Trajan had. But once the dam was breached, the chief engineer was positive the canal would be navigable. After a brief discussion, I gave orders for the dam to be broken.

The generals are in a good humor. Dagalaif and Victor are particularly eager for a decisive battle. Ormisda is nervous: so close to the fulfillment of all his dreams. I then dismissed everyone except Nevitta, who asked to stay behind. Disturbing. Ch.

*Priscus*: What did they talk about? I think Nevitta must have warned him that there was a plot against his life. "Disturbing" suggests this. "Ch" means the Christians. Put the two together and the meaning is plain.

On 24 May the channel was opened and the fleet crossed the three miles from the Euphrates to the Tigris, anchoring half a mile north of the city of Ctesiphon, which rose from the green valley of the Tigris like a mountain of brick whose massive weight seemed quite enough to cause the earth itself to bend. From our side of the river we could see nothing of the city except the walls, which

406

are half again as high as those of Constantinople. At regular intervals, semicircular towers support the thick masonry. Between the Tigris and the city there is an open plain where, during the night of 25 May, the army of the Great King gathered.

Anatolius woke me at sunrise and together we left the camp and went to the riverbank, where half our army was already gathered to observe the enemy. It was a splendid sight. The Persian army numbered almost a hundred thousand men. Or so we now claim. No one ever knows how large the enemy's army is, but we always say that it is three times the size of ours. I think this one probably was. Behind a wooden palisade on the steep riverbank, the Persians were drawn up in battle formation. A crossing seemed madness.

All around us soldiers talked worriedly among themselves. It did not take a skilled veteran to realize how difficult it would be to cross that river under fire and, even worse, to climb the slippery riverbank and assault the barricade.

I turned to Anatolius, who looked as worried as I felt. "We can't cross here."

"Perhaps the Emperor means to move upstream. To cross a few miles to the north then, circling round—you know, the classic Constantine maneuver..." But in spite of his amateur's passion for strategy, Anatolius mumbled into silence. For almost an hour we stared gloomily at the Persians who stared right back. Then one of Julian's heralds appeared, calling the men to assemble. The Emperor would give the day's orders in person.

"Nothing short of complete retreat will satisfy me," I said, while Anatolius wondered what would happen if we simply ignored Ctesiphon and turned south to the Persian Gulf "where the pearls come from. Very rich country, too, from all accounts."

Julian appeared to the assembled troops. He was exuberant: his eyes shone; his cloak for once was clean; his nose was only slightly peeling from sunburn.

"Men, you have seen the army of Persia. More important, they have seen us!" He paused for cheering. There was none. He cut the silence short. Generals who allow an unfortunate pause to last too long are apt to find the silence filled with that one rude phrase which sets off mutiny.

But Julian had a surprise for us. "We are all tired today. It has been a difficult week, clearing the channel, moving the fleet, setting up camp. So today we shall have games. I propose horse racing, with gold prizes for the winners. The betting will be your affair since there are, I understand, a few Petulantes who know about racing odds. I'm sure they'll help the rest of us. Have a good time." He dismissed the men with a wave, like a schoolteacher giving his pupils an unexpected holiday.

Everyone was stunned. If it had been any other general, the men would have thought him mad. But this was Julian who had never lost a battle. Ater the first gasp of surprise, the men delightedly cheered their young leader who could, with such aplomb, order games while the entire army of the Great King of Persia was drawn up only a mile away. To a man they trusted Julian's luck and skill. If *he* was this confident, who were they to worry? So the army did as he told them, and spent the day in races and games.

That night Julian ordered a surprise crossing of the Tigris. The army was divided into three sections. When the first had secured a footing on the far side, the second would embark, and so on. The generals opposed this plan. Victor pointed to the thousand Persian campfires which filled the horizon. "They have every military advantage."

"Not *every*," said Julian ambiguously. "You'll see that I'm right. Tell your men to board ship. I want everyone across by morning."

Four thousand men boarded five empty cargo ships, under the reluctant command of Victor. I've never seen soldiers so frightened. Just before they left, Victor quarreled with Julian on the riverbank. None of us heard what was said but Victor departed in a rage and Julian was uncharacteristically quiet.

The ships disappeared into the darkness. Silence. An hour passed. Julian paced up and down, pretending to be interested only in the remaining ships which were to take the rest of the army across the river once the Persian side had been secured. The army waited.

Suddenly flaming arrows pierced the black night. Victor's men were landing. The Persians were attacking them. First one, then two, then all five of the boats were set afire by Persian arrows. Far off, we could hear Victor's men shouting to one another as they clambered up the slippery riverbank by the flickering light of burning ships. On our side of the river, panic was beginning.

Julian saved the situation with one of his inspired lies. Just as we were all positive the landing had failed and the men were lost,

Julian pointed to the five burning ships and shouted, "That's it! The burning of the ships. That's the signal. Victor's signal. The landing's a success! To the boats! To the boats!"

I don't know how he did it but he made the men believe him. He raced up and down the riverbank, shouting, pushing, coaxing the men onto the landing craft. Then he himself leapt into the first boat just as it was about to leave the shore. The men were now as excited as he. They crowded onto the remaining boats. Some even floated across the river on their shields. Convinced of total disaster, I watched the Roman army disappear onto the black river.

By dawn, to my amazement, we held the riverbank.

The next day Maximus and I, along with the priests and other timid folk, sat comfortably at the river's edge and watched the Battle of Ctesiphon as though we were at the theatre. When we complained of the heat, umbrellas were brought us, and wine. Never have philosophers watched in such comfort two empires collide so fatefully.

I sat between Maximus and the Etruscan Mastara. Anatolius was not with us, for he had bravely chosen to fight beside Julian that day, even though court marshals are not expected to be warriors. We teased him a good deal as he got ready for battle, his tiny mouth a firm military circle in his hopelessly soft face.

"Many years with the cavalry," he said casually. His round stomach jiggled beneath ill-fitting armor as he motioned imperiously for the groom to bring him his horse. With a flourish, Anatolius mounted the horse and fell off the other side. I'm afraid we clerks laughed at our impetuous brother. But Anatolius had his way; he followed his Emperor into battle.

At first we saw everything plain. The Persians were spread out in an arc between the walls of Ctesiphon and the river. Cavalry first; then infantry; then against the wall, like a range of mud hills, a hundred elephants each with an iron tower on its back, containing archers.

The Persian cavalry wear an extraordinary form of armor which consists of hundreds of small iron plates sewn together in such a way that not only is the soldier completely covered by armor but he is able to move easily, the iron fitting the contours of his body like cloth. Their horses are protected by leather blankets. In the hands of a capable general, the Persian cavalry is a remarkable weapon. Fortunately for us, there were at this time no Persian generals of any distinction. Also, the Persian army is not a permanent institution like ours but a haphazard collection of conscripts, mercenaries, noblemen and slaves. At times of national crisis every able-bodied man is impressed into service, hardly the best of systems.

Behind the cavalry, the Persian infantry advanced in close order, protected by oblong wicker shields covered with rawhide. Among the elephants at the rear was the Grand Vizier, while on the walls of Ctesiphon the Great King and his court observed the battle in much the same way we philosophers watched it in our folding chairs on the riverbank. We were too far away to recognize Sapor, though Maximus, as usual, claimed he saw him quite clearly.

"I am extraordinarily farsighted, you know. Sapor is to the left of that tower by the gate. You see the blue canopy? Well, he is just under it, wearing scarlet. Those must be his sons with him. They look quite young . . ." And on he babbled. Actually, all any of us could see was a faint blur of color on the battlements.

But Julian was most visible, riding restlessly along the front line as our army advanced. He was easily identified not only by his white horse and purple cloak but by the dragon standard which always accompanied him.

Our trumpets sounded the advance. The infantry then began its curious stylized march, based on that of ancient Sparta's army: two short steps, a pause, two short steps, a pause, all in perfect unison while the drums beat the tattoo. It is ominous both to hear and to see. Even Maximus was silent as the Roman army advanced. Then with a shout, our skirmishers in the front rank threw their javelins into the Persian cavalry. And the two armies vanished. For an instant I almost believed in Maximus's magic. Where a hundred and thirty thousand men had been perfectly visible to us in the bright sun, there was now nothing but an oppressive cloud of dust. We could see nothing. But from the heart of the cloud we heard trumpets, drums, war cries, metal striking metal, the hiss of arrows.

The battle began at sunrise and continued until sundown. After an hour or two of watching dust the Etruscans grew bored, and withdrew "to pray for victory." Instead, they settled down in a nearby grove of date palms for a drinking party. They were prodigious drinkers. One of my few happy memories of the Persian campaign was the night when all five Etruscans were dead drunk during an important religious ceremony. It was a splendid debacle.

410

They kept dropping sacred vessels and books, while Mastara solemnly assured the furious Julian that "the god has possessed us."

Maximus and I watched the wall of dust all day. The only sign we had of how the battle was going was the position of the dust cloud as, hour by hour, it shifted closer to the walls of Ctesiphon. The Persians were giving ground.

"On 15 June we shall return to Tarsus," said Maximus suddenly; he had been making signs in the dust at our feet with his magician's staff.

"In three weeks?"

"Three weeks? Is that three weeks?" He looked at me blankly. "Why so it is! Amazing to think we shall conquer Persia in such a short time. Alexander hardly did as well. Perhaps I've made a mistake." He studied the dust at his feet. I wanted to break his stick over his foolish head.

"No. The calculation is correct. 15 June. Plain as day. We must tell Julian. He'll be so pleased." He looked vaguely toward the battlefield.

"How do you know that the Emperor..." I emphasized the title. No one but Maximus ever referred to Julian by name. "... is still alive?"

"He has to be. 15 June. I just showed you. Look, in the Sun's Fourth House..."

"And how do you know we shall win this battle?"

"Sometimes you amaze me, Priscus. It is all so plain. Sapor is about to fall, and we shall go home victorious. It is preordained. And frankly I look forward to a return to private life. I'm here only because Julian insisted..."

While Maximus chattered, I stared at the walls of Ctesiphon, waiting for the battle's end. Shortly before sunset, a soft breeze thinned the cloud of dust until we were again able to see the two armies, now in a hopeless tangle at the city's gate. The elephants were running amok, trunks curled, tusks flashing. I am told the Persians use them to intimidate their own men quite as much as the enemy's. Persians as well as Romans were trampled by those hideous beasts.

As the red sun set, the gates of the city opened to receive the Persian army. Our men pursued them. In a matter of seconds, the Persian army ceased to be an army and became a mob of frightened men, all trying to get within the gates. Then it was dark.

411

I cannot sleep. Within my tent, I walk up and down. I am exhausted from twelve hours of fighting—but too excited to sleep, to do anything. I can barely write these lines. My hand shakes with tension.

I have defeated the Great King's army! Twenty-five hundred Persians dead, and only seventy-five Romans! We could have taken Ctesiphon. Our infantry could have entered when the Persians did but Victor stopped them. He was afraid they might be outnumbered inside a strange city. I am not sure that he was right. Had I been at the gate, I would have ordered the men to go through. We should have taken the chance. The Persian army was in flight. That was our opportunity. But Victor is cautious. He was also wounded—an arrow in the right shoulder, not serious. Now we shall have to lay siege to the city. A long business.

I saw the Great King today, and he saw me. Sapor was seated on the wall, beneath a canopy. I was only a few yards away. Though nearly seventy, Sapor looks much younger. He is lean and black-bearded. (Ormisda says that his hair is dyed: Sapor is vain about his appearance, also his potency . . . no one knows how many children he has). Sapor wore a gold crown with a scarlet plume. As a gesture of disdain, he wore court dress! He looked like a peacock, glaring down at me.

I waved my sword arm. "Come down!" I shouted, but in that tumult I doubt if he heard me. But he saw me and he knew who I was. The Great King saw the Emperor of Rome at the gate to his city! The courtiers around him looked terrified. No one made a move. Then I was distracted by the battle around me. The next time I looked at the wall, Sapor was gone.

Before we returned to camp, we buried our dead and stripped the Persian corpses. Many nobles were killed and their armor is much prized by us. Unfortunately, none of the Gauls and Germans can wear Persian armor. It is too small for them. So the best armor in the world goes to our worst soldiers, the Asiatics!

We had a victory dinner in my tent. The generals got drunk. But I could eat and drink nothing. I am too tense. Maximus says the war will be over in three weeks. Soldiers have been serenading me all night. Many of them are drunk but I do not scold them. I go outside and embrace them and call them by name, telling them what fine fellows they are, and they tell me the same thing. Tomorrow I give out war crowns to those who showed unusual valor. I shall also sacrifice to the war god Ares.

Why didn't Victor go into the city?

*Priscus*: The next day was marred only by the sacrifice. After the men had been given their decorations, Julian tried to sacrifice a bull to Ares on a newly built altar. But for one reason or another, nine bulls were found wanting by the Etruscans. The tenth bull, acceptable, bolted at the last minute. When it was finally caught and sacrificed, the liver indicated disaster. To everyone's amazement, Julian threw down the sacrificial knife and shouted to the sky, "Never again will I sacrifice to you!" Maximus looked quite alarmed and even I was taken aback. Flushed and sweating from the hot sun, Julian disappeared into his tent. I can only attribute his strange action to the fact that he had not slept in two days.

The same day Anatolius took me on a tour of the battlefield. He was very soldierly. "Here the Herculani made a flanking movement to allow for the light-armed cohorts of Petulantes to break through . . ." That sort of thing. Anatolius was so pleased with his own military expertise that I did not have the heart to laugh at him as he led me over the dusty ground still littered with Persian dead. I noticed one interesting phenomenon. Persians do not putrefy in the hot sun the way Europeans do. After two days of this climate, a dead European is in an advanced state of decay. But not the Persians. They simply dry up and become hard as leather. I once asked Oribasius about this and he said it was due to diet. According to him, we drink too much wine and eat too much grain while the Persians eat sparingly, preferring dates and lentils to our rich fare. Yet I have observed the dead bodies of lean Gauls—yes, there are some—and though their owners lived austere lives, they decayed as swiftly as their corpulent brothers. It is very puzzling.

The Persians had been stripped of their armor and valuables, except for one who still wore a gold ring. I decided to take it as a souvenir. Even now I can remember the feel of that cold, hard hand as, with great effort, I bent straight the fingers which had been drawn into a brown fist. I stared at the dead man's face. He was young; he wore no beard. I looked at him. He looked at me, eyes glazed as though with fever. Flies buzzed about his head.

"Spoils of war," said Anatolius comfortably.

"Spoils of war," I said to the dead Persian, letting him drop

413

back on the ground with a thump. He seemed unconvinced. The flies settled on his face. I wore the ring until a few months ago when I lost it at the baths. I have become thin lately and the ring fell off in the hot room. Naturally, the attendants never return anything they find.

Two days later, on 29 May, Julian moved the army to Abuzatha, a Persian fort on the Tigris three miles from Ctesiphon. Here we made camp. For several days none of Julian's friends saw him. He was closeted with his military staff. There was disagreement among the generals. Some wanted to lay siege to Ctesiphon. Others preferred to isolate the city and continue the conquest of Persia. A few advised returning to Roman territory. None of us knew what Julian's plan was or even if he had a plan. Nor did any of us know that while we were in camp, he had received a secret embassy from Sapor. I confess that even if I had known, I would not have cared much. Like half the camp, I was ill with dysentery.

*Julian Augustus*                                             *30 May*

The Persian envoys have just left. Ormisda is with them. I sit alone in my tent. Outside, Callistus is singing a mournful song. It is very hot. I am waiting for Maximus. If I withdraw from Persia, the Great King has promised to cede me all of Mesopotamia north of Anatha; also, at his own expense, he will rebuild our city of Amida, and pay in gold or kind whatever we ask to defray the cost of this war. Persia is defeated.

The ambassadors came to me secretly. They wanted it that way. So did I. They were brought to me as though they were officers taken captive in a Saracen raid. No one except Ormisda and myself knows that this was an embassy. The chief ambassador is a brother of the Grand Vizier. He maintained a perfect dignity while proposing a treaty which, if I accept it, will mean that I have gained more of the East for Rome than any general since Pompey. Realizing this, the ambassador felt impelled to indulge himself in Persian rhetoric. "Never forget, Augustus, that our army is more numerous than the desert's sand. One word from the Great King and you and all your host are lost. But Sapor is merciful."

"Sapor is frightened," said Ormisda, to my irritation. I prefer to seem indifferent while envoys talk, to give them no clue as to what I intend to do. But Ormisda has been unusually tense the last few days. Despite his age, he fought like a youth at Ctesiphon. Now he sees the crown of Persia almost in his hands. He is terrified

414

it will slip away. I am sympathetic. Yet my policy is not necessarily his policy.

Ormisda taunted the ambassadors. "I know what happens in the palace at Ctesiphon. I know what is whispered in the long halls, behind the ivory doors. Nothing that happens among you is kept from me."

This was not entirely bluff. Ormisda's spies are indeed well placed at the Persian court and he learns astonishing things. Also, as we conquer more and more of Persia, there is a tendency among the nervous courtiers to shift from the old king to what may be the new. But the ambassador was not of those whom Ormisda could win.

"There are traitors in every palace, Prefect." He used Ormisda's Roman title. Then he turned to me. "And in every army, Augustus." I did not acknowledge this dangerous truth. "But the Great King is merciful. He loves peace..."

Ormisda laughed theatrically. "Sapor wears rags, taken from a beggar. His beard and hair are full of ashes. He dines off the floor like an animal. He weeps, knowing his day is ended." Ormisda was not exaggerating. During the last few hours we have had several harrowing descriptions of Sapor's grief at my victory. He has every reason to be in mourning. Few monarchs have been so thoroughly humiliated.

The ambassador read me the draft of the treaty. I thanked him. Then I told Ormisda to take the embassy to Anatolius's tent, which is next to mine. They will wait there until I have prepared an answer. Ormisda wanted to stay behind and talk to me but I made him go. He is not Great King yet.

I now sit on the bed. The treaty is before me: two scrolls, one in Greek, one in Persian. I have placed them side by side on the lion skin. What to do? If I accept Sapor's terms, it will be a triumph for me. If I stay, I am not entirely certain that a siege of Ctesiphon would be successful. It will certainly take a long time; perhaps a year, and I cannot be away from Constantinople that long. Today the Persian army is no threat, but who knows what sort of army Sapor might put in the field next week, next month?

Everything depends, finally, on Procopius. He is in the north, at Bezabde in Corduene. Or so I hear. There has been no direct word from him.

\* \* \*

415

Maximus was brilliant just now. As always, he went straight to the heart of things.

"This treaty is a triumph: a province gained, peace assured for at least . . ."

". . . a decade."

"Perhaps longer. Amida rebuilt. A fortune in gold. Few emperors have accomplished so much. But then . . ." He looked at me thoughtfully. "Was it just for *this* we have come so far, to gain half a province? or to conquer half a world?"

He paused. I waited. Like a true philosopher, he then turned the matter round, first to one side, then to another. "There is no denying this is an excellent treaty, better than anyone would have dreamed . . . except us, who know what no one else knows. Cybele herself promised you victory. You are Alexander, born again, set on earth to conquer Asia. You have no choice."

Maximus is right. The gods have not brought me this far simply to have me turn back as though I were some Saracen chief raiding the border. I shall reject Sapor's treaty and begin the siege of Ctesiphon. Once Procopius arrives, I shall be free to order a march straight into the morning sun. Yes, to the house of Helios himself, the father from whom I came and to whom I must return, in glory.

*Priscus*: Have you ever read such nonsense? If only I had known! But none of us knew what Maximus was up to, even though he was forever dropping hints about "our plans." But since those plans were never revealed, we were all equally in the dark. When the rumor that Sapor had sued for peace swept the camp, Julian firmly denied that there had been an embassy, and we believed him. I am certain that if the generals had known the terms of the treaty, they would have forced Julian to accept. But Julian and Maximus lied, as did Ormisda, who was not about to end his last hope of reigning in Persia. All three wanted the war to continue.

From the moment of this decision, I trace the rapid decline of Julian. Nothing went right again. In retrospect his actions are those of a madman. But since he seemed so entirely normal at the time, none of us seriously questioned his orders or thought anything he did unusual. We merely assumed that he had information we did not. Also, up until the last day of May, everything he had attempted had proven successful. Even so, the generals were becoming critical. And treason was in the air.

416

# XXII

Midnight. The deaf-mute sits cross-legged at my feet, playing a Persian instrument much like a lute. The melody is unfamiliar but pleasing. Callistus is arranging my armor on the stand beside the bed. Ormisda has just left. He is pleased at my decision, but I am somewhat uneasy. For the first time I find myself in complete disagreement with my officers. What is worse, I cannot tell them why I *know* that the course I have embarked upon is the right one. At this evening's staff meeting, Victor challenged me openly.

"We have not the force, Augustus, to attempt a long siege. Nor the supplies. We also have many wounded." He touched his own bandaged shoulder.

"And no hope of reinforcements." Arintheus automatically follows Victor's lead.

"There is the army of Procopius and Sebastian," said Ormisda. He sat on my right at the conference table, on which our only map of this part of Persia was unrolled. So far, the map has proved completely unreliable.

"Procopius!" Nevitta said the name contemptuously, concentrating in that one word a lifelong contempt for all things Greek. "We'll never see him here. Never!"

"I've sent Procopius orders..." I began.

"But why hasn't he obeyed you?" Victor led the attack. "Why is he still in Corduene?"

"Yes, why?" One is never certain whether Dagalaif is naïve or subtle.

"Because he is a traitor," said Nevitta, the Frankish accent growing harsh and guttural, the words difficult to understand. "Because he and that Christian king of Armenia, *your* friend," he turned malevolently on Ormisda—"want us all dead, so that Procopius can be the next *Christian* emperor."

There was a shocked silence at this. I broke it, mildly. "We can't be sure that that is the reason."

"*You* can't, Emperor, but I can. I know these Asiatics. I never trusted one in my life." He looked straight at Victor who returned the hard gaze evenly.

417

I laughed. "I hope you trust me, Nevitta. I'm Asiatic."

"You're Thracian, Emperor, which is almost as good as being a Frank or a Gaul. Besides, you're not a Christian, or so I've heard."

Everyone laughed; the tension was relieved. Then Victor expressed the hope that we obtain as good a treaty as possible from Sapor. Ormisda and I exchanged a quick glance. I am sure that Victor knows nothing. I am also glad we kept the embassy a secret, especially now that I know Nevitta and Dagalaif are eager to go home. Except for me, no one believes Procopius will join us. I am certain that he will. If he does not...

Salutius proposed a compromise. "We should all assume that Procopius intends to obey his Emperor. Having recently executed a man whom I'd falsely accused of not doing his duty, I favor giving Procopius every opportunity to prove himself loyal. After all, we don't know what difficulties he may have encountered. He may be ill, or dead. So I suggest that the Augustus wait at least a week before beginning the siege, or making any other plan."

This compromise was accepted. Like most compromises it solves nothing while prolonging—perhaps dangerously—the time of indecision. But I said nothing beyond agreeing to delay the siege. I wanted to appear reasonable because I was about to propose what I knew would be a most unpopular action.

"Our fleet requires twenty thousand men to man and guard it. As long as we keep close to the river, the men can do both. But if we enter the interior—either to go home or to pursue the Great King's army—those men must go with us. If they go with us, the Persians will seize our ships. To prevent that, we must burn the fleet."

They were stunned. Nevitta was the first to speak. He wanted to know how I expected to return to our own country without ships. I explained that whether we returned by way of the Euphrates or by way of the Tigris, we would have to go upstream, a slow and laborious business. The fleet would be an encumbrance. This point was conceded to me; even so, I was opposed by the entire staff except Ormisda, who realized that only by burning the fleet will I be able to get the legions to follow me into the interior.

Yes, I am determined now to secure all of the provinces of Persia as far as the border of India, a thousand miles to the east. Alexander did as much. I am convinced that I can do it. Sapor's

418

army is no match for ours. With the harvest at hand, we shall not have to worry about supplies. Only one thing holds me back: Procopius. If he were here, I could set out confident that with Ormisda's help Ctesiphon would fall and there would be no enemy at my back. But I cannot leave until I know where Procopius is. Meanwhile, I must burn the fleet.

Patiently, I answered the arguments of the generals. I convinced none but all acquiesced. As they were leaving my tent, Salutius took me to one side. I could feel the unpleasant heat of his breath on my skin as he whispered close to my ear the single word "Mutiny."

"Who?"

Though the last of the generals had left the tent, Salutius continued to whisper. "The Christians."

"Victor?"

"I don't know. Perhaps. My reports are vague. The men are singing a song that they will soon be home but *you* will not be."

"That is treason."

"The way the words run, the thing sounds innocent enough. Whoever wrote it was clever."

"Who sing it? Galileans?"

Salutius nodded. "The Zianni and the Herculani. Only a few are involved so far. But if you burn the fleet..."

"Salutius, believe in me." I took his hand. "I know things that others don't."

"As you command, Lord." Salutius bowed and left me.

I have spent this night alone except for the deaf-mute and Callistus. I pray. I study Alexander's campaign in Persia. I examine maps and read histories. Helios willing, I shall spend the winter on the border of India. No Roman emperor has ever annexed so great a territory to our world.

*Julian Augustus*                                                    *1 June*

The fleet is burned. Twelve ships were spared, suitable for making bridges. We shall transport them on wagons. I have just sent Arintheus with the light-armed infantry to wipe out the remnants of the Persian army in hiding nearby. I have also ordered him to fire the surrounding fields and slaughter the cattle. Once we are gone it will take the inhabitants of Ctesiphon many months to get sufficient food. That will give us time. No word from Procopius.

*Priscus*: On a hot and windy morning, the fleet was set afire. Flames darted swiftly from ship to ship until the brown Tigris itself seemed to burn. As the sun's heat increased, all objects were distorted by heatwaves. Creation seemed to be ending exactly as the Stoics teach, in a vast, cleansing, terminal fire.

I watched the burning with Anatolius. For once I almost believed in Nemesis. The men, too, sensed that this time their Emperor had reached too far, plunging himself and them into the sun's fierce maw. Ordinarily, any order Julian gave was promptly obeyed, and the more puzzling it was the more certain were the men of his cleverness. But that day he was forced to fire the first ship himself. No one would do it for him. I saw fear in the faces of the men as Julian offered the fleet to Helios.

"Of course we are not generals," said Anatolius tentatively, knowing what was in my mind. "The Emperor is a master of war."

"He can still make a mistake." Neither of us could take his eyes off the fire. What is there in the burning of man-made things which so thrills us? It is like Homer's image of the two rivers in Hades: one of creation, the other of destruction, forever held in uneasy balance. Men have always enjoyed destroying quite as much as building, which explains the popularity of war.

We were still gaping at the fiery river when a group of officers rode past us. One of them was Valentinian, his face scarlet with heat and rage: "Stupid! Stupid! Stupid!" he snarled. Anatolius and I exchanged nervous glances. Was there to be a mutiny of officers? But there was none, despite the grumbling of the tribunes. Incidentally, I have never forgotten that brief glimpse I had of Valentinian, his face swollen with the same rage that was to kill him years later when he died of a stroke while bellowing at a German embassy.

By nightfall, the fleet was gone. In the distance one could see the Persians gathered on the walls of Ctesiphon to watch this extraordinary sight. No one will ever know what they made of it. The Roman Emperor burning the Roman fleet must have seemed to them perfectly incomprehensible. I could hardly believe it myself.

420

We have broken camp and are moving southeast, into the interior. The countryside is rich; there is plenty of water. The men are less apprehensive than they were. They see now that we do not need the river to survive.

All goes well. Nevitta: on guard. Victor. Ch. Close? How? Days grow hotter. May begin night marches.

*Priscus*: Nevitta again warned Julian of a Christian plot. This time Victor was directly involved. I know. I rode beside Julian that same afternoon. We spoke frankly of what Nevitta had told him.

"But if they kill me, who will take my place? There's no one except Salutius and he is hardly a friend to them."

"There is Victor."

Julian smiled coldly. "He would be butchered by the Gauls." Then he frowned. "Nevitta says they have put someone close to me to . . . to do their work. Is it you?" He turned on me and I saw that though his voice was light and playful his face was not. He stared at me with sun-dazzled eyes. Like all of us, his face was burned dark and his eyes were red from sand and sun, the lids suppurating. He had lost weight and one could see the working of the cordlike muscles of his forearms as he grasped the reins. He was a boy no longer, nor even young.

"No, not I." I tried but could not think of a joke to make.

"You'd make a very poor emperor." He was his old self again. We rode on. Before and behind us, the army wound through bright country, rich with coming harvest.

Salutius joined us, wearing a headcloth.

"Look at that! A classic Roman consul!" Julian teased him. But Salutius for all his intelligence had no humor. He explained to us at solemn length why he could not wear a helmet in the sun because the heat made his forehead break out in a rash. Then he handed Julian a letter. "From the senate at Constantinople. To congratulate you on your victory."

Julian sighed. "Too soon," he said, giving the letter back. I recall how the sun shone on the back of his hand and the blond hairs glittered against sun-darkened skin. I also noticed what large nails he had (now that he'd ceased biting them). Curious the clarity with which one remembers the shape of a hand glimpsed years ago, while so many things of importance are lost.

*Julian Augustus*                                                    *5 June*
    Midnight: Fire. Trenches.

*Priscus*: That night the Persians set fire to the harvest. For miles around fields, vineyards, orchards, villages . . . everything caught fire, and night was like day. Although Julian ordered protective trenches dug around the camp, a number of our tents burned, as well as several wagons.

For three days and three nights the fire continued. Whenever I think of those weeks in Persia, I see fire in my mind, smell smoke, feel the terrible heat of sun blazing while fire burns. Luckily, there were springs in the camp and we had sufficient water. We also had food for perhaps a week. But after that, famine. As far as the eye could see, there was black desert. Nothing green survived.

I now shared a tent with Anatolius. This meant that I was more than usually involved in the business of the court. Ordinarily I kept out of such things, for I have always been bored by politics, but now I was very interested in what was going on. We all were. Our lives were at stake. It seemed that everyone had a plan to save us, except the Emperor.

The army was now almost evenly divided between Julian and Victor, between the Europeans and the Asiatics, between the Hellenists and the Christians. Julian of course was strongest because his adherents were, quite simply, the best soldiers. Yet as each day passed in that burnt-out wilderness, the party of Victor became all the louder and more demanding, insisting that the Emperor act. But Julian gave absolutely no hint of what he intended to do. In fact, without this journal we might never have known what was in his mind.

*Julian Augustus*                                                    *6 June*
    Persian cavalry raided our supply depot just before dawn. Several of them killed. No casualties for us. We must expect more of this.

At noon I prayed to Helios. I sacrificed a white bull. The augury was not decisive. What to do?

A sharp encounter with Victor at this afternoon's staff meeting. My quarters are stifling. None of us wore armor. The generals were arranged about me on stools. At my feet sat the deaf-mute; he watches my every move with the alert, loving eyes of a pet dog. I have only to think I am thirsty for him to read it in my face and bring me water.

No sooner had I greeted the generals than Victor took the initiative. "Augustus, we must go back the way we came, through Assyria." Arintheus promptly agreed with him. The others waited to see what I would say.

"That is always a possibility. Of course. Always." I assumed the Mardonius manner: maddeningly reasonable yet perfectly evasive. "But perhaps, Count, you will tell us, first, why you believe we must go back now and, second, why you prefer that route."

Victor looked more than ever like the village bully trying to control himself in the presence of the schoolmaster. "First, as the Augustus knows, we shall soon be short of food. My scouts report that for twenty miles to south and east there are only ashes. To the north there is desert. That leaves us the west, where we came from."

"Have you forgotten that we ourselves burned the fields around Ctesiphon?"

"Yes, we made that mistake, but . . ."

Nevitta made a threatening noise, deep in his throat, like a bull preparing for attack. One may not accuse the Emperor of making mistakes. But I motioned for Nevitta to keep silent. I tried to sound amiable. "But since this 'mistake' was made, what is the point of going from one devastated region to another?"

"Because, Augustus, there are still some regions which we did not burn. We can live off the country. We can also use those forts we captured . . ."

". . . and burned? No, Count, those forts are of no use to us and you know it. So I ask you again: Why do you want to go back the way we came?"

"Because we know that country. We can live off it, somehow. The men will be reassured."

"May I speak, Lord?" Ormisda has ceased to be Great King and is once more Greek courtier, a bad sign. "The army cannot return up the Euphrates because there is no longer a fleet. Nor have we the means to make bridges."

"We can use the ships that were saved," said Victor.

This time Salutius answered him. "Twelve small ships are not enough to cross the Tigris. Like it or not, we are now confined to this side of the river. If we set out for home it must be by way of Corduene."

"Can't we get ships from the Persians?" asked Dagalaif suddenly. "There must be hundreds in the river ports."

"They'll burn them first," said Ormisda.

"I have been making inquiries," Salutius began, sounding as if he were sitting comfortably in his praetorian prefect's chair at Constantinople, surrounded by notaries, instead of sweating in an airless tent with a cloth wrapped about his sunburned head. "And it appears that what ships the Persians have are well out of range. Our only hope would be to build new ones, but of course we lack the materials."

Ormisda finished the matter. "Even if we could cross the Tigris, we would have the same difficulties returning north we have had here. Sapor means to starve us out. He will burn all Persia if he has to. Also, the rains have now begun in Mesopotamia. The winter ice in the mountains has melted. The road that brought us to Ctesiphon is a feverswamp swarming with insects. But of course we shall go wherever the Augustus bids."

"So shall we all," said Victor, "but *what* is his plan?" I looked into the bright eyes of my enemy and saw that he means to kill me. I have known it from the start.

I answered quietly. "Augustus means to consider every possibility before he comes to a decision. He also reminds the council that we have yet to hear from Procopius. There are rumors that he is even now on his way to us here. If he arrives, we shall lay siege to Ctesiphon."

"Using what for food?" Victor challenged me.

"Procopius will bring supplies. Also, to get here, he will have to open up a line of communications from our province of Corduene. That's only three hundred miles away. We don't need to worry about supplies if Procopius comes."

"But if he does not?" Victor leaned forward, a hunting dog who has got the quarry's scent.

"Then we are where we are now. It seems agreed that we cannot return the way we came."

"Because the fleet was burned."

This was too much. I turned on Victor. "Count, you will not speak again until I give you leave." As if struck, Victor blinked and sat back.

I continued. "We can always take our chances in the desert to the north. But it will be a hard march to Corduene." I could see that Ormisda wanted to speak. I nodded.

"The Augustus should know that there are no maps of that territory. We shall have to rely on guides. They may not be reliable."

"Can't we follow the course of the Tigris?" Dagalaif fanned himself with the frond of a date palm.

"Not easily," said Ormisda. "There are many strong fortresses..."

"And we shall be a retreating army, not a conquering one. We would be unable to lay siege to the cities." I let this sink in. Until now no one has mentioned the possibility of our defeat. After all, we have broken the Great King's army; half Persia is ours. Yet now we must talk of retreat because we have been burned out by Persian zealots. It is tragedy. I should have anticipated it. But I did not. The fault is mine. It is hard to believe that without the loss of a single battle one can so swiftly cease to be a conqueror and become the chieftain of a band of frightened men who want only to go home as fast as possible. Is this the revenge of Ares for what I said to him during the sacrifice at Ctesiphon?

Arintheus took my challenge. "We're not retreating, Augustus. How could we be? Why, old Sapor will make a treaty with you tomorrow, giving you anything you want if only we go home." News of the Persian embassy has been in the air for a week. Nothing is secret for long in an army. I suspect the Persians themselves of spreading the rumor, to create discord: why is your Emperor driving you so hard when we are willing to give you gold and territory and a safe passage home? The Persians are expert at this sort of thing.

"Victor seems to feel that we have been defeated," I said. "I don't. I think we must wait a few days longer for Procopius. If he does not come, we shall consider whether to go north to Corduene or keep on south to the Persian Gulf." I said this casually.

It was the first time I have suggested such a thing to the generals. They were astonished.

"The Persian Gulf!" Victor momentarily forgot my ban of silence. He quickly muttered an apology.

Salutius spoke for what, I am afraid, is the majority. "It is too far, Augustus. We are only three hundred miles from Roman territory and it seems like three thousand miles. If we continue any deeper into Persia, we'll be swallowed up."

"The men won't go." Nevitta was abrupt. "They're already frightened. Order them to go south and you'll have a first-class mutiny on your hands."

"But the cities of the Gulf are rich and unprotected . . ."

"They won't go, General. Not now. But even if they would, what's to keep the Persians from burning everything in our path? They're crazy enough to. We'd starve to death before we ever saw the Gulf."

So I have abandoned this dream. For now. I dismissed the council.

I sit on my cot, writing this on my knees. Callistus is preparing the sacrificial robes. The deaf-mute plays the lute. In a few minutes Maximus joins me. In an hour I pray first to Zeus, then to the Great Mother. Where have I failed? Is this the revenge of Ares?

*Julian Augustus*                                                    *7 June*

The omens are bad. The auguries inconclusive. They advise against returning home by way of Assyria, they also advise against going north to Corduene. One indicated that I should go south to the Gulf! But the troops would not obey. They are already close to mutiny. I must bring Victor to heel or face rebellion.

*Julian Augustus*                                                    *8 June*

I have not slept for days. The heat at night is almost as bad as the heat by day. It is like having the fever. We all resemble dried-up cadavers. I lose my temper with everyone. I struck Callistus when he fumbled with the fastening of my robes. I quarreled with Salutius over a trivial matter, and he was in the right. Tonight Maximus was with me. We were alone together because Priscus is sick with dysentery and Anatolius nurses him. While I was having supper, Maximus tried to cheer me up. He achieved the opposite.

"But it's so simple. Give the order to march south. They must obey. You are the Emperor."

"I shall have been the Emperor. They'll kill me first."

"But Cybele herself has told us that you must complete your work. After all, you are Alexander."

I erupted at this. "No, I am *not* Alexander, who is dead. I am Julian, about to die in this forsaken place . . ."

"No. No! The gods . . ."

". . . misled us! The gods laugh at us! They raise us up for sport, and throw us down again. There is no more gratitude in heaven than there is on earth."

"Julian . . ."

"You say I was born to do great things. Well, I have done them. I conquered the Persians. I conquered the Germans. I saved Gaul. For what? To delay this world's end for a year or two? Certainly no longer."

"You were born to restore the worship of the true gods."

"Then why do they let me fail?"

"You are Emperor still!"

I seized a handful of charred earth from the tent's floor. "That is all that's left to me. Ashes."

"You will live . . ."

"I shall be as dead as Alexander soon enough, but when I go I take Rome with me. For nothing good will come after. The Goths and the Galileans will inherit the state, and like vultures and maggots they'll make clean bones of what is dead, until there is not even so much as the shadow of a god anywhere on earth."

Maximus hid his face in his hands while I raged on. But after a time I stopped, ashamed of having made a fool of myself. "It's no use," I said finally, "I am in Helios's hands, and we are both at the end of the day. So good-night, Maximus, and pray for me that it will indeed be a good night."

But I can't believe it is over yet. Our army is intact. The Persian army is broken. We can still go north to Corduene. If Helios deserts me now, there will be no one to restore his worship.

But this is madness! Why am I suddenly in such despair? Why should I die now, at the height of my reign, at the age of . . . I had to stop to count! I am thirty-two.

Afternoon. We are still encamped. Food is running low. No word from Procopius. Yesterday and again this morning, Persian cavalry attacked us. They strike at the outskirts of the camp. Then when we sound the call to arms, they vanish. This is the most demoralizing kind of warfare.

I must soon decide what to do. Meanwhile, I make daily sacrifice. The omens are not good. The auguries confused. I want to put Victor under arrest. Salutius thinks I should wait.

During this morning's staff meeting, there was a sudden racket outside my tent. I heard the tribune who commands my bodyguard shout, "Stand back! Stand back!"

I went outside. A thousand men, mostly Asiatics, surrounded the tent. They begged me to lead them home by way of Assyria. They had been well coached. They shouted and whined, wept and threatened. It took me some minutes to silence them. Then I said, "We shall start for home only when our work is done."

Several jeered at this. I pretended not to hear.

"When we do go home, it cannot be by the way we came. Your general Victor will tell you why." This was a pleasantly ironic move. Victor was now forced to placate the men he had himself incited. He did it very well, explaining why the Euphrates route was no longer open to us. He was plausible, and the men listened to him respectfully. When he had finished, I assured them that I was as eager as they to return to safety. At the proper time we would go; meanwhile, I asked them not to take seriously the Persian-inspired rumors which I knew were going about the camp. They dispersed. I turned to Victor.

"This is *not* the way to force us," I said carefully.

"But, Augustus . . ."

I dismissed him. He has been warned.

Later, I spoke privately to each of the generals. Most are loyal. For instance, Jovian sat on a stool in my tent, his tunic wet with perspiration, his face flushed from wine as well as heat. "Whatever Augustus commands, I will obey." His voice is deep and somewhat

428

hoarse, for he drinks those harsh German spirits which burn the throat.

"Even if I say go south to the Persian Gulf?"

Jovian squirmed uncomfortably. "That is far away. But if the Augustus orders us..."

"No, I shall not order you. Not now."

He was relieved. "Then that means we'll be going back soon, won't we?"

I said nothing.

"Because the longer we stay here, the more difficult it will be. What with the heat, the Persians..."

"The Persians are defeated."

"But the Great King still has a good many soldiers and this is their country, not ours."

"Half of it is ours, by right of conquest."

"Yes, Lord. But can we hold it? I'm for getting out. They say demons ride with the Persians, especially at night."

I almost laughed in his foolish face. But instead I proposed "Pray to your man-god to make them go away."

"If demons haunt us, it is because Christ wills it," he said piously.

I smiled. "I prefer a god who protects those who worship him."

"I don't know about these things, Augustus, but I say let's make terms with the Persians and leave this place. Not that it's for me to decide."

"No, it is not for you to decide. But I shall bear in mind your advice." I dismissed Jovian, more depressed than ever.

I make sacrifice in a few minutes.

*Julian Augustus*                                                    *15 June*

Mastara sees great peril no matter what I do. I sacrificed yesterday and again this morning. There is still no sign. The gods are silent. I prayed more than an hour to Helios. I looked straight at him until I was blind. Nothing. I have offended. But how? I cannot believe that my anger at the war god would turn all heaven against me. Who else will do their work?

Nevitta brings me word that the Asiatic troops already speak of my successor "who will save them." But apparently there is no popular choice. They follow Victor but do not love him. Arintheus? Emperor? No. Not even his boys would accept that. Salutius? He is loyal to me and yet...I grow suspicious. I am like Constantius now. I suspect treason on every side. For the first time I fear the knife in the dark. I make Callistus sleep on the ground beside my bed while the deaf-mute remains awake most of the night, watching for the assassin's shadow to fall across the door to my tent. I never believed that I would become like this. I have never feared death in battle, and I never thought that I feared murder. But I do. I find it hard to sleep. When I do, my dreams are of death, sudden, black, violent. What has gone wrong?

Beside my bed there is a book by Aeschylus. Just now I picked it up and read this at random: "Take heart. Suffering when it climbs highest lasts but a little time." Well, I am near the peak. Will it be swift? or slow?

Priscus and Maximus spent most of the evening with me. We talked philosophy. No one mentioned our situation and for a time I was able to forget that the gods have abandoned me. Yet why do I think this? Merely because the Persians have burned the countryside? Or because of the treachery of Procopius, which does not come as a surprise? Although things are not so bad as I feel they are, the fact that I have this sense of foreboding is in itself a message from the gods.

Maximus wanted to stay behind after Priscus left. But I would not let him, pleading fatigue. I suspect even him. Why shouldn't he be in league with Victor? Everyone knows he has influence over me, and certainly anyone could buy him if they met his price. This is insane. Of course Maximus is loyal to me. He has to be. The Galileans would have his head if I were not here to protect him. I must stop this brooding or I shall become as mad as those emperors who feared the long night of death more than they loved the brief living day. I am still alive; still Augustus; still conqueror of Persia.

Tomorrow we start for home. I gave the order at sundown. The men cheered me. They don't know what a long journey it is from here to Corduene. All they know is that we are leaving Persia. All *I* know is that the goddess Cybele revealed to me that I was Alexander born again, and I have failed both her and Alexander, who is once more a ghost, while I am nothing.

I should have agreed to Sapor's treaty. Now that we are withdrawing, we shall get worse terms.

* * *

*Priscus*: As well as I knew Julian, I never suspected that he was in such despair. The exhausted man who scribbled the journal, and the proud laughing general Maximus and I used to dine with are two different creatures. Naturally, we knew that he was worried. But he never betrayed to us that morbid fear of assassination he writes about. He joked occasionally about the succession, saying that if Rome were to have a Christian emperor he hoped it would be Victor because in a year there would be a million converts to Hellenism. But that was all. He talked as he always talked; rapidly, enthusiastically, late into the night, reading aloud to us from the classics, quarreling with me over Plato's meanings, teasing Maximus for his ignorance of literature. The great magician, having always been in such close communion with the gods, seldom condescended to read the reports of those who could only guess at the mysteries he *knew*.

On 15 June Julian gave the order to go north along the Tigris to Corduene and Armenia. The thing was finished. Even Ormisda now realized that he would never rule in Persia.

At dawn 16 June we broke camp. Julian asked me to ride with him. I did not realize until I read the journal what a good actor he was. That day he was the exuberant, legendary hero, hair and beard burned a dull gold by the sun, arms and legs dark, face as clear and untroubled as a child's; even the constant nose peeling had finally stopped and his head looked as if it had been carved from African wood. We were all quite black except for the pale Gauls, who turn painfully red in the sun and stay that way. There was much sunstroke among them.

As we rode through fire-blackened hills, Julian seemed unusually cheerful. "We haven't done too badly. The campaign has been a success, though not exactly what I had hoped for."

"Because Ormisda is not Great King?"

"Yes." He did not elaborate.

We were interrupted by the tribune Valens. It was the only other time I recall seeing him in Persia. He was not bad-looking, though physically rather dirty, even as soldiers go. He was profoundly nervous in Julian's presence. "Augustus, the scouts report an army approaching. From the north."

Julian dug his heels into his horse's ribs and cantered down the road to the head of the army, two miles distant. Within half an hour, the sky was dark with swirling dust. The rumor went about quickly: Procopius has come! But Julian took no chances. We made a war camp on the spot, with a triple row of shields placed around us. Then we waited to see whose army it was, Procopius's or Sapor's.

We were on battle alert all day. I bet Anatolius five silver pieces at three-to-one odds that the army was Sapor's. Neither of us won. The "army" turned out to be a herd of wild asses.

But that night the Great King's army materialized.


*Julian Augustus*                                              *17 June*

Sapor's army still exists. They are encamped a mile from us. Cannot tell what their numbers are but not so many as were assembled at Ctesiphon. Our troops eager for battle. Had to restrain them all morning. At noon Persian cavalry attacked one of our battalions. General Machameus killed. Though wounded, his brother Maurus fought his way to where the body was lying and carried it back into camp.

The heat is beyond anything I have ever before endured. Though we are all of us giddy from too much sun, I ordered the march to be continued. At first the Persians fell back; then they rallied and tried to stop us. We butchered them. By afternoon they were all of them gone except for a band of Saracens who follow us even now, waiting for the right moment to raid our baggage train.

I write this sitting on a stool beneath a date palm. Everywhere I look I see green circles before my eyes. I am dazzled by Helios. The air is so hot it scorches the lungs. My sweat mingles with the ink on the page. The letters blur. Few casualties.


*Julian Augustus*                                              *20 June*

For two days we have been encamped at Hucumbra, the estate of a Persian nobleman who, luckily for us, did not burn his crops and orchards. Food and water are plentiful. The men are almost happy. I have ordered them to take all the food they can for we must burn this place as soon as we leave it. We shall not find so much food again until we reach our own territory, twenty days' march from here.

432

On the march. The country is hilly and barren. We are about twenty miles to the west of the Tigris, moving north. Early today the Persian cavalry attacked our infantry rear guard. Fortunately, the cavalry of the Petulantes was nearby and drove them off. One of the Great King's counsellors, Adaces, was killed and his armor brought me by the soldier who struck him down. As I gave the usual reward, Salutius suddenly said, "We were good friends, Adaces and I." He then reminded me that the Persian had once been Sapor's envoy to Constantius.

An ugly business tonight. Instead of attacking the Persians at the same time as the Petulantes, the cavalry of the Tertiaci gave way. As a result, what might have been a complete rout of the Persians became only a skirmish. I broke four tribunes but took no other action. We shall soon need every man we have, coward or brave.

We are no longer certain where we are. We move in a line north, but there are no maps to show us where water and villages are. But two days ago, at Hucumbra, an old Persian who knows the province well offered to lead us to fertile country. Ormisda talked with him at length and believes he is not a spy. The old man says there will be three days of barren country and then we shall be in the rich valley of Maranga.

*Julian Augustus*                                                      *22 June*
Battle. Execution. Vetranio. Victory. Where?

*Priscus*: The old Persian was of course a spy who led us straight into an ambush at Maranga, which was not a "rich valley" but a stony place where we were exposed on all sides to the Persian army. Julian was just able to form the army into a crescent when they attacked. The first rain of Persian arrows did little harm. There was no second flurry. Julian was able to resort to his favorite tactical exercise, throwing his infantry at the enemy's archers before they could get proper range.

The fighting went on all day in ovenlike heat. I remained with the baggage and saw very little of what happened. My principal memory is of heat, of blood on white rocks, of the hideous trumpeting of elephants reverberating through the narrow valley.

433

"Execution." The old Persian was crucified when it was discovered that he had deliberately led us into this trap.

"Vetranio." He was commanding officer of the Zianni; he was killed.

"Victory." The Persian army disappeared at nightfall. Their casualties were three to our one. But the men were frightened. The business of the Persian spy had particularly alarmed them. How far out of the way had he taken us? Wouldn't it be better—if riskier—to follow the crooked Tigris north? All these questions were addressed to Julian whenever he appeared among the troops. But he seemed confident as always.

"Where?" Where indeed!

*Julian Augustus*                                                23 June

We are now eight miles from the Tigris. I have decided to follow the river north, though that is the longest and most dangerous route, since we shall have to pass many fortresses. Even so, I am alarmed by this wilderness. We have no idea where we are. The advantage is entirely the enemy's. We are short of food. I have ordered my own supplies given to the men. Ormisda tells me that the Great King is again ready to make peace on terms still favorable to us. Ormisda advises me to accept the treaty. This alarms me most. If Ormisda has given up his dream of the Persian throne, the war is lost.

*Julian Augustus*                                                25 June

There seems to be a tacit truce between the Persians and us. They have completely vanished. We are remaining in camp, tending to the wounded, repairing armor, getting ready for the long journey north. I feel like Xenophon, who also went this way.

A while ago I fell asleep while reading *The March Upcountry*. So deep was my sleep that I did not realize I was dreaming (usually I do). I thought I was wide awake. I was even aware of the oil lamp sputtering as insects passed through its flame and burned. Suddenly I felt someone watching me. I looked up and there at the door to the tent was the tall figure of a man with head veiled; in one hand he held the horn of plenty. At first, I tried to speak but could not—tried to rise but could not. For a long moment the specter looked at me sadly. Then without a word the figure turned and left my tent, and I awakened, cold as a corpse. I leapt to my feet and crossed to the tent opening. I looked out. Except for the sleepy sentry no one was in sight. Small fires glowed in the darkness. I looked up just as a star fell in the west; it came from on high, flared briefly, then vanished.

I awakened Callistus. "Fetch me Maximus. And Mastara. Quickly."

When they arrived, I told them about the star. I showed them exactly where it had fallen in the sky.

Mastara interpreted. "According to the book of Tages, when a meteor is seen to fall in time of war, no battle must be undertaken for twenty-four hours, nor a move of any kind."

I turned to Maximus. "Well at least it was not *my* star."

Maximus was reassuring, but Mastara was firm. "One thing is certain. You must remain here in camp another day."

"But I have given orders. Tomorrow we cross to the Tigris."

"You asked me, Highest Priest, for the word of Tages and I have given it."

I allowed Mastara to go. Then I told Maximus of the dream. He was troubled. "Are you so certain the figure was Rome?"

"Yes. I saw him once before, in Paris, when he ordered me to take the purple."

Maximus frowned. "It could of course be a demon. They are everywhere in this cursed land. Why, even as I walked here tonight, I felt them all about me, tugging at my beard, my staff, testing my power."

"This was not a demon. It was the Spirit of Rome. And he abandoned me."

"Don't say that! After all, in three weeks we shall be home. You can raise a new army. Then you shall complete Alexander's work..."

"Perhaps." Suddenly I found myself tired of Maximus. He means to be helpful but he is not always right. He is not a god, nor am I. Much against his wish, I sent him away. Before he left, he begged me not to break camp tomorrow. But I told him we must move on no matter what the omens tell us.

Callistus is polishing my armor. He says the breastplate straps are broken, but he will have the armorer fix them before we leave tomorrow. The deaf-mute sits at my feet. He plays a Lydian song, very old and very strange; yet one can recognize the voice of Dionysos in the melody. To think, the god sings to us still, though the golden age is gone and the sacred groves deserted.

\* \* \*

For an hour I walked among the tents, unobserved by the men. I gather strength from the army. They are my life, the element in which I have my being. That is the final irony. I who wanted to live at Athens as a student have been eight years a general. Such is fate.

I paused at Anatolius's tent. Through the flap, I could see Anatolius and Priscus playing draughts. I nearly spoke to them. But then I realized that I am hardly the best of company tonight. So instead I sat in front of my tent, watching the sky. My own star burns bright as ever. If it were not for tonight's troubling dream, I would be content. Without reinforcements, we have done all that we could do in this place. But what's to be done with Victor and the Galileans? Nevitta tells me that I am not safe. Yet what can they do to me? If I am openly murdered, the Gauls and Franks will slaughter the Asiatics. If secretly . . . but when an emperor dies suddenly in his youth it is not secret. No, they do not dare strike at me, yet. Curious, as I lie here on the lion bed, I think of something Mardonius once told Gallus and me

*Priscus:* That is the last entry, broken off by sleep, and then by death.

# XXIII

*Priscus:* The next morning Julian gave the order to march west to the Tigris. We were in a dry desolate country of sand and stone. Our slow passage made clouds of white choking dust as we rode toward a series of low hills where waiting Persians watched us, like so many scorpions among the rocks.

I was with Julian in the vanguard. He wore no armor. His servant had not yet repaired the leather straps. "Just as well," he said. Like all of us, he was soaked with sweat, even at dawn. Flies clung to our lips and eyes. Most of us suffered from dysentery. Yet despite the heat and the discomfort, Julian was in excellent spirits. For one thing, he had finally interpreted the dream to his own liking. "The Genius of Rome deserted me. There's no denying that. *But* he left by the tent door, which was to the west. That means this campaign is finished, and we must return home to the west."

"But you said the face was grieving."

"So is mine when I think of what we might have done here. Even so..." As we talked, messengers came to him at regular intervals. Persians sighted in the valley ahead. Skirmishing on the left flank. Count Victor fears an attack.

"No attack," said Julian. "They won't meet us again in battle. They will harass us, but nothing more." He gave rapid orders. The left flank to be reinforced. The Saracens to go to the rear. Count Victor to be soothed. Suddenly a courier arrived from Arintheus: Persian cavalry was attacking the rear guard. Julian promptly turned his horse about and rode to the rear, followed by Callistus.

Some thirty minutes after Julian left us, the van was attacked by Persian archers hidden in the cliffs to the right of the trail. Nevitta called for battle formation. I quickly joined my fellow non-combatants at the center.

Safe among the baggage, I found Maximus calmly combing his beard, unaware we were being attacked. When I told him what was happening, he was not in the least alarmed. "No more set battles," he said, echoing Julian. "Only guerrilla warfare. Nothing to fear."

But Anatolius was roused by this information. "I must join the Tertiaci. They count on me." Then the absurd creature was off, the plump little body kept astride his horse only by the weight of armor. It should be noted that if one is at the center of an army whose vanguard is ten miles from its rear guard, a considerable battle can take place and one not know it. Huddled among the wagons, Maximus and I might just as well have been traveling from Athens to Sirmium as in the midst of a Persian war.

Now this is what happened to Julian. Halfway to the rear, he was stopped by a second courier, who told him that the vanguard was also under attack. Julian started back. He had gone perhaps a mile when the Persians attacked our center. Elephants, cavalrymen, archers swept down from the hills so suddenly that the left flank momentarily gave way. Julian rushed into this action, his only armor a shield. He rallied the troops. They struck back at the Persians. With swords and axes they hacked the trunks and legs of the elephants.

The Persians retreated. Julian rode after them, waving to the household troops to follow him. Suddenly he and Callistus were caught up in a confused melée of retreating Persians. For some minutes both men were lost to view. Finally the last of the Persians fled and Julian was again visible. He rejoined the household troops, who cheered him, relieved that he was safe. Not until he had come quite close did they notice the spear that had penetrated his side.

"It is not much," said Julian. But when he tried to draw the spear, he gave a cry, for the shaft was razor-sharp and cut his fingers. I am told that he sat a long moment staring straight ahead. Then suddenly he hurled his own blood straight at the sun. "It is not much," he said again, and pitched headlong to the ground.

Julian was carried in a litter to his tent. At his own insistence, he was completely covered by a cavalryman's cloak so that no one might know the Emperor had fallen.

When I saw the litter approaching the tent, I thought stupidly: Someone has killed a deer and they're bringing it for our supper. When I realized that it was Julian in the litter, I felt as if I had been struck very hard in the chest. I looked at Maximus. He too was stunned. Together we followed the litter into the tent. Julian was now conscious.

"There is a lesson in this," he murmured, while Maximus leaned over him, as though to hear the words of an oracle.

"Yes, Julian." Maximus whispered prayerfully.

"Always, in war—no matter what—wear armor." Julian smiled weakly at us. Then he turned to the frightened Callistus. "Are the straps fixed yet?"

"Yes, Lord. Yes." Callistus began to sob.

The surgeons meanwhile had cut away Julian's tunic. The head of the spear had entered just below the rib cage, penetrating the lower lobe of the liver. There was almost no blood on the white skin. Julian glanced down at his wound with an air of distaste, like a sculptor who detects a flaw in the figure he is shaping. "Only my hand gives me pain," he said. Then he turned to Salutius who had joined us. "How is the battle?"

"We are turning them back."

"Good. But even so, I'd better show myself. The men must see that I'm still alive." Though the surgeons tried to restrain him, he sat up. "It's all right. I feel no pain. The wound's not deep. Callistus, my armor." He turned to the surgeons. "If you can't draw the spear, at least cut it short so I can hide it under my cloak." He swung his legs over the bed; blood gushed from the wound; he fainted. I nearly did, too. Swiftly, the surgeons worked to stanch the flow.

It was Salutius who asked the surgeons, "Will he die?"

"Yes, Prefect, he will die, very soon." We looked at one another like idiots, amazed, unbelieving.

Nevitta appeared at the tent's opening. "Emperor!" he shouted to the pale unconscious figure on the lion bed.

Salutius shook his head and put his fingers to his lips. With a howl like an animal in pain, Nevitta fled the tent. Salutius followed him. That day the Gauls and Franks, and Celts and Germans slaughtered half the Persian army to avenge their Emperor.

The fighting did not end until nightfall. But I saw none of it. With Maximus, I sat in that stifling tent and watched Julian die.

He was conscious most of the time. He did not become delirious. His mind never wandered. He suffered little pain. For a long time he pretended that all he had suffered was a flesh wound.

"But how?" I asked. The javelin on his side looked absurd, like a long pin stuck in a child's doll.

"I don't know. How?" Julian turned to Callistus, who sat on the ground like a terrified dog, close to the armor stand. "Did you see how it happened?"

"No, Lord. I was behind you. The Persians were all around us. I lost sight of you. Not until we were free of them did I see what had happened."

"At the time I hardly felt it; a light blow, as if I'd been struck by a fist." Julian motioned to the deaf-mute boy to give him water. But at the surgeons' request, he did not swallow.

News of the battle was brought us regularly. When Julian learned that the Persian generals Merena and Nahodares were dead, he was delighted. "They were the best of Sapor's officers. This *is* the last battle. I'm sure of it!"

I confess that for once I was grateful for Maximus's logorrhea. There were no silences that day as he told us endless anecdotes of the various gods he had spoken to. Apparently, all Olympus delighted in his company.

At sundown, the bleeding started again. When it was finally stopped, Julian's face was ashy beneath sunburned skin. "Will you be able to draw the spear?" he asked the surgeons.

"No, Lord." That was the death sentence, and Julian knew it. He nodded and shut his eyes. He seemed to sleep. I sweated nervously. Maximus drew designs on the sandy floor. From far off, the sound of battle grew fainter. Just as Callistus was lighting the lamps, Salutius and Nevitta entered the tent. Julian opened his eyes. "How goes it?" His voice was low but firm.

Salutius placed an ornate bronze helmet at the edge of Julian's cot. "This belonged to General Merena. The Persian army is defeated. So far we have counted fifty of their greatest lords among the dead."

"We won't see that army soon again," said Nevitta.

"You fought well." Julian touched the Persian general's helmet with his good hand. "This war is over."

"But we nearly lost Salutius," Nevitta attempted heartiness. "They had him surrounded. Because of the purple cloak, they thought he was you. So he had to fight just like a Frank to get away. Never thought such an old man could have so much energy."

Julian smiled dimly. "The old man won't be able to walk tomorrow, from stiffness."

"He can hardly move now." Salutius kept up the badinage.

Julian gave a sudden quick gasp. He gripped his sides as though the chest were about to burst. Sweat glistened on his body. The muscles of his stomach contracted in pain.

"Helios," he muttered. Then he added, "Where are we? What is this place called?"

It was Maximus who answered, "Phrygia." And dully Julian said, "Then the thing is done."

Incidentally, I have always wanted to know whether or not that patch of desert was indeed called Phrygia. Knowing Maximus, I suspect him of lying; after all, his reputation as a prophet was at stake. But true or false, it is now a matter of historic record that the Emperor Julian was struck down in Phrygia, as foretold by Maximus and Sosipatra.

Julian turned to the surgeons. "Will I die soon?"

"Lord, we cannot say. The liver is pierced. A few hours..." Callistus began to weep again. Nevitta clenched and unclenched his huge hands as though ready to break to bits bony death himself. Salutius sat limply on a stool, weak from the long day's battle.

"So I have seen the sun—living—for the last time." Julian said this in a matter-of-fact voice. "I should have made sacrifice. Now of course *I* am the sacrifice."

"Augustus." Salutius was urgent. "You must determine the succession. Who is to be our emperor when the gods take you back?"

Julian was silent. For a moment it seemed as if he had not

heard. Then he said, "I must add certain things to my will, personal bequests. Send for Anatolius."

It was Salutius who said, "He is happy, Lord." The classic expression which means that a man has died honorably in battle. I was particularly upset by this.

Julian was startled. "Anatolius dead?" Tears came to his eyes. Then he laughed. "Here I am a dying man mourning the dead! That, Priscus, should appeal to your sense of the incongruous." He became businesslike. "There is a will at Constantinople. Salutius, you know where it is. See that it is honored. Nevitta, summon the generals. Maximus, my friend. I am ready to say good-bye." He grinned and looked suddenly like a schoolboy again. "You know, most of our emperors died too swiftly to be able to prepare a final speech. While the ones who were allowed sufficient time proved disappointing. Vespasian made a bad joke. 'Dear me,' he said, 'I seem to be turning into a god.' Augustus rambled. Hadrian discussed astronomy. None took advantage of the occasion. Well, I mean to be an exception."

Julian nodded to Callistus, who brought him a small chest from which he withdrew a scroll. "As always, the gods have been kind to me. I shall die unique: the first emperor to deliver himself of a well-written (if I say so myself) farewell." He smiled at me. "Yes, I wrote my last words in Antioch, just in case. So no matter what happens to my reputation, I shall always be remembered for this departure." He spoke with such a delicate self-mockery that even Salutius smiled and said, "You have surpassed Marcus Aurelius."

"Thank you," said Julian. Then he shut his eyes and waited. In a matter of minutes the tent was crowded with friends, priests, generals. Almost as if by design, the Asiatic generals stood at one side of the bed, while the Europeans were ranged at the other.

When all were present, Julian motioned for the surgeon to prop him up, a physical effort which caused him some pain. Breathing hard, he ordered Callistus to light more lamps, remarking again to me, "At the end, Priscus, we can be extravagant." I of course could think of nothing to say.

Julian opened the scroll. "Friends," he began. He looked about him. Victor did not stir when Julian's fell on him. "Friends," he repeated. Then he read rapidly, as though afraid he might not live long enough to get to the end. "Most opportunely do I leave this

441

life which I am pleased to return to Creation, at her demand, like an honorable man who pays his debts when they come due. Nor am I—as some might think..." he paused once more and looked about the tent at the faces of his generals, curiously shifting and grotesque in the uneven lamplight... "sad"—he stressed the word oddly—"at going."

He returned to the text. "For I have learned from philosophy that the soul is happier than the body; therefore, when a better condition is severed from a worse, one should rejoice, not grieve. Nor should we forget that the gods deliberately give death to the greatest of men as the ultimate reward. I am confident that this gift was given me so that I might not yield to certain difficulties, nor ever suffer the humiliation of defeat. After all, sorrow can only overwhelm weakness; it flees before strength. I regret nothing I have ever done. I am not tormented by the memory of any great misdeed. Both before and after I was raised to the principate, I preserved my own god-given soul and kept it without grievous fault, or so I think. I conducted the business of the state with moderation. I made war—or peace—only after much deliberation, realizing that success and careful planning do not necessarily go hand in hand, since the gods, finally, must determine the outcome. Even so, believing as I did that the purpose of a just rule is the welfare and security of the people, I was always—as you know—inclined to peaceful measures, never indulging in that license which is the corruption of deeds and of charity." He stopped. He took several long deep breaths, as though he could not get enough air in his lungs.

I looked about me. All eyes were on Julian. Nevitta and Jovian wept openly; the one from emotion, the other from drink. Victor stood on tiptoe at the edge of the bed, like some predatory bird ready to strike. Of that company, only Maximus was his usual self, muttering spells and crumbling dried herbs onto the nearest lamp, no doubt sending messages ahead to the underworld.

Julian continued, his voice weaker. "I am happy that the state like an imperious parent so often exposed me to danger. I was forced to be strong, to hold my own, to resist the storms of fate, even though I knew what the end would be, for I long ago learned from an oracle that I would die by the sword. For this good death, I thank Helios, since it is the fear of those in my place that we die ignobly by secret plots or, even worse, by some long illness.

442

I am happy that I die in mid-career, victorious, and I am honored that the gods have found me worthy of so noble a departure from this world. For a man is weak and cowardly who wants not to die when he ought, or tries to avoid his hour when it comes . . ." These last few words were said almost in a whisper. The scroll dropped from his hand. He seemed to have difficulty in concentrating his thoughts.

"There is more," he said at last. "But I cannot . . . I am . . . I will *not* ramble." An attempt at a smile failed. Instead a muscle in his cheek began to twitch spasmodically. Yet his next words came out clearly. "Now as to the choice of an emperor." Instinctively, the generals moved closer to the bed, the scent of power exciting them much as blood draws wolves to a wounded deer.

Even in his pain, Julian understood precisely the nature of the beasts who encircled him; he spoke slowly and carefully. "If I select someone as my heir and you reject him, as you might, I shall have put a worthy man in a fatal position. My successor would not let him live. Also I might, through ignorance"—this time he did manage a faint smile—"pass over the worthiest man of all, and I would not want *that* stain on my memory, for I am a dutiful child of Rome and I want a good ruler to succeed me. That is why I leave the choice to you. I propose no one."

There was a long sigh in the room. The generals stirred restlessly. Some were disappointed; others pleased: now *their* moment might come.

Julian looked at me. "Did I read that well?"

"Yes, Lord."

"Then I have made the departure I intended." He turned to the generals. "Now let us say good-bye." One by one, the generals kissed his hand for the last time. Many wept. But he ordered them not to. "I should weep for *you*. I am finished with suffering while you, poor devils, are still in the midst of it."

When the last of the generals had gone, Julian motioned for Maximus and me to sit beside his bed. "Now we talk," he said, employing the phrase he always used when he was alone at last with his friends.

Then Julian engaged us in a discussion of the *Phaedo*. What is the precise nature of the soul? What form does it take? In what way does it return to Serapis? I talked philosophy; Maximus talked mysteries. Julian preferred Maximus to me at the end and I could not blame him, for I am bleak and Maximus was hopeful. Together they repeated Mithraic passwords to one another and made cryptic references to the Passion of Demeter. Julian derived a good deal of comfort from Maximus. As usual, I was quite unable to express my affection for him; instead, like a village schoolmaster, I quoted Plato. I was never more inadequate.

Shortly before midnight, Julian asked for cold water. Callistus brought it to him. Just as he was about to drink, black, clotted blood suddenly gushed from his side. He gave a sharp cry and clutched the wound as though with his bare hand he might keep the life from leaving. Then he fainted. The surgeons tried to close the wound. But this time it was no use: the hemorrhage when it finally stopped did so of its own accord.

For some minutes Julian lay with eyes shut, hardly breathing. To this day I remember how the hair on his chest was matted with dried blood, like the pelt of some animal newly killed. I remember the sharp contrast between his sun-darkened neck and the marble white of his torso. I remember that foolish sliver of metal stuck in his side, and I remember thinking: such a small thing to end a man's life and change the history of the world.

At last Julian opened his eyes. "Water," he whispered. Callistus held up his head while he drank. This time the surgeons allowed him to swallow. When he had drained the cup, he turned to Maximus and me, as though he had just thought of something particularly interesting to tell us.

"Yes, Julian?" Maximus leaned forward eagerly. "Yes?"

But Julian seemed to have a second thought. He shook his head. He closed his eyes. He cleared his throat quite naturally. He died. Callistus, feeling the body in his arms go limp, leapt back from the bed with a cry. The corpse fell heavily on its back. One limp brown arm dangled over the edge of the bed. The lion-skin covering was now drenched with blood. No one can ever use it again, I thought numbly as the surgeon said, "The Augustus is dead."

Callistus wept. The deaf-mute moaned like an animal by the bed. Maximus shut his eyes as if in pain. He did not need to exert his gift for seeing into the future to know that the days of his own greatness were over.

I sent Callistus to fetch Salutius. While we waited, the surgeons drew the spear from Julian's body. I asked to see it. I was examining it when Salutius arrived. He glanced briefly at the body; then he turned to Callistus. "Tell the staff to assemble immediately."

Maximus, suddenly, gave a loud but melodious cry and hurried from the tent. Later he told me that he had seen the spirits of Alexander and Julian embracing in the air several feet above the earthen floor of the tent. The sight had ravished him.

After covering the body with a cloak, the surgeons departed, as did the deaf-mute, who was never seen again. Salutius and I were alone in the tent.

I showed him the lance that I was still holding. "This is what killed him," I said.

"Yes, I know."

"It is a Roman spear," I said.

"I know that, too." We looked at one another.

"*Who* killed him?" I asked. But Salutius did not answer. He pulled back the tent flap. Outside the generals were gathering by the light of a dozen torches guttering in the hot wind. Resinous smoke stung my eyes. As Salutius was about to join them, I said, "Did Julian know it was a Roman spear?"

Salutius shrugged. "How could he *not* have known?" He let the tent flap fall after him.

I looked at the figure on the bed. The body was shrouded in purple, except for one brown foot. I adjusted the cloak and inadvertently touched flesh: it was still warm. I shied like a horse who sees a shadow in the road. Then I opened the box from which Julian had taken his deathbed speech. As I had suspected, the memoir and the journal were there. I stole them.

What else? The meeting that night was stormy. Victor and Arintheus wanted an emperor from the East. Nevitta and Dagalaif wanted one from the West. All agreed on Salutius. But he refused. He is the only man I have ever heard of who really meant it when he declared that the principate of this world was not for him.

When Ammianus insisted that Salutius at least agree to lead the army out of Persia, Salutius was equally firm. Under no circumstances would he take command. At a complete impasse, the two factions agreed to meet again the following day.

During the night, Victor took action. Realizing that he himself had no chance of becoming emperor, he decided to create an emperor, one easily managed. His choice was Jovian. In the early hours of 27 June, Victor got the household troops drunk. He then incited them to proclaim their commander Jovian as Augustus. At dawn, the frightened Jovian was led before the assembly by a hundred young officers with drawn swords. The thing was accomplished. Rather than risk bloodshed and civil war, we swore the oath of allegiance to Jovian. Then the new Emperor and his guards made a solemn progress through the army. When the men heard the cry "Jovian Augustus!" they thought at first it was "*Julian* Augustus," and so they began to cheer the miraculous recovery. But when they saw the clownish figure of their new lord, red-eyed, nervous, stooped beneath ill-fitting purple like some exotic African bird, the cheers turned to silence.

That same day, I myself buried poor Anatolius. I found him lying at the bottom of a steep ravine. Until now I have never had the heart to tell anyone that he was not killed by the Persians. He was thrown from his horse and broke his neck. He was a terrible horseman but a delightful companion. I kept his draughts board, which I lost—naturally—on the trip from Antioch to Athens. Nothing is left to me. Well . . .

The rest is familiar history. Jovian made a thirty years' peace with Sapor. He was so eager to get out of Persia and begin a round of parties in Constantinople that he agreed to all of Sapor's demands. He ceded Persia five provinces, including our cities of Singara and Nisbis! It was a disastrous treaty.

We then proceeded to Antioch. En route, Procopius and Sebastian joined us. To this day no one knows why Procopius did not join Julian in Persia. He must have given some excuse to Jovian, but it never filtered down to us. Happily, he himself was put to death, some years later, when he tried to seize the East. So there is a rude justice in our affairs, at least in this case.

Seven months later the Emperor Jovian was also dead. The official report said that he died in his sleep from breathing the fumes of a charcoal stove. To this day, many believe that he was poisoned by Victor, but I have it on good authority that he died naturally. In a drunken sleep, he vomited and choked to death, the perfect end for a glutton. Rather surprisingly, Valentinian was declared Emperor, and that was the end of Victor as a political force. Remember how pleased we all were when Valentinian made his brother Valens Augustus for the East? Such a mild young man, we thought. Well, Valens nearly had my head. He did have Maximus's, and even you had a most difficult time of it. But now the brothers are also dead, and we live on under Valentinian's son Gratian and his appointee Theodosius, who in turn will die, to be succeeded by . . . I sometimes feel that the history of the Roman principate is an interminable pageant of sameness. They are so much alike, these energetic men; only Julian was different.

Toward the end of your justly admired funeral oration at Antioch, you suggested that Julian was killed by one of his own men, if only because no Persian ever came forward to collect the reward the Great King had offered the slayer of Julian. Now I was one of the few people who knew for certain that Julian had been killed by a Roman spear, but I said nothing. I had no intention of involving myself in politics. As it was, I had quite enough trouble that year when Maximus and I were arrested for practicing magic. I a magician!

Fortunately, I was acquitted. Maximus was not. Even so, the old charlatan did manage to have the last word. During his trial, he swore that he had never used his powers maliciously. He also prophesied that whoever took his life unjustly would himself die so terribly that all trace of him would vanish from the earth. Maximus was then put to death by the Emperor Valens, who was promptly killed at the Battle of Adrianople by Goths who hacked the imperial corpse into so many small pieces that no part of him was ever identified. Right to the end, Maximus was lucky in his predictions.

When I was finally released from prison (I wish you luck in your campaign for penal reform), I went straight home to Athens. I locked up Julian's papers in one of Hippia's strongboxes and thought no more about them until this correspondence began.

Lately I have found myself thinking a good deal about Julian's death. You were right when you hinted that he was killed by one of his own men. But by whom? And how? I have studied the last entries in the diary with particular care. From the beginning, Julian knew that there was a plot against his life, and it is fairly plain that he suspected Victor of conspiracy. But was Julian right? And if he was right, how was the murder accomplished?

About ten years ago Julian's servant Callistus wrote a particularly lachrymose ode on the Emperor's death. We were all sent copies. I'm afraid I never wrote to thank the author for his kind gift. In fact, Callistus had completely dropped from my memory until I reread the diary and realized that if anyone had known how Julian died, it would be the servant who was with him when he was wounded.

Callistus of course had sworn that he did not see who struck the blow. But at the time there was good reason for him to lie: the Christians would very quickly have put him to death had he implicated any of them. Like so many of us, Callistus chose silence. But might he not be candid now, with all the principals dead?

It took me several weeks to discover that Callistus lives at Philippopolis. I wrote him. He answered. Last month I went to see him. I shall now give you a full report of what he said. Before you see any of this, I suggest that you yourself write to Callistus for permission. His story is an appalling one, and there is some danger in even knowing it, much less writing about it. *I must also insist that under no circumstances are you to involve me in your account.*

After a tedious trip to Philippopolis in the company of tax collectors and church deacons, I went straight to the house of an old pupil who kindly offered to put me up, a great saving since the local innkeepers are notorious thieves. The only advantage to having been a teacher for what seems now to have been the better part of a thousand years is that no matter where I go, I find former students who let me stay with them. This makes travel possible.

I asked my host about Callistus (I myself could remember nothing about him except the sound of his sobbing at Julian's deathbed). "One never sees your Callistus." My old student is a snob. "They say he's quite rich and there are those who go to his house. I am not one of them."

"Where did his money come from?"

"Trade concessions. Imperial grants. He is supposed to be quite clever. He was born here, you know. The son of a slave in the

448

house of a cousin of mine. He returned only a few years ago, shortly after the Emperor Valentinian died. They say he has important friends at court. But I wouldn't know."

Callistus is indeed rich, his house far larger and more lavish than that of my former pupil. A Syrian steward of breathtaking elegance led me through two large courtyards to a small shady atrium where Callistus was waiting for me. Here I was greeted most affably by a perfect stranger. I don't recall how Callistus used to look, but today he is a handsome middle-aged man who looks years younger than he is. It is obvious that he devotes a good deal of time to his appearance: hair thick and skillfully dyed, body slender; manners a trifle too good, if you know what I mean.

"How pleasant to see you again, my dear Priscus!" He spoke as though we had been the most intimate of friends, even equals! I returned his greeting with that careful diffidence poverty owes wealth. He took my homage naturally. He asked me to sit down while he poured the wine himself, reverting to at least one of his old functions.

For a time we spoke of who was dead and who was living. To people our age, the former category is largest. Nevitta, Salutius, Sallust, Jovian, Valentinian, Valens are dead. But Victor is still on active duty in Gaul and Dagalaif serves in Austria; Arintheus, recently retired to a suburb of Constantinople, has taken to drink. Then we spoke of Persia and the days of our youth (or in my case the halcyon days of my middle age!). We mourned the dead. Then I got the subject round to Julian's death. I told Callistus of your plans. He was noncommittal. I told him that you were in possession of the memoir. He said that he had known at the time that the Emperor was writing such a work and he had often wondered what had become of it. I told him. He smiled. Then I said, "And of course there was the private journal."

"A journal?" Callistus looked startled.

"Yes. A secret diary which the Emperor kept in the same box with the memoir."

"I didn't know."

"It's a most revealing work."

"I am sure it is." Callistus frowned.

"The Emperor knew about the plot against his life. He even

449

knew who the conspirators were." Something in Callistus's manner prompted me to add this lie.

"There were no conspirators." Callistus was bland. "The Augustus was killed by a Persian cavalryman."

"Who never collected the reward?"

Callistus shrugged. "Perhaps he himself was killed."

"But why was this Persian cavalryman armed with a Roman spear?"

"That sometimes happens. In a battle one often takes whatever weapon is at hand. Anyway, I should know. I was with the Augustus, and I saw the Persian who struck him."

This was unexpected. With some surprise, I asked, "But why, when Julian asked if you had seen his attacker, did you say you saw nothing?"

Callistus was not in the least rattled. "But I *did* see the Persian." He sounded perfectly reasonable. "And I told the Augustus that I saw him."

"In front of Maximus and me, you said that you did *not* see who struck the blow."

Callistus shook his head tolerantly. "It has been a long time, Priscus. Our memories are not what they were."

"Implying that *my* memory is at fault?"

He gestured delicately. "Neither of us is exactly young."

I tried another tack: "You have doubtless heard the rumor that a Christian soldier killed the Emperor?"

"Of course. But I was . . ."

". . . there. Yes. And you know who killed him."

Callistus's face was a perfect blank. It was impossible to tell what he was thinking. One can see why he has been such a success in business. Then: "How much *did* the Emperor know?" he asked, the voice flat and abrupt, very different from the easy, rather indolent tone he had been assuming.

"He knew about Victor."

Callistus nodded. "I was almost certain he knew. So was Victor."

"Then *you* knew about the conspiracy?"

"Oh, yes."

"Were you involved in it?"

"Very much so. You see, Priscus," he gave me a most winning smile, "it was I who killed the Emperor Julian."

There it is. The end of the mystery. Callistus told me everything. He regards himself as one of the world's unique heroes, the unsung savior of Christianity. As he talked, he paced up and down. He could not tell me enough. After all, for nearly twenty years he has had to keep silent. I was his first auditor.

A cabal had been formed at Antioch. Victor was the ringleader. Arintheus, Jovian, Valentinian and perhaps twenty other Christian officers were involved. They vowed that Julian must not return from Persia alive. But because of his popularity with the European troops, his death must appear to be from natural causes.

Victor assigned Callistus to Julian as a bodyguard and servant. At first he was instructed to poison the Emperor. But that was not easily accomplished. Julian was in excellent health; he was known to eat sparingly; a sudden illness would be suspicious. Finally, an ambush was arranged with the Persians. Julian has described how that failed. Then it was decided that Julian must die in battle. But he was an excellent soldier, highly conspicuous, always guarded. The conspirators were in despair until Callistus hit on a plan.

"After the Battle of Maranga, I broke the straps of his breastplate." Callistus's eyes sparkled with delighted memory. "Luckily for us, the Persians attacked the next day and the Emperor was forced to go into battle without armor. He and I got caught up in the Persian retreat. He started to turn back but I shouted to him, 'Lord, this way!' And I led him into the worst of the fighting. For a moment I thought the Persians *would* kill him. But they were too terrified. When they recognized him, they fled. It was then that I knew that God had chosen me to be the instrument of his vengeance." The voice lowered; the jaw set. "We were hemmed in. The Emperor was using his shield to try and clear a path for himself through the tangle of horses and riders. Suddenly he twisted to his left and stood in his stirrups, trying to see over the heads of the Persians. This was my chance. I prayed for Christ to give me strength. Then I plunged my spear into his side." Callistus stopped, obviously expecting some outcry at this. But I merely gave him that look of alert interest with which I reward those exceptional students who succeed in holding my attention.

"Go on," I said politely.

Somewhat deflated, Callistus shrugged. "You know the rest.

The Augustus didn't realize he was wounded until after the Persians fled." He smiled. "The Augustus even thanked me for having stayed so close to him."

"It was a good thing for you that he suspected nothing." But even as I said this I wondered whether or not Julian had known the truth. *That* remains the final mystery.

"But what is death?" asked Callistus, promptly losing all the respect I had come to have for him as a villain. He is an ass. He talked for another hour. He told me that Victor wanted to be emperor, but when he saw that this was impossible, he raised Jovian to the purple. Then the notoriously strong-willed Valentinian took Jovian's place and that was the end of Victor. Meanwhile, Callistus was paid off handsomely by everyone. He has invested his money wisely and today he is a rich man. But he will not be a happy man until the world knows his secret. He suffers from what he feels to be an undeserved anonymity.

"By all means tell Libanius the truth. One did what one was born to do." He looked pious. "I am proud of the part I have played in the history of Rome." He turned his face to me left-three-quarters, in imitation of the famous bust of the second Brutus. Then he came off it. "But we'll have to get permission from the palace before Libanius can publish, and I have no idea what the policy is now. Under Valentinian, I was sworn to secrecy."

"Did Valentinian know about you?"

"Oh, yes. He even gave me the salt concession for Thrace. But he ordered me to keep silent. And I have. Until today. Naturally, I hope that we can make the whole matter public, in the interest of history."

Callistus offered me dinner but I chose to take nothing more from him. I said I must go. He accompanied me to the vestibule. He was all grace and tact, even when he chided me for never having acknowledged the "Ode to Julian" he had sent me.

I apologized for my negligence. But then I said, "How could you write such an affectionate work about the man you murdered?"

Callistus was perfect in his astonishment. "But I admired him tremendously! He was always kind to me. Every word I wrote about him was from the heart. After all, I am a good Christian, or try to be. Every day I pray for his soul!"

452

I doubt if Theodosius will allow you to publish any of this. But one never knows. Anyway, *I* am finished with the whole thing and I ask you, please, to keep me out of it.

# XXIV

*Libanius, Quaestor of Antioch, to the*
*Lord Theodosius, Augustus of the East*     *Antioch, May 381*

May it please Your Eternity, I have it in mind to compose a biography of your famous predecessor the Augustus Julian, employing certain of his private papers which have only recently come into my possession.

Since Your Eternity expressed pleasure in my ode, "On Avenging the Emperor Julian," I need hardly mention that I intend to pursue my labor of vindication in precisely the same discreet style as the ode which you so graciously admired. Realizing as I do the religious and political implications of this work, I am impelled not only to remind the Augustus of my perfect (and obvious!) loyalty to his sacred person and sagacious policies but to assure him that I intend to relate this marvelous tale with the conscious delicacy which the subject inspires and the times require.

Lord, those of us who cherish the old ways (yet mean to obey to the letter your just and necessary edicts) will be forever beholden to your magnanimity in allowing me to write with love and candor of a hero whose deeds once blazed upon an astonished and fortunate earth like the sun itself and whose fame in its day (though as nothing compared to Your Eternity's) was Rome's shield against the barbarian. It is my humble wish to reflect that remembered glory in the pages of my own dim but faithful prose.

My cherished friend, the Bishop Meletius, who is now at Constantinople, has told me that he will put my case to Your Eternity with the same high eloquence with which he has for so many decades enlightened the congregations of the East. Accept, then, oh Lord, the homage of one who is old and close to death, and wants nothing for himself but truth, and its telling.

The Augustus has read your letter with the interest anything you write deserves. He has commanded me to tell you that it is not possible at this time to publish a life of the late Augustus Julian.

You refer to Bishop Meletius. He is dead. He was stricken last week during a session of the Ecumenical Council. His remains have already been sent to Antioch for burial. I am, however, at liberty to tell you that before the Bishop died, he asked the Augustus to recognize as legitimate your natural son Cimon. The Augustus is pleased to comply with this holy man's request. The documents are now being prepared by my office and will be forwarded in due course to the Count of the East, who will in turn deliver them to the governor of Syria, at which time you will be officially notified.

It would not be amiss, Quaestor, were you to send the Augustus a complete edition of your works. He would value them.

*Libanius to himself*

I have just come from the funeral of Bishop Meletius, which was held in the Golden House on the island. I don't think I would have been able to cope with the mob in the square if I had not been with Cimon. It seems that all Antioch was on hand to say farewell to their bishop.

The crowd recognized me, as they always do, and they made way for my litter. There was a certain amount of good-humored comment about "pagans" (a new word of contempt for us Hellenists) attending Christian services, but I pretended not to hear. Just inside the arcade Cimon lifted me out of the litter. I have been suffering lately from gout not only in my right foot, as usual, but also in my left. Though I use both a crutch and a staff, I can barely hobble without assistance. Fortunately, Cimon, good son that he is, got me safely inside the church. He was also able to provide me with one of the chairs which had been reserved for the governor's party (the Christians stand during their services and only great visitors may sit).

Of course I saw nothing. I can distinguish light and dark, but little else. I do have some sight out of the corner of my left eye, and if I hold my head at a certain cocked angle I can see well enough to read for a short while, but the effort is so great that I prefer to spend my days in the cloudy subaqueous world of the blind. My impression of the church interior was one of pale circles (faces) and dark columns (cloaks of mourning). The air was thick with incense and the inevitable heavy odor of people massed together on a summer day.

Prayers were said and eulogies delivered, but I am afraid that I wool-gathered during the service. I could think of nothing but that curt letter from the Sacred Palace. I am not to publish. Not even the legitimizing of Cimon can compensate for that cruel blow.

As I sat in the hot octagonal church, the altar to my left and the tall marble pulpit to my right, I was suddenly conscious of the voice of the priest officiating. Like most blind or near-blind people, I am acutely sensitive to voices. Some delight me; others (even those of friends) distress me. This particular voice, I noted with some pleasure, was deep and resonant, with that curious urgency which I always find appealing. The speaker was delivering a eulogy of Meletius. I listened attentively. The words were gracefully chosen; the periods artful; the content conventional. When the priest had finished, I turned to Cimon and whispered, "Who is that?"

"John Chrysostom, the new deacon, appointed last month by Meletius. You know him."

"Do I?"

But the service had continued and we kept silent while the new bishop blessed the congregation. Who was this John "Golden-Mouth"? Where did I know him from? Had he been a pupil? And if he had, would I be able to recall him? My memory is not what it was; also, I have taught literally thousands of men and no one could remember them all. Finally, when the ceremonies ended, Cimon got me to my feet just as the governor of Syria passed us. I recognized him by the color of his robe. The governor paused when he saw me.

"Ah, Quaestor, how good to see you in such blooming health."

The governor is an ass, who means well. "The old tree survives," I said. "But it does not bloom."

However, he had turned to my son. "It is not premature, I hope, to congratulate you on the Emperor's favor."

Cimon was delighted; he craves honor, the way some men crave truth.

"No, Governor, not premature at all. Many thanks. My father and I were both delighted at the Emperor's kindness."

"You must give me some advice, Cimon." And the governor took my son by the arm and led him away, leaving me stranded in the church, blind as Homer and lame as Hephaestos. I confess to a moment of anger. Cimon should have remained with me. He could have made an appointment to see the governor at another time. But Cimon is a lawyer, and one must be tolerant. Even so, I found it difficult to forgive him when I realized that I was now alone in the Golden House, unable to see and hardly able to walk. Leaning heavily on my stick, like some night-creature dazzled by day, I crept toward what I hoped would be the door. I had taken no more than a step when a firm hand took me by the arm.

"Thank you," I said to the vague shape beside me. "I seem to be deserted, and I do need help. I cannot see."

"Any help I give you is nothing compared to the help you have given me." I recognized the voice of the deacon John Chrysostom.

I pretended to remember him. "Oh, yes, John . . ."

"They call me Chrysostom. But you remember me as the son of Anthusa and . . ."

I did remember him. I knew exactly who he was. "My best student!" I exclaimed. "Stolen from me by Christians!"

He laughed. "Not stolen, *found*."

"So my John is the famous Chrysostom the people listen to."

"They listen. But do they understand? After all, I am strange to them. For ten years I have been in the desert, alone . . ."

"And now you've come back to the world to be a bishop?"

"I have come back to the world to preach, to tell the truth, the way my old teacher does."

"We hold a different view of what is true," I said more sharply than I intended.

"Perhaps not so different." We had paused near the door. With an effort, I could just make out the lean face of my old pupil. John has begun to grow bald, and he wears a short beard. But I confess that even were my sight better I should not have recognized him; it has been nearly twenty years since he studied with me.

456

"Before he left Antioch, Bishop Meletius told me of your plan to write about the Emperor Julian." I wondered if John could see into my mind. Why else would he mention the one thing which most concerned me yet could hardly interest him?

"Unfortunately, it is no longer a plan. The Emperor has forbidden me to publish."

"I'm sorry. I know what Julian meant to you. I saw him once. I must have been about fifteen. It was just before I came to you, to study. I saw him the day he left the city for Persia. I was in the crowd, in the forum, standing on the rim of the Nymphaeum when he rode by. I remember the people were shouting something rude..."

"Felix Julian *Augustus*," I murmured, hearing again the chanting of that malicious crowd.

"Yes. I was so close to him I could have touched his horse. And though my mother had told me I should hate him, I thought he was the most splendid man I ever saw, and when he looked my way, his eyes suddenly caught mine, and he smiled as though we were friends, and I thought to myself: this man is a saint, why do they hate him? Later of course I realized why they hated him, but I have never understood why he hated us."

I burst into tears. I have never been so humiliated, or felt so ridiculous. The most famous philosopher of his time, if I may say so, was weeping like a child in front of a former pupil. But John was tactful. He said not a word until the storm had passed, and then he made no reference to my senile outburst. He took my arm and led me to the door. Then he turned round and indicated a high place on the opposite wall. "New work," he said. "I think it quite beautiful." I twisted my head so that I could see — just barely — what appeared to be the giant figure of a man with arms outstretched.

"Can you see him clearly?"

"Oh, yes," I lied. The gold mosaic glowed like the sun itself in the afternoon light.

"It is Christ Pantocrator, come to redeem us. The face is particularly fine."

"Yes, I see the face," I said flatly. And I did: the dark cruel face of an executioner.

"But you don't like what you see?"

"How can I, when what I see is death."

"But death is not the end."

"It is the end of life."

"*This* life . . ."

"Life!" I turned on him fiercely. "You have chosen death, all of you . . ."

"No, not death. We have chosen life eternal, the resurrection of the . . ."

"That is a story to tell children. The truth is that for thousands of years we looked to what was living. Now you look to what is dead, you worship a dead man and tell one another that *this* world is not for us, while the next is all that matters. Only there is no next world."

"We believe . . ."

"This is all we have, John Chrysostom. There is nothing else. Turn your back on this world, and you face the pit!"

There was a silence. Then John said, "Do you see no significance in our victory? For we have won. You must admit that."

I shrugged. "The golden age ended. So will the age of iron, so will all things, including man. But with your new god, the hope of human happiness has ended."

"Forever?" He taunted me gently.

"Nothing man invents can last forever, including Christ, his most mischievous invention."

John did not answer. We were now outside the church. The day was pleasantly warm. People I could not see greeted me. Then my son hurried up and I said good-bye to John and got into my litter. All the way home to Daphne, Cimon babbled about his interview with the governor. He has hope of "governmental preferment."

I am alone in my study. I have already put away Julian's papers. The thing is finished. The world Julian wanted to preserve and restore is gone . . . but I shall not write "forever," for who can know the future? Meanwhile, the barbarians are at the gate. Yet when they breach the wall, they will find nothing of value to seize, only empty relics. The spirit of what we were has fled. So be it.

I have been reading Plotinus all evening. He has the power to soothe me; and I find his sadness curiously comforting. Even when he writes: "Life here with the things of earth is a sinking, a defeat, a failing of the wing." The wing has indeed failed. One sinks.

Defeat is certain. Even as I write these lines, the lamp wick sputters to an end, and the pool of light in which I sit contracts. Soon the room will be dark. One has always feared that death would be like this. But what else is there? With Julian, the light went, and now nothing remains but to let the darkness come, and hope for a new sun and another day, born of time's mystery and man's love of light.

*April 1959–6 January 1964, Rome*

# A PARTIAL BIBLIOGRAPHY

Julian, *The works of the Emperor*.

Ammianus Marcellinus, *The History*.

Libanius, *Orations*: "In Praise of Antioch," "To Julian,"
    "Monody on Julian," "Epitaph on Julian," "On Avenging Julian,"
    et cetera.

Gregory Nazianzen, "Oration Against Julian."

Sozomen, *Ecclesiastical History*.

Socrates, *Ecclesiastical History*.

Theodoret, *A History of the Church*.

Eunapius, *Lives of the Philosophers*.

Pausanias, *Description of Greece*.

Edward Gibbon, *The Decline and Fall of the Roman Empire*.

Jacob Burckhardt, *The Age of Constantine the Great*.

R. A. Pack, *Studies in Libanius and Antiochene Society under
    Theodosius*.

T.R. Glover, *Life and Letters in the Fourth Century*.

J. Bidez, *La Vie de l'Empereur Julien*.

J.B. Bury, *History of the Later Roman Empire*.

Franz Cumont, *The Mysteries of Mithra*.

Norman Baynes, "The Early Life of Julian the Apostate," *Journal
    Hellenic Studies*, Vol. XLV, pages 251–254.

G.E. Mylonas, *Eleusis and the Eleusinian Mysteries*.

M.J. Vermaseren, *Mithras: The Secret God*.

Glanville Downey, *Ancient Antioch*.

Glanville Downey, *Antioch in the Age of Theodosius the Great*.

Stebelton H. Nulle, "Julian Redivivus," *The Centennial Review*,
    Vol. V, No. 3, summer.

# ABOUT THE AUTHOR

Gore Vidal was born in 1925 at the United States Military Academy, West Point, where his father was the first instructor in Aeronautics. After graduating at seventeen from Phillips Exeter Academy, he enlisted in the Army and served in World War II from 1943 to 1946. At nineteen, while stationed in the Pacific, he wrote his first novel, WILLIWAW. His other novels include IN A YELLOW WOOD; THE CITY AND THE PILLAR; THE SEASON OF COMFORT; A SEARCH FOR THE KING; DARK GREEN, BRIGHT RED; THE JUDGMENT OF PARIS; MESSIAH; WASHINGTON, D.C.; MYRA BRECKENRIDGE; TWO SISTERS; BURR; MYRON; 1876; KALKI; CREATION; DULUTH; and LINCOLN. In the fifties Vidal wrote plays for live television and films for Metro-Goldwyn-Mayer. One of the television plays became the successful Broadway play VISIT TO A SMALL PLANET. He has written four other plays, which are AN EVENING WITH RICHARD NIXON; WEEKEND; ROMULUS; and THE BEST MAN, which ran for two seasons on Broadway. His books of essays include ROCKING THE BOAT; REFLECTIONS UPON A SINKING SHIP; HOMAGE TO DANIEL SHAYS; MATTERS OF FACT AND OF FICTION; and THE SECOND AMERICAN REVOLUTION. Vidal wrote one volume of short stories, called A THIRSTY EVIL